MW01035861

THE LOST IMMORTAL

THE INFINITE DIARY TRILOGY BOOK 1

Tony Huston

Wayfarer Press

DEDICATION

To my mom, Cindy, who has always been my biggest fan, and who will undoubtedly be gifting this novel to everyone she knows whether they want it or not.

PROLOGUE

SHE LUNGED FROM BEHIND the door, ambushing me as I entered the chamber. Her blade was swift, thrice piercing my back ere I could blink. White-hot pain set my blood afire, and I pitched along the table. There I fell into our supper, toppling the wine upon which we'd sipped but moments ago in the candlelight. I reached for my wits, groping for them amidst the glorious shock of her attack, but she was relentless. Again and again did she drive her weapon into my flesh as if a hateful whirlwind had sprouted hands and taken up arms against me.

Under the force of her blows did I roll from the table, crumpling to the floor, but her bloodwork was yet unfinished. She was astride me in a blink, savaging me anew. Only then could I see that her weapon was not a dagger as I'd assumed. Nay, twas the ivory comb I'd gifted her that very day, its handle having splintered into a keen point. Why the comb was thusly fractured, why my fine gift from lands exotic had been fashioned into the tool of my death, was unbeknownst to me. I could but gasp as she drove its crimson tip into my lungs, stealing the same breath that oft whispered to her in the night. It punctured my heart, hushing the rhythm that beat only for her. My innards ruptured; my ribs cracked. Limp and helpless, I could but wait for death.

In that dimming twilight, however, my eyes could yet see, and my ears could yet hear, the closing blackness having not yet stolen their purposes. Thus, in that final moment, I drank her in. My lust-beaten devil of jealousy, draped in a reddening gown of white. Her raven hair whipped the night with each plunge of that misused comb, and mean contortions marred her olive cheeks. Those amber eyes, vibrant as the hills of autumn, saw but did not see, so consumed were they with mindless wrath. Yea, this tempest of beauty and rage was a fine liquor, and I tasted long and deep of her. And in those final seconds of life was I jolted by a sudden truth. The truth that I loved this woman more madly than I'd ever loved another.

Twas only then that I was wracked with panic. Only then, when confronted by the realization she might vanish. As you well know, you who are me, those who vanish are rare, but in our countless eons, it has happened. That we wake from death only to discover a soul we'd once known has been blanked from the world. A pawn snatched from the cosmic

1

chessboard by the fickle hand of fate. None can recall these lost souls, nor even affirm their names. They are but gone, leaving you and I as the world's sole witness to their existence. For centuries thence are we haunted by the memories of their ghosts. Thus, as Seraphina seized my last breath did it occur to me she might vanish, condemning my resurrection to wander the earth in a cruel and futile search for her phantom. I knew fear then. The miserable taste of true and unbridled fear, the likes of which I'd not suffered in millennia. That I might forever lose my fiery jewel had been a nightmare undreamt, but now the notion was a crystallized terror, a spectral knife one thousand-fold more agonizing than the one she pumped into my chest. In our short time together, she has hoisted me from the pits of unfathomable despair, re-igniting a life dulled by a torturous soup of meaningless epochs. She is the first in centuries to strum the chords of my soul as though I were a dusty lyre salvaged from an ancient cellar, returning me to past and joyful melodies. Only in that very moment of death did I know I truly loved her, and that I have held her at arm's length in betrayal of my heart. Yet now I might lose her to infinity. Twas a fear that scorched my blood like none before. Thus, for the first time in thousands of years, I yearned to live.

CHAPTER 1

THE KNOCK STARTLED HER. At first, she thought it was her imagination. No one ever knocked on her door, not at home. At the office, sure. Lots of people interrupting her there. Not here, though, where she hid from the loud, needy world in her cozy fortress of solitude. Maybe this was just a trick of her mind, an auditory hallucination induced by hours of reckless caffeine drinking and monotonous typing. She remained silent, fingers poised over the keys, ears perked.

The knock repeated. Bolder and more insistent, too strong to be one of her elderly neighbors. So who was it? She wasn't expecting a delivery, and solicitors were not permitted in the complex. Had someone from the university decided to pop in? That'd be a first—and a last, too, after the scolding she would give them for showing up unannounced. At least that's the fantasy she conjured in her mind. In truth, she would tolerate the intrusion like a timid mouse.

Staring at her laptop, she battled indecision. Give into curiosity and answer the door, or ignore the interloper and continue working?

The doorbell this time. Then a faint voice. "Doctor Grace? Are you there? It's rather important." A man, Italian accent. Not one of her colleagues then. Nevertheless, it sounded like a professional matter. Intriguing, but also rude. She would never dream of appearing at a stranger's home out of the blue to talk shop. She considered staying quiet until he retreated, but she feared he'd just accost her later at a more inconvenient time. May as well get it over with now.

She rose from her chair, knocking off a stack of folders that had been teetering on the edge of her desk. With a curse, she began gathering them, but each time she pressed one folder against her chest, two more escaped her grasp, sliding across the hardwood.

The doorbell again.

"*Mon Dieu!*" Giving up on the folders, she tossed the few she'd gathered onto a side table where they flopped among the other clutter. On her way to the door, she stopped to check her reflection in the mirror. Yikes. The she-thing from the library. Oh well, nothing she could do about it now.

"Ah," she heard the stranger say as she turned the deadbolt, *"molto bene."* She opened the door a foot wide, squinting the sudden sunlight from her eyes. There stood a portly man in a gray suit, blazer unbuttoned, a loose tie around his ample neck. He removed his fedora, set his briefcase down, and extended a meaty hand. "Doctor Valory Grace, I presume." His relief was obvious. "It is an honor to meet you. My name is Doctor Rafael Moretti. I am the Deputy Chief of Staff for the Italian Ministry of Cultural Heritage." Like a wizened cherub, his grin was fat and red-cheeked where it was not smothered by an ashy beard. His nose was a fleshy bulb, his hair a tidy horseshoe ringing a bald pate. The broadness of his smile turned his eyes to friendly slits etched with crow's feet. "I hope I have not startled you."

She shook his hand without opening the door further. "I was working," she said, only afterward realizing it was an aloof thing to say. "Sorry, I mean that I wasn't expecting visitors. What can I do for you, Doctor Moretti?"

Moretti placed his fedora over his heart. "My sincerest apologies, Doctor Grace, I know I have come uninvited. But, due to the nature of my visit, it is necessary."

"Why? What is this about?"

Moretti was hesitant, casting a sidelong glance as if the empty breezeway might be peopled with well-hidden eavesdroppers. When he spoke this time, it was in Italian. *"La questione è piuttosto delicata, Dottoressa. Possiamo parlare dentro? Per favore?"* The matter was sensitive, and he wanted to talk inside.

A list of excuses to decline zipped through her mind. None were socially feasible. "Yes, of course. *La prego di entrare, Dottore."*

"Grazie mille."

Before she closed the door behind him, Valory glanced over the guardrail of the walkway. In the car park below, a man in a dark suit was leaning on a Mercedes lighting a cigarette. He slipped the lighter into his pocket, looking up at her. She shut the door.

Turning, Valory was suddenly embarrassed. Only then when she saw Doctor Moretti checking out her apartment did she realize just how chaotic it was. Books upon books piled here, spread open there. Loose papers scattered over the couch. Coffee mugs lying about, some of them accompanied by crumb-filled plates. A whiteboard where a normal person's television might be, dense with scribbles and symbols. "Sorry about the mess," she said. "If I'd known you were coming—"

"No no no, Doctor, please," he said, waving her off with his fedora. "I am the one who is imposing. Besides," he chuckled, "you should see my office."

"Kind of you to say. Please have a seat," she said, clearing off a spot on the couch. *"Caffè?"*

4

"*Si,*" he said, sinking into the cushion, "but only if it is already brewed. I don't want to be a trouble."

"Trust me, if these eyes are open, there is freshly brewed coffee nearby."

Doctor Moretti's deep-chested laughter and plump red cheeks brought visions of an Italian Santa Claus to her mind. Except that one always knows the exact date that Santa will arrive at one's chimney. As Valory went into the kitchen, she considered the nature of his surprise appearance. The Italian Ministry of Cultural Heritage? She'd never worked with them, and she was quite sure the university had no open collaborations there. So why would they send their Deputy Chief of Staff to her private residence, bypassing all official channels in this clandestine manner? She'd find out soon enough, but she feared she'd have to withstand a volley of small talk beforehand. Though not as bad as the French, Italians liked taking their sweet time. Valory had endured many an aimless conversation with sociable European academics before being allowed to sample the goods. If only all people were as businesslike as the Germans.

"I must say, Doctor Grace—"

"Just Valory, please," she called as she felt along the top shelf, hoping to find a clean mug. "Or Val if you're into brevity."

"*Bene.* And call me Rafael."

"K."

"I must say, Valory, I was a bit surprised to learn that a thirty-four-year-old woman lives in a retirement home."

"Assisted living. There's a difference."

"Ah yes, of course. But," he grunted, pulling a hairbrush from beneath his rear end, "after some rumination, I see that it is quite a prudent choice. I'm sure your elderly neighbors are quiet as mice. No parties or loud music. You don't have to maintain the grounds or repair anything. You can escape your office and focus on your work here without hassle." He chortled. "I think the rest of us have all missed a fine, eh, how do the kids say—a life hack, hm?"

"You've discovered my secret. Cream and sugar?"

"*Si, grazie.* The only thing I don't understand is how. Must not a person be of a certain age to live here?"

"Normally, yes, but old people love me. They accept me as one of their own." She handed him the coffee before taking an adjacent chair. "Kidding, of course. I mean they are rather fond of me—they say I have an old soul—but the truth is my colleague at Oxford pulled some strings to get me in here. She's chummy with the administrator."

"Ah, I see." He sipped his coffee and nodded approval. "I think, not long from now, I may be living in a place such as this. Not to work in peace, but because I will be too old to face the world anymore, eh?" Another Santa chuckle hid his eyes. Valory smiled politely but said nothing. It was then she

5

noticed Rafael had placed his briefcase behind his legs as if protecting it. Something important in there. "I can see you are anxious for me to get to the point," he said after a second sip. "I cannot blame you. I understand this is all quite unexpected."

"Well, since you mention it."

"*Molto bene*. Down to business then. First, Valory, I must confess I've done a bit of homework on you."

"Homework? On me?"

"*Si*. And two words kept coming to mind as I read about your career—quietly remarkable."

"Oh. Thank you."

"Let's see how good my memory is. As I recall, you began attending Harvard at sixteen, eventually attaining your doctorate in historical linguistics."

"That is correct."

"And, as a student, you also worked as a judiciary translator."

"Yes," said Valory, tightening. "I'd thought that to be a rather obscure part of my life. How did you know?"

"I found an old article about you in the *Harvard International Law Journal*. It said you were a *wunderkind*, that the courts held you in high demand. You could speak any language thrown at you—a dozen interpreters rolled into one. Such recognition opened many doors for you, hm?"

Valory bristled. Was Rafael casually hinting at her stint with the D.I.A. during the Iraqi War? Her translations of intercepted communications had led to people dying—not something she was proud of. Nor was it something Rafael should know about, yet she was beginning to suspect he did. "You certainly have done your homework, Doctor."

"We are academics. Our entire lives are homework."

"Can't argue there."

"Now, I also know after graduating, you held a position at the Max Plank Institute for Psycholinguistics in the Netherlands. While there, it is said that you gained a reputation as a resurrector of dead languages. You assisted teams around the world with reconstructing extinct tongues using what little evidence had survived. Your uncanny comprehension even earned you the moniker 'Language Jesus.'" Rafael was tickled by the nickname.

Valory nodded, a bit embarrassed. Yes, she'd contributed to such projects throughout her career, sometimes bridging linguistic gaps that had eluded other experts for decades, but she'd never liked 'Language Jesus.' Sounded sanctimonious. She'd been trying to ditch it for years.

Registering Valory's discomfort, Rafael moved on. "I also learned that you've consulted on numerous archeological and anthropological ventures worldwide."

"I've traveled a little, yes."

"And currently, you're a researcher for the Centre of Study of Ancient Documents down the road at Oxford."

"You're on a roll, sir."

"An impressive career, especially for your age. As I said—quietly remarkable."

"Thank you."

"May I ask how many languages you speak, Doctor Grace?"

"Valory."

"*Mi dispiace*, Valory." He sipped his coffee, smiling.

"Fluently? Seventy-five modern languages, give or take. Semi-fluently, another ten or fifteen, depending on your definition of semi-fluent. Honestly, I don't keep an exact count."

"*Oddio!* You say that without the slightest braggadocio."

Valory shrugged. "It's not as mind-blowing for me as it seems to be for others. It doesn't feel extraordinary."

Rafael popped with surprise. It was the first time Valory had seen the entirety of his irises. "Surely you are joking! I speak four languages, and those took me years to learn. Your achievement is remarkable!"

"I suppose."

"Almost a hundred modern languages. *Oh mio.* I hesitate to ask how many historical languages you know. You might give me an inferiority complex, no?"

"We don't want that," she said, hoping to match his genial energy. "Guess I'll just have to keep that to myself."

"No no, I can't resist, you must tell me. How many, please?"

"Well, let's just say that if it was written on papyrus, painted on a wall, or carved into stone, I can read it."

"Amazing," Rafael half-whispered. "What is your secret? How do you retain so much knowledge?"

Valory shrugged again. "The mysteries of this world are never-ending." She managed a lighthearted tone, but she prickled with annoyance. Minutes ago, Doctor Moretti said he would get down to business, but all he'd done since then was engage in sycophantic posturing, back-door interviewing her for a job for which she hadn't asked. Now he wanted her to explain the freakish neurological complexities that made language comprehension as natural for her as a sunrise. Good thing she'd lied to him. If she'd told him the real answer—that she could speak more than a thousand modern languages, far and away surpassing every other hyperpolyglot on the planet—he might have blown a fuse. She'd learned to perpetrate that lie long ago, understating her abilities just so she didn't have to deal with peoples' amazement.

"Say something in Swahili!" they'd demand.

7

Sighing, she'd respond, *"Kitu katika Kiswahili,"* which translated to "Something in Swahili." That game had gotten old in her teens.

This man had come to Oxford all the way from Rome when a simple call to her campus office would have sufficed. Why? What matter was so sensitive, and what was in that briefcase he was protecting? *Spill the beans already, Jack.*

Valory felt a poke of guilt, for Rafael had noticed her edginess. He sat forward, dowsing his cheerfulness. Doctor Grace the party pooper strikes again. Would she ever be able to fake the graceful social etiquette that made people like each other? "What are you working on now, Valory? If I may ask?"

More questions. Managing a smile, she fetched a handful of folders from her desk, the same ones with which she'd fumbled earlier. She withdrew several high-res scans of weathered stones carved with faded lettering. "The Centre is collaborating with the Department of Antiquities in documenting a neglected corpus of Hellenistic inscriptions. Thousands of documents and artifacts with alphabetic scripts in syllabic, Phoenician, etcetera. I'm serving as principal researcher. For instance," she said, handing a print to Rafael, "this image shows a section of a stone altar bearing a prayer for Ptolemy V Epiphanes. One-ninety BCE."

Moretti wrapped a pair of glasses around his ears, face crunching as he squinted through the round lenses as if they blinded rather than aided him. "Fascinating," he muttered, inspecting the scan. "There is much historical overlap between the Ptolemaic era and ancient Rome. I am surprised that you and I have not met before in some official capacity. Our work is certainly intertwined."

"I suppose so."

"Translating and cataloging these must be keeping you quite busy."

"Definitely. And I have hundreds to get through." Hint hint.

"Tell me," he said, peeking over the rim of his glasses, "might you be willing to set these aside for a little while?"

"Set them aside?"

"*Si.* Say, if a golden opportunity appeared on your doorstep?"

"Well, that might be difficult. We're working on a one-year grant, so I don't have much time to . . ."

She trailed off as Rafael slid a stack of books out of the way and put his briefcase on the coffee table. He spun the numbers on the combination lock but stopped short of opening the case. "Valory, if I may ask, what led you to your profession?"

"Led me?"

"Well, clearly, you love languages. Their evolution, their etymologies, their cultural significance. You have pursued such studies from a very young age. It is a field of academia that most of the world finds dry and boring, but

8

not you. My guess is you would not be happy doing anything else. So, what is it? Why do you love it so much?"

Valory measured the question. How could she answer without sounding like a freak? Doctor Moretti wouldn't understand the truth. No one had ever understood, not even other hyperpolyglots. As an adolescent, she had tried to explain it to her mother, to her sister, and to friends. How confronting a new word tickled her mental pleasure center. How absorbing a dead language gave her a rush akin to a lover's caress. When other teenage girls were going on dates and navigating social pitfalls, she was running her fingers along glossy pictures of ancient Egyptian hieroglyphs, reveling in a quasi-erotic miasma as she uncovered their dusty meanings. In the innocence of girlhood, she thought everyone shared such feelings. How could they not? Was not the mastery of words and language an intoxicant like no other? Did not everyone long to weave that magic tapestry underpinning the whole of humanity? No. No, they didn't, she had learned. Hers were not natural feelings. People thought she was weird. Looney bin weird. Quasi-erotic? Best not to say things like that. Ever. Just bottle it up and move on.

Rafael sensed that he'd hit on something personal. Even so, he did not retract his question. For whatever reason, he wanted an answer. *Fine. Give him the watered-down version.*

"Language is everything to me," said Valory. "I see it as humankind's most vital and most beautiful invention. Without it, we'd have never evolved beyond simple societies, let alone built great and complex economies. Civilizations could not have recorded their collective wisdom, nor have educated their citizens, nor have kept an accurate historical record. We'd have no Plato, no Dickinson, no Shakespeare. No way for our brightest scientific minds to build upon the achievements of their predecessors. No one ever thinks about that," she said. "The modern age just takes it for granted, but the truth is that today's world would be unrecognizable without complex language and the written word."

Rafael nodded, pleased. "I knew I chose the right woman. *Saluti*, Doctor Grace."

He opened the briefcase, producing some thin cotton gloves. He gave a pair to Valory before putting on his own. Then he removed a protective foam layer and spun the case around so Valory could see. Lying there, snug in another layer of fitted foam, was a fragment of dried clay riddled with timeworn markings. At first, Valory assumed it was a cuneiform tablet like others she had examined from ancient Sumeria. Like those Sumerian tablets, this one had been made by forming marks in wet clay and then letting it bake dry in the sun. Such tablets were several thousand years old and contained the first true writing system in human history. One look at these markings, however, revealed they were not Sumerian. Nor were they proto-writing symbols from any civilization with which she was familiar. The markings on this fragment were unrecognizable to her. *That* was shocking. She'd studied every letter, symbol, glyph, and pictogram in antiquity and could identify them in an instant. But not these. The characters before her were beautiful and new, rudimentary yet artistic, like a clay-bound predecessor of calligraphy.

"First reactions, Doctor Grace?"

"It's an unknown language isolate . . ." She heard the breathlessness of her own words as she painted the relic with her eyes.

"Brilliant!" said Rafael, clapping his meaty palms. "My little team spent months of comparative study determining that, and here you've done it in mere seconds. *Assolutamente brilliante, Dottoressa. Si*, it is an isolate as you say. Whatever this language is, it bears no genealogical relationship to any other known language."

Valory steadied herself, unsure if she could believe what she was seeing. "Where was this found?"

"I'm afraid I can't discuss that. But I will say this. By our estimates," said Doctor Moretti, pausing for impact, "this writing predates even Sumerian. We put the date at approximately 8000 BCE."

"You're saying this is ten thousand years old? But that would mean . . ."

"Yes. It means we must revise history. For this written language holds the new title for the earliest in all of humankind. And you, Doctor Valory Grace, are one of the first in the modern world to lay eyes upon it."

Had Valory been standing, she'd have swooned. She looked at Moretti, who nodded, granting permission. Trembling, she placed a fingertip on the dried clay, dragging it slowly along the archaic impressions. Through the thin glove, her skin dipped into the grooves, lingering for a moment on each character. In her career, every extinct language she'd studied had been unearthed long before her arrival. But here, beneath her quivering touch, was a true and shining mystery. Not just for her, but for the entire human race. Now Valory had a chance to start from ground zero. The buzz in her brain was almost audible. Could this be a hoax perpetrated by some skillful counterfeiter? No. No way. The fragment was authentic. She could *feel* it. As she caressed the ancient characters, they seemed to lift out of the dried clay, slipping into her skin, crawling into her fingers, tingling up her arm, into her blood. They beckoned her. They whispered. In the silence, she could almost hear their words. *Let us have a lusty dance, sweet Valory. Bring us deep into your soul. Revel in the taste of our secrets . . .*

She snatched her hand from the tablet.

"Are you alright, Valory?" asked Rafael, reaching out to her. "You look flush."

"Yes," she said, suppressing embarrassment. "I'm fine, thank you. This is just a bit of a shock, that's all." She tried to smile at him, but she couldn't take her eyes off the fragment.

10

"You have many questions."

"I do. The first being why would you bring this here?" She heard the reproachful tone of her voice, walking it back. "I mean, I'm honored that you did, but this is a priceless and fragile relic. It could be damaged, it could be stolen. Lost forever. Does your Ministry know you're traveling with this piece?"

Rafael chuckled. "You're right to chide me, of course. I promise I would never do such a thing under normal circumstances, but this situation is far from normal, as I hope you will soon discover."

"I'm all ears, Doctor."

"Yes, well, unfortunately, there is much that I cannot say, not at this stage. What I can tell you is this." He rested his fingers on the edge of the briefcase. "What you see here is just a morsel. There is more."

"More?"

"*Sí.*"

"More like this? Inscribed with this language?"

"*Sí*, and many other things."

"Such as?"

"Valory," said Rafael, enjoying her enthusiasm, "it pains me that I can't answer that right now. My government demands complete discretion, you understand. But if you agree to the job, all will be made clear. Once your security clearance has been approved, that is."

"So you *are* offering me a job, then."

"Indeed, and it is this. I would like you to lead the study of these historical relics," he said, tapping on the briefcase. "I believe you are uniquely capable of deciphering and documenting what we've discovered. In fact, you are one of the few people on Earth who qualifies for this project."

Valory peered at the fragment, an eager lump in her throat. "That's why you brought it here. You knew if I saw it—if I touched it with my own hands—I wouldn't be able to refuse."

Rafael smiled like a boy caught stealing from the cookie jar. "So you will accept?"

Deep within her, a voice was crying *Yes! A thousand times yes!* But she forced a practical response. "When would I start this job?"

Rafael tugged at his tie. "We must leave tomorrow, I'm afraid."

"Tomorrow. You're kidding."

"I wish I was. Unfortunately, I am on a very strict schedule here. Again, I can't—"

"Can't go into details, right. Could you at least say where I'd be going?"

"To the site."

"The site where you found this tablet?"

He nodded.

"An active excavation?"

"Eh, yes. In a sense."

"Uh-huh. And I assume the site is in Italy since the Italian Ministry of Heritage is in my home."

"I'm so sorry Valory, but I'm unable to reveal that information until you pass clearance. If you decline this job, you cannot know where the site is. For that matter, whether you accept or not, I must ask you not to tell anyone about this meeting, or what I have shown you today."

"Right. Super-secret Italian stuff." Valory exhaled, coaxing herself away from the rush that was coursing through her. When she was sure her legs would hold, she walked to the dinette table and thumbed through the Oxford folders. "Doctor Moretti—Rafael—I admit I'm sufficiently tantalized, but I can't just up and leave the university tomorrow for some mysterious job in God knows where. We're three months into our grant, I can't bail on my colleagues."

"Yes, your work at the Centre is of course very important." Rafael grunted, rising from the couch. "But, at the risk of sounding melodramatic, this is a once-in-a-lifetime opportunity. There is no doubt you will forever regret it if you decline. For I humbly swear," he said, raising his right hand, "the site in question is a treasure unlike any I have ever seen. And that is saying something considering my experience."

"Yes, I'm sure." She turned from her folders, thinking. Past projects had taught her that so-called dream offers such as this were often riddled with gotchas, and that she had better clearly define her conditions. "When you say you want me to lead the project, you mean I'll have a team?"

"A small one, yes."

"So the course of study will be at my discretion, right? No hidden overseers?"

"That is correct. This project will be all yours." He watched her ponder this as she looked at the fragment. Smiling, he said, "To tempt you a bit more, let me just say that the site is in pristine condition. Never looted. It is rich with well-preserved texts the quality of which academics like us can only dream. The artifacts we are discovering there have the potential to change the world. You can be a part of that, Valory."

She held his gaze for a moment, letting his words resonate. There, on the coffee table nestled in the briefcase, the oldest written language in existence begged to be explored. She laid her fingertips upon it, resting them on those words that someone, somewhere, had pressed into clay ten thousand years ago.

Let us have a lusty dance, sweet Valory.

CAPITOLO 2

SHE WHIPPED HER DARK chocolate hair into a ponytail, checking the full-length mirror one last time. The woman looking back was more GI Jane than traveling academic. Black button-down utility shirt, North Face hiking pants, broken-in trail boots. It was the same outfit she'd worn for previous fieldwork. Thanks to Rafael's caginess, she was unsure whether to dress for a dig or a desk, so she opted for the former. Now if she could only salvage her face: hermit-pale skin, eyebrows in need of a good plucking, a lone roaring blemish on her cheek. Coupled with her pronounced cheekbones and delicate chin, she looked more vampire than human. Her eyes aided that impression. A plush shade of hazel, they were her best feature, but after an anxious night, the bags they carried seemed packed for a round-the-world trip. She could almost hear her sister, Violet, berating her. *Jesus, Val, it's called concealer, hello? You know you could be pretty, right? If you tried?*

"Well, Vi," muttered Valory, smoothing her shirt, "we can't all be beauty queens like you. This is what the world gets today."

Rafael was in the living room waiting. He'd arrived at 6:00 A.M., a full hour earlier than the agreed-upon time. Being familiar with the relaxed attitudes of Italians, Valory had been expecting his arrival an hour late, not an hour early. Miffed, she scurried to get ready while he gently pressured her by calling out things like, "Hopefully we can make it to the site by the afternoon."

In the car park awaited the same Mercedes and the same man Valory had spotted yesterday. The man burned the last of his cigarette and flicked the butt to the pavement. He was tall and thin, mid-thirties, with a gel-swooped mane of dark hair. Rather handsome in his black suit. Too bad he smelled like a smokestack.

"Valory, this is my associate, Mr. Trentino. He'll be driving us to the airport."

"Hello," said Valory. Trentino shook her hand but said nothing. He only nodded, his dark eyes not so much acknowledging her, but scanning her. Sizing her up, as if determining whether she might cause trouble at some point. He dismissed her an instant later, concluding she was harmless, even uninteresting. *Great to meet you, too*, she thought.

13

Trentino leaned against the car, pulling a pack of Camels from his inner coat pocket. *"Il tuo telefono, per favore."* He wanted her cell phone.

"Uh, perché?"

He lit a cig and took a drag, squinting at her over the glowing tip of the filter. *"Per favore,"* he repeated, the words wreathed in smoke.

Valory turned to Rafael, who was loading her luggage in the boot. "Rafael, why does he want my mobile?"

Rafael closed the boot, straightening his fedora. "You must forgive Mr. Trentino's lack of etiquette. He is here for our security. Just a precaution to protect us and our precious cargo," he said, nodding toward the briefcase in the back seat. "Consider him a bodyguard."

"Okay. Why does the bodyguard want my mobile?"

"He wants to disable your GPS and location sharing, as he has done with mine. So that no one can track us to the site. Is this alright, Valory?"

Seemed like paranoia to her. Nevertheless, she unlocked her phone and handed it to Trentino. He began swiping through the interface, cigarette hanging from his lips.

"Who would be watching us?" asked Valory, looking around the car park. In the eastern breezeway, Mrs. Battersby was out for her morning stroll, scooting along behind a walker. "Graverobbers? Activists? Are we in danger?"

"No no, of course not," said Rafael, waving off the mere suggestion. "You are in no danger, Valory, I assure you. It is just that if word about the site gets out, then our job," he said motioning back and forth between them, "could become, well, impossible."

"Impossible."

"Si. Again, I cannot say more until you gain clearance, but you will understand soon. I promise."

Trentino returned her phone, then walked around and took the driver's seat.

"Shall we?" said Rafael, opening her door.

On the way to the airport, Valory mustered the nerve to do what she'd been dreading all night—ring her director at Oxford, Professor Chloe Meadows, to inform her that she was taking an impromptu sabbatical effective immediately. Meadows was flummoxed. Not only had she been blindsided by the news before she'd even put cream in her morning coffee, but Doctor Grace declined to give her a satisfactory reason for this bat-out-of-hell departure. At Rafael's insistence, Valory was not allowed to explain why she had to leave, where she was going, or when she'd be back. As a result, the call was rife with one-word answers and awkward silences. When it became clear that Professor Meadows had no choice but to 'deal with it,' she wished Valory a chilly farewell, saying, "Let's hope your position is still here when you return."

14

They boarded an eight-passenger plane called *The Falcon*. Only then was their destination revealed—Verona, Italy. That made little sense to Valory. Verona's historical secrets had been plumbed long ago. Surely it could not have suddenly produced the pristine archeological site of which Rafael spoke. The characters on the clay tablet came nowhere near to matching up with that region's attested proto-literate languages. So why Verona?

The mystery would have to wait. For now, Valory was just happy to discover they'd be flying private. She'd only flown private twice in her career, but those two flights had ruined her for commercial. Being stuffed into a long metal tube with coughing, gum-flapping hoards is the stuff of an introvert's nightmares. But she didn't have time to admire the wood grain table pullouts or the swiveling leather bucket seats, because the minute they were settled, Rafael assigned her a dreary task. Paperwork. Loads and loads of paperwork. Background checks, security clearances, work visa applications, non-disclosure agreements, the list went on. All loose papers, nothing digitized. Everything had to be completed by the time they landed so they could be delivered to a ground agent who would transmit the forms for expedited processing. A team of bureaucrats was on standby, ready to reduce a months-long approval marathon to a matter of hours. For that reason, Rafael insisted that there could be zero—*zero*—mistakes in the paperwork. Any minuscule error might slow down the approval, and they had no time to waste. No pressure.

Once Rafael had stated as much, however, he relaxed. He sat opposite Valory, sipping on wine and ever loosening his tie. While she plodded through the forms, he chatted in Italian, rambling about his wife, his kids, and his dogs while looking out the window and chuckling at his own jokes. When Valory asked for silence so she could concentrate, he apologized, went quiet for five minutes, and then started back up again. Trentino was in the adjacent seat losing his cool as the flight wore on. Two hours in, he was tugging at his tie, tapping his foot, and clicking his tongue. Nicotine fits, Valory suspected. He was already falling apart, and they still had another two hours in the air.

Valory stifled the urge to snap at the men, trying to focus on the forms. But even those annoyed her thanks to the grammatical errors. The errors weren't surprising in and of themselves—grammatical slips existed in every written work, everywhere in the world, in all languages—but the authors of these forms were in sore need of an Italian 101 refresher. Valory wasn't allowed to make a single mistake, yet whoever wrote these forms was screwing up the conjugation of pronominal verbs like they were on drugs or something. Between the whirlwind exodus out of England, the annoying men, and the mistake-riddled forms, Valory was quietly fraying at the seams. She revolted in the only way she could, by striking through the errors and

15

writing corrections in the margins. Rafael did say there could be zero mistakes in the paperwork, did he not?

One of the forms caused her to pause and reflect. It was an extended background check, requiring details about all her closest colleagues, friends, and family members. She finished the friend section in a jiff. Not much to speak of there. Then she listed her parents, Randy and Victoria Grace, the odd couple who shouldn't have lasted but somehow did. Dad was a free-spirited artist of varying success who forever encouraged his family to take chances, tune into the spiritual marrow of the universe, and to unshackle themselves from the chains of preconception. Mom was a button-down professor of neurology at Stanford University whose incisive intellect was a natural BS-crusher. As she filled in the pertinent details, Valory found herself wandering into a childhood memory of her parents. She was at the dinner table, listening to them talk about the human brain. Dad was in a paint-smattered shirt, championing the brain as the most powerful work of art in the universe, shaped and sculpted by a passionate, unseen Creator. He used his fork like a sculptor's chisel to emphasize his point. On the other side of the table was Mom in her cardinal red Stanford sweater, smiling as she called the brain an imperfect mass of wrinkled gray lumps, molded over eons by unfeeling Evolution. Their debate was spirited but lighthearted, with a loving respect for one another's viewpoints. That discussion was a perfect microcosm of their relationship. Despite being opposites, they had persevered. They still lived in Sunnyvale, California in the same home in which they'd raised Valory and Violet.

Ah, Violet. She was another story. Valory's non-identical twin, Violet was smart, beautiful, and outgoing. A teenage popularity queen growing up. But she was also flighty and thrill-seeking, often snubbing her intellectual gifts as she strayed into the fast lane. While adolescent Val buried her face in books, Vi was sneaking out her bedroom window, lured by the siren song of the Californian underground. She drank. She did drugs. She had sex. She spent nights in jail. Occasionally, she would disappear for days, panicking the family. Then she'd return home sickly, burned out and terrified of whatever brink she had teetered upon. Mom and Dad did everything they could to set her straight: rehab, therapy, private school, the whole nine yards. With her family's untiring love and support, Violet would begin to thrive again. Her health would return, her grades would improve, and her soul would quiet down. Everything would be normal. Until one day, boom. She'd vanish into a fresh downward spiral. That was the pattern.

It was tough for Valory to think about Vi. To call their relationship tempestuous would be putting it mildly. Best friends one minute rivals the next. Replay *ad infinitum*. She didn't like to dwell on it. Too many bitter memories there. In the part of the form that asked for Violet's current address, she wrote *non lo so*—I don't know—and she didn't. The last time they'd spoken was after Violet graduated. She'd managed to stumble her way through college, somehow overcoming her self-defeating vices long enough to earn a bachelor's in genetics. Valory attended a small party in her honor, and for much of that time, the twins were happy in each other's company. Then Valory asked the wrong question. "So why genetics, Vi?"

"Why not genetics?" Violet shot back. "What, you think I'm not smart enough to understand molecular biology?"

"No, that's not what I'm saying at all." Valory looked around the party, embarrassed to see a few people watching. She lowered her voice. "I only meant that all those years growing up, you never talked about genetics, or anything academic, really. You weren't exactly an aspiring scientist."

"Here we go," Violet said, swigging the remainder of her cocktail. "Crazy runaway Violet can never be as smart as the high and mighty Valory Grace, kid genius."

"No, I didn't—"

"Yeah yeah yeah, you didn't mean it like that. You, Mom, Dad, Aunt Linda, none of you ever mean it like that. But every time you look at me, it's in your eyes. 'What'd our pretty little fuckup do this time?' You think I don't see it? Well, I do. I see it, Val, I've seen it my whole life." She snatched a fresh drink from the bar, downing half of it before speaking again. "None of you know how tough I've had it. What it's like to be me. You were Mom and Dad's perfect little prize, and I was a liability."

"That's not tr—"

"Well guess what, sis? I earned this degree all by my crazy little self. My money, my hard work, my brainpower. I proved you all wrong, so suck on that."

With that, Violet stormed out of her own party. That was five years ago. Since then, she'd been off doing her own thing. No one knew for sure where she'd gone. There were rumors she'd begun working for a genetics lab in Prague. Who knows. The only certainty was that she was done with the Grace family, and that was fine. Heartbreaking, but fine.

They landed at a small military base outside of Verona. When they alighted, Rafael was met by two suits at the foot of the stairway. He handed Valory's paperwork over to one of the men, who hastened into the terminal. The other man introduced himself as Marco Savelli, saying he'd come to relieve Trentino. The two could have been brothers. Same dark suit, same sunglasses, same swagger of a dutiful bodyguard. Savelli, however, was more rugged, sporting a no-nonsense buzz cut and a tight-lipped scowl, his cheeks marked by pits and creases. And unlike Trentino, Savelli was armed. Valory could see the pistol in a vest holster under his blazer. The sight of the firearm unnerved her. Not something an historical linguist sees on a typical workday. Even more unsettling, Savelli seemed to be a little too focused on her. She thought he was looking at her—*studying* her—with a sort of restrained resentment. With the dark glasses, it was hard to know for sure. Maybe she was just imagining it, her distaste for guns seeding her with paranoia. Savelli turned to share a few brisk words with Rafael. Trentino pulled a Zippo from his pocket and lit a cigarette the moment his foot hit the stairway, burning through it in seconds and flipping another from the pack. He left without so much as a nod.

They walked to a nearby helipad, where they were to board a helicopter for the final leg of the journey. As they approached, the pilot stopped them and delivered bad news; the winds were too high near the site, making it too risky to fly there. They'd have to take ground transport or otherwise wait until tomorrow morning to try again. An argument exploded between Savelli and the pilot, with lots of barking and inflated hand gestures. Then the argument died as quickly as it had erupted, and the men shook hands as if nothing had happened.

They pivoted to the car park, where they boarded their ground transport—an army-green four-wheel drive tactical jeep the size of a small tank. The driver, a *marshal* named Buccini, loaded their luggage in the cargo area before taking the wheel. Savelli took the passenger seat while Valory and Rafael clambered into the back. Valory felt like she was climbing to the top of a jungle gym, taking a massive step up to the running board, then grabbing the interior handles and pulling herself into her seat. Doctor Moretti wasn't as nimble. He tried twice to heave himself into the cab, only to sink back down to the pavement. On his third attempt, cheeks bulging red, he managed to shimmy his way in, belly-flopping onto his seat before righting himself. Panting, he closed his door and motioned for the driver to go. The engine roared to life, and they lurched forward, finally en route to the mystery site.

"Are you okay, Rafael?" Valory had to raise her voice over the noise of the engine and the drone of the tires.

"*Si, grazie.* Only my pride is wounded." He dabbed his forehead with a hanky. "*Oddio.* Believe it or not, Valory, there was a time when I was handsome and fit. *Un uomo forte.* A million years ago, maybe, but it's true, and I have pictures to prove it." Chuckling, he fanned himself with his blazer flaps. "You were smart to wear your field clothes. This suit is smothering me. I think it has shrunk, no?"

Valory smiled, waiting. Surely he would fill her in now. In the last thirty hours, she'd left her job at Oxford and had flown to Italy with barely a scrap of information to go on. The reams of paperwork had been completed, and now they were in an off-road beast heading to this supposed golden egg of a site. She hadn't even been told where she'd be staying. So yeah, it was time for Rafael to drop the cloak and dagger stuff. Where were they going and for what was she risking her career? What was this site shrouded in so much secrecy? But Rafael was in no rush to brief her. He sat cleaning his glasses, starting over when the jeep hit a bump and he dropped them.

The meaty tires rolling on the tarmac filled the cab with a dull roar as they sped north out of Verona. The interior smelled like a leaky fuel canister in a military surplus store. Through the window, the eastern outskirts of the city receded into the distance.

Valory had always wanted to visit Verona. The picturesque town was not only bursting with medieval charm and history, but it was also the setting for two of Shakespeare's plays: *The Two Gentlemen of Verona* and *Romeo and Juliet*. Valory had heard that Juliet's house still stood in the city and that one could visit the very balcony where she had been wooed by Romeo. There, lurking in the orchard beneath the balcony, Romeo had looked upon Juliet and uttered his famous line: *But soft! What light through yonder window breaks?* That scene was, perhaps, the most romantic in all of literature, and one of the few that had rendered her doe-eyed as a young girl. In truth, Valory understood the balcony in Verona was only a contrived tourist attraction, and that the star-crossed lovers never actually existed. Still, she wanted to see it. Call it silly, but she wanted to stand on that balcony and imagine having her own Romeo look up at her on a moon-drenched night, marveling upon her beauty, renouncing his family just to be with her. Not very scholarly of her, perhaps, but even scholars were allowed flights of fancy.

When the spires of Verona had faded to dots, Valory decided she could not extend her courtesy any further. "Rafael," she half-yelled over the noise of the ride, "maybe it's time you clued me in?"

Rafael had been looking at his smartphone. "Sorry?" he said.

"*Ho fatto tutto ciò che mi è stato chiesto.*" She'd done everything he asked. "*E ancora non so nulla di dove stiamo andando.*" And she still knew nothing about where they were going. Her switch to Italian was not deliberate, but rather a byproduct of exasperation. There were times she didn't know what language was going to pop out of her mouth until she started speaking. "Aren't I owed a little disclosure?" she continued in English. "Or am I to be blindfolded until the last possible second?"

Before answering, Rafael looked toward the front seat at Savelli. Savelli turned, eyes hidden behind dark sunglasses, and brandished a satellite phone at them.

"I am sorry, Valory," said Rafael. "But we must wait for your clearances to process. Until we get the call on that satellite phone, I am not permitted to brief you."

That's when it dawned on her. Savelli was not just a bodyguard. Just then, Rafael had looked to him for permission. Which meant Savelli was some sort of authority. Same for Trentino. Neither Savelli nor Trentino had presented credentials or offered any extraneous information. So that meant

19

what? Who were they? Secret agents or something? Why would men like that be mixed up in an archeological dig? For that matter, why was the Italian military involved?

What the hell had she gotten herself into?

KAPITEL 3

THEY DROVE FOR HOURS, winding their way north into the region of the Italian Alps known as the Dolomites. The scenery was breathtaking, a backdrop of sky-kissing crags merging with rolling green foothills and glittering lakes. Valory rolled her window down, relishing the crisp, unspoiled air and the lack of traffic. The urge to hop out of the jeep was strong. To settle into a lakeside cabin where she could live in solitude, studying, fishing and hiking in her own tract of paradise. Wordsworth eat your heart out.

They gained elevation rapidly as they drove deeper into the mountains. The street signs and kilometer markers disappeared, and the road became unpaved and rough. After navigating a rocky bend, the driver inched uphill, watching for something. He soon spotted a narrow turnoff, camouflaged by foliage and an overhang of rock. He turned there, onto a semblance of a path. Minutes later, the jeep was dwarfed on both sides by snow-packed canyon walls. Blanketed in shadow, they ascended a steep grade, so steep in parts that Valory wondered if the jeep might tip backward. They plowed forward carefully, bouncing and whipping side to side as the tires hit rocks and dipped into crevices, forcing the passengers to hang on for dear life. This was no road in any real sense of the word. It felt like being in one of those commercials where a heavy-duty truck gobbles up terrain on which no sane person would drive.

Valory grew frustrated. She was being battered like a bean in a maraca, and no one was telling her anything. The satellite phone still hadn't rung. Not knowing where they were going was driving her crazy. Just what could be up here? There were very few ancient civilizations that had built their societies on the mountaintops. The people of the Tibetan plateau. The Incas of Machu Picchu in the Peruvian highlands. Some various mountain tribes of lesser renown. Yet here she was being shuttled into the Dolomites at a current elevation of eight thousand feet and gaining. There was no way that humankind's first written language had originated from these barren heights. Could it have? What sort of pristine, world-altering site could be atop these rugged crags? The entire thing was becoming harder to swallow by the minute.

Marshal Buccini stopped the jeep for one blessed moment to blare the horn at a herd of mountain goats hopping along the rocks. An alpha goat with impressive, curved horns stood in the path dead-eyeing the jeep while the others crossed, then he, too, scurried off.

After another half hour, the southern canyon wall dropped off, and the late afternoon sun greeted them again. A gorgeous view of the valley yawned below. Valory strained to see, but her view was quickly obscured by a wall of pines. Following a few more miles of rough climbing, the jeep lurched to a stop. There was a fallen pine lying across the rock bed, making it impassable. The tree had to be cleared before they could continue. It was too heavy for Savelli and *Marshal* Buccini to move with pure manpower, so they had to use a winch to maneuver it from the path with the jeep. Valory stood off to the side with Rafael on the high slope, shivering in the gusty mountain breeze.

As Savelli called out instructions to Buccini, Valory drew a long breath, noting how much thinner the air was here. She checked her cell phone. No reception. Just a red X and a rapidly draining battery. Sighing, she powered it down. "Rafael, any chance you'll tell me what's going on now?"

"I would love to, Valory, but my government—"

"Was supposed to have called by now. That's what you said. I filled out all the paperwork, and I was supposed to have been cleared already." Valory felt her face going hot, even in the cool wind. She didn't like pressing people, didn't like forcing the issue, but she had a nagging sense of being played for a fool. In the last few hours, this shiny diamond of an adventure had lost its luster, leaving an imitation gemstone in its place. "Look at this," she said, jutting her hands at the jagged alpine expanse. "Am I to believe there is an ancient archeological site ten thousand feet up in the Italian Alps? It just sounds absurd. And why is the military involved in this? Who is Marco Savelli? And Trentino? Can't you tell me something? Please?"

Rafael sighed, bobbing his head in agreement. "You are right, Doctor Grace. Though I was given strict orders, it is quite unreasonable to keep you in the dark. I will tell you what I can now and fill in the gaps later after you're cleared. Should be soon. I don't know what's taking so long," he said, watching Savelli readjust the winch on the base of the deadfall.

"Agh!" Savelli doubled over, clutching his hand to his chest. He'd gotten it caught in the winch when Buccini took the slack out of the cable. He flung a string of curses at the young *marshal*.

Rafael led Valory a bit farther down the road, out of earshot. "Let me see, where to begin?"

"How about telling me about the site."

"Yes. Well, it is a secluded structure, strategically hidden within a cauldron of these very peaks." Rafael checked his watch. "We are not far now. Once we get going again, we'll be there in an hour or so. Hopefully before dark."

"What kind of structure? What civilization lived there?"

"Well, we have some thoughts, but my team is very small. Without expertise of your caliber, we can't quite quantify what we've found."

"Okay, so what is it? A villa? Cliff dwellings? Caves?"

Rafael measured his response. "I'd better not talk about that until you're cleared. How about I tell you why the military is involved."

"Okay."

"The truth is, Valory, my government feels that ownership of the site could be called into question. What I mean is that even though the site is located on Italian soil, it wasn't always so. We believe that certain other parties—if they knew of the site's existence—could produce proof of provenance."

"You mean another government could claim control of the site."

"Precisely. So you see, we mustn't leak the slightest detail. If these other parties discover what we have found, well, I don't think I need to tell you what could happen, Doctor Grace."

No, he didn't need to tell her. It was beginning to make sense now. Valory had seen governments contest archeological finds before. Their battles to gain dominion of ancient sites or artifacts could bring large-scale excavations to a grinding halt while the matter was debated in international courts, sometimes for years. Fame, tourism, and riches were the spoils of ownership. While chest-puffing politicians disputed the tiniest claims, archeologists and historians were forced to sit on their hands, allowing time for thieves to rob the site of precious treasures. So yes, it was all clear to Valory now. The secrecy, the cloak and dagger stuff . . .

"And even the rushed time frame," she said, finishing her thought aloud. "You need me here immediately because once winter comes in the mountains, the site will be covered in snow. It will be inaccessible."

Rafael tapped his nose.

Valory zipped up her coat as the breeze nipped at her. "Which countries would have a possible claim?"

"The region in question has, historically, changed hands many times. Before the Kingdom of Italy's ownership, it belonged to Archduchy of Austria. Prior to that, to the Kingdom of Bavaria, which is of course modern-day Germany. In earlier centuries, it has belonged to a great many entities. The Frankish Empire, the Holy Roman Empire, the latter of which fractured into a multitude of nations. You start to see the point, eh? Luckily for us, the site is so remote and unreachable that we doubt it has ever carried strategic importance to anyone. We think it has gone unnoticed for centuries, and we'd like to keep it that way. At least for now."

"And yet someone lived there, unknown to the rest of the world."

"Indeed. It will make more sense when you see for yourself." Rafael looked over his shoulder, ensuring Savelli was still out of earshot. "Best if I don't say any more about it. For now."

"Well, who is Savelli? Can you tell me that?"

"*Agenzia Informazioni e Sicurezza Interna*. In English, we just say homeland security. *Agente* Savelli is the principal agent in charge of the site. He and Lorenzo Trentino, among others, have been assigned to monitor our operations at all times. You know," chuckled Rafael, "because we academics can't be trusted."

"Right," nodded Valory, "I understand. I wish you could have explained this before. I wouldn't have freaked out on you."

"Yes, but I was ordered to say nothing until you were cleared. I'm sorry, Valory."

She blew into her hands. "Can you tell me what else you've discovered there? Besides the tablet?"

Before Rafael could answer, the jeep's engine roared as it dragged the deadfall to the side of the rock bed. "*Bravo!*" yelled Savelli, clapping as the trunk was cleared.

"Looks like it's time to go," said Rafael. "Allow me to beg for your continued patience, Valory. Soon you will have clearance and we will reach the site. Then you will come to know much more than you bargained for."

***

The call finally came. *Agente Principale* Savelli answered the satellite phone, exchanged some words with the caller, and then hung up. He turned and told them Valory's clearance had been approved. Rafael, however, explained that they were just moments away, so rather than spoiling the surprise with more debriefing, he implored Valory to wait a few more minutes so she could relish the full impact of laying eyes on the site for the first time. "Is it so much more satisfying that way," he said.

The road that wasn't a road leveled out somewhat before spilling into a rugged plateau. To the north, a bend of fractured rock needles jutted skyward like the fangs of a dragon, their tips glowing orange with the onset of dusk. To the south, the plateau fell off into a valley surrounded by ashen peaks. Here, the crew was stopped by a blockade. Two jeeps identical to theirs were parked hood to hood across the path. Just beyond those stood a compact military encampment. A handful of uniformed soldiers milled about among the canvas tents and storage containers. Two of them approached, peering into the window at the newcomers. After some credential flashing and a few brusque pleasantries, one of the soldiers held up a basket. "*Telefoni, per favore.*" Valory was not thrilled about turning over her cell phone, but Rafael had warned her earlier that this was coming, and it was not up for negotiation. Part of securing the site meant no cameras or recording devices of any kind other than those controlled by the *Agenzia*. Once Valory and Rafael had turned over their phones, the soldiers backed the jeeps out of the road, and the crew continued.

Beyond the encampment, near the edge of the plateau, a squatty cluster of crumbling stone remains came into view. They appeared to have once been small houses. Mostly just piles of hewn stone now, but a few of the structures were still somewhat intact. Here a partial chimney still stood, there a cross timber had not fully rotted. She could make out a defunct chicken coop as well as a few leaning posts and rusted wire mesh that had probably been the perimeter of a livestock pen. At first glance, there was nothing remarkable there. Just the unspectacular ruins of a tiny village. Was this the so-called golden egg of a site?

"Rafael," said Valory as the jeep rounded the bend, bypassing the remains, "are we not stopping? That village . . . " but she trailed off, for when she looked back at Rafael, he was smiling at her, waiting for her reaction. Then she saw it. The jeep had just cleared the last needle, and they were now driving into a sloped cauldron ringed by a crown of snow-capped pinnacles. There it was, nestled within the crags. Her jaw went slack . . .

A castle. An enormous, majestic, impossible castle. Not built with individual stones, but rather carved right from the rock as if the hand of God had chiseled away the mountain summit until only the castle remained. Camouflaged by the surrounding spires, it loomed under the amber skies, lording over a glacial lake in the valley far below.

CHAPITRE 4

CERVANTES HAD BEEN STANDING by the hotel room door for a half hour—in the dark, dead still, waiting—when he finally heard a key card slide into the digital lock. The lock disengaged with an audible click. Schulz was right on time. And by the way he opened the door, it was obvious he suspected nothing. There was no caution in his entry, no wariness. No one ever guessed that an intruder might be lurking in their hotel room, especially at a swanky place like the Waldorf. But Cervantes had half-hoped Lukas Schulz would be smarter. Like himself, Schulz was former special ops. *Kommando Spezialkräfte*, Germany's equivalent of a US Navy Seal. Such men were highly trained in situational awareness, and with the way this situation had gone down, Schulz's senses should have been tingling. But no, he was a stag beetle bumbling into a spiderweb. There'd be no struggle then. That was good, but also a bit of a shame. Under different circumstances, Cervantes would relish the opportunity to face off against a fellow elite like Schulz. To beat him down. To break him, slowly. To watch the realization dawn in his battered eyes that he was being toyed with by a superior fighter. A moment like that—that snapshot in time where a man first begins to acknowledge he is about to die—those are the moments for which Cervantes lusted. This, however, could not be one of those moments. The job had to be flawless. There could be no signs of struggle in the room and no marks on Schulz when the *Polizei* found his corpse. Men who commit suicide generally don't get their asses whipped beforehand. Schulz had to go down quickly and quietly. No sedatives either, lest the tox report come back dirty. That left Cervantes with his least satisfying weapon—the stun gun.

Schulz closed the door behind him and reached for the light switch. Just before he touched it, Cervantes planted a lightning storm into his kidney, the darkness crackling with white light. Schulz dropped like a telephone pole.

***

Many people would say it was a beautiful night in Berlin. April 23rd, 2024, the night of the Pink Moon. Astronomers and hippies were making a big deal out of it, but it wasn't pink to Cervantes. He struggled to remember what pink looked like. He'd gone completely colorblind in his late teens, and he now saw the world only in shades of blacks, whites, and grays. To him, the moon was bright, round, and white—just your run-of-the-mill rock in the sky. People loved to obsess over trivial stuff like that, assigning meaning to every humdrum event, every random occurrence. Anything to take their minds off the surefire fact they were going to die one day.

He peered through the scope of the Mauser bolt action rifle. It was aimed at a penthouse seven hundred thirty-seven yards from his position. The mark would be coming out onto the balcony after 20:00 hours, as was his custom. He'd sit in that garden chair on the right. The line of sight was clear. The only problem was, according to the last entry in Schulz's log, the scope was zeroed for one thousand yards. To dial it in for this range would require a round of test shots, which would draw attention. That meant Cervantes was just going to have to *feel* this one. At least the night was mild. No crosswinds. At this distance, the Coriolis effect was negligible. Two shots would probably be enough, but he figured he could squeeze off three if needed before the mark even realized what was going on. The mark wasn't military. He wouldn't know why a flowerpot next to his head exploded while he sipped on his brandy. He was just some environmental attorney who had become a big problem. Jonas Krause was his name. A well-known and popular man in Berlin, someone to whom people listened. He was trying to force the relocation of the Salvador's manufacturing plant that was supposed to have broken ground outside of Berlin months ago. The fiery, charismatic Krause was using the courts as a weapon, rousing public support for his cause, and denouncing the overreaching American 'imperialist' who sought to taint German soil with his new gigafactory. Or something like that. Cervantes didn't care. All that mattered was that the Salvador wanted Krause dead, and it had to look like someone else killed him.

That's where Schulz fit in.

Cervantes looked at Schulz in the corner. Gagged and bagged on his knees, hands cuffed to his ankles behind his back. Mouthing desperate, muffled words to Cervantes through the gag. Trying to beg. He didn't understand what was going on nor why he was in this position. He didn't know a damn thing. He was an innocent victim in all this. An unwitting pawn on the Salvador's chessboard.

Months ago, while the Salvador's people were digging up dirt on Jonas Krause, they discovered Krause was having an affair with Schulz's wife, Heidi. Krause's own wife had recently given birth and had been 'closed for business' during the last several months of her pregnancy. That didn't work for Krause. He was not only a high-powered lawyer, but a high-powered horndog. One who couldn't bear to stay chaste for more than a few weeks. He set his sights on Heidi Schulz, a paralegal working in his firm. It was a convenient arrangement, and things heated up quickly. As the affair carried on, Lukas Schulz noticed something about his wife was off. He recognized the changes in Heidi's demeanor, saw the little signs that suggested something was up. Suspecting an affair, he hired a PI. The PI confirmed his suspicions, delivering the damning evidence only a few days later. Schulz confronted Heidi, and it blew up from there. Lots of fighting, crying, and bottle-smashing. Lots of storming out on each other. All the agonizing consequences one should expect from the foolish enterprise called love.

While Schulz's marriage circled the drain, the Salvador saw an opportunity. His spooks checked into Schulz further. Found out he was ex-military. Discovered he had several firearms registered in his name. One of those was a Mauser bolt action rifle, the perfect weapon for, say, sniping an arrogant attorney who'd been banging his wife. But Schulz was law-abiding. As devastated as he was, he wasn't going to do the deed on his own.

Enter Cervantes.

It was a silver platter set-up. The hardest thing about it was the brain-numbing flight from Los Angeles to Berlin. Once he was there, it had been a cinch to establish Krause's routine. Mr. Important lived in the penthouse of the poshest hi-rise in Berlin, and he spent every Wednesday and Friday evening sitting on his balcony with his wife, sipping brandy and making eye-love to his laptop. The Waldorf Astoria Berlin was within eight hundred yards of said hi-rise, and the south-facing rooms provided a perfect perch. Schulz, the jilted husband, already owned a suitable sniper rifle. Silver platter indeed.

That morning, Cervantes had broken into Schulz's house after the quarreling couple had left for their respective jobs. He found the gun safe, cracked it. Stole the Mauser, the log, and a Ruger 9MM, leaving the other firearms untouched. Then he checked the search history on his laptop. The humiliated husband had already done plenty of cyber-snooping on Krause. Perfect. Taken with the hard evidence provided to Schulz by the PI, motive and intent could be established. No need to plant further evidence. Cervantes left, covering any signs of his break-in.

Later, he used a burner to call Schulz at his job.

"*Guten Tag, hier spricht Lukas Schulz.*"

"I have information you can use against Krause."

"Who is this?"

"Reserve room 3024 at the Waldorf tonight. Be there at 19:30 hours sharp. Come alone. I'll meet you there at 20:00 hours. Copy?"

"What is this? Who are you?"

"Someone who wants to help. You copy or not?"

"Yes, but why—"

"Tell no one or I take my information elsewhere."

That was all it took. Once Cervantes had confirmed Schulz's reservation, he went to the Waldorf early and broke into the room, bypassing the joke of a lock. Then he set up his perch at the window and awaited Schulz's arrival. Now it was 19:45 hours and all was in readiness. The Mauser—registered in Schulz's name—was mounted in a bipod, pointed at Krause's balcony, in a room reserved by Schulz, while Schulz was bound like a pig three feet away. Soon, Schulz would 'commit suicide.' After he'd slain his hated rival, Jonas Krause, of course.

Cervantes checked the scope. Still no one on the balcony. He could see Krause's wife, Giselle, wandering around inside the penthouse, newborn baby in her arms, but Krause himself was nowhere to be seen. If he followed his normal routine, he'd be out on that balcony in the next twenty minutes or so.

Cervantes panned left, down a couple of floors, until his narrow field of view settled on a lit apartment. There, near the window, a middle-aged woman sat in a leather recliner reading one of those *How to Be a Master of the Universe* type of books, judging by the cover art. Businesswoman then. Probably single. Career before relationship kind of lady. Cervantes observed the way she was engaged in the book, holding it with both hands about a foot from her face. From this angle, he figured he could take both her hands off with a single shot. She wouldn't even realize what had happened, not at first. She'd just very suddenly find herself looking at two blood-squirting stumps rather than the pages of some jerk-off book. He imagined that snapshot in time when her eyes were seeing a horrid new reality, but her brain was lagging, unable to make sense of the impossible thing that had just happened.

He panned right. Another apartment, someone's living room. A skinny Asian man was watching a music video and dancing around in his underwear. In the adjacent bedroom, his wife or sister or whoever was lying on the bed, tapping away at her phone. Neither of them seemed to care what the other was doing. Living separately, together. If he put a bullet through one of their brains, how long would it be before the partner realized there was a corpse in the other room?

Cervantes continued glassing the floors. Curtains drawn there. Lights off there. From his line of sight, he could see maybe ten other apartments, but no activity. Disappointing. Wait—there. A beautiful young woman was emerging onto her balcony. Fresh blonde ringlets. Low-cut evening dress. Jewelry sparkling in the lights of the city. She was dressed for a fine dinner, or an opera, or whatever. She was smiling, smartphone in one hand, glass of wine in the other. Setting the glass on a table, she began photographing the so-called Pink Moon. A tubby older man in a tux stepped out and joined her, wrapping his arms around her from behind. Together they looked up at the moon, talking and laughing. As she snapped pictures, his lips roamed over her neck, hips swaying on hers. He reached down. Lifted her dress, put his hand up there. She was annoyed. At this high magnification, Cervantes could see her little fake smile. She did not enjoy his touch. Nevertheless, she put on a cattish show of arousal. Moments later he was inside her, pants around his ankles, his round belly smashing against her back while she gripped the railing, dutifully moaning.

Cervantes' chest heaved, trigger finger trembling. Such an opportunity. What would satisfy him the most? A bullet in the man's heart just as he climaxed? Watch the pig die at his precise moment of ecstasy? Or should he fire straight into the woman's moaning mouth, so that the pig would suddenly find himself defiling a corpse? Which shot would bring the sweetest rush?

Breaking from the scope, he loosened his collar and breathed, trying to quell the heat in his veins. The pig and his slut were not the job. The job was Krause. Don't screw it up. Don't fail the Salvador. Calm down. Breathe. Focus.

Schulz had sensed something was up. He'd stopped blubbering through his gag, and he was listening to Cervantes' rapid breathing, head cocked. The sight of Schulz perking up, trying to gain an informational advantage, was enough to yank Cervantes from his fantasy. Composing himself, he returned to the scope.

Giselle was there now, sitting on the balcony. Breastfeeding the infant. Krause hadn't yet joined her, but he was home now. His shadowy projection played on the bedroom curtain as he changed into his evening clothes, unaware that he was minutes away from eternal night. While he waited, Cervantes aligned the reticle with Giselle's face. She was nothing like her social media pictures. He was expecting the glamorous socialite who had bagged Krause, not this pale, bloated woman with a bun of ill-kempt hair. And there, nestled in her chest, suckled the newest Krause. Cervantes didn't know if it was a boy or a girl, and he didn't care. Nor did he care that he was about to make it fatherless. He'd been fatherless, too. So had the Salvador. Now, the two of them were barreling down a road to greatness. So maybe having a father wasn't the end-all-be-all everyone pretends it to be.

Cervantes hissed through his teeth, for the baby's soft melon of a head perfectly filled his reticle. Like it was made for it. If he took this shot, the melon would explode, and the bullet would continue into Giselle's heart. Mother and infant would leave the world together and never even know it. Seemed like poetry.

Krause finally stepped onto the balcony. Not the high-powered, silver-spooned adulterer, but a weary, paunch-bellied working father. Wearing an open blue robe with peejays beneath, he kissed Giselle and the baby, then he took the adjacent seat. Setting his brandy on a side table, he opened his laptop on his thighs and began reading, his face illuminated by the screen.

The magic moment had arrived.

Cervantes press-checked the rifle, pulling the bolt and feeling the brass in the chamber. Then, breathing long and deep, he placed the reticle on

Krause's forehead. Gravity would pull the shot down into his chest. He caressed the walnut stock with his gloved hand before letting his finger hover over the trigger. He drew one long breath, exhaled, and fired.

The round punched through the sliding door behind Krause, six inches to the right and three inches high. Giselle turned her head at the sound, but Krause didn't flinch. Too absorbed in his work. Cervantes chambered the next round and adjusted his aim, counting the scope's tick marks left and downwards to compensate for the miss. When it felt right, he breathed, exhaled, and fired. Krause jerked from the force of impact, the laptop sliding off his knees. He slumped forward, clutching his chest briefly before his arms fell to his sides. Giselle didn't believe it at first. She thought he was playing a joke on her. When she finally realized what had happened . . . yes . . . oh, yes. With the distance and the noise of the city below, Cervantes could not hear her screams, could not hear the baby crying, but the black and white movie before him needed no soundtrack. Giselle's mouth was open in full-throated terror, convulsing as she struggled to suck in enough air to scream those magnificent screams. He drank it in. Savored her horror-twisted face. Tasted her utter disbelief. The familiar feeling of bliss zoomed through his blood like tiny dragsters were using his veins as a racetrack.

Sadly, he could not revel in his euphoria. He had to finish and get out. Forcing himself from the scope, he drew the Ruger from the small of his back and flicked the safety. Then he squatted by Schulz. "The man who ruined your life has a bullet in his heart. That should please you."

Schulz attempted no reply. Still hooded and restrained, he remained silent.

"You know what needs to happen now, don't you?"

No answer.

"And you know what will happen to your family if you don't?"

Schulz's head dropped. Still, he said nothing.

"To your brother, Paul? Your sisters, Mina and Elsa? Your mother, Rebekah? The old man, Elias?"

Schulz trembled, sucking in sharply.

"Or it could just be you. Right now. In the temple, with your own hand. Honorable. You do that, my associates and I will be on the next flight out. But if I don't call them in the next five minutes, the Schulzes will be wiped from the face of the earth. Slowly, one at a time. Spread out over months. They'll live in constant fear until the last of them is gone."

Schulz pitched forward, sobbing.

"Good. You do get it."

Cervantes watched him sob. This big, strong, German *Kommando*, now just a sack of blubbering *Wienerschnitzel*. Pathetic. Everything he ever was, reduced to nothing in the blink of an eye, all because of love. Anyone—literally anyone—could be controlled, fully and completely, just by going after their loved ones. Cervantes would never understand such a weakness. Fearing no altercation, he removed Schulz's restraints, hood, and gag. He packed these items into his bag and went to the door. From there, he slid the Ruger over to Schulz.

There were no associates. That was a lie. The Salvador trusted Cervantes and Cervantes alone for this kind of op. If Schulz knew this was a one-man job, however, he might use the pistol to fire on Cervantes. Try to fight his way out. He'd fail, but then Cervantes would have to kill him himself, after which he'd have a lot of staging to do to ensure it looked like suicide. That would introduce the chance of the cops sniffing out foul play. Even the most skillfully staged suicides never looked quite right. Better to make the man do it himself for that natural and authentic look. Bluffing about associates ensured this outcome.

Standing on shaky legs, Schulz picked up the pistol. Looked at it, then looked at Cervantes, who was but a shadow in the darkened foyer. Finding his inner stoicism, he stood up straight, muttering something in German. With one smooth movement, he raised the pistol to his temple and fired.

Cervantes drank the moment. The last shallow breath from the lump on the floor, the splatter of gore on the mirror, the tangy scent of gunpowder and blood. He closed his eyes, tuning into the lightning strikes of ecstasy flashing through his veins. Then, throwing his bag over his shoulder, he opened the hotel room door and poked his head out. All clear. He pocketed his ski mask and gloves, then stepped into the hall and strolled away.

CAIBIDIL 5

AS SHE WALKED UP the rough slope toward the castle, a gust of wind knocked Valory off balance, but she barely noticed. She could only gawp. Never had she laid eyes on a sight like this. Most of her career had been spent at a desk. Her occasional field work had been dry and predictable, but *this!* Vaguely, she was aware of Rafael beside her dishing out the mysterious details she'd been waiting to hear, but now his words were vaporous. They drifted from his mouth and dissipated in the chilly winds. For God's sake, there was a castle here! Hidden in plain view in the forgotten heights of the Italian Alps. Carved right out of the rock, like Mount Rushmore or Ad Deir in Petra. It was as gorgeous as it was absurd.

While *Agente* Savelli and *Marshal* Buccini met with the soldiers, Valory and Rafael approached the outer wall where an enormous gate stood open in the barbican. Stout bastions framed the sides of the barbican, with two taller bastions marking the east and west corners of the wall. Long banks of snow were sloped against the walls and upon the surrounding cauldron pitches. Beyond the gate, at the north end of the courtyard, loomed the keep, its monolithic walls dotted with windows and streaked with the grunge of time. There wasn't an individual stone to be seen. The keep was one solid piece, its foundations merging with the bedrock below, its rear structure flowing into the steep pitch of the summit. From the rear of the keep, a solitary tower speared the heavens.

When the group came within fifty yards of the gate, Valory stopped to take it all in. She reached for her phone to snap some pictures, only then remembering it had been confiscated. That's when Rafael's voice finally penetrated her fog of awe. "Right about here is where we usually land," he was half-yelling, his coat beating in the wind. "When the conditions are right, we use the helicopter. Otherwise, the route we just took is the only way to get here. I do apologize for putting you through that grueling ride."

"Huh? Oh, yeah. Sure."

Rafael smiled. "Impressed, Doctor Grace?"

"I think dumbstruck is a better word."

"Indeed. When I first saw this place, I, too, was dumbstruck. I still am."

"How old is it?" asked Val, squinting into a fierce gust. She spit a lock of fluttering hair from her lips.

"Construction began in the Middle Ages, but it didn't end there." Rafael held his hat to his head while he spoke, leaning into the wind. "It was in a constant state of work over centuries. You will see influences from the Renaissance and Baroque periods. Upgrades, additions, repairs. The craftsmanship was superior, no matter the date of the work. Just look, even after it has been abandoned for many years, the castle is in excellent condition. In fact, when we first ventured inside, we concluded that a small earthquake had damaged some of the interior artifacts, but the castle itself was remarkably unaffected. Quite an achievement."

"*Det är det verkligen*," Valory half-yelled as they resumed their approach.

"Pardon?"

"What?"

"I didn't understand. Was that Dutch?"

It took Valory a moment to realize she had, for whatever reason, answered in Swedish. "Oh, sorry. I said, 'It certainly is.'" Abruptly, the wind died off, allowing her to speak at normal volume. "So, I guess my next question is who? Who built it, who abandoned it? Who maintained it for all the years in between? And why?" Her brain was kicking back in, recovering from its bout of stupefaction. Now her thoughts were full speed ahead. "I can't imagine a tactical reason for this fortification. There's no populace to protect. You can't control trade or traffic from way up here. You can't defend a kingdom. So, this was what, a vanity project? Whose? And how does a ten-thousand-year-old language fit in?" she asked, gesturing at the castle. "Surely the clay tablet you showed me didn't originate from here, that'd make no sense."

"Exactly!" said Rafael "How great is it to feel that sense of wonder? Could you have ever guessed you'd be posing such questions about a place like this?"

"Can't say so, no."

"Nor me. We are truly lucky. The honest answer to your questions is we don't know. We are lacking specific expertise. This is why you are here. You, Doctor Grace, are our ass in the hole."

Valory smiled. "I hope you mean *ace* in the hole, Doctor." The Italian word for ace was *asso*, so it was an excusable gaffe, but she couldn't resist a little poke.

"What did I say? Ass? Oh, dear. *Mi dispiace, cara mia*. Ace, of course."

"No problem," she laughed. A real laugh, not a *This is where I'm supposed to be friendly* type of laugh, but a genuine laugh. She was starting to freeze her tail off, but she didn't care. She was energized. Excited. It had been a while since she could say that.

"Well then," said Rafael with a clap of his hands, "let us go get out of the wind and go inside the keep, eh? When you see what is there, Valory, I wager you will never want to leave."

***

From his vantage point atop the keep, *Agente Speciale* Enzo D'Arezzo watched as Doctor Moretti and the new lady passed under the barbican into the courtyard. Seemed everything had gone as planned. D'Arezzo wasn't sure if that was a good or bad thing.

It was difficult to tell in the mask of twilight, but the woman looked decent enough. Much more attractive than the Mouse anyway. The soldiers in the camp were probably making lewd comments about her right about now, describing what they'd do if they had five minutes with her. Yet they'd said the same thing about the Mouse, whose endowments were lacking. Slim pickings up here at the top of *Italia*.

D'Arezzo heard Moretti yelling over the wind, directing the woman's attention to the stables in the western bailey. D'Arezzo's English wasn't great, but he could tell the woman was surprised to see the two horses in those old stalls, their heads jutting over the doors. Moretti explained that horses were the best means of short-range recon up here in this rough terrain.

Then Moretti pointed to the series of wooden structures along the eastern wall. Those, he explained, had been livestock pens in prior eras, but now they were being used to house the generators that powered the equipment inside the keep. *Capitano* Ricci was there, cursing at one of the generators. He'd just replaced a gasket, but it hadn't done the trick. The generator sputtered and died, earning a kick from Ricci.

After pointing out the high-altitude garden and some architectural details, Moretti led Valory to the stairs at the base of the keep, disappearing from D'Arezzo's view, and he from theirs. With the next lull in the wind, he lit a cigarette. Moretti despised people smoking in this place. He nearly popped a vein once after he'd found Trentino lighting up inside the keep. Like the stone was going to catch fire or something.

D'Arezzo turned and gazed up at the woman towering over him. With her flowing robes and sinuous figure, she was once a beautiful statue, but now her bronze skin was layered in the greenish-black grime of centuries, and both of her arms had fallen off. The details of her face had smoothed over time, but her eyes were still in decent condition. D'Arezzo took a drag, looking at those eyes. Though her expression never changed, he couldn't help but feel she was glowering at him. No doubt just an illusion born of his conscience, but still, it was creepy. Walking past her, he looked up at the tower which rose from the keep. Tomorrow would be his last time going up there, at least for a while. Now that Savelli was here, D'Arezzo could leave

35

this place for a few blessed weeks. Get back to the city, where curvy women, good restaurants, and warm beaches waited. For a little while, maybe he could forget the things he'd had to do in that tower.

***

Rafael reported that the wooden door of the keep was original. Darkened and distressed by time, the thick wood was reinforced with rusted metal plates. After the castle had been discovered last year, Rafael's engineer had only to perform a bit of careful work on the hinges to get the door working smoothly, a testament to its craftsmanship. Still, Rafael exerted considerable force to push it open, and it groaned like an old beast roused from a deep slumber. Smiling, he bade Valory enter.

She found herself in a vestibule. The vestibule was in architectural harmony with the exterior of the castle in that it had not been constructed with individual stones, but rather hollowed out of the gargantuan block of rock that was the keep. A single entity, flowing together as one contiguous, seamless structure. But before Valory could begin to admire the engraved arches sweeping up from the floor, or the candelabra hanging from the ceiling, or the fine wooden armchairs, or the paintings with gilded frames, her gaze was drawn to the north wall. For there stood two arched portals, beyond which gleamed the Great Hall.

As if she'd levitated there, Valory found herself in the hall, gaping. Three stories high and half a soccer pitch in length, the room overawed her senses, not only with its size but with its unending opulence. Marble floor tiles, carved columns, candelabras, paintings, sculptures—there was nowhere to look without being dazzled by ancient treasures. Portable lights had been arranged throughout the hall, illuminating many areas, but many artifacts remained tantalizing shadows lurking in pockets of darkness. She could see that one such nook contained piles of broken marble and frames, probably damaged pieces from the earthquake Rafael had mentioned. Overhead, the second and third-floor balconies overlooked the entire hall.

Rafael was talking, but again, Valory was not hearing him. Her attention had been captured by the far end of the hall. There, on a raised dais flanked by columns, stood two thrones. With their tall, fearsome spires, the thrones dominated the room. Even from this distance, she could see the intricate gold and silver inlays in the woodwork. And . . . what? It couldn't be. Squinting the uncertainty from her eyes, she confirmed the most striking sight of all—one of the thrones was occupied.

"Pardon?" said Valory, barely realizing she was responding to Rafael.

"I said, didn't I tell you? Once in a lifetime opportunity, eh?" Rafael was beaming at her. "*Santo Dio*, look at you. You have just been given a thousand Christmases at once, I think, and you haven't even seen the texts yet." His chuckle echoed throughout the hall. "I am very pleased to see you so excited, Valory. Please, have a look around. I insist."

Embarrassed for having reduced herself to a slack-jawed yokel in the presence of a new colleague, she cleared her throat and nodded toward the dais. "Who is she? Sitting on the throne?"

Rafael snapped his fingers. "Let's go say hello to her, shall we?"

As they walked, she marveled at the columns lining the grand walkway to the dais. Spanning floor to ceiling, they were as round as mature oaks. Each column was carved with a bas-relief narrative—a picture story—spiraling up from the base. To read the story on a column, one would read the carvings on the lower level, then go to the second-floor balcony to read the middle, and then read the conclusion on the third floor. Valory wanted to start reading the bases, but the multitudes of other works competed for her attention. She was no art historian, but she guessed the pieces here were centuries old, and there were enough of them to fill a wing in the Louvre. Numerous paintings hung on every wall, massive in size. Most seemed to be from the Renaissance era. There were marble statues throughout the hall as well. These were placed randomly as if to make the hall appear populated with courtiers. Some were broken or cracked, but having been sheltered within the keep, the majority had survived the centuries well.

"Here we are," said Rafael as they climbed the steps of the dais and reached the thrones. "Doctor Grace, allow me to present Her Majesty the Queen Maria Rossi."

The 'queen' was a sculpture of a young woman seated upon the throne. She'd been carved wearing a jewel-encrusted crown and holding a scepter, her elaborate gown flowing to her feet. Her face was flawless. High cheekbones, full lips, and a slender nose for which women of the modern era paid good money. Her hair spilled from the back of the crown into a twisted faux braid such as worn by the ancient Greeks. Though her small form was dwarfed by the throne itself, she seemed to fill it with the sheer dignity of her regal expression. The sheen of the polished marble had tinted with time, but even so, the queen cast a dominating presence over the hall. Valory gazed into the smooth, blank orbs of her eyes, wondering who she was. Rafael had called her Maria Rossi; that name was a placeholder, Italy's equivalent of Jane Doe.

"She's stunning. You don't know her real name?"

"No, but we have some clues. Look here." Rafael wrapped his glasses around his ears and leaned in, pointing at a symbol on the queen's robe. It was a cross with a diamond in the center, encircled by the letters K-R-S-L. "This represents the Carolingian dynasty of the ninth century. So that suggests she is from Charlemagne's lineage, but who? This is not the face of any known Carolingian queen."

37

"Hm. And what about this?" asked Valory, pointing at another symbol on the other side of the robe. Three crosses were arranged in an inverted pyramid, the head of a panther in the center. "I recognize the pyramid of crosses. That's from the Kingdom of the Lombards, but unless I'm mistaken, the Lombards never used a panther."

"That was our assessment as well. Except that it took us weeks to make the Lombards connection." Rafael smiled. "You're very good, Valory. I am anxious for you to begin your work here. The sooner you begin translating texts, the sooner we will solve mysteries like this. Who was she? Why was this place built? Who were the artists of all these amazing works? I think you can help us find answers."

"I hope so," she answered, staring into the queen's eyes. So beautiful. Why was she sitting here all alone? Why was her king not sitting on the second throne?

"Goodness, I do apologize for rushing you here, and for arriving so late," said Rafael, checking his watch. "My government has placed a premium on scheduling. Their condition was that if I wanted to recruit you, I had to get you here immediately. If we'd been able to take the helicopter as I'd planned, we'd have been able to put in a full day's work."

"Uh huh," she murmured, lost in the queen.

"I'm sure you are tired and hungry after such a long journey. Perhaps you would like to retire for the night and start fresh tomorrow."

"What?" said Valory, tearing her attention from the throne. She held her hands to the magnificence all around her. "How could I think about retiring after seeing this? I could probably stay up for two days straight just wandering this hall."

"Ah yes." Rafael looked around, appreciating the hall anew. "I know what you mean, but we've lost the sun, and it is about to get very cold very fast. These old bones are already fussing at me," he chuckled. "I'd like to get you settled into your bedchamber so I can get to my own."

"My bedchamber?" asked Valory, hazel eyes popping wide. "I'm staying inside the castle?"

"Of course, *cara mia*. Where did you think?"

"I thought . . . I mean I just assumed that—"

"That I'd put you in a tent out there with the soldiers? No no, Valory, *no lo sognerei*. We are academics. Our delicate bodies are not made for sleeping on rocks." He laughed, patting his round belly. "No, I've had a chamber prepared for you. Not as comfortable as the Hilton, perhaps, but much better than the encampment."

Valory was shocked. She'd stayed at excavations overnight on a couple of occasions, and the accommodations had been meager, to say the least. She wanted to ask the practical things about the chamber—Is it structurally safe? Is it warm? Does it have a place to study and work? Will it have electricity?—but instead, she just smiled. She was going to live in a medieval castle, studying the most fascinating texts of her career. All she could manage to say was, "Wow."

"You can settle in, have some dinner, some wine. And maybe," said Rafael, a twinkle in his eye, "I can give you a bit of bedtime reading. To satisfy your excitement and whet your appetite for tomorrow, hm?"

Physically, Valory was exhausted. Mentally, she felt like she'd been shot up with a gallon of caffeine. The castle and its treasures were one thing, but now Rafael was giving her a private chamber and some 'bedtime reading.' Something to start working on tonight. Something ancient. If the castle was an overdose of caffeine, then the promise of laying eyes on the oldest language in human history in mere moments was an injection of hardcore narcotics.

Grabbing a couple of flashlights from a folding table, Rafael led Valory to a spiral stairwell in the corner of the keep. The chamber that would be Valory's was on the same level as the Great Hall's middle balcony. Panting up the narrow stairs, Rafael muttered something about going on a diet.

The hallways were dark. Though there were sconces along the walls with silver torches in them, Rafael explained that lighting them was forbidden, citing the possibility of setting fire to the artifacts in the vicinity. Fireplaces with screens could be used in the bedchambers, however, and in fact, were required to stave off freezing nights. Otherwise, the only approved light sources in the keep were flashlights, propane lanterns, and portable lights with guard shields. "And no cigarettes!" huffed Rafael. "If you see anyone smoking a cigarette in any part of the keep, please inform me at once."

They walked by several doors, all of them closed save one. From that one, dancing fingers of firelight reached into the hall. Valory glanced into the room as they passed. There was a man in there, tall and gaunt with an unkempt head of white. He was bent over a desk, holding a magnifying glass over the pages of a textbook. He looked up, meeting Valory's gaze for a second before she cleared the door.

"Here we are," said Rafael, pushing open a heavy wooden door. It was blackout dark inside. "*Momento*, let me turn on the lamp." He walked in, shining his flashlight. As Valory followed, she stepped on something. Pointing her flashlight down, she saw a couple of extension cords running into her room. Bundles of these cords ran down the length of the hallway, with two or three branching off into each room. "There," said Rafael, switching on a portable light stand. "Electric is a scarce commodity here, I'm afraid. We supply two extension cords to each room, and we ask that you only use them when necessary. Why don't you have a look around while I get your fire going."

As Rafael went to the fireplace, Valory smiled. A real medieval bedchamber. She ran her fingers along the intricate patterns in the oaken bed frame. The bedposts loomed ten feet high, topped by an imposing canopy. The bed had been there unmoved for ages, but whatever type of bedding it had once contained had been replaced by a modern folding mattress. The twin-sized mattress was dwarfed by the regal oak frame and topped with a goose-down comforter. Valory's suitcase had been placed over the comforter, delivered earlier by *Marshal* Buccini. An original foot bench rested in front of the bed, also carved with beautiful floral designs.

There was a small table on the south wall with a Renaissance-style crossover armchair tucked underneath. Beside those was an assortment of propane-powered equipment: a lantern, a stove, a portable hot water shower, and other camping gear. There was also a five-gallon jug of water, some snacks, and a pile of MREs. Valory was pleased to spot a coffee maker among the goods. Inspecting the room further, she noticed a narrow door leading into the garderobe—a medieval toilet. The skinny door—just two wooden planks bound by iron—squeaked when she opened it. The inside was no bigger than a telephone booth. Her nose wrinkled reflexively as she stuck her head in, but she realized there was no smell. Her flashlight revealed a smooth stone bench with a foreboding hole in the center. To the side were stacked several rolls of biodegradable toilet paper and hygiene wipes.

"Don't worry, it is very deep," called Rafael as he poked at the fireplace. "You don't have to worry about odors. If you are uncomfortable using the garderobe, there are portable latrines outside. They are managed by the soldiers."

"No," answered Valory, "this will be fine. I think." She had to banish an image that popped into her head—sitting there in that hole, stuck, slowly getting sucked into the netherworld below.

"Now then," grunted Rafael, pushing himself up, "your fire is ready. You will need to tend it throughout the night to keep the chamber warm. There are bundles of firewood here, and we can bring more as needed. Just remember to always place the screen in front of the fire, *si?*"

"Yes, of course. Thank you, Rafael."

"Please make yourself at home. If you need help using any of the equipment, or if anything is not to your satisfaction, just let me know." He checked his watch. "*Agente* Savelli has offered to bring you some food and wine. He should be here shortly. In the meantime," he said, eyes disappearing into his smile, "I will go and fetch your bedtime reading, hm?"

With that, he left Valory to her new environs. Walking around, she admired the many pieces of period furniture: the bed, the foot bench, a wrought iron floor-standing candelabra, a gilded chest, and a faded tapestry on the west wall. Antique dealers would lose their minds in this room alone, not to mention the rest of the keep. Perhaps most amazing of all was the fact that, like everything else, the chamber was one solid structure, hollowed from the rock of the mountain and flowing seamlessly into the rest of the castle. She didn't have to be an expert to realize that, from an architectural standpoint, such a feat involved genius-level planning and execution unlike anything else in antiquity. How had the builders achieved such a thing? Even the Egyptian pyramids were a doddle compared to this gargantuan mountaintop sculpture. The only disappointment, if it could be called that, was that there were no windows.

Valory examined the tapestry, trying to determine what story it told. The colors were faded, the threads ragged, but she could still make out the gist of it. The tapestry was quite busy, with lots of people dancing, singing, and playing instruments. There were several animals in the scene as well: a dog, a large cat, a peacock, an owl, and other birds. In the center, under a decorative canopy, lounged a dark-haired woman in a white dress, probably the host of the party.

While she continued soaking in the chamber, *Agente* Savelli entered. His appearance put her on guard. He'd not been very accepting of her since they'd met. But he appeared a little more relaxed now, even genial. *"Buona sera, Dottoressa. Vengo portando regali."* He said he came bearing gifts, and indeed he did. He set a covered plate on the table, then withdrew a bottle of wine from his bag. Speaking Italian, he said the wine was a light-bodied *Valpolicella*, perfect for pasta and meatballs. Then he lifted the cover on the plate, revealing that very dish. As he uncorked the bottle, he explained that they were forced to keep it simple up here on top of the world, so don't expect anything too fancy. The cooks were just soldiers from the encampment, and their recipes were limited. "But the wine," he said, switching to heavily accented English, "there is always wine. Otherwise, we are revolting, yes?"

Valory held in a laugh at the expense of Savelli's *faux pas*. His obvious meaning was that they would revolt—not that they would appear physically revolting—in the absence of wine. She loved those kinds of little language idiosyncrasies. *"Grazie mille, Agente Savelli,"* she replied. *"Questo andrà bene."* She said it would be fine, and it definitely would. If he thought this was a simple meal, she didn't want to tell him about her regular diet. Most nights, while hunched over a laptop, all she could manage for herself were grilled cheese sandwiches with Doritos.

Resuming his businesslike attitude, Savelli used a small camera to take Valory's picture, explaining that they took photos of everyone at the castle for security reasons. She found that a little odd but didn't question it. Then he produced a laptop, a USB hard drive, and a larger digital camera. All of them were marked as property of the Italian government. She was required to write her translations on the computer and take accompanying photographs of every piece she worked on. Everything was to be saved to the external drive (and nowhere else). The drive would be confiscated periodically and switched out for a fresh one. Routine security stuff. There was no internet up here, so if she required reference material, she would need to request it from Rafael, who would have it fetched from the Ministry. If she needed to make a call to the outside world, she could use the satellite phone. But fair warning, the *Agenzia* monitored all calls, so do not expect privacy.

With a blunt nod, Savelli left her to her dinner. After a couple of dainty bites, she began Hoovering the food in, the taste making her realize how just hungry she was. She'd had nothing but a few snacks since leaving Oxford this morning. Had she been in England this morning? Seemed like weeks ago.

Just as she finished her meal, Rafael returned, panting, rolling a metal case along behind him. Italian Santa bringing her yet another gift. "Ah, I see Agent Savelli has been here. May I?" he asked, pointing to the wine bottle.

"God yes, of course."

"*Grazie,*" he said, pouring himself a cup of *Valpolicella.* He swigged the whole cup and poured another, refilling Valory's as well. "*Mamma mia.* Getting around this castle is thirsty work, *signora.* My heart can't take much more of it." He took another drink, savoring the flavor. He seemed to lose himself in thought for a moment, bottom lip sucking the wine from his mustache. He snapped back when he saw Valory eyeing his case. "Ah! Forgive me, *cara mia.* I was lost there for a moment."

He placed the case on the table and put on a pair of cotton gloves, handing a second pair to Valory. Then he opened the case and withdrew a large felt cloth which he laid across the table. Gently, he produced four clay tablets, one at a time, and lined them up. They were much like the fragment he'd brought to her apartment, only complete and unbroken. Inscribed upon them was the unknown language isolate. Ten thousand years old, if Rafael was correct.

Valory leaned over the tablets, heart skipping a beat. The rough edges, the dull, sandy color, the words of a long-dead human inscribed there, eager to tell her a story. Slowly, she ran her fingers along the individual characters. The hardened grooves and punches were more defined than those from the fragment. Much less degraded. These tablets had been well-cared for. More striking, however, was the alphabetic script. As she'd observed in her flat, the script was complex and artistic. More like creative ornamentation than written language. In addition to the predictable grooves and dots which had been pressed into the tablet with a stylus, there were also fanciful extractions—swoops and curves where the clay had been removed with a tiny scoop or some other utensil. This was in stark contrast to the other earliest scripts in history, such as Phoenician and Cuneiform. Those scripts were simple and utilitarian, easily formed and easy to pass down to new learners. They were exactly what one might expect from humankind's first attempts at writing. The writers of this language, however, had given no mind to the speed of writing nor ease of teaching. That was rather shocking. Though the language was beautiful, why make it so difficult to produce? It was a mystery that brought a reverent smile to her lips. Letting her fingertips linger in the indentions of the oldest writing ever, she began to feel flush. Tingly. Already, the tablets were whispering to her, swirling in her mind's eye. Tickling her insides.

She withdrew her hands. Not because she wanted to, but because Rafael was watching. After composing herself, she asked in the most professional tone she could muster, "These were all found here at the castle?"

"Yes. In the library."

"The library?"

"*Si.*"

"There's an actual library here? With more tablets?"

"*Si*, and it is unlike any library you have ever seen or will ever see again. Full of tablets, tomes, scrolls—there is enough down there to make ten careers out of."

Valory gaped at him. "Can we go see?"

Rafael's smile was tinged with weariness. "Valory, the library will be all yours, but not tonight. Half an hour from now, I will be dreaming of my wife and family. I knew you would be anxious, though, which is why I brought you these."

She spread her arms, placing her hands on the edges of the far tablets as if she might pull all four of them into her bosom. "What can you tell me about these in particular?"

"Well," said Rafael, "first let me say that the library is arranged in chronological order. By which I mean, the oldest works start in the northeast corner. As you walk west down the aisle, they are more recent. When you reach the end, you start over from the next row. Oldest to newest on every aisle."

"Sure."

"In that northeast corner, where the earliest works are, there are stacks of these tablets."

"Stacks?"

"Stacks upon stacks."

"Whoa."

"*Si*, and these four in particular," he said pausing for dramatic effect, "are from the very first stack."

"Wait," said Valory, rapt. "Are you saying that these four tablets are the first of the first? So not only do I have the oldest written language ever," she said, jutting a finger at the characters, "but I have the first edition so to speak?"

Rafael shrugged. "We think so, but I leave it to you to study and confirm."

Valory leaned back in her chair as if she'd just run a marathon. "I can't—*bu her saniye daha inanılmaz hale geliyor.*"

"Pardon?"

"Hm? Oh, jeez, that was Turkish. Sorry. I said this gets more incredible by the second."

He chuckled, patting her shoulder. "You are something special, Doctor Grace. So. Consider this an appetizer, *si?* Tomorrow, when you're rested, you'll get the main course."

"Tomorrow, yes. I'm sorry to keep you, Rafael."

"Not at all. By the way, please don't mistake my intentions. I am not expecting you to translate this language anytime soon. I know it could take months or even years of study. I just wanted you to have a small reward after such a crazy day."

"Thank you, Rafael. For everything. This is all . . . thank you."

He bowed. "And now, I bid you *buonanotte.* My room is two doors down if you need anything."

The moment he closed the door behind him, Valory went to work. The next time she looked up, it was 6:00 A.M., and she'd translated every tablet. What they said was jaw-dropping.

チャプター 6

SITTING CROSS-LEGGED, CERVANTES BREATHED long and deep, concentrating only on that simple act. When his chest was full, he exhaled—smoothly, measuredly, completely—until pushing out every last molecule of oxygen. This cycle had he been repeating for an hour. His eyes were closed, his back straight, but he had lost any real sense of his naked body. There was nothing in the world but his breath.

When he opened his eyes, the Las Vegas morning was warm on his face, its heat penetrating the window of his hotel room. Outside, the flamboyant energy of the Vegas strip was neutered by the sunlight, its sidewalks devoid of revelers. He gave himself a moment to adjust to his bright, colorless world. Then he stood, raising his hands over his head. He began bending over backward, millimeter by millimeter, hands drawing ever closer to the floor until his palms laid flat upon it. He held this arched bridge position for several minutes—an upside-down U—until his anterior muscle chain was screaming. Then, tightening his core, he lifted his feet off the floor, straightening his legs until he was balancing a perfect handstand. From there, he began repping out handstand pushups.

The room was expensive, with lots of luxury touches for which Cervantes could not have cared less. He'd have been just as happy in a shack out in the desert, but the Salvador would not hear of it. He wanted the best of everything for Cervantes, at least when it suited the mission. Sometimes, though, it was just irritating. To get any real training done, Cervantes had to push all the fine furniture against the wall or stack it on the bed to clear out floor space to move, and there was still not enough room. Nevertheless, he began his jiu-jitsu warm-up drills.

Anyone walking into the room at that point may have guessed they were witnessing an epileptic having a mild seizure. A naked Hispanic man on his back, shimmying backward along the floor by rocking from side to side and pushing himself with his feet. It was a drill called the shrimp, essential practice for maneuvering beneath an opponent. When he'd gone the length of the free space, Cervantes reversed direction, scooting forward on his back while mimicking the action of pulling an opponent into his guard. Then came the side shrimp, using only the small of his back to twist and wobble

45

sideways toward the door, his feet and arms raised in the air. The shrimp variations were core intensive, and he worked up a full sweat in minutes.

He had not expected to be in Vegas now. From Berlin, he'd been on his way home to Beverly Crest via LAX, where he was to meet with the Salvador. A few hours after leaving Berlin on a private charter, however, the pilot had given Cervantes the news—they'd been diverted to Las Vegas. No further explanation was given, nor expected. It was the Salvador's wish, case closed. But Cervantes knew the likely reason. The Salvador was a determined man, but over the years, he'd learned the art of patience. Though he could force the issue when needed, he also knew that sometimes, it was best to just sit back and wait for a perfect opportunity to present itself. When it did, he'd strike like a coiled viper. The fact Cervantes had been diverted to Vegas probably meant that the Salvador had identified such an opportunity and was now executing a long-considered plan.

There was a brief layover in New York followed by the final leg to Vegas. A spook had met him at the airport. New guy. There was no small talk. The man gave him a fake ID, two burners, a set of rental car keys, and a card key for a hotel suite. Then he left without a word. That was last night. Cervantes had driven to the suite and waited a few hours, but the burners never rang.

Now, as he crab crawled backward across the floor, one of them rang. He flipped to his feet and answered it.

"You've done well," came the voice on the other end. "As always."

"Thank you, Salvador."

"Dominic, you know you don't have to call me that."

"I know, but I want to. If you don't mind." Salvador meant 'savior' in Spanish, and that was who he was to Cervantes—a personal savior. After what happened in Afghanistan, he could not view him as anything else.

"If you feel strongly about it, then sure." The Salvador's voice was silky smooth, like drinking fine wine on satin clouds. His timbre was deep and calming, his words fat with buttery pleasure. It was not difficult to see why people responded to him the way they did. Why they were eager to get close to him, to do things for him. In person, the effect was magnified tenfold. "The reports began filtering in last night. The police are not looking beyond Schulz. You were flawless."

"Did you expect otherwise?"

"Not for a second. Anything extraneous I should know about? Any loose ends?"

"Negative. Everything is accounted for."

"Excellent. Once again, I find myself marveling at your abilities. You're truly a god among men."

"You are the one people revere, Salvador."

"I think you're a little premature on that. But yes, one day it will be so. I believe that. When that day comes, you'll stand beside me. Not in the shadows, but openly."

Openly, the eyes of the world upon him. Such a thought was impossible to imagine. Cervantes had operated in the underbelly since the day of his fake suicide, his entire life masked. Could the Salvador create a reality in which his deeds were not only known, but accepted? Even expected? "That will be a great day."

"Listen, I apologize for the diversion. I was looking forward to finally reuniting, but as you know, circumstances in my world change quickly these days."

Cervantes remained silent.

"Even now my time is short. But before I brief you on the new mission, tell me, is there anything you need? Anything at all I can get for you? Professional or otherwise?"

"Negative, Salvador. I'm ready."

"Good. Here, I'm sending you a photo. Tell me if you remember her."

Cervantes tapped the incoming image. A young woman. Head tilted sideways. Long, straight hair, likely blonde. Big, bedroom eyes with false lashes. A glossy smile. Yes, he remembered her. Misty Givens. An actress who had once been an up-and-comer in Hollywood. After gaining popularity in a few supporting movie roles, she'd been given a lead in a film whose name Cervantes couldn't recall. He did remember that that film had flopped, losing the studio millions. That was several years ago. He couldn't recall even hearing her name since then. Not that he would have. He had no interest in films, nor the pomp and glitz of Hollywood. He couldn't have named a single movie at the box office right now, but he remembered Misty Givens, and he had a good idea why she had to die.

"I remember her."

"She's become a problem. A personal problem."

"Understood."

"It needs to be done tomorrow."

"Where?"

"She's there now, vacationing in Vegas. Tomorrow, she's going out to Red Rock Canyon, seventeen miles west of the city. A day hiking trip. Do it there."

"Copy that." Cervantes immediately saw the reasoning. Out of the city, in the remote desert wilderness. People got lost all the time in places like Red Rock. They hiked off-trail and never found their way back. Or they took unfortunate tumbles, breaking their necks on the way down. No one around to see or hear them. Sometimes, their corpses weren't found for days.

"She probably won't be alone."

"Who?"

47

"A boyfriend, Zack Miller. Bodybuilder. He's big. Strong. No formal combat training, but he loves to brawl. He spent some time in jail after a bar fight four months ago. Broke some guy's jaw, put him in a coma." The Salvador paused. "Will that be a problem?"

"Of course not."

"You understand I had to ask. I can't tell you what time, or which part of the canyon they'll be hiking, so you'll have to play it by ear. Improvise."

"Yes, Salvador." Cervantes had learned not to ask questions like *How do you know all this? How can you know she'll be at Red Rock tomorrow?* The Salvador just *knew*. If he said that the moon would not rise tonight, it wouldn't.

"Dominic," said the Salvador, his honeyed voice becoming deeper, richer, "something is in the air. Something I can't quite put into words. I feel . . ." he went silent for a moment, "I don't know. It's like a thousand doors are slowly opening, just a little wider every day, and a shine of unimaginable power is beginning to spill out, bathing us in its glow. You and me. I know that sounds strange."

"No, Salvador. It doesn't. That power will be yours."

"Ours, brother. It will be ours."

The line went dead. Cervantes broke the phone and tossed it into the dumpster on his way to the sporting goods store.

***

He arrived at Red Rock at 07:00 hours while the fee station was unmanned. A short way down the road, he pulled into the first overlook and parked. Any traffic coming into the park would pass by the overlook, so he only had to wait. Not that he expected Misty Givens anytime soon. She was the kind of woman who didn't make a move before 11:00 hours. No discipline, no urgency. After sleeping in and then making a dawdling Starbucks run, she'd spend an hour applying make-up and trying on 'cute' hiking outfits to ensure her social media pics were perfect. That was the impression she'd given Cervantes years ago when the Salvador had had his brief fling with her. He'd be surprised if she got to the canyon by 13:00 hours. He was in for a long wait. Still, he arrived early just in case. Since there were no rangers on duty yet, his face wouldn't be seen.

His face. Dropping the visor, he popped open the mirror. The man looking back at him was monochromatic—a black-and-white photo come to life. Short black hair. Dark, expressionless eyes. Light skin, nearly white. Angular, clean-shaven cheeks. Plain. As plain a face as any man could ever have. A face no one looked at twice. It was a trait he cultivated. The more forgettable he was, the more effective his work. Even the hiking clothes he'd bought yesterday were boring and drab. Lots of khaki. A wide-brimmed sun hat. A small Camelbak. He'd be a ghost out there, even to the few people who saw him.

He flipped the visor up and settled in.

***

Misty surprised him. At 10:00 hours, she and her boyfriend drove past the overlook in a black F150, much earlier than he'd anticipated. Had she matured in the last few years? Or had the boyfriend goaded her along? No matter. Possibilities like this were why Cervantes always arrived early. After letting another vehicle pass, he pulled out of the overlook, tailing the truck by a quarter mile. Winding through the curvy cliff roads and open sandstone expanse, there was no chance he would lose them. He could keep a safe distance back, with a car or two in between.

The mid-morning Nevada sun was a blazing pinhole in the fabric of an unspoiled sky. The temperature was in the sixties, with an incoming high in the low eighties. No humidity. There was a desolate beauty in places like this. As Cervantes drove past cactus-speckled boulder fields and gray limestone cliff faces, he wondered what secrets laid among the baked earth and the scrub brush. Might there be bodies buried out here, disappeared in the glory days of a mafia-controlled Vegas? Victims of a yet unknown serial killer? A slew of cold cases lurking six feet beneath the saguaros and the brittlebush? Yeah, probably.

As he tailed Misty, the sparse traffic became sparser. That was good. The more remote they were, the less chance of other hikers muddling the op. Cervantes checked his park map. This far out, there was only one trailhead to which the couple could be driving—Turtlehead Peak. That was also good. According to the trail map, the Turtlehead would provide several optimal scenarios. Cervantes would hike along behind them and make his move at the right moment when the most natural opportunity presented itself. He had no weapons with him save a utility knife and a garrote wire, and he would only use those if the situation got out of hand. This job had to look like an accident.

He parked his rental several spots down from Misty. She and the boyfriend had already exited the truck and were gearing up for the hike. As Cervantes had predicted, she was not dressed for function, but rather to impress. Betty Boop tennis shoes, black tights, a trendy t-shirt with shiny letters, a bandana, and oversized movie star sunglasses. He wanted to kill her already.

Then there was Zack. Big bastard. Schwarzenegger in his prime big. He wore a tank top and hiking shorts, flaunting hyperinflated muscles crisscrossed by thick, squiggly veins. Six foot four, smothered in facial hair and tattoos, the man looked like he swigged a gallon of steroids with every meal. If things went south, Cervantes was going to have to take this beast down. A ropy man of five-ten versus a goddamn minotaur.

Cervantes made a show of filling his Camelbak with water and snacks, allowing the couple time to finish their prep and begin hiking. Misty's yammering was shrill and excited as she checked her reflection in the truck window. She tucked a strand of blonde hair into her bandana, then pulled it back out when she decided it looked better that way. Zack hulked beside her, waiting impatiently. He glanced at Cervantes, disinterested.

There was one other car at the trailhead, an old Nissan Sentra. This meant there was at least one hiker on the Turtlehead right now, maybe more. Cervantes would have to keep that in mind. If those hikers stumbled into his job, they'd have to go, too. That would strain the narrative to incredulity. One couple vanishing on the trail was rare, but normal. Two separate couples vanishing on the same trail on the same day would create unwanted suspicion.

At long last, just as Cervantes was beginning to think they'd never leave, Misty and Zack began their hike, walking into the trailhead and quickly disappearing around a cactus-strewn bend. He waited. He'd give it a few minutes before he followed, to maintain his distance.

It had been what, five years since the Salvador's little dalliance with Misty Givens? It was hard to believe now, but back then, the Salvador hadn't been so careful. He'd been transitioning from handsome young *wunderkind* to visionary business magnate. His wealth and power had grown daily, his sphere of influence spreading like a fast-moving lava field. For a self-made man who'd begun life as an orphan, it was like suddenly being crowned an emperor. *You are better than everyone else, and this proves it.* With that intoxicating rush of success, he began to indulge his power, wielding it in ways that were damaging to his long-term interest. Like hosting secret investor parties where he paid black women to serve his rich white guests while wearing nothing but bondage manacles. Or by pitting homeless people against one another in an all-out brawl, the last bum standing winning a thousand dollars while the Salvador and his elitist club laughed.

Then there were the ladies. The Salvador loved ravishing the ladies, especially the forbidden ones. The married ones, like Misty Givens. Misty was a bubbly beauty who wielded her physical assets like a modern-day Marilyn Monroe. She had just risen to stardom, landing her first leading role. Hollywood's newest darling. When the Salvador met her, he became infatuated. He wanted her, and in his power-mad haze of superiority, he would not be denied. The fact that she had recently married was no hindrance, but rather an accelerant feeding his lusty fire. The Salvador charmed Misty into the sheets, not even bothering to hide the tryst from her husband. Naturally, the marriage hit the rocks. Yet even then, as Misty had fought to win back her husband's trust, the Salvador asserted his newfound dominance, taking her whenever the urge struck. Of course, after a couple of months, he lost interest. That toy no longer pleased him. He ghosted Misty, leaving her standing in the ruins of her marriage. Her career flamed out soon after.

Cervantes was kept busy back then. Covering for the Salvador, cleaning up his messes. The body count was much higher in those days as the Salvador fought a sea of rivals on his way to the top. It hadn't been easy. The man's ballooning ego could make things prickly, but he wizened in the ensuing years as his public profile mushroomed. With his hot-blooded power trip out of his system, he began to focus on his burgeoning empire and his future aspirations. To that end, he had recently become engaged.

Misty, on the other hand, was desperately trying to recapture her short-lived glory. This hiking trip was a social media farce designed to showcase her love of nature. Look at me, I'm so green, I respect the environment, I eat plants. Hollywood loved that type of crap.

But why did she have to die now, years after the affair? Cervantes suspected Misty had orchestrated her own death. No doubt she knew of the Salvador's meteoric rise. No doubt she blamed him for ruining her marriage and flunking out of Tinseltown. Now he was a household name with global business interests and a new fiancée. Misty probably believed she was owed some payback. Decided she could extort him. Give me a million dollars or I'll go to the press about such and such. Make me rich or I'll expose you for this or that. Cervantes didn't know what she had on him, what piece of evidence she might have saved from their affair. A damning video of his bondage party? A sex tape showing the Salvador's perverse preferences? Maybe nothing. Maybe Misty was bluffing, hoping that the Salvador would pay up without question. He was rich enough that he wouldn't blink at a million dollars of hush money. Cervantes suspected the latter. If Misty really had a winning hand, she'd have already played it. Even so, the Salvador couldn't afford to leave such a mess unattended. At the very least, Misty had the power to make things uncomfortable for him with his fiancée. Whether she had something or not, she had to go.

Cervantes strapped on his Camelbak and hit the trail. Gravel crunching beneath his boots, he wound his way along the bend. The trail began gaining elevation immediately, as expected. The trail guide rated the hike as strenuous and warned of an immediate lung-busting ascent. Later, there would be a long ravine that had to be scrambled as well as a precarious stretch of trail that paralleled a steep ridge, both of which the guide described as dangerous. They sounded like perfect places to have an accident.

Cervantes caught sight of Misty and Zack sixty yards ahead. They hadn't gotten very far. They were upslope, stopped in the shade of a giant rock shelf. Misty was taking photos of tiny flowers growing out of a bed of cacti. Zack had his thumbs in his backpack straps, waiting. To maintain his distance,

Cervantes sat on a rock and retied his boots. As the hike wore on, he had to repeat this often. Misty didn't seem to be able to take ten steps without stopping for pictures.

After two miles, the couple reached the ravine mentioned by the guide. Cervantes waited in the skinny shade of a juniper tree, watching from afar. The ravine wasn't as steep or as lengthy as he'd hoped and was therefore not an optimal kill box. If he flung Misty down the ravine, she might survive. He'd need to wait for a better spot.

While he lurked, he observed the couple scrambling the slope, grabbing rocks and fissures to help themselves up. Misty was weak and uncoordinated. That was obvious. As she slipped and struggled on the scree like a newborn fawn, Cervantes knew she was going to be a simple kill. But Zack was sure-footed, moving with power and awareness. At one point, while he waited for Misty to take a selfie, he pulled a watermelon-sized boulder off the ground and, out of boredom, hurled it down the slope. The bastard was strong, but strength wasn't everything. A man-beast of that size had weaknesses that could be used against him. But even a bull with ten swords stuck in his back can gore a matador to death. Cervantes had to use caution. Best case scenario, he could just push the happy couple off a ridge together and be done with it. That way they'd only sustain damage consistent with an accidental tumble down the mountain. There'd be no challenge in it, but the job was not to find a challenge. The job was to protect the Salvador.

After the couple cleared the ridgeline, Cervantes followed, springing up the ravine like the nimblest of mountain goats. Cresting the ridge, he saw Misty following Zack up and around a steep bend. He tailed them, making it a point to stay a bit closer now. In another half mile, the trail would come to the perilous highline ridge mentioned by the guide. Perhaps he could make his move there.

The sun was straight overhead now, beating down on his hat. His scalp was hot, but the rest of him was cool enough. A nice breeze and a lack of humidity made for a perfect hike. Having achieved an elevation of six thousand feet, he was being treated to sweeping panoramas of the high mountain desert. Now and again, tiny four-legged wildlife scampered across the sand. Overhead flew red-tailed hawks, drifting on the wind as they scanned the desert surface for prey. In another life, Cervantes might have called this place beautiful. Could even see himself living here, away from the cattle of society. In this life, however, he was entwined with the Salvador. Though they were not blood-related, and though their mothers didn't know each other, Cervantes and the Salvador were brothers. They'd been born on the same day, in the same hospital, just minutes apart. As newborns, they had likely rested in the same hospital nursery, mere inches separating them. Yet they only met many years later, at the Marine Corps School of Infantry at Camp San Onofre. Brought into life together, separately, yet reuniting at the most fortuitous time possible. It was no coincidence.

After a half mile, the trail leveled off, winding its way among the rocks and the marigolds. There, standing on a precarious ridge, were Misty and Zack, with the mountains and the big blue sky as their backdrop. Misty was attaching her phone to a selfie stick, preparing to take more pictures. Zack was irritated. He was sick of all the posing and stopping. As Misty fumbled with the stick, Zack fussed. "No, not like that. You have to put the thing in the—no, I said not like that!"

"Well, I'm trying!"

"You're not doing it right. You're about to break the damn thing."

"No, I'm not! Just shut up for one second, jeez."

"I wanna get out of here before midnight for fuck's sake."

"Just . . . here, I got it, okay? It's done. Now be quiet and take some pictures with me."

It was perfect. The two of them were standing only feet away from the edge of the cliff, where it would be easy. Hell, there was even a sign beside them reading: WARNING: FALLING HAZARD. DO NOT GO BEYOND THIS POINT.

They'd gone beyond the point.

Cervantes' breath quickened. Not from his labors, but from this moment. He was about to snuff out two lives for all eternity. Maybe he'd catch a glimpse of the horror in their eyes as they fell. That limitless fear, the sight of which electrified his soul. Just walk up to them as if to help. Get them to turn and look at the view. Hurl them into oblivion. Even when it was this easy, it was magnificent.

The couple posed with their backs to the cliff edge, Misty holding the selfie stick out in front of them. She was all white teeth and sunglasses. She struck several poses while she click-click-clicked. Zack was a scowling ox. He never smiled, never moved.

"You know what would be a great photo?" called Cervantes. He hoped his voice was steady, though he could taste the adrenaline in his mouth. "If you face the canyon and put your arms around each other. I could take it for you."

"Oh my god," said Misty, "that would be so cute! Thank you, yes, we'd love that." Cervantes walked over to them, noting Zack's beard-choked grimace. The big man loomed over him as he took Misty's phone, his bullish musk clashing with her too-sweet perfume. "Just press the red button," she said, adjusting her bandana. "Oh, and if you don't mind taking a couple of long shots and a couple of close shots that would be awesome."

"Sure."

"Thank you so much. Come on, Zack. Stop grumbling."

Cervantes took several steps back as the couple posed facing the cliff, their backs to him. Zack draped his arm around her shoulders, and she placed hers behind his waist. "Think you could scoot a little nearer to the edge?" asked Cervantes. "It'd make for a more dramatic photo."

Zack half-turned his head. "Are you nuts?"

Misty scooted him forward. "Come on, he's right."

"No, he's not. It won't make a shit of difference."

"What, is my big bad boy scared?" she teased. "Come on, just a little bit. Right here, there you go. Trust me, this is gonna look awesome."

"There," said Cervantes. "That's good right there."

Zack shook his head as the couple posed as before, only this time they were a foot closer to the cliff, their backs nice and square to the ledge. One savage push would be enough. Heart turning backflips, he tried to steady his breathing. He'd slain a lot of marks, but never like this. He'd shot them, he'd knifed them, he'd strangled them. He'd crushed one guy in a car compacter. But never this. This would be new—a flying death for two.

Holding the phone up, Cervantes faked taking the pictures. When the cops searched her SIM later, they could not be allowed to find photos of the couple standing by the ledge. They'd want to know who took those photos, taken right before their plunge. Couldn't have that. So he scooted ever closer, faking the photos and saying. "That'll be a good one. Keep holding, let me get a little closer."

A little closer.

He looked back at the trail to ensure no one was there.

A little closer.

Now.

Crouching, Cervantes dropped the phone and sprang forward like a sprinter off a starting block. He thrust his hands into their backs with explosive force, Misty with his left, Zack with his right. But just as he made contact, Zack ruined it. The man-beast had heard Cervantes' quickened footsteps and had started turning to look. That skewed his torso just enough to throw the angle off-kilter, keeping the shove from landing full force. Though jarred by the impact, with his stubborn mass and his deft reaction, he was able to spin on his feet and grab a fistful of Cervantes' shirt, preventing himself from falling. Misty was not so lucky—she flew like a wounded duck.

Zack saw her fall, heard her yell, but he was not the type of man to spend even a microsecond in shock. Powering himself away from the cliff, he unleashed fury on Cervantes, roaring and punching. Cervantes, shirt clutched in Zack's massive fist, could only focus on weathering the onslaught. He dodged, jammed, and deflected, avoiding direct blows and testing for leverage as the men spun around and around in a cloudy carousel of limbs.

"You motherfucker!" bellowed Zack, arm working like a jackhammer. "I'll kill you! I'll fucking kill you!"

Cervantes knew this could not continue. Zack's roaring would draw the attention of any hikers within earshot. And out here, sound carried for miles. He also knew he would not be able to end the bout by trading strikes. Zack's size and reach advantage could make for a prolonged fight, which would not do. He had to get the minotaur down into the dirt where he could use ground skills to defeat him. Tricky when he was being tossed like a rag doll.

Seeing a sliver of an opening in Zack's batshit assault, Cervantes jabbed his Adam's apple, choking off his roars. But to leverage that brief window, he'd had to sacrifice his own defense. Even as he popped Zack's throat, the big man's right fist smashed him full in the eye.

When Cervantes regained his wits, he found himself on his back with stars swirling in his vision. Zack was on top of him, a bearded blitzkrieg trying to pound him into the rock. The punch to his throat had stolen his breath, but not his reckless fury. But even during those few seconds in the twilight zone, Cervantes had maneuvered for position, his fighting instincts taking over. His legs were wrapped around Zack's waist, ankles crossed against his back—a full guard. From there, Cervantes controlled Zack's mobility, hampering his attack while squirming for a better position. Zack's blur of fists rained down, but even when they landed, they were ineffective, castrated by Cervantes' expert guard.

Zack's offense began losing steam as he incinerated his short supply of cardiovascular endurance. Cervantes had been expecting this. When he felt it, he struck. In a series of moves that may have looked like magic to a layman, he slithered out from under Zack, using his inflexible mass against him, and then he swarmed him like a squid engulfing its prey. Seconds later, Zack was shocked to find himself on his back locked in a vicious armbar. Unable to escape the lock, he flailed in the sand, desperately trying to punch and kick his way out of his helpless position. Cervantes heaved with the might of his entire body, applying maximum leverage against the elbow until he heard a deep, sickening pop. Zack roared in pain.

Cervantes released and back-rolled clear of the scrum. As Zack floundered, clutching his arm to his gut, Cervantes picked up a basketball-sized rock. He carried it over to Zack, who was attempting to stand. Cervantes front-kicked him in the throat, putting him back in the dirt. Then he raised the rock overhead and smashed it down on his face. The beast went limp.

"¡Pendejo!" hissed Cervantes, kicking his victim. "¡Saluda al diablo de mi parte!"

He began rolling the big man toward the cliff edge, straining against his weight. Moaning through shattered and bloodied teeth, Zack did his best to resist, but he could not stop the inevitable. He regained awareness as his body cleared the ledge, meeting Cervantes' eyes just before plummeting to his death. Sucking hot wind, Cervantes watched the tattooed mass slam against the cliff face, pinwheeling off a jutting rock. A moment later, he exploded on the canyon ground, ten feet away from the ruins of Misty Givens.

He looked, panting, savoring the sight. The familiar rush tingled through his blood, like tiny fireworks popping off in his veins. His godly reward for murder. But he had no time to enjoy it. Looking back, he snatched Misty's phone from the sand, cleaned off his prints, and tossed it off the cliff. Then he set about cleaning the site. Zack's blood was everywhere, and it had to be scooped and scoured away. There could be no signs of a struggle here, lest the rangers suspect foul play. Before Cervantes could begin in earnest, however, he noticed her. There, by the trail, stood a hiker. A lone woman, hiking poles holding her steady while she gaped at Cervantes in disbelief. She'd seen. She'd seen the fight, had seen the murder.

Now she had to disappear.

MOKUNA 7

VALORY JERKED UPRIGHT. DAZED, she sat quietly, waiting for her mind to de-fog.

"Doctor Grace? Are you awake?" Rafael's voice, followed by a knock. She realized where she was then. The castle. The bedchamber. She looked around the dark, wiping drool from her chin. The fire had turned to a pile of embers. Frost wreathed her breath. She was sitting at the table, still in yesterday's clothes. Her laptop glowed before her, flanked by the clay tablets. It was all real. Not some wild and crazy dream. She was in a castle, and she'd fallen asleep while translating the earliest written language ever.

Another knock, louder this time. "Yes," she called. "I'm up. Come in."

The door swung open with a groan. Rafael entered holding a propane lantern. He'd ditched the suit and was wearing comfortable field clothes with a jacket. He looked at Valory, then at the unused bed. "Oh, *cara mia!* You have not slept a wink!"

"Oh. No, I guess not."

"This is my fault, I am so sorry, Valory. I should not have given you the tablets last night. Now you have not rested at all."

"No no," she said. "I'm fine."

"Ach, I feel awful. Please, go back to sleep. There will be plenty of time—"

"No," she said with a little more vigor than she'd intended. "I'm fine. Better than fine." She stood, unable to contain a smile. "You won't believe what I've translated."

"Translated? You don't mean the tablets."

"I do, actually," she said. Rafael stared at her, wondering if she was joking. Or perhaps still asleep and talking nonsense. "Can I show you?"

"You are serious? You've translated them already?"

"Well, you gave me exactly what I needed. But first, I have to ask. Are you positive these tablets are ten thousand years old?"

"Thereabouts, yes. Fossil fragments in the clay were carbon dated to that age."

"Good. Okay, look at this." She snatched his lantern out of his hand as he stood open-mouthed. Casting the light upon the table, Valory swept her free hand over three of the tablets. "These three are practice tablets. You can see that the author was still feeling out this invention of his, trying to adapt some existing oral language into writing. Look here, this first tablet shows the same set of characters, repeated several times. Most of them show gradual modifications as you read from left to right, probably as he sought to further differentiate the characters. He was trying to standardize his new alphabet. Determining the angles of the strokes, the lengths of the arcs, how deep to inscribe them into the clay, things like that. Interestingly, the script gets more artistic as he goes, as if simple forms aren't meeting his internal vision."

"Like he had an artist's soul."

"Quite an anomaly for the time period, right? And look here. See these faint indentions around this grouping? He mashed out this entire area and started over, probably because he'd messed up. The world's first typo." Valory's cheek-to-cheek smile contrasted with her reddened, sleep-starved eyes.

"Yes, I see."

"The second tablet is dedicated mostly to phonetics. He's tying sounds to his new alphabet. Of course, we can only guess at how it sounded. But look at this third tablet," she said, steamrolling Moretti's response. "This is where he starts stringing everything together. Writing simple sentences, sizing the distance between the characters, the words, the margins, things like that. It's mostly just basic content. For instance," she said, pointing at a word grouping, "this says 'the sun hides behind the clouds today.' This next grouping says 'Two elk were felled in the hunt.' I'm not sure if it says elk. It's something like that, an elk or a deer or whatever. There's no way for me to know the species. I just wrote elk and notated it."

"I see. But how were you able to—"

"But this one," said Valory, laying her fingers on the fourth tablet. Her face lit up in a way that few people had ever witnessed. "*This* one, Doctor . . ."

"What? What does it say?"

"Here, just read the translation for yourself."

She spun her laptop toward Rafael, then stepped away and watched him. Her typed translation of the tablet was there on the screen, waiting. Wrapping his glasses over his ears, Rafael leaned in and began reading.

Men have known me by many names
This day they call me Alikai
I make these marks as a gift to you
For you are me and we are one
No one can know our sorrow
Nor why we make these marks

For men wither and die with the seasons
While you and I yet live on
Him who we call friend
With whom we hunt and feast and sing
Turns to dust beneath our feet
She with whom we laugh and love
Who whispers to us in the night
Is lost in the winds of time
Their faces fade from memory
Their voices vanish like dreams
Until we wonder if they ever drew breath at all
Always has it been and always shall it be
Thus we make these marks to remember
Hardened in the earth they shall persist
A thousand winters hence shall you read this
You who are me
And you will know what we did
And what we said
And you will be reminded of those
With whom we shared our time
You will read of things that were done
By others and by us
For we shall make these marks without fail
From this moon onward and forever.
I shall be your companion from the times that were
As you shall be mine from the times that will be
With these marks shall we make a bridge
Over the river of eons that divides us
Let us be one another's savior
In this world where we do not belong

Rafael pulled away from the screen, but Valory pre-empted his reaction. "Can you believe it? I mean, okay, let's exclude the content for a moment and focus on the technicals. Right off the bat, we have a written language developed for the sole purpose of communicating a stream of consciousness. That's in stark contrast to other ancient writings which evolved from accounting practices." She spat a twist of wayward hair from her lips. "We know the very earliest marks were more akin to chicken scratching, written to keep track of sheep, measures of barley, jars of oil, stuff like that. Those first markings were conceived out of necessity to manage growing economies, *not* as a record of speech. Over many centuries, they evolved into ideograms, pictograms, and so on, eventually leading to true written languages like Sumerian."

"*Si, certo.*"

"But this isolate is unique, and not just because of its artistic nature. It didn't evolve from an accounting system or anything else. It was a deliberate

59

invention, someone's focused brainchild." She paused, waiting for Rafael to ooh and ahh, but he only looked on, waiting for her to continue. "Don't you see, Doctor? This author totally bypassed centuries of writing evolution, creating this highly artistic, novel system in his own little bubble. That's like . . . I don't know, like Einstein developing relativity without ever having heard of physics!"

"Interesting," mumbled Rafael, inspecting the tablets as if he'd never seen them before.

Valory was disappointed in his subdued reaction, but she plowed forward. "So how did this guy do it? How did he create the first written language in a vacuum, thousands of years before the rest of the world? And why is the script so artistic when rudimentary impressions would have sufficed?"

"Do you have a hypothesis?"

"Well, we clearly have a very gifted individual here. A genius for his time. This could be a stretch, of course, but I'm thinking he could even be a high-functioning autistic. A savant."

"Oh? Why do you say that?"

"Just a hunch, really, but look at the content." Valory spun the laptop back toward herself. "First of all, it has a poetic feel to it, don't you think? I mean it's choppy and lacks any real structure, but we can forgive him for that. Point is, he saw things differently from his contemporaries. He's introspective and creative in a time when those qualities were probably not valued or recognized like they are today. Look here, he refers to his marks as a bridge over a river of eons. Granted, he didn't use the word eons. His literal wording is 'a river of time so vast it cannot be known.' I felt eons conveyed his point. In any case, that's one sophisticated metaphor, don't you think?"

"Certainly."

"And he's very sad. That's obvious. At its heart, the text is just one long lament. And why is he so sad?" Valory looked at Rafael as if she were dropping an epiphany bomb on him. "Because he thinks he's immortal! Either that or he has created a work of fiction, which I'm not buying. This man is alone. He feels like an outsider, like gifted people often do. So much so that he has fabricated this delusion of immortality. He invented the first written language from scratch, *specifically* to send a message to his future self, just so he could read it years later and feel like someone shares his unique experiences and understands his pain. This tablet is a sympathy letter to himself. He never wanted or expected anyone else to read it. There wasn't even a such thing as 'reading' back then."

"I see."

Do you? She wanted to yell. *Because someone forgot to tell your face!* "Doctor Moretti, don't you think this is amazing? I'm telling you that not only have we discovered the father of written language, but also that he was possibly a savant with delusions of immortality. Does that not blow your mind?"

"Oh yes, yes. My mind is quite blown, I assure you. Apologies, *cara mia*. I just wasn't expecting . . . may I ask how were you able to translate all this so quickly? With so little source material? I don't mean to offend," he said, frantically waving off the idea. "Please know I'm not questioning your findings, Valory. It's just that I've been doing this for forty-three years, and I've never seen anyone do such a thing. My esteemed colleague, Professor Mancini, began examining these tablets last summer, and he has made, shall we say, only moderate progress. Then I bring you here, and in one night, you've deciphered this language? Using only these samples?" he said, gesturing toward the four tablets. "That seems eh, what is the English word for it? I've lost it." He snapped his fingers, trying to jog his memory. "*Sovrannaturale*. How do you say that?"

"Preternatural," answered Valory quietly, the word feeling like a bubble that floated off and popped in the distance.

"Yes! Preternatural, thank you." With that, he waited for her explanation.

She might have expected this. Sooner or later, everyone wanted an explanation. *How did you do that? That's not possible. How do I know you're not mistaken? I don't believe it. Where are your workings?* The watered-down version she'd given Rafael yesterday wasn't going to cut it now. Not after this. She should have been more thoughtful in how she disclosed her findings. Now she had to give him something palpable or he might distrust her translation. If he doubted her expertise—if he thought she was making things up and that she couldn't have deciphered the inscriptions in one night—then he might dismiss her from the project. After having been exposed to all this, that would be devastating. But the dead honest truth? No. She could never tell him that. Could never tell him about last night . . .

***

Rafael closed the door behind him, leaving her alone with the clay tablets. There they were, laid out on the table, waiting. The firelight licked the chamber walls, popping and crackling. Despite the hour, Valory dove into the work. The tablets had been calling to her the second they'd been uncased. She'd just been waiting for Rafael to leave.

Breathing deeply, she reached for the first tablet. Placed her gloved fingertip on the upper leftmost character. Let the flesh of her pad fill the groove. She lingered there for a moment. Then, slowly, she pulled her fingertip from top to bottom, never breaking contact. The character slipped inside her. Through the glove, it slid beneath her skin, into her bloodstream,

61

caressing her flesh from the underside. There, in her very essence, it undressed itself. She could feel it. She could *smell* it. Gleefully exposed, it danced like a thing alive, weaving among a vast store of color-splashed letters from all the languages of the world. This one was greenish-yellow and slick in her mind, with the aroma of fresh rain on a grassy meadow. She inhaled it as if she were standing in that meadow with her arms open wide. She knew it then. She *knew* it. The mark had found its home within her. No need to make notes, no fear of forgetting. The mark had become hers, forever.

She barely felt herself moving to the next letter. Her finger just flowed to the right, sinking into the adjacent groove. On the tablet, this was a curl-swept swoosh with a dot hovering above it, but in her mind, it was light pink, fluffy like cotton, and it smelled of magnolia. She absorbed that mark, too. Then she moved to the next mark, and the next, and the next, each of them tingling with color, aroma, and texture unique to all others. As she became more familiar with the graphemes—their style, their technique, the intent behind their making—she began playing the tablets like a pianist, clocking their centuries-old forms as her fingers roamed the pitted surfaces. When she had absorbed all the characters on the tablet, she played with them like new and exotic toys in her mind. She swirled them into a myriad of configurations as if assigning them dance partners. If they didn't dance well with one partner, she matched them to other partners, and to others, and to others, until their pairings were fluid and graceful. With every dance, a piece of the puzzle was solved, a fragment of meaning uncovered. Slowly in the first few hours, quickly in the next few, and then all at once. By sunrise, the mysterious, ancient tongue had rendered its lost provenance unto her, and she could hear its voice over the very bridge of eons which it conceptualized. The language was hers.

The fire had dwindled. The air was frosty. Valory slouched at the table, unaware of the hours that had passed. In the charged aftermath of her session, she felt something new. Something she'd never felt with any other project— the essence of a man. Just a faint feeling to be sure, but amidst those words she'd pulled from the fog of time, he was there, alone, kneeling upon the ground, making his strange letters in the soft clay. Though she couldn't see his face, his skin color, or any meaningful physical detail, she knew it was him. Him, the father of written language. Working his stylus, unaware that he was creating the most beautiful, most vital innovation in the history of humankind. On some level that Valory could not explain, she connected with him. She heard his voice. Resonated with his pain. Felt his genius, his naked loneliness. For she was alone, too. She felt the aching pain of her own genius, much like he had. This man, this Alikai, whispered to her from the darkness of ages past, for she alone had deciphered his message. In a way that both baffled and excited her, she was . . . *touched.*

$$***$$

"Valory?"

"Hm?"

"Is everything alright?"

"Oh. Yes, sorry. What were you saying? Oh, right," she said, her world becoming solid again. "My translation."

"It's okay if you're too tired. I don't mean to pressure you."

"No, it's fine. Honestly, I don't think I'll be sleeping much in the next few days. Not with stuff like this to work on." Composing herself, Valory calculated her next words. She was going to have to give Rafael more than she wanted, but she didn't have to give him everything. "Rafael, have you heard of synesthesia?"

"Synesthesia? I'm not sure I have."

"It's a rare neurological condition in which stimulation of one cognitive pathway involuntarily activates a second cognitive pathway."

"Ah. And that means?"

"Well, it can manifest in several ways depending on the person. For me, it manifests as grapheme-color synesthesia. That is, when I see or hear language, I experience it in colors. Internally."

"Ah, yes! Now that you mention it, I believe I have heard of this. It is common among . . . certain types of geniuses, no?"

Valory nodded, warming with embarrassment. She'd caught his near slip—Rafael had almost said the A word. And yes, it was true. A great number of synesthetes were autistic. That's why it was never easy telling people about her gift. The few times she had, they'd tended to treat her differently afterward. They'd speak to her in a more calculated way. Or they'd watch her when they thought she wasn't looking, as if observing a gifted gorilla in a lab. The stigma of autism was awkward and unwieldy, a perpetual elephant in the corner of Valory's life. Was it any wonder that she preferred to keep her synesthesia quiet?

"Yes," said Valory. "I don't see myself as a genius, but yes, many synesthetes display capabilities unattainable by the average person. Myself, I've been a synesthete since I was a toddler. I don't remember much about those early days, but my parents tell me I absorbed language and vocabulary like a sponge on steroids. Their words. Mom said as a baby, my eyes would open wide anytime I heard someone speaking. She said I'd just lay there listening, trying to mimic what I'd heard."

"*Che carino.*"

"In my twos, I never showed the slightest interest in any other type of activity. Just language. I was always trying to read books that were beyond my age level, or I'd watch TV, mimicking the characters' dialogue and accents. When my parents turned it off, I'd just bumble around repeating what I'd heard until bedtime."

"I see, go on."

"Well, to fast forward a bit. I read and mimicked speech incessantly, developing language skills beyond my years. By the time I was three, I could speak English at a teenage level. That's what my parents tell me anyway. I can't really remember."

"Sure."

"My first real memory with a foreign language was when we were at the grocery store, and I overheard this elderly couple speaking Spanish for the first time. I was enthralled. Sitting in the shopping cart, I absorbed every word." Valory fell short of revealing that their words felt cottony, or that they surged like a zesty river of rainbows through her young mind. *No need to go overboard here.* "After eavesdropping on them for a few minutes, I began repeating everything they said, which kind of freaked them out. When my mom recognized how fascinated I was, she brought me home and turned the TV to a Spanish station." Valory shrugged. "I was fluent in Spanish a few months later."

"*Oddio,* is that true? How old were you then?"

"Five, I think."

"Goodness, that is remarkable."

"After mastering Spanish, I just started devouring any language I could get my hands on. TV, radio, books. Verbal or written. Wherever I could find a new tongue, I went after it. French came next, then Italian, then German. I learned them all and just kept going. When I was eleven," said Valory, smiling at the memory, "I made Dad take me to a Vietnamese church just to sit and listen to the sermons. We got some weird looks from the congregation, but I loved it. To me, their language sounded like birds singing." *And were like colorful feathers fluttering in my mind.* "I began imitating them to the point of obsession. After a few weeks, I began speaking Vietnamese to the congregation. They were pretty shocked."

"I can imagine," chuckled Rafael. "What a sight that must have been."

"Doctor Moretti, I can't explain why my condition has equipped me or motivated me to understand language. I just know that being able to see it in colors is like a cheat code. They help me memorize, catalog, and compare with ease. I just get it, you know? Language makes perfect sense to me in a world where little else does. I'm rubbish at everything else. I have no other real-world skills. No hobbies except maybe yoga. No serious relationships. But I know language from the inside out. This," she said, touching the clay tablet nearest her, "makes perfect sense to me. The man who wrote it—" she caught herself, stuttering when she realized she was going flush with the memory of being 'touched.' "The uh, the man who wrote this . . . I know his message. And I stand by my translation."

"Yes yes, of course, my dear. I am so sorry, I think I have offended you. That was not my intention, I swear."

"No, it's okay. You're right to wonder."

Rafael slumped forward. "Valory, I feel like such a poor host. First, I make you endure that ride in the jeep, then I keep you up all night, and then I question your fantastic work, and it truly is fantastic. I'm sorry if I seemed underwhelmed. Look, let us start fresh, hm? I came to fetch you for breakfast. *Per favore*, when you're ready, please join me there. The Dining Hall is on the same level as the Great Hall, just take the north corridor and you'll run into it. You remember how to get down there?"

"Yes, thank you. I'll be on my way in a moment."

When Rafael left, she slumped into her chair, exhausted. Not from her sleepless night, but from that conversation. Getting real with people was tiresome enough. Revealing deeply personal details about herself made her feel like her body cavities had been pried open and examined with a flashlight. It was embarrassing to know others suspected her of being autistic. Especially because some people still thought so. That's why she didn't tell Rafael the truth—that colors only constituted a fraction of her perceptual experience. There was no need to tell him that letters had aromas and textures, or that words stimulated her on a level that no man ever had. Nor did she wish to justify the fact that she much preferred being alone with her studies rather than interacting with other humans. She'd learned to hide such things long ago. For, whenever she talked about the smell of the letter R, or how the French word for apple, *pomme*, felt like a cool, yellow breeze—those were the kind of things that caused people to look at her like a freak. The second glances, the furrowed brows, the whispers. She didn't recognize those expressions as a youth, lost in her own vibrant world of language as she was. Violet often called her a weirdo, but that was to be expected among bickering twins. Valory was in her teens when she began to realize Vi was right. People did think she was a weirdo. Like, everyone. For a teenage girl, it was a mortifying realization. One that led to her clamming up for good. From a certain point on, she had become quiet, shy little Val. The meek, mousy bookworm with a universe of color swirling in her mind. Reclusion became the comfortable baseline of her existence. Yes, she was still obliged to interact with others, but at least the when and the where were usually up to her.

Her colleagues at Oxford had learned to accept her idiosyncrasies, but still, whenever she met them in person, the unspoken question was always written on their faces—*You know every language in the world, yet you don't like talking to people?* The irony was not lost on her. Why the *Rain Man* of language would prefer to be alone in an old folks home rather than use her gift out in the world, not even she could not explain, and she had grown tired of trying. If she was ever forced to tell anyone about being *touched*, she'd probably just jump off the nearest cliff.

Taking a moment to reflect on her conversation with Rafael, she couldn't help but wonder—why hadn't he been more shocked by her translation? Even if he'd been skeptical, she'd have expected more of a reaction to her hypothesis about the savant with delusions of immortality. He hadn't even flinched at that bombshell. Most curious.

FEJEZET 8

AFTER A SPIT BATH, a change of clothes, and a half-hearted attempt to apply a bit of make-up, Valory threw on her jacket and made her way down to the Great Hall. Emerging from the spiral stairwell, the view stopped her in her tracks. Though it was cold and devoid of people, the hall glowed. The morning light shone through the high windows, dust drifting in the slanting sunbeams. The walls, the columns, the statues—everything was bathed in a soft, magical radiance. It was almost holy. Only the portable light stands and the extension cords snaking along the marble tiles marred the scene. Still, those items could not detract from the majesty before her. For a moment, she just stood and absorbed it.

To her right, an arched entrance to the north corridor loomed. Valory was supposed to take the corridor to the Dining Hall—she could hear the voices of Rafael and others echoing down the hallway—but she couldn't resist spending some time meandering the Great Hall alone in the morning allure. There was so much to see. The fine details that had been muted by darkness last night stood now illuminated. The gray veins in the marble flooring. A hairline crack in the hand of one of the courtiers. A curled bit of ragged canvas on a nearby painting. All the things that made the dream real.

Valory found herself being pulled toward the centerpiece of the hall—the queen. She was soon standing on the dais before the throne, admiring her. This young, beautiful woman, immortalized in marble, ruling over her vast hall of treasures. Beside her, a second throne, presumably the king's, but for some reason empty. Only this mysterious queen presided here, adorned with crown and scepter. Kissed by the sunlight, her white face was flushed with morning amber, eyes teased with sleepy life. Valory could imagine that the queen was slowly becoming real, fed by the sun's warmth, and that she might soon rise from her throne and speak. Oh, that she could. What would she say? What language would she speak? What histories might she reveal?

"She is very beautiful, no?"

Valory turned, startled. Behind her stood a thin woman engulfed by a heavy pink winter coat. She was fair-skinned with a dark blonde ponytail and glasses, and she held a laptop against her chest with both arms. Her smile was timid and awkward. She had spoken softly with a heavy French accent.

"Yes," said Valory, "she is quite beautiful."

"I am sorry, I do not try to startle you." The woman stepped forward and offered her hand. "My name is Janelle LaFleur. I am here for to appraise and document the artwork in the castle."

"Ah," answered Valory, recognizing that Janelle was not fully fluent in English. "*Enchanté. Je m'appelle Valory Grace. Je suis ici pour traduire des textes.*"

"*Enchanté,*" said Janelle. Her handshake was so gentle that it was almost non-existent. "*Merci de parler français,* but I try to practice my English, so it's okay, yes?"

"Of course. Well, I'm happy to help if you need it." Valory was disappointed that Janelle wanted to speak English. French was her favorite, hands down. It was a soft and flowy Romance language, and she experienced it as vibrant swaths of pastels, like an Easter party in her head.

"Thank you. You are American, yes? I am asking this because your French is very good. I am not hearing American accent."

Valory shrugged. "Language is kind of my thing."

"Ah, *oui, très bien.* Then you are here for to study the text? Like old books?"

"I am, yes, but I've only seen a few samples so far. Doctor Moretti—I assume he recruited you, too?—he's taking me to the library today."

"The library?" With Janelle's accent, the question sounded like *Zeh librarEE?* "I do not know there is library here."

"No? Have you been here long?"

"Mm, about three weeks."

And they haven't told you there's a library? "Well, according to Doctor Moretti, it's vast and incredible."

"Ah," said Janelle, nodding. "Sure, sure. You are arriving here yesterday, yes?"

"Yes, last night."

"Can you believe all this?" Janelle held her arm toward the hall. "When they bring me here, I am thinking it is so amazing. I cannot believe my luck."

Valory nodded. "Same here. I'm still pinching myself. It must be exciting being among the first to study all this amazing art. There's so much of it," said Valory, gesturing around. "You must have your hands full."

"It is a dream that comes true. I cannot even express." Janelle's cheeks were flush, her posture tight. Kind of mousy. Valory sensed a fellow introvert, perhaps with a touch of social anxiety. Shy and meek, Janelle had likely taken a big step in coming over and introducing herself. That is just not something with which introverts are comfortable. They must work up the courage to face even superficial encounters. Valory could testify to that.

"I know what you mean," said Valory. "I've been here one night, and I've already worked on the most exciting translation of my career."

"Yes, that is my feeling, too. I am eh . . ." Unable to finish her thought in English, Janelle switched to French, saying that if it wasn't so cold up here, she'd think she had died and gone to Heaven.

Valory agreed, sharing a laugh. "So, what can you tell me about our queen here?"

"*Elle est très magnifique, no?* She is the best sculpture in the castle." Janelle stepped onto the dais to stand beside the queen. "She is made of Calacatta. Do you know of Calacatta?"

"Doesn't sound familiar."

"It is marble from the Carrara region of Italy. The finest marble in the world. Rare and expensive. It is the stone preferred even by Michelangelo. These others," said Janelle, pointing at random marble courtiers positioned around the hall, "their stone comes from many quarries around Europe. Some come from Carrara, but they are not Calacatta. Only the queen is Calacatta. This says she was very special to the artist."

"I see."

"Not just this," said Janelle, "but she is perfect."

"Perfect?"

"Yes. Because you see, in all sculptures, there are always mistakes. Tiny imperfections, eh, design flaws, things like this." *Sings like ziss.* "For example, you know Michelangelo's *David*, yes? Well, *David* has a design flaw. His center of gravity no is balanced. This makes extra pressure on the ankles, and this has made some cracks. If you tilt him a little," said Janelle, leaning sideways, "he will break at his feet."

"Yikes."

"Yes, this is how I mean. Even the masters are not perfect. Mistakes are found in all sculptures, including the others in this hall. But the queen . . ." she looked upon the queen's face with hushed reverence. "She is perfect. No imperfections, no design flaws, nothing. She is a very rare masterpiece. Whoever made her might be the greatest sculptor of all time."

For what seemed like the hundredth time since she'd arrived, Valory was stunned. The greatest sculptor of all time? Whose masterpiece was way up here in a secret, forgotten castle, which also happened to house the most ancient language in human history? That didn't make much sense. Then again, very little about this place made sense. Valory leaned in close, studying the queen's cheeks, her hair, and the blank orbs of her eyes. She was no art expert, but as far as she could see, Janelle was right about the lack of surface imperfections. There were no nicks, no gouges, no scarring. The swooping lines of her dress flowed with stark realism, and even her fingernails were flawless. Every inch of her was as smooth as glass, her

69

patina reflecting the amber glow of the morning. "Janelle," she said, "I do believe I'm speechless."

"*Oui,* speechless. This is me, too." As Valory continued to inspect the queen, Janelle, feeling encouraged, chanced a more personal topic. "I like to say, Valory, I am happy to see other woman here in the castle. I am feeling, eh, what is this word? *Dépassé en nombre?*"

"Outnumbered."

"Yes, *merci.* Outnumbered."

For a half second, the English word outnumbered took on a darker hue in her mind, deepening from its usual sandy beige, before returning to normal. The French translation, *dépassé en nombre,* remained a frothy pastel blue. Words did that sometimes. "So you're saying there are no other women here?"

"There was one woman the day I was arriving, but I only see her, I never meet her. They say she had to leave. Family reason or something like this." *Sumzing like ziss.*

"I see." Valory hadn't thought about it before now, but it was true. There had been no other women in sight since she'd begun her journey to the castle. It was nice to finally meet one, and a kindred spirit at that. Pale, studious, quiet—she and Janelle, it seemed, were two sides of the same page. "Well in that case," said Valory, "let's not be strangers. I'm not entirely sure how my days are going to look yet, but maybe we can eat dinner together some nights. Talk about our work, compare notes?"

"Yes." Janelle nodded, pleased with the suggestion. "Yes, I would like this."

A piercing whistle cut the silence of the hall. It was *Agente* Savelli, standing in the portal to the north corridor. He called to Valory, voice echoing. "*Dottoressa, per favore, ti stiamo aspettando.*" They were waiting for her.

"*Va bene,*" she called, then said to Janelle, "*À bientôt, oui?*"

"*Oui,* goodbye."

Savelli waited as she walked toward the portal. She wondered if his brusque attitude may have cooled by now, but as she neared, she saw he was all business. Annoyed, even. "*Per favore,*" he said matter-of-factly, "this way."

The marble tile ended where the corridor began. Valory followed Savelli, mindful of the electrical cords running along the floor. As she walked, she again found herself marveling at the stonework—the floor, the walls, the arches, the friezes—everything blending into everything else with no seams to be found. At some point, she hoped to discover how such a thing had been done.

The Dining Hall was a vaulted room with a long table of oak flanked with high-backed chairs, eight per side. A fireplace big enough to warm

Valory's Oxford flat three times over stood cold and dark on the west wall, its stone mantel carved with elaborate friezes. Thick tapestries were draped along the other walls. A pair of iron chandeliers were suspended from the ceiling, though they held no candles. Rafael and a group of men were standing near a portable light in the far corner, speaking together. At their end of the table, a host of period tableware had been gathered. Plates, platters, silverware, ewers, candlesticks, all centuries old, the stuff of antique dealers' dreams. They were not being used for breakfast but rather seemed to have been carefully moved out of the way. And over there in the corner, were those instruments? They were half-hidden by darkness, but Valory thought she could make out a lyre and a drum, maybe a flute lying on the stone. Had troubadours entertained noble diners in centuries past?

Savelli was already huddling with the others. Having only seen such a setting in movies, all Valory could manage was a head shake. Her 'this is amazing' muscles were too fatigued to endure another round of slack-jawed awe.

On the end of the table nearest Valory, a breakfast spread had been set up. There were pastries, cold meats, and *biscotti*, with water, juice, and coffee. She poured and decorated a cup of coffee, then turned to view the tapestry behind her. Against a field of deep red, there was a raven-haired maiden in an extravagant dress standing beneath a royal canopy. The queen from the throne room? At her feet lounged a large black panther. Surrounding the canopy were evergreen oaks and cypress trees, with a multitude of birds in the crimson skies. The tapestry was in excellent condition.

A whispered argument caught her ear. Savelli and Rafael had stepped away from the others and were engaged in a heated exchange. She couldn't hear what was being said, but they each darted a glance at Valory, confirming her suspicion—they were arguing about her. Why, she couldn't begin to imagine.

"Doctor Grace," called Rafael, breaking away from Savelli. "Please come over here. Let me introduce you to everyone."

Valory immediately forgot about the argument. Time to steel herself. Meeting new people was not easy. Asking her to meet a *group* of people all at once was like asking her to stroll across hot coals. *Come over here and let complete strangers ply you with questions, false niceties, and boring stories while you try your best not to appear aloof.* It was so draining. She could spend ten hours straight studying language without so much as a yawn, but ten minutes in forced conversation with strangers zapped her batteries for hours afterward. No wonder Janelle was hanging out alone in the Great Hall. Stepping toward the group, Valory manufactured smiles and eye contact.

Speaking Italian, Rafael introduced the men from left to right. First was *Capitano* Alfonso Ricci, who commanded the onsite military detail. He nodded but said nothing. Beside him was *Tenente* Pietro Esposito, who coordinated equipment and rations for those staying inside the castle. He stopped chewing a pastry long enough to say hello. Then there was Dario Bertinelli, a portly structural engineer who had worked on a slew of historical restoration projects in Italy, including several at the Colosseum. Dario's friendly smile was missing a tooth. She already knew Marco Savelli, of course, grim and pockmarked. Next to him were fellow *Agenti Speciali*, Gianni Moreno and Enzo D'Arezzo. D'Arezzo was scheduled to depart soon now that Savelli had returned. There were always at least two homeland agents stationed on-site, and usually three. Lorenzo Trentino, the chain smoker who'd driven them to the airport yesterday, was on another assignment for several weeks. Valory noted with some discomfort that all three agents were armed, catching occasional glimpses of the pistols inside their blazers.

Though overwhelmed by the number of people she was meeting, there was one thing Valory enjoyed—the sensations of spoken Italian. The language was fiery red in her perception, shot through with vibrant purple and green gradients. It had a spicy, slightly alcoholic scent. The more people speaking it at once, the stronger it flowed. It had been a long time since she'd been mind-deep in those perceptions—there weren't many Italians at Oxford.

"And also," said Rafael, continuing the conversation in Italian, "we have an art historian and curator here, who I'm told you've already met."

"Janelle," said Valory. "Yes, I just met her in the Great Hall."

Savelli cleared his throat at that comment, and Rafael tensed. Something uncomfortable there, something about Janelle. That seemed weird. What problem could Savelli have with the shy little art mouse?

Rafael ignored Savelli's prompt. "Well then, the only two you haven't met are my colleagues, Emilio Mancini, professor emeritus, and his nephew, Rollo Stephano. They hail from the University of Florence but have graciously agreed to help us here. They are probably already in the library. Professor Mancini will be your primary research partner."

"Really?" said Valory. "An emeritus professor is okay working under my direction?"

"Eh, yes." Rafael rubbed a meaty palm along his bald spot. "He is old and simply relishes the opportunity to be in the field again. You will need his help. But please, have some breakfast and get to know the others, *si?* We shall go the library after."

"Could we just go now?"

"Now? Don't you want to enjoy your coffee? Have something to eat?"

Glancing at the group of men, who had resumed talking amongst themselves, Valory shook her head. "I'm not hungry. And I'm anxious to see this library."

"Ah. Well then, who am I to keep you from work? Let us go to the library!"

Rafael excused the two of them. Dario Bertinelli, the engineer, smiled at Valory, saying he was pleased to have met her. Savelli eyed Rafael with keen purpose.

Halfway down the corridor, Rafael stopped and faced her. "Valory, I must tell you something."

"Okay."

"We have certain strict directives from the *Agenzia Informazioni e Sicurezza Interna*. This site, for reasons we discussed yesterday, is classified as top secret by the Italian government. As such, we are instructed to, eh, compartmentalize our efforts."

"Compartmentalize. Meaning?"

"The contractors that we bring here, like you and Mr. Bertinelli and Ms. LaFleur, and others, we are asked to eh . . ."

"Yes?"

"You are asked not to share information with each other. Your expertise, your research, these kinds of things. They do not want anyone leaving here knowing everything there is to know about this place and what they've seen. For security purposes, you see?"

"They're forbidding researchers from collaborating?"

"I know it is harsh, but this is what my government demands."

"But collaboration is the bedstone of academic progress. We don't learn in vacuums. Your government must know that."

"Yes, they know the restriction is not ideal, but they feel it is necessary, at least for now. To that end, I must ask you not to meet with Ms. LaFleur or any other contractors unless you are supervised by one of the homeland agents."

So that's why Savelli's knickers were in a bunch. He'd seen Valory talking to Janelle, perhaps even heard her explaining her findings about the perfect queen. That was an apparent no-no around here. How ridiculous. "So, I am to keep my research to myself."

"Well, you may of course collaborate with Professor Mancini and his associate since you are working on the same project. Just no one else."

"That doesn't seem like overkill to you? I mean, this is not a nuclear missile facility."

"I agree, but these are our orders. I am sorry, Valory."

"So anytime I want to talk to Janelle, an agent has to be present."

"I'm afraid this is non-negotiable. Believe me, I have tried."

Great. The only two women in the castle had to have a man there telling them what they could and couldn't say. Just great. Times like these were where Valory wished she had a bit of her sister's spunk. Violet would give everyone here a tongue-lashing over such an injustice. Instead, Valory asked "Any other rules?"

"Actually," said Rafael, "this goes without saying, but you are not to remove anything from the keep. Artifacts, keepsakes, what have you. Everything here is property of the Italian government."

"Of course."

"Also, I must ask you not to go into any part of the castle that you haven't been given explicit permission to enter. This level is fine. And, of course, the living quarters, the library, and common areas like the hall and the courtyard. But please do not proceed to the upper levels of the keep, nor to the, uh, the tower." Rafael appeared squeamish with this last request. "For your own safety, and for the national security reasons I have mentioned."

Valory figured it couldn't hurt to take a shot. "What's in the tower?"

"I'm told there is some sensitive information up there. Only the homeland agents are allowed access." Rafael hesitated before continuing. "I must stress this rule, Doctor Grace. Please, please do not venture anywhere off-limits. They take this very seriously."

Valory felt like they'd closed Disney World after riding a single ride. She'd been expecting to tour the entire castle. There would never be another opportunity to explore an untouched wonder like this for the rest of her life, and she'd just been told she would only be allowed to see a portion of it. "Well," she sighed, "if this library is half as spectacular as you say, I suppose I'll cope."

"Thank you for understanding. Shall we?"

They continued toward the library, taking the spiral stairwell down. The level beneath the Great Hall, which was the ground level, housed the kitchen, storage areas and the servant quarters. Rafael explained that most of the agents and civilians were bunking on that level. Valory felt a poke of guilt. Her lavish bedchamber was much roomier than the servant quarters. Why had she been given VIP treatment over the others?

Using his flashlight in the frosty darkness, Rafael led her down one more level, explaining that they were now under the castle. This level had been carved out of the rock beneath the keep, ensuring it was always cool and free from outside elements. Perfect for preserving ancient tomes. Valory zipped her jacket as they stepped onto the landing. There was an oak door set into the wall, banded with iron. Three electrical cords ran beneath it.

"Here we are," said Rafael. He placed his hand on the wrought iron handle. "Ready, my dear?"

"Ready."

The hinges squealed as Rafael pulled the door open. He stepped aside and bowed, letting her pass. Two steps in, she gasped, bug-eyed and frozen in place, barely hearing her own breathless whisper:

"Holy shit."

BAB 9

THE UNLUCKY HIKER SAT on a rock, knowing that the balance of her life was being weighed. In the calculating eyes that measured her, she saw no empathy or compassion. This man regarded her not as a real person, but as a logistical problem. Hands trembling on her knees, her pack and hiking poles on the ground beside her, she prayed. Under her sun hat, her eyes were glassy, one milky from a cataract.

A breeze ruffled Cervantes' blood-flecked shirt. He tapped her ID against his palm, dead-eyeing the frightened lamb. Rosemary Velasquez of Henderson, Nevada. Age sixty-three. Pretty fit for an old lady. Lots of pictures on her phone: an old man in a wheelchair, a few daughters, a bunch of grandkids. There were several shots of her drinking margaritas with friends at a Mexican restaurant, the kind with hokey crap all over the walls. The old bag was enjoying life, a good reason to kill her if he didn't already have one. But could he?

She'd seen the murder. Had come around the trail just before Cervantes smashed Zack's skull. The sight of that vicious act had frozen her with shock. When Cervantes spotted her, she tried to run, but he easily caught and subdued her. Now she had to be dealt with. Therein was the dilemma.

Her corpse could not be found here. Not today, on the same day Misty and Zack had had their luckless tumble. The cops wouldn't buy it—three bodies, same day, same location. Two freak but separate accidents. That kind of thing just didn't happen. No, it had to be somewhere else. But where? How? He couldn't kill her here and drag her body down to the parking lot. There were bound to be other hikers on the way to the summit right now. They'd probably be arriving soon. He couldn't sneak a corpse past them. Even if he managed to tote it down off-trail and load it into his trunk, Rosemary's car would be left in the parking lot. It'd be found alongside Zack's truck, again raising suspicions. Cervantes considered asking the Salvador to have an operative fetch the car, but asks like that were displeasing to the Salvador. If you couldn't handle the task given to you, using only the resources allocated, you became a problem. The Salvador did not suffer self-inflicted problems gladly, even when it was Cervantes.

"Rosemary, Rosemary, Rosemary." He shook his head, clicking his tongue at her. "You had to pick today of all days."

"Please," she pleaded, voice wavering, "I have a family."

"No shit," he scoffed, scrolling through the pictures on her phone. Smiling, everyone smiling. Why does everyone pretend they're so goddamn happy in pictures? "I'm sure they'd make a stink if you went missing."

"My husband, he had a stroke. He's in a wheelchair. Please, he needs me."

"*¿Por qué estás aquí si él te necesita?*" Why are you out here if he needs you?

"*Por favor, por favor.*" Her head dropped into her hands. "I swear I won't say anything. Please."

Cervantes spit at her feet.

This job was supposed to have been fun. A quick trip into the beautiful high mountain desert to fling two wastes of flesh off a cliff—the first opportunity he'd ever had to make people fly. The satisfaction should have been as sweet as sugar, but it had all gone to hell. The worst part? It was all his fault. First, he'd mucked up Zack's murder. That sack of steroids managed to twist away from the cliff at the last instant, ruining the swift, easy kill and even managing to deliver a haymaker to Cervantes' eye. What should have been over in one second instead lasted for two minutes—enough time for Rosemary to wander into the mix. Therein laid Cervantes' other failure—he hadn't done his due diligence before the kill. He should have hiked past Misty and scouted ahead to ensure no one was descending from the summit. Had he done so, he'd have discovered Rosemary up there, on her way down, and he could have adjusted his timing, but he'd gotten excited. Eager. That had made him careless. Now he had a rapidly swelling eye and an old hag who had seen everything. Had seen the kill, had seen Cervantes' face, had heard his voice. She could tie his likeness to Misty Givens. Could instigate a search that might lead to the rental car. From there it might be possible to draw a circuitous path to the Salvador. Doubtful perhaps, but still possible, and even the tiniest possibilities were unacceptable. Rosemary should be slain here and now, but doing so would fail the mission. Now this withered loose end would have to live.

Cervantes scooped up a rock and hurled it full force at a boulder. It splintered, the deep thump echoing across the mountain. Seething, he faced Rosemary. She'd flinched at his sudden outburst and was now cowering, hiding her face.

"Well, lady. Today is your lucky day." Using a bandana, he wiped down her ID and flung it at her. "Here's what's going to happen. Pay attention. I'm going to call my associates. I'm going to give them your name and address. They're going to monitor you and your family. Hey!" he yelled, snapping his fingers. "You hearing me?"

"Yes," she said, looking up at him in tears. "Just please don't hurt my fam—"

"Shut up and listen. You and your family will be monitored. The police frequencies will be monitored. If any of this gets reported—today, tomorrow, ever—guess what's going to happen. Guess!"

She shook her head, unable to meet his gaze.

Cervantes brandished Rosemary's phone and began swiping through the images, shoving them into her face. "This wheelchair husband of yours? Dead. These lovely daughters, dead. Your grandchildren, dead. You hear me? We don't fuck around. We'll kill them all. *¿Me entiendes, Rosemary Velasquez? ¡Respóndeme!*"

She sobbed, nodding. "*Sí, entiendo.*"

Cervantes had worked himself into a fury. This was all his fault. Storming off, he finished cleaning the site, scooping up bloodied sand and rocks and putting it all into his pack. Then he raked the sand with a fan of branches where it had been pushed into heaps by the floundering combatants, afterward dotting the surface with rocks and twigs to blend with the surroundings. After a thorough inspection of the doctored site, he stood over Rosemary. "I'm keeping this," he said of her phone. "You tell everyone you lost it out here. And all these beautiful faces," he said, showing her a picture of her grandchildren, "they're going straight to my associates. One word about any of this, they all die."

Cervantes turned and jogged back to the trailhead. After he'd put some distance between himself and Rosemary, he stopped, wiped down her phone, and hurled it deep into the scrub brush. Then he continued his descent, cursing himself the entire way.

ROZDZIAŁ 10

VALORY STARED DOWN THE nearest aisle, speechless. She hadn't known what to expect from a mountaintop library in a secret medieval castle, but it wasn't this.

The average person might not be impressed. This library looked nothing like the dazzling gold and white-hued Admont Abbey Library in Austria, replete with frescoes and sculptures. Nor was it akin to the Renaissance-inspired Handelingenkamer of the Netherlands, with its lofty glass dome, elaborate spiral staircases, and iron-wrought dragon heads keeping watch from overhead. No, this library was simple and utilitarian. As Rafael had said, it was carved from the bedrock beneath the castle. As such, the walls, floor and ceiling were of gray stone, smooth and undecorated. The bookshelves were shaped from the stone, acting not only as double-sided shelves but as structural supports, their chunky slabs spanning floor to ceiling instead of columns. As with everything else in the castle, the shelves melded into the rest of the stone—one giant, seamless mold of a room. But what had stunned Valory was the light. Down here, she'd been expecting a dark, cavernous gloom requiring flashlights and propane lanterns. Instead, the library was swathed in gentle illumination. How, she couldn't say. There were no windows, no skylight, no torches, no candles. Yet the entire room was aglow, and it seemed to come from everywhere. Tomes upon tomes lined the shelves, caressed by a subtle luminescence as if by magic.

The room was enormous, extending farther into the mountainside than the levels above ground. Peering down the aisle, Valory could only just see the far end, the two bookshelves converging into a distant point near the north wall. She walked over to the next aisle, and it was the same. So was the next aisle, and the next. All the shelves were filled with thick, dusty tomes, kissed by that tender radiance.

"How?" whispered Valory, more to herself than to Rafael.

"I assume you mean the light. *Gloriosa, no?*" Rafael stepped into the nearest aisle, beckoning her to join him. "Look there, near the top of the shelves. See the holes? There in the stonework?" He pointed at a line of baseball-sized holes that had been bored into the casing of the slab. Each hole glimmered with pillowy light. "And here," he said, pointing at another line of holes on the adjacent slab. "These are on every aisle, spaced throughout the library. They lead to larger shafts lined with polished metal, which, as we can see here, is perfect for refracting and diffusing sunlight. So there is no single light source. It is just everywhere."

"Ingenious," said Valory. "You illuminate the library with indirect sunlight. So you've got dry, subterranean climate control for preserving the tomes, and natural light for reading to eliminate the inherent danger of using fire."

"Precisely."

"How did they do it, though?" asked Valory, passing her hand below one of the holes. "If this is all one contiguous maze of stone, how could they have drilled these holes with such precision? How did they fit the polished steel inside?"

"Good question," said Rafael. "The answer begins on the roof of the keep. Up there, there are a series of what we've been calling suncatchers. They look like big flowers, but the petals are mirrors and the pistils are large magnifying glasses. They are positioned to follow the sun's arc through the sky, directing and amplifying light through the shafts and into the library. It is an ingenious system. All we had to do was clean it up a bit."

Though she was no engineer, Valory's mind was drawn to the ingenuity. If a Middle Ages castle builder could do this, why had it not been replicated in any other number of castles throughout Europe? A technology such as this would have been prized among royalty and clergy, who forever sought glorification. Back then, being able to proclaim *I have an underground library infused with God's light* would have elevated one's renown to new heights. It is the sort of thing for which vainglorious Renaissance kings such as Henry VIII and Francis I would have emptied their treasuries to build. Yet here it existed in secret isolation.

Valory was unable to ponder the architectural feat any further, though. Before her was the project for which she was recruited—archaic books. Thousands of them. Rows upon unending rows, tempting her like the treasures of a thousand civilizations. They were not standing upright like modern books, but rather laid flat, stacked atop one another in the manner of bygone eras to better protect their fragile innards. Drawing closer to the nearest tomes, she closed her eyes and inhaled. The smell of musty leather and ancient vellum was like opening a long-forgotten chest in the corner of an old attic—intriguing, and rife with promise. Valory could feel her soul being tugged toward the pages through her nose, so tantalizing was the scent. She wanted to pull down any random volume and dive in, but she sensed Rafael was not ready to turn her loose just yet.

"Ah," he said, squinting down the long aisle toward the center of the room. "I believe I see Professor Mancini at the table there. *Per favore seguimi, cara mia.* I would like to introduce you."

Rafael led her down the aisle, passing countless books along the way. Thick ones, thin ones. Some were covered in plain leather, some in decorative fabric. There were bindings of leather thongs, bindings of rings. Ornamentations and metal corner pieces. These were not modern mass-produced books but rather works of art handcrafted in times when books were not just collections of words, but attributes of God. Each of them called to her, begging her to stop and take them into her hands. To lay them open and ingest them. The pull was strong. It took a herculean effort to tear her gaze away from the shelves and just keep going.

After walking the length of half a football field, they emerged into an open area in the center of the library. There sat a ten-foot-long oaken reading table flanked by Renaissance-style armchairs. Piles of modern research books were scattered along the table with a couple of unlit propane lanterns. There were two men there. One was in his mid-thirties, a thin and studious-looking Italian who was photographing the pages of a beefy tome. The other man was the one Valory had seen last night as she'd followed Rafael to her bedchamber. This was Professor Mancini, she presumed. Lean and silver-haired, Mancini's face was sunken and gaunt, frozen in a permanent scowl behind a set of thick glasses. He looked up from the volume he was reading, dark eyes regarding Valory with unveiled disapproval.

"Allow me to introduce Professor Mancini, retired from the University of Florence. Professor, I hope I am not interrupting. I would like you to meet—"

"*Si si, certo*," growled Mancini, remaining seated. He continued to peer at his text while he spoke. "*La donna che è venuta per salvarci tutti.*" The woman who has come to save us all. "Come, Rollo," he continued in English, beckoning to the younger man, "we can go home now, it seems."

Flush with embarrassment, Rafael smiled weakly at Valory. "Apologies, *cara mia*. Might you excuse us for one moment?"

"Of course." Valory stepped back into the aisle and began perusing the books there. So this is how it was going to be. She might have expected it—not like it was anything new. Thanks to her unrivaled gift, her career had been filled with colleagues who resented her. People like Mancini who had spent their lives studying ancient languages and cultures, only to have a quiet young woman come along and surpass them. Solving mysteries that had befuddled them for years, showing what they'd done wrong, making corrections to their published works. It never sat well with the older generations. Not to mention the young academics who were eager to make names for themselves. The ones who'd fancied themselves the brightest in their field, only to be upstaged by a kid genius. When Valory enrolled in Harvard at the age of sixteen, some of her older classmates boiled with jealousy and had no problem showing it. As a result, Valory learned to keep her head down, work in her little corner, and try to ignore the pettiness of others. Her work was for the good of the world, and she would not cave to petty egos. That's what she'd tell herself, anyway. In practice, it was difficult. Hurtful. Isolating. Perhaps being scorned by so many had contributed to her introversion. Or perhaps people were just assholes and she preferred being alone.

Professor Mancini was standing now, arguing with Rafael, flinging his bony hands at his portly counterpart. While Rafael spoke in harsh whispers, Mancini made no effort to muffle himself. In Italian, he yelled things like "We don't need her!" and "She is only a girl!" and "Why don't you trust me!"

Valory tried to block it out. She walked back up the nearest aisle, scanning the stone bookshelf. If she'd had gloves on, she'd have run her fingers along the spines as she strolled. It was almost painful keeping her hands to herself. She stopped when she spied a particular collection of volumes. Unlike the others around them, the corners of these volumes were fitted with elaborate end pieces, and there were jewels embedded on the boards—rubies, sapphires, and pearls lined with gold and silver. Treasure binding, the practice was called. This suggested the books had been commissioned by someone very rich or very pious. Probably both. Breathlessly, Valory realized she was looking at true rarities of antiquity. Precious few treasure bindings had survived to the modern day. What subject matter did these volumes contain? When might she find out?

"Hello, Doctor."

Valory turned to see Stefano Rollo approaching, an uneasy smile on his face. "Hello."

He gestured toward the ongoing argument. "I apologize for that. The professor is an acquired taste. Don't worry, he will come around." His English was good, his Italian accent unintrusive. "I am Stefano Rollo. People just call me Rollo."

"Doctor Valory Grace, pleasure to meet you."

"Yes, Doctor Grace. Your reputation precedes you. Welcome to the mystery that I call *Il Castello Della Lupolina*."

"*Lupolina?*" asked Valory, catching Rollo's meaning. In English, *lupolina* translated loosely to 'nonesuch.' Rollo was playing on the fabled Nonesuch Palace, the fairytale-like castle constructed by King Henry VIII of England in the sixteenth century. The egoistic monarch had spared no expense on that palace, its lavishness ensuring there was 'nonesuch' like it in the entire world. "Very clever, I like that."

"Thanks."

"So you're a colleague of Professor Mancini?"

"Yes. No. Sort of. I'm a historian, but mainly I'm here because I'm his nephew. Emilio does not trust his colleagues at the university. Actually, he doesn't trust anybody."

"I see."

"My job, officially, is to help provide historical context to the works being translated here," he said, nodding toward the bookshelves. "But really, I'm functioning as more of a documentarian by photographing and storing these books electronically. Doctor Moretti wants to ensure they are all digitized as soon as possible. In case some disaster were to occur, we'd at least have digital backups of the content."

"So you're photographing every page of these books, front to back?"

"Yes. As you can imagine, it is time-consuming, but I'm making good progress. I began last season, and I've completed much of this level."

"This level?"

Rollo smiled. "There are two more levels to the library," he said, pointing down. "Has Doctor Moretti not told you? The stairs are over there on the west wall."

"Two more levels," whispered Valory, astonished. As if this one wasn't already a treasure trove beyond comprehension. "We certainly have our work cut out for us, don't we?"

Rollo's response was preempted by Professor Mancini, who shouted, "Bah!" Slamming shut his reference text, he stuffed it into a satchel and stormed off, leaving Rafael at the table. "*Vuoi una bambina, che puoi averla!*" yelled Mancini. If you want a little girl, you can have her, he'd said. Disappearing down the adjacent aisle, his footfalls echoed off the stone as he huffed away.

Rafael joined Valory and Rollo, massaging his temples. "Doctor Grace, I am so sorry. I thought we had already worked through all of that. It seems I was wrong."

"I can't say it's not upsetting, but it's nothing I haven't faced before."

"Well, I am saddened to hear that. It is a poor testament to academia. I should have known better, to be honest. I have known Professor Mancini for many years. He is my oldest and most trusted colleague, but he is, eh . . ."

"Spirited," offered Rollo.

"Spirited, yes. That is a kind way to say it. My mistake was telling him that you deciphered the isolate in just one night. This, he could not accept. But, as I say, I know him better than anyone. He will come around. Just give him some time."

Sure, thought Valory. *I'll just cave and adapt to the biases of others while they continue spewing bigotries against my age, gender, and expertise until they tire of it. Sounds like a plan.* "Doctor Moretti, back in Oxford, you told me you wanted me to lead this project. Is that still the case?"

"Yes, it is."

"Well, if Professor Mancini is on board with that, I'm glad to work with him."

"Thank you. I promise he will be as sweet as a kitten once he adjusts."

"Very good. Now," she said, unable to keep a smile from creeping into her lips, "about these two lower levels."

БӨЛІМ 11

AGENTS MARCO SAVELLI AND Gianni Moreno stood atop the keep, sipping coffee and warming their bones in the morning sun. Though there was still a chill in the mountain air, there was no wind and no cloud cover, so they were pleased to bask in the heat. Nights in the castle got old quickly. No TV, no internet, no excitement, no women—no life. The cold was the worst part. The small fireplace in their shared chamber was almost worthless. First, you had to tend it throughout the night, poking it and adding more wood now and again to keep it burning. Before you could do that, you had to get out from under your blankets and walk across the stone floor in the frigid air. And you only did that once you argued with your partner about whose turn it was to tend the damn fire. Even when the fire was putting out maximum heat, it wasn't enough. You always had to flip your body, warming your back for a bit while your front got cold, and vice versa. They'd had some space heaters delivered earlier in the season, but Moretti banned them immediately. They didn't have the proper shields, and as such, presented a fire hazard. They were still waiting on replacements. When or even if those would arrive was anyone's guess. The whole situation was enough for Savelli to demand reassignment, but he may as well demand a trillion euros. Wasn't going to happen. Besides, this was his first time serving as *Agente Principale*. There was no way he was going to complain. This was a 'prove yourself' assignment. If Director Teruzzi came to think Savelli couldn't handle it, he'd be demoted. He had no choice but to suck it up and make the best of it.

Below, a military hostler was putting the horses through their paces, their hooves clopping on the ashen stone of the courtyard. The horses looked restless. Whinnying, tossing their heads, trotting ahead of their reins. *They probably hated it here, too*, mused Moreno. Like himself, they wanted to get back to a nice, warm barn at sea level.

Beyond the castle walls and the slope leading into the plateau, the mountain dropped off into an enclosed glacial valley. It was a gorgeous view. Once you'd seen it a dozen times, though, it was just 'whatever.' Last year, Savelli joined a recon team that had explored the valley basin and the surrounding areas. From down there, he discovered you could not see the castle. Even if you looked at the exact spot where you knew it should be, all you saw was jagged, snow-dusted rock. Clever as hell.

Both agents turned, hearing a noise behind them. Beyond the weathered statue of the woman in the flowing robes, the tower loomed. A crashing sound had come from within, followed by breaking glass. The agents didn't react. They just turned back toward the valley.

A few moments later, the wooden door at the base of the tower swung open, and *Agente Speciale* Enzo D'Arezzo emerged. Teeth gritted, he heaved the door, slamming it shut and locking it tight. Then he stalked over to join his colleagues, tapping a cigarette out of his pack.

"What happened?" asked Moreno in Italian, nodding at a thin two-inch cut on D'Arezzo's forehead.

"What the fuck do you think happened?" snapped D'Arezzo. He sucked a quarter of his cigarette down in one long draw. "Thank God my leave starts tomorrow. You two can spend the next few weeks fighting over who has to go up there." He yanked a tissue from his pocket and began wiping the blood from his brow. "To hell with this place."

Moreno shook his head, staring at the valley. "I still think we should have pushed back on the Grace appointment. If she ever finds out about . . ." He left the sentence unfinished, only nodding at the tower. Then he drew his finger across his throat.

"Shut up," said Savelli. "Both of you. I don't like the situation any more than you, but this is the job. Stay sharp, follow your orders. Keep the American away from the tower and we won't have a problem."

More smashing sounds echoed from within the tower. D'Arezzo shook his head. After another long drag, he flicked his cigarette and walked away.

ISAHLUKO 12

Title: Clay Tablet Diary Entry #2
Date: Holocene est. 8000 BCE [Citation|Carbon dating req.]
Subject(s): Tribal dynamics, religious beliefs. Region/race unknown
Language: Unknown isolate
Material: Clay tablet, inscribed front and back
Condition: Fair. Some hairline cracks and chipping
Note: Actual dimensions of item are 24.6 x 18.8 cm. 32 lines [18 front/14 back]. Upper margin of 3 cm.; lower margin of 2 cm.; left margin of 2 cm.
Location discovered: Classified

The woman Kahiliva shared my bed yesternight
Stealing into my camp under the harvest moon
While the others slept
Kahiliva is sweet and fair of skin
With eyes as dark as a starless night
And she loves me
For she thinks me blessed of the gods with eternal youth
Though in sooth I am ancient and weary of life
I have beseeched her to find another mate
But she will not listen
She is the daughter of the chieftain Malikai
Who would forbid our union if he but knew
For I am no longer pleasing to this folk
The tribe is suspicious of my earth-drawn marks
And of the tired wisdom that weighs
On my eyes and my voice
Yet touches not my face
Which has not withered in all the seasons
That these men have called me kin
They whisper that I am kept young
By the wicked spirits of this land
Soon I shall feel their spears in my heart
This I know
For I have seen such fears in all men
Countless times in lands near and far

Yet poor Kahiliva will not abandon me
For she is naïve and believes
That I may one day give her children
Though I tell her my seed is unfruitful
And no woman has grown fat with child
Who has shared my bed
In my endless winters upon this earth.

Title: Clay Tablet Diary Entry #3
Date: Holocene est. 8000 BCE [Citation|Carbon dating req.]
Subject(s): Tribal dynamics, religious beliefs. Solar eclipse. Region and race unknown
Language: Unknown isolate
Material: Clay tablet, inscribed front and back
Condition: Fair. Some chipping, bottom left corner broken
Note: Actual dimensions of item are 23.1 x 17.9 cm. 29 lines [18 front/11 back]. Upper margin of 3 cm.; lower margin of 2 cm.; left margin of 2 cm.
Location discovered: Classified

Two days ago the moon devoured the sun
Such that darkness overtook the land
In the midst of day
And all men were struck with fear
Falling to their knees and begging mercy
From the heavens
Women wept and wailed
Shielding their young from a doom unknown
But then the sun returned its light unto us
And brother cast blame upon brother
They shouted words of fury
And laid their hands on one another in violence
Until the woman Shalika gave finger to me
And laid bare my secret tryst with Kahiliva
Saying this had brought great wrath upon the tribe
From the heavens
And they arrested me in righteous anger
And Kahiliva too
That we may pay the toll demanded by the gods
Thus were we burned to death
In a sacrifice of fire
But my earthen marks were well-hidden
And those they could not locate
Nor destroy
And so appreciate these marks now
You who are me

And remember sweet Kahiliva
The gentle spirit who loved us
Whose eyes were the soul of the night

The language was a rainstorm on a savannah. It flowed with the colors of dark, gloomy clouds and green lemon grasses, dashed with spectral rainbow flares. Certain graphemes had the aroma of fire-cooked game drifting on the wind, hinting at undertones of magnolia. Such were the unique sensations of the world's first written language.

Valory clicked Save, rereading her translation. Then her gaze fell upon the clay tablet, letting the fanciful inscriptions dance in her mind. A tear slid down her cheek.

She was alone. Down on the third and lowest level of the library, which held the most ancient writings not only in the castle but in all the world. Like the first and second levels, the third was illuminated by the magical lighting system. The temperature, though chilly, was at least dry and constant, and could be staved off with a coat and gloves.

After a brief tour of the lower levels with Rafael and Rollo, Valory had gotten straight to work, starting with the earliest clay tablets. Four of them were missing from their spot, still resting on the table in her bedchamber. The others were stacked on the stone with animal pelts laid between them for protection. The next three tablets in the series had been practice, the author further refining and expanding the vocabulary. These she had studied and documented over several hours before moving to the diary narratives. Now, on the oak table in the middle of the library, the tablets laid upon beds of foam. Beside them, the government-issued laptop glowed with Valory's fresh translation.

She had translated many horrible things in her career. Some from antiquity, some from the modern era. In her brief stint with the D.I.A. during the Iraqi War, she had uncovered messages about savage beheadings and people being blown to bits by IEDs. She'd found the same type of language in the earliest writings: stories of torture, burning people alive, and beheadings. Always beheadings. Humans hadn't changed much, it seemed.

But this. These words from Alikai, this sad, delusional, desolate genius from thousands of years ago. She felt him. Felt his unthinkable pain, the emptiness of his heart. Felt the giant vacuum in his soul from where humanity had fled. His poor, bittersweet relationship with Kahiliva—the woman who dared to love him—sacrificed to flames for nothing but the unending fear and ignorance of Man. Obviously, he had not died in the sacrifice. How he had escaped his fiery fate, the tablet didn't say. Since he'd suffered from delusions of immortality, he'd probably just fabricated the part about burning alongside Kahiliva. A sort of connective fiction tying his delusion to his affection for her. But the suffering he'd felt that day was clear.

Through his writing, Alikai's crushing loneliness was palpable. A real thing that had crawled out of the clay, through Valory's fingers, into her arms, sinking into her belly. Now she was pregnant with his despair. Soul-wrecked.

She leaned over and put her head into her hands, letting the tears fall into her gloves. Feelings long repressed were now awakened, stoked to life by this gloomy tale of genius scorned. As Alikai was distrusted and maligned by those who didn't understand him, so had Valory been. Professor Mancini was only the latest in a life filled with those who sought to denigrate her. To minimize, deride, and exclude her for her strange gift. It was something with which she'd been forced to live since childhood. As such, it had crystalized as the normal course of her life. In her heart, she had constructed a cage in which to store the negativity. The rejection, the isolation, the pain of not being 'normal.' She was good at storing things away. Focusing on her studies had kept those feelings locked up, but Alikai had busted open the cage. Even as she pulled his story from the forgotten depths of time, he likewise unmasked her, revealing her as something of a modern-day counterpart. A social castaway forever falling into a bottomless pit of seclusion.

There were hundreds if not thousands more clay tablets lining the shelves of the library. After drying her tears, Valory photographed the tablets with her assigned camera and attached the jpegs to their corresponding translations. Then she gently replaced the tablets, affixing a catalog tag to each. Gathering herself, she drew the next tablet in the series from the shelf, praying that it was a continuation of Alikai's story. She wanted to know more.

There was no way all the tablets on these shelves were his creations. There were just too many for one man to produce. Eyeing the inscriptions on the next tablet, however, she knew they were made by his hand. Same ornamented writing, same angles, same margins, same depths. Upon seeing the words, the rainswept savannah flowed into her mind again, brimming with the scents of the grasslands. This tablet had some damage to small portions of the text and was of poorer condition, but that didn't dampen her eagerness. Less than an hour after placing it on the foam, she had completed the translation.

Title: Clay Tablet Diary Entry #4
Date: Holocene est. 8000 BCE [Citation|Carbon dating req.]
Subject(s): Tribal dynamics, religious beliefs. Region and race unknown
Language: Unknown isolate, origins unknown
Material: Clay tablet, inscribed front and back
Condition: Fair. Some missing/damaged text and scarring

Note: Actual dimensions of item are 24.0 x 18.1 cm. 26 lines [18 front/8 back]. Upper margin of 3 cm.; lower margin of 2 cm.; left margin of 2 cm.
Location discovered: Classified

> I took leave of the settlement of Malikai
> \<damaged text\>
> \<damaged text\>
> Roaming to the lands of the north
> Where it is said that dangerous and warlike tribes dwell
> Having evil hearts and long filthy beards
> Who worship false gods and vengeful devils
> But I suspect they are no worse than others
> For men always make villains of
> Those who are not themselves
> Malikai and the elders have banished me
> Recalling not that they slew me in fire
> Alongside fair Kahiliva
> Recalling not that my legs melted while they jeered
> My death is never remembered
> As you know well
> You who are me
> We suffer the pain and anguish of dying
> Yet then we live anew
> As though our last breath was never gasped
> And none remember our death save us
> \<damaged text\> or why we alone must suffer
> What choice have we but to pack our sorrows
> And drag our unnatural life to lands unknown
> In search of final death
> Which will never come

Valory sniffled, tagging the tablet and storing it back in its original place. She considered grabbing the next tablet in the series, but her eyes burned, and her shoulders slumped in fatigue. She'd still only slept a few winks since traveling from Oxford. Now, on top of her weariness, her emotions had been ridden to the ground by the weight of Alikai's elegies. Tuning into her body for the first time in days, she suddenly felt like she was wearing a leaden cape.

She packed her equipment and began the long trek to her bedchamber. Two flights to the top level of the library, then a long walk to the west portal, a two-floor climb up the spiral stairwell, then a lengthy stroll to her bedchamber. It behooved a person to be fit around here.

On her walk across the top floor of the library, Valory spotted Professor Mancini in one of the aisles, jotting notes while squinting at a shelf of books. He saw her but didn't acknowledge her. Just turned back to his notes. A

90

silent snub of contempt. It stung more than it should have. In her current state—spiritually shellshocked by Alikai's story—the affront cut deep. Holding back a fresh set of tears, she hurried to her bedchamber, where she slid down a tunnel of dull, aching thoughts into a fitful slumber.

KAPITTEL 13

CERVANTES MEDITATED.

Regular people had many motives for meditating: to reduce stress, to improve sleep, to reaffirm their purpose, to feel closer to God. Pick a reason, any reason. But regular people were fatuous. They treated meditation like a novelty, a toy they could pick up and play with until they got bored. Then they'd push it aside and forget about it, only picking it up again at their next yoga class, or spa retreat, or when the rigors of their fenced-in lives overwhelmed them.

Dominic Cervantes was different. His meditations were a set-in-stone requirement. They served one goal and one goal only—to keep him from killing. Because that's what he'd do without the Salvador and meditation. He'd kill everyone.

The urge had been there since childhood. As a malnourished waif growing up in the drug-riddled slums of Oakland, he didn't understand it. It was just there, a feeling that played in his mind like a light that couldn't be turned off. If he saw a stray dog on the street, he visualized killing it. If he saw a group of men huddled in an alley smoking crack, he wondered what they'd look like with slit throats. It felt normal to him, as natural as breathing. The six-year-old Dominic didn't know any better. Only as he began executing his desires did he come to realize that his urges were considered vile.

Like when he killed the cat wandering the slums. The cat was feral and would never venture close enough to catch. So he baited it with a live mouse he'd trapped in a jar. He set the jar near a trash bin that the cat sniffed around every so often, and he hid around the corner, waiting. When the cat came by and pawed at the jar, Dominic snuck up and struck, stabbing it with a shard of glass.

He was proud of that first kill. He'd fashioned a weapon, set a trap, and waited patiently. Then he'd struck with speedy silence, performing the deed without a whiff of instruction. All on his own. When the glass point punctured the cat's skin and he felt the jagged edge grinding against tiny little bones, fireworks went off inside him. Tingly bursts of pleasure, like he was being rewarded by God.

Little Dominic brought the dead cat into the multi-tenant hovel where he and his mom were staying at the time. He stepped over a man sleeping at the door. Cut his bare foot on a broken bottle of Mad Dog 20/20. Wandered the halls until he found his mom in the corner of a trash-strewn room. She was leaning on the man next to her, drooling, glassy eyes staring into space. That rubber thing was tied around her arm.

"*Mira mamá*," he said, holding up the cat by the tail. She didn't stir. "*Mamá. Mamá*, wake up. Look what I did." He shook her shoulder, and she blinked, looking at him through a haze. "Look, Mama. I killed it."

It took her a moment to register what she was seeing. Through her stringy hair, she took turns opening wide and squinting at the furry, blood-soaked bundle dangling from her son's hand. When she realized what it was, she shook her head. "No, Dominic," she mumbled. "That's bad. You can't do that."

"But it's okay. I killed it. I was really good."

"No. You shouldn't kill animals."

"Why?"

"*No es bueno, bebito*. It's bad."

"But when I killed the rat, you said it was good."

"*No, esto es diferente. No entiendes, bebito*. It's really bad." Just then, she inhaled sharply, looking in bug-eyed ecstasy at something only she could see. "*Ay Dios mío. Ay Dios mío.*"

"*Mamá?*"

"*Dios mío.*"

The man she'd been leaning on was awake then. An unshaven, shirtless skeleton of a man. Head tilted as if the weight was too much for his neck, he peered under heavy eyelids at Dominic and his grisly prize. "Whoa. Like, what the hell is wrong with you, little man?"

From the opposite corner of the room, a lady named Rosa chimed in, hissing at the boy through yellow teeth. "You're a sick *culito*, you know that?"

Dominic paid little heed to their disgust. His mom, those people, something was wrong with them. They weren't thinking straight. When they felt better, they'd see what a good job he'd done. But that never happened. In fact, on the days she was lucid, his mom got angry whenever he killed something. She never listened to Dominic when he told her how wonderful and natural it felt to take a life. Sometimes, she even cried.

Over the months and years that followed, the same scenario kept playing out. Whether he killed a cat, a dog, a raccoon, a bird, or whatever, people were disgusted. Those looks they gave him when he wandered around dragging a gashed carcass behind him. The way his mom flipped out when she found him in the condemned building down the road, surrounded by a makeshift shrine of his kills. Even the other slum kids—who cursed and shoplifted and got into fistfights—even they ostracized him after he set fire to that litter of puppies behind the Lucky Mart. Little by little, the realization sunk in. Young Dominic began to understand that he was a freak. Soon after, the colors of life began fading. Slowly, over many years. He managed to pass his CCT before boot camp, but by his second year in the military, he was completely colorblind.

Cervantes felt himself slipping out of his meditation. It was tough today. Tough to focus, to clear his head. There was a lot of noise up there. Yesterday's job was a semi-failure, and that knowledge was eating at him like maggots had hatched in his brain and were gnawing their way out. Zack Miller and Rosemary Velasquez—they were the maggots. He could hear them in his head, for the sounds of their feasting was his nagging guilt. He could feel them up there, for their scuttling legs were the tingling pricks of humiliation. The pressure of his failure grew stronger by the hour. That shouldn't have been the case. He'd killed yesterday and killing was supposed to relieve the pressure. Killing and meditation. If he'd done his job properly, there'd be no maggots, no pressure. His meditation would be deep and calming, resetting him for the day and staving off his murderous desires. The Salvador had taught him this. *Meditation quiets the mind and allows you to focus,* he'd said years ago. *It elevates you from an aimless animal beholden to its instincts to a finely honed instrument of domination. Only when we are calm and focused can we be everything that we are meant to be.* Without the Salvador to guide him, Cervantes would have been dead long ago, or at best, serving consecutive life sentences somewhere, such a slave had he been to his killing lust. Now, he could feel the old him clawing his way to the surface, eager to rectify his mistake with a spree of carnage. Right here, right now, in this flashy Vegas hotel. *Just walk through that door and kill everyone you see.*

He launched himself from lotus with a tortured roar. They were having sex in the suite next door. Disgusting, carnal, human sex, moaning and yelling and banging the wall in the middle of the damn day. They'd started while he was meditating, and he couldn't block it out anymore. He yelled at them, calling them filthy, beastly cattle, and he smashed a crystal lamp against the wall, but that didn't stop them. They didn't even pause.

Having nothing professional in the room, Cervantes scooped up the biggest shard of broken crystal, and he broke the fat end into a sharp point. Forgetting that he was naked, he stalked toward the door.

The burner rang. He stopped, looking over. The driver who'd met Cervantes at the airport gave him two phones, one of which had already been used and destroyed. This one was the post-op burner. Picking it up, he let it ring again before tapping Accept.

"Dominic."

"Salvador," he breathed, and he fell to his knees as though he'd been injected with a sedative.

"Brother. How are you?"

Cervantes didn't know what to say. Still emerging from the mists of his wrath, he was unfocused and off guard. He stuttered that he was okay.

The Salvador let the line go quiet for a moment. When he spoke again, it was like he *knew*. "Dominic. You are not alone. You will never be alone. I am with you, now and always. You believe me, don't you?"

"Yes," he whispered. "I believe you."

"Good. Because I believe in you. And I get the sense you're being much too hard on yourself about something."

"I have failed, Salvador."

"Is that so?"

"Yes."

"Tell me."

"There was a woman. She saw me do it. I didn't scout ahead. I didn't know she was coming."

"And taking care of her would have raised suspicions."

"I had to leave her." Cervantes slumped over, touching his forehead to the carpet. "I've failed the mission."

There was a moment of silence before the Salvador replied. "You think she'll talk?"

"I don't know," Cervantes answered, voice muffled by the floor. "I told her what would happen if she did. But, as you say, loose ends topple empires."

The Salvador drew a long, deep breath. Being familiar with his mannerisms, Cervantes knew that he was looking inward, a faint smile touching his lips. "Dominic, how often do think about November of oh seven?"

Cervantes sat upright. The Salvador was asking about the so-called Shinwar Massacre in Afghanistan. "Now and again."

"Hell of a day for MARSOC, right? One minute, we're cruising through Spinpul, everything's quiet. Next minute, suicide bomber drives right into the convoy. Boom. Got us. Then his buddies swarm the streets and ambush us. *Us*, Marine Raiders, by far the superior warriors. Say what you want about those dirt worshippers, but they had balls of steel. Gotta give 'em that."

Cervantes remained quiet.

"That was the first time you showed the real you," continued the Salvador. Deep-timbred and buttery, his voice was the vocal equivalent of reclining in a chair with a glass of brandy. "You'd been hiding until that day. In plain sight. Hiding from the team, from me, even from yourself. Up to then, you'd been this dark, quiet Marine. Always keeping to yourself, yet always watching everyone around you." He chuckled. "You gave the other men the heebie jeebies."

"Yes," acknowledged Cervantes quietly. "They called me Creeper."

"That they did, but not me. I knew you were special. That's why I partnered with you when no one else would. I kept telling the men, you guys just wait. One day, the man you call Creeper is going to shock you. And after that ambush, when the real you came out to play, they never called you that again."

"No."

"What you did to that ambush party, none of us had ever seen anything like it." The Salvador assumed the tone of an awestruck storyteller. "There we were, gridlocked, trapped in the street. Sparky and Hammerhead were burning in the lead Humvee. We were pinned down, heavy fire whizzing at us from all directions. Everyone arguing about an intelligence failure, scrambling for cover, unable to coordinate a response. We didn't know if we were going to make it. And then . . . *you*."

Cervantes squirmed. This was the part of the story where he'd lost control. Though the Salvador was speaking of it with reverence, to Cervantes, it was embarrassing, smacking of mental weakness.

"You break cover," said the Salvador, "and you just rush right out into the open. Our jaws drop. I'm thinking you'll be dead in two seconds, but no. You just start snuffing out Hajis one by one. They're unloading on you but everything's missing. You're a one-man whirlwind, spraying in all directions, every round plugging a skull like it was on a line. Hajis on the rooftops, behind cars, around corners, doesn't matter. They poke their heads out—boom—they eat a bullet. They duck and hide—boom—you tag them through the wall. You're just stupid accurate. You're going wild, just yelling and shooting. The street is exploding with crossfire but you just stand there unscathed, splitting skulls like the angel of death."

Cervantes found himself inside the memory, transported by the Salvador's narrative. The afternoon sun beating down on streets filled with dust and smoke. Bullet-riddled junkers lining the curbs. Dingy plaster buildings with blown-out windows and exposed rebar. The smell of explosives and gas and blood. A chorus of assault rifles singing their song of death: pop-pop-pop-pop-pop! He remembered *feeling* the battle. Every round screaming through the air. Every hot, panting breath from every Afghani. Every racing heartbeat of every living thing in the area. He felt it all. Knew where everything was and where it was about to be. Felt each bullet as it snapped into the chamber, exploding through the muzzle, and he rode upon each of those bullets until it was lodged in a brain. Then he felt that brain die. He was a sweaty, psychotic, raging conductor of death.

"You paved the way, single-handedly. After that, we were able to clear the gridlock and get the hell out of there. But you weren't quite done, were you, my friend?"

No, he wasn't. After drinking long and deep from the chalice of madness, Cervantes had worked himself into a bloodlust. What followed was a blurry memory, just a series of crimson-soaked snapshots. The convoy rumbling through the streets. Robed militia taking potshots from the roofs. And civilians. Lots of them, throwing rocks at the jeeps. Yelling, screaming, crying. Cervantes couldn't restrain himself. He fired on them. Women, children, old men, they were all one giant blur of a target. He sprayed them until his last mag was empty. When the jeeps stopped again due to an obstruction, he jumped out and ran into a throng of civilians, unleashing a hand-to-hand onslaught. Knifing anything with eyes. Punching, kicking, spitting, snapping bones. He'd been so engorged with murderous ecstasy that he didn't even feel the bullet that bit his shoulder.

"When you leaped out of the Humvee that second time," said the Salvador, "we followed you. We couldn't let you do it all yourself. Not again. We knew it wasn't right, but we were inflamed by your passion. Your anger was our anger. Right or not, we wanted a taste of that vengeance."

Phone still to his ear, Cervantes rose and walked to the window. The late afternoon sun showed on Vegas, and the streets were becoming busier. In a few hours, they'd be packed. "Salvador, why are you telling this story?"

"Listen, Dominic. What you did that day was supernatural. There's just no other word for it. It confirmed what I'd long suspected—that you were earmarked for greatness. When I found out later that you and I had been born at the same time in the same hospital, I knew our fates were intertwined. But you were raw. Unhinged. You broke free of that prison society had built around you, but you had no control. No discipline with your dark gift. You were wild, lacking depth and subtlety.

"But look at you now," continued the Salvador, pride in his voice. "Disciplined. Calm. Calculating. You've learned to make peace with yourself and with your gift. Because of that, you're now the deadliest man in the world, brother."

With his free hand pressed against the window, Cervantes closed his eyes. "Because of you, Salvador. Only because of you."

"Yesterday, in the desert, you were not the berserker Marine Raider who was court-martialed for inciting a massacre. When that old woman saw you, you didn't do anything rash like the old Dominic would have. You were thoughtful. Intelligent. Restrained. You weighed the facts, considered all the options, and you came to the proper conclusion."

"I did?"

"Yes, you did. Killing her then would have been problematic. Your only mistake, as you said, was that you should have reconnoitered the area first."

"Yes. Forgive me, Salvador." The apology hung in the air for a moment. A long moment, until the words grew so fat that Cervantes could almost see them floating in front of him.

When he continued, the Salvador's tone was businesslike. "The good thing is you can still rectify the situation. Tonight."

Cervantes opened his eyes, puzzled. "But the police will retrace her movements. They'll find out she was at Red Rock yesterday. On that same trail. Won't they be suspicious?"

"Let me worry about that. Tonight, I want you to drive to Henderson and take care of our little Miss Rosemary Velasquez, copy?"

"Copy that. I'll prepare right now."

"Good. After that, brother, I'm bringing you home."

The line went dead.

Cervantes continued standing there for a moment. Then he flopped into a nearby chair, breathing relief. There he stayed for several minutes, letting the Salvador's words work their magic on his noisy mind. His rage and his guilt receded. The edges of his focus become sharp again. In a matter of hours, this would all be fixed.

He began gearing up to leave, his thoughts turning to how he was going to approach the job. Only as he walked out the door did he realize he'd never mentioned the name Rosemary Velasquez to the Salvador, nor that she lived in Henderson.

MUTU 14

SOMETIME AFTER MIDNIGHT, THE last of the house lights went dark and the teens hanging out at the corner dispersed. By 01:00 hours, there were only crickets. Still, Cervantes waited. Bathed in black, he sat in the rental listening to news radio.

The neighborhood was decades old judging by the vintage architecture. That kitschy Fifties neo-modern look. The houses sat on cactus-strewn, oversized gravel lots with plenty of space between properties. It was the kind of airy development they didn't build anymore. But everything was run down and dumpy. Cars on blocks, rusted appliances lying in yards, cheap wind ornaments. Having watched the street for a couple of hours, Cervantes observed that the residents were mostly either retired people who'd been living in these houses most of their lives, or younger, poorer people who could only afford dilapidated places like these. Rosemary Velasquez's house was halfway down the block. There, in the driveway, was her old Nissan Sentra, the paneling and sidewalls still layered with desert grime. Beside the Sentra was a white van with a handicap placard in the window.

Cervantes itched to make his move, but he would wait a while longer. Patience and observation were key in this cleanup mission. No one could see him approach the house, nor leave it when the deed was done. To that end, he had ensured there were no security cameras mounted on the nearby porches. That was the good thing about an old neighborhood like this. Elderly people didn't embrace modern technologies, and poor people couldn't afford them.

"Breaking news from KTNV in Las Vegas." Cervantes turned up the radio. "The bodies of two hikers have been recovered from a remote section of Red Rock Canyon just west of Las Vegas. Early reports say one of the hikers has been identified as Hollywood starlet Misty Givens. Givens and her partner, Zachary Miller, were found by a park ranger who noticed the couple's vehicle had been left overnight in a parking lot. Their bodies were discovered at the base of Turtlehead Ridge, a popular but dangerous hiking trail where several others have died in recent years. Misty Givens is best known for her role in the 2016 film, *Boys and Wives*. We'll bring you more details as they become available.

"Nasdaq futures are up in early trading on reports that better-than-expected earnings—"

He flicked the radio off. It had been a day and a half since he'd done Misty and Zack, yet it felt like months. Dwelling upon his mistakes slowed the passage of time as if every second was a wad of gum pulled and stretched to three feet long. He could not even enjoy the memory of that moment when Zack was going over the edge. When his eyes snapped into full, panicked awareness of what was happening. Rosemary had forever sucked the joy out of that moment.

At 02:00 hours, Cervantes made his move. He slunk to Rosemary's house, hugging the darkness. Snuck into her backyard. Put on gloves and a ski mask. Searching the area, he found a spare key in the fake rock by the door. Then he opened the breaker box on the side of the house and cut the power. Seconds later, he was inside.

The interior of the house was like many he'd visited in his youth. Ratty couch, Jesus candles on the windowsills, crosses and knickknacks on the walls, pictures of family everywhere, the faint scent of zesty spices from a thousand home-cooked meals. In the corner, the moonlight shone on a small shrine to Our Lady of Guadalupe. He'd seen that shrine many times before. This was the house of every neighborhood *tia* who had briefly cared for Dominic whenever his mom fell into a smack-induced coma. It was the house of every *vecina* who'd taken pity on the shirtless waif sleeping alone on the street. Rosemary Velasquez was one of those kind souls who would have taken Dominic into a house just like this and stuffed him full of homemade tamales, maybe giving him a fresh change of clothes that had once been her son's. That's the feeling he got as he looked around, his mind conjuring unbidden memories of those days. He was nothing back then, just a skinny little weirdo, belonging nowhere and wanted by no one. It was a chapter of his life he strived to forget. But now, in Rosemary's time capsule of a house, he remembered. This is where he'd come from. *Casas* like this— and people like Rosemary Velasquez—were why he hadn't wasted away and died in the gutter. He was alive not because of his smacked-out mother. Nor because of his father, whom he'd never even met. No, he was alive today because of people like Rosemary.

Cervantes stood in the darkness, dead still, something tickling his conscience. Something new. A feeling, suddenly, that he didn't want to kill her, that she didn't deserve it. That felt bizarre. Rosemary hadn't helped him when he was a boy. She only reminded him of others who had. He owed her nothing. So why was he hesitating? Why was he staring at a moon-kissed family photo, the lingering scent of cayenne and chile powders dusting his nostrils? Was it because of empathy? *Is that what this is—empathy?*

As a youth, Cervantes didn't know what empathy was. It had never been explained to him in a manner he could understand. Going into his teenage years, all he knew was that the adults in the neighborhood were constantly horrified by things he said, things he talked about doing. He'd figured out that he was a freak, but he could never figure out why. No one ever sat him down and gave him a satisfactory explanation as to *why* it was wrong to kill, or to talk about killing, or to laugh when someone got killed. Instead of explaining, they just avoided him. He heard the words people used—empathy, sympathy, compassion, sensitivity—but the concepts behind those words made no sense.

During a short bout of sobriety, Dominic's mom had taken him to a church to meet the pastor. Some old man in a robe. He had a bulbous, pockmarked nose, Cervantes recalled, and he smelled of menthol. This man spoke with Dominic in one of the pews, asking lots of questions and trying to guide him toward God. Cervantes couldn't recall the specifics of the conversation. Mostly, he was just looking around in awe of the cavernous ceiling and the giant Jesus on the cross. He'd been about eight then. At that time, he didn't realize why he was being made to speak with this pastor, nor did he register anything strange about their talk. All he knew was that afterward when the pastor spoke with his mom, she broke down crying. Dominic didn't understand what was wrong, and his mom wouldn't explain. It was only years later, when the adult Cervantes gained a clinical understanding of the concept of compassion, that he thought back and reconstructed that day. He realized that his mom had come to understand that Dominic was very troubled, and she had taken him to the church for help. Pray the devil away. But whatever answers Dominic gave the pastor stunned the man. He could see the pastor's face now in his mind's eye, gaping at Cervantes in bewilderment. Dominic didn't recognize that expression at that time. Emotions just did not register back then. But now, the memory and the meaning behind the pastor's reaction were clear.

The day after, his mom made him sit down with her. She hugged him, telling him she loved him no matter what. That he was always going to be her baby. It was nothing but a foggy memory now, more feeling than recollection. For reasons he couldn't grasp, his mother just held him, rocking him back and forth. She'd never done that before. Then she sang him a Spanish lullaby, running her fingers through his hair while he lay against her chest. He couldn't recall the words of the lullaby, but he remembered thinking she had a pleasant singing voice. Clear, kindly, maybe even motherly. After he processed the strange event, he realized it had been kind of nice. Even though he was too old for lullabies at that age, it affected him deeply. Because for that one brief moment in time, he'd known what being loved felt like.

After that day, his mother never sang to him again. The drugs were more important. For the remainder of his childhood, only strangers like Rosemary showed him kindness.

So there he stood, surrounded by Rosemary's family pictures, her cheap furniture, and her holy symbols, feeling like he'd been there before. Feeling like Rosemary would have pulled young Dominic off the streets if she'd seen him all those years ago. He pictured himself sleeping a night or two on that old couch with a homemade shawl draped over him. Saw the young him being served a hot meal at that scuffed-up dining table while Rosemary asked where his mom and dad were. Maybe, if he'd asked her to, she'd have sung him a Spanish lullaby.

As a clock ticked on the wall behind him, he felt himself losing the desire to kill her. A realization hit him—*that* was compassion, *that* was empathy. He finally understood because he was feeling it for the first time. After all these years, it had just become real.

And he hated it.

It was a slime oozing into his soul, sapping his strength, his will. Muddling his thoughts, steering him away from his task. Away from victory. It may as well have placed a white flag of surrender into his hand. For what were compassion and empathy if not the very weaknesses which separated victor from vanquished? What conqueror ever gained power by doling out acts of sympathy and kindness?

Scowling, Cervantes scanned the living room again, this time seeing it for what it was—a hovel for an enemy of the Salvador. Embarrassed for having let the slime seep in, he stalked into the kitchen and thumbed through the knife block, selecting an eight-inch chef knife. He had not brought any weapons of his own. This job had to look like a two-bit burglary gone wrong. He flicked the knifepoint with his gloved finger, ensuring it was up to the task. Cheap, but good enough.

He walked down the hallway to the back bedrooms. The first room was a hoarder's delight, piled full of boxes and junk. Next was the guest bedroom—musty but clean. Finally, he stepped up to the master bedroom, pushing the door open slowly.

There she was. Rosemary Velasquez, sprawled out on the bed. Sound asleep. Her hair was covered by a nightcap. One leg stuck out from under the covers. Her husband, the stroke victim, was off to the side, lying on his back in a recliner. His wheelchair was folded up next to the wall.

Cervantes smiled, but only on the inside. This bitch, this bringer of turmoil who sought to come between him and the Salvador, would now pay the eternal price. He couldn't just slip the knife under her breastbone, though. He was supposed to be a small-time burglar who would only commit murder if the homeowner woke up and caught him in the act. That's what this scene had to look like—a sloppy, amateurish homicide that shouldn't have happened.

Walking to the dresser, he rifled through the drawers, welcoming the ruckus it made. He dumped the contents of a jewelry box onto the dresser, causing a clatter of cheapo rings, bracelets and watches. Rosemary stirred. She raised to one elbow, looking at her husband as if he'd made the noise.

"*Hola*, Rosemary Velasquez."

Her head snapped around. Even though the room was dark, she knew who was standing beside her bed. "*No,*" she whispered weakly. Then she found her voice. "*¡No no no! ¡No dije nada! ¡No dije nada!*" She scrambled to the other side of the bed. Cervantes let her. Tripping over her nightgown, she began crawling on the floor in abject fear. "*¡No dije nada! ¡Por favor, no dije nada!*"

Cervantes stalked her, allowing her to get up and scurry toward the door. Just as she was about to go through, he slashed her back. She pitched to a knee, but the strength of her fear brought her back to her feet, and she ran. Tingling, he slashed her again, whipping her blood onto the hallway wall. She stumbled, knocking pictures from their hooks. She cried for help, scratching her way forward. He let her crawl into the living room. Let her think she had a chance to get away. There, she collided with her religious shrine, falling to her back as her nightgown turned dark with blood. She turned her eyes to him from the floor. Gave him the look. That beautiful, terror-soaked look that said *I am about to die*. He sucked it in like he was smoking a pipe, the flavor of her despair roiling in his lungs. He smiled. A real smile this time. Then he savaged her. Again and again, slicing, thrusting, piercing, his soul riding a rocket of bliss.

When it was done, he spent several minutes descending from orbit, staring at her corpse. Watching the blood pool beneath her body, blacker than the black around it. The maggots in his brain died along with her. Everything was right again.

Almost.

The old man was awake in his recliner. Making noises, trying to move. Cervantes found him flopping around, trying to grab a nearby phone. He'd shit himself, and he was drooling. Pathetic. Cervantes grabbed a handful of his hair and jerked his head back. Stared into his droopy eyes. "You're disgusting, you know that? How could you let yourself get like this? Like a goddamn baby." Throwing his head away, he placed the point of the knife under the man's ribcage. "You should have done this yourself a long time ago." He shoved the blade in until half the handle was buried in the abdomen. The old man gasped, then went still, the light fading from his eyes.

Yes. Everything was right again.

CAPÍTULO 15

VALORY WOKE IN A fetal position beneath her goose-down blanket. After laying there for a moment, she pushed the light button on her watch. It was 1:30 P.M. She'd slept for fourteen hours.

She sat up, blinking into the darkness. With no windows or active light source, her chamber was as black as a subterranean cavern. She'd been so drained last night that she hadn't bothered to start a fire, thus not even a faint ember glowed under the mantel. Shivering, she felt her way along the wall and into the garderobe. She mustered her courage, then sat her bare bottom on the cold stone, gasping as she shimmied into position over the hole. How did medieval women ever get used to this? Before tomorrow, she resolved to fashion a cloth cover to lay over the stone.

Feeling her way to the table, she lit the propane lamp, squinting into the sudden light. Then she plugged the coffee maker into the power strip and started a brew. While she waited, she laid a spare blanket on the floor and began her morning yoga routine. Yoga and calisthenics had become a vital part of her life. Not that she loved the exercise, but being a studious introvert meant that ninety percent of her time was spent in sedentary seclusion. Without daily exercise and stretching, she'd not only be as pale as a ghost, but she'd grow to be plump and rigid as well. That would cause a slow cascade of health problems as she aged, which meant less time for sedentary seclusion. She was never quite sure if that was a good thing or not.

It was her mother, the Stanford neuroscientist, who'd convinced her to train her body daily. "Feed your hippo," was one of Doctor Vicky Grace's favorite sayings. "Feed your hippo every day, and it will reward you tenfold." She meant the hippocampus, a component of the limbic system located in the medial temporal lobe of the brain. During exercise, she'd explained, the neurons in the hippocampus begin popping off like firecrackers, which enhances creativity, memory, and spatial cognizance. "You see, dear, normally, the hippocampus shrinks with age, bringing mental decline with it. But studies have shown that daily exercise prevents shrinkage and boosts cognitive function even into your golden years. That's why I jog every morning."

Valory took her mother's lesson to heart. If she was going to spend her life in chairs with her nose in books, she'd better feed her hippo.

Her father agreed but espoused a different perspective. "Forget that scientific mumbo jumbo, Val," he said, ribbing Mom. "Do it for your soul. Yoga, exercise, movement, these are all physical pathways to spiritual truth, honey. They connect you with your deeper self, and to the universe. I practice every day, and the revelations I gain bleed into my art."

They were always doing that, Mom and Dad, agreeing on things from opposite perspectives. Odd couple indeed.

As Valory struck a Warrior One pose, she found herself drifting into some random verbal language exercises. These often tickled her brain at unexpected times, their colors prompting her to speak as if they had wills of their own and were just using her mouth as a tool. Today, the sentence that formed in her head was "I don't want to work, I just want to bang on the drum all day." She voiced this first in Hindi, assuming a Bagheli dialect. She repeated it in Japanese Kanto. Then Danish Jutlandic. In this manner she carried on, fluently voicing numerous dialects such that she could fool native speakers the world over.

After a camp wash and an MRE breakfast of runny eggs and sausage, Valory packed her equipment and began her trek to the library. She stopped when she stepped into the Great Hall. It felt different now. She had experienced the hall under the shroud of night and in the gentle blanket of morning. Each of those settings had a unique ambiance. But now she beheld a fresh afternoon setting, and she was dazzled all over again. The hall was alive in midday sunlight as if the very stone had awakened from slumber. Were it not for the modern equipment scattered among the columns and the sculptures, she might have sworn she'd stepped through a time portal into the active court of a medieval monarch.

There was one occupant of the hall other than the marble queen. Janelle LaFleur was atop an eight-foot rolling stepladder along the south wall inspecting the surface of a painting with some kind of electronic device. She was absorbed in her work and didn't notice Valory's entrance. The sight of her made Valory uneasy. They were under orders not to speak to one another unless a homeland agent was present. Such was the draconian rule of law in the castle. It was silly, but Valory had never been a rule breaker. She considered starting now. It really was a dumb order, going against everything academia stood for. Surely the other experts had broken it a time or two?

After a bout of indecision, Valory decided it was best not to rock the boat, at least for now. Instead, she walked through the cadre of sculptures and bas-relief columns over to the queen. She felt compelled to pay homage to her each time she passed through the hall. It was her castle, after all. All these people camping out here—the scholars, the soldiers, the agents—they were trespassers. If Valory was going to be sauntering around every day plundering the castle's secrets, she could at least pay the queen a bit of respect.

Standing before the throne, Valory observed the monarch's flawless marble face. In the warm glow of the afternoon, she exuded a whole new countenance. That of a sun goddess, blooming with ocher life. Tonight, when darkness took the hall, she would again become the dreamy moon queen, mysterious and pale. Had the castle purposefully been designed that way? With the windows positioned to glorify the queen's beauty no matter the hour? Or was it just a coincidence? Valory mused as she ran her fingertips along the queen's smooth cheek, down her neck and along her shoulder. She traced the contours of the diamond symbol on her robe, the crest of Charlemagne, and wondered if she had been an unknown daughter of that celebrated Frankish emperor. If so, then what of her other symbol, the crest of the Lombards? The Lombard people were of Viking descent, having migrated from ancient Scandinavia into the regions now known as Italy. Why was the queen's robe emblazoned with both crests? Did she represent a royal union between the Franks and the Lombards?

"*Bonjour!*"

Valory turned to see Janelle waving at her from atop her ladder. Her smile was toothy and inviting. She climbed down, beaming as if she had something exciting to share. Valory returned the wave, fretting. Rafael made it clear that fraternizing with the others was forbidden, yet Janelle was now motioning for her to come over. Had she not been informed of the rule? Did she just feel so lonely that she was willing to risk it? There was no one else in the hall, so perhaps they could sneak in a chat if they were quick. The thought of being caught made her heart thump—to fraternize would be to rebel.

Stop being a wuss. Her sister, Violet, in her head again. *It's a ridiculous rule, sis. What are they gonna do, fire you? You're the only one that can read those texts. Wield your leverage.*

Valory was saved from the dilemma when the door groaned open, illuminating the vestibule. *Agente Principale* Marco Savelli appeared at the entrance to the hall, buttoning his blazer. He stopped there, looking at them. His eyes narrowed to suspicious slits.

Valory turned and hastened to the library.

***

Savelli shielded his eyes and leaned into the downdraft, suit whipping as the helicopter wobbled into the air. *Agente* D'Arezzo was in the cockpit next to the pilot putting on his headphones. He didn't look back. Lucky bastard. D'Arezzo's leave was beginning. Savelli, however, was on his first assignment as *Agente Principale*. He didn't get leaves.

As the helicopter crested the toothy peaks and pitched into the clear skies, Savelli straightened his blazer and inspected the cargo it had delivered. Mostly personal packages for the civilian eggheads. These arrived every so often to provide preferred creature comforts. With his pocketknife, he cut open a sturdy box addressed to Dario Bertinelli, the engineer. Inside were two bottles of whisky, a carton of gourmet cream-filled pastries, and a couple of pornographic magazines. Typical Dario. Savelli held the whisky bottle to the sunlight, checking for contraband. Once, on another assignment, he'd found a camera pen wrapped in cellophane hidden in a Coke bottle. The bottles were clean. Unscrewing the cap on one, he took a little sip, and then one more. Good stuff. He had a quick flip through one of the magazines. Good stuff, indeed.

Returning the items, he shoved the box aside and checked the next one. It was addressed to the old man, Professor Mancini. Nothing but books in there. One look at the first title and Savelli wanted to shoot himself. *Structural Lexicology and the Greek New Testament: Applying Corpus Linguistics for Word Sense Possibility Delimitation Using Collocational Indicators.* How boring did someone have to be to read such babble? He nearly fell asleep just reading the title. Opening the book, he ensured it hadn't been hollowed out to conceal a cell phone or any other compromising item. He repeated this for the other books in the box.

Scoffing, he pushed it aside and checked the next box, a small one addressed to Janelle LaFleur. Inside were packages of French candies, several art collector magazines, and an envelope full of photographs. Savelli rifled through the photos. Most of them showed Janelle's cats in various poses. Some of the photos had a woman in them, Janelle's friend, or sister, or whoever. Caring for the cats while Janelle was on assignment here. Whoever it was had no clue where Janelle really was. Like all the Ministry contractors, Janelle had been forbidden to tell anyone where she was going or how long she'd be gone. All care packages had to be sent to the Ministry and would then be retrieved by the *Agenzia* for delivery to the castle. Savelli tossed the pics back into the box and moved on to the next. After he'd inspected the contents of every box, he motioned for *Tenete* Esposito to deliver them to their recipients.

The day was gorgeous. A crisp, gentle breeze, a warm sun, and a blanket of clear blue heaven. Only the snowbanks piled along the castle walls reminded him that winter hadn't quite left the mountains. Downslope of the cauldron, in the military encampment, a group of soldiers were returning from field exercises. Busy work to keep them active. Two soldiers detached from the group and clopped toward the castle atop the horses. Savelli appreciated the intrinsic beauty of the sight—two riders trotting against a backdrop of azure sky and a pristine glacial valley. He supposed if he had to babysit a bunch of scholars, there were worse places in which to do it. Just as he thought so, one of the horses defecated on the stone.

Savelli strode back to the castle. He quickened his step as he passed under the barbican, looking up at the gate as he did. The iron spikes lining the bottom of that gate always made him uneasy. Dario had assured him the gate could never crash down on its own, but such assurances were little comfort when a row of rusted spikes loomed in the shadows above your head.

Along the eastern wall of the courtyard, the chorus of generators droned from the old livestock pens. A soldier was on his knees, making repairs to one of the motors. The area smelled like fuel and oil. Last time he was here, Savelli had spotted a soldier smoking a cigarette near the fuel canisters, so he tore him a new *stronzo*. That resulted in an argument between himself and *Capitano* Ricci for dressing down the soldier personally rather than referring it to the proper chain of command. Savelli insisted that as *Agente Principale*, his authority under the *Sicurezza* office was absolute, and he would dress down anyone he damn well pleased. In truth, due to the site's unique circumstances, even he was uncertain who the top dog was here. There was a constant tug of war between Ricci, *Sicurezza*, and the Italian Ministry of Cultural Heritage over who had the final say about specific matters at the castle. So-called clarification from the highest levels of government was anything but.

Savelli arrived at the stairs of the keep and took them two at a time. He pushed on the thick, banded door, entered the vestibule, and then heaved the door closed. When he passed under the portal into the Great Hall, he stopped. The two women were in there, unchaperoned. The Mouse was by the east wall among the paintings. The Librarian stood near the thrones. They were separated by half the hall, but the guilt in their eyes was obvious. They'd been on the verge of fraternizing. Savelli let the uncomfortable moment linger, letting the women see his displeasure. Then the Librarian turned and hastened toward the north portal. He watched her. Watched her hips sway in her well-fitted hiking pants. Long brown ponytail swinging to and fro. Skin as milky as the statue with which she'd been standing. Perhaps she wasn't beautiful, nor tanned, nor the most well-endowed, but she had nice eyes, and she was not without her charms. Hell, up here she was a beauty queen. Not like the Mouse, who was now awkwardly climbing her ladder to return to her paintings. There was nothing to get excited about there.

Savelli crossed the hall, hoping there was some lunch left in the Dining Hall. He didn't enjoy instituting the no collaboration rule. Mostly because he didn't have the resources to enforce it. There were only two or three homeland agents onsite at any given time while there were perhaps a dozen Ministry contractors along with a handful of federal contractors. The agents couldn't be everywhere monitoring every interaction, and Savelli wasn't about to make himself look incompetent by begging his superiors to reinstate the same number of agents he'd been granted last season. So, he'd instituted the rule, honor system style. He'd had no choice. The Incident last month had almost led to complete disaster. Had it played out to its worst conclusion, this top-secret site could have become worldwide news, and Savelli's failure would have been career-ending. Therefore, things had to change, despite Moretti's vehement objections.

Moretti was another problem. The man was a blithering egghead with no mind for the stakes here. He protested every security measure, every order, every restriction. He wanted open collaboration, he wanted phones, he wanted internet, he wanted specialized equipment of every kind. Who cared if such equipment had been manufactured by foreign interests and might have been implanted with surveillance technology that might expose the site? Not Moretti. Everything he could do to hamper Savelli's job, he did. His worst offense was bringing the Librarian here. Valory Grace. He'd demanded approval to recruit her, and unfortunately, his case was strong. There was no one else qualified to decipher the tomes in that library. Professor Mancini had proven to be almost worthless. Still, the appointment stunk to Savelli.

Director Teruzzi had enthusiastically approved Doctor Grace's nomination. He insisted it was a beautiful coincidence that, if managed properly, could not only substantiate provenance but could also be used as leverage for the most important objective of all. Pursuing that latter objective was distasteful. Savelli didn't like it, nor did his men. And so far, their efforts had proven ineffective. Teruzzi, however, ordered them to press on.

Still, during weekly briefings, Savelli never missed an opportunity to warn the brass about Doctor Grace. Her presence at the castle was a ticking time bomb. If she somehow managed to get a look inside that tower, it would be Savelli's mess to clean up.

Moretti didn't know the details—didn't know who was in the tower, nor what had happened during The Incident—but if things blew up, he'd be culpable. And if it came down to Savelli putting a bullet in the Librarian's head to maintain secrecy, Moretti could bet his fat ass he'd be forced to watch.

BÖLÜM 16

BAG OVER HER SHOULDER, Valory pulled on her beanie and Isotoners as she made her way down the aisle. The library, awash with sunlight, wasn't as frigid as it had been last night, but it was just nippy enough to cover up. She fumbled with the gloves, letting slip a mild French curse when she struggled to wriggle her fingers into the right holes. As she did so, the laptop bag slipped off her shoulder, and she jerked awkwardly at the hips to keep it from hitting the floor.

She stopped to compose herself. Confronting Mancini was not going to be easy, but it had to be done. She was the head of this project, and Mancini had to accept that. Or at least acknowledge it. She could see him farther down the aisle now, sitting at the center table, surrounded by a fortress of modern texts. His hair was wispy and unkempt, the strands exploring the air like a sea anemone. As Valory had dressed, she rehearsed what she was going to say to him, settling on something dignified and tactful. Now, with the old man in sight, her little speech was slipping from her brain like a tire with a slow leak. *If I could just write him an email.*

Needing a reset, Valory paused, turning to the bookshelf on her left. It was a good place to gather herself, for there rested the beautiful treasure bindings she'd spotted yesterday. In an ocean of otherwise typical leatherbound tomes, these stood out, their embedded jewels glinting in the soft luminescence of piped-in sunlight. Rubies, sapphires, pearls, the boards were packed with gems set in gold and silver. There were twelve books in all. It was rare to encounter even one treasure binding in antiquity, so to have a dozen lying before her, untouched for centuries, was the stuff of fantasy. Again, she wondered who had commissioned them and for what purpose. Most treasure bindings were religious in nature—gospels used for imperial coronations and the like—but Valory had a hunch these were different. The fact that there were so many of them, far removed from any historical seat of governance or clergy, suggested some other purpose. She was eager to find out. Nothing was stopping her—she was free to pick and choose her plan of study—but having already engaged with Alikai's diary, she felt obligated to continue translating his work first.

Right now, though, it was time to deal with Professor Mancini. Find out what he had been working on and, if necessary, redirect him. She hoped it wouldn't come to that. Crabby old men did not like such things. She looked down the aisle at him. He was at the table scribbling notes. In her mind's eye, she was already seeing his reaction to her olive branch. His croaky protests, his exaggerated Italian hand gestures, his bushy white brows scrunched over dark, angry eyes. *Maybe I should put this off*, she thought. *Just get back to my clay tablets and worry about Mancini tomorrow.*

Or maybe you should stand up for yourself and show this jerk who's boss. Violet's imaginary voice again. It had been creeping into Valory's thoughts more and more since leaving the safety of her Oxford flat. She'd had no need of it there, buried in her own little study cave, but since venturing into the real world, her twin sis had become mouthier. Just a mental coping mechanism, but it helped to remind Valory that Violet wasn't just some wayward druggie wild child. She had strengths. She knew how to stand up for herself. How to ask for—no, demand—what she wanted. Where Val was weak, Vi was strong. Playing *What Would Vi Do?* was a helpful exercise in times like this. *March straight up to him and lay down the law*, continued Vi's phantom. *Right here, right now. So what if he gets pissed? At least he'll know you're not a doormat.*

"Not a doormat," muttered Valory. Looking at Mancini sandwiched among his books, she breathed long and deep, then began walking toward him. *Here we go.*

Mancini looked up as she approached, the fuzzy sunlight accentuating the wrinkles of his face. To his left, his closed laptop sat atop a stack of modern books. Farther to his right, one of the library's ancient leather-bound tomes laid open in a wooden cradle. Several more piles of contemporary texts were stacked around him. The scene gave the illusion of an old man being devoured by a beast made of books.

"*Buon pomeriggio, Professore Mancini*," said Valory. "*Come sta?*"

"Ah," he said, returning to his notes, "*Il nuovo capo è venuto per usurpare il vecchio povero.*" The new boss has come to usurp the poor old man.

Valory chose to ignore the comment. Speaking Italian, she began her prepared remarks, saying that she was pleased to be working with him, that she was excited to begin contributing to this historic project alongside him, and that she was sure that the two of them, together, would produce a benevolent corpus of research for the betterment of humankind. But she fumbled the words, their colors blurring in her mind, their textures melting into amorphous blobs. She paused and faltered, shades of her social phobia threatening to derail her. She flashbacked to instances in her life when she'd teetered on the edge of incoherence. That time she'd given a stuttering presentation at Harvard. The meeting where she'd blubbered to a roundtable full of strangers. That meek confrontation where she'd tried to ask a rude neighbor to stop parking in her assigned spot. All were humiliating memories of the great linguist reduced to a frightened dullard. Now, just like that, her simple, well-considered speech had become a scatterbrained exercise in verbal endurance. All she could do was slow down, gather herself, and push through it, red-faced and humbled. Midway through her performance, Mancini seemed to realize how nervous she was, and he stopped writing so he could watch her. As if she wasn't feeling enough pressure. When she finally uttered the last, merciful syllable, she stood in silence, waiting for his response.

For a moment, Mancini only stared, bushy eyebrows furrowing over his glasses. When he spoke, it was in heavily accented, gravel-throated English. "Your Italian is very good. You have a cultivated Tuscan dialect. I hear not even a faint American accent."

Valory remained silent. Not quite the response she'd expected.

"The stuttering notwithstanding, you could pass for a true Italian, I think."

"Thank you."

Mancini removed his glasses, cleaning them with a cloth as he leaned back in his chair. "Most Americans don't bother to learn another tongue. Too arrogant and lazy. They think the whole world should speak English, but where do they think their language comes from, eh? From God? Bah!" He flung his hands away from his ears in a *They are crazy!* type of gesture. "Americans think they own the world, but they barely know their own history."

Valory wasn't sure what was happening. Mancini seemed to be both complimenting and insulting her. She glanced toward the far end of the table. Rollo had come back from wherever he'd been, and he was preparing to photograph a volume that was lying open in his cradle. "Yes," she said to Mancini, "well I'm happy to continue in Italian if you'd like. *È una lingua molto bella.*"

"*Sì,* it is very beautiful, unlike English. Such an impure, hodgepodge language. Like three species of pigs grunting at each other, eh? Nevertheless," he sighed, putting on his glasses as he returned to his work, "we have been instructed to write our translations in English. So we may as well speak it." With that, he fell silent over his notes.

"Uh, Professor," said Valory, clearing her throat, "Doctor Moretti tells me you began your work here last summer."

"Mm."

"I'm quite interested to know what you've studied in that time. I've barely arrived and I'm already, well, shocked really, by what I'm seeing. I can only imagine what you've uncovered."

"Mm, yes. There is much here."

She waited, thinking he would elaborate, but he just scribbled his notes, every so often checking the reference book to his right. His handwriting was sloppy, and his hand trembled as he wrote. "Anything notable you'd like to share? Bounce off me?"

"Later, perhaps. I am busy. Check with Rollo."

There was the familiar blow-off, undisguised. She'd seen plenty of those in her career. She swallowed a nervous lump, wondering if she should just let it go. Wishing Violet was there for support. Rollo was at the far end of the table listening to their conversation. Having an audience only unnerved her further. Steeling herself, she had another go. "I have some translations to add to the official record. Some clay tablets from the lower level. I assume you've developed a classification system for the library?"

Mancini stopped writing, his pen shaking over the paper. He pursed his lips but said nothing.

"Professor?"

"What?"

"The classification system?"

"*Si si*, classification, I heard you." He looked at her, tapping a bony finger to his temple. "Don't worry, it is all up here."

"You mean . . . in your head?"

"That's right. Safe and sound."

"Ah. Well, uh, with respect, Professor, that might not be the best way to facilitate collabora—"

"Listen, *signorina*," he said, throwing down his pen and rising from his chair, "I have been doing this since you were just a dream in your father's eye, *capisci?* I was publishing papers while you were in diapers. Everyone knows my work. So don't you worry about classification, I said I am taking care of everything." With that, he banged his fist on the table and walked off.

Valory made no move to stop him. She just let him storm past her, thankful at least that the confrontation was over. She gave herself a moment, blowing a long breath to steady her nerves.

"Don't let him get to you," said Rollo, walking over. His thin frame was inflated by a padded coat, and a Nikon hung around his neck. "He's all bark. You spoke to him as well as anyone could have."

"*Ne čini se tako.*"

"Come again?"

Valory shook her head, realizing she'd answered in Croatian. "Sorry. I said it didn't seem like it went well."

"No, trust me, you were very patient compared to his other colleagues. You didn't take the bait."

"Right, the bait," said Valory. She never took the bait—scurrying off was much easier. "So you're saying he picks arguments like that with everyone?"

"Yeah, almost everyone. It is his way of handling his, uh . . ." Rollo trailed off. It seemed as if he'd stopped himself from saying something he shouldn't. Instead, he smiled. "My uncle is very proud, that's all."

"I see," said Valory. "So, Rollo, may I ask what you're working on right now?"

"Of course. As I mentioned before, my job here, other than providing historical context, is to digitize these works, page by page." He flipped his camera's LCD screen so she could view it, and he began advancing through his photos. "These are from the book sitting in my cradle over there. For what it's worth, I have my own informal classification system. I'm happy to share or to convert to one of your choosing."

"Great, Rollo, thank you." She squinted at the images as he flipped through, but the text was too small to read on the LCD screen. She could not make out the language. She could only see that it was handwritten and that the text appeared strangely unharmonious. "What is the title of this one?"

"There isn't one," shrugged Rollo. "None of the books I've photographed have had a title. They are all like this, hundreds of them. Blank boards, no flyleaves. The writing begins on the first page, no title, no author, no date, nothing."

"*Niente di niente?*" Nothing at all?

"Nope. Not so far."

No identifying marks. Strange. Valory walked to the other side of the table where Professor Mancini had been working. Adjacent to his notes, one of the tomes rested in a wooden cradle, swathed in the gentle illumination of the library. Probably crafted in the Renaissance era. Bound in cracked leather, its boards were laid open, revealing stiff sheets of eggshell-colored vellum parchment. Holding her ponytail against her chest, Valory leaned over to examine the text. As Rollo had mentioned, it was handwritten in black ink, and it covered the parchment from top to bottom, leaving narrow margins. The ink strokes suggested a quill pen had been used. None of those factors were surprising. What was surprising was the language—or rather languages. There was more than just one. There were lots of them, representing different eras from regions all over the world. The result was an alphabetic medley, lacking uniformity or a common genealogical foundation. It was as if the author had crammed a dozen tongues into a jar, shaken them up, and then constructed each section with whatever he pulled out. It gave the pages a clunky and confusing appearance, and it caused some curious infighting between the colors and textures billowing through her mind. Homing in on each segment in turn, Valory found one written in Primitive Norse, a language that was cold in her mind, giving her the sensation of brain freeze. The next segment was in Old Welsh, which smelled of seafoam and pond lilies. The next was Archaic Greek in a myriad of beiges which felt like slick tile. Then back to Norse.

Perplexed, she glanced through the following page, further identifying a jumbled soup of tongues. Vulgar Latin. Demotic Egyptian. Dalmatic, once spoken in modern-day Croatia. Here and there, a single sentence would begin in one tongue and transition to another halfway through. One passage was even written in Sumerian, recognized worldwide as the (previously) first-ever written language. Historical samples of Sumerian existed today only in clay and stone. Yet here it had been adapted to ink and parchment.

Valory was aghast. A collection of extinct languages, separated by vast centuries and geographical origins, mish-mashed together in a single volume? Not even the famed Rosetta Stone was as diverse. That renowned slab of stele, discovered by a Napoleonic soldier in 1799, was carved with three languages, and it had given modern linguists the key to deciphering ancient Egyptian hieroglyphs. It had changed history. Yet lying before her now was something just as wonderful, perhaps more so. The tongues here predated the era in which this book had been crafted by centuries. Renaissance scribes could not have possessed a command of all these languages, especially Sumerian. The Sumerian language had only been unearthed by modern scholars in the nineteenth century, several hundred years after this codex had been created. It was an isolate that had not spread into the genealogy of any other language. So why was it here? Just what the hell was she looking at? Some kind of joint effort by a team of Renaissance scribes? Sitting around taking turns writing passages in extinct languages that should have been unknown to them? That seemed absurd.

Valory began to compare the scripts to one another, narrowing her focus to specific sections to separate their colors and textures. The Old Norse sections were written in bold, blocky Runic. The Vulgar Latin was written in epigraphic majuscule script. The Dalmatic in Croatian Glagolitic. Diverse and independent orthography, suggesting a host of authors. Yet, as she examined the text, a common paleographic thread slowly emerged. A subtle, nearly imperceptible pattern revealing an underlying uniformity in the writing style. Factors such as the length of the strokes, the widths of the curves, the spacing of the characters, and the pressure applied to the nib of the quill. Everything was consistent from the top of the parchment to the bottom. It was a handwriting pattern that suggested . . .

"This was all written by a single person," whispered Valory. She couldn't believe her own words. One author wrote all this? No way. That was just wrong. Who would write like this? Who *could* write like this? If this book had been crafted in the Renaissance period, then the languages on these pages had already been long extinct. How had a single scholar of that era accomplished this? For what and for whom was it written? What audience could have understood it?

"What did you say?" asked Rollo, turning off his camera.

"Huh?"

"I thought I heard you say something about an author."

He may as well have been speaking from another dimension, for his voice was just a distant hum on the fringe of her consciousness. Ignoring him, she reached for a nearby box of gloves and fumbled for a pair. After pulling them on, she laid her fingers gently upon the edge of the leather boards and read some of the passages. Every language on the pages was familiar. She'd experienced their unique sensations many times over. She had published studies on some. She could translate them in real time, no reference materials required. She ate them with her eyes, sucking their juices into her mind, their ancient flavors more satisfying than a butter-soaked filet mignon.

"Doctor Grace?"

It appeared to be a diary. Like Alikai's clay tablet diary, but with greater linguistic complexity. The author was writing of his travels, recording the names of people and places he'd encountered. Words he'd shared, things he'd seen. Slipping from one language to another, the quill strokes betokening a rapid writing style, as if the hand that created them was playing catchup to a gushing waterfall of thoughts. There was no explanation behind the use of so many tongues and scripts. The narrative was written as if the author regarded the multitude of languages as a single, global mega-language.

Valory forgot about Mancini. Forgot about Rollo and the treasure bindings. She even forgot about the clay tablets. She was tingling all over, as if her skin were conducting a low voltage of electricity, its current made of playful hues and scents. Before her was a gorgeous linguistic mystery unprecedented in all of antiquity, written by one hand, possessing a command of ancient writing that should have been impossible.

"Doctor Grace!"

"What?" she said, startled.

"What's wrong? Are you okay?"

Valory could only stutter as she tried to find the words.

"*Oddio.* You've found something big. Please, you must tell me!"

"Well, I'm not quite sure what to make of it. It's just so . . . wait a minute," she said, pulling herself away from the book. "You mean your uncle hasn't told you?"

"Told me what?"

She stared at him, disbelief halting her tongue. Then she reached for Mancini's research notes, the ones he'd been jotting about this very tome. Maybe the old codger had already learned something about the author or the text. Her disappointment was instant. Mancini, it appeared, had just been copying passages from the modern handbook he'd been referencing: *The Mouton Companions to Ancient Egyptian*. Valory had whipped through that handbook as a teenager and had found it uninspiring, useful only for beginners. Flipping through the rest of Mancini's notes, she saw pages and pages of copied text, sprinklings of his own unhelpful thoughts mixed in. His handwriting exposed a trembling, unsteady hand. This wasn't research, it was busy work. She suddenly understood why she'd been recruited to take over.

"What is it?" asked Rollo, his excitement growing. "Has my uncle discovered something? Why wouldn't he tell me?"

"I'm not sure," said Valory, still struggling. She felt her mind being pulled in a dozen directions, each thought wilder than the last. The oldest works in this library—the clay tablets—were diary entries. Her translations had shown that. Now, here in the upper level where the most recent works rested, was another diary. It couldn't be related to those much older tablets, could it? At least not in the incredulous way that was poking her intuition. Doubting herself, she returned her attention to Mancini's tome. Gingerly, she grasped the righthand parchment and turned the page. Staring back at her were two more pages crammed with forgotten tongues. "Oh my."

"What?"

She ogled the text, grappling with a hunch that she dared not entertain. "Rollo, let me see the book you're working on." Before he could answer, she was striding toward his workstation at the far end of the table.

"Yeah, sure," he said, hastening behind. "It's open there in my cradle."

The nip in the library was negated by Valory's excitement, the enchantment of the lighting system forgotten. Her mind was now engorged with these codices. Rounding the table, she leaned over the tome Rollo had been photographing, holding her ponytail to her chest. It, too, appeared to have been constructed in the Renaissance era. Written upon its yellowed parchment were more exotic languages. At a glance, Valory picked out Old Welsh, Breton, and Mycenaean Greek, the latter of which hadn't been spoken in thirty-five hundred years. But the book was only around four hundred years old! She turned the page. Sumerian again. Old High German. Old Hungarian. Even Early Middle English, the language of Renaissance England. The handwriting matched. The same author had penned both books. Spot-reading some of the passages, she confirmed that this tome, too, was a diary. Just like Mancini's book. Just like the clay tablets.

"Rollo."

"Yes?"

"*Wie viele dieser Bücher*—sorry, I mean—How many of these tomes have you photographed?"

"Mm, since last year? Like eight hundred, I think."

"Are they all like this?

"Like what?"

"This," said Valory, jabbing her finger toward the book. "Written in all these languages. Are they all like this?"

"Well, yeah. I think so."

"You *think* so?"

"I'm sorry, Doctor Grace," he said, and Valory swore he'd spontaneously become fifteen years younger, his expression like a clueless teenager's. "There are so many books to get through. Unless my uncle points out something specific, I don't really pay attention to the text anymore. I just click and turn, click and turn. But yes," he said, seeing her exasperation. "I think they are mostly like this."

"Well, what has your uncle deciphered? Where is his work?"

"Uh, well I know he has translated some Latin inscriptions, and some Greek, and some fourteenth-century Italian. But he doesn't tell me much. He turns in his completed work to *Agente* Savelli."

"Unbelievable," she muttered.

"Why, what is it? My god, Doctor Grace, you're torturing me! You must tell me what you've found."

Valory shushed him. Mancini had translated some Latin, some Greek, and some Old Italian? That's it? Any Mediterranean-based historical linguist could do that. The familiar realization overcame her. The realization that she was surrounded by lesser minds and that she would have to do everything herself. It was both exasperating and thrilling.

She had planned to resume working on the clay tablets in the depths of the library. Not anymore. After seeing these books, she was unable to resist them. Focusing on Rollo's cradled tome, she tuned out everything else and began reading the diary. She was looking for something. For what, exactly, she couldn't admit to herself. There was no possible way that her hunch was true, so she did not entertain it. Except that she did. And when her hunch was all but confirmed by the text, the mild electrical sensation she'd been feeling became a surge that brought her to her tiptoes.

"Doctor Grace," said Rollo, helping to steady her. "Are you sure you're okay?"

"Rollo," she said, voice quivering.

"Yes?"

"Help me take this book to my chamber."

CAPITULUM 17

PROFESSOR EMILIO MANCINI STOPPED at the foot of the spiral stairwell to gather his strength. The stairs were the worst thing about working at the castle—too steep, no elevator, no handrails. It was two flights to the main level, and they were not regular flights. The narrow walls made him feel claustrophobic, and they seemed to curl around forever. An esteemed seventy-four-year-old professor with arthritis should not have to suffer such conditions. If this project were not the most important of his and Rafael's careers, he'd have quit on day naught.

He raised his right foot to the first step, then brought his left foot to that same step. He repeated the action for the next step. In this manner, he puttered his way up. If he led with his left foot, a tingling pain would shoot from his lower back down into his leg. That issue had started five or six years ago. As it had gotten worse, he'd had to change the way he moved, the way he did certain things. He never went to the doctor about it. They'd just try to convince him he needed unnecessary surgery. No, all he needed was his pool back home. The heated pool in his beautiful garden. A long soak in that, with a nice glass of *Valpolicella*, and presto, no more pain.

Huffing, he reached the main level and rested against the wall of the throne room. It was bright in there, the afternoon sun exploring every nook and cranny. Closing his eyes, he allowed his heart to settle. He realized how sleepy he was. So sleepy he could take a nap right here. The temptation was strong. He felt heavy, his bones weary. Maybe he could just sit and doze off for a few minutes.

The keep door groaned open, followed by men's voices. So much for a power nap. From here, Mancini couldn't see the men in the vestibule, but he could hear them yelling.

"*No no, apetta, apetta! Spostalo un po 'a sinistra!*"

"*Non posso!*"

"*Si, puoi! Afferralo lì!*"

The men were trying to fit something large through the keep door and were having difficulties. One of the voices was Rafael's. Forgetting his nap, Mancini shuffled past the sculptures and columns so he could see what was going on. Rafael and a soldier were in the vestibule while Dario and another soldier were outside. Between them, wedged in the door, was a wheeled contraption that looked like an overgrown lawnmower. The team was having trouble turning it to an angle that would fit it through. Mancini wondered what the contraption was, then decided he didn't care after the men began shouting like they were all archenemies.

Mancini walked to the far side of the throne room, the unpleasant bickering motivating his haste. When he reached the west portal, he stopped, furrowing his brow. Where was he going? He'd known just a minute ago. He was going . . . Well, he'd remember in a moment. For now, just get out of the Great Hall, away from the squabbling.

Wandering down the west corridor, he stopped to admire a small painting. The subject was a dark-haired woman, proud eyes piercing the viewer. Probably a portrait of the marble queen. The colors had faded with time, or at least he assumed they had. It was a bit dark in the corridor, and he couldn't tell for sure. Maybe the painting was vibrant, maybe not. He didn't much care. The only colors he cared about nowadays were the ones in his garden. The red-orange fire bursts of his Alpine lilies. The deep, royal purple of his viola pansies. The whimsical blues and yellows of his evening primroses. His wife, Mia, had created an oasis behind their home, and it was the loveliest place in the world. Right about now, she was probably out there, talking to the flowers, pruning and fertilizing them. In a few hours, she would be soaking in the heated pool wishing he was there with her. He longed for it to be so. Lounging there, together, in their little fragrant slice of heaven. It wouldn't be long now. Just finish up and few things here and he would go. Maybe he'd ask for the satellite phone so he could give her a ring. *Keep the water warm, my dear. I'll be home soon.*

Mancini's stomach rumbled, and he remembered where he'd been going. The Dining Hall, of course. Felt like ages since he'd eaten breakfast. He hoped there was still something there. By mid-afternoon, everything had usually been picked over.

After a wrong turn or two and a bit of backtracking, he found the hall. With its vaulted ceiling and sumptuous trappings, the hall was reminiscent of a church. Only instead of pews, there was a long oaken table, and instead of a pulpit, there was a massive, frieze-lined fireplace. *Agente* Savelli was seated at the table with a *caffè* and a *biscotto*, typing on a laptop. "*Professore*," he said, nodding at Mancini.

Mancini grunted. He was not fond of Savelli. The man was always looking. Always suspicious. Always pressing his heavy hand on the scholars like a pit-faced Mussolini. This place would be much more tolerable without him. Shuffling to the other side of the table, Mancini poured some coffee, trying to keep his hand from shaking. But Savelli noticed. He always noticed.

"Look at this," said Mancini in Italian, taking a mini sandwich from a platter. "Here we are doing the most important work in the country, and this is what we are given to eat, eh?" He slipped into one of the high-backed chairs, brandishing the sandwich at Savelli. "I tell you, this food makes me long for my wife's cooking. Mia's *baccalà alla vicentina?*" He kissed his fingertips. "*Mamma mia.*"

Savelli half-smiled but said nothing. He only watched as Mancini sipped his coffee and ate the sandwich. There he goes, watching again. Always watching. Mancini wondered how well he was concealing his trembling hands. Savelli's gaze only made him more self-conscious.

"So tell me, *Professore,*" said Savelli in Italian, "how is your work progressing?"

"Very good."

"Very good?"

"That's what I said."

"Sure, okay." With his finger, Savelli toyed with the edge of his laptop. "It's just that you haven't turned in a report in quite some time." He shrugged. "Is everything okay?"

"Yes, I told you, it's fine."

"Good. So I can expect your report soon then?"

"Sure, why not? You can do as the Americans say—expect in one hand, shit into the other, see which fills up first. Perhaps that will entertain you while you sit around doing nothing. Meanwhile, I will continue doing actual work which will change the world. How does that sound, hm?"

Savelli grimaced, jaw going tight, eyes locked on the old man, watching as he chewed.

"Oh," said Mancini around a mouthful of sandwich, "I need to use the satellite phone."

"For?"

"Not that it is any of your business, but I wish to call my wife. I need to speak with her." He pointed a gnarled finger at Savelli. "And don't you even think about listening in. Get your fascist jollies elsewhere."

"I see," said Savelli. He considered his next words. "*Professore,* don't you think you are forgetting something?"

"And what is that?" he answered, grabbing a second sandwich. "You want me to beg? Oh, please great and noble agent of Italy, may I pretty please use your phone? Perhaps I can wash your car and press your suit while I'm at it? Bah! I am no one's prisoner here."

Savelli bristled at this, looking toward the door. "*Professore,* you should be more tactful with what you say. You might give some people the wrong impression."

"Oh, I am to be told what I can and can't say now? Maybe you've forgotten that I am one of the world's foremost scholars. I will not be treated like a child, especially by a gun-toting troglodyte. Now why don't you make yourself useful and fetch me the phone."

Savelli shifted in his chair and straightened his tie. He made no move to leave. Then he answered Mancini in measured tones. "*Professore,* when I asked if you were forgetting something, I meant that it is not possible to call your wife."

"And why is that?"

"Because she died three years ago."

Mancini froze in mid-chew, looking at nothing.

"Don't you remember? The pneumonia? The funeral?"

He did remember. *Now* he did. It all came back to him as if someone had just opened a door, revealing a room filled with anguished memories. They hit him all at once. Mia in the hospital bed, a tube in her mouth, barely coherent. His hand wrapped around hers as she passed. A cloudy funeral attended by a handful of old friends. The beautiful garden she'd crafted, wilting and dying no matter what he did to save it. He'd tried, he'd desperately tried, but he didn't have the touch. Moretti had been at the funeral, his arm around Mancini's shoulder as they lowered Mia into the ground.

"*Professore?*"

"What."

"Don't you remember?"

"Of course I do," he answered quietly. His hands trembled as if he was freezing. He hid them under the table. "I meant that I wanted to call my daughter, Alessa. I misspoke."

Savelli nodded, watching the old man as he stared at his plate. "Well then. I shall bring you the phone." Standing, he buttoned his jacket and gathered his laptop, looking once more at Mancini before leaving him to his thoughts.

CUTUBKA 18

VALORY REREAD HER TRANSLATION. Then she reread it again, checking it against the source material with a fine-toothed mental comb. For several hours she proofed her work, absorbing the colors and scents of each character, both individually and in the overall context, daring herself to discover errors. Drastic, fundamental errors that would invalidate her work. Because the alternative—that everything she'd translated from the codex was accurate and true—was the stuff of science fiction. A giant slap to the face of reality. If she took this to peer review, she would be placing her career in jeopardy.

Yet, she knew it was true. The colors never lied. And if her hypothesis were correct, she would find a ton of supporting evidence in the library. That was her goal now. To go back to the library and find the proof to make this all real. She would do that before she even thought about bringing this bombshell to Moretti.

Rising from her chair felt like breaking out of a cocoon. Five days. For five, restless days had she holed up in her bedchamber, hunched over her laptop translating the tome she'd snatched from Rollo's cradle. Hours upon hours of sitting, sinking ever further into a disbelieving haze as she unlocked one revelation after another. She only attuned to her physical body when her tummy roared with hunger, when her bulging bladder caused her to tap dance in her seat, or when she jerked awake after drifting off. Now she felt the full effects of her five-day cerebral cyclone. Stretching tall, her spine popped like a xylophone, her yawn a silent scream to the heavens.

With her blood flowing again, she stood over the tome examining the text she'd translated. What a thrilling experience. The alphabetic kaleidoscope fluttering through her mind, the exotic languages tickling her soul. It hadn't felt like work. More like she'd been wrapped in the embrace of the mysterious author, his breath warming her ear, exposing secrets meant only for her. A foolish flight of fancy, perhaps, but exciting. Every word stoked her appetite for more. More of this man's strange tongue-weaving, more of his eon-leaping whispers. Even her fleeting naps had tingled with his voice, audible only to the deep pleasure centers of her mind. More than once, she had awoken with her hand between her legs.

The time was 11:38 P.M. Aside from the gaseous breath of her propane lamp, the castle was dead quiet. During the day, Rafael had come by her chamber. He was eagerly awaiting her translation, having been told by Rollo that she'd 'flipped out' after seeing this particular tome. But Valory had shooed him away, irked that he'd broken her flow. *Agente* Savelli had come by a few times as well. Routine checks, and to collect her completed work. Though Valory was expecting this, it stung, because she was not allowed to keep copies of her translations. As instructed, she'd saved her work to an external hard drive. Savelli confiscated that drive, giving her a replacement. Everything she'd accomplished to that point was gone. The most exciting work of her life just whisked away. She hoped once the *Agenzia* ensured there was nothing in her translations that would endanger their directives, they would return it for proper academic treatment, but she was not certain of that and had no recourse otherwise. She consoled herself with the knowledge that she could at least go back to the source material.

The cold was biting now that she was no longer mind-melding with her work. For the first time in hours, she noticed her frosty exhalations. Felt the iciness of her cheeks. It had been a while since she'd tended the fire, and it was now just a sleepy pile of orange. She should have gone to bed then. Just stoke the fire and crawl under that warm goose-down comforter for a few hours. But she couldn't. Not yet.

After ensuring the fireplace shield was in place, she stuffed her laptop into her bag. Donned her coat and beanie, threw the bag over her shoulder. Grabbed the propane lamp. After one last look at the magnificent tome lying in her cradle, she left the chamber, pulling the door open just enough to squeeze through.

It was dark and freezing in the corridor. Being an interior hallway, there were no windows. The lantern cast a bubble of soft light around her, but beyond that was blackness. No light shone from beneath Mancini's door nor from Moretti's. Valory knew that if she switched off her lantern at that moment, she wouldn't be able to see a foot in front of her face. *Do I really want to do this right now?* she thought, but it wasn't a real question. There was no 'want' here. There was only 'need.'

She trod slowly, minding the electrical cords along the floor. Someone had pulled them out of their neat bundle along the wall and strewn them into the walkway. Valory remembered hearing soldiers out here some hours ago arguing about replacing a cord that had been accidentally cut. Seemed they hadn't tidied up afterward. Once she passed the mess, she made her way to the spiral staircase and descended into the blackened depths of the keep.

Crossing the top floor of the library, she took the far stairs down to the third level. By the time she set her things on the table, her body had warmed from the walk. She made a mental note to do some jumping jacks every ten minutes or so, maybe some squats or jogging in place. Anything to generate body heat.

In the glow of the lantern, Valory spotted something new in the library. Between the table and the nearest stone shelf rested a machine that looked like a bulky yellow lawnmower. A ground-penetrating detection radar. These were often used in archeological digs to look beneath the ground without actually digging. By beaming electromagnetic subsurface variance data to a visual display atop the device, it negated the need to physically impact the site. The fact that the radar was here, on the bottom level of the library, meant that Dario speculated there might be something farther down. Another level, a chamber, a hidden compartment, something. That was exciting. She'd walked the entire floor the first time she'd been down here and hadn't seen any sort of access to a lower floor. She wondered why Dario suspected otherwise, but it would be against the rules to ask.

"Okay," she whispered, rubbing her Isotoners together. "Back to the good stuff." Picking up her lantern, she trekked toward the northeasternmost corner of the library, where the earliest clay tablets were stored. The works were arranged in chronological order, and she would begin her task with the oldest material.

She walked through the darkness, the stone shelves looming on both sides. It felt like a narrow tunnel in the underworld, her frosty breaths the ghosts of tortured souls. She glanced behind her as she walked, imagining disembodied eyes peeking at her from the void. She quickened her pace.

Arriving at the northeast corner, she tapped into the exhilaration of being among the most ancient writing in human history. Piles upon piles of Alikai's clay tablets sandwiched between matted animal pelts, running down the aisles into the darkness. The tablets Valory had translated were already affixed with catalog tags. Following the shelf south would lead her forward through time into the later works. As she went, she would pick works at random, spot-checking them for specific information. Information that would support the outlandish hypothesis she'd been forced to conceive after translating the tome. To wit:

That Alikai truly was immortal.

That he had not only written the clay tablet diaries, but every single work in this library.

Over the course of ten thousand years.

She shivered. A bit from the cold, a bit from the creepiness, but mostly from that thought. An immortal human being! The idea was madness of the highest degree, at least until a couple of weeks ago. But after deciphering the clay tablets and the tome, she could not deny the evidence. As a researcher, she had to go where the evidence led and nowhere else, no matter how kooky the emergent data. Maybe, as she spot-checked the works from earliest to latest, she would find counter clues to refute her absurd hypothesis. Maybe she'd root out tell-tale discrepancies or uncover the fingerprints of an elaborate hoax.

But if she could prove Alikai was immortal . . .

Even better, if she could find evidence that he was still alive . . .

And if he *was* still alive, where was he?

Pants swishing, Valory hurried down the aisle, past the tablets she'd already translated. Past the thousands of others like them, walking forward in time by decades, perhaps centuries. She'd almost reached the northwest corner of the library when the works changed from clay tablets to stretched animal skins and flattened bark. Here, she set her lantern down and removed the top work from the nearest pile. It was an animal's hide pulled taut across a wooden backboard, bound by decomposed leather braids. She tilted it sideways, letting a layer of dust fall away. She refrained from blowing off the rest, lest she expose the ancient skin to the moisture of her breath. Kneeling, she set the board on the floor and held the lantern near, observing the faint writing scrawled upon the skin. The words were written not in ink, but in blood, blackened and faded by time. Some of the blood had become nearly invisible. Though not easy to read, there was no mistaking the author. "Alikai," she whispered. "It's you."

To Valory's eye, there was no doubt. Before her was the same language invented by Alikai, written in the same style. Though the characters had been adapted from grooved impressions to flat text, from specialized styli to quill dipped in animal blood, they carried an identical paleographic signature. The writing was more evolved than that on the tablets, with greater complexity, refinement of letterforms, and density of spacing, but this was definitely Alikai's work. The technicals were evidence enough of that, but the technicals paled in comparison to her *experience* of examining his work. Greens and yellows dancing in the rain. The sizzling juices of wild game cooking over a fire. A sunflare with a rainbow halo. These sensations were seen not with her eyes, nor smelled with her nose. Rather, they frolicked in her essence. For a moment, she went blank and just let herself feel this unique, beautiful language.

But why had Alikai changed mediums from clay to hide? Maybe because he had migrated to a region where clay was difficult to source. Or perhaps he'd simply decided to try something new, something easier. Whatever the case, this relic lent legitimacy to her immortality hypothesis. Human life expectancy in 8000 BCE was around thirty-five years. Valory had just walked by thousands of Alikai's clay tablets. That was a lot for one man to create, even if he'd started at a young age. If all those tablets had indeed been created by him, his implied lifespan would be well beyond thirty-five. She couldn't let excitement cloud her study, though. There was still much to examine, and Valory had to make every effort to debunk her own hunch, lest she face the scorn of academia.

A smile touched her lips as she gazed upon the language isolate. The isolate that she alone deciphered, despite Mancini's year-long head start. She was the only person on Earth who could read it. It was hers. Hers and Alikai's. She had already thought of a name for the language—Immortalese. That wouldn't fly in academia, of course, but it was harmless for current purposes. Pleased with her own whimsy, she pulled a magnifying glass from her coat pocket, then she leaned into the soft lantern light and examined the portions of text that were still legible. After reading it, she pulled down another skin, and another, and another, absorbing them all. As suspected, the writing was a more linguistically complex continuation of Alikai's somber journal to himself. Descriptions of his travels, people he'd met, and events he'd experienced. All penned with an undertone of existential dread, a continuous questioning of the meaning and value of his endless life. Most of the content might be considered boring and depressing were its author anything but an eternal human being. The fifth skin she read, however, was eye-popping.

Three nights ago, the sky was split asunder, and the ground trembled. I came from my bed in haste, running down the hillside to see. From the ridge, I looked upon the camp, my sight aided by a luminous moon. There I beheld a river of mud crashing down from the mountains, frothing with trees and boulders and debris, bringing fast destruction to my clansmen below. From my lofty point I watched the carnage. He that was called Vallju was crushed with his wife and their goats. Though their mouths were wide with terror, I could not hear their wails over the roaring earth. Then Uhkku vanished, and Iidda, and their daughter Isa, all swallowed by that storm of soil. Scarcely had I drawn another breath before the entire camp was overwhelmed.

I felt little grief in watching my clansmen perish, and I suffer no shame to say it. They, as all people, are but faceless hordes, living and dying in droves between the blinks of my eternal eyes. Instead, I stood in jealousy of their swift deaths. For my brothers had just achieved a bliss that I will never know. Then a thought befell me. Never in my ill-fated centuries upon this world had I been slain by such a thing as this river of earth. As you know well, you who are me, we have died in all the ways a mind can fathom. We have leaped from the highest lofts, we have thrown ourselves into lakes of fire, we have had our head lopped off, we have tasted every death in the lands and seas, and always have we arisen. But before us now was a new and untried scheme that might finally appease fate and deliver us unto oblivion.

Thus did I hasten down the hill and hurl myself into that wild torrent of mud and rocks and trees. The earth filled my throat, the rocks cracked my bones, my flesh was pierced a thousand times, and I was slain.

Yet then I woke, unscathed. The landslide roared still but had missed the camp, rumbling instead through the meadow adjacent. Vallju breathed still, and Uhkku, and lidda, and Isa. Their yurts stood untouched, their bodies unswallowed. None of them knew that I had just seen the entire clan devoured by the earth.

Yes, there stood we, you and I, hoodwinked yet again by happenings that only we have witnessed, whilst others remain in blessed ignorance.

Two days later was I beset by a greater mystery. I came to realize that a child known as Sahkar, who had been among this clan since his birth, no longer existed. His parents were there still, and his sisters, living and breathing all, but of Sahkar, none could remember. None, save me. I beseeched his mother to remember that she had birthed Sahkar some twelve seasons gone, yet she would not hear it. She and the elders only looked upon me with confusion.

This is a rare thing, as you know. The complete disappearance of a soul who once walked and breathed and laughed, who shared with us songs and feasts. Vanished, with not even a name to remember. The why and how of these vanishings remain unknown. No answers have been revealed, no explanations have descended from the heavens nor risen from the seas. There walks no man upon the earth who has experienced this mystery save you and me. For whatever reason, we stand as the solitary butt of this cosmic jest.

And so, remember this child called Sahkar. We shall record his name and the names of others like him who have gone from living to never-weres. If the world shall not remember him, and if cruel time shall not count his days, then shall we. Perhaps one day, in some form, these vanished souls shall give us some understanding of this accursed immortality.

Valory sat back, feeling the texture of the language in her mind, trying to evaluate what she'd just experienced. There was so much to unpack here. While reading, she'd been trying to identify this clan and its placement in history. There wasn't much to go on, but the names mentioned—Vallju, Uhkku, Sahkar, et al—were suggestive of the Komsa, a pre-Viking hunter-gatherer tribe that inhabited ancient Scandinavia. The Komsa did not leave behind a written language, but they still had descendants living today whose naming conventions bore resemblance to those in the text. Without more data, however, Valory could only speculate.

The other elements of the story were the most outrageous she'd read yet. The entire village annihilated by a landslide, but then it wasn't? A child vanishing from existence as if he'd never been born? Valory had no idea what to make of these statements, other than that they sounded even nuttier than the notion of immortality. Alikai believed his tale was true—she knew that—but it was too fantastical to give him the benefit of the doubt.

Most disturbing were Alikai's casual admissions of repeated suicides. In his words, he'd leaped to his death from the highest lofts. He'd dove into lakes of fire (magma?). He'd eagerly flung himself into a landslide. He even wrote of decapitating himself. He wrote as if these suicides were just a normal part of his life. Such unimaginable despair. Was that the price of immortality? To become so twisted by the eons, so incomprehensibly alone, that you committed heinous acts of suicide in futile attempts to escape?

Part of her hoped this was indeed just an elaborate hoax. Perpetrated, perhaps, by an endless stream of masters and apprentices whose epoch-spanning goal was to create a vast library of bullshit to fool the world by forever fabricating a product called Alikai. But who would do such a thing, and for what purpose? To hide it all at the top of a mountain in hopes that some linguist would one day cry on her knees as she read it? In a way, the hoax theory was more absurd than the possibility of an immortal man.

Valory shook off the gloom of Alikai's story. Now was not the time to indulge that sorrow. To solidify her hypothesis, she needed to press on. She took the skin to the center table and typed out the translation. Then she affixed it with a catalog tag and returned it to the shelf.

Blowing warmth into her hands, she looked down the aisle. The darkness beyond her lantern's glow was like a black hole. Deep, impenetrable, final. As she pushed into it, lantern held high, the library seemed to allow grudging illumination. The sounds of her footsteps seemed intrusive, the swishing of her pants an irritant. Valory imagined spectral faces leering at her from the gloom, annoyed by her warm lungs and frosty breaths. She quickened her pace.

Past many aisles she walked, noting the various mediums stored upon the shelves as she pushed forward through the millennia. She spotted thin sheets of tree bark and stone tablets on the later-era shelves along with more clay and animal hides. In one section rested the decomposed remains of organic material such as palm fronds and other flora. Alikai had likely used these as temporary agents before transferring his notes to hardier mediums. The question looming large in Valory's mind was, *How were all these works transported to this castle?* Alikai had obviously traveled over vast regions while writing his diary, but there's no way he could have toted all these relics around with him. How did they wind up here centuries later? Who brought them, and who stored them in chronological order?

Toward the east side of the library, she began seeing the first papyrus scrolls stacked on the shelves. Papyrus, from which evolved the modern word paper, was a thick, gray-yellowy sheet made from the papyrus plant, a reed native to the swampy deltas of the Nile River. It was produced exclusively in ancient Egypt for hundreds of years until it was adopted by scribes in the Mediterranean and beyond. That meant Valory had advanced to the era of the written word. By the time Alikai had penned these scrolls, cultures across the world had developed written language. Alikai had front-run those cultures by centuries all by himself, but the mortals had eventually caught up. Seemed like a fine place to connect the next dot.

Valory set her lantern down and removed the top four scrolls from their pile. These she carried to the center table, taking care in untying their leather cords and unrolling them, one by one, placing felt-bottomed weights on their edges to hold them flat. Passing the lantern over them, she recognized the handwriting as Alikai's, but the language was not Immortalese. It was Classical Latin, the language of ancient Romans. Meaning Alikai had most likely written these from somewhere within the Roman Empire, and he had learned to write in the region's prevailing tongue. Not only that, but his style here matched the Latin she had translated from the tome in her bedchamber. This hinted at an exciting confirmation. That Alikai was a language chameleon. A profound hyperpolyglot like herself.

A glance at the content of the scrolls revealed what Valory had now come to expect—more diary entries. Like all forms of Latin—Old Latin, Vulgar Latin, Medieval Latin, etc—Classical was like a vibrant garden in her mind, blooming with the colors of oleander, violets, irises, and others. The texture was like fertile soil running through her fingers, with an aroma to match. As she perused the scrolls, one stood out in that the handwriting was different from the others. Still Alikai's but lacking the stately epigraphic script of the other three. His handwriting on this scroll was sloppier. Loaded with misspellings. Like he'd been impaired when he wrote it. As Valory sat down and began to read the faded ink, she gasped with a realization—Alikai had been drunk!

Ho, brother of ages to come! Hail to you, whose visage I loathe to see! Yours is a face most tiresome and ugly which never leaves my mirror, nor changes, nor stays dead when slain. Oh, how I long to shit upon that face, yet I cannot raise my ass to its height, nor force it down to my ass. Even if it could be done, what good shall it be? Shit piled upon shit is but a great deal of shit! So let me drink you away then. Yea, only sweet wine makes your face tolerable, this I swear by all the gods!

Hark now I say! Hear of this event which has just transpired, and for which I was roughly treated by smelly monkeys with beards. There I stood in the popina with a gaggle of slaves and whores and outlanders, casting my coin about, buying wine for the wretches, and trying by all the gods to drown myself in it. Then one fine wretch asked of me, Do you not wish to be sober for the parade, Alaksandus? And said I, What parade? And said he, The pope himself shall be in procession on the Sacred Street this day! Then this wretch asked how I had not heard of this, for it was common knowledge in the city. To which I answered that I find greater meaning in my piss than in the doings of popes, and a more pleasant smell.

So gave these dirt lickers hearty laughter, and they challenged me to make proof of my boast. This of course was no challenge at all. For as you know, you who are the future and uglier me, there stands no challenge upon this earth for one who is forever dead and alive at once.

And so! We clutched as many ewers of wine as could be carried, and we stumbled toward this so-called Sacred Street, which is only dirt and stone like any other. Spirited crowds were gathered there, and colorful banners were aflutter, excitement hot in the air. At length, the procession appeared, and cheers filled the street. Fathers held their babes aloft to harvest blessings from this man in silly garb called Pope Innocent. He sat on a palanquin carried upon the shoulders of men, surrounded by priests and guards and horsemen. He waved from his cushioned seat and signed the cross unto his adoring masses.

Here now did I amble into the road before the parade where flowers rained into the pope's path. There I let my breeches drop unto the stone, and I made a fine yellow soup for all to behold. And it streamed well from my dangly, and seemed never to stop, for I had saved it all for this moment.

Oh, what fine sport transpired! The procession halted, and all eyes fell to me and my snake, which spilled yellow venom. Thereby was I cursed and spat upon as I laughed at a thousand horrified faces. Here was I accosted by the angry soldier monkeys. As they bore me away, I shouted my love toward the Pope. Then I saw his lips hurl an insult at me. *Mentula caput!* said he.

Valory gasped, covering her mouth. *Mentula caput* was Latin for dickhead.

Thereafter was I to be taken and soundly beaten, but I made sport of the bearded monkeys, for I was in rare high spirits, feeling fine and devilish. Even well into my cup did I presage their every move, their every thought, and thus I slipped from their grasp again and again, clouting their heads whilst they pawed at the air where I'd stood a blink ago. Oh, how I danced as I felled them like fools! When they could sup no more from the plate of humility, I took my leave, whilst upon the

ground they lay panting and befuddled. Ha! Monkeys! Baboons! Ass
lickers!

Yea, all of this has transpired just one hour ago, and now I give this
story to you, you stubborn and undying hag-man. Best you appreciate
it. For now, a headache bears down upon me, promising punishment
which no soldier can equal.

Valory reabsorbed the text, ensuring her Latin was true. The name
Alaksandus had thrown her momentarily, but this was just Alikai's *nom du
jour*, a name he'd taken to mesh with Roman society. As his very first clay
tablet had specified, *Men have known me by many names*. Satisfied that this
was Alikai's work, she sat back and processed the story. Pope Innocent?! If
memory served, he was pope sometime in the fifth century CE. Unless of
course Alikai—Alaksandus, rather—was speaking of a later Pope Innocent.
Several popes had taken that title throughout history. Whatever the case, the
story was remarkable. A firsthand account of a papal procession in the
ancient Roman Empire was huge, especially as recounted by an immortal
who clearly bore no reverence for the Holy Father.

Also, the drunken frat boy shenanigans showed that Alikai still
possessed the earmark of humanity. His previous writings had shown him to
be a devastated soul—lonely, depressed, and ostracized. This one showed he
could still have fun, even if that fun was a bit mean-spirited. Truth be told,
Valory found guilty pleasure in Alikai's mischiefs. His good mood made her
happy.

The last part of the scroll was intriguing as well when he continually
slipped from the grasp of the soldiers. Here he implied he possessed some
sort of precognition, claiming to know their every move, their every thought,
even before they did. As such, he was able to avoid punishment, leaving
them humiliated. Under normal circumstances, Valory would dismiss such
a claim as pure nonsense, a fictional element to his tale conjured by his wine-
addled brain, but not now. That tome sitting in her bedchamber contained
the same fantastical claim. This scroll, written centuries before that tome,
strengthened the claim. To wit, Alikai had developed a certain prescience
from his eons of existence. Like he could see into the future. Hard to wrap
one's head around that.

The other three scrolls, though containing interesting historical
references, were drab by comparison. Those, she rolled up and returned to
the shelf. The pope scroll, however, she formally translated and saved it to
the USB drive with her other work. *Just wait until Rafael sees this.*

A glance at her watch made her groan. It was four in the morning. Where
had all that time gone? Her goal, though having progressed, still was not
complete. If she could just get to the second level and continue for another
few hours, she might be able to strengthen her hypothesis to the point of

132

certainty. She considered soldiering on, but seeing the clock yanked the remaining energy right out of her. She needed sleep. A bath. Food.

On the way back to her chamber, she pondered everything she'd translated. Landslides. Changing realities. Drunken hijinks. A cursing pope. The unique personality of an immortal hyperpolyglot slowly taking form over centuries worth of narratives. She thought of the tome in her bedchamber and the shocking information she'd uncovered there. Thought about the ways all these writings tied together over thousands of years. The discoveries they yielded were so bizarre, and yet she was slipping into them like fresh-out-of-the-dryer pajamas.

As she walked through the Great Hall to the stairwell, she stopped, looking at the thrones. They were but moon-softened silhouettes spearing the pre-dawn miasma. Valory had deciphered many spectacular things in the tome, none of which she'd been able to share with Rafael yet. Now, one of those things sprang to the forefront of her mind, urging her to perform one last act before bed. Adjusting her bag on her shoulder, she diverted herself to the throne, eyes glued to the queen. Starlight glinting off the jewels in her crown, robes flowing to the foot of the throne, the queen was alluring in the darkness. Valory held the lantern toward her, laying silky light upon her alabaster skin. She stared at her. Wondered what her voice sounded like. Wondered how she walked, how she moved. Above all, how she'd captured the heart of an immortal. Because that's exactly what she'd done. That was one of the many revelations Valory had gleaned from the tome in her chamber. This marble queen was Alikai's lover.

"Your Majesty," whispered Valory, setting her bag on the floor. She tried a little curtsey, adding an awkward head bow at the end. She felt a bit silly speaking to a statue in the dark, but that silliness was tinged with accomplishment. Right now, no one in the world knew more about the queen than her. That would change when she shared her report, but at this moment, Valory was the only person who knew her name. "I think a more formal introduction is in order now that I know something about you. Uh, if it pleases you, my name is Doctor Valory Grace. Well met, and glory to you, Queen Seraphina."

KAFLI 19

AGENTE PRICIPALE SAVELLI MARCHED into the deepest level of the library, caring little for the significance of its contents nor the magical light in which it basked. Cap-toed Oxfords echoing off the stone, he strode past the shelves, looking between the aisles for Dario Bertinelli. He'd grown annoyed by the engineer's nonchalant work ethic. The man was supposed to have delivered his written report yesterday, but surprise surprise, he hadn't. Now Savelli had to track him down and extract his input before the helicopter arrived.

He found Bertinelli sandwiched in an aisle in the southeastern quadrant, inching forward while peering at the readout on his ground-penetrating radar. Like he was studiously mowing the library floor. "*Signore Bertinelli,*" barked Savelli, startling the portly engineer. "*Hai confermato che c'è una livello nascosta o no?*" The question was abrupt and pointed, leaving no room for Bertinelli's windiness—Had he confirmed that there was a hidden level beneath this one or not?

"Ah," said Bertinelli, hand over his heart, "*Agente Savelli, mi hai spaventato.*" He'd scared him.

"*Il livello? Si o no?*"

Seeing that Savelli was in no mood for a chat, Bertinelli pointed at the tablet mounted on the top of the radar. The tablet displayed the variance data that had been mapped up to that point. To Savelli, it only looked like a mess of zigzagged lines. Continuing in Italian, Bertinelli explained the readout. "See these lines going across here? They indicate the denseness of the substrate below. As you can see, the large gaps of white in the pattern show us that there is quite a bit of open space there, deep down. Probably a large chamber. The denser forms here and here are other solid masses."

"What are the masses?"

Bertinelli shrugged. "That is not what this tool tells us. It only tells us something is there. These patterns here are amorphous and could be anything. But these others? Their angular nature tells us they are manmade objects. Could be more shelves, could be furniture. Maybe something else entirely."

"Well, how do we get down there? Have you found the access yet?"

"Not yet. There is no access point on this level." Bertinelli's missing tooth caused him to whistle when he spoke, like there was a sleepy bird in his mouth. Sometimes the whistling made it difficult to take him seriously. "Whoever built this place didn't want anyone down there, it seems."

Savelli pulled at his tie. "There must be a way. They wouldn't just carve out a hidden level for no reason."

"Possibly. If there is an access point, it might lay somewhere else on the mountainside. Beyond the castle perimeter, perhaps. Once I finish mapping the rest of this level, I can send up the drone to survey the surrounding slope for the most likely locations. Maybe there is a hidden hatch or gate or something."

"Why can't we just blow a small hole into the floor here?"

Bertinelli looked at Savelli as if he'd just ripped up the Italian Constitution right in his face. "Are you crazy? We cannot do such a thing."

"Why not?"

"Why not? *Christo!* Why not just bomb the Pantheon?! *Agente* Savelli, you are standing in a true wonder of the world. Do you really want to compromise its structural integrity with explosives?"

"Then you tell me, what can we do?"

Bertinelli exhaled as if he'd just avoided falling off a cliff. "At most, we could drill a small hole into the stone and drop a borescope camera down there. But even that wouldn't tell us much. The space down there is too vast to obtain detailed imagery. It is best if we *patiently* look for an access point."

"Fine," huffed Savelli. "I'm flying to headquarters shortly. I'll be gone for a few days, so notify *Agente* Moreno if you find something on the slopes. He will arrange a detachment to accompany you for a physical inspection. And hey," he said, poking at Bertinelli's chest, "I want your report on time from now on. *Capisci?*"

Savelli stormed away, not waiting for a response. Bertinelli flung a stubby middle finger at his coattails.

On the top level of the library, Mancini and his nephew were working at the table, if it could be called work. In Savelli's opinion, Rollo's presence was far from essential. Certainly not important enough to merit a top-secret security clearance. His only contributions seemed to be taking pretty pictures of books and calming his crazy uncle, who had no clue what he was doing. With the decline of his mental faculties over the last year, Mancini's reports had become increasingly nonsensical, lacking actionable data. Whenever Savelli broached the subject with him, the old man went ballistic. Doctor Moretti only made the issue worse. He knew damn well Mancini's mind was cooked, but he remained loyal to his old friend. Still placed his trust in him, still insisted that he was one of the world's best. It was obvious bullshit— the man kept forgetting his wife was dead for Christ's sake—but Moretti had refused to dismiss him. Instead, he'd brought in Doctor Grace to take the reins.

Savelli stalked past Mancini and Rollo with only a cold glare of acknowledgment. At least they'd submitted their reports yesterday on time, useless as those reports were. Same for the art connoisseur, Janelle LaFleur. She was eager to share her findings, but those findings, though competent, had not contributed much to the prime directive. In fact, since The Incident, there had been only minimal progress toward finding the one vital piece of information the brass coveted more than anything else.

Savelli found himself giving half-hearted thanks for the newest addition, Doctor Grace. While he still strongly opposed her appointment due to the additional security risk, her work had proven to be an unexpected boon for the *Agenzia*. Not only had she consistently delivered her findings on time, but she'd stunned the brass by punching out the precise kind of information they'd been hoping to see. This had been unexpected. Considering the sheer number of works in the library and the glacial pace of discovery up to that point, no one had anticipated the immediate value of Grace's presence. A day ago, she'd submitted her translation of a tome that Rollo had been photographing. Submitted was, perhaps, the wrong term. Savelli had gone by her chamber to get her report, but he'd had to rouse her from a deep sleep. She'd been burning the candle at both ends and was too zombified to explain her findings. Instead, she'd gotten out of bed, fetched the USB drive from her bag, and mumbled something about it being incredible before crawling back under the comforter. After reading the report, Moretti had nearly soiled himself with shock. Savelli, however, didn't understand what was so revelatory about the translations. He could see there was some potentially useful information there, but Moretti was acting like the world had just flipped. At the appointed time, Savelli phoned the General Director, Vincenzo Teruzzi, to read him a handful of excerpts. Next thing he knew, he'd been commanded to return to headquarters with the totality of the experts' reports, especially Doctor Grace's. Her name was heating up the offices of the director, and they wanted to scrutinize her findings. Not only that, but Savelli was to bring Moretti with him for perspective analysis.

Savelli was left puzzled by this order. What was contained in Grace's translations that demanded an immediate face-to-face with the director and his team? Much of her work was ancient and dusty, having nothing to do with modern intelligence affairs. The only aspect of her research that Savelli considered relevant was that it reinforced what everyone already suspected—there exists an immortal human being. Ergo, there exists the possibility of Italy discovering the key to biological immortality. A mind-blowing concept, to be sure, but nothing new. The events of The Incident, among other things, had already slapped their collective faces with those possibilities. And some people (like himself) still suspected that this entire thing was just one giant scam and that everyone involved was allowing themselves to be suckered by the desire to live forever. He found it strange to be in the minority on that belief.

To understand what he was missing, Savelli had swallowed his pride and asked Doctor Moretti about the matter, trying his best not to sound thickheaded. Thankfully, Moretti had been too excited about the material to flaunt any kind of intellectual superiority. Savelli found him in his bedchamber, re-reading Grace's work with an awed half-smile. Then, after Moretti sat him down and walked him through the translation, he got it. He understood. Grace had uncovered some important data which might hastily advance the success of this project. First, she'd confirmed that the author of all these works was likely the owner of this castle and that this owner, while gallivanting through Europe, had likely left a trail of documentation: old immigration reports, town ledger entries, port authority records, etc. These might be discovered and researched by the Ministry and could lead to proof of provenance. Second, Grace had uncovered an eye-popping connection to one globally famous historical figure which, if publicized, could earn global accolades for Italy. It was the third revelation, however, that had stoked Teruzzi's interest. Savelli was still irked for not deducing it himself. He should have seen it. Even though he couldn't quite swallow this whole immortal nonsense, he still should have understood that this piece of the puzzle might constitute the most actionable evidence to date. *Mamma mia*, was it a big one.

***

A small group had gathered in the Great Hall, milling among the sculpted courtesans and marble columns. There was some kind of buzz in the air. Something going on. Janelle watched from afar, having been sitting at one of the portable tables when everyone began trickling into the hall. She'd been enjoying the latest issue of *Cahiers d'art*, a French artistic and literary journal that had arrived a few days prior, but the steady influx of occupants had split her attention. The two *Sicurezza* agents were present, Marco Savelli and Gianni Moreno. A suitcase and a briefcase rested at Savelli's feet. Talking with the agents were *Capitano* Ricci and *Tenete* Esposito as well as a third soldier who Janelle didn't know. Their conversation was brisk and businesslike. Nearby were Moretti, Mancini, and Rollo. Moretti held a suitcase. The trio was standing nearer the thrones than the others, and they seemed excited about something regarding the queen. Well, except for Mancini, who was scowling. Janelle's Italian wasn't great, and many muddled voices reverberated in the hall, so she couldn't make out what anyone was saying. A few other people loitered as well, but she didn't

137

know who they were. All men. More Ministry contractors, probably, but Janelle had never been introduced and had only seen them once or twice.

Aside from Dario Bertinelli, the only person missing was Doctor Grace who'd been zonked out all day. Had Valory been among the group, Janelle might have wandered over to find out what was going on. Without her, however, she felt far from bold. Not only was Valory the only other female at the castle, but she was also the only one who spoke fluent French. Moretti tried, but his French was thick and uncouth. He usually just chose to speak to Janelle in English, and his accent there didn't jive with her fluency. Professor Mancini knew French, but the old man made no effort to speak with her. No one did. In fact, she often sensed that her work here was not as important as anyone else's. Maybe it was just her own shyness, but she sometimes felt like an afterthought at the castle. Like no one expected much of her, nor cared about her studies here. That's why she wished for a friendship with Valory. The two of them seemed to be cut from the same cloth. Though they'd only really spoken once thanks to the no collaboration rule, their paths had crossed many times: in the corridors, in the Great Hall, in the dining room, in the courtyard. Every time they saw each other, they exchanged a wordless yearning, a look of promise. Something that said *We must talk soon, despite this stupid rule.* At least that's what Janelle hoped. Being an art-loving loner in a castle full of extraordinary art was getting to be a bit depressing. She'd discovered so many exciting things but had no one to share them with.

The chop-chop-chop of an approaching helicopter filtered into the Great Hall. The group made rapid farewells and began to disband. The agents, the soldiers, and Moretti made a hasty exit through the vestibule. On his way out, Moretti glanced over and saw Janelle at the table. He hesitated as if he might come over and share a quick word, but *Agente* Savelli hurried him along. Moments later, the thrum of the helicopter faded away.

Janelle was again alone in the hall, sitting in silence.

ГЛАВА 20

SENATOR HARRISON KIRK EXITED his black Cadillac, stepping into a throng of dignitaries and assorted suits. The Republican presidential candidate smiled, nodded, and shook scores of outstretched hands as he made his way to the towering double doors of the mansion. This fundraiser was a biggie for his campaign. All the ultra-rich conservatives in California were attending, eager to support Kirk in a bid to neutralize the heavy-handed Democrats running the state and the country. For Kirk, this fundraiser on exclusive Lido Isle in Newport Beach was like a supercharged ATM.

From thirty yards away, Cervantes watched the senator. Noted his thick white eyebrows, his rigid posture, his camera-ready smile, and his Propecia commercial looks. Same as most pretentious politicians. But Kirk was different. According to the Salvador, if all went well, Kirk would be the next President of the United States of America.

How would it feel? Cervantes had never slain a mark as high as United States President. He wondered if the rush would be any more intense. He'd offed plenty of well-known people, but they always felt the same. Just another exhilarating flavor of wonderful. The U.S. President, however, was the most powerful person in the world. Even if he never did anything remarkable during his tenure, Kirk's legacy would endure for the simple fact he was President. And if a bullet split his skull, he'd achieve even greater renown, because then he'd be remembered on the same level as Lincoln and Kennedy. That enticed Cervantes. You can't say the names Lincoln and Kennedy without saying Booth and Oswald. President and assassin entangled together for all time.

Kirk and Cervantes. Had a nice ring to it.

Breathing long and deep, Cervantes tugged on his vest and scratched his new stubble, reminding himself why he was here wearing this ridiculous valet outfit. Thomas Rockwell. He was the target tonight. Rockwell, the power behind the curtain, the man pulling Kirk's strings. Rockwell had the dirt on Kirk, big time. Cervantes had no idea what that dirt was, but he knew it was so filthy that the senator had no choice but to be Rockwell's human silly putty. Armed with that secret, Rockwell had spent the last couple of years grooming Kirk, holding the dirty secret over his head, shaping him into a stooge that would negotiate any political obstructions to Rockwell's business interests.

But tonight, Rockwell's life belonged to Cervantes.

A Mercedes pulled into the drive. "You got this one?" asked a young valet named Diego as he scurried to the next car. Cervantes acted like a good servant, opening the car door and nodding to the VIP who emerged. The man disregarded Cervantes as he buttoned his blazer and looked toward the mansion, eager to ingratiate himself with Kirk via his giant pocketbook. Cervantes parked the car and hurried back for the next one.

It had been easy to assume the valet job. He'd done it a couple of times in the past. Find out the name of the valet service being employed, appropriate one of their uniforms, show up to the gig, and slip into the rotation. He was seldom questioned. When he was, he always had answers prepared and names to drop. Easy. A man in uniform could get away with murder, literally. Cervantes had posed as a cop on two occasions. Site security on others. A construction worker once. People just accepted the uniform at face value. For this job, he'd begun growing a beard to complement his disguise, but he was already wishing he hadn't. The hair was rough and itchy. He couldn't wait to shave.

Twenty minutes passed before the target's vehicle pulled into the drive—Rockwell's luxury tour bus. A silvery behemoth, the bus was Rockwell's limo fortress, his preferred method of intercity travel. Bigger and flashier than anyone else's ride, it was a way for Rockwell to suck all the attention away from his rivals. He often invited common people to come aboard and have a look around. His social media feed was full of pictures of regular schlubs enjoying themselves in his bus, sipping champagne and delighting in conversation with the man himself. For Rockwell, that kind of public goodwill was golden.

The bus hissed to a stop. The door opened and Rockwell emerged alone, as expected. Cervantes watched from afar, risking only the occasional glance. Staring down a target was a good way to arouse suspicion, especially when that target was Rockwell. The man was *aware*. That was his natural state. He observed. Clocked his surroundings. Looked everyone in the eyes. Traits he had cultivated in the military and the cutthroat world of business. You couldn't sneak up on him, mentally or bodily. With that kind of surefire awareness, Rockwell could pose a challenge for Cervantes. He'd have to be at the top of his game tonight. No Zach Miller-type slip-ups.

Rockwell strode toward the mansion. Unlike Kirk, he didn't stop to chat and shake hands with the other dignitaries. While he welcomed their overtures with a sparkling smile, he made them walk with him as if he were on a mission and they were his subordinates playing catch-up.

The gaggle of suits disappeared into the mansion, and Cervantes returned his attention to the bus. That was where this was going to happen.

He couldn't do Rockwell inside the mansion. It had to be on the bus when he was alone. With a hydraulic groan, the bus lurched forward and wound its way through the palm treed drive to the east side of the property, where it would be parked until Rockwell departed several hours later. When Rockwell boarded, Cervantes would be inside waiting.

He spent another half hour doing his 'job' until the last of the guests had arrived and their cars had been valeted. Then, when the dusk melted to black, he made his move. Taking a glass tumbler he'd set aside earlier, he jogged toward the eastern lot as if he were fetching a car. One of the local police officers patrolling the grounds noticed and promptly dismissed him, returning to his smartphone.

Rockwell's driver was a sixty-something-year-old man named Cornelius. Cervantes knew that Cornelius usually lounged in the bus watching TV while he waited on Rockwell. There was never a need for him to alight. TV, bathroom, internet, everything he needed was right there. But Cervantes had to force the old man to exit the bus for a few minutes so he could slip in undetected. Anticipating this, he'd come prepared. Slinking up to the rear where there were no windows, Cervantes removed his shoes and socks. Then he scaled the back panel, hoisting himself on the embossed runners with fingertips and tiptoes. On the roof, he peered into the skylight, confirming that Cornelius was within. The old man was spread out on a black leather couch watching ESPN and talking on his phone, surrounded by oak cabinetry with silver finishes. He'd taken off his blazer and loosened his tie. Nice and relaxed.

Dropping back to the shadows, Cervantes placed his valet vest over the tumbler, then grabbed a nearby rock. As quietly as possible, he smashed the tumbler into pieces. Then he began tapping the shards into the outer back wheel of the bus with the rock. Gently, he embedded the shards into the rubber. When he was satisfied that the bus looked as though it had driven over a pile of broken glass, he took the largest remaining shard and worked it deeper into the tire, driving it in until air began seeping out. Then he tossed the rock, picked up his vest, and climbed back up to the roof.

It took a while for Cornelius to notice the air pressure notification from the bus's computer. Cervantes watched him get off the couch, heard him say, "Hang on a minute, Reggie, I gotta check on something." He exited the bus, leaving the door ajar. Checked the driver's side tires first, then circled to the passenger side. "Aw, now what the hell is this? Son of a bitch. Yeah, Reggie, I gotta let you go, partner. Got me a flat. I'll holler at you later."

Cervantes lay on the roof while Cornelius prepped the spare. He listened to the old man curse as he struggled to withdraw it from one of the storage bins. Some tools clanked down. Something dropped onto the old-timer's foot. More curses. The tire, the tools, and the bus were all one big son of a bitch if Cornelius was to be believed. After setting a block under the adjacent tire, he got into the cab and drove the bus forward onto the block, lifting the damaged tire off the ground. When he began removing the lug nuts, Cervantes belly crawled toward the door, then slithered from the roof directly into the bus like a snake into a tree hollow.

The inside of the tour bus was like a nightclub for dataphiles. Mood lights and media screens, liquor bottles and stock tickers, black leather and pattern analysis charts. Rockwell liked to stay plugged in, in style. Cervantes skulked along the narrow aisle to the back of the bus, into what might be called the master bedroom. On one side, there was an array of elegant cabinetry with recessed lights. A trio of monitors above the dresser was tuned to the major news networks. On the other side was a leather loveseat that could fold out into a bed. Over that hung a mini-U.S. Marine Corps flag with the words *Semper Fi* inscribed in gold. Cervantes inspected the room, ensuring that nothing in it would hamper his plan. There wasn't much space to operate—just a few feet of clearance between the couch and the cabinetry—but he could work with it. He slid the closet door open, revealing several fine suits on a rack. He tossed his vest into the closet along with his shoes. When he slid the door closed, he left it open by half an inch. No doubt Mr. Hyperaware Thomas Rockwell was going to notice that half-inch gap when he returned. Cervantes was counting on it.

"Son of a bitch!" yelled Cornelius from outside. Then another man's voice drifted in, joining Cornelius. He couldn't quite make out what the two were saying, but he guessed someone had come over to help. One of the cops, maybe. Cervantes listened, hoping the newcomer was not Rockwell returned early for some reason. That would kill this plan immediately. Cervantes had not yet had time to prepare himself—mentally—an extra step that he wouldn't need if the mark was anyone other than Rockwell.

Satisfied that the newcomer posed no threat, Cervantes chose his hiding spot. Just outside the entry to the bedroom was a bathroom, and beside that was a narrow closet containing towels and other toiletries. Below the bottom shelf was a space just big enough for him to squat in. While Rockwell was suspiciously examining the gap in his bedroom closet door, Cervantes could emerge from this hiding spot and sneak up on him, sinking a garrote wire into his neck. The garrote wire was the optimal weapon here. Not only because it was silent and easy to sneak past security, but also due to the tight quarters. Between the bed and the dresser, there was little space for the victim to employ tactical evasive maneuvers. It would be over in moments. Nice and quiet. Cervantes ensured the closet door made no sound when he opened it. No squeaky hinges. He'd brought a small tube of lubricant with him just in case, but it wasn't needed.

He scratched his neck where the beard was itching—why had he even bothered with such a flimsy 'disguise?'—then he pulled the garrote wire from beneath his shirt collar. He'd fashioned it to look like a necklace, complete with a holy cross pendant. Security hadn't given it a second look. Removing it from his neck, he ripped off the pendant and pocketed it. Then he gripped the tiny handles in his palms and yanked on them, feeling the deadly tautness of the thin carbon fiber cable. Satisfied, he prepped his body, performing an assortment of strength and flexibility poses on the marble floor, noting the novel experience of that floor being slanted from the tire jack. When he heard Cornelius finishing up the job, he squeezed down into the lower cubby of the bathroom closet and closed the door. Time to begin his mental preparations.

***

"One does not simply fuck with Thomas Rockwell."

A business rival had actually said that tonight. Out loud, into the mic for all to hear. It was a meme. A fucking meme floating around the internet with Rockwell's name in it. The rival had known exactly what he was doing by repeating it in front of the entire assembly. Daniel Kauffman, fourth-generation oil baron, eighty-seven-year-old billionaire and friend of Senator Kirk, still playing the game as if he would live forever. Kauffman had flicked that meme into the crowd with a smirk on his sagging face, garnering a round of chuckles. He'd delivered it as if he were innocently acknowledging Rockwell's ballooning profile. The hidden message, of course, was that Rockwell was secretly positioning himself as their future leader, so they'd better start falling in line right now. This to a room of high-powered elites who did not take kindly to such overtures. Every person at that fundraiser tonight was a shark. Not just sharks, but goddamn megalodons, brimming with razor-sharp teeth and global policy-swaying power. People like them fumed against the type of strongarm tactics to which Kauffman alluded.

The worst thing about it was that Kauffman was right. That is the sentiment Rockwell wanted to foster—*Do not fuck with Thomas Rockwell*—but not yet. There were still years of groundwork to lay before he became nakedly aggressive. But the cat was out of the bag. Among the youth of America, the notion that Rockwell was undefeatable had manifested into that meme, buoyed by his rapid successes in accomplishing the impossible. He wasn't even familiar with the origin of the meme. His social media lead had had to explain that it came from a film called *Lord of the Rings*. The original line was "One does not simply walk into Mordor," spoken by actor Sean Bean. That line had been appropriated into many whimsical forms: One does not simply eat one Pringle, One does not simply watch Netflix for five minutes, One does not simply talk to their dog in a normal voice. And now One does not simply fuck with Thomas Rockwell. If even the skeletal remains known as Kauffman were picking up on that, then things had been moving too fast. Were the situation left unchecked, there'd be a bullet coming Rockwell's way. It was time to get in front of this.

The bus pulled up as Rockwell strode down the walkway, and Cornelius emerged. "Welcome back, sir," he said. "Your scotch is on the sofa table."

"Why's your shirt dirty, Cornie?"

"Oh, nothing to worry about, sir. Just a little tire trouble. All good now."

"Tire trouble."

"Yes, sir. Just a little flat. I took care of it."

Rockwell did not enter the bus. Steely eyes narrowing, he looked around the grounds. He saw a couple of cops walking near the security gates. A valet was jogging toward the back lot, a sheen of sweat on his face. A few suits were gathered near the mansion, talking about Rockwell but trying to make it look like they weren't. Another valet, a young woman standing twenty feet away, was trying to build up the nerve to ask him for a selfie. She'd already snapped a picture from afar, thinking she'd been inconspicuous. "Which tire?"

"Pardon, sir?"

"Which tire was it, Cornie?"

"Back passenger. Picked us up a little glass somewhere."

"Back passenger." On the other side of the bus from the only ingress.

"Yes, sir. Everything alright, sir?"

Rockwell didn't answer. He continued to scan the grounds, locking eyes with anyone who looked his way. He peered into the manicured shrubbery, into the tree branches, into the dark shadows of the gardens. Nothing there. Perhaps he was being paranoid—just Kauffman getting into his head—but it was damned coincidental that this 'flat tire' happened on the night he'd given his security detail off.

"Mr. Rockwell?" It was the female valet, sheepishly inching toward him. Cute little thing. Hispanic, long ponytail, nice eyes. "I'm so sorry to bother you, but I was hoping I could get a selfie?"

Rockwell smiled diamonds at her. "Course you can. Get over here."

"Thank you so much."

"My pleasure, Ms . . . ?"

"Marianna."

"Marianna. Now that's a lovely name."

"I mean Martinez. Ms. Martinez. Marianna Martinez. Oh, God, I promise I'm not this ditzy."

"No need to convince me. You're one smart cookie, I can tell."

"You can?"

He nodded, cupping her shoulder. "Let me guess. Pre-law?"

"Wha—how did you—?"

"Just a hunch. I knew it was either pre-law or pre-supermodel," he said with a wink. Marianna melted. Rockwell knew that she was fantasizing about joining him on his bus, where she would do anything—*anything*—that he wanted. "Come on, let's get that selfie."

He pulled her in close. As she fumbled with her smartphone, she muttered, "God, you smell so good."

After she snapped the picture, Rockwell said, "How about one more with you kissing my cheek."

Marianna happily concurred.

"Thank you so much," she gushed. "This is totally going to be my wallpaper."

"You're very welcome. And hey," he said, "one little piece of advice before you go."

"Oh, okay."

He stepped in close. "Don't be eighty years old and wonder why you never stood up to him. This is your life, Marianna. You own it. Live it fearlessly, your way." He lingered for a moment, smiled at her, then turned toward the bus.

Marianna stood frozen, gawping.

"Let's roll, Cornie."

"After you, sir."

Cornelius followed Rockwell up the stairs into the bus, then entered the cockpit and closed the privacy door behind him. The bus began moving, winding down the drive past the gates and into the breezy California night. Rockwell, however, remained near the door, staring into the disco data center that was his bus. Scrutinizing it. Trying to see if something, anything, had changed. A liquor bottle out of place. Dirt on the marble. Fingerprints on the glass. Anything. And he listened. With his ears, his eyes, his skin, his mind, he listened as if his senses were invisible tendrils exploring every surface, every nook, every cranny. He picked up nothing. Nevertheless, he doffed his blazer, unlocked the desk cabinet, and pulled the Glock from the drawer.

*　*　*

Cervantes had turned it all off: his anticipation, his kill lust, his thoughts, his being. He was only his shallow breath and his auditory canals, floating in nothing. He knew Rockwell was approaching, his Oxfords squeaking on the tile as he cast a net of hyperawareness over the bus. Cervantes only knew this peripherally, not directly. Like a comatose patient with fleeting, nebulous images of his former life, he was just a deactivated brain with a few essential synapses still firing. This was the key to assassinating Thomas Rockwell—going blank.

One or five minutes later—time was vague in his stripped-down cognizance—he heard Rockwell's footsteps draw equal with his hiding spot, where they stopped. Whether Rockwell was sensing his presence behind the

145

door or peering at the half-inch gap Cervantes had left as bait in the bedroom, he didn't know. Could not allow himself to ponder it. He had to remain blank.

The bus rocked gently as it hummed down the road. Cervantes was aware of the ambient thumps and squeaks of the rolling behemoth. Ice clinking in a glass. The gentle rush of an air conditioner. The faint buzz of a fluorescent light. Moments ago, he'd clocked the sound of Rockwell racking the slide on a pistol. Now Rockwell was standing on the other side of the door, inches from Cervantes' shoulder. Somewhere in the deep space of his consciousness, he knew that he very well might be seconds away from taking a bullet to the head.

Finally, Rockwell continued into his bedroom. The sound of his movement suggested he was shuffling forward in firing position, aiming at the baited closet. The pistol meant Cervantes was going to have to disarm Rockwell first, then look for an opportunity to use the garrote wire.

The magic moment was now.

He opened the door. Slithered out soundlessly, crouching. Rockwell's broad back was facing Cervantes, his shirt stark white against a bus full of gray and black gradients. He was reaching for his bedroom closet with his left hand, preparing to sling it open and target whoever was hiding in there. Doing so had caused him to bring his pistol in closer to his body. Rockwell's focus was on the door, his weapon within easy reach.

Measuring the move, Cervantes shot forward, clutched Rockwell's arm, pulled him off balance, and twisted the Glock from his palm. Before the pistol hit the marble, he kicked Rockwell's foot out from under him and rammed a knee into his face. With his prey stunned, Cervantes whipped the garrote wire from his pocket and looped it over his head. But, even dazed, Rockwell managed to get his hand inside the loop at the last instant, rendering it ineffective, and he twisted to face his attacker. The man was excellent. So began a shitstorm of grunting, jabbing, kneeing, and spitting as the combatants grappled in the tight quarters of the bus, slamming against furniture while slipping on the slick tile. Cervantes remained in relative control, neutralizing Rockwell's offense with a Muay Thai clinch, stymying his attempts to gain leverage. Rockwell, however, was a capable combatant, breaking the clinch and forcing Cervantes to change tactics. Snarling, they went toe to toe with a tight whirlwind of fists and elbows, feeling for arm bars and choke holds. But Cervantes had only been toying with his victim. Letting him think he had a chance. Now it was time to finish. Relishing the moment, he dismantled Rockwell's defense, dazing him with a rapid combination of strikes followed by a ferocious knee to the groin. When Rockwell doubled over, Cervantes snatched the garrote wire from the floor and sunk it into his neck. But the man wasn't quite licked. He powered to his feet even while Cervantes clung to his back, pulling the wire into

Rockwell's throat with his entire body. Breathless and choking, eyes bulging against crimson cheeks, Rockwell slammed Cervantes into the closet door, shattering the mirror. Cervantes was unphased, legs wrapped around his victim's waist like a high-powered magnet. With his final, desperate attempt, Rockwell heaved himself into the air and fell backward, crushing his assailant against the floor and bashing his head on the dresser. The impact winded Cervantes and threw starbursts into his vision, but the wire remained deep in Rockwell's throat, drawing blood. Finally, just before Rockwell lost consciousness, he tapped Cervantes' leg.

Cervantes released the wire and dropped his legs, allowing Rockwell to gasp for breath on top of him. Half a minute passed before Rockwell had the strength to roll to the side, wheezing and rubbing his throat. He rose to his knees, shirt flecked with blood. Cervantes grabbed Rockwell's hand and helped him up.

"Goddammit," coughed Rockwell, shaking his head. "You really got me. Well done."

"Thank you, Salvador."

"Did you have to use the garrote wire? Jesus. I won't be able to speak properly for a week."

"You said to make it as unexpected and as real as possible."

"And you sure as shit did." Rockwell walked to the mirror over the sink, inspecting his war zone of a throat. "Deb's going to have to buy me some turtlenecks," he croaked. "I hate turtlenecks."

"If you want to fend off a real assassin, that's what it could be like. You have to be better."

"Don't rub it in." Rockwell noticed the bathroom closet door ajar. Saw Cervantes' hiding place. Shook his head again. He spit blood into the sink, then met Cervantes' dark, impassive eyes. "As usual, I stand in awe of your abilities, Dominic. You were invisible. No one else on this planet could get the jump on me like that."

Cervantes nodded. "I am what I am because of you, Salvador."

"Nice beard, by the way," quipped Rockwell. Then the two men embraced. "Welcome home, brother."

***

The bus cruised north on the 405 toward Beverly Crest. The thirty-four-year-old golden boy lounged on his leather sofa swirling a Macallan Red and talking on his phone. He'd cleaned himself up and changed suits, looking again like the burgeoning celebrity over whom the press drooled. Stylish dark brown hair, deep blue eyes, a confident, clean-shaven smile, muscular build, uncanny professional acumen—the man had it all. Before he'd become engaged, *Business Insider* had named him the most eligible bachelor of the year.

Only Cervantes knew that there was more to the Salvador than what the world saw. Only he knew about the Salvador's gift. It was that gift that had saved Cervantes' life after the events of the Shinwar Massacre. Not once, but three times. Besides his old sensei back in Oakland, no one else had ever given a shit about him.

The main television monitor was tuned to Fox News, the second to CNN, and the third to a YouTube channel called Eat the Mania, a popular millennial pop culture show that the Salvador used to keep in touch with his own age demographic. Above the monitors, two digital stock tickers scrolled through the futures and cryptocurrency markets. Cervantes sat in a chair opposite, hands in his lap. Just watching the Salvador. The way his eyes flicked among the monitors, registering all the relevant information there even as he remained engaged with his caller. Aware of everything. Plugged in. While he conversed, he looked at Cervantes now and again, acknowledging him, appreciating his presence. The nonverbal equivalent of saying "I see you, brother."

The memory of that fateful day long ago flashed in Cervantes' mind. Post Shinwar, after it was announced that his squad would be investigated for rioting in the town proper and slaughtering innocent civilians. After that announcement, the writing on the wall became clear—everyone was going to point their fingers at Cervantes to save their own skins. Even though he'd saved the team and his battle competencies were off the charts, he'd never been accepted by his fellow Marines. Not really. He was the Creeper, the loner. The freak who stared at corpses. Though they all recognized his superior skills, nobody ever truly wanted him there. Nobody except the well-respected Rockwell, who was forever smoothing over social miscues between Cervantes and the rest of the men. But Cervantes had been distrustful of Rockwell back then, always rejecting his overtures of friendship.

When news of the impending investigation reached him, Cervantes was still in medical recovering from the bullet he'd taken to the shoulder. He knew the others were going to betray him. Only a matter of time before he'd face a court martial. He'd be tried and convicted. If the charges were as severe as expected, there was even a chance he'd be sentenced to death. But he didn't care. He determined he'd just get it over with, by his own hand. This world wasn't made for him. Never had been. By that point, he wasn't even sure if he was human. Ashamed of what he was, rejected by all, sick of the mockery of his existence, he decided to end it. First chance he got, he would hang himself.

He went into the latrine at 03:00 hours while everyone else slept. Grimacing from his shoulder wound, he tied a length of cordage around an exposed rafter and fashioned a noose. He was seconds away from his final kill. That's when Rockwell found him. He just showed up, inexplicably, bleary-eyed, wearing a t-shirt and boxers. Barged into the latrine as if he'd known exactly what was happening.

"Cervantes," he said, "you don't have to do this."

"The hell are you doing here?"

"I've heard you, man. I've felt your pain. I'm here to help you."

"Fuck off."

"I need to tell you something. Something I've wanted to tell you for a long time."

"I said fuck off, *cabrón!*"

"Look, just hear me out, okay? Give me sixty seconds, Raider to Raider. If you don't like what I have to say, I will fuck off as hard as any man has ever fucked off. Deal?"

Cervantes hesitated. His instinct was to jump down, whip Rockwell's ass, and then resume hanging himself, but that wouldn't work. His bum shoulder would thwart him. Also, anyone in earshot would wake up. They'd come rushing in, robbing him of suicide. Then he'd be restrained and placed on a twenty-four-hour watch like some goddamn zoo animal. "Spit it out then."

Rockwell reached toward Cervantes. Looked at him with those bottomless eyes. Locked in on him, unafraid of who he saw. He was the only one who'd ever done that. "I've felt everything you're feeling, Dominic. I know your pain. Your isolation. Your big question."

"The hell are you talking about?"

"You lie awake at night saying why me? Why I am different? Why am I cursed? You feel like some kind of alien. Like there's no place in this world for you."

Cervantes had never heard those words said aloud. He'd thought them a million times. Had anguished over them in the endless night. But they'd never been verbalized by himself or anyone else. How did Rockwell know? He was exposing Cervantes' innermost thoughts, bringing them out into the open, giving them a vulnerable gravitas they'd never had before. "How do you know that?" asked Cervantes quietly.

"I was just like you, man." Rockwell inched forward as he spoke, his voice deep and warm, an auditory hot tub. "My mother died after giving birth to me. My father killed himself soon after. I was alone. Spent my early years in a group home. Bounced around a few foster homes, started running the streets. Almost died a couple times. I felt like no one wanted me, like I didn't belong anywhere. That pain you've been feeling your whole life?" Rockwell tapped his hand on his own heart. "That was my pain, too."

"Great. You done?"

149

"I have the answer you've been looking for, Dominic. I know who you are, and it's fantastic. You, my friend, are meant for greatness."

"What?"

"Your skills, the things you can do, no one else on this earth can match them. No one can defeat you. The men saw it back there in Spinpul, but I've known since the day I laid eyes on you." Rockwell drew within a foot of Cervantes, looking up at him on his chair, never breaking eye contact. "You're right to think you're not human, Dominic. You're much more than that. You're a god. And you have a purpose far beyond what any normal man can dream of."

"What purpose?"

Rockwell smiled. "It's right there in your name. To dominate. To wield dominion over everyone. With me. Hey," he said, raising a finger to Cervantes' chest, "if the world will not accept you, brother, then it will *bow* to you."

Cervantes sank into Rockwell's gaze. He'd never been good at reading emotions or facial expressions, but with Rockwell, he didn't have to. In his colorblindness, Rockwell's azure blue eyes were balmy gray pools, deep with honesty. Sincerity. Purpose. Suddenly recognizing such traits in another person floored him. Somehow, Rockwell had done something no one else ever had. He'd *connected* with Cervantes, and he was fully accepting of what he saw. Not even Sensei Lam, who was the closest thing Cervantes ever had to a father, had accepted him on this level. Something happened then. A gentle soothing of his mind, of his heart. Like a warm blanket had just been laid over his freezing soul. He removed the noose. Stepped down from his chair. "What am I supposed to do?"

"First, let me help get you out of this court-martial mess," said Rockwell. "When that's behind us, I'll let you in on my plan. And your place in it."

"Plan?"

"Look, here's the thing, Dominic. I have a gift, too. Different from yours. I've only realized how to focus that gift in the last couple of years or so, but it's clear now. It makes perfect sense. You and me, two exceptional men meeting how we did, that's no coincidence. It's destiny. Let me teach you." Rockwell leaned in until their foreheads were nearly touching. "Hey," he said, "I *see* you, brother."

That was it. The moment that forever changed the course of both of their lives.

Rockwell would go on to serve as a character witness at Cervantes' trial. The trial was big news, garnering extensive media coverage and drawing scores of liberal protesters who portrayed Cervantes as a baby murderer among other things. The verdict appeared to be a foregone conclusion. In fact, everything seemed to be going the prosecution's way until Rockwell took the stand. As he gave his testimony, making eye contact with every juror, the overall tone of the trial changed. Even Cervantes felt that. In the end—somehow, against all odds—Cervantes was cleared of the most heinous counts, leaving him only with a Bad Conduct Discharge. It was the best possible outcome, and it should have been the long shot of the decade. As the defendant, Cervantes had had a front-row seat in court and still had no clue how Rockwell pulled it off. All he'd done was . . . *talk*. When he asked later how he'd done it, Rockwell answered, "Same way I got you out of that noose, brother. I focused my gift."

That was the second time Rockwell had saved him. The third time was what he referred to as his awakening. When Rockwell had taught him about his purpose. How to focus, to meditate. How to hone his deadly gifts in pursuit of that purpose. He did not have to join the dreaded 1st Civilian Division. Instead, he could work for Rockwell, who had somehow just become stupid rich. Soon after, Cervantes saw all the pieces of the puzzle slip together. Like a blind man struck with super vision, the reason for his existence was suddenly clear. He was no longer a neglected waif shunned by society, nor a murderous freak who stared at corpses. He was a knife with which Rockwell was going to cut out the evil heart of the world. That was when Rockwell became the Salvador.

Cervantes watched as the Salvador doled out directives to his caller. Admired his presence, his confidence. He'd come a long way since those days in the Marines, amassing power and wealth faster than anyone should be able to. With his aggressive entrepreneurship, he'd become a business dynamo, a media darling, a pop culture icon, and Senator Kirk's puppet master. All because of his gift. Cervantes was often astonished by how much that gift continued to grow. Over the years, the man had become downright supernatural. A week ago, he'd extracted Rosemary Velasquez's name and city of residence from Cervantes' head *over the phone*. That was new, and kind of freaky. In the past, the Salvador required face-to-face interaction to read a person. Just how powerful was he now?

"Just remember, Steve," said Rockwell, throat raspy, "We need to launch those sats within Kirk's first hundred days. His political honeymoon period. That means a clean beta in the first quarter. No excuses. No, don't worry about that. I have faith Kirk is going to win. You just keep development on schedule, and you call me the second that it's not. Right. See you next week. And hey, tell Julie and the kids that Uncle Tom says hello, okay?" He pressed End, then looked at Cervantes. "I've got two speaking engagements and a live interview with *America Tonight* in the next few days," he croaked, rubbing his throat. "Seriously, did you have to use the garrote wire?"

"Actually, I think it's an improvement."

"Hey, what was that? Did you just crack a joke?"

"Maybe," said Cervantes, blank as a new chalkboard. "I'm a very funny man."

"Right," chuckled Rockwell, leaning toward the bar to refill his tumbler. "This is a fifty-thousand-dollar Scotch Whisky. Aged five decades. Sure you don't want to try some?"

"I'm sure." The Salvador knew Cervantes didn't drink, but he always offered anyway. The Salvador almost always knew what people were going to say, but he still engaged in the pretense of authentic conversation. Like Cervantes, he had to hide his gift.

"So," said Rockwell, swirling his liquor, "let me tell you. What you did in Berlin? That was huge. Krause is out of the way, and his replacement is bought and paid for. That puts the Faraday factory back on track. I know you don't care about the nuts and bolts but having that factory will allow us to dominate the European EV market. You gave us a massive win, and I want you to know that."

"Copy."

Rockwell nodded. "It's good to finally see you again, brother. I didn't mean to keep you in the field that long. Tell me, how are you?"

"I think you know."

"Sure, pretty much," he shrugged. "But I'd still like you to tell me. After all, I'm one of the privileged few who ever gets to hear your voice."

"Mm," said Cervantes, "or maybe you have a job for me you know I won't like, so you're feeding me prompts to make me feel like it's my idea."

Rockwell tilted his gaze, a devilish half-smile on his lips. "You," he said, pointing a finger at Cervantes. "You're good. Maybe you know me a little too well."

"Who is it? That Kauffman guy you were talking about?"

"No, not Kauffman. Crusty fucker. Don't get me wrong. I'd love to take him out, but after tonight, it would just raise suspicion. We're just going to let Mother Nature take its course there."

"Then who?"

"Man, do I love that one-track mind of yours. Sorry to disappoint you, but we're still in recon mode."

"The target is in hiding?"

"Something like that." As Rockwell sipped his scotch, the bus hit a pothole, causing him to spill a bit. "Damn it, Cornie," he muttered.

"What does that mean?"

Grabbing a napkin from the bar, Rockwell wiped the liquor from his shirt. "What we have is sketchy. European intel is working to substantiate. All we know is that the target might be in possession of . . . let's just say some extremely desirable information. If that information is legit, I want it." He dead-eyed Cervantes, his charming demeanor gone. "And when I say I want it, I mean I'll launch an all-out war to get it. And I'll destroy anyone else who knows of it."

Cervantes noted the steeliness in the Salvador's gaze. The abandonment of his charisma and geniality. He hadn't seen him like that for years. He was ready to go to war? Cervantes thought that part of his plan was still far into the future. This job, whatever it was, had piqued the most ferocious part of his soul. "You can't say that and just leave it. Tell me the rest."

Rockwell resumed his relaxed posture, took another sip. "Like I said, it's still quite speculative. Could turn out to be smoke."

"But you don't believe it's smoke."

The Salvador's piercing eyes and subtle head shake said much more than words.

"Then tell me."

Swirling his scotch under his nose, Rockwell entertained his own thoughts for a moment. When he spoke, there was a restrained yearning in his voice. "Dominic, remember when I told you I felt something indescribable in the air? A feeling? Like the door to unimaginable power was slowly creeping open right in front of me?"

"Are you saying this job is that door?"

Rockwell didn't answer. Instead, he seemed to lose himself in a daydream, staring into nothing. That wasn't like him. The Salvador never zoned out. He was always here, always aware. Cervantes watched him, waiting. Finally, the Salvador muttered something odd. "Trust in dreams, for in them is hidden the gate to eternity."

"What?"

"Hm?" said Rockwell, returning from his torpor. "Oh, nothing. Just an old saying."

"Salvador, the job?"

Rockwell smiled, crossing his legs. "Tell you what. We're not ready to move on her, but I'll let you ask one question. I'll answer truthfully, but that's all I can give you right now."

Cervantes shook his head. "You still have me begging, even when I knew that was your angle."

Rockwell shrugged. "You going to ask or not?"

"Fine. You said 'her.' So the target is female."

"Is that a question?"

"And you mentioned the European team. So the job is somewhere in Europe."

"Asking without asking. I do believe I'm rubbing off on you, brother."

"Give me a name," said Cervantes, indulging the Salvador's little game. "And a city," he added.

"Name and city. Jesus, Dominic, that's like eighty percent of the current intel."

"You said you'd answer."

Rockwell regarded him with toying blue eyes. "Alright. But for the sake of maintaining my damaged sovereignty," he said, massaging his throat, "you only get a country, not a city."

"Fine. What country?"

"Italy."

"Italy. We've never done anything there." He paused, hoping the Salvador might elaborate. He didn't. "Okay, Italy. And her name?"

Before he answered, Rockwell crunched a piece of ice, plummeting into a thousand-mile stare. Then, as if sampling the flavor of the word, he drawled, "Grace."

ODSEK 21

BEL RAGAZZO NICKERED, RUBBING his bulky head against Valory. She scratched behind his ears as he leaned into her, forcing her off-balance. *Not head shy, this one*, she thought, bracing herself against the horse's muscular neck. Of course, she knew you're not supposed to let a horse rub his face against you. That is not affection, but a display of dominance. But Valory didn't care. Bel Ragazzo was not her horse, so she didn't have to deal with the consequences of his bratty behavior. He was just a big ol' sweetie pie as far as she was concerned, only hankering for a little attention. "Who's a good boy?" she cooed in Italian, petting his face. "Who's a big, beautiful boy, hm?"

The sun was just beginning to drop behind the crags, dashing the western skies with a canvas of pinks and yellows. To the east, foreboding storm clouds loomed. Cold gusts whipped the castle, abusing an Italian flag on the roof of the keep. Out for a brisk walk, Valory had noticed the two horses watching her from their pens, their long necks jutting over the wooden gates. Magia, the black mare, pinned her ears back at Valory's approach, showing the whites of her big, dark eyes. *Stay away from me*, the mare was saying. Bel Ragazzo, however, welcomed her with a snort of eagerness. The gelding's body language said, *Come here, lady! Let's visit!*

Fetching a stiff-bristled dandy brush from the tack pen, she began brushing Bel Ragazzo's chestnut coat, which he was pleased to allow. It had been about twenty years since she'd been around horses when she'd taken riding lessons with Violet. More accurately, she'd been forced to take lessons. *You can't spend your entire life cooped up in a tiny room with your face in books*, her father had insisted. *Your body's going to rot, and that genius mind of yours will follow.*

But Val knew the real reason behind her parents' sudden equestrian interest, and that was Violet. Vi had recently returned from a stint in juvie, arrested for vandalism and underage drinking. To help get her back on track, the Graces engaged her with a healthy, active hobby. And to ensure it didn't look like a punishment, they made Val participate under the ruse of sisterly bonding.

Neither of the girls had shown the slightest interest in riding horses before that, and Violet never quite took to it. A few weeks in, she was cursing the steeds as big, stupid, smelly beasts. But Valory grew to enjoy the lessons. Horses were much easier to befriend than humans. They didn't lie, make fun of your pimples, or call you a quiet little weirdo, and they didn't glue the pages of your books together while you were at gym class. Horses were majestic creatures with unique personalities. Sure, some were obstinate, but if you put in the work, you could connect with them emotionally, developing a fun and rewarding relationship. Even with the stand-offish ones like Magia.

The lessons lasted for six months. Then Violet vanished again, running off with some eighteen-year-old, pill-popping dropout. They planned to 'go to Mexico together,' where they'd work on a farm or some such nonsense.

"*Sei cosi bello, bambino,*" said Valory, baby talking Bel Ragazzo. "*Sta diventando freddo e vento. Vuoi la tua coperta?*" It was getting cold and windy, did he want his blanket? She wondered if the hostler would be upset at her for doing his job, but he was nowhere in sight. As she considered blanketing the horses, the keep door groaned open and *Agente* Trentino emerged. He cupped his hand against the wind and lit a cigarette. As he took a drag, he looked down on the courtyard without really looking. Trentino didn't seem to have the same steely watchfulness of Savelli, the same 'nothing gets past me' attitude. To Valory, he seemed preoccupied with a million matters, his external focus limited to the tip of his cigarette. Just the vibe he gave off.

Yesterday, Trentino had helicoptered in while Valory was sleeping. Savelli and Moretti had boarded that same helicopter, departing on urgent business. Upon learning the news, Valory felt like a child running downstairs only to discover her Christmas gifts had been swiped from under the tree. She'd been planning on sitting down with Rafael and discussing all the wonderful things she'd translated from the tome and the other works. She wanted to watch his face as he read her report, but he was gone. Now all she had was *Professore* Mancini, which meant she had no one. Rollo, maybe, but sharing her findings with him might be in poor taste. Ostracizing the highly regarded Mancini while working with his nephew? Not exactly the most professional behavior.

A moment after Trentino emerged, Janelle LaFleur stepped out onto the landing beside him. Her appearance was slightly comical, a skinny, glasses-wearing waif engulfed by a heavily padded, pink winter coat. Like the Easter Bunny had a child with the Michelin Man. Janelle waved down at Valory, then she asked Trentino if it would be okay if the two ladies spoke. He nodded.

As Janelle descended the stairs into the courtyard, Valory felt a pinch of anxiety. True, their conversation would be supervised by an agent, so they'd be following the rules. But they'd have to think about what they said before they said it, lest something *verboten* slip from their mouths. She felt a little spineless worrying about it—especially since Janelle didn't appear to have the same qualms—but she couldn't help it. There just wasn't a rebellious bone in Valory's body.

"*Bonsoir*, Valory," said Janelle, a smile peeking over her purple scarf.

"*Bonsoir*, Janelle. *Comment ça va?*"

"I am very well, thank you." Janelle motioned toward the colorful hues in the sky. "Such beautiful evening, no?" *Zooch byootiful eveNEENG, no?*

"It certainly is. Looks like you're well-prepared for the cold."

"Ah, *oui*," said Janelle, patting her big pink coat. "I am not friends with cold," she laughed.

Bel Ragazzo threw his head against Valory and snorted. *Hey, why have you stopped brushing me?* he seemed to say. "You'll have to excuse this big lug," she said, flinging her ponytail away from the gelding's slobbery mouth. "I think he's a little attention-starved."

"Ah, you are expert with horses?"

"Expert? No, I wouldn't say that. My sister and I took lessons as teenagers. Have you ever ridden a horse?"

"No. Well, I ride a pony one time, when I was the little girl."

"Sure. Well, maybe one day the hostler will be nice enough to let us ride these guys. I could show you if you want."

"*Oui*, this sounds fun."

"Here, let me introduce you." Valory looked into Bel Ragazzo's bulbous eye and said in Italian, "Bel Ragazzo, *questa è la mia amica*, Janelle." Then she turned to Janelle, switching to French. "Janelle, *c'est mon nouvel ami*, Bel Ragazzo."

"*Ciao,* Bel Ragazzo," she said, petting the gelding's neck. "He is very handsome. What about the other one there?"

"That's Magia," answered Valory. Magia was watching the ladies from her pen. "She's a little standoffish. Might take a while to earn her trust."

As the ladies lavished attention on Bel Ragazzo, the chat fizzled. Two newly met introverts did not induce sparkling conversation, it seemed. They both noticed the uncomfortable silence, and they wanted to break it, but the very realization of that circumstance caused their brains to sputter even more. An exchange of awkward smiles was all they managed. Finally, just as Janelle was about to excuse herself, Valory found her wits. "So, um, where are you from, Janelle?"

Janelle seized the lifeline. "Ah. Well, originally, I am from Bordeaux, but now I live and work in Paris."

"Nice. Is that where you studied art?"

"Yes. I studied at the *Université de Paris* under Professor Laurent."

As Valory asked more questions, Janelle's tongue loosened. She continued in English for a bit but switched to French as she got on a roll.

157

She'd grown up in modest conditions with two older brothers. Dad was a mechanic. Mom was a primary school teacher before health problems forced early retirement. No one else in the family had the slightest inclination for art, so Janelle's interest was a headscratcher. Recognizing her talent, her parents did whatever they could to support her passion. After taking first prize at an art fair with one of her paintings, she was hooked for life.

Valory was just about to begin drawing parallels between their childhoods when a dust-smothered jeep rumbled into the courtyard, passing beneath the gate. Pebbles popping under the tires, the jeep pulled to within ten meters of the keep, and *Tenete* Esposito alighted with two other soldiers. Trentino skipped down the stairs and met the group at the rear of the jeep, inspecting numerous boxes of supplies. After a quick check, Trentino approved the shipment and went back inside the castle, the soldiers laboring behind him with boxes in hand. They, too, disappeared into the keep, leaving only the whooshing wind, the fluttering of the flag, and the hum of the generators in the eastern bailey. Valory and Janelle looked at each other, a nervous thought ping-ponging between them: *We are alone and unsupervised.*

Valory quietly brushed the horse. Janelle pulled her beanie over her earlobes and hugged herself against the cold, shifting her sparse weight between her feet. Each of them focused on the horses, darting uncertain looks at the keep. Bel Ragazzo snorted.

The last inch of sun was sinking behind the mountains in the west, resulting in a brilliant, last-gasp starburst fanning over the crest. Distant thunder rumbled in the east. A rapid advance of freezing, stormy darkness was at hand. Valory wondered if Janelle had the same urge as her—to scamper away like frightened mice before anything bad happened. Then, somewhere in her mind, Violet poked a metaphorical finger into her chest. *There you go thinking like a wuss again*, she said. *Maybe, for once in your life, you should grow a set.*

"Hey, Janelle?"

"Yes?"

"I still don't see the hostler. Would you mind helping me blanket these horses before the storm arrives?"

"Yeah, sure."

The ladies grabbed the heavy, padded blankets from the tack pen, draping them over Magia and Bel Ragazzo. Janelle struggled with the weight but managed to pull her ends into place. "There we go," said Valory, patting Bel Ragazzo. "Nice and warm for the night."

They lingered a moment, Valory making a show of tidying the tack. Janelle asked if she needed any more help, and Valory said she didn't think so.

"Okay," said Janelle, drenched with indecision. "Well. I guess . . . unless there is something else . . . I will uh . . ."

"Yeah."

" . . . retire to my chamber."

"Right. Sure."

"Okay, then. *À bientôt, oui?*"

"*Oui. À bientôt.*"

Janelle began walking toward the keep, two skinny legs under a muffin top of pink padding. Valory felt a sinking feeling. Though the two had only just met, Janelle was her closest thing to a friend at the castle. Not a colleague, but someone who might understand her on a personal level. Watching her leave, not knowing when they might get to talk again, kindled a lonely desperation in her.

"I know the queen's name," blurted Valory.

Janelle turned. "What?"

Valory looked up, half-expecting to see Trentino's dour eyes aimed at her from a window or something. Nobody there. She drew near enough to whisper to Janelle. "The marble queen. I know her name. And a lot more, too. A whole lot more."

"Really?"

"It was in a tome I translated. I can hardly believe what I've read."

"*Mon Dieu,* you must tell me!"

"I'll do better than that," said Valory, heart pole vaulting into her throat. "Agent Savelli has confiscated my original work, but I kept a copy of the translation," she whispered. "Secretly." She paused once more before jumping off the deep end. "How about we meet in your chamber at midnight?"

БӨЛУМ 22

Title: The Infinite Diary Series (Volume & Entry #TBD)
Date: Renaissance period, est. 1594-1615 CE
Subject(s): Aléxandros (aka Alikai, Alaksandus, et al)
Language(s): Unknown isolate, Early Modern English, Old Hungarian, Lombardic, others
Material: Codex, leatherbound boards & leather bindings, ink, vellum
Condition: Good. Fragile bindings, vellum intact
Note: Actual dimensions of item are 31.5 x 23.8 cm. 120 pages. Written with quill and ink. Upper margin 6-8 cm.; lower margin of 6-8 cm.; left margin 8-10 cm.
Location discovered: Classified

Context: The narrative alternates between many languages. Preceding each transition, the original language is notated in brackets. -V.Grace

[Early Modern English] This eve finds me at the Tabard Inn, deep within this bustling and malodorous town of London. Here the streets are narrow and boisterous, and the stench of civilization piles heavily upon the tongue such that the taste cannot be spit out. Yet are the folk lively and accepting of such conditions. **[Old Hungarian]** We arrived two days ago, István and I, and have been obliged to dally whilst repairs are made to the coach. To István have I given coin aplenty, that he may partake of things that such hives offer. Let him lay his eyes upon flamboyant spectacles and his lips upon wily women, thirsts which cannot be slaked at the castle. **[Early Modern English]** Meanwhile I sojourn here, finding no interest in the entertainments of Man. The delay is expected, as are all unexpected things. For we have mastered the dance of happenstance, you and I, and I have thusly vouchsafed for lost hours. Forsooth, he who devises a flawless plan is the sport of Fate. Thus the repairs hamper not our pilgrimage. Midsummer Day is more than a fortnight hence, and our destination lies only a few days west. We shall ride anon. **[Lombardic]** Nothing shall stop my annual trek to that place. Should I die a thousand times betwixt here and there, ever shall I rise and go to her, just for the fool's chance of seeing her again.

[Early Modern English] Presently, however, in the firelight of this Tabard common room, I think of you. You who are me. Brothers of eternity are we, coursing with devil's blood, singing lamentations unsung by any other. **[Unknown Isolate]** I wonder how many centuries will pass before you take up this parchment and sup with me at the table of Time? For oft have I returned to the writings of he who was once me, finding comfort in remembrance of his days. So shall you, the man who I will become, give eye to this writing centuries hence and find solace in my words. What shall you remember of these days in which we now dwell? Little, I wager. Our eons are but hours bleeding together like paints on a palette. For untold years have we tread upon all the lands of the earth, yet our minds are as feeble as any man's and cannot cradle the memories of millennia. **[Early Modern English]** Tis only this diary that saves us from an infinite and terrible insanity. Yea, this diary, the record of my soul, stands second only to the remembrance of sweet Seraphina who lives forever in my heart. To her I give present and solemn thanks. For, by her grace, I have met a fellow worthy of my quill here in this very town of London. Of him and our meeting shall I write hereof.

As in some past summers, István and I debarked in the port of Dover, for I fancied a visit to the towns of Canterbury and Dartford on the road to London. Some days we rested in each of those places in the least offensive accommodations. In Dover, whilst abed in the silent and cavernous night, a yearning that you know well, you who are me, crept into my bosom and seized my heart. Twas the familiar flame that burns hotter as we draw ever closer to that great henge of stone, where last we beheld her face. **[Lombardic]** Hoping that we might see her there again drives us madder by the second. Yea, tis true that we see her in our mind's eye at all times, in all the seconds that flutter from present to past. Tis also true that I have fashioned her likeness in all earthly mediums a thousand times over, and that oft I look upon her semblance with sorrowful joy. Yet on that fateful day long ago, in that grove of towering monoliths, she appeared in the flesh, I swear it. No painting was she, nor sculpture from my hands, nor flimsy ghost in the breeze. She was flesh, as solid and whole as the lover who embraced me centuries ago. There in that glade, I beheld the watery moonlight in her eyes, the gentle breath of wind in her hair, the fluttering of her dark dress. Behind her, endless stars poured down upon the henge like a veil of diamonds made only for her. Whence I sank unto my knees in disbelief, I felt her hand upon my head, I did. Strike me not with words such as hallucination or madness. She came to me, and I shall hear no word against it. To know that such a miracle might yet occur in a matter of days, no matter how improbable, is a mournful hope no lover can bear. Only you know of what I speak. You who are me. Only you feel that yearning madness that sets upon us, year after year, as we close upon the henge lusting for but one last caress of her ivory hand.

[Early Modern English] Twas this very fever that sprang me from my bed in Dover. In the dead of night was I compelled to fashion a semblance of my Sera, there and then, lest my desire scorch me from within. But I had no paints, nor clay, nor materials of any kind with which to craft her. Thus in haste did I gather the soot from the fireplace, and I made her face upon the wall of my accommodation, rubbing the ash thick and heavy into the grain until my fingertips were more splinter than flesh. **[Lombardic]** Whence she'd been made, spanning floor to ceiling upon the wall, I fell to my knees in a sweat and looked on her. Thereby was my poor heart was given piteous reprieve. For, even scrawled from dust and ashes, she was celestial.

[Early Modern English] Alas, the next morn, whence the proprietor's woman saw my work, she made quick tattle to that proprietor, who immediately revoked my patronage for damages wrought. **[Old Hungarian]** István and I were banished with great pageantry, sending tongues and rumors wagging through the streets.

[Early Modern English] The next town on the road was Canterbury and thence Dartford. In both was I compelled to draw my Sera, as I had in Dover. I was unwilling to resist. The waiting, the foretaste, twas a thing alive, moving my hand of its own will, goading me to make her everywhere. In Canterbury did I accost a poor and reedy artist, and I bade him sell me his paints, in return gifting him a fistful of gemstones. With these paints, I made swift likenesses of my queen in all the places where my gaze might settle. Upon the coach, upon the tabletops at the taverns, on a well in Dartford, and others. The townsfolk whispered that I was touched in the head, for I speckled their towns with visions of Seraphina wherever it so pleased me. My doings stirred distrust and confusion among the folk, and dutiful István was obliged to pull me from the angers of some who were offended.

So twas that tales of my madness reached London before us as if they'd ridden a mean gale to the heart of this city. Whence we arrived at the Tabard, where I presently sit, the innkeeper asked if I was that man who had wielded strange magics in those prior townships, causing painted women to appear upon walls, laying curses upon the shires. Such errors are the way of all peoples, as ever. **[Unknown Isolate]** Even before the rise of towering empires, whence the land was roamed only by fragmented tribes, people have impregnated the world with myth and folly.

Here is where I remind you of the fellow we met two nights ago, in this very spot where I write. **[Lombardic]** And herewith shall you remember that our meeting was by the grace of Seraphina.

162

[Early Modern English] Whence he entered the Tabard, I knew he was searching for me. We know these things, do we not? You who are me. With but a single glance, we know the mind of a man as if we'd molded it ourselves. **[Unknown Isolate]** For we have looked in his eyes a billion times over. We have watched him since he hunted the savannahs. We have listened to his lies, those he tells others and himself. For days unending have we divined his deepest purpose such that it now lies open before us like a book that we ourselves have authored. Precious few surprises spring from the well of infinity. **[Early Modern English]** Thus, as this particular fellow entered the Tabard, we knew what he was about. Though he made jovial words with the barkeep, and though he pretended nonchalance in his fine doublet and green velvet stockings, I knew his business. He had come in eager search of me, that he may meet the man who packed the streets with rumors. Behind his eyes twinkled wonderment and questions, his humours aglow with the swaths of a passionate artist. Simmering with curiosity had he sought me out, tracking me here to the Tabard. All of this I divined with a blink.

Gazing about the common room, he looked upon those who were dining, upon the bard who played his lyre, and upon those townsfolk who sang with unmelodious merry. These he paid little heed. Thence upon me his eye rested, here in this chair near the fire, as I sketched a portrait of Seraphina with coal and parchment. And he was taken aback, for I sat in wait for his gaze, and met it directly. So did I raise my hand and beckon him to join me. Behind him did he look and, seeing none other, pointed at himself and mouthed the word, "Me?"

[Old Norse] As you know, you who are me, we do not suffer conversation willingly. We have heard all things men have to say and wished rather that our ears might rot off than listen to the selfsame prattling of eons. Yet on some rare occasions do we encounter a man such as this one. Receptive and observant was his air, with a pliant mind unbound by its own narrow experience. **[Aeolic Greek]** One such as he is a hundredfold more mindful than his brethren, for he discounts nothing and entertains all things in good faith, even against his rigid teachings. These infrequent men intuit that truth is not a thing of certain and singular nature, and thus they stand unshackled to the bedrock of prejudice. Tis only this kind of man, untricked by his transience, who does not think us inhabited by devils should we speak of our curse. With these men, you and I might share words.

[Early Modern English] As he neared my table, I leaned and held my open palm near the floor, and he was puzzled to see it. Thence was he bumped by a merrymaker, and the ale cup tossed from his hand, which I thence caught in my own. He looked upon me with astonishment, and spoke, "Good sir, how came thee to know I wouldst spill my cup, and precisely where it wouldst fly?"

To which I said, "Thou shalt ponder another question in days to come, sir. To wit, wouldst thou have spilled thy cup had I not held forth my hand?"

In silence, he worked upon this thought, and he asked how I had come to know such things. I replied that life is but a lake that ripples, and I have ridden those ripples forever. With this, I filled his cup from my pitcher and bade him sit. Here he speculated as to what stunt was afoot, his curiosity fuller than the cup I pushed toward him. Studied he my youthly face, pondering how a lad half his age was comported with the grave and poised air of one much older. Above all was he delighted, for he knew he had found who he sought.

Before he sat, in the manner of English gentry, he made a pointlessly formal introduction and named himself William Shakespeare. In return . . .

Janelle shot a look at Valory, open-mouthed. There was no need to ask which part she'd just read. Valory just nodded, motioning for her to continue. After looking back and forth between Valory and the laptop, she refocused on the page.

. . . and named himself William Shakespeare. In return, I gave the name Aléxandros as my own, and I allowed him to indulge in further pleasantries as beloved by this city kind. In these pleasantries, he remained reserved, making no quick point in fear of offending my sensibilities, which were yet unknown to him. Thus I spoke, "Sir, a torrent of questions pours forth from thine eyes whilst thy mouth remains locked by formality. Hath no caution in thy tongue, for thy questions are known to me. Prithee ask."

He was loosened by this and spoke, "If it pleases thee, good sir, what mean thee that mine questions are known to thee? For in troth hath we never met, lest my memory be a traitor most scandalous."

[Unknown Isolate] To this I answered that I have tread this world for millennia, and have seen all things, and have met all people, and have suffered all interactions in such abundance that I now stand saddled with foreknowledge. Should I choose to give focus to the present, always can I divine the next moment as if it were past rather than future.

[Early Modern English] With my claims did his logic wrestle, and he yet suspected I was naught but a traveling swindler. He thought on the ale cup then, and how my hand had laid in wait for it ere he'd been jostled. I let his mind work in silence, reckoning with these improbabilities and

164

formulating a new query, which I knew would be, "If the future is known to thee, pray tell what shall I ask next of thee?"

Thence he made this very question, in approximation, to which I answered, "Thou dost wish to ask of mine sketch." Intrigued was he, and he confirmed this was his mind. I thence spoke further of his unvoiced thoughts. I predicted his wish to know if my present sketch was the very same that had stirred the townsfolk of Dover and Canterbury and Dartford, and if I was, in sooth, that strange man who had left these drawings upon those townships. "For thou dost believe," said I, "if I be that eccentric fellow of rumor, that mine character shall provide fodder for thine art, which I daresay lies in dramatic verse."

He confirmed these were his very thoughts, and he was struck tongueless with the prospect that I dispensed not deceit, but genuine truth. I thence gave over my sketch of Seraphina to his studious eye. He perused her countenance, and he spoke well of her beauty and my skill. Said he, "But drawn in rough and blackened coal, thy hand hath wrought thy lady as fairly as the moon upon a bed of stars."

His fine words basted me with bittersweet flavors, for they painted the memory of my sweet Seraphina that night in the henge, whence she did appear to me under such a bed of stars. To that place traveled I anon, unbeknownst to this William, and he beheld the sugary sorrow of my eyes as my mind revisited that Midsummer's eve of yore.

"Prithee, noble Aléxandros," said he, "if it pleases thee, give tell of thy lady faire. For thy love glitters in thine eyes more brightly than the sun upon a king's treasury. Of she who hath captured the undying heart of an immortal, I wouldst know all things."

Still was he not convinced that I was immortal, only indulging me in trade for my story, but of my true love, there stood no challenge in him. Besotted was he with the institutions of love and passion and chivalry, this was as clear as the purest stream. Equally was he intrigued by the tale of tragedy and loss which he hoped might spill from my lips. Such tales, afire with the pits and pinnacles of emotion, were the lifeblood of his art. And in his desire of my words, he offered unto me a fleeting gift, as was my selfish motive all along. To wit, that I should tell my story to someone who might actually believe it. To be heard by sympathetic ears, and not be shunned as a fool by dullards who know all things, is the best we can hope for in this life, you and I.

[Lombardic] Thus I began my tale. Beginning not, of course, with the inconsequential epochs before Seraphina, but on the very day I met her. For on that day, all that was nothing became an everlasting treasure.

I shall not repeat the story here, for tis reproduced at length already, as you know, in the twelve. That telling is, in sooth, our dearest jewel upon the earth, and you know it well. **[Early Modern English]** Here only shall I say that I regaled Master Shakespeare into the dark hours, and he was a rapt and goodly listener. Well pleased was I to watch his reactions, his enormous empathy. Full and bewitched were his chestnut eyes, absorbing my tale as much as his ears, so open and wanting were they. I was moved as I had not been in decades, for he began to participate in the joys of my tale, and to suffer through the losses. So it came to be, as I plied him with a richness of story that could never be born of lies, that he swooned over its heart-wrenching truth. As he gave himself thusly, he was no longer a target upon which to spear my woes, but a rare and fleeting friend.

Therefore, I broke from my tale and afforded him the ears of reciprocity. I asked of him, whom did he love, what wished he from this life, what grievances did he bear, and other inquiries. These things I asked for his profit, not mine. For I knew his answers and could have listed them myself, in approximation. To wit, twas known to me that his marriage was sour and resented, and that he oft sought passion in the sheets of others. Such was a token written in his air, which speaks truth even as lips lie. Spoke he of the rude reception handed to him whence he'd come to London from the country and had begun to ply his art. This, also, was a thing known to me, as I have witnessed resentments toward better minds for all the days of my existence. Thence delved he into the fine points of his craft. To wit, he recited lines from his works, gave tell of his fellow players, and demonstrated his skill for enthralling a crowd. To his heart I gave ear, as he had given me, thus offering him all the humanity I could gather from the bone-dry well of my soul. Of this was he thankful, and he gazed upon me, seeing more than just another young man. Twas apparent he had become taken with me and wondered if a tryst might come to pass between us. Such a thing, however, he dared not speak aloud.

At length, I resumed my tale of Seraphina, and it stood yet incomplete whence the fire in the common room faded. Thus did I invite Master Shakespeare to my accommodation, that we may speak further into the night. There he produced from his satchel a pipe and cannabis, of which we partook equally. We sat upon the floor, and he heard my voice more than any person had in centuries, for my throat was ale-coated, my tongue loosened by herb. Of Seraphina I gushed like a sot, making tell of her joyously unpredictable ways. Rare merriment snuck into my voice, fueled by those imbibements and by William's quick friendship, and I even laughed. For I spoke of the first time I was slain by Seraphina's hand. Hot and vicious was her temper, said I, and in beautiful madness did she stab me lifeless with her dagger. I laughed at this until I was breathless, and thence did I laugh for the realization I was laughing, for tis a thing I'd not heard from my own lips in decades.

William sat appalled and confused, which tickled my bones ever the more. Said he frothily, "What mean thee the 'first time' she slew thee? Dost thou infer that she slew thee a second?"

At this, through my laughter, I held up seven fingers.

Said he in answer, "Seven? Thy lady faire sleweth thee seven times?" Thence quipped he, "Thou didst not take the point, methinks." At this, we broke from words and only laughed for a spell, til a pounding came upon the wall, and an angry wench cried for silence.

Twas a fine thing to make merry again, and to share time with a goodly soul. Unexpected and welcomed. Remember it, you who are me. Remember laughing with William now, and let it bring a moment of satisfaction upon you.

The last of my story did I recount, telling of Seraphina's terrible death and my powerlessness to prevent it. Thus the throes of tragedy reclaimed my heart. We fell to somberness, and fair William held his arm around my shoulder, his long, brown hair against my cheek, and twas very well. Thence did I reveal that my destination was the famed henge of stone in the English countryside, for twas there that Seraphina's spirit appeared to me once, on Midsummer's Day, many years after her death. "Yearly do I trek there," said I, "on the anniversary of her appearance, burning to see her again, but it has not come to pass." My merriness was thence fled, replaced again by the cold temperance of joyless eons.

Twas nearly dawn then. Fair William was leaned upon me, his heart beaten by my tale. He knew words would not console me, though he longed to do so. As slumber overcame us, I knew that he bore me friendship and love.

In the light of the afternoon, William took his leave. Thanked me did he for granting him an inspiration that he should never forget, and he bade me Godspeed and blessed fortune in my quest to rendezvous with Seraphina. Spoke he, "Always shall I remember not only thy tale, but thy golden hair and thy dew-drop eyes. Verily, dear Aléxandros, thou art more lovely and temperate than the very Midsummer Day that thou dost pursue. If thou art in troth immortal, tis surely blessed to ride such beauty into eternity." Thence was he away.

With his face fresh in my mind, I made a sketch of Master Shakespeare in coal, that I may forever remember he who gifted me with fleeting compassion and rare cheer. You who are me, you shall find him pressed into the pages of this book, once tis made. Look upon him and remember.

Janelle fired her question at Valory like an eager child. "Do you have this sketch of Shakespeare?"

"Shhh," hissed Valory. "We don't want anyone to know I'm here, remember?"

"Sorry," whispered Janelle, checking the door of her small chamber. "Do you have it?"

Sitting cross-legged on Janelle's cot, Valory smiled at her counterpart's enthusiasm. "Unfortunately, no. It wasn't in the book."

"But it must be somewhere, no? Maybe it falls out. Have you search the library? What is it?" added Janelle when Valory giggled.

"It's just nice to see someone as excited as I am."

"*Bien sûr, oui*, I am excited! This discovery, *c'est énorme!* Because we do not know what Shakespeare truly looked like. He was never drawn or painted in his own lifetime, you know? The images we have of him today were made long after his death. *Sacre bleu*, this sketch could fetch millions!"

Valory nodded. "Trust me, I'm keeping my eye out for it. At least we have a written physical description. Not only that," she said, pouring wine into each of their cups, "but we now have the world's only firsthand account of a real conversation with William Shakespeare. His actual spoken words. More incredible—if our immortal author is as prescient as he claims—we even have his thoughts!"

"*Bordel de merde*," whispered Janelle, the fireplace glowing in her glasses. Valory giggled again. *Bordel de merde* translated literally to 'shitty brothel.' It was as close as the French came to 'holy shit.'

"*Oui*," agreed Valory, "This diary brings the greatest English writer of all time into stark focus. His real personality is here. His emotions, his behavior, his empathy. We learn that he drank alcohol and smoked cannabis. We get hints about his promiscuity. My god, we even have one of his beloved puns!"

"What pun?"

"Ah, you may have missed it. It was when he said 'thou didst not take the point.' From when he was stabbed by Seraphina."

"Ah yes, I see this now. Queen Seraphina. *Mon Dieu,* why did he love such an angry woman?"

Valory shrugged. "He must have seen something in her to be so head over heels. I hope to find out as I translate more of his diary."

The time was 12:45 A.M. The castle was dark and quiet. Only the occasional rumble of thunder could be heard from without. Janelle's bedchamber was much smaller than Valory's, with a tiny chair and a table big enough only for one. No garderobe either. These rooms, one level below the Great Hall, had probably housed servants in past times. Valory felt guilt-riddled—her own chamber was lavish compared to Janelle's.

With a reckless gulp of wine, Janelle scrolled through the document again, rereading some parts. "Oh, and this! These words Shakespeare says—thou art more lovely and temperate than the very Midsummer Day that thou dost pursue—I am recognizing this. Is this not a poem or something?"

"Ah, very astute of you to catch that. Yes, he writes something similar in his most famous sonnet, Sonnet 18." Valory sipped her wine, then she cleared her throat, sat up straight, and recited the poem from memory.

> "Shall I compare thee to a summer's day?
> Thou art more lovely and more temperate:
> Rough winds do shake the darling buds of May,
> And summer's lease hath all too short a date;
> Sometime too hot the eye of heaven shines,
> And often is his gold complexion dimm'd;
> And every fair from fair sometime declines,
> By chance or nature's changing course untrimm'd;
> But thy eternal summer shall not fade,
> Nor lose possession of that fair thou ow'st;
> Nor shall death brag thou wander'st in his shade,
> When in eternal lines to time thou grow'st:
>   So long as men can breathe or eyes can see,
>   So long lives this, and this gives life to thee."

Janelle, enraptured, sighed. "*C'est très beau*," she whispered. "You are memorizing this?"

"I was enamored with his work as a teenager," said Valory, warmed by a fuzzy memory of being curled up under a blanket with *The Complete Works of William Shakespeare*. "His way with language is mesmerizing."

Nodding, Janelle pointed at the translation. "So then, what means all of this? Your immortal, he is Shakespeare's subject for Sonnet 18?"

Valory shrugged again. "That might make sense. Shakespeare scholars have long theorized that his sonnets were not addressed to a mistress but to a secret male lover. We don't see that kind of sexual relationship here, but maybe the great bard was just in awe of our immortal. Hence the line, 'thy eternal summer shall not fade.'"

"Of course," drawled Janelle, seduced by the thought. The legendary bard had addressed his world-famous love sonnets not to a woman, but to an immortal man?!

Valory watched Janelle lean back in awe. The shy little art mouse had been livelier in the last ten minutes than ever. "I must say, Janelle, I didn't expect you to focus on Shakespeare. I thought you'd be asking about all the artwork Alikai says he made of Seraphina."

"Alikai?"

"Oh, right, he calls himself Aléxandros here. His name changes over the centuries. I 'met' him as Alikai. I guess it has stuck."

"Ah, yes. This is all making sense now." Janelle rose from her chair and paced around her cramped quarters. "Valory, I am noticing strange things about the artwork in this castle, but I was never sure. I am not knowing how to explain it. Now it is like, eh, smack in the face, no?"

"What is?"

Janelle returned to the laptop, leaning toward the screen. After scrolling a bit, she located a specific sentence and read it aloud. "I have fashioned her likeness in all earthly mediums a thousand times over." Then she rose, lost in thought.

"What is it?"

With a knowing smile, Janelle refilled both their wine cups and then instructed Valory to drink up. "Now," she said after Valory drained her cup, "put your coat on. Let's go."

"Go where?"

"It is my turn to share something fantastic."

SURA 23

EVERYTHING WAS STUBBORNLY LOUD: the patter of their footsteps, the swish of their clothing, their very breaths. Janelle's chamber was just down the corridor from the *Sicurezza* agents, so they had to sneak past en route to the Great Hall. Using flashlights—which they covered as they tiptoed past the agents' chamber—they skulked like fugitives, hearts pounding. In the back of her mind, Valory knew this was a stupid idea and there'd be consequences if they were caught, but her wine-soaked id was in control now.

As they ascended the spiral stairwell, a clash of thunder startled Janelle, causing her to trip and fall to her knees. She giggled, clamping her hand over her mouth. As Valory helped her stand, she began giggling as well. There they lingered for several moments, shushing each other between bouts of muffled laughter.

Setting foot in the Great Hall sobered them somewhat. Being in this antediluvian wonder while the storm raged outside reminded the ladies of their purpose. "Over here," whispered Janelle, leading Valory to the eastern wall. She waved her flashlight across the row of paintings that were angled off the wall, the chunky, gilded frames yielding a dull reflection. The varnish on the boldly colored oils had browned with time, but the artwork itself was superb. With their size and grandeur, the works reminded Valory of a wing in a metropolitan art museum. "These works here?" said Janelle, switching to French. "They were painted in the Renaissance period, yet none of them are signed." Janelle seemed to think this was an exciting fact. When it was obvious Valory was waiting for more information, she continued. "The Renaissance is when artists began to sign their works to differentiate themselves from their peers. Before that, art was a guild activity, not so much about individual creativity."

"Ah," whispered Valory, responding in French, "I think I knew that somewhere deep down. It's just a little tough to connect the dots right now if you know what I mean." The ladies suffered another giggling fit, covering their mouths as their laughter took on a life of its own. Valory was a bit annoyed with her own constant tittering. It was not appropriate or smart, and her cheeks were hurting from all the smiling. But it was fun. When was the last time she'd gotten buzzed while hanging out with a new friend? In a castle? During a storm?

"My point," whispered Janelle when they'd recovered, "my point . . . what was my point? Oh yes! My point is that these works should be signed. The artist is a master. He should have wanted to separate himself."

"He? As in one person?"

"Yes. That is what I mean." Janelle turned to Valory, her mousy features sandwiched between her beanie and scarf. "I believe that one artist made every single work in this castle!"

"What?" breathed Valory, beginning to grasp where Janelle was headed.

"Every painting, every sculpture, every tapestry, every relief. Everything. One artist." A flash of lightning from the high windows lit Janelle's face, highlighting her toothy smile.

Valory scanned the shadows of the Great Hall trying to guesstimate how many pieces were there, let alone in the rest of the castle. There had to be thousands. Though not an expert in the field, she knew that the variety of mediums and quantity of pieces were much too numerous for a single man to master and create in his lifetime. Unless it was an immortal lifetime. "This is all Alikai's work?" she whispered, running her fingers along a nearby marble courtier. "Not just the library, but . . . everything?"

"Everything. I wasn't sure until I read your translation. There was no smoking gun, you know? No signatures, no notes, no materials lists, nothing. Still, I always suspected it. His style is so unique and unified. Most of his work is dark and moody, underscored by a powerful loss and loneliness. I knew it had to be one artist, I knew it!"

Valory looked into the blank eyes of the courtier. He was an eighth or ninth-century nobleman, solemn and dignified. There was a Lombard crest on his surcoat, similar to the one on the queen's dress. "So his art is just like his written works. No signatures, no dates, no titles."

"And doesn't that make sense? Why would an immortal care about dates? I mean, if you live forever, does the calendar even matter?"

"I suppose not." Valory had wondered why Janelle didn't flinch at the idea of an immortal diarist. Now she knew—Alikai's writings had simply confirmed Janelle's pre-existing suspicions. "My god, I can't imagine living with no regard for the passage of time."

"What?" asked Janelle, puzzled.

Only then did Valory realize she'd spoken in Hindi. How had she drifted into that tongue? Resetting, she repeated herself in French.

"Same here," said Janelle. "Luckily for us, Alikai spent his days creating all this magnificent art. And can you guess his favorite subject?"

Valory stood for a moment, peering at the paintings to find a common subject. She had never really studied them closely. She'd been consumed by the library since she'd arrived. Now, shining a flashlight on them as she walked, she began to see it—the paintings were telling a story. A story about a woman. There she was, prominent in every work. Her energy leaped from the canvases. Raven-haired, smoldering eyes, fiery-willed, gorgeous. From the east wall to the south, then to the west, the paintings followed this woman from youth to womanhood, concluding in a portrait wherein she was crowned and cloaked in royal finery. Valory turned toward the marble queen who, from here, was just an enthroned shadow dusted with starlight. Everything had just fallen into place. "Seraphina," she breathed, the name riding vapor from her lips. "Of course. This is for her." She spun, gazing around the hall in new appreciation. "All of it. The castle, the art, everything here. Alikai made it all for Seraphina, the love of his immortal life."

Hearing that sentiment aloud, Janelle teared up, hands covering her mouth. Barely able to get the words out, she whispered, *"C'est tellement romantique, je pourrais juste mourir."*

At that moment, Valory experienced a blossom of pastels in her mind's eye, born from the French language, and it was beautiful. Swirling pinks and yellows and light blues fluttering with Janelle's words. It hadn't even been a profound statement. Janelle had simply said, It is so romantic, I could just die.

Valory swayed, knees growing weak, cheeks hot with the urge to mirror Janelle's tears. The wine, this starry-eyed revelation, this long-missed companionship. Together, it was an emotional bath she'd not taken in years, if ever, and it snuck up on her. She only realized she'd lowered herself into its steamy waters after she was neck deep, the heat stealing her breath. As Janelle wiped a tear, Valory did something she hadn't done to anyone in ages. She hugged her. And Janelle hugged her back. Arms pressed around each other's bulky coats, the ladies laughed and cried, tumbling down a rabbit hole of unanswerable questions. What was it like to be loved so passionately? By someone who had seen everything? Experienced everything? Who had known countless women in countless lands, only to dedicate his eternity to a single mortal woman? Somehow, Seraphina had seized the heart of a god. The mind-boggling depth of his yearning, his devotion, was glorious and heart-wrenching.

Another crack of thunder broke them from their embrace. They composed themselves, both a little embarrassed. They looked around the hall, fearful that someone may have entered while they'd been lost in the moment. "So," said Janelle after they'd straightened themselves out, "would you like me to walk you through the paintings? Interpret the story as I think Alikai intended it?"

"I would," answered Valory, "I really would. But I think I should wait."

"Really? Why?"

"Somewhere in the library, Alikai has written of his life with Seraphina. He mentions it in the tome after he meets Shakespeare. I'd like to find that story and translate it first. Just so I'm sure my interpretations aren't colored by extraneous speculation, know what I mean?"

"Ah, yes, of course."

"I'm sorry, I don't mean to say that your findings are only speculative. I just like to go into my work with as much of a blank slate as possible."

"No, I do not take offense. I like having a clean canvas, too." Janelle smiled at this, pleased with her little art pun. "But since we've come this far," she continued, whispering to the point of near silence, "let me show you the studio."

Valory, her gaze having drifted to the enthroned Seraphina, snapped back to Janelle. "What studio?"

***

As they reached the top floor, they paused on the landing to rest. Janelle leaned against the stone. Valory put her hands on her knees. The steam of their panting evaporated in the glow of their flashlights. Plodding up three flights of spiral stairs at altitude with blood full of alcohol was not the easiest task. As the fire in her legs receded, her buzz morphed into anxiety. The edges of this fuzzy little venture had just become sharper, the reality of their disobedience starker. She was slinking around in a part of the castle she'd been forbidden to enter, in cahoots with a person with whom she'd been forbidden to collaborate, while a raging storm accentuated their crime. If she were caught now, she could claim no innocence. Downstairs, there'd been an element of fun and games baked into her secret rendezvous with Janelle, but this was downright defiance. A part of her wanted to end this foray here and now. Just sneak back to her chamber and pretend it never happened. Yet Janelle was leading her farther into the frigid darkness, emboldened by wine and—to Valory's estimation—naivety. The art mouse just didn't seem to appreciate the gravity of their venture.

And you're being a coward. Violet's devil-on-the-shoulder presence said. *Everyone's asleep, you won't get caught. Besides, you're doing nothing wrong. They are wrong, their rules are wrong. You know that, sis.*

As Valory gulped the thin mountain air, she wondered if the reverse was true. If Vi—wherever she was out there in the world—ever heard Val in *her* head. A voice of reason and sanity when she was doing something stupid. Like that time she was busted driving drugs across state lines for a 'boyfriend' who didn't give a flip about her. Did she maybe stop and think for one second, *What would Val think about this? Would she do something this idiotic?*

At least I'm doing something, Vi would say, *instead of sitting at a desk reading lame-ass books all my life.*

"Shut up, Vi."

"What?" whispered Janelle.

"Nothing."

"Come on. The studio is just ahead."

The studio had a sliding wooden door suspended from rails. Janelle motioned for Valory to grasp a wrought iron handle and help her pull it open. "Slowly," she whispered. "Or it will squeal like crazy." Together the ladies leaned against the handles, opening the door just enough to squeeze inside. "*Et voila*," said Janelle, shining her flashlight into the room. "*Bienvenue dans l'atelier d'Alikai.*" Welcome to Alikai's studio.

Lightning flashed through a long row of windows, strobe-lighting the studio. Spanning the width of the keep, the vast room was crowded with artisanal workshops. Nearest the ladies, along the southern wall, was the sculpting shop. There, a semi-circle of stone pedestals rose from the floor, an oven-sized block of marble resting atop the largest pedestal. The block had been chipped away on one side as if abandoned after an hour of shaping. Hammers, chisels, and other tools were strewn about the area, and chunks of waste material laid in course heaps on the floor. Scattered around the area were assorted busts and sculptures, some beautiful, some half-finished, some damaged. Along the northern wall, built-in stone shelves held a host of other tools and materials.

A gust of wind raised a sharp howl outside the studio. Marble shale fragments crunching under her boots, Valory walked among the pedestals, removing her glove to run her fingers along the various tools. She hefted a meaty chisel, cold to the touch, and turned it about in her hand. "So this is where the magic happened."

"*Magnifique, no?*" whispered Janelle. "This is the way Doctor Moretti's team found it. Aside from the pieces I've handled, nothing has been moved for decades."

Valory thought of her father, an artist since his youth, and wished he could be here to see this. He'd flip his lid. She had not inherited his artistic ability, but being amidst the sculpting shop got her juices flowing. The urge to start chipping away at the marble, just to see what she could create, was tempting. "So do you think Alikai created his perfect Seraphina sculpture here?" She placed her fingertips on the largest stone base. "Right here on one of these pedestals?"

"After reading your research, yes," said Janelle in French, unable to express her excitement quickly enough in English. "Yes, I do." She shined her flashlight on an upended clay bust lying on the floor. "I was uncertain before that. This studio is so big and so versatile that, at first, I thought it was a shared workspace of some kind. Like a school or a retreat where artists from all over Europe would gather to learn and hone their crafts, but that seemed dubious. I couldn't shake the feeling that this was the studio of a single artist. First, because the underlying style and tone of the pieces here were so consistent. So beautiful yet tortured."

"Beautiful and tortured, just like his writing."

"Exactly. Second, the subject was usually the same." She kneeled and gently rolled the clay bust toward Valory, revealing Seraphina's face. "Now, thanks to your work, we know with certainty this is Alikai's studio. His and his alone."

Valory squatted to examine the bust. "Queen Seraphina," she whispered, running the back of her fingers along the cheek. The clay was not as smooth or flawless as the marble queen downstairs. "Why is this bust made of clay?"

"Sculptors often fashion preliminary models from clay before they transfer the design to marble. Because clay is much easier to work with, you know? If you look over there," said Janelle, shining her light toward the shelves on the northern wall, "you will find many clay models of the courtiers from downstairs. All preliminary designs. He used that defunct pulley elevator in the corner to transfer materials from the ground level."

Valory gazed at the jumbled shelves, moving her flashlight along the heaps of models, buckets, tools, and whatnot. Everything was so messy and disorganized. *Like my apartment*, thought Valory. She envisioned him rifling through the mess, grabbing this and that as he prepared to fashion his next masterpiece. Though she still had no clue what he looked like, she could imagine his somber eyes and world-weary spirit as he moved about the studio.

"Come on," said Janelle, snapping her from her vision. "Let me show you the paint shop." She led Valory farther into the studio where the starlight shone on a group of stout wooden easels and stools arranged in a row near the windows. Paint bottles, rolls of canvas, brushes, palette knives, and other tools rested in dirty piles on nearby shelves and rolling carts. Everything was flecked with careless splotches of time-darkened paint: the floors, the walls, the easels, even the glass of the windows. Along the northern wall stood a framing station with woodworking tools and lengths of frame stock. "This is where he created his paintings. I have matched the paint residue here to the paints used in the rest of the castle. As you can see," she said, gesturing toward the framing tables, "he designed his own frames as well. A master of many talents."

"Indeed, he was," said Valory, wondering if she should have said 'is' instead of 'was.' If Alikai could not die, as his diary suggested, he should still be alive, right? "It makes sense that his work is so brilliant. If you practice something for thousands of years, becoming a master is a foregone conclusion."

Valory had little time to admire the shop before Janelle scooted her along. "Come over here," she said, walking farther into the vast darkness toward the eastern wall. "Look at this textile antique. A high-warp loom."

The loom was set against the east wall, a towering wooden contraption that looked more like construction scaffolding than something upon which tapestries were woven. The frame was eight feet wide from gable to gable, spanned by a series of rollers, and it nearly reached the ceiling. Shriveled strings of fabric hung from one of the beams, and a muddle of bobbins and beaters laid in and around the frame. A simple bench stood over the treadles. Sitting there weaving on that behemoth, Alikai had probably looked like a dwarf playing a pipe organ.

"This is amazing, Janelle." Valory sat on the bench looking up at the loom. Imagined herself working the treadles and bobbins. She thought of the tapestry hanging in her chamber, which depicted people dancing, singing, and playing instruments. At its center, she recalled, was a beautiful, raven-haired woman in a white gown overseeing the festivities—Seraphina. She knew that now. Alikai had woven that tapestry on this loom, sitting right here on this bench. Yet another tribute to the love of his life. The castle and everything in it, in fact, were tributes to his marble queen. It was so obvious now that Valory felt humbled for not seeing it sooner. "How long did it take to weave a tapestry?" she asked, running her hand along one of the spanners.

"Like the ones we see here in the castle?" said Janelle, taking pleasure in sharing with a colleague. "Eight or nine months, and that's with a team of weavers. But one man, alone? Much longer. Some tapestries could have taken him years."

Valory tried to remember how many tapestries she'd seen hanging around the castle and tried to calculate the hours Alikai had spent sitting at this loom. Then she thought about the wealth of paintings, all the sculptures, all the tomes and scrolls. She couldn't begin to imagine the centuries he'd spent creating so many works. And that was just the castle's contents. The man had been alive for eons before the castle was built. Were there other locations in the world where he'd plied his many crafts? Might there be more of his artwork sitting in undiscovered locations? More books, more clay tablets in other mountaintop hideaways? Might the man himself be living in one of those places, still writing? Still sculpting Seraphina? Just how ancient was he? He couldn't have existed before the rise of Homo sapiens. His life had to have begun sometime after the onset of modern human evolution. If that were earlier rather than later, Alikai could be more than a hundred thousand years old! So when was he born? Who were his parents? Did he have siblings? How had he been conceived? Immaculate conception? Had his DNA been manipulated somehow? If so, then by whom—or what?

These were bizarre thoughts, and they led into a rabbit hole from hell. Walking herself back, Valory recalled her first impression of Alikai. After reading his first four clay tablets, she'd pegged him as possibly autistic. Now, she wasn't sure. A genius, yes. He was still that in spades, but his genius was not due to some neurological divergence that made him different

177

from 'normal' people. It was acquired. His talents, his words, his art, his tortured soul—these seemed to be natural manifestations of living forever.

A fierce gust beat upon the windows, whistling through cracks and holes in the glass. Some loose panes tapped against the stone casing, buffeted by the angry winds. The ladies exchanged nervous smiles, drawing closer to one another. Valory felt the tug of her bedchamber. The alcohol had lost its celestial charm, and cold reality was tightening its grip. They were wandering around in a frigid, storm-lashed castle in the dead of night. That was nerve-wracking enough, without the knowledge that she was violating orders.

Janelle saw Valory check her watch and took the hint. "Perhaps we're pushing our luck."

"Agreed. This is beyond fascinating, but we should probably quit while we're ahead."

"Yes," nodded Janelle. "But before we go, let me show you one more thing. I think you will enjoy it."

Leading Valory to the northern wall of the paint shop, Janelle set her flashlight on a shelf, then removed a stack of deteriorated canvas rolls from atop a chest. The size of a footlocker, the chest was bland and unimpressive. Plain oak, a flat top, no lock, carvings or décor of any kind. Kneeling into the dust cloud she'd raised, Janelle opened the lid. "Before your research, I wasn't positive of what I'd found here. Now, I believe the answer is obvious." She reached inside with both hands, carefully withdrawing two thick stacks of individual canvas sheets. Setting the stacks on the nearest table, she stepped aside and motioned for Valory to have a look, smiling.

The sheets were oil paintings, tattered, unframed and unmounted, lying atop one another like they were any old stack of paper. Valory held her flashlight over the top sheet, the cracked, centuries-old paints reflecting faded colors. The subject of the painting was a handsome young man, head turned to the left in a traditional three-quarter portrait view. His shirt was ragged, hanging loose around his shoulders. His dark blond hair was long and wavy, pulled into a slack ponytail. Strikingly, his eyes were different colors. His left was the amber of rich honey, his right, the blue of a tranquil sea. Exploring her vast and colorful language stores, Valory summoned the name for this ocular condition—heterochromia—a word that flashed like a silver spotlight in her mind. Heterochromia was rare among humans, and it gave the man a mysterious allure. At first glance, his age was difficult to determine. Although his rounded chin and soft cheekbones gave him a youthful appearance, his expression told a different story, one of inconceivable desolation. To Valory, this young man seemed to be melting with despair. Tortured. As if . . .

A shiver raced up her spine.

Gaping, she locked into those mismatched eyes, and she was empty. Her mind, so analytical, so full of thoughts and theories and languages, went dark. Her lungs froze. Her heart ceased to thump. All she could do was stare at this youth whose ancient soul was as grave as the stormy night. Janelle was speaking, but the words didn't exist. Nor did the studio—it had vanished, leaving only Valory and Alikai staring at each other in an endless tunnel. Here was the face of the immortal. The genius. The artist. The inventor of the written word. Young and ancient. Dead and alive. Beautiful.

Exhaling her long-delayed breath, she lifted the painting to look at the next canvas sheet in the stack. It too, was a portrait of Alikai. As was the next sheet, and the next, and all of them, each depicting him in different clothing and hairstyles. Janelle's voice began to fade up in her perception again. ". . . can state for certain that these are all self-portraits," she was saying in French. "Alikai must have painted one every so often. Like his other works, there are no dates. However, I've analyzed them with my spectroscope, and I know them to be from the early Renaissance onward. I'm guessing he painted one at least every year."

"Yes," whispered Valory, the word cracking in her throat. Breathing, she reset and tried again. "Yes, that makes sense. Just as he documented his life in writing, he documented his appearance through portraits. Probably hoping to see aging over time." She hoped her voice was steady because her flesh was tingling, her hands trembling as she sifted through the portraits. One showed him with a short beard. In another, he wore a hood. She wondered why Alikai had stuffed the paintings in a plain chest, hiding them away from the rest of his art as if they were just trivial nothings. If the world came to know what these were, it would be electrifying.

"Oh, this one is interesting," said Janelle as Valory came to a portrait that was more vibrant than the others. "He was in a good mood when he painted this one, I think. Possibly drunk. You can see he uses an abstract background and free-flowing brush strokes, bordering on sloppy. He is feeling quite careless here."

"And he's smiling," added Valory, looking closer. There it was—a small, enigmatic smile. Almost undetectable, but it was there, playing at the ends of Alikai's full lips. His own little *Mona Lisa* impression. And it was thrilling. All the other portraits were marked with the gloom of eternal imprisonment, making this more colorful piece downright jubilant by comparison. It warmed Valory's heart. Why had he been in a good mood that day? Of what or whom had he been thinking?

Janelle watched as Valory was absorbed by the portrait, staring at Alikai as if he were a long-lost lover. After several moments had passed, with only the sound of the wind gusting against the windows, Janelle spoke. "Um, Valory, would you like to take that portrait with you?"

"Really? Wouldn't that be against the rules?"

"Maybe, but . . ." Janelle locked her lips and threw away the key, a flash of lightning bouncing off her glasses.

अध्याय 24

SHE DREAMED OF HIM that night. Tucked away in her chamber, with the storm raging beyond the castle walls, she dreamed of Alikai.

He came in her deepest slumber when the corporeal world was farthest from her sensory grip. From the billowing hues of centuries, he emerged, reaching for her. Touching her with the rainbow vapor of time, breathing the breath of prescience upon her cheeks. His voice was a thousand voices, his words born of a thousand tongues, an intoxicating resonance of languages harmonizing throughout the meadows of eternity. Ethereal and physical, spirit and flesh, he wrapped himself around her, meeting her gaze with those beautiful, mismatched eyes. She felt him. Merged with him. For the briefest moment, they were inside one another.

Then he was gone.

She tried to stay asleep, to remain inside the dream, to follow Alikai into the nebula. But vile wakefulness was upon her, leaving her grasping at will-o'-the-wisps. In the cold darkness of her chamber, she whispered furtive pleas in all the languages of mankind, begging for his return, lusting for his heady presence for yet a while longer. Her body thrashed to make it so, and her hand worked with a fury between her legs while she imagined him within her still. But the climax of her physical body was only a consolation prize compared to his phantasmal touch.

***

Something shifted. Something subtle, yet monumental.

Something new.

He opened his eyes, but he could see nothing, nor did he wish to. The darkness was complete, the cold all-consuming. Ice crackled in his marrow. Without, the wind howled a mournful lament, its empty breath mimicking the timbre of his existence. These were the corporeal shades that frittered against the forsaken shores of his consciousness. Where he was, he did not know. How he'd gotten there, he did not remember. Even if he knew these things, it wouldn't matter. Where and when and how had long ago become meaningless notions. Soon would he perish, waifish, frostbitten, his stomach empty and frozen. Then he would live again. Where and how this unending cycle occurred—indeed, whatever happened anywhere—mattered not.

Yet this new thing stirred him, simply by the novelty of its presence. For there was nothing new in the world. Not for him. All things had he seen, had he felt, had he known through and through. All things under all the skies, millions of times over. The totality of earthly experience was ancient and monotonous. New was impossible. Yet here it was, this unique, emergent sensation. He tuned into it. Reached out with his being, melding with it. He allowed it to explore him, and he it. This vibration, this *she*, faint and soft. It fell not upon his ears, nor his skin, but upon the infinite cosmos of his soul. He was a taut string upon a lyre, and he had just been gently strummed in a whispering field of forever.

He knew.

This novel vibration, this *she* who echoed in his being—he knew what she was. How he knew was unknowable. He cared nothing for that mystery. All that mattered was the portent she heralded.

He laughed then. A joyous and terrible laugh, his cracked lips ringed by a shaggy, frost-laden beard.

Finally.

The end had begun.

KAPITOLU 25

"MR. ROCKWELL? MS. WOLFE has arrived, sir."

"Thanks, Andrew. I'll be along in a minute."

As Andrew left the room, Rockwell pulled up a banking app on his phone and sent him a generous cash gift. Tomorrow was Andrew's birthday. The soon-to-be twenty-eight-year-old was a bit of an oddball, but he'd been Rockwell's personal assistant for four years. What he lacked in confidence, he made up for in unquestioning diligence.

After the money was sent, a notification chimed. Rockwell opened his home security app and pulled up the video of Angela Wolfe arriving at the guard station moments earlier. Zooming into the frame, he observed her facial expressions as she interacted with the guard. Saw her shoulders lifted toward her ears. Noted her forward position at the wheel of her Lexus, an aggressive posture that said *I'm nervous but in control*. He watched the tightness of her jaw as she said, "Angela Wolfe from *America Tonight*, here to interview Mr. Rockwell," with all the charm of a drill sergeant. This woman was not here to lob softballs at the superstar entrepreneur. She was out for blood.

"Thomas, honey," said Debbie with playful annoyance, "I can't do this if you keep looking down."

"Of course, sweetness." Rockwell set the phone down, jutted his chin up, and pulled his mock turtleneck collar down. "Have at it."

"Thank you." Deb dabbed at his throat with her make-up sponge, concealing the blacks and greens of his ghastly bruise. "Ach, this is so gross. I really wish you'd take it easy with that sparring of yours. You could get seriously hurt."

"I just want to be able to protect the most important people in my life," said Rockwell, appreciating her with his eyes. It was a practiced look, designed to charm. The lingering hoarseness of his voice did not temper his allure.

"That's so sweet, honey, but maybe just let the bodyguards protect us? I don't like seeing my handsome fiancé all beaten up." When she was satisfied that his throat looked as good as it was going to, she pulled the turtleneck up and adjusted it into place. By itself, the collar hid the wound almost fully.

The concealer was just in case the fabric got pulled down unexpectedly. "There we have it," she said, dusting his shoulders. "Good as new."

Rockwell rose from his desk and went to the mirror. Tilted his head this way and that. Deb had done a fine job. Even where the edge of the bruise peeked over the neckline, he could not see it. The make-up hid the discoloration and blended perfectly with his skin. "Just look at that," he said. "You can't even tell. Reason number five thousand I can't wait to marry you."

"What would you do without me?" Deb pulled a bottle of Fraser Fir from her bag and removed the cap. "Here's the cologne you asked for," she said, shooting a test spray into the air and giving it a sniff. "I still don't know why you wanted this one. You've never worn it before. And it's cheap. You suddenly on a budget?"

"Just thought I'd try something new. Come on, hit me."

As Deb sprayed him with the cologne, Rockwell 'helped' her by doing a playful little dance into the mist, as if the scent was making him come alive. "Oh, yeah, Tommy likes that."

"Ooh, nice moves there, Tommy."

"Get a good look, sweetness. You're the only one who gets to see them."

"I'm so privileged."

"Help me with my jacket?"

She helped him put his blazer on, and then she wrapped her arms around him from behind, looking at his reflection and admiring the way the royal blue mock turtleneck matched his eyes. She stood on her tiptoes and kissed his cheek, then wiped her lipstick away with her thumb. "You're all set. Go get 'em, tiger."

"Come with me. I want them to meet you."

Deb resisted at first, as he expected. The limelight was not her thing. But he pulled her gently along—with his smile as much as his hand—and she caved. He knew she would. Deborah Kristiansen was an easy read. She was one of the most wholesome, honest, and giving people he'd ever met. A caring and empathic soul whose avowed purpose was to Do Good. She volunteered her time with hospice patients, underprivileged youths, and relief shelters, and that was just for starters. Her philanthropic schedule was as busy as Rockwell's calendar, the difference being that she never sought attention or compensation. She did what she did because it was good. She was the perfect fit for his long-term plans.

Before Deb, Rockwell's voracious sexual appetite had been driven by a desire to bed the best of the best. The hottest celebrities. The trophy wives of his rivals. Random women he'd see in public, even (especially) when they were with dates. Many Saturday nights had ended with him pouring champagne over naked, writhing supermodels. Deb was his first 'real' woman. Not a fantasy of flesh or power, but a beacon of purity. Perhaps she was not the most attractive woman in the world, but pretty enough. Long, light blonde hair, warm green eyes, hourglass hips on a slender frame. Yes, she was pretty, but it was when you spoke with her that her true beauty shone. In live conversation, no matter who you were, she engaged with you. Cared about what you said, what you felt. Complimented your strengths and your passions. Encouraged you and offered help if you were down. Interacting with her was the verbal equivalent of a Swedish body massage. When you experienced her in that way, when you felt her angelic charms up close and personal, you experienced true human resplendence. Deb was the rarest of souls, and she had fallen in love with Thomas Rockwell. It was not by chance. Sometimes, he felt bad about what he was doing to her.

Together they walked down the hall, chatting as they descended one of two sweeping staircases. Rockwell's mansion was neomodern and white, clean and glossy, peppered with paintings, sculptures, and Murano glass chandeliers. Deb had begun to add her own touch, replacing some of the more masculine décor with bright and welcoming pieces. After all, this was going to be her home, too, once they married.

They crossed the ivory great room, passing through fifteen-foot-tall vanishing glass doors that opened into a breathtaking veranda replete with artisanal furniture and an illuminated bar. There they joined a small sea of people who were preparing for the interview. *America Tonight* did not conduct live on-location interviews of this nature, but Rockwell had declined to travel to the studio in Manhattan, citing a packed schedule. His business dealings left him scant time to spare, thus he could only facilitate the interview at his home on this day at this hour. Being the ratings cow that he was, *AT* agreed to come to him. This was all his design.

The camera crew had arrived several hours prior and had already set up for the shoot on the veranda. To the puzzlement of the crew, their director, John, had agreed to Rockwell's set requests. Strange. As a rule, directors did not take stage direction from the interviewee. Yet, after speaking with Rockwell, John ordered the crew to face the cameras west toward the hilly California coastline and to abstain from additional lighting. To the crew, this setup was far from optimal. For Rockwell, it was perfect. During the interview, the sun would be setting toward those hills, creating a dusky backdrop with the sky playing on the infinity pool behind Rockwell's chair. Through methodical experimentation, Rockwell knew that if you were in that specific chair at that specific time of the day, the reflection off the glass doors bathed you in a subtle glow. A soft, fuzzy illumination. The other chair, where Angela Wolfe would be sitting, didn't quite catch the same angle. When the interview started, Rockwell and Wolfe would be lit equally by the same light. Then, as the sinking sun dashed the California skyline with swaths of pink and yellow, Wolfe would dim while Rockwell would take on a faint, subliminal radiance. His smile would dazzle. His eyes would pop like sapphires. All live, all premeditated.

Rockwell made it a point to introduce Deb to the *AT* crew. She didn't know it yet, but he had big plans for her. It was time for her to start learning how to be around the media, how to interact with them. He did not coach her—didn't need to. He knew as she became more comfortable in their presence, her natural golden demeanor would begin to flow. After exposing her to a few such situations, her reticence would vanish, and she'd start beguiling the press in the manner he always intended—First Lady-like. Together, they would be Thomas and Deborah Rockwell, the world's most recognizable philanthropic couple, a force of good for humankind.

Rockwell was a gracious host, making it a point to greet each member of the crew personally. He poured a glass of iced tea for the boom mic operator. He complimented the assistant cameraman on his shoes, a vintage pair of Air Jordans. He helped the imaging tech bundle a heap of wires. To each of them, he asked, "Have you met my fiancée, Deb?" and he introduced them. The crew members were flabbergasted. They'd interviewed big people before—presidents, secretaries of state, even royalty—but those people never acknowledged them. The crew was the lamppost in the corner. Now, though, this superstar business titan was engaging with them on a personal level, treating them as equals.

As Rockwell deftly managed the crew, he reached out to Angela Wolfe. He'd been stealing glances at her as she sat near the illuminated bar being prepped for the camera. Mid-thirties, fit, dirty blonde hair, hawkish features. She was studying a binder of notes, her demeanor dead serious. He reached out to her not with his hand, but with his mind.

A couple of weeks ago, he had never heard of Wolfe. She had only joined *America Tonight* last year, having previously worked as an investigative journalist for a Chicago-based media company. In that role, she'd exposed a multimillion-dollar insurance scam backed by a trio of corrupt local politicians. She had impressed some important people with that story, and now she was here on the big stage. Interviewing Rockwell was to be her big splash. Her *Here I am, world!* moment which would catapult her into the mainstream. She was determined to take full advantage. Her focus was like a lighthouse beacon—bright, intense, unwavering. That focus, however, was only surface noise. Though it gave her a loud, heated aura, it had no substance. No primal scent. No honesty. It was the comfort blanket under which people shielded themselves from the hardest truths. It proved no obstacle to Rockwell. He crept under the blanket like a spider into a sleeping bag.

As he invaded Wolfe, that familiar ecstasy set in. A feeling of whizzing through hyperspace, titillated by the energy of a million passing stars. There was nothing more intimate than exploring a person's essence. Their soul, their subconscious, whatever one wished to call it. He preferred essence. To him, essence was an ether upon which all life was woven, existing beyond the perception of physical senses. In the depths of a person's essence was written the story of her life. All the memories, all the secrets, all the pits and summits of her existence, naked and exposed to Rockwell. To him and him alone. As far as he knew, he was the only person in the world with this ability.

Wolfe's essence was layered and convoluted. Most people were like that, splashed with a myriad of colors and aromas born of their life experiences. The types of tentpole memories everyone possessed. Fond reflections of childhood swirling in careless yellows and greens. Sharp, pungent moments of teenage embarrassment streaking in shades of violet. The hot pink cyclone of a tepid love affair racing and frolicking. If Rockwell wished, he could focus on one color, one scent, one thread, and from those he could reconstruct memories from Wolfe's past. He did not experience these sensations through any corporeal means. They were just *extant*. Filaments in his mind revealing the vibrant fabric of her life. He was not interested in her brighter moments, though. What he sought was the dark substratum of Wolfe's essence, wherein lurked her long-banished traumas. Traumas that she no longer remembered in her day-to-day awareness, but which still pulled her strings like an unseen puppet master. Everyone retained such traumas, but most people buried them deep into mental voids, hoping never to confront them again. Over the years, Rockwell had become adept at diving into those voids and coaxing out the devils like a clam diver harvesting pearls.

In Wolfe, he didn't have to search long. As he explored her, he registered a faint, foul scent lurking beneath a childhood haze. As if clearing a layer of fallen leaves from a forest floor, he swept her brighter memories aside until the foul scent was exposed. He grabbed onto this sapor like a rope he'd discovered under the leaves, and he followed it into the forest, pulling it up from the brush under which it had been concealed. Deeper he went, Wolfe's innocent youth fading into a darker, murkier essence. There was a bitter taste there as if Rockwell had bitten into old black licorice. That's when he knew he'd found it. Savoring the sensations, he explored this dark sliver of Wolfe's childhood, listening, watching, feeling. Within seconds, he'd harvested everything he needed.

***

She watched him. Making his rounds among the crew, introducing his wife to everyone, smiling, laughing, complimenting. Being effortlessly cool and gracious. She'd heard that about him—that he was a genuine people person who you couldn't help but like—but that perception was likely a subterfuge. Self-made gazillionaires like Thomas Rockwell didn't achieve such dizzying success by being nice. Many high-powered CEOs and politicians met the clinical definition of a psychopath. They lusted for power and behaved like absolute fascists in attaining it. For that type of person, relationships with other people were transactional in nature. If you couldn't help them rise to glory, you were discarded. Yet, necessity had taught these people to disguise their ruthless behavior beneath a veneer of charm and charisma. That was Rockwell. Wolfe was certain he was much dirtier than his squeaky-clean public image suggested. Well, not *certain*, but she had dug deep enough to know that he was not the angel he pretended to be. The main topic of tonight's interview was Operation Uni-Fi, Rockwell's ambitious plan to provide free satellite-based internet access to the entire world. A noble and seemingly impossible cause, and symbolic of most of his efforts, but how would he react when she mentioned the names Jonas Krause and Misty Givens? Both had recently died. Both had ties to Rockwell, one professionally, one romantically. They were distant ties, true. There was no proof he was involved in their deaths, and Wolfe knew she was just chasing a risky hunch. But while investigating his past, she had discovered a long list of corpses in Rockwell's wake. Nothing sticky. Nothing solid tying him to anything, but her gut instinct was hot with certainty. This guy was as dirty as they came, and he was damn good at hiding it. She couldn't stand rich megalomaniacs who treated the lives of others like disposable commodities. Her goal was to become known as the fearless woman who took down those kinds of assholes. So, sure, she'd make the network happy and interview Rockwell about Uni-Fi, but if (when) the names Krause and Givens slipped into the conversation on live TV, so be it.

Rockwell looked at her, then he broke from the group and began walking over. Wolfe steeled herself. No doubt he was about to lay on the charm, but she would not let him push her off her game. She rose and put her binder down as he approached.

"Ms. Wolfe, hello. Such a pleasure to finally meet you." Rockwell's voice, deep and purring, resonated along her skin. He took her hand, enveloping it in both of his. His palms were warm like he'd been holding them over a campfire.

"The privilege is mine, Mr. Rockwell. And please just call me Angela."

"Alright, Angela. And I'm just Tom."

"Okay, Tom. Thank you for inviting me into your home today. It is quite stunning."

"Thank you. Hey," he said, his baritone dropping to a whisper, "want to know a little secret?"

"Sure."

Rockwell glanced around, then leaned in close. "I drew up a rudimentary blueprint for this house as a kid while I was living in a group home."

"Really?"

"Mm hm. I felt lonely and isolated there. So one of my little hobbies was hiding in the closet with a flashlight drawing up master plans for the big shiny mansion I would build one day," he chuckled. "I never expected to fulfill that dream. I count that blessing every day."

Wolfe was taken off guard. The thought of an unloved orphan doodling his dream house alone in a dark closet was not something she'd been expecting to confront while speaking with Thomas Rockwell. It hit an unfamiliar nerve. Still, she couldn't let it affect her process. This mission required a hard heart. "Well, I knew you were a lot of things, Tom, but I didn't know you were an architect."

Rockwell laughed, delight frothing in his ocean-blue smile. "Hey, don't tell that to my actual architect, okay? I think he'd rather flee the country than work for me again." He mimicked a little boy's voice, "Hey, mister, I said I wanted a basketball court in my living room! Get it right!"

Wolfe returned the laugh and then wished she hadn't. She could not allow herself to like this guy. "So, um, Tom, since we still have a few minutes, shall we go over a few talking points before the interview?"

"Absolutely. But before that," he said, growing earnest, "I just want to say that I'm very impressed by what you did in Chicago, Angela. And I'm so glad I have a chance to thank you face to face."

"Thank me? Why?"

"Well, I'll tell you," said Rockwell, pouring her a glass of water from a nearby pitcher. "Back in my mid-twenties, I very suddenly found myself in a situation where I had a whole lot of money but no idea what to do with it."

"You're referring to the initial fortune you made mining Bitcoin?"

"You've done your homework. I like that. Yes, I was one of those first dweebs who took a chance on Bitcoin when it was worth mere pennies. Man," he said, shaking his head, "that was only about eleven years ago, but it feels like a hundred."

"Well, the gamble obviously paid off."

"That's what I'm getting at. There I was, this lucky Marine who had no idea how business worked. All I knew was that I wanted to use that newfound wealth to make the world a better place. So I dove in head first, partnering up with whoever would listen to me. I stalked a lot of CEOs back then, pitching some ambitious ideas at them while they wondered aloud how I'd gotten in the door." He laughed, shaking his head. "Long story short, I made a few good decisions, but it was my *bad* ones . . ." Rockwell exhaled as if he'd sidestepped a catastrophe, "my bad decisions almost cost me everything. I learned the hard way that business and politics are saturated with bad actors who will do anything to make a little more money or gain a little more power. They'd steal bibles from a nun if they thought it gave them an edge." He pointed at her. "That's why you're special. That insurance scam in Chicago was a nasty bit of business that destroyed people's lives." He placed his hand over his heart. "I fell prey to my share of such scams. I know how devastating they are for the victims. But you put in the tireless work to expose those guys, and for that, I sincerely admire you. I only wish I'd had you on my side in those early years."

Wolfe felt her resolve wavering. She'd come here ready to make this man squirm on live TV. Take him down a notch. Bring an internet shitstorm to his proverbial doorstep. Now here she was holding back tears, and she couldn't quite understand why. Usually, she was immune to flattery and flowery language—that was part of the job—but somehow, he was getting to her. "That's very kind of you to say, thank you."

"Hey," he said, cupping her shoulders, "you're the best at what you do, and this world is better for it. I don't know if you need to hear this or not, but . . . I'm very proud of you, Angie."

***

She was now his.

She didn't know it yet. In Angela Wolfe's rational mind, she'd only shared a brief, personable conversation with Thomas Rockwell. A little sappy, but nothing too out of the ordinary. What she didn't know was that she'd just been gently mindfucked.

Wolfe's hard-as-nails attitude had begun to crack the second Rockwell came near. Before he'd even spoken to her, she'd smelled his cologne. The Frasier Fir Deb had sprayed on him minutes before. The cologne Wolfe's father wore. As Rockwell shook her hand, he saw her nostrils flare as she detected its strong, piney scent. Though she gave the scent no conscious thought, her essence had been suckered. The olfactory sense—the sense of smell—was a direct line to the essence, bypassing all logic and activating the oldest and most meaningful memories. When Wolfe had smelled that pine, she'd instantly associated Rockwell with her father.

Next, Rockwell told had her a 'secret.' A deeply personal story about himself in the group home. Then he'd talked about his scrappy naivety and bad decisions in his early career. This hadn't been idle chat, but deliberate incisions of dark psychology. Telling secrets about oneself and revealing character flaws—underscored with humor—gave a sense of relatability and genuineness. Rockwell had told those anecdotes to erode her fiery hot focus.

He'd gone on to lavish Wolfe with praise for her achievement in Chicago. He acknowledged how hard she'd worked and explained how valuable that work had been for him personally. That was bullshit, just more psychology. He'd simply played the part of the rich, famous man delivering soul-affirming praise to someone who had no clue how desperately she needed to hear it.

190

That had led Rockwell to her emotional jugular. After he invoked the thought of her father, after he shared his personal failings, and after he praised her valuable work, he made physical contact and said the words: *I'm very proud of you, Angie.* That was the moment she cracked.

Angela was the seventh of eight children born to William and Kara Wolfe. Six boys, two girls. Rockwell knew this from the report given to him by his private intel team. The same team that had dug up William's entire life and discovered which cologne he preferred, among other data. Rockwell didn't need the report, though, for Wolfe's essence conveyed a much more complete picture. As he'd delved into her mind, focusing on its deepest, darkest pits, he tapped into her early memories. He saw it all. A house full of siblings, loud and rambunctious. Everyone competing for everything: food, clothes, privacy, the best grades, the highest achievements. And the most coveted prize of all—attention from Mom and Dad. But the parents were always busy, and there was never enough love to go around. It was a mock survival situation, and poor Angie was the runt of the litter. The bonds she craved were constantly yanked from her tiny hands, for she was always trumped by her louder, more demanding, more ruthless siblings. Years upon years of inattention, bordering on neglect, piling up in her psyche, settling in her essence like layers of sediment. Writing a sad, empty story that would go on to seed the entirety of her life. In a way, she'd been an orphan, too. Just once, Angela wanted her daddy to tell her what he'd told the boys. Just once, she wanted to sit in his lap, smelling that spicy, pine-scented cologne, and she wanted him to put his arms around her and say the words he'd said to Mark and Jacob and Toby, but never to her. Those unspoken words looking for a voice in the mists of her essence: *I'm very proud of you, Angie.*

* * *

At first, Wolfe made a valiant mental effort to stick to her plan. To ask the tough questions, to shed light on some of Rockwell's morally questionable business maneuvers. To talk about Jonas Krause and Misty Givens so she could make Rockwell flounder live in front of America. Those questions were there during the interview, burning the tip of her tongue, but for some reason, she couldn't pull the trigger. It just didn't feel right anymore. As they discussed Operation Uni-Fi, her image of Rockwell as a conniving megalomaniac began to feel silly. Sitting across from her smiling, joking around, talking about his fiancée and his future aspirations for a family—he was so genuine. He'd even called Deb into the shot so he could show her off to the nation. The guy just seemed like a boy scout, as did his fiancée, who was obviously a wonderful person. So why had she ever been so angry with him? How had she conjured such an evil image of this good-

191

hearted man? Perhaps she needed to take a step back and examine her investigative biases.

She left Rockwell's house with a smile on her face. The segment was a hit. *America Tonight's* social feeds had been blowing up since the interview started, and early sentiment suggested a roaring success. The name Angela Wolfe was being spoken all over the nation. Sure, she'd bottled that killer instinct, but still, she'd achieved exactly what she wanted.

NDZIMA YA 26

ROCKWELL WENT INTO HIS garage, flicking the switch to the door lift. As the hangar-like doors rumbled open, he strode past his silver luxury bus. Then past the Rolls Royce, the Ferrari, and the Hennessey Velociraptor, finally climbing into a modest golf cart. He set his phone and a rifle case in the passenger seat, then he drove into the California night, winding his way along the expansive palm-lined driveway before exiting the security gate and turning onto a gravel path leading into the hills. It was a breezy evening. The dark, rolling hills twinkled with the house lights of distant, wealthy neighbors. The wind felt cool rushing against his skin, along his face, through his hair. He enjoyed the moment. These days, he was seldom alone, and he found precious little peace and quiet. This little jaunt down the hill, surrounded by nothing but stars and the chirping of crickets, was surreal in its rareness. It helped to focus him and prepare him for this next task.

His destination was a house a couple of miles down the hillside. It was a property he owned. Not outright, but through a specialized REIT managed by a small investment firm underwritten by a subsidiary of Rockwell Industries. Rockwell had set up the deed so as not to tie himself to the house. No one needed to know he owned it, not even his future wife. That's because a dead man lived there.

Gravel crunching under the tires, he soaked in the night until his phone vibrated again. It had been blowing up after the interview. Business colleagues and political allies calling to congratulate him, to suck up to him. Even Angela Wolfe texted him, thanking him for the opportunity and for trusting her with his personal number. He answered that text, knowing it would strengthen their new connection.

Grabbing the phone, Rockwell dismissed the many notifications and pulled up trending recaps of his interview. As he drove, he played a highlight video that had just been posted. There he was on the veranda, bathed by a twilight backdrop, the reflection in his infinity pool doubling the illusion. Wolfe was talking about the nation's perception of him as a modern-day Renaissance man, giving a brief recap of his career. After his military service and his beginnings as a Bitcoin miner, he'd flourished at a torrid pace, launching or investing in a plethora of global endeavors. First, he'd expanded his Bitcoin operations, setting up renewable energy mining farms in several countries. At the same time, he'd launched Flex, a fintech company that bridged payment channels between traditional currencies and cryptocurrencies, like PayPal on steroids. From there he'd branched into a bevy of other projects. Some were practical, like Faraday, his company in Berlin which supplied specialized software and batteries to the burgeoning European electric automobile market. Others seemed kooky, like Aeternus, an anti-aging genetics lab with the stated goal of 'solving death.' Perhaps most eyebrow-raising of all, said Wolfe, was Operation Uni-Fi, his effort to gift free high-speed internet to every citizen of Earth. How could he expect to pull off such a costly and impossible task? He was already facing a bevy of lawsuits from infrastructure and service providers even as he worked toward a beta launch next year. Was he really expecting to succeed? How would it all work?

Rockwell answered with his signature laid-back enthusiasm. The genius Nikolai Tesla, he said, had had a dream to provide free wireless energy to the world. He'd been smart and determined enough to succeed, but the powers that be would not hear of it. Those early industry titans wanted to enrich themselves by metering energy usage to the people, thus they conspired against Tesla. Using their vast power and resources, they rendered him penniless, his dream forgotten. Today, everyone paid a monthly bill for something that had evolved into a basic human need, and this was as wrong as paying for oxygen. But, said Rockwell, he would succeed where Tesla failed. The internet was the singular most revolutionary invention since electricity, and the next logical step was to take it into space, where a fleet of satellites could deliver internet to every part of the globe, even those parts that were without service now: third-world countries, far-flung settlements, poor communities, etcetera. The internet, he argued, had become ubiquitous with human rights, and he would disrupt the establishment in whatever way he needed to deliver it. Legacy providers, he said, would do well to join his team instead of fighting him.

"But who will pay for these satellites?" asked Wolfe. "Won't it cost billions to provide a free service of that magnitude?"

He answered that he and a consortium of venture capitalists were footing the initial costs and that the rollout would proceed in manageable stages. Later, once Uni-Fi was in full swing, the satellite network would be monetized in various, innovative ways. Average consumers, though, will never have to spend a dime if they choose not to.

How was he going to get past the legacy providers? They were already piling up lawsuits in efforts to block Rockwell at every turn.

"To answer that," said Rockwell, "I would tell the American people that if they support my vision of free internet for all, and if they don't want to see it buried like Tesla's noble dream, the best thing they can do is to go out this

194

November and vote for Senator Kirk for President of the United States. Kirk is the visionary we need, not just because he supports Uni-Fi, but because he has real, actionable plans to address the unprecedented issues plaguing our great country."

Rockwell turned the phone off, refocusing on the winding gravel path. He wasn't sure if he liked that last line. Sounded hacky. He'd have to workshop something better. Something more subtle. The important thing was he'd nailed the interview, and now Wolfe was butter melting in his hands. A determined enemy was now in his corner. That was his gift.

It hadn't always been so easy. Rockwell had wrestled with his gift for many years before honing it into the manipulative tool it was today. While growing up as an orphan, his extraordinary ability had been nothing but a curse. He hadn't understood it. Hadn't known what it was, nor why he was the only one who possessed it. He was called Thomas Kerry back then, born to Melody Kerry and Joseph Smith, an unmarried pair of nobodies. Melody, a waitress and want-to-be actress suffered a prolonged death after giving birth to Thomas. Joseph was a troubled drifter with no education or job. There weren't many details about them or their relationship. By all accounts, they'd only had a brief fling, conceiving the future bastard Thomas Kerry before parting ways. When Joseph later learned that Melody had died after giving birth to his son, he committed suicide rather than face that responsibility. They found him with enough heroin in his blood to kill two men. Young Thomas had not been told that story by his group home carers. He only uncovered it years later after doing some research as a teen. He changed his name to Rockwell soon after.

In his formative years in the group home, little Tommy didn't know he was different. Certainly, his carers noticed he was prone to saying strange things, but anything coming from the mouth of a five-year-old could be written off as the fancy of an innocent and active imagination.

Miss Gardner, why are you all purple?

Miss Garcia, how come you smell like rubber?

Miss Perry, you look like you're wearing a hat made of rainbows.

One question caused the soft-spoken Miss Perry to stop and stare at Tommy in befuddlement—*Why is your hair so loud?* he'd asked her. That was how he experienced adults back then. They abounded with colors and scents and noises, constantly shifting, waxing and waning. Sometimes these sensations were meek and unintrusive, but sometimes they were so intense that Tommy had to squeeze his eyes shut and clamp his hands over his ears to keep his head from hurting. The other orphans, though loud and rambunctious, emanated a more singular aura. They were just bright like there were light bulbs inside their ears.

The real problems began when Tommy got a little older. At the age of eight or nine, he started to realize there were hidden treasures in all those colors and scents and noises. He found that if he stopped and remained quiet, and if he focused on those sensations, they would begin to form fun little images. He didn't see these images with his eyes but with something else. Something inside him, like an eye *behind* his eyes. It was weird. He was never able to explain it to people. When he tried, bad things had happened. Like the time he'd been living with his second set of foster parents, Mark and Lucy Abberton. One evening, when Lucy was reading him a bedtime story, he stopped listening, instead focusing on the pinwheel of swirly colors emanating from within her head. To his surprise, he began to experience a scent like rotten eggs. This odor led him to swaths of darker colors, and he watched as they melded with her normal blues, greens and yellows. This new, tangled palette coalesced and morphed into the image of a pale white man with green eyes. The man's pants were down, and he was guiding little Lucy's hand toward his privates. Tommy heard the man's voice in the image but couldn't make out the words. It was all muffled like he was speaking underwater.

"What is the man saying to you, Miss Lucy?"

"What man, honey?" Lucy asked, setting the book aside.

"The man with the green eyes," he answered as if Lucy should know who he was talking about. "I can't hear what he's saying."

Miss Lucy smiled, patting him on the leg. "Who do you mean? There's no one here besides us."

"No, not right now! I mean when you were a little girl. When the man with the green eyes put your hand on his thingy. What is he saying?"

Well. That went poorly. Miss Lucy's aura turned pitch black as she gaped at Tommy. Then she fled to her bedroom and locked herself in. When Mr. Mark came home later, he and Miss Lucy spent the rest of the night arguing. There was lots of crying and confusion. Lots of perturbed glances at Tommy. He was at a loss. He knew he'd done something to upset Miss Lucy, but what? No one would explain. In the following days, the Abbertons became distant, leaving Tommy to wonder yet again why people didn't like being around him. A few weeks later, he was shipped to a new set of foster parents.

As he passed through a handful of foster homes over the next few years, he came to understand that no one—not one single person anywhere—could see the colors. They couldn't smell the smells, couldn't see the images, couldn't hear the sounds. Why not? Did it mean he was some kind of freak? If he tried explaining his gift to anyone, they looked at him like he was crazy. But the sensations kept happening. Kept getting stronger. More tactile, more defined. By the time he was an adolescent, everyone around him had become a walking pile of open books, exporting the stories of their lives through a kaleidoscope of sensations that only he could experience. It wasn't pleasant. Everywhere went, it was like people's minds were screaming at him, drowning him in gushing rivers of their own humanity. There was no one with whom he could talk about it. No one to explain, no one to make sense of this frightening thing that was happening to him. If only he'd had a mentor. Someone to teach him how to relax, to meditate, to focus. To block out the noise and home in on individual slivers rather than being bombarded by full essence. He'd had to slowly figure it out, all on his own. Even today, he didn't feel he'd reached the full potential of his gift. If he'd had a guide when he was young and struggling, there's no telling how powerful he'd be today.

Rockwell pulled into the back patio of the house and grabbed the rifle case from the seat. This house was modest compared to his polished citadel of a mansion. It was a five-bedroom Mediterranean-style property with a red tile roof, typical of the region. There were no cars in the drive, no décor in the yard, no lights in the windows. Nothing that would give a passerby any clue about who lived there. The outdoor patio light was on, but only because it had an automatic sensor. Walking past the heated pool, he arrived at the carved double doors but stopped short of inserting his key. Instead, he tried the handle. Yep, unlocked. Shaking his head, he entered.

He didn't turn on the lights. There was no need. He knew that if he looked, he'd see a couch that hadn't been sat on, a TV that had never been plugged in, and a bedroom that had seldom been slept in. Were it not for the weekly cleaning crew, there'd be a layer of dust over everything. Walking through the dark, Rockwell made his way down the hall, descended into the basement, and came to a magnetized door in the corner. He stood before the facial recognition pad and then entered when he heard the click. Beyond the door, a set of stairs led into a custom-built subterranean complex.

He emerged into an underground firing range. Walking through the control corridor, he glanced down the darkened lanes, noting their cleanliness. Much different than the last time he'd been here. Even the bullet traps had been cleared. Nice and tidy.

Beyond the firing range was an armory, the north and west walls chocked full of knives, swords, pistols, machine guns, and assault rifles. The east wall held the fun stuff: a rocket launcher, a grenade launcher, a flame thrower, even a six-barrel Vulcan cannon. The room smelled like oily bullets.

Passing through the armory, Rockwell opened the far door and stood on the threshold, looking into the dojo. Cavernous and airy, the dojo was lit only by shielded candles lining the walls, causing a dance of shadows upon every surface. Cervantes sat alone in the center of the floor. He was in lotus, his back to the door, wearing a plain t-shirt and billowy black pants. He didn't acknowledge Rockwell's entry. Rockwell set his rifle case down, put his heels together, and bowed. Then he removed his Derbies and walked across the tatami, sitting to the left of Cervantes. Placing his hands on his knees, he assumed lotus and began to focus on his breathing. Together, in the flickering darkness, they meditated.

Dominic Cervantes was legally dead. A tragic case. Shunned Marine with PTSD covers himself in thermite and sets himself ablaze in an abandoned building, leaving his dog tags, a box of personal memorabilia, and a short note near the remains. The authorities searched his computer afterward, finding the search phrases *What is the hottest burning substance* and *How to make thermite*. It was an open-and-shut case. But the corpse—just a crumbling husk of powder after being consumed by thermite—was not Cervantes. It was just some bum who'd been plucked from the streets.

His 'death' had not been critical to the plan. More of a symbolic procedure. 'Killing off' the old Cervantes was a way of ensuring that his new life belonged to Rockwell. To the Salvador.

Rockwell inhaled until his lungs were full, then released in a slow, deliberate breath. He repeated this until the external world melted away, his mind quieting. It felt good to meditate again. It had been too long since he'd had the opportunity to resharpen his focus. Meditation was the tool he'd used to grow into his gift long ago as he transitioned to manhood. By silencing his fears, his questions, his confusion. By abandoning his primal lizard brain and connecting with his higher self. In blocking the grimy baggage of his own humanity, he had learned to decipher the language of divinity—the all-revealing essence. With continual meditation and practice, he'd evolved into something more than human. Here and now, however, he did not let himself sink into the pillowy oneness of introspection. Not fully. That was because of the man sitting next to him.

Cervantes was his brother. Not by blood, but by *something* else. A strange, metaphysical connection that Rockwell had never been able to put his finger on. The two of them had been born in the same California hospital, minutes apart, to different parents. Yet they had only met many years later when they'd each needed what only the other could provide. That was not just some quirky coincidence. There was a meaning behind it, Rockwell had always been sure of that. For, like himself, Cervantes was something more than human. The import of their connection would someday make itself known. Someday soon. Even so, he had never been at ease with Cervantes. Though they were 'brothers,' Rockwell was unable to relax in his presence. He always maintained an edge of awareness. A hint of frostiness. Why?

Because Dominic Cervantes was one scary motherfucker.

In Rockwell's entire life, he had never experienced an essence like his. Most people flowed with color and sound, with aroma and life, emanating an aurora borealis of human emotion. Not Cervantes. He was black. Just black. When Rockwell focused on him, there was no light, no sound, no life. Just an all-consuming darkness, wretched and foul. And his odor. That disgusting stench, pungent and overwhelming. Rockwell could withstand these sensations when he had to, but if he focused on Cervantes too long, that dark void would settle into his own essence, taking root, slinking into his soul. Its vileness was enough to make Rockwell gag. That had happened once on their first tour in Afghanistan. There, in the barracks, Rockwell was practicing his gift, delving one by one into the minds of his fellow Marines as they put away personal items and organized footlockers. In the essences of these men, he saw the typical things: wives they'd left behind, fears they'd yet to confront, joys they'd cherish forever. When he came to Cervantes, sitting there on his bed staring at nothing, something new happened. Tuning into him, he felt a rush of putrefaction, like he was being blasted by a hot wind sweeping down from a mountain of three-day-old corpses. The funk was thick enough to chew. He leaned over and puked on the side of his bed. Some of the other Marines turned to him, asking if he was alright, offering him water, but all he could see was Cervantes' dark eyes staring at him from behind a shroud of soul-rot.

"Have you come to spar?"

The words startled Rockwell. He'd thought Cervantes to still be deep in mediation. It irked him to be caught off-guard—Cervantes was the only man on Earth who could do that. "I have not."

"You should," replied Cervantes, still in lotus, eyes closed. "Your technique on the bus was sloppy. You're getting soft."

"Thanks for the reminder. But I just don't have the time right now."

"Then you've come to tell me you're leaving."

"I have. Tomorrow. I'll be gone for about a month." Rockwell didn't elaborate. He knew Cervantes didn't care. Didn't like to clutter his brain with non-actionable information. Sometimes, Rockwell wished he could live as black and white as that, but destiny was a harsh mistress. Tomorrow would kick off a whirlwind international business trip. First, to Pennsylvania to meet with Senator Kirk and his campaign team. Rockwell had not been pleased with the campaign's strategy in recent weeks. An intervention was overdue. After that, a two-day stint in Jackson Hole for an economic symposium. The SEC chairman, George Boseman, was delivering the keynote address regarding the administration's stance on the parabolic rise of cryptocurrencies. This new type of digital money was decentralized in nature (by the people, for the people) and was therefore resistant to governmental control. As such, Boseman and his big bank lackeys were desperate to bury it in regulation. Rockwell would not let that happen. He'd made his initial fortune through Bitcoin (by stealing his friend's mining rigs and digital wallets after he died, but no one needed to know that), and he championed cryptocurrencies because the government couldn't wrap its dirty little fingers around them. To America's youth, he was the Bitcoin godfather, ushering in a new era of incorruptible money that leveled the playing field for long-suffering millennials. Rockwell was looking forward

199

to getting Boseman in a room, one on one, to have a 'friendly chat' about these regulations. After that, on to Berlin to deal with business relating to Faraday, and then to the Aeternus genetics lab in Prague to discuss the latest progress with the head researchers. On his way home, he'd stop off at the Uni-Fi development facility in Redmond, Washington, where he'd tour the manufacturing floor and meet with the orbit control teams. He'd have no time off, nor barely even an hour to himself. That was the cost of ambition. "When I get back, I'll be touring wedding venues with Deb for another week. So this will be our last face-to-face for a while."

Cervantes drew one last long breath, then did a forward roll and popped to his feet. "What about the job?" he asked, stretching his arms overhead, his shadow looming upon the walls of the candlelit dojo.

"I haven't given you a job, brother."

"You know what I mean, Salvador. Italy. The Grace woman."

Rockwell rose from lotus. As he flexed the circulation back into his muscles, he noticed Cervantes' bed in the far corner of the darkened dojo. It was a simple sleeping pad like those used on backcountry camping trips, a tiny inflatable pillow resting upon it. No blankets. "Jesus, Dominic. You know there's a sixty-thousand-dollar bed up there in your bedroom, don't you?"

"I do."

"I have the same one. It's refreshing. Like sleeping on marshmallows. Have you even tried it?"

"No."

Rockwell shook his head. He knew it was pointless. If he wanted Cervantes to sleep in that bed, he'd have to put a corpse on it. "Follow me, brother. I have a gift for you." Putting his shoes on, he bowed at the dojo entrance and grabbed the rifle case before continuing through the armory into the firing range. He flicked on the lights, set the case on the shelf in the nearest lane, and popped it open. "The Russian AK-15 assault rifle by Kalashnikov," he said, stepping away so Cervantes could examine it. "Gas-powered, seven-point-six two-millimeter rounds, recoil compensator. Fires seven hundred rounds per minute. This one's equipped with a forty-millimeter single-shot grenade launcher. Go ahead, have a feel."

Cervantes pulled the rifle from the case, turned it over, measured its weight. He pulled the magazine, saw it was full and slapped it back in. Adjusted the butt stock, flicked the safety, and assumed firing position, aiming down the lane. Rockwell covered his ears just before Cervantes squeezed off a handful of rounds, punching a cluster of bullseyes through the target.

"It fits you," said Rockwell, uncovering his ears. "Then again, every weapon fits you."

"Good rifle," said Cervantes. "Thank you, Salvador."

200

"My pleasure."

"But you haven't answered my question."

"What question is that?" asked Rockwell, feigning confusion. But Cervantes was in no mood for games. He just stared at the Salvador, devoid of emotion. Standing there in his t-shirt and loose pants, he looked plain and innocent. Were it not for the rifle at his side, he might be some average Joe at a 7-Eleven. "Alright, alright, I won't torture that one-track mind of yours any longer." From his blazer pocket, Rockwell withdrew an envelope and handed it to Cervantes. "Your itinerary. You fly out in two days."

Setting the rifle down, Cervantes opened the envelope and read the contents. "Verona, Italy. But this is just transport and quarters."

"Yep. A safe house is being prepped at that address as we speak."

"Where's the target info?"

"My team is still pinpointing her coordinates. We're getting close. For now, I just want you on standby at the safe house, ready to mobilize on my command. All details will be given at that time."

"Roger that."

"Dominic," said Rockwell, growing steely, "this one's going to be a little different. Not your standard hit-and-run. The job might be tricky."

"Why?"

"One, because there's a geographical element involved. Getting to the location will be challenging. Comms will be spotty, maybe nonexistent. You'll understand when I brief you."

"Okay."

"Two, it appears our target is protected by the feds. Maybe even an army platoon. You'll need to find a way to access her and retrieve the information."

"The target is military?"

"No, not military. Just a researcher." *A researcher who just may hold the key to immortality.* Rockwell sipped on the savory juices of that thought. Human immortality seemed outlandish, or at least it had before he founded his genetics project, Aeternus. His research team there had done some fine work in (theoretically) furthering life expectancy. Thus, he knew where humanity stood in its understanding of reversing the aging process. Under normal circumstances, if some rando approached him with supposed evidence of a man who couldn't die, he would have laughed in that person's face. Yet, the way this tip had come through was . . . kismet. He didn't quite know how, couldn't quite quantify the feeling, but when he'd received this tipoff, something had clicked. Something internal. It was the same type of sensation he'd experienced when he'd met Cervantes all those years ago. Rockwell's destiny was tied to this job the same way in which it was tied to Cervantes. He felt that in his essence. "Dominic," he said, drawing to within inches of him, "this job could be the big one. Worth all the marbles. I need you to be at the top of your game. No mistakes. You copy?"

"Affirmative."

"I feel I should tell you. I almost sent the Bloodhawks instead of you. I was this close."

Cervantes grimaced. The Bloodhawks were an illicit private army for hire. The Salvador had used them a couple of times, most recently to drive a Congolese warlord out of a contested mining region. He'd needed control of that region to secure the supply chain of specialized minerals to his gigafactory. "*¿Qué carajo?* Why would you send those fucking mercs over me?"

"Doesn't matter. What matters is I chose you. That proves I have the utmost faith in you, brother. I just need you to understand that we may never get this shot again. Anything goes wrong, that could be it."

"Yeah, I said I copy."

"Hey. Look at me." Dead-eyeing Cervantes, Rockwell reached into him, diving into the putrid black ocean of his existence. There, within his essence, he *pulsed.*

Cervantes' eyes popped wide, heart skipping a beat. The Salvador was inside him. Deep, deep inside, in some visceral part of him where nothing had ever been. He went blind. He went deaf. All he could perceive was the godly presence within him, muddling his sense of control, blurring the lines between his soul and his physical body. *Pulsing* with complete power. It was all-consuming, stretching on forever. Then, mercifully, the sensation subsided, leaving Cervantes gasping as he returned to the corporeal world. He felt the Salvador's hand on his shoulder, holding him steady. As his vision faded up, he was shocked to realize he was seeing color. Just for a second, like the Salvador was enveloped in a puffy rainbow cloud. Then it washed to black and gray, leaving him colorblind again. Disoriented, he came to see the Salvador's steely eyes boring into his, inches from his face.

The Salvador spoke then, his purring voice echoing in the charged aftermath. "Do *not* fail me, Cervantes."

Cervantes fell to his knees. "*!No te fallaré!* I will not fail you, Salvador! I swear it!"

PENNOD 27

THE STORM SYSTEM LOOMED over the Dolomites, as cold and gray as the slopes below. Winds and hail lashed the castle walls in sharp gusts, chaperoned by throaty thunder. The system wasn't going anywhere. Valory had overheard *Agente* Trentino on the satellite phone yesterday trying to receive weather updates. The reception was sporadic, but from his limited conversation, she gathered that this foul weather was forecasted to hang around for a few days. Rafael and *Agente* Savelli were therefore delayed in returning to the castle. Even ground transport was too dangerous.

The storm troubled some of the other Ministry contractors like Janelle and Dario, who were anxious about being stuck at the top of the mountain. Being unable to come or go freely and unable to send or receive messages unnerved them. Valory, however, didn't care. She was in a zone. A nuclear war could have erupted outside and she'd have said, "Yeah, yeah, I'm working. Just let me know when it's over."

That dream she'd had the night before last—wow. Just wow. 'Dream' was too flaccid. It was much more intense than that. Physical, spiritual, even erotic. She had never used drugs, but she couldn't help but liken her experience to being high on mind-expanding narcotics. Something that broke down the barriers of your consciousness and ushered you into a loftier, nebulous reality. That's where she connected with Alikai, inside that nirvana. Connected. Not met, not saw, not guessed at from afar, but connected. Like her soul was liquid mixing with his, only for an instant, before separating and re-entering the supercharged flesh of her body. Afterward, everything changed. She couldn't say how or why, couldn't even verbalize what had happened, but when she awoke, she knew two things with certainty. One, Alikai was still alive. He was out there, somewhere. Two, Valory was going to find him. How, where, when, she didn't know, but she was certain that the answer would present itself in the continuation of her studies. At some point, she'd find the key that would lead her to him.

Destiny. That was the word for it.

After the dream, she'd zoned into her work, anxious to discover Alikai's tale of his time with Seraphina. He loved her like no man had ever loved a woman, for he was not a man. She didn't know what he was—some kind of demigod? An archangel? An alien with no memory of his origins? Those all sounded bizarre, just ridiculous non-theories that could never be advanced in academia. Yet, he was something more than human, and he loved Seraphina more than any of the countless women he had known in his immortal lifetime. Valory wanted to know why. Why had he chosen Seraphina above all others? What was so special about her that she'd captured his undying heart? What did she have that had driven him to devote his eternal existence to her? And the biggest question prickling her from the shadows:

Could I do the same?

Throwing her blankets off, she scurried barefoot across the floor to the fireplace, removed the protective screen, and chucked some more wood on the pile. The time was 4:07 A.M. Aside from the groans of the storm, all was quiet. Valory had only slept in spurts, still buzzing from her meta-dream hangover. It was a lot to process. This was the real world, where mystical woo-woo dreams were nothing but fantasies of the scientifically illiterate. Yet here she was in an immortal's castle, suckered into such a fantasy after dancing an otherworldly tango of souls. His ethereal chant had felt like a deliberate reverie tailormade for her. After waking from that dream, she lay in bed for hours, glowing in the aftershock. Wondering if she was crazy. Wondering how she could live in this new world where the supernatural was real.

When she'd finally gotten out of bed, she'd hastened to the library, only barely greeting Janelle as she passed her in the Great Hall. But she wasn't successful in locating the story of Alikai and Seraphina. She spent all day spot-checking the tomes from the medieval era, when the two had likely met, but the works were too numerous. Today, while the storm blanketed the castle, she would continue her search.

There was no point in returning to bed after stoking the fire. Her mind was already in the library. While she brewed some coffee, she withdrew Alikai's self-portrait from under her bed, studying him. He was quite dashing if not for the centuries weighing him down. The aged canvas and the faded paints accentuated his gloom. Wavy blond hair, fair skin, a pillowy bottom lip. The man was GQ handsome. The fact that his dew-drop eyes (as Shakespeare had described them) were different colors only added to his allure. One, a golden amber, the other, a gallant blue, both burdened by an existence that no one else could possibly understand. She imagined his soft lips moving, speaking to her in a thousand ancient tongues, whispering what he'd do if he was there with her now. Telling her how he would touch her . . . what tricks he had learned over his vast years . . . Suddenly flustered, Valory lay back and pleasured herself.

***

204

She zipped her jacket as she walked to the center table. With the storm holding the sun hostage these last couple of days, the library was colder and dimmer than usual. Coats, flashlights, and propane lanterns had become full-time necessities. *Professore* Mancini was already there, a heavy coat draped upon his thin frame, a bubble of light glowing from his lantern. He was copying text from a scholarly handbook, keeping up the charade of contributing something of value.

"Ah," said Valory, attempting a smile as she set her bag down, "*buon giorno, Professore.* You're at it early again I see."

He responded with a gravelly, uncommitted mumble. Valory noticed a coffee cup near him, and she wondered if she should say something. Food and drink were not allowed in the library, as they could damage the delicate works therein. She decided to let it go. Mancini had felt undermined by her presence even before she arrived, and he'd only grown more obstinate since then. Every day, his dark eyes became a little more resentful, his interactions with her more abrupt. She was running circles around him, and he knew it. Everyone knew it. Still, he continued to pretend to be useful. She supposed she felt sorry for him. *Whatever. Let the old man have his coffee.*

Hands wrapped around the warm base of her lantern, she headed to the far mid-north sector of the library. That was where the works from the eighth and ninth centuries were stored. Or at least that was her educated guess based on their construction and content. As usual, Alikai had not dated his entries. This section extended deep into the side of the mountain, running perhaps a hundred meters farther than the base of the keep above. It had a bit of a disconnected feel to the fore of the library. A little darker, a little spookier. It was comforting to know Mancini was there at the table, another living, breathing body in the vicinity.

Perusing the stone shelves, she found the marker she'd planted yesterday. A folded piece of paper she'd stuck between two piles of tomes, jutting into the aisle to remind her where she'd left off. Pulling the marker, she began inspecting each codex, gently removing them from their stacks and spot-checking the text within. Reading Alikai's diary entries never got old. Even when they didn't contain the specific information she sought, it was thrilling. His handwriting, his facile use of languages, his globetrotting stories, his unique perspective and experiences. Much to Valory's surprise, she found thirty-odd tomes written in Ancient Chinese on bamboo parchment. Though these weren't what she sought, she couldn't resist spending a little more time with them. It wasn't often she got the chance to translate something so exotic. Most iterations of Chinese were windy shades of gold and auburn, and the graphemes smelled like the intricacies of a forest. It was a gorgeous, experiential language. What had Alikai been doing in that part of the world? Reading the characters from the top down per the manner of Chinese script, she found a fascinating account of Alikai interacting with Emperor Xuanzong, who ruled in the early eighth century.

He came unto me in the garden adorned in red silks, and we stood among scented flowers in bloom, a small stream trickling by. "Alixei," said he, "I know that it was never your intent to linger here or to take profit in our conflicts. Yet you have been of great service to my people. I shall reward you and let you be on your way if that is your wind. However, if you stay and train my generals in war and wisdom, your rewards shall be without end. This I propose to you now."

Here did I look upon Xuanzong, putting on a show of respect due his station. "Your Imperial Majesty, your affairs are now well in hand. Your want of me is only a comfortable pillow upon which to lay your head. For in teaching you to lead, I have taught you the pinnacle of all lessons; the lesson of how to make leaders. Stay true to this, and your honorable guidance will bear the fruits of a mighty empire."

The next day did I take my leave upon a treasure-laden wagon pulled by his four strongest draft horses. Though I cared little for these rewards, the grateful emperor would have been insulted had I refused. Thusly did I roll away from his palace and into the hinterlands.

Wow. Another face-to-face with a famous historical figure. Pope Innocent, William Shakespeare, and now Emperor Xuanzong of ancient China, who knew Alikai as Alixei. But, whereas Alikai's encounters with the pope and Shakespeare were fleeting, his relationship with Xuanzong seemed to have been one of mentor and student. The other tomes likely contained the story of this relationship. Incredible. In mentoring such a powerful ruler, Alikai had influenced world events, and yet Valory could recall no mention of him in any of the period's historical documents. How many other monarchs had he mentored in his existence? What other world events bore his fingerprints? Might she discover the answers in other tomes? The excitement of knowing she might make an entire career of finding out was exhilarating, but she couldn't dwell on that. Above all, she wanted—needed—to find the story of Seraphina. She placed the codex back on the shelf, letting its shiny golden hues fade from her mind.

Valory spent the better part of the day searching through the tomes, breaking only for the annoyances of using the bathroom, exercising, eating, and replacing the empty propane bottle on her lantern. She also ventured into the courtyard once. Just to see the dreary storm that was making the others so nervous and to visit the horses.

In a dark corner of the Great Hall, she snuck in a few words with Janelle, telling her about her mission to find Alikai and Seraphina's love story.

Janelle was bursting with anticipation. Valory sensed that there might be another forbidden rendezvous in the ladies' future.

Back in the library, however, she began to lose steam. Two days of poring through the medieval era texts had yielded no mention of Seraphina. Was she in the wrong section? Had she miscalculated the time period or the age of the tomes? When her watch showed 6:12 P.M., she sat down at the table, closing her eyes and clearing her frustration. Mancini had already finished for the day, and Rollo was packing his things. When he had gone, Valory just sat in the dark, listening to the faint, steady drumbeat of the storm. She found her thoughts drifting to The Shakespeare Tome, as she had come to think of it. It was still hard to believe that Alikai had spent a full evening in friendship with *the* William Shakespeare. The man was not only the greatest writer in all English literature but a flat-out hero of the language. He'd invented over seventeen hundred words, phrases, and names, many of which were still common vernacular. He'd done this with creativity and playfulness, forever experimenting and cooking up delightful wordplay. The man was simply a genius. Now, however, he was only Valory's second favorite genius behind Alikai. Imagining those two in that London inn talking about Seraphina was a glorious daydream. She recapped what she'd translated, wondering if perhaps she had missed some clue that might lead her to the written narratives she now sought. The two men had sat in the common room drinking ale for a while. They'd gone up to Alikai's room. They'd drunk some more, laughed it up, smoked a bit of weed (hard to forget that image), and talked until dawn. Seraphina had been their main topic of conversation, but Valory just couldn't think of any details she may have missed. She was just about to abandon the thought process when . . .

For on that day, all that was nothing became an everlasting treasure. I shall not repeat the story here, for tis reproduced at length already, as you know, in the twelve. That telling is, in sooth, our dearest jewel upon the earth . . .

An everlasting treasure. The twelve. Dearest jewel . . .

The twelve treasure bindings.

Almost falling from her chair, she snatched her lantern from the table and made a beeline to the southeastern quadrant of shelves where rested the treasure-packed volumes. She had noticed them on her very first trip into the library, lying there amidst the sea of regular tomes, their bejeweled surfaces glinting under the piped-in sunlight. At the time, before she knew that every work in the collection had been written by Alikai, she'd suspected they'd been created for religious purposes. The bulk of treasure bindings in antiquity were crafted for use in imperial coronations and other ceremonies. She never dreamed that this unique set of volumes held the world's only tale of immortal love and devotion.

207

Holding her lantern before her, she hastened down the aisle where she'd first seen them, waiting for the glimmer of rubies, sapphires, and pearls to reflect in the lantern light. There they were. Twelve of them, stacked in three dusty piles, a fur pelt separating the volumes. The exhilaration of seeing them again, this time knowing what they likely contained, made her lightheaded. Why Alikai had placed them here with the Renaissance period works was a bit curious. The lovers had met centuries earlier, meaning their story should be within the medieval texts. But she didn't have the patience to care right now. She just wanted to read.

She set her lantern down and reached for the topmost volume in the first stack. Handling it as if were the world's rarest Fabergé egg, she brought it down and cradled it near her chest, feeling the coldness of the precious stones through her gloves. It weighed almost three times that of the other volumes, so decked out with gold and gems as it was. She gulped with the realization she was now holding a tome worth a million dollars, maybe more. She walked it slowly to the table and laid it in a wooden cradle. When she was sure it was well supported, she darted back down the aisle and grabbed the lantern, returning to the book with girlish zeal.

Holding the light near the cover, she observed the embedded stones. They were arranged in dazzling swirls around a central golden plate. Upon that plate was engraved the Roman numeral one, confirming this was the first book in the series. Gently, she pinched the gold-set corner piece and opened the board, relishing the creak of the binding. She gasped, her hunch confirmed—the manuscript was illuminated!

Illuminated manuscripts were the most beautiful written works in antiquity. Their pages were decorated with intricate illustrations and vibrant colors. They were like treasure chests filled with words and images instead of gems, their shiny paints reflecting upon the parchment. Religious in nature, illuminated works were costly and time-consuming to produce, only affordable for the rich and pious. This tome, however, was no bible or prayer book. It was, as Valory was giddy to confirm, Alikai's diary of his time with Seraphina. On the first page, he'd painted a floral background of reds, blues, and yellows with a sinuous black panther at each corner. Upon the bed of flowers laid a royal crest of gold and silver. Centered within the crest was a portrait of Seraphina. She was a twilit angel, a celestial nimbus highlighting her dark, flowing hair, pinpoints of silver light twinkling in her soft, bronze eyes. With imperial cheekbones and full lips turned in a half smile, she was regal and heavenly. Beneath her, in bold Lombardic, was written her name, followed by the words *In loving memory.*

For a moment, Valory sat enraptured, staring at the woman who owned Alikai's heart. Somewhere back there, in some swept-away pocket of her mind, she compared herself to her. Seraphina was much prettier, even if Alikai had been generous with his depiction, but Valory didn't hold it against her. She was used to playing second fiddle to Violet in the beauty department.

The next two pages were also illuminated, and the entire text was written in Lombardic. Yet another juicy discovery that was now hers to claim. The bulk of the Lombardic language was lost to time. Precious few fragments existed in antiquity, mostly in old Latin law codes and other extraneous documents where the language had been cited. The most Lombardic text she'd ever seen was in the Shakespeare Tome, where he'd sprinkled it in when writing of Seraphina. Those entries alone had gone some way toward completing the historical record of the language. Now, using these volumes, Valory would likely be able to fill in all the knowledge gaps and bring the entire tongue back from the dead. Language Jesus strikes again.

With a slow and measured exhalation, Valory settled in and began translating the lavish text. As with Alikai's other journals, this one began without a foreword or a date. Color-splashed Lombardic characters she'd never seen slipped into the linguistic powerhouse of her brain, drifting into place like a puzzle she'd solved thousands of times before.

Title: The Infinite Diary. Tribute to Seraphina, Codex 1 of 12, Entry #1
Date: Renaissance period, est. 1594-1615 CE
Subject(s): Aléxandros (aka Alex, Alikai, Alaksandus)
Seraphina (presumed), Adrian, Count of Orléans
Language(s): Lombardic
Material: Codex, treasure binding, vellum parchment
Condition: Excellent
Note: Actual dimensions of item are 33.5 x 24.5 cm. 167 pages. Written with quill and ink, illuminated. Margins vary due to illumination.
Location discovered: Classified

The moon was but a sliver whence last I dabbed the ink. This night, it hangs fat over the land, pale as the clans of the north, and I write by candlelight in these borrowed accommodations above the tanner's abode. Naught has beckoned my quill since I have come to this place called Bath in the country of Wessex. The diary of he who was once me has reminded me that I set foot here centuries ago whence twas the Roman city of Aquae Sulis. The memory of that visit, however, my mind cannot raise. Twas not my aim to wander here again, yet in numbness of spirit have I come.

The city is as others in the region. Its bones are Roman still, but the Saxon culture is taking root, slowly devouring the old ways. And though its peoples are as fine as any, I have been no more aroused in the city's midst than if I stood upon a mud pile. This day, however, the gray embers of my soul were fanned, if only a little, by a new wind. Thus shall I tell you who are me of the slight interest I have gained from this day.

This morn found me lounging in the steamy waters of the old Roman spa, surrounded by others who sought its healing vapors. I was not there in search of healing, but merely to blank my tortured thoughts for a spell. As I languished, a lad of twelve winters pulled me back to the present, asking if I should like to be pleasured by him for coin. I waved him away, and he propositioned the next man. Ere I could empty my head once more, excited whispers fell from those who milled upon the balcony above. As one, they hastened to overlook the road, a single word basting their lips over and again: sin-eater.

This stirred me. I had heard tell of these sin-eaters during past travels in Wales but had yet to meet one. Thus did I robe myself and enter the muddy road. There, among others who had flocked to watch, I beheld a funeral procession snaking toward the church, the coffin pulled along in a horse-drawn cart. At the front, a priest in grey robes chanted and rang a handbell, but twas the back of the procession that had drawn the crowd. For there, alone, walked the sin-eater. A woman of twenty winters draped in black, a cowl shadowing her face. At her bosom, she clutched a golden cross adorned with jewels, her ivory fingers red at the knuckles. She trudged ten paces behind the procession. Those who marched nearest her turned to look at her often, mindful that she kept a distance.

Whence the procession passed, the common folk disbanded, muttering of this sin-eater. Yet my fancy was to follow her. In the execution of her duties, I reckoned I might see something new and of momentary interest. For that which is new, even but only slightly, stands as a short-lived tonic to eternal repetition.

The job of a sin-eater is to absorb the sins of the dead by eating a ritual meal at their funeral. Thus is the soul of the deceased absolved, whilst the sin-eater is thereafter burdened with those sins forever. Tis but self-mollifying superstition, as always, yet these folk question it not. You who are me may presume that a grim stigma lies upon sin-eaters. They are dreaded for the numerous sins they have accrued, yet also praised for the service they perform. All wish to be absolved by sin-eaters, yet none wish to consort with them.

The procession slopped through the mud and arrived at the church. From some paces away did I watch as the coffin was carried inside, the mourners following. The sin-eater stood alone, waiting in silence. Once all were within, she joined them. Before I entered, I spared a moment to consider whether I might change from my tasteless robe, now splotched at the hem with mud, and to cover my feet. Thence the thought was gone.

I sat in the back, ignoring those who cast disdainful eyes upon me. Among the family and friends of the deceased did I endure the ceremony, but my gaze rested always upon the sin-eater. Cloaked in black, she stood near the chancel whilst the priest fluttered pacifying words upon the mourners. Though her eyes were hidden under the cowl, her full lips and smooth cheeks betokened a woman not only of youth and beauty but of determination. Indeed, I can know many things about a person with but a glance, though they hide behind cloaks, words, or shadows. Such is but one of our accursed traits, brother, as you know. Here I knew that this lass had suffered greatly, more so than any common woman. Life had beaten upon her like a soldier's dummy, bashing and scarring her spirit. This profession of sin-eating was not her true lot, but only a temporary means to an end, and the road to that end was paved with vengeance. This I saw in her humours.

Whence the time came for the sin-eater to perform her rite, the mourners became uneasy. Many looked away whilst others signed the cross. The priest placed bread and wine inside the casket atop the deceased along with a payment of coin. Thence he stood away, and the sin-eater came upon the coffin. Holding her golden cross above her head, she spoke this prayer. "I give easement and rest now to thee, dear man. Come not down the lanes or in our meadows. And for thy peace, I pawn my own soul. Amen." Though speaking in this tongue of West Saxon, her voice was heavy with an exotic southerly accent. I knew that she hailed from the land of Lombard across the channel, for I had lived there in prior days and had learned their tongue as I'd learned countless others. I mused as to what brought her here, so far from that country.

Here, two men entered the church as quietly as they might. One was a Frankish peacock, a self-important noble. Adorned in gold threaded finery, with hair as long as a horsetail, he slipped into the row opposite me, his underling following. There they examined the proceedings, giving studious eye to the sin-eater. Twas known to me that they were hunting this woman. Though they strived to hide their goal behind etiquette and subtleties, they could not hide it from me. Their humours prickled with excitement, for they grew surer by the second she was who they sought.

With her prayer done, the sin-eater set her cross upon the chest of the deceased. Thence she drew back her cowl, the dusty, golden light of the clerestory falling upon her face. Her hair, fine as silk and dark as midnight, dropped about her olive cheeks. Her eyes, though fawn-like and comely, shone with a pride fierce and unwavering. She was a tortured soul, robbed of all that life might offer, angry and desolate from an endless winter of pain. No other might see these things, but for me, twas a truth as clear as the snowmelt.

This sin-eater began to consume the ritual meal, causing restlessness among the mourners. To them, she literally and willingly imbibed the very soul of evil. Were it not for the absolution she provided, they'd have rather stoned her. The Frankish gentles opposite me, however, grew ecstatic. In their eyes, I saw triumph and certainty. They'd been hunting this woman for some time, and at long last, they'd found her. In moments, whence the service was ended, they meant to slay her and take her head to the Kingdom of Francia. This I knew as I know many unhappened things.

The service concluded, and the mourners shuffled from the nave. I, too, departed, leaving the Franks to their prey. I had now seen this business of sin-eating, and it stirred me little. I would return to my bath, where I fancied an attempt to drown myself. A futile attempt would it be, of course, but oft do I try still on the chance that, perhaps, this time shall end differently. Yet, as I made my way, the sin-eater caught my eye again. Briskly did she stride past, cursing at the mud sucking upon her feet. Her cowl was over her head, her cloak wafting in the wind. The Franks were in pursuit. Their number stood now at three, and each thumbed a broadsword at his side. Homed upon the sin-eater, they slogged after her, quickening their pace as she began to run.

What drives us to help another? I ask you, you who are me. What point lies within it? Everyone around us, though living and breathing, shall be dust whence next we blink. Thence shall they be at peace, their sins eaten, whilst you and I yet live this farce of life, unhelped by gods or men. Tis a cruel riddle. We care nothing for this unending existence, yet others care dearly for theirs, though death shall ultimately negate all for which they strive. To me, they are but mayflies, who live but a single day. Should I deign to help a mayfly survive a few more moments? What value lies there? What means anything anywhere? Perhaps, brother, whence you read this scroll centuries hence, you shall have invented an answer.

I cannot say why I chose to help this sin-eater avoid the chop. There was, I wager, no choice in it at all, other than perhaps to stave off eternal boredom. Mayhap I likened her tortured bearing to mine and thus bore her sympathy. Or mayhap this pompous Frank offended me in some human way that I'd not acknowledged. As with all things, it mattered not. Simply did I find myself moving to her aid.

From the street did she gain the stone path to the east gate and fled sprightly toward the quay. The Franks gave chase, the noble among them shouting, "Stop! In the name of God and Emperor Charlemagne, I command you to stop and face justice!" They pushed peasants and goats from their path and made much commotion. The sin-eater yet fled more swiftly.

I followed this lot to the wharf, where I beheld the sin-eater trying to steal a horse that had just been led off a boat. She pushed the handler aside, but as she attempted to mount the steed, the Franks laid their hands upon her, dragging her down. She spat on them and called them swine, screaming and kicking and punching as a tempest of robe and limbs. The coins she'd earned from sin-eating spilled to the stone. Thence, as

213

the woman flailed, she caught a Frank hard in his groin, and he sank to his knees.

Here did I speak, standing now but paces from the fray. "You shall unhand her now, gentlemen," said I. "Immediately." My command, of course, was destined to be ignored, yet I made the pretense of extending choice.

The nobleman, struggling with his wild package, said, "Stand away, sir! This be the emperor's business!"

"Very well," said I, "say not that I offered no peace." Thence did I kick his leg from beneath him whilst yanking his horsetail hair, and he thudded upon his back near his fellow. The third fellow, who yet rough-handed the sin-eater, took my fingers deep into his eye sockets. He wailed, blinded.

The sin-eater, seeing this unexpected reprieve, leaped to that blinded fellow and stole his blade from its scabbard. Thence did the nobleman regain his feet along with he who'd been groined, and everyone looked upon me with my robe and muddied feet, unarmed, and struggled to make sense of my presence.

"Vile peasant!" cried the noble in a deep Frankish accent. "You now look upon Adrian, Count of Orléans! And you presently stand in interference of God and Emperor Charlemagne!"

"Aye," said I, "so have I heard."

"We've no patience for you! Return to your pigsty this instant, or you shall be skewered for your crimes!"

"Waddle hither then, peacock, and fan me with your feathers."

Thus, he and his man advanced upon me with a mind to spill my innards. Of a normal day, I should welcome such an act in hopes that it should cause my very last death. But here my aim was to assist the sin-eater, thus I danced the dance of survival. They attacked as one, stabbing and hacking in smug expectation of quick victory, but they were struck with disbelief. For again and again did their steel miss my flesh, each thrust by less than a hair, and they could not guess how I evaded their every move. How might we explain it to them, brother? How might we convince a mortal that we have heard his echo so many times that he now stands as but a tired repetition of himself? Might he comprehend that we see his shadow seconds before he thinks to cast one? That we can pinpoint the precise location of his blade from tip to pommel in moments yet unseen? Shall we tell him that he is but a ghost of our memory which betrays his every action and reveals his every thought? Which forespeaks his words before he thinks them? Shall any man hear that his life is naught but a slavish reverberation of a past that only we can see?

With curses spitting from their tongues, the Franks hacked and hacked, their steel whooshing by my ears, always missing by the width of a grain. Whence I'd grown weary of the sport, I stole the peacock's blade from his hand and smote his own cheek with the flat, thence did I kick him from the wharf into the river. His man, learning no lesson, stabbed at me again. Him did I sidestep, cutting his ear off as he stumbled past. He collapsed, blood spilling through the fingers he held to his head.

With these Franks momentarily bested, I turned to the sin-eater. The point of her stolen blade was aimed at me, a firestorm of confusion burning in her eyes. "Who are you?!" she demanded, her Lombard accent thicker now. "Why do you aid me?! Speak!"

I let the Frankish blade clang to the stone, and I looked upon her. Said I in her native tongue of Lombardic, "Best tarry not, little mayfly."

Thence was I away.

After translating the last sentence, Valory leaned back in her chair and stared at the tome. She'd experienced a build-up of energy as she worked the narrative—a colorful sugar rush—and now she was floating. Here then was Alikai's first meeting with Seraphina, and oh what a meeting! She was a sin-eater? That was an obscure and rather ghoulish profession which, to Valory's knowledge, had never left Wales. She hadn't seen that coming. More striking, Seraphina was being pursued as a fugitive by the order of Charlemagne. The King of Francia and Emperor of the Holy Roman Empire. How about that for having an enemy in the highest of places!

Awed, Valory inspected the image Alikai had included at the end of the section. In paints of vibrant hues, it depicted Seraphina being pulled from the horse by the Franks while Alikai walked onto the wharf in a mud-splotched robe. The image was too small for facial details, but the subjects were obvious. During the reading, Valory had turned about thirty pages, the narrative consuming a greater number of pages than usual due to the abundance of supplemental images and fanciful designs. *If only Janelle could see this!*

After letting the sugar rush subside, Valory began translating the next entry.

ПОГЛАВЈЕ 29

Title: The Infinite Diary. Tribute to Seraphina, Codex 1 of 12, Entry #2

This day finds me preparing to move from this place with the night. Leaving had not been my plan but has rather been spurred by the sin-eater of whom I have writ. Tis her will that ushers me from Bath, and of this I now give tell.

After saving her from those dutiful Franks, I returned unto my lodging, beating the rumors which were beginning to flood the lanes. As I walked, I beheld the sin-eater galloping away on the horse she'd thieved, dark hair whipping in the wind. She saw me as she rode, setting one last puzzled look upon me whilst making flight to the gate.

Two morns later, which is this day, a young lad rapped upon my door. He handed a letter unto me, sealed with wax, and I divined from his humours that he had received it from the sin-eater. I took it from his hand, but he yet lingered with expectance. "Say why you loiter, boy."

"Begging your pardon, sir, but the lady did say I would be paid for this delivery."

"Did she now?"

"Aye, sir."

This almost brought a smile unto me. Twas quite cheeky, the sin-eater promising coin which was not hers to promise. Yet I fetched my purse and withdrew a handful of silver, giving it forth. The lad looked at the coins in his palm, his smile as wide and as toothless as the Thames, and he was away.

Here have I transcribed the sin-eater's letter, which was writ in the Lombardic tongue and scripted with brave elegance:

Dear Man,

I am she for whom you intervened by the wharf. For your assistance, I offer my gratitude. However, though your aim was noble and true of heart, you have left me charged as a fugitive of this land, in which I am a foreigner without rights. You did not slay the Franks who criminally assaulted me, thus am I yet hunted by them and the court of Wessex. Furthermore, my dutifully earned wages were lost during your intervention, and I am unable to continue my virtuous work in the name of God for fear of capture. Thus have you rendered me completely without means. Now shall you make amends, as your actions have birthed this quandary. Tomorrow eve, you shall follow the northeasterly road from Bath into the hills. I shall rendezvous with you on the road at a place and time of my choosing. With you shall you bring to me all necessary equipment and rations for travel and as much coin as can be gathered. I care not how you acquire these provisions. These things you shall do in restitution for the ills you have brought upon me, and you shall say no word of this matter to any soul, living or dead.

Thence did I truly smile. I have come to expect all things from all people, and too rarely find myself surprised. Yet did this letter surprise me for its brazen tone and wicked twists of truth. Jupiter's bones, how dare I suspend my apathy long enough to rescue this mayfly from a certain and violent death! What flaming cheek have I!

Twas delightful.

In gratitude of that delight shall I follow this sin-eater's orders. Perhaps a second meeting with her shall produce another smile, which might otherwise elude my lips for centuries to come.

NODALA 30

Title: The Infinite Diary. Tribute to Seraphina, Codex 1 of 12, Entry #3

This eve finds me in the hills of Wessex camping beneath the stars. By the light of campfire and lantern do I pen these words, whilst across from me slumbers the sin-eater. Here is what transpired yesternight.

With all provisions aboard did I drive my wagon into the night, as was the sin-eater's amusing order. Some miles down the road, with a thick fog settled over the land, I came to sense her presence among the dark and misty trees. Though she made no words, cracked no twigs, and rustled no bush, I knew she lurked in the growth watching my wagon rumble along. How can we explain this, brother of ages to come? To know things that no man can know is but a mainstay of our existence, and not even we can say why. We conjure no sorceries and receive no knowledge from the skies, yet we know a thing as if we were remembering rather than observing it. Let it be called the byproduct of eternal life. Yet still, knowing she was there, I did not rein my horses nor call out for her. Such an insight would have vexed her, for she was a woman in grave fear of her circumstance, desperate to regain control. Thusly, for her profit, did I continue to drive with an air of ignorance.

At length did she emerge from the forest, light of foot, and stole to the back of the wagon. As she climbed aboard, quiet as a mouse, I gave no tell that I knew of her presence. I allowed her to sneak beneath the bonnet and place the cold edge of her dagger to my throat. "Stop the coach," commanded she in the Lombardic tongue, "or I shall open your neck."

This I obeyed.

"Tell me all you have brought," said she, her breath warm upon my ear, her hair brushing my shoulder.

"All that I have," answered I, also in Lombardic. "Blankets, food, mead, lanterns, bow and quiver, all that is needed."

"And what of coin?"

"Look there, in that small chest at your feet."

She gave it a glance, never moving her dagger. "This best not be trickery."

"Dear lady, my tricks are better spent elsewhere."

She studied me, inspecting my goodly clothing and well-made boots, a fine change from muddy robes. After some indecision, she left my throat and opened the chest. A nest of gems and coins glittered darkly in the starlight, and she gasped as she let a handful run through her fingers. "But this is a princely sum! How have you gained this, you who stood barefoot in muddy robes yet three days gone? Are there burgled men in pursuit of you this very moment? For that matter, how do you know Lombardic?"

I turned to her, and she thrust her point toward me in distrust. She wore the selfsame cloak and dress of wool as whence she'd fled from Bath, now torn in places. Her white cheeks were as pearls smudged with dirt, her eyes shimmering as a silver glade. "Perhaps the greater question be this, madam; How did you suspect I could provide these supplies if you thought me but a muddy beggar?"

She mused on this, having given it no prior mind. Thence she sheathed her weapon and regarded me keenly. "You are no beggar. In His infinite grace, God has struck me with revelation, and this is how I knew to write you. He has sent you to aid me on my path."

"Of course," said I, allowing the divine explanation. In sooth, I knew that she had been desperate and had writ to me for lack of other options. I had pulled her from certain death, and I had spoken her tongue, all much to her surprise. With a night or two alone, hunted and starving in the woods, she had no choice but to ask more from the one person who had aided her. Thus had she skirted the town, finding a farm boy to bring me her letter. This I saw in her troubled memory. "Shall we drive onward, madam? For I assume your horse is lost."

She nodded, and we went forth into the deep of night.

"Yes, divine intervention is afoot," said she, rummaging through all that I had packed. "Why else would God send a rare man who speaks my tongue? Though you are not native, still you speak it well. You have been to my country of Lombard, yes? You have spent time among my people?"

"Twas my home for a spell, yes."

"What are you called, man?"

"You may call me Aléxandros, madam, if you please."

"Aléxandros. You are Greek then?"

"The land of my birth is but a memory lost in time. This name have I given myself."

This gave her pause from her rummaging, and she looked upon me as I drove. "Well, what of your parents? What are they called?"

I grew somber at this question. For as you know, you who are me, if ever we had parents, their memory is a flame long snuffed. No piece of them lives in our heart. No mother's sweet kiss upon our cheek, no doting father's lesson in hunting. Oft do I wonder if we were ever a child at all. Our earliest memories have been long erased by the eons, and so do they continue to disappear with every sunset. Cruel is the fate that gave us a mortal mind in an immortal body. Here is why we write, brother—to remember. But these things I wished not to voice, and so I gave her but a careless response. "I knew my parents not."

She fixed upon me a sour eye, caring not for the riddle. "Very well, Aléxandros. It matters not where you were born or to whom. It matters only where you are going." She climbed to my side and looked down upon me. "The hand of God is at work this night. In His eyes, you have proven yourself a true ally of Lombard. Thus, your place is now with me." Standing tall and proud, she made her regal proclamation. "I am Queen Seraphina of the Lombards, daughter of Desiderata and Emperor Charlemagne. You, Aléxandros, were sent to help me win back my country."

CAPÍTULO 31

"THIS IS BULLSHIT."

"Is that right?"

Senator Kirk skipped the packet across the table. "It won't play, Tom. Not a chance."

"How do you figure, Harry?" asked Rockwell, but it wasn't a real question. He was just letting Kirk blow off steam.

"Isn't it obvious?" said Kirk. "Look, first you bend me over the barrel with this whole Uni-Fi fantasy. Now you want me to push deregulation of the EV market? Subsidies for environmentally sustainable crypto mining?" He jabbed a finger toward the packet. "Everyone knows that's nothing but a wish list for your own interests. Christ, have you forgotten the platform I'm running here? If I push this crap, it'll look like I work for you."

"You do work for me." Rockwell filled both of their tumblers. "In the grand scheme."

"The hell I do. You're coming on too strong." The senator snatched his Scotch from the conference table and walked to the window. "You want all this shit? You run for President."

"Thirty-four-year-olds can't run for President, Harry." Rockwell leaned back in his chair, smoothing his tie. "Besides, I'm just a little orphan boy, and you're one of the great American Kirks. You guys are long overdue for landing POTUS, aren't you?"

Kirk sucked liquor through his teeth and then shook his head. "You're having so much fun, aren't you. National media falling at your feet. Millennials think you're some kind of goddamn messiah. Meanwhile, you got me straddling both sides of the aisle here, chasing piss down a river. It's time you backed off, Tom. Just back off and let me do my thing."

Rockwell watched Kirk as he ran his hands through his silver hair, scowling out the window at the assorted media vans and lookie-loos. The wall adjacent was dotted with award plaques and photos of Kirk with assorted political and sports figures. The late Prime Minister Margaret Thatcher here, boxing champ Evander Holyfield there. A US flag hung flaccidly from a pole in the corner. They were at Kirk's Allentown office, which was normally quiet and peaceful. Since he'd announced his presidential candidacy, though, his life had become a festival of obnoxious reporters, stalking him everywhere, preventing him from having any semblance of a private life. Thank God Rockwell kept his little visits off the books. If the media knew he was sitting in this office right now, there'd be a veritable circus on his lawn. A female reporter saw Kirk in the window and waved at him. He took a gulp of Scotch and closed the blinds.

The man was frazzled. He'd never wanted this. Had never even wanted to be a public servant, much less a senator or a president. Everything he'd achieved had been at the behest of his family. The Kirk dynasty was a throwback to the wealthy families that emerged from the Industrial Revolution, those early titans of the American iron and steel industry. In the last forty years, the Kirks had been seeding Washington with their entitled spawn in a relentless effort to become the world's most powerful modern empire. There were Kirks all over the political arena, much like the Kennedys or the Bushes, but they hadn't won a presidential seat yet. Their most recent attempt was eight years ago with Senator William Kirk, Harrison's cousin, but he was a flop. Sputtered out during the second round of primaries. But the Kirks were positive this was their year. Harrison wasn't the sharpest tool in the shed, but he'd never had to be. Good looks, well-placed donations, and name recognition won most of the battles. All he'd had to do to win his senatorial seat six years ago was show up, smile that handsome smile, slap an alarmist twist on some tried and true conservative mantras, and bask in the glow of victory. Now here he was running for President of the United States, the wheels of the machine greased by his family and by the vigorously ambitious Thomas Rockwell.

A couple of years ago, though, Kirk had been prepared to tell his family that he was sick of politics and would not be running for reelection. He'd been ready and willing to accept his punishment: ostracization, removal from the boards on which he served, and even litigation. The Kirks would flay him like a fish. Just as they'd done to his cousin, Ted, who had spurned their efforts to place him in Congress. After he refused to play ball, Ted was harassed until he changed his surname to Fields. He was now a real estate agent in Connecticut or something. Not exactly living his dream life, but at least he was no longer under the draconian heel of the Kirks. Harrison had been ready to accept a similar fate, and he'd been positioning himself accordingly. He was going to tell his mafia of a family to stick it where the sun doesn't shine, and he'd be free to finally live his own life, for better or for worse. That's when he'd met Rockwell. The man had shown up at a fundraiser in Pittsburgh and had made it a point to engage in one-on-one conversations with Kirk and other VIPs. After that, somehow, Rockwell knew everything. Like, *everything*. Things that even the most hard-nosed liberal mud rakers hadn't dug up. These weren't things like Kirk's old gambling addiction from twelve years ago. That had already been exposed and splashed all over CNN, and his campaign had weathered it and moved on. No, these things were impossible to know, because Kirk had never told a soul. He'd had no cohorts. There were no living witnesses. No evidence existed, or so he had thought. Yet Rockwell knew it all as if he'd been at Kirk's side the entire time. And one of those things—one very particular secret that Harrison had been hiding—could bring the entire Kirk dynasty to its knees if it were made public. As for the dynasty, Harrison could probably have lived with the guilt of their destruction. But his own career—his legacy, his marriage, his kids, everything that ever meant anything to him—that could all be ruined in one swift stroke from Rockwell, forever.

Harrison tended to forget this fact when the pressures of his situation overwhelmed him. He liked to forget that Rockwell was pulling his strings. So, now and then, when he was triggered, he pushed back. Tried to assert himself, to win back a shred of dignity.

Rockwell rose from his chair and adjusted his jacket. "Harry," he said, walking around the table to join Kirk, "You've been working very hard. I want you to know I recognize that." He gripped Kirk's shoulder. "And soon, you're going to be the greatest Kirk ever. The Kirk of the Kirks. The gold standard by which all future Kirks are measured. When that happens, you can do whatever you want to your family. You'll have their nuts in a vice. Castrate the lot of them, if you want."

"Big whoop. I still won't be free of you." He drained his tumbler. "How about you just quit patronizing me, goddamnit. I've been doing this shit a lot longer than you, and I'm telling you, the RNC won't stand for your little wish list."

"They will stand for whatever I tell them to stand for."

"Why?" asked Kirk, meeting his toying gaze. "You telling me you've got the goods on them, too?" After a coy shrug from Rockwell which all but confirmed the answer, Kirk went slack, his mind working through the ramifications of such a thing being true. If Rockwell had serious dirt on the major players in Washington, he would be, for all intents and purposes, invincible.

"You seem surprised," toyed Rockwell. "Did you think you were the only politician with a skeleton in the closet?" He paused, locking into Kirk. "A five-foot-nine underage skeleton that gave great head?"

"Shut up," hissed Kirk, checking the door.

"Maybe we could get the whole party together and have a sort of round table confessional. Get it all out in the open."

"Shut up, goddamnit! I got it, okay? Just . . . let's move on."

Smirking, Rockwell slithered into Kirk's essence, probing for malice or deception. There was some rotten stuff in there. That was true of most politicians and businesspeople at the elite level, which often made subversion a cakewalk. But Kirk was more like a fish being forced to live in the desert. This overprivileged dynasty boy had never been at ease with his lot. Family business and politics were soul-sucking bore-fests. His true passion, the one that had been beaten out of him as a young man, was music. In a deeply buried streak of royal purple which smelled of field lilies, Rockwell experienced Kirk's fondest memories from those long-gone days. Sitting around with friends in a garage, snorting lines and shredding guitar. His original personality—the one he'd been born with—was like a wild stallion. He wanted to jam, to travel, to screw. He wanted to experience life at full throttle, throwing caution to the wind. He wanted to be Freddy Mercury, not Ronald Regan. But the Kirk family arsenal didn't stand for that. When he'd had enough of his son's shenanigans, Daddy Kirk burned all his instruments and shipped him off to military academy. He'd been a reluctant stooge for the empire from then on, his spirit ever strangled.

Killing off his true self had given birth to a set of sideways tendencies in Harrison. A rebelliousness that may not have manifested if he'd been allowed to live his own life. There'd been a streak of pointless shoplifting for which he'd never been caught. A nasty phase of prescription painkillers. The gambling addiction. The most unexpected twist, however, was his indulgence in his long-repressed homosexuality. The fact that he liked men was one that he had hidden for a long, long time. Because, in the Kirk family war room, there was no place for faggots. Above all perversions, that was the worst. The Kirks had learned to tolerate many unnatural practices to comply with the modern phenomena of diversity and political correctness. Minorities holding leadership positions in their companies, for instance. Allowing 'go green' initiatives to affect their policies was another. But being a homo was intolerable. There were no openly gay employees working for any Kirk industry, and there certainly were none in the family. Not the Kirks. Therefore, Harrison stifled his curiosity at a young age. Married a woman. Had three kids. Only in the last few years had he indulged his true self. He'd done his damn duty, and it was time to finally get a taste of what he'd always yearned for. It was dangerous, he knew the risks. Consequently, he was oh-so-careful. More careful than he'd ever been with anything in his life. There was not even a sliver of a chance that anyone knew what he was doing when he went out of town on 'business' and hired young male prostitutes from the streets, but Rockwell did. Somehow, that bastard not only knew, but he could describe the trysts blow by blow. The clothes he'd been wearing, the words he'd spoken, everything. Worst of all, he knew about Kyle.

The kid was sixteen. A handsome, well-built Asian who liked to jabber. He recognized Harrison, even with his disguise, but he only mentioned it afterward. Harrison was shocked. Being made was too much for him. There was a fight, first verbal, then physical. In the end, Kyle was on the hotel room floor dead, his skull having been smashed against a nightstand. In the middle of the night, Harrison dropped the body out the window into the alley below. Then he went down and heaved it into a dumpster, covering it in refuse. He was sure he'd gotten away with it. The room had been booked under an alias, and he'd come disguised. There'd been no security cams. No one had seen anything, and street people don't talk to police anyway. The murder didn't even make the news.

Then, almost two years later, Rockwell showed up, and the son of a bitch knew it all. Knew what the kid had been wearing. Knew about his thick Asian accent. That he had a tattoo on his chest. That his lip curled when he smiled. There was just no explanation for it. Kirk could only assume that Rockwell had filmed his escapades with remote spying equipment and now had the video in his possession.

In Kirk's essence, Rockwell saw only fear. No cunning plan to escape his situation, no backroom meetings with dark web hitmen. No, he was playing ball like a good little Kirk, as he'd been trained to do since his youth. He was, honestly, rather pathetic. His only real course of action, if he wanted out, was suicide. But Kirk had a strong survival instinct. He would rather be alive and reviled than dead. The only potential issue was that Kirk could make a mistake due to his own stupidity and ruin everything, but Rockwell had contingencies in place were that to occur. He had contingencies for everything. Barring the unforeseen, Rockwell would soon be pulling the strings of the President of the United States.

Rockwell's phone chimed. It was the intel he'd been awaiting, a deep dive on the Grace woman. "I think we're done here, Senator. Unless you need clarification on anything?"

"Clarify this," said Kirk, thrusting his middle finger at Rockwell. Then he slammed his tumbler down, grabbed his briefcase, and stalked away. When he opened the door, a throng of aides and sycophants began clamoring for his attention. "One at a time, please," said Kirk, closing the door behind him.

The second he was gone, Rockwell's smirk vanished. He slammed his fist on the table, staring daggers at the door as if Kirk was still there with his gnarled middle in the air. *You insolent, mouthy son of a bitch!* he wanted to yell. *You want to flip me off? I will end you! I will end your entire existence!* He yanked his tie and swigged his Scotch, imagining himself beating the living shit out of Kirk. The toughest part about his plan, without a doubt, was the gamesmanship. Even though he was a decorated Marine who possessed abilities of which normal men could only dream, he couldn't just outright destroy these entitled bastards and take what they had. Not yet. He had to play the game. That meant suffering the impudence of his pawns.

There was a knock, and Rockwell composed himself. "Come," he said. His men entered. Osborne and Barrera, two Veteran Marines who'd served in Afghanistan, now his well-paid and willing security detail. They were fine men—not psychopaths like Cervantes—and they much preferred making good money in service of Rockwell, whom they held in the highest esteem, rather than slog it out in the 1ˢᵗ Civilian Division. "Sir," they each said, taking their positions at the door.

"Gentlemen," said Rockwell, still simmering.

After them, Andrew stuck his head in. "Shall I have Cornelius bring the car to the back, Mr. Rockwell?"

"Yeah. Thanks, Andrew."

When he was gone, Rockwell took a deep breath, straightening his jacket. Then he sat down, grabbed his phone, and pulled up the intel on Grace. He looked closely at her picture, taken from her university ID badge. Read about her parents in Sunnyvale. Dad the artist, Mom the neuroscientist. Her fraternal twin with whom she hadn't spoken in years. The elementary school she'd attended, her childhood friends, her first car, her academic record. Everything his spooks had been able to gather was there. A remarkable history, he supposed, but nothing that changed his plans. Then, just as he was about to close the report, he saw it. There it was, just a tidbit of information that burst like a fireball in his essence. He stared at it, jaw hanging. For a moment, he could only sit frozen as one giant piece of the puzzle wiggled into place.

అధ్యాయం 32

Title: The Infinite Diary. Tribute to Seraphina, Codex 1 of 12, Entry #4

Should I peer through the eyes of a human, I might say much excitement has occurred since last I penned this journal. By my truth, a mortal would be well pleased with the happenings of the last few moons. Well, so am I, if only a little. You who are me shall understand, even thousands of years from this day, how golden is an occasion that sauces our humours. To once more feel the blood coursing in our veins, if only for a second, is a thing most fine. Yea, on this day, I take renewed liking of the sun's warmth upon my cheek, the earthy scent of the hills in my nose, and the taste of spiced mead upon my tongue. Here is what has transpired.

I, along with she who has named herself Queen of the Lombards, made but a few hours of sleep, thence we rode the next day and into the night. Seraphina was certain the Franks were in lusty pursuit now that they'd had their foul hands upon her, and she possessed an urgent will to lay miles betwixt them and us. For many moons had they tracked her, chasing her from Francia, thence across the strait and into Wessex. With some skill and luck had she stayed always beyond their reach, fleeing whence the winds portended their arrival. To the far north, she flew, finding brief haven among the Picts. Whence rumor came that the Franks approached those Pictish lands, she sailed west to Ireland and later escaped to Wales, where she learned her art of sin-eating to earn coin others feared to earn. From there, as the Franks drew near again, had she fled back to Wessex.

"I was in Bath but a fortnight whence they tracked me to the church," said she as we rumbled upon the moon-soaked road. "Methinks they'd only just arrived, for I heard no whispers of their presence among the townsfolk."

"The townsfolk held their whispers from you," said I, "in fear of your occupation."

"That is likely so," said she, wrapping herself in furs I had brought. Though summer, the deep of night was cut with a chill. "Tis no matter. We must look forward now. I mean to restore the Kingdom of the Lombards, which was usurped by my father, Charlemagne, who is but a devil clothed in riches. Whence my birthright is regained, and his head is impaled upon a pike, only thence shall justice be served. So swear I in the eyes of Almighty God."

To these boasts I said naught and merely drove into the forest. She looked upon me for a spell, starlight in her eyes, with only the creaks and clatter of the wagon for company. Thence said she, "You are a peculiar man, Aléxandros. You stand not in wonder of a queen, nor do you ask of my claims. Yesternight, you flinched not at the edge of my dagger upon your throat, as if you care nothing for your life. Your words are few, yet your bearing betokens vast experience. Your lineage can you oddly not remember. And as well," said she, "you move about unlike any other man. The manner in which you bested Adrian and his puppets was as queer as witch-fire. Impossible, I might even say."

To this, I replied only that yes, I am odd, and left it in silence thereafter. For I was well familiar with this dance. In her mind was she working through all she had seen. Were I to explain now, the truth of my immortality would find no purchase in her reasoning. She, as all mortals, must be allowed to wander the maze of happenstance, arriving at acceptance in due time, prompted by no other.

At length did she relax, falling to troubled sleep.

The question prickled me again—why have I deigned to aid a mayfly and a batty one at that? This plot of hers, to alone conquer Emperor Charlemagne, was as nutty as a field of scrotums. She truly believed she was his daughter, this I could see, and she was convinced Lombard was her birthright. There was no question in her conviction, nor her fortitude. Yet even if her claims were true, she was but a lone woman, destitute, with a gaggle of Franks pursuing her relentlessly. Why her father would rather see her slain than dancing in his court, I could make a fine guess, but her scheme of vengeance was fruitless. Without a mountain of support, she would soon find herself a head shorter. So why do I continue to help? Perhaps I am drawn to her madness. Forsooth, over the eons, it has been only the hijinks of the mad that have soothed me from the doldrums of eternity.

The morn saw us camped off the road beyond a small village. Whilst Seraphina slept as the dead, I felled two hares for our breakfast and prepared them over fire. The scent did wake her, and she savaged the meat as might a bony street waif. As well, I gave unto her a loaf of peasant bread, which vanished quickly into her belly, and she was well satiated. We broke camp then, continuing our flight from the Franks. Here I spoke. "Well then, Your Royal Majesty, Queen Seraphina of Lombard, shall you tell me the tale of your kingdom lost?"

She did look upon me then, and I knew that none had ever addressed her as royalty, and she was well pleased by its ring. Though her clothing was in ill repair, and though her hair was tangled, and her skin tanned with dirt, she sat forward upon the bench with a stiff and regal carriage as though the crown of Lombard glittered bravely upon her head. Thence did this story come from her lips, which she told long of wind, but which I have reduced to its bones here.

Her mother was Desiderata, who was the daughter of Desiderius, King of Lombard. In the year 770, Desiderius gave Desiderata to King Charlemagne of Francia for marriage with intent to forge goodly relations between the two countries. "But," swore Seraphina, "Charlemagne was a treacherous snake. For but one year later, he divorced my mother in sinful defiance of their holy contract with God. Such blasphemy did he commit to marry a thirteen-year-old Swabian wench called Hildegard." In the speaking of this, Seraphina spat upon the ground.

Desiderata was banished from Francia, returning in disgrace to Lombard, where the blame of divorce was heaped solely upon her, with none upon villainous Charlemagne. "My mother was reviled for her failure to please Charlemagne, though she was a true and devoted wife. Whence she returned to Lombard, her own people spat upon her, piling the ills of our land upon her innocent shoulders. Even her own father, my grandfather the King of Lombard, wished to punish her. He stripped her of land and title, sending her to live in an abbey in the country. There is where my mother came to know that I was in her belly. Thus was I born in sin, a bastard of Charlemagne."

With this she fell silent, seething with inner fire, and began to rock gently. Thoughts long hated rained in her eyes, her hands clenching. "Upon my birth, she wrote to Charlemagne, begging for his grace. She wished for me to live a royal life and to betroth a noble husband with property and title. At length did the king respond, calling her a liar and me the bastard of some other man. He swore that if she persisted in her trickery, he would exact justice. Justice, he says!" This did Seraphina yell at the forest as if it were the villain of her tale. "Whence I had lived but one winter, Charlemagne invaded Lombard and captured the capital, Pavia. My mother and I fled from his armies, finding wretched lives in the south. Soon was my country and birthright dissolved, and we lived in servitude and poverty. My birth was never acknowledged by my father, nor even my grandfather."

She looked upon me then, seeing that I was little affected by her tale. My indifference roused her ire. For, of a sudden, she slapped me across the cheek. "Your stillness calls me liar!" said she. "Yet know you nothing! Pry not into my soul then, if you stand as the enemy of truth!"

This strike, of course, could I have deflected, yet I permitted it. For twas not struck against me, but rather against those who had usurped her fate and driven her to ruin. To react to her misplaced anger would only spur it further, thus did I continue driving the wagon in quiet amusement, letting her humours find peace of their own time. I enjoyed the moment of surprise she had offered with her unprovoked attack. Here is why I value the mad, for they do things undone by the sane. Fine little surprises, brother.

"I did not mean to strike you," said she after a moment, lips pursed with the bitter taste of swallowed pride. "You have been of great aid to me." She thought of saying more, but rather left it, and we rode in silence for a spell.

The remainder of her tale, and the story of why Charlemagne's men now pursued her, was left unsaid. Some moments later, she changed the topic. "Well then, quiet Aléxandros, I have told you of my lot, now you shall tell me of yours. Why do you not remember where you were born, or to whom? You must know something."

"Aye," said I, "I know many things. Yet are none of them the thing I wish to know above all others."

"And what be this thing you wish to know above all others?"

"How to be dead."

"Ha! But that has a simple answer!"

"For you, yes. For me, nay. Though I have died countless times over countless eons, always do I live again. I am immortal."

She looked upon me as though I were the mad one. Thence she took aim at ridiculing my claim, but rather stayed her tongue, her thoughts turning to those odd things she had noticed of me: my lack of fear, my quiet bearing, the manner in which I'd defeated three skilled swordsmen with only my bare hands. Her eyes grew narrow then, and she sought to test me. "Immortal, you say. So if I were to open your belly with my dagger—"

"I would die, and you would watch me die, and you would think me a dead liar. Thence would I breathe again, belly unopened, and I would be here at your side as if naught had occurred. No memory would you have of this, and you would deny it if I asked. Only I know the truth. This is my curse."

She studied me as a physician might a patient, considering whether to sink her blade into my gut in experiment of my words. Tis not oft that we tell another of our curse, as you know, you who are me. Futility lies that way. Should we tell a cow or a man, the glassy-eyed result is ever the same. Yet are there two sorts of folk who may at least entertain the outlandishness of our claim—those who are genius, and those who are mad. This sin-eater, Seraphina, is little of the former, and a heap of the latter. Thus had I wagered the telling of my condition.

Herewith did she amuse me further. For instead of naming me fool or liar or madman, she began to ply me with queries most un-queenly. "So you age not?"

"Only in mind. Never in body."

"So you are in sooth an old man."

"The oldest in all the world."

"That explains your dull and boring humours, so oddly wrapped in handsome flesh. Are you a god then?"

"I have been falsely named one in eons past. Yet am I only a man who cannot stay dead."

"Hm. Did you meet Jesus of Nazareth whence he walked the earth?"

"Nay."

"Well, that is disappointing," she murmured. "Have you ever ridden a unicorn?"

"Nay," said I, taken off-guard, "for there exist none."

"That is false. I have seen their horns peddled by traders from the north. They are crushed into powder and put in soups to cure all manner of ills."

"Of course."

"Could the same be true of your flesh? Should I eat it, or drink of your blood, might I become immortal?"

"Nay."

"What if your head were lopped off and magically sewn upon another man? Would that man become immortal?"

At this, I was but speechless, having never been asked such a thing.

"Wait!" said she. "Here is a finer question. If your head was sewn to that man's body, you would have his phallus. Might you feel guilty? You know, playing about with another man's jewels?"

I thought on this. "Nay, for they would be his hands, not mine."

"Clever. How low dangles an immortal phallus? Let me see it."

Here did I laugh, and let it heartily fly as I had not in ages. For this was a conversation I'd not held in the entirety of my memory. At first was she offended by my laughter, for her queries were earnest. Thence she laughed as well, and she reached into the hold and drew forth a bottle of mead, which we shared until there was none.

Valory smiled as she studied the artwork Aléxandros had included at the end of the entry. It was a front-on view of the wagon as if the viewer were sitting on one of the horses backward looking at him and Seraphina. She held a dagger in her right hand, stern eyes upon him, black hair falling over her chest. He faced straight ahead, a tiny smile on his lips. The trees loomed over them from both sides, a white moon peeking through the leaves. The scene was somehow joyous to her. This was the second work she'd seen in which Alikai was smiling, and it was heartwarming. The depiction gave a sense that he knew, and yet didn't know, that he was sitting beside his new love. Though dark and moody in tone, the image whispered with hope.

She took a moment to appreciate the sensations of the Lombardic language. The characters were broody, flowing with hard-bitten grays and somber blues. There was a metallic, steamy undertone to them. The scent of glowing orange steel being dipped into water, as if Valory was standing in a medieval forge.

She took a little break. Did some exercises, fetched a little lunch, exchanged a few words with Rollo. Then she went back to work.

HAADSTIK 33

Title: The Infinite Diary. Tribute to Seraphina, Codex 1 of 12, Entry #5

For a time we rode in goodly humours, enjoying mead and forging whimsy. Our destination was Swindon, though there was no true reason for it. Nothing awaited us there. Seraphina was full of boasts and promises, saying she would restore Lombard and slay Charlemagne with her own hand, but this was a fantasy. Though she had yet to reveal why she was hunted, there was little doubt her goal was for naught. She hadn't a true plan, nor gold for an army, nor support from the duchies. In sooth, it was likely that none of the former Lombardic nobles even knew she existed, nor would recognize her lineage. Still did I indulge her. She was at worst a reprieve from endless boredom, and at best fine company.

We had just uncorked a second bottle of mead whence I drew the horses to a halt.

"Why do we stop?" asked Seraphina.

"Behind us," answered I, "your Franks approach."

In a panic did she turn to see. "What?! Have no sport with me, Aléxandros. There is naught behind us but a long and empty road."

From my pack, I withdrew a scrying glass I'd fashioned and gave it unto her. "Point this end to the far hills," said I, "and place your eye into this end."

I aided her with this, and she was startled to see the distant road brought near in the glass. "In the name of God, what sorcery is this?!" said she, moving the glass away from her eye. "I see the far hills in this tube! How?!"

"Keep your eye in the tube and wait, milady." Whilst she did, I fetched a length of rope from the wagon and hopped to the ground, where I set about tying it around a tree by the road. "See them yet, do you?"

She gasped. "Dust is raised upon the far hills. The Franks are there! They come!" With the glass still upon her eye, she drew a dagger with her free hand and stabbed the air before her.

"They are distant yet, Your Majesty. You cannot harm them."

"How did you know of them? They are yet unheard!"

"I know many things."

"They ride with evil purpose," said she, peering into the glass. "They will be upon us. We must flee!"

"Nay," said I, "we shall end this now." Testing my knot for fastness, I dragged the rest of the rope across the road. Thence did I heap dirt and leaves upon it to hide it from Frankish eyes. "Drive the wagon forward by a field's length. Keep within their sight."

"Why? What will you do?"

I looked upon her, she who stood panicked in the wagon, fumbling with my glass. "Put that away and trundle now forward, Your Majesty. You shall serve as bait for these peacocks."

She did as I bade, and I took the loose end of my rope into the trees. Soon was Seraphina far upon the northerly road, whilst the dust of the Franks grew larger from the south. Their number was five now, three in the fore and two behind. Count Adrian rode front and center. He had sighted Seraphina and spurred his steed to a gallop.

A yawn did stretch my mouth as I waited for them. The mead, it seemed, had slowed my humours. Whence the riders were upon me, thundering on the earth, I pulled the rope taut and held it through a fork for leverage. Here did the foremost horses trip upon my trap, letting fly their riders who tumbled through the air, crashing as human boulders unto the road. The rear horses pulled up just in time, their riders cursing with surprise.

With the horses sputtering and whinnying, the Franks came to understand my trick. Here did I step from my hiding place, sauntering into the cloudy confusion. "Good morrow, gentlemen," said I, speaking their Frankish tongue. "Shall we have another dance?"

One of Adrian's men, he who'd lost an ear in our prior dance, was broken-legged upon the road and could offer no fight. Adrian himself was lying upon the earth, his vision swirling as he looked upon me. His other man, the one whose eyes I'd gouged in Bath, had escaped dire injury and was gathering his wits. The two rear riders, unharmed by my trick, dismounted. One came unto me with naked blade whilst the other fetched bow and arrow from his saddle.

"Slay him!" barked Adrian in Frankish, head pained by the heat of his rage. "Slay this man now!"

The bladesman, seeing me unarmed, gave unto me an able thrust, but he took my fist into the ball of his throat, thence my foot into his groin, and he curled into the dirt. Thence came this fellow whose eyes I'd gouged, his sockets puffy and bruised. With vengeance on his mind did he attack, but I gouged his poor eyes again with even better force. He fell away from the dance.

Here sunk an arrow deep into my breast. Twas was a goodly shot, passing betwixt my ribs and into my lung. From afar did I hear Seraphina cry out, for she watched now my certain death. With strength ebbing did I fall unto my knees, and Adrian Count of Orléans came upon me in his golden threads, drawing his blade. Said he with a sneer of victory, "In the name of God and Charlemagne, I hereby send you to judgment!" Thence he ran me through, letting spill my life. Slowly did the sun's light fade, and I was slain.

Whence life returned, I was stood again on the road. The archer who'd slain me moments ago was nocking his shaft as before, yet this time was I prepared, moving from its flight in the last instant. Thence did I snatch a small rock from the ground, hurling it unto my killer. Twas a fine throw, too, for as he screamed the words "God and Charlemagne!" the rock went into his widely opened mouth and down his throat. Dropping his bow, he clutched himself and choked most violently.

Only Adrian was left to fight, and he was quickly upon me with unsheathed blade. For but a moment or two did I let him tire, missing me time and again with blows he was certain should land. Here I noticed one of those oddities privy only to me. Before I was slain, Adrian's eyes were of greenish hue. Yet now were they as brown as mud. Oh, devilish little changes, brother. Oft do they appear after we have died, oft but not always. Have you solved this mystery yet, you who are the future me? Have you discovered why some poor souls vanish from existence after our death?

Whence brown-eyed Adrian was spent did I draw my dagger and cut his golden clothes from his body, bit by bit, as he flailed at me with breath much labored. "Stop!" puffed he as I slashed his pantaloons away. "What in hell's fire are you about?! I am nobility! Stop! I command it!"

Soon was he naked but for his gloves and boots, gasping for breath upon his knees, his finely stitched feathers upon the dirt in shreds. Around us were his men littered in various states of ruin, blinded, choking, and broken of limb. He whose throat I'd punched was regaining his feet, so I punched it even harder, and he made love to the ground.

Herein strode Seraphina, dagger in hand, wild-eyed with triumph. "So then!" said she in the tongue of Wessex as she came to Adrian, haughty and beautiful. "Here is how it ends for the dog Adrian, slave to a false and unholy king!" She lifted his chin with the edge of her steel. "Grunt your last oinks, pig, that I may send you to Hell!"

Adrian blubbered upon his knees, begging for his pasty life. Seraphina did feast upon his words like a gourmet dinner, goading him to serve ever tastier courses, but I knew she would not slay him. We know these things, brother, as we know many others. Though she had yet to tell me why she'd been hunted by these men, the answers were written on the scroll of her soul. In the reading of those answers, I saw murder. Yea, she had slain someone close to Charlemagne, and she had fled thereafter. As well, I knew that murder haunted her, its memory whispering to her in the abyss of her tortured dreams. Though she pressed her edge into Adrian's throat until it bled, she would not finish the deed. In her failure to do so, she would live forever ashamed of her weakness. Thus, to save her as well as I might, did I intervene.

"Majesty," said I softly, coming to her side. "It does not befit a queen to soil herself with bloodwork. Prithee, let this man be."

"Nay, Aléxandros. The crimes of him and his master are beyond redemption. He mustn't live."

"Fret not, for he shall die as all others. But until he does, let him live in humiliation, stripped of title and dignity as were you. We shall leave him a pauper, reviled until the end of his days. Would this not be a better punishment?"

She gave this a musing, and she was tantalized. "And just how shall we do that?"

As I gave tell of my plan, she smiled most naughtily.

CHƯƠNG 34

Title: The Infinite Diary Series. Tribute to Seraphina, Codex 1 of 12, Entry #6

The next morn, we rode into the Saxon city of Swindon and sold the Franks to a slave trader, delivering them gagged and naked in binds of rope. Seraphina had hacked away their fine, leaving them ragged and wretched of sight. Using my own parchment and quill had I forged a legal court order in stately Frankish writ and pressed Adrian's very own seal upon it, having found it in his pack. My lie was that Seraphina and I were hunters of runaway slaves. We'd been commissioned to recapture these men, sell them back into slavery, and return the profits to Adrian's estate. These men, I'd writ, had been Adrian's property, but had revolted some months ago, fleeing to Wessex. "And this one," said I to the slaver, "claims to be Adrian himself, for he is desperate to evade justice with never-ending lies." Thus were the lot sold, save for him with the broken leg and missing ear. His sale was rejected for his lameness, and he was taken elsewhere. Their horses we sold to farmers, earning more coin.

Seraphina was well pleased as she watched Adrian squirm, tied to his new fate, begging through his gag. Soon would he and his men be beaten with rod and lash until they submitted to their new lot. One day, perhaps, the trick might be discovered, and Adrian might be free again. But on such a day, he shall find no path to Seraphina.

Quickly did we go, driving the wagon east toward Lundenwic. Sera, as she bade me call her, was of a mind to return to her former lands and rouse support for her cause to reinstitute Lombard. I did not spoil her fantasy. The empire was mighty, and Charlemagne was cunning, protected, and loved by his people. Opposing him was Sera, who had naught but a new bag of coin which was not plump enough to buy soldiers, nor even to buy well-placed whispers in courts of influence. Yet was there no call for me to fling her newfound joy upon the fires of truth. She could at least live freely for a spell.

That eve, camping under the stars east of Swindon, I drew my citole from the wagon and strummed a lively tune. I played not for my own enjoyment, but for Sera's, for she was blissful. Her belly was as full as her purse, and those who meant her harm had been vanquished. How long had it been since she was safe and with means, and no longer alone? Such comforts were but far-flung dreams for her. This present and unexpected joy had given her wings. Thus did she dance. Twirling and leaping, long black hair fanning into the night, she reveled in my tune, a white smile parting her olive cheeks, laughter gliding from her lips. And I watched her, for she was lovely.

Once that tune was strummed, I played a Lombardic drinking song that I'd oft heard in taverns there, and she shrieked with delight to hear it. Sweating under the moon did she doff her dress, keeping only her white smock upon her lithe frame, caring little for modesty. Even I, who long ago grew numb toward physical delights, did appreciate the protuberance of her pink nipples through her fabric and the tantalizing dark shadow betwixt her thighs. Yet she was careless of this and danced with abandon. So great was her merry, so speedy her pirouetting that I had little choice but to strum faster, matching her spirit. Thence did I find my voice, singing as I'd not in decades, the dull embers of my soul stoked by her pleasure. Some of the lyrics had I forgotten, thus I made my own, which pleased her.

Whence her heady fervors were spent, she collapsed next to me, breathing frost through her smile, and she drew a fur upon herself. I fell into an easy tune, calm and reflective, my fingertips but whispering along the strings. Here did we drift into sleepy conversation.

"Aléxandros," said she, gazing up at me, hands behind her head as she lay.

"Yes, Your Majesty?"

"May I call you Alex?"

"If you wish."

"Tell me of yourself, Alex."

"What wish you to know?"

"Tell me of something you have done in your everlasting time upon this earth. Something you hold dear in your heart."

"Dear in my heart." Her wish, of course, was that I speak of things warm and kindly. This night was her spirit liquored and fine, and she craved only goodly words. Thus did I attempt to repress my dour nature, for her profit. "Dearness is only for mortals whose lives are but fleeting," said I, failing immediately in my aim. "Yet can I say I have given some things unto this world which others may hold dear."

"Such as?"

"Look there," said I, "at my wagon."

"What of it?"

"Twas I who made axles for wheels, thousands of winters gone, that I may transport my writings and crafts. Though I remember little of it now. I am only reminded from reading the words of he who was once me."

"What is your meaning? The wheel was your invention?"

"Nay, not the wheel, but the axle and its mount. The first of their kind did I forge, thence did I trundle the lands in a rolling wagon, gawked at by all. Thereafter was my creation copied in kingdoms near and far and stands now commonplace. I suppose one may call that dear."

"Very well," she sighed. "Axles. What else?"

"I was the first to make written language, which I formed upon clay. This idea, too, was copied, first by the Sumerians."

"Dear God, bore me no longer, old man, I beg you. Tell me something better. Your eyes, for instance. Why are they of different color?"

"I cannot say, my lady, for they are not of my making."

"Can they see in the dark? Or through walls?"

"No better than yours."

"Well, what of women then? Tell me that. Have you loved?"

"Love," whispered I, tasting the ashen remnants of that feeling. "Aye. I have loved women of yore. Though I remember them little. The eons are too vast."

"Come now, handsome Alex. Not even an immortal is so dull. You must remember who you loved."

Here again did Sera wish not to hear the unpleasant truth—that love was a recipe of mortal life, cooked by idle chefs in a broth of primal humours. Beneath the bittersweet flavors of love was but a primitive goal—to spawn heirs. And the unspoken aim of spawning heirs is the seeking of immortality, which I already possess and wish I did not. Therefore are life and love but misguided ironies. Yet none of this did I speak aloud, for such words may only crush a mortal's spirit. "As I say, my true memories of love suffer from the staleness of centuries. Only fragments can I summon, as if slivers of a broken mirror. Though I look upon a sliver, it offers no meaningful reflection. Tis only through the writings of he who was once me that I may reassemble the slivers and look upon the memory of past lovers. He reminds me of their names, and their faces, and of times we shared, and of words they spoke. Yet my own mind, here and now, knows little."

Here did she scowl at my words. "Boo, sir. Boo and hiss. I pray that he who was once you possessed greater cheer."

So turned the spirit of our evening from fine to morose, and Seraphina's thoughts grew heavy. Despite my will against it, I had done it. Yet still did she seek further words.

"Why did you not kill them?" asked she. Her meaning was the Franks. I could have slain them in Bath, and again on the road, or even in Swindon. Yet I did not, and I stayed her hand from doing so as well. "If you are immortal, I daresay you care little for their lives, or any lives for that matter. Yet you only made fools of them and let them live. Why?"

Here I strummed a chord or three in thought, her lashes brushing the moonlight whilst awaiting my reply. "Perhaps we should not speak of such."

"But I want to know. I *must* know."

"If I say, you may not understand. And if you understand, you shall wish you did not."

"Have you so little faith in me?" Drawing playful sternness upon her face, she sat up and said, "As your queen, with the power vested in me by our Heavenly Father, I command you to tell me."

"Very well," said I, "but say not that you were never warned." So did I make tell, knowing it would bring even moodier ruin upon the night, yet knowing she would have it no other way. "Every day," said I, ceasing the strum of my citole, "every hour, every second, through and through, I perceive a great tunnel of time. Centuries piled upon centuries, flowing through my mind, mixing until they are incomprehensible. Tis like galloping upon the fastest steed in all the world, so fast that all existence becomes naught but a blur of colors whilst I sprint across the lands. Yet they are not lands. They are my memories."

"Go on," said she, propping her head upon her elbow.

"All that is me is ingrained within those blurs of time. They are filled with folk I have known, with deeds I have done, with tongues I have learned, and with love I have shared. Yet are such memories but endless repetitions muddling together on the fringe of my perception. Though they be embedded in the frail mind of this man who sits before you, they offer no solace unto him, for they are but fractured artifacts of immortality."

Sera was silent for a moment, only looking upon me, and I knew pity for me bloomed within her. Only now was she awakened to my state, if but by an inkling. Tis impossible for any mortal to fully sympathize with our condition, as you know, brother. Their minds, as ours, are not built for eternity, nor the understanding of its curse. Yet shall we receive this sympathy gladly, for tis the rarest of things, and it pleases us. "I know not what to say," said Sera, compassion weighing her eyes. "Is there aught I can do to help?"

"Nay, Your Majesty."

"But, though your words be remarkable, still have you not answered my question."

"Indeed, the Franks," said I, putting my instrument aside. "Bear with me. I have told you of my tunnel of time. Now shall I tell you the worst of it. Unless that is, you heed my counsel and choose the finer peace of silence."

She considered this, fearing what I might say next. "No," said she, finding timid resolve. "Tell me. Please."

I knew I should not. Even with this sin-eater, who was tormented by deep injuries yet unvoiced, and whose broken mind was better prepared for insanity than saner persons, I knew I should not make tell even by her askance. Yet, in selfishness, I did. "Very well," said I. "Think, if you will, on this great tunnel of mine, surging always in my mind. And tell me, if you please, what one might see at the farthest reaches of a common tunnel."

"Well, you see the end. In the distance."

"Aye. The end. Or, as I think of it, an escape."

"An escape from what?"

"From life, of course. Into blissful oblivion." Here was I beset by the dead ache of living, overcome by this pointedly cruel reality that belonged to me alone. Any grain of happiness I had heretofore experienced in Seraphina's company fled as I let these words poison my lips. "All things in existence whiz forever through the tunnel, rushing toward that escape. All things arrive there in but a wink of my profane perception. To wit, should I see a newborn babe, I see him as a boy, thence a man, thence a withered corpse. This do I see in but an instant. Not with my eyes, but through colors of shattered memories. For I have witnessed his birth and his death so many times that he is but ether racing through my tunnel." I let her grapple with this for a moment before continuing. "Do I look upon a tree," said I, nodding at those behind me, "I see a sprig, thence a sapling, thence a sturdy trunk, thence a rotten husk laid over, all in a blink. Shall I come upon a newly built manor, it but crumbles to dust in the prison of my mind, melting into never-ending hues of untouchable memory. All things come and go without end. Only I am left behind, drowning in life. Though I yearn for death with all my heart, willing myself to arrive at that distant escape, it remains ever beyond my grasp. I can but watch as fragments of myself go there without me. All my joys and accomplishments. The lives of those I love. Those whom I call brother, sister, friend. They pass me by, pouring into that heavenly end whilst I forever rot in life. And I am jealous of them all," said I, hearing the human spitefulness in my voice. "Call me hateful if you will, or petty, or foolish, but I can no longer bear to see a man die. Be he a good man or foul, I shall not slay him. Never again. Not because I am compassionate, but because I am wretched. For, in a dying man's eyes, I see only the great, unbreakable chains of my existence, mocking me for all eternity."

Sera's eyes leaked, the firelight dancing in their wetness as she looked upon me with even better pity. No words could she utter whilst she handled my pain. She only reached for my hand and held it in hers. Looking upon her tears, I felt a fool for having burdened her with my sorrows.

With a sigh, I took her hand as she had taken mine. "Forgive me. I have forgotten myself, as I am wont to do among mortals. Let us return to merrier words."

Yet Seraphina was not done with the darkness. "Alex. What mean you *again?*" I turned from this, but she persisted. "You said you will never slay again. Does that mean you have done it?" Her voice dropped to a whisper. "You have killed?"

Though I gave no answer, I needed not. Twas written upon me such that any mortal could read it. In silence did I stare at the fire, watching the thin column of smoke twist into the night.

"Please, Alex. It would help me to know."

I knew of what she spoke. Though she fancied her secret unknowable, I knew. That she herself had slain a man was an echo ringing in her humours. This slaying which she had done, this murder, was a devil in the night, pitchforking her slumber without mercy. To hear me speak of committing the selfsame act could, for her, be a salve of bonding. Thus, for her sake, did I oblige. "Yes, Your Majesty," I said. "I have killed."

"How many?" asked she.

It so happened that a coyote howled in the distance, his song as desolate as my soul. "Thousands. Hundreds upon hundreds of thousands."

Title: The Infinite Diary. Tribute to Seraphina, Codex 1 of 12, Entry #7

I left her in the Saxon village of Reada ingas.

There, in a room at the Bull Inn, I took my leave whilst she was abed, thrashing and weeping, the past haunting her sleep. My chest of riches did I place by her side with other necessities. Thence into the night did I fly.

My decision to leave her was inevitable. For she was besotted with me, or rather with a romanticized specter of me, as though I were a troubled but goodly man whom she longed to save. This I knew, even if she did not. But I cannot allow her to love me. Though she had piqued my empty soul for a time, and though I'd had fine moments in her company, our companionship mustn't flourish. Pain and misery that way lies, as you know, brother. We must only spare her, for our deed is done. We have saved the mayfly, and she will thusly live a few more blinks. Let her find another who can put a child in her belly, and who will die alongside her. On both counts, I am incapable.

Seraphina's aim is to travel east to the port of Lundenwic where she might book passage to the mainland. There may she bumble for some years in search of supporters of old Lombard and of her claim. Whence in time she abandons such futility, she may finally find her true destiny which, I hope, grants her peace. So do I return to the West to ensure we shall not meet again.

Now, brother, I shall visit one of our many troves, which lay hidden across the world, and which store our writings and treasures. This I mention to you, as often I do, so that we never forget the existence of these troves as we forget so many things. Were they ever forgotten, so would be our correspondence and thus, our sanity. To this end have I consulted my master list which I carry always, and of which I keep copies in all my troves. These are written in my own language, which is known by no other. The list has reminded me that I once constructed a trove near Salisbury, north of that well-known henge of stone in the English country. To there I go anon.

Adieu, then, to Her Royal Majesty, Queen Seraphina of the Lombards. Let us wish her Godspeed in her quest, which she swears is for throne and country, but which we know is truly for acceptance.

Valory turned the page, eager to find that perhaps Alex had decided to return to Seraphina, but he hadn't. The rest of the tome was dull, covering his travels into the west alone. Dull was a strong word considering the author, but the narrative definitely fell off a cliff after the couple split. Pages and pages of Alex speaking with farmers and moaning about eternity proved quite boring in comparison to the burgeoning relationship about which she'd been reading.

Her wooden chair creaked as she sat back and rubbed her eyes. Though fatigued, she was buzzing over the diary. There was some heavy stuff in there—the pain and torment of Alex's curse was beyond compare—and yet it was lovely to get to know him and Sera better and to be part of their unfolding love story. Perhaps most intriguing was Alex's description of his curse. The way he perceived life and time, through a tragic funnel of lost memories, was just so heartbreaking. Like Sera, she had begun to gain an inkling of understanding of what it was like to be immortal. Through his words, she had begun to grasp the depths of his pain, even while knowing she could never truly understand.

Standing and stretching, Valory mused over the rest of the narrative. The idea of the system of secret troves intrigued her. That explained how Alex had been able to collect and keep so many written works over the centuries. He buried them all over the world and just dug them up from time to time to read about his past. Had he dug them all up and brought them here? Or were there yet undiscovered troves dotting the world? And what was that about killing hundreds of thousands of people? He wrote about that without a hint of further explanation. Like, no big whoop, let's move on. He certainly did not come across as a mass murderer. What could he have meant?

Those were questions for later. Right here, right now, Valory wanted more Seraphina. Allowing a slip of professionalism, she began turning several pages at a time, scanning for Sera's name, but no. Just more existentialist dreariness, like a medieval Edgar Allen Poe. Seraphina was right, Alex could be a real buzzkill. When she reached the last page, still finding none of the good stuff, she closed the tome and stretched her arms overhead. That was enough for today. Tomorrow, she'd finish translating this volume and then dig into the next. *And you'd better go back for Seraphina, mister.*

SKYRIUS 36

THE EVENING SKIES WERE BLUSTERY as the plane touched down in a private airfield west of Verona. A storm system over the mountains had forced the pilot to fly a more circuitous route, but Cervantes hadn't noticed the additional time in the air. He'd been lost in thought, thinking about the Salvador. About the *pulse*.

The Salvador had been inside him. Not inside his brain, but inside his *existence*, if that made the slightest bit of sense. Cervantes had been utterly consumed by his presence. It was like being tased. When fifty thousand volts are coursing through your body, you're nothing but a slave to the lightning storm surging through your veins. That taser may as well be God. Well, that was what the Salvador's pulse was like. Cervantes suspected that, if he'd wanted, the Salvador could have done more than just pulse. Had he dialed it up a little more, something bad—something permanent—could have happened to Cervantes.

He'd never flexed on him like that before. Sure, there'd been times when he'd felt the Salvador in his head, but those felt like harmless whispers in his mind. What had spurred this sudden show of force? Thinking back on the events of the last week, he settled on the likely answer—the Salvador was reasserting his dominance. That had to be it. On the bus, Cervantes had defeated the Salvador with relative ease. That had been by his own order, to stage a mock assassination to keep the Salvador sharp in the event of a real attempt on his life. Cervantes had executed that order too well. He could have killed him if he'd wanted, a fact which likely did not sit well with the Salvador. After that, Cervantes had badgered him about the Grace job, at various points almost demanding information. Perhaps the Salvador had become angry. Perhaps he'd begun to view Cervantes' behavior as defiance. He never quite knew how the Salvador saw him. Sometimes they were brothers and equals, destined to rule the world together. Other times they were master and subordinate. Whatever the case, the Salvador's all-consuming pulse made two things clear. One, the Salvador was in charge, and he was not to be fucked with. Two, he was dead serious about this job. More so than any prior job. He wanted Grace with every fiber of his being, and the pulse was a way of demonstrating that.

But when had he become that powerful? Hell, after the Salvador's show of force, Cervantes had briefly seen colors. Real colors, the likes of which he hadn't seen in twelve years. How?

A car was waiting for Cervantes at the airfield, or rather for his current alias, Mr. Fernandez. It was a white Fiat Panda, a common vehicle in Italy. It wouldn't earn a second glance. A paper map rested in the driver's seat with the keys. Chucking his duffel into the back seat, Cervantes began the hour-long drive to the small town of Pescatina northwest of Verona. The location of the safe house. From there, he'd stage his hunt for the Grace woman.

The landscape became hilly as he wound his way toward the stormy Italian Alps, the twinkling outskirts of Verona fading from his rear-view mirror. When night fell, his surroundings became invisible, lost under a nocturnal blanket. The radio was tuned to a talk show, but it was in Italian. He flicked it off, preferring the soulless drone of the tires on the dark, empty highway.

The safe house was a rustic two-story country manor outside the Pescatina city proper, fenced in by gray stone. With its vine-covered walls, shuttered windows, and tiled roof, it had the look of a vintage Italian lord's estate. Cervantes unlocked the gate, swung it open, drove inside, then closed and relocked it. Then he drove up the gravel path, winding through a field of evergreen corks and cypresses before parking near the front landing. The door and the windows were reinforced with new metal bars, and security cameras speckled the property. Apparently, the Salvador planned for him to hole up here once he'd obtained Grace's research, or evidence, or whatever he was going after. The Salvador hadn't yet made that clear. Per standard operating procedure, Cervantes had to wait for his call to receive mission objectives.

Inside, he flicked on the lights and looked around the first floor. He paid little heed to the traditional furniture and décor, noting instead the location of the back windows and door as well as the entry to the basement. He went upstairs, bypassing the master bedroom and entering a parlor that had been converted into an office. There, next to a desk with a trio of monitors, were two equipment lockers. A satellite phone rested atop one of them along with a handheld GPS and an array of power chargers. Setting those items aside, he opened the lockers. The first held a modular tactical vest, an ILBE rucksack, black fatigues, high-powered binoculars, MREs, and other assorted gear. The second held the Russian AK-15 which the Salvador had gifted Cervantes, along with pistols, knives, frag grenades, flashbangs, and ammo. Cervantes inspected each weapon one by one. Disassembled and reassembled the firearms, then took them outside for a few test shots. Satisfied, he returned to the parlor and began packing his gear.

The satellite phone buzzed. The caller ID showed as Private. He picked it up and tapped Accept, holding it to his ear.

"I trust all the gear is up to spec?"

"Affirmative, Salvador."

"Any complications?"

"Negative." He sensed something different in the Salvador. There was an edge to his customary relaxed confidence. A controlled urgency. "We're good to go."

"Great. Listen, Dominic. I hadn't planned on briefing you so soon. I was going to let you settle in, but I have something to share, and it can't wait. I've just sent you Grace's profile. Read through it and tell me what you see."

Cervantes switched to speaker, then tapped the incoming text and selected the attachment. Mission coordinates and supporting topographical info. He glanced over that—roughly what he was expecting—then scrolled down to Grace's picture. A white woman in her mid-thirties. A shade of hair that he assumed was brown, pulled into a ponytail. Pale skin. Pillowy eyes. Maybe she was pretty, maybe not. He'd never been interested in such things. He scanned her personal details, wondering what had struck such a nerve with the Salvador. He didn't see it at first. Only when he scrolled through a second time did it leap out at him. Squinting in disbelief, he stared at the info, blinking at it as if it might change. "How?" he whispered without meaning to. "Is this true?"

"It most certainly is, brother."

"But . . . what does it mean?"

"It means I was right," declared the Salvador. "I was dead right, Dominic. I told you this was coming. I've been feeling that door of power opening, deep, deep down. I know it sounded like some mystical hippy bullshit, but this intel is validation. Grace is the key to that door. Not just her research, but her. The woman herself."

Cervantes enlarged Grace's photo, hoping that doing so would explain this bizarre information. "I don't copy, Salvador. What's going on?"

"Let me ask you a question, Dominic. What do think when you hear names like Julius Caesar? Genghis Khan? Atilla the Hun?"

"Say again?"

"What comes to mind when you hear those names? Come on, first word off the top of your head. Go."

"I don't know."

"Conquerors. That's the word. They were the greatest conquerors the world has ever seen. Right or wrong, loved or hated, that's the way history remembers them. Conquerors." The Salvador's inflection suggested he'd power-clenched his fist. "The world won't allow uncompromising men like them anymore. They're a thing of the past. But even as a kid, they always enthralled me. These men who dominated millions. They forced the world

248

to kneel, no matter the obstacle, no matter the era, no matter the forces aligned against them. They crushed anyone who defied them. Still," said the Salvador, pacing as he spoke, "even though they accomplished the impossible, in the end, they were all defeated. You know why?"

"No."

"Because they were mortal, that's why. They had superior minds, ironclad wills, and loyal armies at their beck and call, but their flesh was as mortal as every jackoff who has ever lived. No matter what they did, they were destined to fail in the end, their empires dismantled. Because once they died, the roaches regained control. But," said the Salvador, teeming with intrigue, "what if they'd had more time? Like thousands of years? You think they'd have let their accomplishments fall to ruin? Hell, no. Had Caesar lived for centuries, he just may have conquered the whole of Europe. Maybe more."

"Salvador, why are you—"

"Listen, Dominic. We lead short lives. Eighty years if you're lucky, that's all you're going to get. And you're only at peak physical and mental efficiency for a fraction of that time. Then poof, dead forever. So what can you do, huh? If your goal was to conquer the entire world, what do you have to do to have even a remote chance of succeeding?"

"Hurry up?"

"Right. That's goddamn right. You have to spend every second of every day striving for that goal, because next time you blink, you'll be pushing up daisies. You don't have the luxury of taking it slow. You can't plant seeds. You gotta get out there and fire bazookas up people's asses. Take what you want by any means necessary. Today. Not next week, not tomorrow. Today. But," said the Salvador, too excited to pause, "what if I weren't constrained by time? What if I had *all* the time? I'm talking hundreds of thousands of years living forever at the top of my game. You know what that could mean?"

"You wouldn't have to rush."

"Go on."

Cervantes hesitated. He could tell that the Salvador wasn't really asking for his opinion. He was just trying to get him pumped about this mission. He had a real hard-on for this one. "How about you just tell me, Salvador."

"Think about it, Dominic. If mortality wasn't a factor, I could use my gift to achieve things that no one ever imagined. I'd spread the Rockwell empire systematically, one tiny bit at a time, so slowly and with so little violence that no one would notice. Just subtle, almost imperceptible aggressions that, over centuries, lead to uncontested global power. It'd be like building a fence around a herd of wild horses. You know that lesson?"

"What lesson?"

"You start with a single fence post. Totally harmless, just one post out where the horses roam. They don't bat an eye at a single post, right? Don't even know what it is. A year later, you install another one. They don't give a shit. You go on like that for hundreds of years, slowly adding more pieces to the fence. Generations of horses die off over time. The new generations see the fence as the norm. They've grown up with it. Hell, they like being inside the perimeter. They find it familiar and comforting. You just keep doing that over thousands of years until the fence is complete and they're all enclosed. By that time, they're not wild horses anymore. They're sheep. Your very own docile little sheep who you've provided with the safety of a fenced-in home. You are the only master they've ever known. They don't even question it. No bloodshed, no violence, no strife. Just backdoor evolution." The Salvador's next words were a forceful whisper. "We can build a fence around the entire world, Dominic! With our gifts and with unlimited time, we can create what no other conqueror has ever been able to—a *planetary* empire!"

Cervantes walked to the window and stared out into the darkness of the yard. "Permission to speak freely, Salvador?"

"You think I sound crazy." Cervantes felt lame for having asked permission—the Salvador always knew what he was thinking. 'Speaking freely' was unnecessary. "It's okay, Dominic. I know how it sounds. But I ask you, have I ever been wrong?"

"No," said Cervantes, smushing a mosquito between his thumb and the window. "But this is different. Everyone dies. Everyone is *supposed* to die. Even you. That's just the way it is."

The Salvador's reply was twisted with distaste. "No. I don't accept that, and neither should you. Why do you think I founded Aeternus Genetics? You think I spent millions of dollars and pilfered the world's best geneticists so they could sit around sticking their thumbs up each other's asses? No. Their sole mission is to extend the human life span, or even to solve death altogether—for me. They don't know that part yet. They think I'm doing this for the good of humanity, but I own every bit of their research. Not only will I never make that research public, but I will actively suppress any other teams with similar goals."

"Are they close?"

"Not really. Been nothing but baby steps so far. I don't know if they'll ever succeed. That's why I need Grace."

"Why?"

"Because she is part of a team that has discovered the existence of an immortal man."

"Come again?"

"I said there's an immortal walking this earth. Right now. He's out there, and if Grace isn't with him now, she can find him."

Cervantes thought, but didn't say, *You've got to be kidding me.*

"I'm not kidding you, brother. Hey, I know how it sounds, but trust me. This is as real as that bullet you took to the shoulder. What's more, Grace has a connection to the immortal."

"What do you mean?"

"I mean like you and me. She shares a bond with him the same way you and I do. And thanks to this intel," the Salvador paused, his next words dripping with desire "we know that she's bonded to *us*, too."

Cervantes sank into the desk chair, grappling with the insanity that had just been laid upon him. Blankly, he looked at the data sheet again, focusing on that innocent-looking, yet shocking tidbit of information:

December 7, 1985, 9:46 P.M.
Santa Clara Valley Medical Center
Sunnyvale, California

It was Grace's birthday and place of birth.
The same date and hospital as Cervantes and the Salvador.

ISAHLUKO 37

WITH A GRUNT, PROFESSOR Mancini took the final step to the landing, leading with his good foot. His satchel slipped off his shoulder, spilling his textbooks and his thermos. Grumbling, he bent down, slowly, in stages, and he gathered everything into the satchel. When all was situated, he straightened his coat, heaved the door open, and entered the library.

Holding his lantern out as he shuffled down the aisle, he came to the center table and put his things down, glad to finally be rid of the weight, and glad to be alone. That was why he began his workday just after 4:00 A.M., to enjoy a few peaceful hours before Rollo and Grace showed up to annoy him. Yesterday, Grace had arrived much earlier than normal. He hoped that was an isolated occurrence.

Pouring himself a coffee from his thermos, he noticed that a felt cover had been laid over one of the book cradles, so he lifted it. Resting beneath it, closed, was one of the treasure bindings. *So Grace was studying that now, eh?* He shook his head. That little girl had been jumping around from floor to floor, codex to codex. Like a human hummingbird zipping through one flight of fancy after another, eschewing diligent and systematic work in favor of whims and fantasies. She may have been duping Moretti and Savelli, but she wasn't duping him. He just needed a little more time to prove it—to expose her work as fluff, and to prove his as essential. Then they'd see how foolish they'd been to trust her inexperience over his vast decades. Yes, time would vindicate him.

Sinking into his armchair, he considered that time was not on his side. Sure, he was relatively healthy, but how many more years could he reasonably expect to be around? There was much work to do here, more than he could accomplish in his remaining life. It was a personal struggle for sure. The Ministry was depending on his research, but it was unfair to leave Mia at home alone all this time. Although she knew how important his work was, and although she encouraged him to see it through, he couldn't help but feel that his priorities were mixed up. Shouldn't they be together now enjoying their golden years in the home they built? Is that not the most important thing in life, more so than a bunch of dusty tomes? Why in the hell was he here?

Drat. He'd forgotten to pack sugar packets. He always did that. Mia would have packed it for him. She wouldn't have forgotten. She always took care of him. The two of them should be in the garden right about now, decorating their coffees and sitting in the patio chairs, ready to watch the sunrise. That had become one of their favorite routines in the last few years. The gentle rays rising over the hills, dawn's light falling upon his Alpine lilies and purple pansies. Chatting together, watching the world awaken. Sometimes, she poked fun at him for the weird garden gnome he insisted on displaying in the flowerbed. It was more of a gargoyle than a gnome, she always said. They laughed about it.

"Ah, there you are, love," he said as Mia walked into the room. "Could you be a dear and fetch some sugar for me? I forgot again."

"Excuse me?" said Mia.

"Yes, I know, forgetful me. My mind was elsewhere, as usual."

"Uh, are you okay, *Professore?*"

"Now why would you use my formal title?" he said, chuckling as he turned the page in his textbook. "Have I done something to . . ." but he went silent as he looked up at Mia. She wasn't Mia. She was the girl. *Dottoressa* Grace. Standing there in her coat, bag and lantern in hand, staring at him. "What . . . where is . . . ?"

"*Professore?*"

Hands trembling, Mancini fumbled with some random items on the desk. "Yes. Yes, of course, I'm alright." Mia wasn't here. Mia was dead. He was here in this castle because she'd left for Heaven. There was no reason for him to return home.

"Are you sure?"

"Don't badger me, please."

"Oh, sure. Sorry." She kept standing there, uncertain what to do next. After a moment, she spoke again. "So, um, *Professore*, did you happen to see the treasure binding I'm working on? It's illuminated. Really beautiful. Would you like to—"

"I said I'm fine!" he barked. "Now leave me alone. Please. I . . . I have work to do."

She lingered another moment, looking at him. Probably relishing his humiliation. Saving it up as ammunition to use against him. Get him kicked off the project, the only thing that held meaning for him now. Finally, she went about her business. Mancini withdrew a tissue and dabbed his eye.

***

As soon as Rollo entered the library, the girl put him to work. He had not yet photographed the tomes in the top floor southeastern quadrant and had therefore not digitized the treasure bindings. Getting up to stretch,

Mancini watched the two of them gingerly bring the first volume to Rollo's cradle. The girl kept darting nervous glances at Mancini. He could tell that she wanted to say something to him about his coffee, how he shouldn't have it here in the library. She probably thought he didn't notice, but he did. Everyone always underestimated him. Thought he was too old to see and hear things, or that he didn't understand, or that he was feeble and might spill his coffee on the delicate tomes. Even his longtime friend Rafael underestimated him, even though he of all people should know better. And the *Sicurezza* agents, well, they just ignored him. He often overheard them talking about classified topics around the castle. Sometimes, they knew he was nearby but just assumed he was too old and harmless to pay any heed.

Rollo photographed the volume, beginning with the exterior. The girl aided him with this, propping up lights and shifting the codex into various angles so he could capture every surface. Then, opening the cover, she showed Rollo how she wanted the individual pages photographed, directing him to take close-up shots of each section of illuminated artwork in addition to the usual full-page photos. While he worked on that, she said, she would begin translating the second volume.

"*Zio,*" said Rollo to his uncle after he'd snapped a few photos, "*hai visto questi? Sono incredibili.*"

Mancini only grunted in reply. Yes, he'd taken a peek at them, and yes, they were incredible. But he preferred to adhere to a systematic study plan, not chase shiny things around like some child. Just a little more time, and he'd expose her. A little time and the right opportunity. He'd pick his spot, and he'd set everything right.

As Mancini settled back into his studies, he heard the door to the library groan, followed by footsteps. *Agente* Trentino emerged from the gloom of one of the aisles like a ghost in a suit. Pale and weary-looking, he gazed down the length of the table, sleep-starved eyes resting on Mancini, Rollo, and Valory in turn. He carried a briefcase, and there was an unlit cigarette dangling from his lips. Setting his case down, he withdrew a slim digital camera from his coat pocket. "*Dottoressa,*" he said.

When the girl looked up, he snapped her photo. "*Uh, perché stai scattando la mia foto?*" Why was he taking her photo, she'd asked.

Trentino ignored her, slipping the camera back into his pocket. Then he spoke to the three of them as one. "*Ho bisogno dei tuoi rapporti adesso. Tutti voi.*" He wanted their reports immediately. And he'd used the informal, which offended Mancini considering the agent was addressing respected academics.

"Um," said the girl, "*non accenderai quella sigaretta, giusto?*" He wasn't going to light his cigarette in here, right?

Trentino only snapped his fingers in answer, holding his hand out to receive her portable drive. Valory saved her morning updates, disconnected her USB drive, and handed it over. Trentino gave her a fresh drive from his briefcase in return. Rollo followed suit. Then the agent walked over to Mancini, who ignored him. The old linguist merely continued writing notes.

"*Professore*," said Trentino, looming over him. He snapped his fingers in his ears. "*Il tuo rapporto. Andiamo*." Your report. Let's go. He'd used the informal again.

Mancini told Trentino to get his hand out of his face.

Already tired and testy from who knows what, Trentino said that Mancini hadn't turned in a report last time and that his lateness could not be tolerated again. Mancini ignored this. Just sat there writing as if the agent wasn't there. Trentino nearly bit his cigarette off. "*Il tuo rapporto!*" he barked. "*Andiamo!*"

That was it. Mancini couldn't stop himself. Everything he'd been feeling rushed straight into his mouth. The usurping of his position, the disrespect, the forgetfulness that made him feel like such a fool. Being perceived as irrelevant. Being seen but not seen. His old bones aching as he hobbled around the castle. His once prestigious career tottering toward a whimpering, inglorious end at the hands of troglodytes and amateurs. And Mia, his poor Mia. She'd left him, gone forever. He'd never hear her voice again. Face burning, he rose from his chair as fast as his old muscles would allow and stood nose to nose with Trentino, shouting at him with eye-popping ferocity. Unphased, Trentino returned fire, his smokey voice overpowering Mancini's, a roadmap of veins in his forehead. The two went at it for a full ten seconds, attacking the air with their gestures, spittle flying as they came within a hair of physical violence. Then Rollo was between them, his shouts joining theirs, demanding that they cease this idiocy. Trentino shoved Rollo out of his way and stalked off, sweeping Mancini's books off the table as he left. At the other end of the table, Grace stood horrified, hands over her mouth.

"Leave me alone!" shouted Mancini as Rollo tried to help him sit. "Get out of here, both of you!" Hands trembling, he fumbled with his handkerchief, trying to wipe sweat and tears from his face. His silver hair, wild and unkempt at the best of times, stood on end as if he'd been electrified.

"Uncle, let me help—"

"I said no! Go away!" His dark eyes locked in on Grace, and he scowled. "You! This is all because of you! Everything!"

"Uncle—"

"Everything was fine until you came! It was fine! Why don't you just go away! Get out of here!"

"Uncle Emilio!" shouted Rollo. "That's enough!"

"No! It's not enough! You're always taking her side! You work with her like she is your family, not me! You treat me like I'm senile! Well, let me show you how senile I am!" Leaning on the table, breath raspy, he pointed at Grace. "You want to know the truth, girl? Huh? I'll tell you where to find the truth. Go look in the tower!"

"Uncle!"

"Get your hands off me, Rollo!" He straightened his jacket, then swept a gnarled finger between the two of them. "You think I don't hear things, but I hear! You think I don't know, but I know! I am not the fool everyone thinks I am!" He turned his narrowed gaze back to Grace, voice dropping to a growl. "I heard them, I heard everything. You just get a look in that tower, girl. Trust me, you want to see who is there."

"Don't listen to him, Doctor Grace. He's gone mad."

"Have I?" barked Mancini. "Do it, girl. Look in the tower. Ask them about The Incident. Ask them!"

"Okay, that's it. Let's get you to your chamber. Come on." Rollo grabbed hold of his uncle and dragged him from the table. Though he resisted at first, Mancini surrendered, too exhausted to fight, and he let himself be led away. Just before they disappeared behind the aisle, Rollo looked over his shoulder. "I'm so sorry about this, Doctor Grace. Please do not take him seriously. Please."

BAB 38

THE DAY WAS BRILLIANT, a cheery sun beaming from the depths of a crystal sky. The weather system had cleared yesterday evening, and the occupants of the highest castle in the world were finally being rewarded for enduring a week of gloom. A temperate breeze graced the courtyard, a reprieve from the lashing winds. For Valory, it was a perfect morning, despite the smell of fresh horse manure. Baby talking Bel Ragazzo, she brushed his coat until it was clean and shiny, relishing the enjoyment in his big brown eyes. "All done," she said in Italian, giving the horse a pat on the neck. Then she went toward Magia's stall, showing her the brush. The mare was reticent, big round eyes boring into Valory's. "Is today the day?" she asked. "Are you finally going to let me beautify you?" Magia only stared, though she appeared less edgy than the last time Valory had tried to groom her. "I promise it'll feel goooood," she cooed. "Let's give it a shot, hm?" Swinging the stall door open, she inched toward the mare. She began running the brush along her shoulder. "See? I'm not so scary, am I, girl?"

There were more personnel milling around outside this morning, thankful for the sun. As she'd begun tending to the horses, Valory had seen Janelle and a host of others emerge from the keep to enjoy the warmth. Now a group of soldiers was standing by the generator bay, laughing and cutting up. Even *Capitano* Ricci was among them, relaxed and in good spirits for once. There was another man she hadn't met jogging in the courtyard. Valory had seen the man around the castle a few times but wasn't sure about his field of expertise. From bits and pieces of conversation she'd overheard, she guessed he was a geologist, maybe a seismologist. Mid-fifties, slim, dark skin. The two had only exchanged a head nod or two, wary of the compartmentalization rule. After stopping for a series of jumping jacks, he jogged through the gate and out of the castle perimeter.

Agents Moreno and Trentino were standing atop the keep, torsos visible over the battlement, blazers billowing in the wind. Trentino was smoking. From here, Valory could hear faint bits of their conversation, and she pieced together they were waiting for the arrival of a helicopter. Agent Savelli and Rafael were returning, having waited for the storm to clear. She wasn't sure if she was looking forward to that. After yesterday, she had questions for

Rafael, most of which she was afraid to ask. As she brushed Magia's coat, Professor Mancini's words were like ghosts rampaging through her head.

Look in the tower. Ask them about The Incident. Ask them!

She looked to the tower spearing the heavens atop the keep. She had always considered it majestic, the grandiose exclamation point of this hidden world wonder. But now, after Mancini's cryptic message, she was seeing it in a new light. It seemed foreboding. Mysterious. Dirty. The gray stone from which it had been carved was streaked with grime. She had always looked past the layers of aged muck, seeing the tower through rose-colored lenses, but the spire seemed ominous now, even menacing. She hadn't noticed before, but there was a window near the top of it. Though the window faced a wondrous view of the valley, it had been packed and sealed with fresh mortar. The contrast between the mortar and the rest of the stone was stark, and she was irked she hadn't seen it before. It raised a frightening realization. If someone was up there as Mancini implied, then they were being held prisoner. Surely it wasn't Alikai. Why would they imprison him? Why would they hold him there instead of in some secure government facility?

But if it *was* him . . .

She lost herself in a scenario where she'd get inside the tower. She'd walk through the tower door and there he'd be. Not in some weird dream, but face to face, in the flesh. They'd look into one another's eyes. They'd touch hands. They'd speak in languages no one else knew. When she pictured them kissing, butterflies erupted in her tummy.

"*Ehi!*" came a voice, startling her. It was the hostler, a soldier named Lannuzzi. "*Cosa stai facendo?*" he demanded. "*Non dovresti farlo. Scappa.*" You're not supposed to be doing that. Get away.

"*Mi dispiace*," she said, giving him the dandy brush. Then she scuttled off, making her way toward the keep stairs. Leaning on the wall by the landing, she let the sun warm her. There was little she could do right now, whether Alikai was up there or not. It seemed unlikely, considering the source of the info. *Professore* Mancini might have been a great historical linguist once, but now he just wasn't able to produce competent work. His mind was failing him. He'd even mistaken Valory for his wife, Mia. How could she take him seriously about the tower and this so-called Incident?

She ascended the stairs. Stepping through the giant, banded door, propped open by a melon-sized rock, she walked through the vestibule and into the Great Hall. There she stopped, taking a moment to admire the magnificent view for what seemed like the millionth and the first time simultaneously. The midmorning sunlight spilled into the hall like floating honey. The paintings and marble courtiers glowed. Even the dust particles flashed an occasional sparkle, drifting in sunbeam rivers. Valory inhaled, taking it all in. She would not be here forever, and taking pictures was forbidden. This scene would live only in her memory.

Walking across the hall, past the sculptures of nobles and the tables of equipment, she approached the first marble column, the one just left of the dais. From her towering throne, Queen Seraphina of the Lombards looked on, her expression conveying complete control. Valory smiled. In his diary thus far, Alex—she wanted to start thinking of him as Alex—had written of Seraphina as being fearful, impetuous, and slightly bonkers. Yet the woman sitting on the throne was anything but. Under her jeweled crown, she bore a look of regal confidence and wisdom. A great artist could do that—capture a person's true essence through art. At some point, she expected to read about how Alex had experienced those qualities in her.

For now, she wanted to view the columns. On her first evening in the castle, she had noticed that the bas-relief sculptures embedded in the columns were telling a story. Her hunch was that that story was a retelling of the diary narrative. After a few moments of examination, her hunch was confirmed. The first sculpture nearest the base showed Seraphina standing behind a coffin, her cross raised above her head. Performing her duty as a sin-eater. From there, the story spiraled upwards around the column. The next carving, flowing seamlessly from the former, depicted the Franks chasing her through the streets of Bath, a church with a bell tower in the background. The next showed her being dragged down from her horse near the wharf, the Franks surrounding her. In the next relief, Alex was there. He had carved himself as something of a fighting monk, dispatching the hapless Franks while his robe billowed around him. A tiny Seraphina looked on from the background. For whatever reason, Valory smiled, bringing her hands to her face. She couldn't quite say what had provoked her warm feeling. Maybe it was the expertise of Alex's artwork. Or perhaps it was because the column provided corroborating evidence of her translations, which was always a fuzzy feeling for a scholar. Along the length of the column, the reliefs continued, but she didn't want to 'read' the full story here. Nor did she want to view the story in the paintings, as Janelle had pointed out. Not yet. She wanted to continue translating the treasure bindings without the influence of these other mediums. When she completed the last volume, she would return to the hall and read the art.

The chop-chop-chop of a helicopter filtered into the hall, growing louder. Through the upper windows, the copter descended from a field of blue sky into the basin outside the castle walls. Her Italian Santa Claus was finally returning. Valory still had no idea why he'd had to leave so abruptly. The day after he left, she'd asked *Agente* Moreno about it, and he'd responded with, "That's classified."

Agents Moreno and Trentino entered the Great Hall from the northern corridor, having come from the roof. They strode across the marble on their way to receive Rafael and Savelli. If they noticed Valory, they paid her no mind. She stood near Seraphina, waiting as they exited the keep. A few minutes later, they returned. Rafael and Savelli were with them, carrying luggage and briefcases. Valory waved, hoping Rafael would stop and have a quick chat before he settled in, but no. All the men were dour as they made a beeline toward the corridor. Rafael glanced at her, but he only gave her a little nod as he marched on. The way the agents surrounded him, it almost looked like he was their prisoner. The four of them were gone a moment later, leaving Valory to wonder just what the hell was going on.

ISI 39

Title: The Infinite Diary. Tribute to Seraphina, Codex 2 of 12, Entry #1

As the sun touched the westerly horizon, I spied the great stones in the field. I cannot say how many years have passed since last I set foot in the henge, but I daresay they have not changed. Still are they collapsed and overgrown, serving none of their past use. Of them and the question of their purpose, I gave no mind. Although the quarrying and transporting of such behemoths was a fine achievement, they are now only rocks long abandoned.

With dusk near, I turned my mind to setting up camp amidst the stones. On the morrow would I continue north to the trove, but now did I build fire and bed. Here there were signs of many past campers, for twas a fine spot, shielded from the wind by the chunky slabs. With my camp made, I set upon cooking supper, but I was stopped. For I came to know that a rider approached from the east from whence I'd come. Though I heard no hooves on the wind nor felt the shaking of earth, I knew that a horse should be galloping soon over the hills. We know these things, brother, as if they are memories rather than present happenings. Thus I waited, watching. Thence the rider appeared, just a dark spot against the horizon. This rider grew steadily larger, cloak billowing, and I knew that twas Queen Seraphina of the Lombards.

As you know well, you who are me, I am little stirred by ever-roiling fortunes. The sight of a dragon upon the horizon might cause me surprise, but not a man or woman. Yet I felt something in the sight of this sin-eater. Her presence did stir me. Whilst she covered the distance, I mused upon this oddity.

Seeing my wagon, she spurred forth harder, riding upon the wings of anger. As she drew near, her mare sweaty and foaming, she screamed at me some unkind words in Lombardic. Straight upon me she rode, nearly trampling me, face twisted as a raging windstorm, and she dismounted before her horse had even stopped. Her dress was new as was her cloak, but both were dirtied from the road. Her long, black hair had been braided, and a fine new dagger was upon her belt. In the dusky air did she charge me as a rabid badger, laying into me. "How dare you!" she shrieked, piercing the silence of the meadows. "How dare you abandon me! You venomous, disloyal snake! You stupid boring clod! Why did you leave me alone?! Why?!" In this manner she carried on, scratching my cheeks with her nails, raking my eyes, kicking my shins, and beating my chest. Soon was I as fit as a stuck pig, face bleeding as though attacked by crows. Yet still was she about it, pummeling my docile form until she was winded and voiceless. Thence was her spirit spent. "How dare you," she croaked, giving a last, lifeless punch unto my chest. She rested her forehead upon me, weeping, too fatigued to savage me further. "Insidious toad," finished she weakly.

Blood ran down my cheeks, falling into her hair as she wept, her shoulders heaving. Gently did I place my finger beneath her chin, tilting her eyes unto mine. They were as two little universes drowning in the yellow-orange ether of dusk. And in those universes, I saw all that she had suffered, all that had formed her madness over the hardened years of her life. So very hurt was she, so very rejected, and so terrified of her path to redemption. The loneliness pouring from her soul was as mine. But whilst my loneliness was the dull, stillborn ache of eternity, hers was the fiery hot blaze of a falling star, and ever as intense. In such a state had I abandoned her. "Seraphina," I whispered, looking into those broken eyes, "I am sorry." I gathered her into my arms. "I am long numbed to the sympathies of mortals. I think of my pain only, forgetting that which I give unto others. Forgive me."

She sank into me, drawing her arms around my neck, and her tears soaked my jerkin. "Why did you leave me?" she sniffled. "Do you hate me as do all others?"

"No, Sera. I cannot hate you. You have roused me as I've not been roused in thousands of moons."

"Then why?"

"Forsooth," said I, looking into the doused flames of her soul, "my fate is endless whilst yours is not. Should I stay in your company, I shall only bring deep sorrow unto you." Even as I said such words, our curse came upon me, brother, and I saw her withered and dead as though a century had just whisked by. Thus was I compelled to look away. Though her decay was in my memory, and not in my sight, still I could not look.

"But I have forbidden you to leave me, Aléxandros," she said, pulling my gaze back to hers. "I have told you, you are my very own angel, sent by God Himself. Perhaps I will die one day, and you will not, but until that day, your destiny lies with me. So shall we revel in it."

Thence stood she upon her toes and kissed me. Softly, her palm upon the back of my neck, and twas fine. We looked upon each other, me well bloodied, she with tear-stung eyes, and she kissed me again, fiercely. Her passion erupted, from warm to scorching hot in but an instant, and she moaned whilst tasting the blood from my lips. Her flesh grew red, her breath hot in my mouth. So did she remind me I was still a man. For, stoked by her fervor, I carried her into the stone henge, twilight falling about us.

Our lovemaking was timid in its onset. For Sera's soul was in turmoil, haunted by circumstances yet unrevealed to me. Yet I knew, as I know many things, that she'd never lain with a man by choice. Though burning with desire, her humours abounded with fear, shame, and uncertainty, and for such reasons did I not press myself unto her. Yet the well of her passion burned hotly, and she was soon upon me with a long-repressed hunger that would no longer be denied. Thence were we making love like the last man and woman in the world. Quiet, then loud. Pleasant, then coiled in sweet agony. Troubled, then rife with abandon. Thusly was I released from the chains of my tortured thoughts, my mind riding the clouds, my flesh rejoicing in pleasures long unremembered.

Thence, brother, came a true and unexpected gift.

Astride me was she, loving my flesh with all the might of her lithe body whence she found her apex. She flung moans of pleasure toward the stars, legs quivering. Her passion brought forth my seed, and I moaned in harmony with her. After, I was well spent upon my back, pleased with this primal sliver of humanity. Yet thence did her humours change as if by a lightning strike. For even as she descended from her pinnacle, she wailed, turning black and treacherous. Ere I knew what she was about, she snatched her dagger from the ground and plunged it into my heart.

Here, brother, I use a word that no longer has a place in my experience: shock! Aye, I was shocked into life as I watched her atop me, madness wracking her humours as she stabbed me again and again, her cries rolling along the monoliths. Even as I bled and died beneath her, she did not cease her onslaught.

Oh, what a mad and brilliant woman have I found! Shock, brother, shock! To feel such a thing again was magic most pure, conjured by this unlikely sorceress! Remember it now! Feel it again! So human a thing to feel, and we felt it, brother! Can you remember it now, as you read these words thousands of years hence? Remember! For we've had no such thrill in epochs untold! Here had this woman tracked me down and forbidden me to leave her, forcing her love upon me, thence sinks cold steel into my heart. Oh, what joyous misprediction! What mad tenacity! What a fine woman!

Whence I was alive again, she was crying and beset with hysteria as before, and her dagger was held over me, ready to strike, naked breasts quavering. Yet she stayed herself and did not carry forth the deed.

"Do it!" yelled I, eager to feel more human things. "Do it, I say! Slay me again, my queen!"

My voice pulled her from the fog of her madness. Panting, she looked down on me, and to the weapon in her hand. This she tossed away, the horror of her thoughts fueling her anguish. Thence she lay upon me and wept.

TSHOOJ 40

Title: The Infinite Diary. Tribute to Seraphina, Codex 2 of 12, Entry #2

Under the moon we lay watching the stars drift across the sky. Her head was upon my chest, my arm around her. Here did she wish to explain why she drew her weapon upon me, swearing that twas not her true will. Rather had she been assailed by a rush of evil memories, stealing reason and forethought from her mind. Over this, I assured her I was not begrudged. As well, I did not reveal she had slain me moments ago, and that she was now speaking to my resurrection. I said only that I had enjoyed her outburst more than she could know and bore her no grievance. Yet still did she wish to say her peace. Thus shall I recount the remainder of her story, revealing why Count Adrian had been in relentless pursuit of her these many moons, and why she slew me.

Whence Charlemagne invaded Lombard, Sera and her mother, Desiderata, were living in an abbey, their lives devoted to God. That abbey was in the country north of the capital, Pavia, and thus was in the direct path of the approaching forces. Fearing Charlemagne's promise of 'justice,' Desiderata fled south with Seraphina, carting what food and provisions could be spared by the abbess. Seraphina was but a babe of one winter and formed no memory of their flight.

Over many months, Desiderata trekked south to the border of the Eastern Roman Empire. The road was fraught with peril. "My mother told me of the hardships we faced," said Sera. "An unwed woman roaming the lands alone with a child was sinful in nature, and many shunned our plight. Those whom she told of my blood, revealing I was the daughter of Charlemagne, only charged her with lies and madness. Oft were we destitute, stealing warmth and food from open barns and homesteads. So said my mother."

Whence finally they settled in the southern Duchy of Benevento near the Roman Empire, they were no better off. Desiderata, insisting she was once a princess of Lombard and queen of Francia, was believed by none. She was forced to work in a tavern to make what ends she could.

There she and Sera lived in a storage room among casks, crates, and rats. At this time came official news that Lombard was conquered by Charlemagne and had been annexed into his empire. Lombard, Sera's birthright, was no more.

"That tavern is where my earliest memories were made," said she. "Whilst my mother broke her back working for bits and scraps, I played among the patrons and in the streets, running about with other children. In those days was I unaware of our plight and only lived as a little girl, questioning nothing of our poverty. I did not understand why she always gave me food to eat whilst taking little for herself. Twas a normal life to me, save for one thing; always, in the quiet mornings, would she teach me how to be a queen."

Lessons upon lessons, said Sera, were taught unto her. Proper speech, regal composure, courtly etiquettes, reading and writing, goodly pastimes of the court such as weaving and dancing, all of these did Desiderata teach her daughter daily and without fail. Even as Sera grew sick of these things did her mother force her to task. "For one day," said Sera, recalling her mother's oft-repeated words, "you shall be a queen. This do I swear, my sweet Sera."

As the years passed, misfortune befell Desiderata and Seraphina, and they were mired in poverty. Desiderata was accused of stealing from a traveling Roman patron and, as punishment, was forced into slavery until her debt was repaid. Thus were she and Sera remanded to this merchant's estate, both of them made to perform menial chores, day and night. "And this merchant, Thaddeus, came to enjoy raping my mother," said Seraphina. "For she was his property and had no recourse against him. Betimes did I see him take her with my own eyes whilst I hid. Oft did I see my mother bent along a table, weeping softly whilst fat Thaddeus had his way." Here did Sera's fingers scratch deep into my chest with restrained rage. "Yet always did my lessons continue. Through every misfortune and every crime against us, my mother yet molded me into royalty."

In time, Desiderata managed to escape from slavery, fleeing with young Sera again. Their hardships continued for many years whilst from farm to farm they traveled, depending on the kindness of strangers to sustain them. Betimes, however, they were shown little compassion, and rather was Desiderata forced to skirt the law to stay free. One elderly farmer suspected they were runaway slaves and had a mind to alert the authorities. This old man did Desiderata overpower, binding him in rope and stealing all that was needed for their continued flight. They rode to the coast, making passage south to lands across the sea.

266

"During this time," said Sera, "my mother grew touched. She began to mumble unto herself and to yell in her sleep. She ceased to bathe and once pulled a great tuft of hair from her head. Her dream to make me a queen appeared as a raving fantasy to all who might listen. All the while," said Sera, "she took degrading jobs for coin. What once was so beneath her royal stature had become the norm. All so that I may live and one day recapture my stolen birthright."

Whence Sera had seen sixteen winters, Desiderata gained a mind to act. By this time was Sera well-trained in courtly affairs and could pass for aristocracy. With the coin Desiderata had saved and stolen, she bought Sera a fine lady's dress, scented oils for her hair, and paint for her face, and she made her beautiful. Thence north to Francia did they travel, concocting false names and purposes to avoid sending rumors ahead of them.

"My mother's will was but to appear before Charlemagne and present me, his true and deserving daughter. Her reason was that many years had passed, and whatever ill feelings he'd possessed of yore had now faded, and that he would welcome his child into court. Thence I should be reinstated into his line of succession. I knew little of such matters, thus I saw no fault with her plan. I could not have known twas foolish. Yet had my mother grown ever more touched, and she was no longer able to know fine ideas from bad."

Their return from abroad to Francia was fraught with obstacles, aided little by Desiderata's slow descent into madness. Encountered they foul weather, hostile terrain, constant lack of coin, erroneous bearings, and the like. With these obstacles did young Sera contend, for her mother was ever more incapable. A full season passed whilst they wend their way to the far north, and Sera was seventeen by the time they reached Aachen, the seat of Charlemagne's governance.

"My mother wished to march straight upon the steps of Charlemagne's imperial residence and demand an audience. Yet did I counsel a more tactful approach. I beseeched her to first write a letter to make a formal request. For even I knew that an emperor should dislike brash demands from his former wife. With reluctance did she agree."

So was this letter penned and sent, but no response was returned. Thence did the ladies come to know that Charlemagne was away on campaign, personally leading his armies into lands afar to unite all Germanic peoples and extend the Holy Roman Empire. Thus were Desiderata and Sera compelled to await his return. More than half a year passed whilst mother and daughter labored for coin in anxious wait. Their hardships were just as they were in years prior, making ends meet with menial work. Thus were their daily lives difficult, and hope grew dim.

As well, Desiderata grew yet more touched, oft forgetting where they were or why they had come. Here she was lucid only but half the hours in a day. Betimes, the circumstances were unbearable, sapping Sera's desire to carry forth. Yet did her mother emphatically deny any suggestion of abandoning her plot.

Seraphina had seen nearly eighteen winters whence news came that Charlemagne was to return to Aachen and that a victory parade was to be held in welcome. Upon the hearing of this, Desiderata acted swiftly. Here did a smile touch Sera's lips as she spoke. "I had never seen my mother so cheerful and beautiful. She donned her old queenly garb, which she had kept all those years in pursuit of this day, and she was most splendid. News of my father's arrival seemed to banish her demons, and she was good of mind and merry. 'By the end of this day,' she said, 'you shall be a princess, my love. All that we have worked for shall bear the sweetest fruit you have ever tasted.' She hummed as she brushed my hair. We laughed as she painted my face and helped me dress. So excited were we. Our troubles were done. Little did we know," she said, turning dour, "of the horrors awaiting us."

Desiderata and Seraphina did not attend the parade. Rather, they came to the courtyard of the palace of Aachen to await Charlemagne there, where a quieter meeting might take place. Yet were they approached by his guards and ordered to stand away from the emperor's path. "But my mother was a former queen and knew how to speak to these men. With a regal comportment that touched me most proudly, she scolded the guards and proclaimed my title, and she ordered them to give way. This they obeyed with some confusion, so royal was her air. My chest was afire with pride, for my mother was truly a queen."

Thence came the emperor's lavish coach, which was drawn to the steps before the palace. "Whence Charlemagne came down from the coach and I saw him with my own eyes, he was as a god to me. Have you ever seen an emperor, Alex? With your very own eyes?"

"Aye," said I. Yet I did not say I was once considered one long ago.

"Thence you know of how grand my father appeared. He wore robes adorned with gold and jewels, and the crown gleamed upon his head. He was so tall, a head taller than the next tallest man. I remember his finely oiled beard, his long curls, regal and kingly. Everyone bowed and catered to him, and twas as if all the motions of the world were his to control. He was, as I have said, like a god. But the most surprising thing to see," said Sera, "was that I was the very spit of him. My eyes were his, and my nose. Our faces were alike, save for age and gender. Even through his beard, the similarity was plain to all. Thus I knew that I was his daughter, the daughter of an emperor. And I was breathless, for my mother never told me of such likenesses." Thence did Sera's fingernails dig into my chest as her thoughts blackened. "But my mother's madness got the best of her. For she called out to him, unable to withhold her dark grudge from the past. To him, she said these words that I shall never forget. 'Charles! Look upon Queen Desiderata, your one and true wife in the eyes of God Almighty! And behold your firstborn! Your true daughter, Princess Seraphina, who holds divine right to your favor!'"

Here did Sera pause in her telling, reliving the moment. "Well," said she, "he did look upon us, and upon me, as did his many advisors. Yea, Charlemagne and his entire procession stopped to make sense of what had just been proclaimed. And there, of a sudden, I felt like the center of all the world, for all eyes fell unto me. At once was I appalled by my mother's accusing tone, yet so exhilarated that I thought I might fly. Twas a far-flung dream from all I had known."

So did Charlemagne see his daughter, and he knew from looking upon her countenance that she was of his loins. For a moment, it seemed all might be well, and that he might grant the audience that Desiderata had worked to achieve over their long winters of hardship, for his gaze held interest and curiosity. "But thence a voice cried out from the palace entry. This was Fastrada, the current wife of my father, who had come to receive her husband. She was little pleased with my mother's declaration. Cried she, 'False and conniving botch of a woman! How dare you sully this day with such cretinous lies! I, Fastrada, stand as the one and only wife of the emperor!'"

Here all the devils of Hades went to work. Desiderata went abruptly mad at being thusly challenged on this day of all days. With complete loss of bearing did she leap at Fastrada, attacking her with fists and nails. The guards accosted her mother and dragged her off Fastrada. Yet she would not settle, and was like a wild boar, so they struck her. Still did she fight, so they struck her again, and again, and again until she was bloodied and beaten on the cobblestone. Sera cried for them to stop, but the guards accosted her as well. One man held her whilst another laid his fist into her gut to silence her. "And in just that instant," said she, her tears wetting my chest, "all was ruined. All those years of hardship, all the lessons in royalty, all my mother's pain and sacrifice, snuffed as if naught but burning parchment. Thence were we thrown in the dungeon."

In those hours after, young Sera was inconsolable, her pain as deep as an ocean trench. The shock of what had occurred was beyond her belief, and she pled with God to wake her from her cruel nightmare. Yet was it not to be. She and her mother were held in separate cells, weeks passing as they awaited judgment. "My cell was cold and damp. I was given few comforts, with no word of my mother's fate. Every day I expected the king to send for me so that he may look upon my face and hear his daughter's plea. I desired but to tell him of all we have suffered, as I am telling you, and to plead for his good and willing favor. For surely his heart and his conscious were close to God. But he never summoned me." Instead, said Seraphina, another came for her. This was Pepin the Hunchback, Charlemagne's first son, who was unsavory of face and deformed of body. Pepin had been among the throng upon the palace steps that day. Watching the fray, he had taken a fancy to Seraphina, his half-sister. "Whence he came to my cell," said Sera, "he paid the guard to take his leave so that he could be alone with me." Here did Sera taste shame and disgust upon her tongue, speaking through tears. "He . . . forced himself upon me. This vile, horrid half-man. He beat me and stole my maidenhead. Hence, I knew my father did not love me."

Many a night did Pepin come with endless coin in trade for the guard's discretion. There in the cell, he grunted over her, violating her, doing all that he wished, and Sera could only scream for help that would never arrive. Of all the trials she had suffered, all the years of hardship with her mother, there was nothing so twisted and horrible as the darkness-hidden crimes Pepin committed upon her. Here did Sera cease her tale, only hiding her face and weeping for a spell before continuing. "One night, whilst he had his way, he whispered unto my ear, his foul breath upon my cheek. He said that my mother was dead. That she had been beheaded that very morning for her attack on Queen Fastrada. My fate was yet decided, but he said I should worry not, for he would visit me every night until my case was heard. At that moment, hearing such horror, anything that remained of my heart was shattered."

With this half-man upon her back, laughing and grunting, her soul went numb, blanked by emotions too excruciating to receive. She knew little of what happened next, her agony preventing the memory. Whence her wits were returned, she saw Pepin the Hunchback dying upon the stone, holding his gushing neck. His own knife was in her hand, stolen from his belt. Yet she could not believe her own hand had done such a deed, and only did she stand in disbelief for a time. Thence came the footfalls of the guard. Thus, she lay beside Pepin as if dead, concealing the dagger. He came into the cell and reached for her, thence did she stab him many times, as fast as she might, and he joined Pepin upon the floor to die. In a panic did she gather what she could, stealing Pepin's rings and gold. She escaped through a sewer grate, wading through rancid muck before fleeing into the night.

"I have been a fugitive ever since. I am charged with the murder of Prince Pepin and the guard, as well as the theft of Pepin's royal jewels. Those jewels did I trade for secret passage away from Francia. Count Adrian, who is the brother-in-law of Charlemagne, had been in constant pursuit of me with his men until God sent you to intervene." With this, she gazed at me with the weight of regret in her soft eyes. "Forgive me for holding a knife over you. You are the first man since . . . At that moment, I was back there, in that dungeon. He was atop me, grunting and sweating. Laughing." She buried her face in my chest. "Twas him I meant to harm, not you. Never you, my sweet Aléxandros. For you are the harbinger of my salvation."

Title: The Infinite Diary. Tribute to Seraphina, Codex 2 of 12, Entry #3

As I put nib to parchment by the firelight, I take some solace. For this day has been the finest I have seen in seasons untold. Here to my right sits pretty Seraphina, wrapped in fur, reading a scroll I penned hundreds of years ago. That scroll is one of many we have unearthed from my trove this day, and she would not be denied the reading of it. Tis writ in Latin, which was taught to her by Desiderata, and thus is she enthralled by the words of he who was once me. I cannot recall a time whence we have allowed another to read our correspondences, brother, and tis heartening. Whilst Sera reads those words of old, I pen newer words unto you. Let me tell you herewith of this day.

This morn, after sunrise, I gave lesson to Sera in the art of hunting grouse. Though she had hunted with bow in days past, her form was poor, her technique sloppy. Thus did I teach her the finer points. With some practice, she loosed a fine shot, spearing a grouse in the head, as I instructed, so as not to waste the meat. Well pleased was she with her success, and the delight upon her face was fine. Thence did I field dress and cook the bird for our breakfast. Yet did she begin to panic, for she only just realized she had abandoned the chest of riches I had given her, so distraught had she been over my disappearance. The chest was left in her room in Reada ingas and was likely stolen by now. Thereby did she fret, whipping herself with insults for her own carelessness, and she had a mind to hasten back there. Yet I told her worry not, for tis only a chest of shiny rocks struck and filed into pleasing forms. That these rocks are valuable is a shared delusion of which men have convinced themselves to sustain cities and hierarchies. In eons of yore, such rocks were only curiosities, bearing little consequence. For lack of something better, men agreed to pretend these curiosities were of great worth. Over time, they forgot they were pretending. But of this notion she cared naught, fretting only that she would be unable to restore Lombard without those rocks.

Here did I gain some clarity of will. To wit, many hundreds of years have passed since I abandoned my kingdom and resumed wandering this earth without aim. Such roaming have I done since forgotten times, before ever a brick was laid to form a city, before shiny rocks ruled men's hearts, whence but disparate clans hunted the forests and ever migrated ahead of the seasons. My only wish, the only thing I ever sought in my wanderings, was death. Failing that, I have merely sought that which may cause me to forget my misery for a while. A nigh impossible task for one who has seen all things millions of times over. Yet it occurred to me this morn that Seraphina's company had eased my waterfall of misery, if only by a drop or two. Why, I asked. Why had she delivered me unto finer humours? It had naught to do with her beauty. For although she was beautiful, so had many women been over the eons. Nor had it to do with her wisdom, nor her power of reason, for she had little of those. Yet had her very nature pulled me from endless torment into the present moment. And the present, dear brother, is the only place that joy might be found. Past and future crush me from both ends, their march unstoppable. But the present, if given proper due, cannot be crushed. Seraphina had forced me to crawl away from my tunnel of time and to live in this very moment before my eyes, a scarce feat. This had she done with her madness of wit, her unpredictability, her lethal tantrums, and her flights of emotion. After eons among mortals who had morphed into a selfsame blur of stale repetition, Sera had proven a breath of air that I yearned to breathe. Yet this was not all that drew me to her. For, too, her misery was kin to mine. She and I were alone, castaways of this world, our lives but farces of what should have been. Thus were our sympathies for one another a bittersweet tonic which we might sip together from the selfsame chalice.

Thus I came to know that I would give myself unto her as she wished. I shall be her angel from God, and I shall accompany her for as long as she wills it. If her mind is to embark on an impossible quest to overthrow the most powerful emperor in the world, I shall but stand as her fellow fool.

Whilst she fretted over the chest of riches that might now be stolen, I loaded the wagon and bade her ride north with me to my trove. For once twas unearthed, she would be most pleased with the surprise that awaited, and she would never think on her lost treasure again.

North of the henge did we ride for two full turns of the cup, and we came upon the clearing wherein my trove was buried. Twas near the bank of a small tributary of the River Avon in a patch where few men tread. Here did I settle the wagon and fetch my shovel, and I bade Sera tend the horses whilst I dug. Half the day was done whence I had cleared away enough dirt to open the trove. Sera brimmed with curiosity, for this was, to her, as a treasure hunt in the wilds. Anxious was she to see what an immortal had hoarded over the centuries. To remind you, brother, this trove was dug by he who was once me, and twas a fine job. Once the portal was cleared of earth, it could be opened, and the trove could be walked into as a small underground house, for twas framed with timbers against the weight of earth resting above.

We came into the trove, and there under layers of fallen dirt were numerous crates and chests, sealed with wax to protect against the elements. These were surrounded by all manner of pieces resting in loose disarray: marble statuettes, jade figurines, painted potteries, clay busts, gilded reliquaries, and all the like, many fashioned by the hands of he who was once me. Sera looked upon these items with joy, blowing the dirt from their surfaces and hoisting them for perusal. Some she carried into the sunlight to see them clearly, and her lips gushed questions upon me. Whence did you make this? For whom? What inspired you? How did you come to such talents? As well, she demanded to know why I'd hidden these things away, for they were as excellent as any she'd ever seen. Yet was she little satisfied with my vague and forgetful answers, naming me a dullard.

Here did I pry open my crates, revealing my past writings: tablets of stone and clay, leatherbound parchments, scrolls, and the like. Some of these did I remove with a purpose to read them in reminiscence of my former life, and to soothe myself with the words of he who knows my heart. Sera was as a child among a field of toys, gasping as she ran her fingers along my works. Much of these could she not read, for they were writ in varied languages I'd learned over eons. Yet did she unravel a scroll which was writ in Latin, and this tongue she knew from her mother's lessons, as I have said.

For a spell did we read, she from her Latin scroll, me from the stone tablets. Yet could I give little mind, for Sera's lips worked as much as her eyes, flinging questions upon me about what I had writ. She asked of the folk of whom I'd writ, and of the meaning behind some of my words, and other queries of this kind, but always was she disappointed with my answer, which was oft "I cannot recall."

At length did I withdraw a group of chests from the back of the trove and bade Sera pry them open. Whence she did, she beheld the treasures I'd collected over many centuries. Coins of gold, silver, and copper, stamped with the faces of ancient kings near and far. Precious stones of reds and greens and blues. Necklaces of pearl and ivory. Rings, brooches, coronets, all glittering in the light of the afternoon. She stood as frozen as a victim of Medusa, mouth agape as she looked upon these trinkets.

"Seraphina," said I, drawing her gold-struck eyes unto me. "If you wish to win back your kingdom, you shall require baubles as these to buy allies and armies. So let us bring them along."

I watched the color of her emotions play upon her. Til now, her quest had been but a fever dream racing through shattered memories. Yet with this gift of treasure, the dream had just become real. Thus, I waited for the question I knew she would ask. "So . . . does this mean you agree to aid me?"

"Aye."

"You will win back Lombard with me? My home?"

"Is that not what you have commanded, Your Majesty?"

"I . . ." said she, but could speak no longer, muted by emotion, and she was as an innocent doe gazing up at me. Thence did she embrace me with all her might, aching with joy upon my bare chest. "You are truly my angel, Aléxandros," whispered she. "Well and truly. For that will you sit beside me as King of Lombard, this I now swear under God." Thence did we share lips, wet with her tears, and but held one another for a spell. I felt the thump of her little heart beating against my skin, and I held her closer to feel it even better.

"Alex?" said she after a moment.

"Yes, Your Majesty?"

"Whence have you last bathed?"

"Forgive me. It seems my labors have left me odorous."

Fetching scented soap and sponge from the wagon, I led Sera to the stream, and we removed our garb, setting it to soak. Thence did we bathe under the lengthening shadows. We ran the sponge along one another, making merry as we washed away the dirt of her past. Sera was of brilliant humours, long hair clinging wetly to her breasts, beauty alight in her eyes as she spoke of the magnificent life that should soon be ours. Playful and cheery was she, the light of dusk glowing upon her wet skin, and I was surprised to feel my loins burn with desire. Soon were we making love in the stream in the manner of drunk and unfettered teens. And this time, she was not bedeviled by the memory of that dark dungeon.

Now, as I write, the hour is late. Sera is at my side, reading my scrolls with sleepy eyes. We shall camp here this night. On the morrow shall I refill the dirt over my trove and we shall be away toward Lundenwic. At this moment, I only await her slumber, for I wish to draw her image upon parchment whilst she is unaware, with her humours at peace.

275

Brother, I implore you now—let us never forget this one.

CAPITOL 42

WHEN SHE WAS FIVE, Valory almost died. She remembered it clearly. She was alone in the den, watching TV. Mom was in the other room folding laundry or something. A Spanish talk show was on, and Valory merrily repeated all the dialogue as she danced around in her little pink jammies. Now and again, she ate a grape from the bowl on the coffee table. The grapes were dark purple and fat. Even now, she could recall the image of them sitting there plumply in that white porcelain bowl. She'd pluck one off and suck on it for a bit, cheek bulging as she mimicked the show. Next thing she knew, she was on her knees, choking.

She never forgot that feeling of panic upon realizing what was happening. That overwhelming sense of doom bearing down. Such a weird thing to feel as an innocent child who knew nothing of the reality of death. Vi walked into the den then, seeing Val on her knees clutching her throat. She scoffed at first, thinking it was a bad joke, but then she started screaming for Mom. Then a strange thing happened. Val's panic faded, and she eased into a calm, submissive peace. She stopped struggling. She just lay on her back and waited for the end, which suddenly wasn't so horrifying. The morning sun beaming through the windows began to dim. Vi's screaming drifted into the distance. Ironically, the last thing she heard was the guy on the TV saying, "*Adios, hermanita.*"

Moments later, she was sitting upright, wheezing, her mom at her back performing the Heimlich. The grape came flying out of her mouth, rolling along the hardwood. Then Mom and Dad hugged and kissed her like there was no tomorrow. She remembered Dad's chest tattoos smushing against her face as he embraced her, the scent of oil-based paint filling her nose. No more grapes in the house from that point on. To this day, she would not eat them.

Valory stared at her fresh translation, glowing on the laptop, that childhood memory creeping into her mind. Something about Alex's story had summoned it from the cubby hole where it had laid undisturbed for years. Alex's all-consuming focus on death—his desire for it, his endless experiences with it, his legitimizing it as something to crave rather than fear—exhumed her near-death experience from the depths of her memory.

She reread the section where Sera had murdered him. To imagine such a vicious scene—in the middle of world-famous Stonehenge, no less—was wilder than the wildest thing she had ever read. The text, shining with inks of brilliant gold and silver in the mystic light of the library, was at odds with the narrative. Such a beautiful work of art to be paired with an act so unconscionable.

This was her third time reading Alex's description of himself dying. The first was when he'd thrown himself into a mudslide while living among ancestors of the Komsa. The second had been from this very tribute when the Frankish bowman's arrow had pierced his lung. Now this, a disturbed queen killing him seconds after a bout of lovemaking. He had, of course, come back to life every time. What did Alex experience in the moments when he was dead? Thus far, his narratives had not addressed that question. He'd only written that he'd died, and then he was alive again. What about the in-between? Did he have a transitional moment of otherworldly consciousness, drifting down the tunnel of light commonly reported by near-death patients? Or was there only the sweet oblivion he so craved? Did it all happen too fast to register? Blink once, I'm dead, blink twice, I'm alive? When Valory had choked on that grape, the world had faded to black, but there remained a fuzzy ball of light in the distance linking her to the world of the living. She was lucky that light hadn't winked out. But what about Alex?

The historical treasures contained within the narrative were incredible. Personal accounts of Charlemagne, Fastrada, Pepin the Hunchback, Desiderata, Count Adrian, not to mention Seraphina herself, an unknown daughter of that famous emperor. Historians could have a field day with these texts.

And Seraphina. At the beginning of his story, Alex had quickly pegged her as 'mad,' and he was right. This woman was clearly unstable, as was her mother, but what would her modern-day diagnosis be? Psychopath? Sociopath? Those seemed unlikely, for although Sera had shown a shocking proclivity for sudden violence common to those psychoses, she also displayed love, empathy, and humanity. You don't see those traits in psychopaths. So then what? Manic bipolar? That offered a better fit, but Valory was no psychologist. She felt a desperate desire to share the narrative with her mom. Doctor Victoria Grace, the acclaimed neuroscientist, could certainly offer an educated opinion on Sera.

And what was this business about Alex having been a king?

"Have you ever seen an emperor, Alex? With your very own eyes?"

"Aye," said I. Yet I did not say I was once considered one long ago.

In a previous entry, he had written something similar. That he'd left his kingdom to resume wandering the lands. Yet he had not elaborated. What could he have meant? And how about the passage where he claimed to have

278

slain hundreds of thousands of people? How could that even be possible? The questions were piling up in multiples of the answers.

The dimming of the ambient light told her that evening was settling over the castle. The suncatchers on the roof were catching less sun. Whipping her ponytail out of the way, she fired up a nearby propane lantern. Aside from its vaporous hiss, all was silent. Professor Mancini had left a few hours ago, and Rollo an hour after that. Rollo had finished photographing all the treasure bindings before returning to the regular volumes (if anything here could be called regular). Valory hoped that he would finish this level before the season was over. She didn't know what was going to happen once winter swallowed the mountain, but she suspected she'd be sent home and re-summoned to the castle next spring. The thought of leaving was dreadful. Although she enjoyed her position at the Centre of Study of Ancient Documents, that may as well be a pile of old toss compared to this. This job was destiny. It was meant for her. She felt like Alikai wanted her here, deciphering his diary. The dream . . . that night he'd come to her. She could not imagine having that dream away from the castle. Maybe she could convince Rafael and the *Agenzia* to let her continue translating the tomes from her Oxford flat. She didn't need the physical tomes, she could just work off of Rollo's imagery. She'd promise to treat the digital material as if they were the most holy relics in the world. She'd use encrypted hard drives, keeping it all top secret. She'd be oh so careful. She'd swear oaths to anyone and everyone who asked. They wouldn't even have to pay her.

"Valory?"

"Oh my god!" She nearly leaped from her chair, recoiling from Rafael. *"Ты сукин сын!"*

"I'm so sorry," said Rafael, hiding his amusement. "I didn't mean to frighten you. I thought you heard me coming."

Valory fell into the backrest, clutching her heart. *"Иисус Христос.* I feel like I just lost ten pounds."

"My apologies, *cara mia.*" Rafael chuckled. "I was hoping you had a moment to talk. Unless I've scared you speechless."

"No," she said, exhaling. "I'm alright. I've been wanting to talk to you for a while now."

"What was that language you spoke just then?"

"Hm?" she said, sitting up. "Oh, that was Russian."

"Ah. And what did you say?"

Valory sheepishly curled her bottom lip. "I insulted you."

"Is that so?"

"Yeah. It was pretty bad, actually. Sorry."

"Well, I suppose I deserved it." He wrapped his glasses around his ears and leaned over the cradle where rested the opened treasure binding. Its extravagant borderwork gleamed in the lantern light. "My goodness, will you just look at that illumination. *Che bello. Semplicemente magnifico.*"

"You can say that again."

"Is this Lombardic?"

"It is. The most complete collection of Lombardic text in the world, in fact." She raised her shoulders to her ears, smiling. "By the time I'm done translating these twelve tomes, the language will likely be restored. Yee!"

Rafael's eyes vanished into his grin. "That's why they call you Language Jesus. Outstanding, Doctor Grace."

"Thank you."

"I'm sorry I've been away. But I've read your translations and I've been anxious to talk about them. *Oddio*, they are amazing. The Shakespeare entry alone, *non posso crederci!* And your discovery of the identity of our marble queen*, che emozione!*"

"And how about the fact that this is all the work of an immortal? That's got to take the cake."

"Yes," said Rafael with a flash of discomfort. "I must admit, Valory, I was encouraged to withhold information on that particular subject—top secret, you know—but the cat is out of the bag, isn't it? Let's discuss everything."

Valory had been dying to sit down with Rafael and geek out over her work. Now that the opportunity was finally here, she gushed. They talked in-depth about everything she had documented, with Valory leaning heavily into Alex and Sera's love story. Rafael hadn't read the latest updates since she had only just finished, so she gave him the skinny version which, an hour later, turned out to be the obese version. Then, with the falling darkness encasing them in a bubble of lantern light, they went to Rafael's chamber. Sitting near the fire, surrounded by centuries-old antiques and accouterments, they talked about the Shakespeare entry, each of them trying to out-amaze one another with the implications of presenting this shocking text to the world. They discussed both technical and fanciful topics, scholarly and whimsical until Rafael began to yawn, his eyes sagging. Valory sensed she had overindulged, and that the courteous doctor was beginning to humor her, but she couldn't leave just yet. On the heels of this lighthearted chat, she thought she might get some answers to the questions that had been troubling her.

Growing serious, she weighed her words. "Rafael. Any chance you'll tell me what's going on around here?"

"*Scusa?*" he asked, but his expression betrayed him. He knew what she meant.

"Look, I'm nervous. So are the other contractors. We know something's up, and it's freaking us out a little. *Siamo in pericolo?*" Are we in danger?

Rafael ran a hand along his baldness, checking the door. There was no one else around, but when he spoke, it was in German, his most fluent second language behind English. "*Ich werde mit Ihnen ehrlich sein.*" I will be honest with you. "*Die Agenten vermuten, dass diese Seite kompromittiert wurde.*" The agents suspect that the location of the site has been compromised.

"*Was?*" Valory whispered. "*Von wem?*" By whom?

Rafael hesitated. Then he whispered that a powerful third party—a non-government entity—was suspected of receiving information not only about the castle's existence, but its location. This party was being monitored by the *Agenzia*. At this time, however, there was nothing to fear. The *Agenzia* was on top of it and had already begun beefing up security protocols— extending the boundaries of a no-fly zone over the site and blocking the turnoff that leads to the only path up the mountain, among other measures. None of this would affect Valory's job in any way, nor the other contractors. They were to carry on as normal. There was no danger.

In reply, Valory whispered, "*Nichts ist niemals in Gefahr.*" It was an old German proverb meaning 'Nought is never in danger.'

"*Das ist wahr,*" Rafael said, acknowledging that sentiment. He continued the conversation in German. "Agent Savelli is quite on edge. Because of this news and other things."

"What other things?"

Rafael appeared pained. "I'm afraid I have spoken out of turn, my dear. Forgive me, but I think I have broken enough rules for one night."

"Well," ventured Valory, "what about The Incident? Can you shed any light on that?"

Alarm flashed in his dark brown eyes. "Who told you about that?"

"Does it matter?"

Rafael shook his head, looking down. "Please, Valory, trust me when I say it's best to forget about that."

"Why?" When he turned away, she pressed him. "Please, Rafael. This is kind of frightening. I'm starting to feel like I shouldn't be here. Like, I don't know . . . like maybe I should leave." That was a lie. Valory wouldn't leave Alikai's castle unless she was dragged out kicking and screaming, but she figured she might coax a little more information from Rafael with the threat. It worked. If he'd been alarmed before, he was downright aghast now.

"No no no, Valory, please don't leave. This project needs you more than anyone else. Even more than me, I'd guess. Listen," he said drawing closer to her, "let me say only this. The Incident was something that happened before you arrived. It was uh, a security breach of sorts. Savelli and his men brought it under control, and it's over. There is nothing to fear, I promise you," he said, hand over his heart. "Can we leave it at that?"

Tucking her hair behind her ears, Valory figured she'd take one more shot. Still speaking German, she said "*Hat es etwas damit zu tun, wer im Turm ist?*" Does it have something to do with whoever is in the tower?

For only the second time since she'd met him, she saw the entirety of Rafael's eyes as he gaped at her, appalled. Then, realizing what he must look like, he reset himself. "I'm sorry, Valory, I really am, but I can say no more."

The chamber was colder now, the fire having dwindled. Their shadows had ceased to dance upon the wall and were now just static blobs morphing together. For a moment, she just looked at him, hoping for . . . something. Just a little more info. When the silence became uncomfortable, she tried again. "Rafael, if I may say one more thing?" She did not wait for his agreement. "If I've heard you correctly, you and the *Agenzia* have known all along that Alikai is immortal. Even before my translations."

"Ah. Well, yes, it was suspected."

"May I ask how you knew?"

Clearing his throat, Rafael folded his fingers across his belly. "I suppose it is fitting that you mention that now, Valory. It leads to what I must show you next."

"Okay."

"Have you by chance taken a glance at the very last set of works yet? The most recent?"

"No, not yet. I started with the oldest clay tablets and have been translating the Renaissance-era tomes since. Why?"

"Well, when we first began our studies here last year, we thought it prudent to examine the most recent of the library's contents first. Professor Mancini reasoned that the most modern works would be more easily translated than the scores of extinct languages in the tablets and tomes."

"Sure."

"However, that was not the case. The most modern works, it turned out, are the most indecipherable we've encountered in our careers."

"In what way?" asked Valory, drawn to this new challenge.

"I don't think I could even begin to explain. It is best to see for yourself. Take a look at them tomorrow. I'll just say that the Professor was at quite a loss when he scrutinized them. All except, that is, for this one item." With that, Rafael opened his briefcase on the table. From within, he withdrew three sheets of browned parchment encased in protective plastic. "The time has come for you to see this. It is a letter that was found with the most recent works." He handed the sheets over. "It is written in modern German, which Emilio and I can both read. It explains why we've always suspected we were dealing with an immortal. I can't let you keep it," he said as he got up to stoke the fire, "so please read it now."

Intrigued, Valory re-lit her lantern and held the parchment in the light. As Rafael had indicated, the letter was written in modern German, dancing in shades of mauve and taupe in her perception, crisp and coarse upon the fingertips of her mind. But this letter was different from the other works in the library. It was not in Alikai's handwriting. The script here was looser and less refined. *A diary entry from someone other than Alex?*

"Valory," said Rafael, "I must stress that this letter is between us. You are instructed not to share what you read with anyone. The only reason I'm allowed to show it to you is because you discovered the truth about the immortal on your own."

"Sure," she answered. "Mum's the word." With that, she dove in.

Dear Meister Alexander,

Here writes your humble servant, Jürgen Ziegler, who has cared for your person and affairs for thirty-seven years. I remind you of my name and station should this letter find you centuries from now, at which time you may have forgotten me, a thought I dread above all others. It is with a guilt-ridden heart that I write you now. For all the failure and misfortune that has delivered us to this point lies upon my shoulders.

Today is the second of September in the year of our Lord, 1952. Though I am aware you care little for dates, I prefer to record one here, so that if you ever return to your castle, you will find this letter and know the day and the circumstance of my pitiful resignation. It has been one full year since last I saw your face. For the sake of your poor memory which struggles with the curse of eternity, I will recount the details of our last month together and of the predicament that forces me from your service.

Remember, *Meister*, if you can, that I came to you in April of 1951 while you were shut away in your chamber, suffering with a terrible malaise. To brighten your spirits, I showed you a newspaper article about a scientist at the University of Princeton. This man was my countryman, endowed with great intellect, and he had revolutionized our understanding of the very nature of time itself. This is what you have always asked of me, *Guter Herr*, to bring you word of any modern science that may help to solve the mystery of your immortal nature. This article stirred you from your malaise. As I read it to you, your eyes opened, and your cheeks flushed. You rose from your bed and said, "*Herr* Ziegler, you shall bring me to this man of science. I will speak with him."

I answered that this man, though a fellow German, lived now in America across the Atlantic, and that a journey there would be long and uncomfortable and might only bring disappointment. To which, *mein Herr*, you replied, "My dear man, you have just perfectly understated the entirety of my existence. Now go and arrange a visit."

I traveled to Verona to send a telegram requesting a meeting, and some days later received a decline. In your uncanny wisdom, *Meister*, you foresaw this and, in anticipation of such, you had given me a king's ransom from your personal treasury which was to be donated to the university in exchange for a meeting. Though your word was 'bribe,' and not donation. I executed this donation through the banks as you instructed, and some days later, the meeting was approved. So I returned to the castle to make preparations for our journey. I gave the servants instructions to direct their activities for six months if our task should take that long, though I never expected that it should. Two days later, we rode the horses down the mountain, taking with us only light provisions and luggage, with plenty of treasure to trade for future necessities. We rode to the port of Genoa to book maritime passage to America. I suggested hiring an automobile to transport us to the coast faster, but you declined the convenience, *mein Herr*, calling motorized coaches queer and unnatural contraptions, second only to airplanes, which you call ghastly beasts of the sky.

The voyage across the Atlantic lasted three weeks and a day, most of which you spent in your cabin or staring out to sea. During this time, I gave you parchment, ink, and coal, as you like it, *Meister*, but your hand was still, never once moving to write nor to sketch your queen, and you spoke little.

When we docked in New York, you were displeased with the noise and rambunctiousness of the port. Machinery chugged, steam hissed, and automobiles whizzed along crowded motorways. These modern things troubled your mind as always, and you lamented the loss of the old world and its pastoral silence. This I could only assume as you spoke in a tongue that I did not understand.

That night, at the hotel, we dined on the roof. You looked to the sky and cursed the overwhelming lights of the city, for they had swallowed the stars, causing you to feel morose and disoriented.

The next morning, I hired an automobile to take us to New Jersey. You despised this journey, *Meister*, but the only other options were the train or bus, both of which you despised even more. At length, however, we settled at the Nassau Inn in Princeton. I surmised this was the best lodging for you as it was within short walking distance of the university.

Per your will, *Meister*, I sent word of our arrival and finalized the meeting arrangements. Two days later, I accompanied you through the campus until we came upon the Institute of Advanced Study. There, *mein Herr*, you instructed me to return to the hotel where I was to await your return. This I obeyed with some reluctance, as I did not wish to leave you.

When you returned to the hotel late that night, you were in such a state! So awful a state as I'd never seen! You would not speak to me, nor tell me of your meeting, and I fretted. Your expression, if I may say, was one of mania. Your speech was indecipherable, and I only understood bits and pieces, for you seemed to speak in ten languages at once, and never to me, but only to yourself, who you called 'the future me.' You even laughed, *Meister*, and it was horrible, to be honest. You had not laughed in the thirty-seven years that I'd been in your employ, and its peculiarity took me off-guard. It was a sound which froze me in my boots, for it was not the laugh of humor, but of hysteria. Oh, how I fretted for your state, *mein Herr*, so dearly I fretted. You would not settle, instead pacing and babbling, and I fretted. For some time, this carried on. Then, God have mercy, you recovered some modicum of sanity, and you asked for parchment and ink, for you wished to write. This brought me hope, for you had not written words or created art in many years, and I supposed a return to this activity might be of some solace to your poor heart. I did not even care that you called me István, who was a former manservant of yours. In that moment I could have forgiven anything so long as you returned to your long-disregarded writing. Before I fetched your materials, I asked if you might rather have a typewriter so you may put your thoughts to paper faster. You answered that a typewriter was a deplorable and dispassionate device and that I was a 'noble churl' for offering. So I fetched your materials and, seeing that you laid fast into your parchment, I retired for the night.

Alas, in the morning, you were gone. Your bed had not been slept in, and your fresh suit hung in the closet. All your belongings had been left, including your writings, which laid still upon the table, the ink barely dry. I could not read them, *mein Herr*, I could not. They were only cryptic codes to me, and you had left them there with only my ignorant eyes to make sense of them. Your money, for which you have always cared little, was thrown upon the floor, and you were gone. My *Meister*, my dear man, my lonely genius, you were gone as if from the earth, and the task of finding you was futile. I did try, I tried so very earnestly, searching the hotel, the university, the bus station, the parks, and all the like. You were gone, *Meister*, gone. After some days, I notified the police, and for weeks I anxiously awaited word you had been found. Yet it never came.

There is great reluctance in my hand now to write what I must. For it is the most awful conclusion to be drawn. That is, *mein Herr*, that after three months of waiting for you, I could wait no longer. The money we had brought was spent, and the task of finding you had grown hopeless. If I hadn't returned to Italy then, I may have never afforded it later, and the servants would have abandoned the castle for lack of master and duty. Oh, how it pained me to go. How it tortured me to know you were out there, alone, in this modern world which you despise so much with no one to guide you, nor to understand you as I do. Oh, dear *Meister*, I was most aggrieved to leave, but leave, I did. With me, I brought your last writings and the rest of your effects and have dispositioned them here at the castle exactly as you prefer.

Now here I sit in my chamber, with only your phantom whispering in the shadows, vanishing when I turn to look. It has been a full year since I returned from America, and you have not come home. I have already dismissed the servants, for I cannot in good conscience retain them if they have no *Meister* to serve. Only I remain. Dearest God in Heaven, I do not know what has become of you, Alexander. Though I know you still live, I fear that I shall never see you again. For I have fallen ill, *mein Herr*. My seventy-fifth birthday was two weeks ago, and I spent it here, alone, slowly dying, clinging to the hope that you may yet come home.

I blame all things upon myself. I accept all responsibility. I will die in shame for having failed to serve you in America, *mein Herr*, and for the state of your fine castle, which shall lay abandoned once I have perished. If ever you find the death you seek, please find me in Heaven so that I may beg your forgiveness, which I do not deserve. Of course, only do so after you have reunited with your one true love, the queen of your heart. Until then, it has been an honor and a privilege to serve you, my dear, wise *Meister*. For only I, Jürgen Ziegler, a poor carpenter from a small village in Germany, have been the personal servant and friend of the world's only living god, who saved my family from bankruptcy, and who held me when my wife died, and who gifted me with a life of purpose, knowledge, and magic.

Your humble servant and friend,
Jürgen Ziegler

Valory lowered the parchment, wiping a tear before it fell.

"We found Mr. Ziegler in his bed upstairs," said Rafael, pouring two cups of wine. "There was a deteriorated photo of his wife in his hand. Very sad, very sad." He signed the cross, then gulped his wine.

Reading through the document again, Valory digested it further. She was glad to confirm that Alex had used the castle as his home and not just as a tribute to Seraphina. That had not been a given up to this point. Also, he had developed a strong personal relationship with one of his servants, Mr. Ziegler. Before Ziegler, she had only known Alex to develop a real human bond with Seraphina and, perhaps, his former servant, István. Alex's lack of close relationships paralleled Valory's introverted nature, which pleased her in the saddest way possible.

Perhaps most troubling, the letter revealed Alex to be at odds with the modern world. By Ziegler's account, Alex shunned innovations like cars, planes, and typewriters. Valory felt she understood why. For many thousands of years, Alex had lived an arcadian life of little variation. Indeed, the man had been around since Homo sapiens were still only far-flung tribes of hunter-gatherers, according to his diary. For almost the entirety of his existence, society had been simple and quiet. Unchanged for vast eons. Then, in what must have felt like a blink of an eye to Alikai, there was a revolution of industry and technology that sharply upended all he had ever known. To 'suddenly' be living in such a different and noisy world must have been very disorienting to him. She could only imagine how he must feel now in this age of internet, smartphones, and space travel.

Finally, and most surprising, Alex had not only been to America but had become lost there! If Rafael was correct, this letter represented the last written work in the library. This meant Alex had either never returned to the castle or, if he had returned, he had just quit writing.

"This is beyond incredible." Valory took the cup of wine Rafael handed her and sipped it. "Who is the man Alex wanted to meet in America?"

"We don't know. This is all we have."

"Wait a minute," said Valory, realizing something else. "You said you found this letter straight away. So that means you guys have known the whole time. You, the agents—you've known this castle belonged to a lost immortal from day one."

"Suspected is the better word, I think," said Rafael, refilling her cup. "This was just one letter, after all. Alone, it was not sufficient proof for an immortal human being. However, as we continued the investigation of the castle, certain findings bolstered the idea. Soon, the notion became quite obsessive. This is why the *Agenzia* agreed to let us bring in experts for more thorough research." He flashed a sleepy smile. "You, Doctor Grace, have provided the confirmation they've been seeking."

Rafael returned Ziegler's letter to his briefcase. Valory sipped her wine, thinking. She supposed Rafael and the *Agenzia* could be forgiven for keeping her in the dark. Not that she was happy about it, but being here was apology enough. This raised a new question, though. If the *Agenzia* had been gunning for proof of an immortal, did that mean Alex was *not* the one imprisoned in the tower? Because what more proof would you need if you had the man himself?

Then again, what if Alex had come home during the Italians' occupation, at which point they'd imprisoned him? Maybe they were keeping him there, away from the world at large, until they could figure out how to duplicate his immortality. Maybe they were testing his resurrection ability with controlled killings. Systematic experimentation to find out what makes him immortal. What a horrible mental image. Could they be so heartless?

"So then," said Valory, devising an impromptu test, "has Italian intelligence opened an investigation in America? To try and track down Alex?" This was a perfect way to mask her real question—Is Alex the prisoner in the tower?

"I could not say," answered Rafael. "I have not been informed of such an investigation. They only tell me what they must."

Valory nodded, losing herself in thought again. It was weird picturing Alikai in mid-century America. That image of him didn't mesh with his ten-thousand-year-old writings. Nor with his castle, his queen, or his art. She thought about his self-portrait she'd hidden under her bed. His wavy, dark blond hair, his beautiful, mismatched eyes, his nearly imperceptible smile. She just couldn't imagine that guy walking the busy streets of 1950s New York in an era-appropriate wool suit and fedora. This letter from Mr. Ziegler had turned her antediluvian image of Alikai on its head. She pictured him standing outside a drug store looking through the glass, marveling at brightly packaged products that were foreign to him.

Rafael's voice cut through her daydream. "And this is why," he was saying, "I must now redirect you."

"Redirect me?"

He rose from his chair like an old bear, casting a fat, warbly shadow on the tapestry behind him. "Valory, the *Agenzia* did not expect you to come in and start uncovering such meaningful data so quickly. They had become accustomed to the pace set by Professor Mancini, you see. As such, they were happy to let you settle in. They assumed it would take months or even years to make headway with the material."

"Uh-huh."

"But now that Director Teruzzi sees the gift he has in you, and since you know the secret of the immortal, he would like to utilize you to his greatest advantage. By focusing your studies, you see."

Valory grew queasy. It sounded like Rafael was about to take her off the Seraphina tomes. "Focus my studies."

"*Si*. He wants you to translate these most recent works as soon as possible. The hope is that those works will contain modern information that is most pertinent to their objectives."

Something sickening slithered into her stomach. He *was* taking her off the Seraphina tomes. "You're saying I'm working for the *Agenzia* now. Is that what I'm hearing?"

"Well, this project is entirely under their jurisdiction and funding. Technically, we've been working for them all along."

The sickening thing in her stomach spread, seeping into her blood. There were still ten treasure bindings to translate. Ten more tomes filled with the story of Alex and Sera, and she had been anxious to study them first thing in the morning. With this new directive, however, she might not be able to study them until next season, if at all. "But you told me I was free to direct the course of study on this project, Doctor. That's what you said when I agreed to the job."

Rafael made a sympathizing grimace. He made attempts to placate her, but she only half-heard him. The disappointment was burning a hole into her heart, for the truth of her situation had just become crystal clear, and it was this:

Her work would never see the light of day.

Everything she had translated—all the amazing information she had uncovered and saved to controlled hard drives—was being sent not into the hands of other scholars, but into a black hole of government secrecy. The *Agenzia Informazioni e Sicurezza Interna* cared nothing for the institute of academia, at least not in this case. They'd brought her here to advance their own interests, seeking not so much proof of provenance, but the key to immortality. The realization was crushing.

She heard the spectral voice of Violet echoing through the vapor. *Don't you dare let them steamroll you like this, sis! This is bullshit and they know it! You're in charge of that library and these are your discoveries! They need you more than you need them. Use your leverage, Val!*

"Will that be okay, Valory?" said Rafael on the tail end of a pacifying speech.

She set her wine down. Rose from her chair. For one frigid moment, she only stared at him, trying to muster the courage to tell him exactly what she thought. Instead, she spun on her heel, heaved the door open and stalked away.

ПОГЛАВЉЕ 43

SOMETHING SHIFTED.

Had he been in the city, so bustling and noisy, he might not have noticed. For it was only a subtle feeling, a heated whisper drifting on the contours of the night. He'd only become aware of it after he'd stepped out of the car and slung his pack to the dirt. Cervantes stood listening to the hush of the mountains, breathing the damp, piney scent of the forest. From somewhere in the woods, a small creek trickled. This area, far down a seldom used dirt road, was as remote as possible while still having a route to the target. There was no one else around for miles. No human cattle. No blubbering, self-important meat sacks ruining the lifeless beauty of the evening. He remained motionless, tuning into . . . whatever this was. This murmur on the wind. Though he'd never felt it before, it was familiar. Invigorating. His muscles seemed denser, his awareness sharper. It was . . . *power*. He closed his eyes, feeling it.

Dominic, remember when I told you I felt something indescribable in the air? A feeling? Like the door to unimaginable power was slowly creeping open right in front of me?

This is what the Salvador was talking about. Cervantes felt the door now, too. Ten minutes had passed when he realized he'd been standing there in a haze, adrift on the feathery sensation. He didn't understand what it was, but he didn't have to. The Salvador knew.

He ensured his car was hidden under a canopy of trees, invisible to the helicopters patrolling the area. According to the Salvador, the patrols were new, having only been deployed after the Italians received intelligence concerning a leak. Also, new military presences had been established along all possible access points into the mountain. Cervantes had passed one such blockade on his way here. For that reason, he'd been forced to park miles away from the mountain and would need to hike to the first waypoint.

He wiped his prints from the car. In this far-flung clearing, two hundred yards off the dirt road, there was little chance of it being discovered. Even if it was, it could only be traced to an alias unconnected to the safe house. Still, Cervantes had to take all precautions. The Italians were on high alert. If the worst happened, he might need to kill feds and military personnel to get to

Grace. Serious crimes. His car, if found and reported at any stage while he was on the mountain, could tie him to those crimes. The rental had to be scrubbed. He wiped the door handles, the steering wheel, the shifter, and the center console. Inspected the seats and the floorboards with a flashlight and a magnifying glass, removing one of his own small hairs while leaving a couple of long, curly ones that weren't his. He spent an hour going over everything twice.

He performed a gear and weapons check. Examined his rifle, holstered his pistols, sheathed his knives. Noted the waypoints on his handheld GPS. After shouldering his rucksack, he donned his helmet and flicked on the night vision goggles. The display seemed brighter than normal, so he turned down the brightness control. Then he hiked into the night. He would only travel in the cover of darkness to avoid being spotted by patrols or resupply units. Considering weather, terrain, and unforeseen obstacles, he estimated a three-day hike to reach the site, maybe four. Penetrating perimeter security would likely take some additional time and ad-hoc planning. The return trek would take about two to four days depending on the success of his objectives and the response of the Italians. To be on the safe side, he had packed enough rations for eight days, and he could set wild game traps to supplement his supply if needed.

He had to bushwhack the first few miles as he navigated dense forest, but the NVGs and the machete made quick work of it. In this manner would he continue until he reached the first waypoint. There, he'd begin his ascent up the mountain. His blood warmed quickly from the exertion, negating the chill of the nighttime foothills. He felt good. Damn good. His body was strong, his mind buzzing. That feeling in the air—that novel sense of power—seemed to give him a little extra something. He felt as if he could take the entire band of Bloodhawks by himself.

The Bloodhawks. Bunch of rejects. The fact that the Salvador had considered sending that band of second-rate mercs on this all-important mission still stuck in his craw, but the Salvador had come to his senses. In fact, he may have only been dangling the Bloodhawks in Cervantes' face as a motivational tactic. To get him fired up and focused. The Salvador liked to do that kind of thing. He thought about his last conversation with him. They'd spoken several hours ago, just before the mission launch, for a last-minute briefing.

Dominic, this mission could define not only the rest of our lives but also the very future of this world. It's what we've been waiting for, and it all hinges on you. Succeed, brother. Succeed at all costs.

CHITSAUKO 44

THE SILENCE HUNG IN the air as if were a living, breathing thing. It made the room fat, the oxygen thick. Voicelessly urging them to do what must be done. They tried to deny its reality, yet they all knew it whispered the truth.

"You are certain you heard him say those words. Those exact words."

"Yes," replied Trentino, speaking Italian. "He yelled it as I was leaving the library. He knows, Marco. I'm not sure how, but he knows."

Savelli turned his back on Trentino and D'Arezzo. Facing the corner, he sighed, running his hand through his hair. The storage room felt small. It was crammed with old stonemasonry and woodworking tools: benches, workhorses, hammers, chisels, saws, compasses, a lathe and the like. The clutter made it feel like the walls were closing in. His suit felt tight. He was suffocating. He'd been forced to call a meeting here in this disused extremity of the castle, far away from everyone and everything else because a certain fact had just become clear—this keep had ears. If the decrepit old professor had overheard a sensitive conversation or two, there is no telling who else might have and what they might know. Savelli wanted to kick himself. He thought back on all the times he'd noted voices bouncing off the stone. How whispers seemed to float down corridors. How you could hear doors groan open two floors away. He'd often heard the civilians' faint conversations through the walls, the floors, the ceilings. Yet he'd not snapped to the fact that his team might be leaking restricted information in the same manner. Again, it was Savelli's fault. He should have recognized the threat and taken steps to neutralize it. Cursing, he turned to Trentino, his face half-lit by a small lantern. "You think he's told the others?"

"I don't know," said Trentino, tapping his thumb against this leg like a tiny jackhammer. He needed a cigarette. "Maybe. But if we do this tonight, it won't matter. The others will get the hint."

Savelli turned back to the corner, leaning on an old grindstone. Shook his head. Scoffed at the debacle this whole thing had become. His first assignment as *Agente Principale*, and here he was deciding a man's fate due to his own negligence. A living, breathing grandfather with a family and a long, prestigious career. The majority of *Sicurezza* agents never had to confront such a situation. Savelli, however, had been forced to confront

292

many things that he and his superiors had never anticipated. This site was different from any other in Italy. It presented a unique set of circumstances that eroded protocols and lulled the agents into complacency. It felt like mischievous imps were running around undermining Savelli's every move, laughing in dark corners. The Incident had been the worst event. Even though his damage control efforts had been successful, the fact remained Savelli had failed to contain the initial situation. For that, he was lucky to have only received a formal rebuke. The rest of his time here felt like a never-ending parade of smaller, more discreet screwups. So far, none of those had reached the director's ear, but if he didn't right this ship, that would change. Inquiries would ensue.

"*Signore*," said Trentino, "The man is a loose cannon. You know that. At this point, his fat mouth is a matter of national security. We can't afford to wait. You have *carte blanche* here, give us the order."

Savelli kicked the remains of an ancient crate, shattering what was left of it. Two strides brought him to the door of the storeroom. He stopped there, holding the handle. After a brooding pause, he looked at the agents over his shoulder, face shrouded in darkness. "It's my mess. I'll do it."

***

The jeep waited in the courtyard, a crescent moon looming overhead. D'Arezzo was at the wheel, engine running. He didn't look back as Savelli opened the rear door and tossed Mancini's suitcase in.

"Get in," said Savelli.

"What's the emergency with my daughter?" *Professore* Mancini appeared every bit the disheveled old man who had just been roused from slumber and prodded into the cold night. He wore his big coat over his pajamas. "Why won't you tell me what the Ministry said?"

"The message wasn't specific." Savelli helped Mancini into the jeep if manhandling could be called helping. "I'll call them once we get down the mountain when we have a better signal." He climbed in to sit beside the old man. Then he straightened his jacket and stared straight ahead, stone-faced.

D'Arezzo drove the jeep across the empty courtyard through the barbican, taking care not to rev the engine, and they slowly ambled around the wall of rocky spires camouflaging the castle. Passing the remains of the tiny old village, they drew near the military encampment. All the lights were off. There was no activity among the canvas tents and equipment. D'Arezzo navigated around the other jeep, which was stationed at the checkpoint. Squinting through the window as he cinched his jacket, Mancini grumbled, "Where are the guards?"

Savelli remained silent.

They passed the checkpoint and then began their drop into the steep, craggy road that was not a road. Within moments, the jeep occupants were being jostled all over the cab. Mancini tried to prop himself against the interior any way he could, but he was weak, and he bounced against Savelli on his left, the door on his right, and the seat in front of him. "Slow down! For God's sake, slow down!" Agent D'Arezzo did not heed the old man's pleas. Blessedly, about a mile down the mountain, he stopped the jeep, pulling into a narrow shoulder near a rocky cliff. Panting from the exertions of protecting himself, Mancini righted his glasses and looked around, ready to chew out D'Arezzo for his driving. Then he saw the cliff just a few meters beyond his window, and the words died on his lips.

"Tell me who is in the tower, *Professore*."

"What?"

"You told *Dottoressa* Grace you knew our guest in the tower," said Savelli, dark eyes boring into the old man from the shadows of the cab. "Tell me who it is."

"I . . . I didn't . . . I just . . ." Mancini looked to D'Arezzo in the front seat, futilely hoping for protection.

"Say it, *Professore*. Give me a name."

Mancini grasped his chest, struggling to breathe. He looked to his right again, eyeing the moonlit rocks that marked the edge of the yawning cliff.

He said the name.

Savelli and D'Arezzo exchanged eye contact through the rear-view mirror. "And how do you know that?"

"I heard Trentino tell him," said Mancini, nodding at D'Arezzo. "I heard him through the walls. Please, Marco."

"Who else have you told?" demanded Savelli. "I want to know every single person who knows that name. In the castle and on the outside. Tell me now."

"No one."

Savelli inhaled long and deep, spearing Mancini with a smoldering gaze. When he spoke, it was with a tooth-grinding growl. "Don't lie to me, old man. I will interrogate everyone you know, starting with your daughter, Alessa. And I promise you I will get answers, no matter what it takes. Answer me. Who have you told?"

Mancini trembled. "No one," he said between machine gun breaths. "I swear . . . I told . . . no one."

"No one at all. Are you sure that's your answer?"

"Yes."

"What about Rollo? Moretti? What did you tell them?"

"Nothing . . . nothing . . . please . . ."

Savelli's eyes were like scalpels dissecting the old man from the inside out. Mancini squirmed, but he didn't change his response. Savelli turned away. Facing straight ahead, he sighed, grappling with what came next.

Minutes passed while they sat in darkness, the engine idling with a low rumble. Mancini began to regain his composure. His breathing slowed, his tremors lessened. Maybe this was all over. They could just go back to the castle now. He'd behave until he could leave. Just leave this damned place and go home to his garden, to his memories. He never wanted to be home more than this very moment.

Letting out a long, slow breath, Savelli exited the jeep, slamming his door behind him. He stalked around to Mancini's side. "No," said Mancini. "No, please. You can't do this."

"Out," said Savelli, opening the door.

"Please don't. I swear I will be better, I swear." The pale glow of the cab's overhead light fell over the Professor's face as he cowered within. Frail, feeble. Behind his glasses, he was welling up. "Please, Marco, please. I'm not ready."

Savelli wilted. He shouldn't have looked into the old man's eyes again. Those scared, sagging, watery eyes. What he'd planned on saying at this moment wafted away on the cold mountain air. Instead, he reached his hand to Mancini. "Come Emilio. Your wife, Mia. She needs you now. You shouldn't keep her waiting."

Mancini looked inward, the seconds ticking by like hours. Then, with a tear sliding from under his lenses, he nodded. Looked at his suitcase but didn't take it. Grasping Savelli's hand, he climbed down from the jeep, the cold rock biting through his slippers. Standing with the cliff edge before him, he looked toward the moon, a brilliant crescent surrounded by stars. He smiled. His hands ceased to tremble. It seemed an eternity passed before he felt the boot on his back. Then he was falling.

A RESTLESS MIND TROUBLED her, foiling peaceful slumber. When she did manage to drift off, the wispy tendrils of half-dreams and muddled thoughts had her tossing, waking her in starts. In those moments, she lay staring at the fire, anxious. The secrets, the tower, The Incident, the third-party threat—these had turned her academic adventure into a dark, thorny pit. Most unsettling, perhaps, was that most of these things had been festering under her nose all along. She was now simply becoming aware of them.

Tenete Esposito and two other soldiers were clearing the great table when Valory entered the Dining Hall. The sight of them gave her pause, but she made herself relax as if wandering in for breakfast. The truth was she'd been on a mission to find Janelle. Searching the castle but making it look like she wasn't. Thankfully, Janelle was there inspecting the friezes on the fireplace, *biscotto* and *caffè* in hand. Seeing Valory, she started to smile and wave, but Valory shook her head, her stern expression saying *Do not acknowledge me.* It took Janelle a moment to get it, brow furrowing behind her glasses. When she did, she put on the worst poker face ever.

"*Mi dispiace,*" said the *tenete* when he saw Valory walking to the table. He said they'd already packed most of the food, but she could have a *biscotto* if she wanted.

"*Sì,*" she answered, "*un biscotto va bene. Grazie.*" Ignoring Janelle, she poured herself a coffee. When the soldiers' backs were turned, she withdrew a folded paper from her pocket and, ensuring Janelle noticed, set it on the table behind a pitcher. Without looking at her, she tapped on the paper— *This is for you*—then she grabbed a *biscotto* and left the hall. Just as she was about to cross the threshold, she glanced back and saw Janelle putting the paper in her pocket. The soldiers never noticed.

Her heart thumped like mad as she walked to the library, the enormity of her act only just setting in. Passing secret notes in grade school was one thing, but passing them here, right behind the backs of those who might arrest you for treason? She couldn't believe she'd actually done it. She never would have under normal circumstances, but 'normal' was a concept that had begun losing its grip the morning Doctor Moretti had appeared at her doorstep.

Two more soldiers passed her as she crossed the Great Hall. She nodded and smiled, trying to appear casual. The note. She prayed that Janelle would not be careless with the note. No telling what might occur if it were discovered. Valory hoped her attempt at encoding it was enough to prevent such an event. She'd written the note in argot, a slangy version of French only understood by lifelong French natives. Natives and Doctor Valory Grace. In that cryptic pseudo-language, she had written: *Need to talk. Meet me in the studio at midnight. Burn this note, tell no one.* She felt the need to add 'Burn this note' to ensure Janelle understood the gravity of what was being asked. At times, the art mouse seemed oblivious. It probably—no, definitely—wasn't smart to initiate a second secret rendezvous with Janelle right now, but Valory was feeling squeezed in, even desperate. She needed to know what Janelle knew, what she may have heard. She needed a friend.

Valory hastened into the stairwell, the narrow passageway giving her a sense of protection she hadn't appreciated before. The narrow, helical stone walls were comforting. Soon, she would be back in the library, where she felt most in control. There, she would begin her new task of translating the most recent works since she was apparently now taking orders from the Italian homeland director. Things had become so weird. A threatening type of weird, like a ghostly scythe drawing closer to her neck, felt but unseen. Professor Mancini's cryptic message had been the catalyst of these fears, kickstarting the suspicions in her mind. Suspicions that were, Valory now realized, justified. *Somebody* was being held prisoner in the tower. That secret wasn't so secret anymore. Something to do with the so-called Incident, whatever that was. Whether or not Alikai was that prisoner was a question that haunted her sleep. That, and the news of this third party that had learned of the castle. The *Sicurezza* agents had clearly been rattled by that development. Whoever this party was, the agents regarded it as a justified threat.

The situation with Doctor Moretti had taken an ambiguous turn as well. Though he was a civilian, it seemed he was acting as an extension of the *Agenzia*, his task being to assuage the fears of the contractors and, seemingly, to ensure they stayed in the dark. That's the sense Valory was getting, anyway. She knew nothing with certainty, which just made everything worse. To whom was his true allegiance here—the idealistic institute of academia or his short-sighted, secretive government? What else did he know that he wasn't telling her?

The morning was cloudy, creating a dusky wash of light in the library. As Valory reached the central table, she greeted Rollo, who was just getting to work. *Professore* Mancini, however, was not there, nor were his things. That was a bit odd. The old man was always the first one there in the mornings, sitting in his usual chair. Yet here it was, 8:02 A.M. and no Mancini. Maybe he was ill. Valory felt ashamed for hoping so. Without him there, the library had a lighter, more pleasant atmosphere. Maybe he'd take the whole day off.

After situating her things, she made her way to the northwest sector of shelves, where the most recent of Alikai's works were stored. When she'd first explored the library—that seemed like a lifetime ago!—she'd breezed through this sector, noting that it ended with two and a half rows of empty shelves. Presumably, had Alex remained here rather than getting lost in America, he'd have filled the vacant space with more codices over time. As it stood, the space seemed destined to remain empty. Alex's last works, lying in haphazard stacks upon the shelves, were thin, shoddily assembled portfolios rather than the beefy tomes with which Valory had become accustomed. Their covers were plain leather, boardless, with careless bindings. It was as if Alex had grown disinterested in creating his usual quality constructions. She pulled the top book off the last pile, tilted the dust off, and carried it to her workstation.

She didn't know what to expect as she laid the book into her cradle. Rafael had stated that these works were the most indecipherable that he and Mancini had ever seen, and she'd been wondering what he could have meant by that. To her, there was no such thing as an indecipherable language. When she opened the cover to view the first page, however, she understood. The text was absolute chaos. It took a few moments just to grasp what she was seeing. Scrawled upon the pages were languages upon languages, both modern and ancient, running atop one another in slipshod fashion. Exotic fragments of long extinct tongues penned in a wealth of disparate, sloppy scripts. There were languages there that he hadn't used in other tomes: Middle African Nagumi, Aka-Kol of ancient India, Cumbric of the British Isle. Here and there, whole sentences curved across the page, running over others. Characters were misshapen, words were misspelled, and blots of ink bled in the spaces. There were notes scribbled in margins, headers, and footers, many with arrows pointing into the main body of text as if Alex had been saying *This goes here.*

Breaking the chaos into the smallest possible units, Valory deciphered some bizarre configurations. For instance, she identified the word university, but it was split into two distinct languages. The first half of the word was written in modern Russian, the second half in Czech. The result was the bastard *Универ-zita.* There were structural and grammatical oddities everywhere. Absolute chaos.

Peering at the page, she tried to attune the colors in her mind's eye. But instead of the characters dancing in their usual harmony, they were at odds. Clashing, rejecting one another. Their textures and aromas were fleeting, or even missing altogether. Nothing made sense.

She turned the page, but if she'd hoped for more clarity, she was disappointed. The text was a free-for-all cage fight between a thousand combatants. A novel sense of panic slithered into her bloodstream. For the first time in her career, Valory felt blind.

I can't read this.

She'd not had such a thought since childhood when she'd first encountered Chinese. That complex language, so different from the Romance and Germanic languages that she had studied up to that point, had taken her much longer to learn. This drunken mishmash was worse.

After allowing herself a quick freakout session, however, Valory calmed, clearing her head. She could do this. Settling in, she focused on the text, morpheme by morpheme. It was tough at first. But over the next few hours, Alex's dyslexic system began to make sense. The colors began to dance, the textures to solidify. The textual lunacy unraveled, and Valory began reconstructing the diary into a sensible narrative. It was obvious that Alex had suffered a nervous breakdown, immortal style. The eons had finally delivered him into insanity. The thought made Valory sick. She did not want to picture Alex like that. Still, she soldiered on, decoding the un-decodable. Once she felt comfortable enough, she began typing a cohesive translation in English. So sloppy and inarticulate were his thoughts, however, that she was forced to take ample creative license: guessing his intent, reorganizing his sentences, fleshing in missing bits, and omitting nonsensical ramblings. In doing so, she was able to fashion a translation that was in harmony with his previous works.

One curious tendency Alex showed here was his use of the phrase 'One Stone.' From the context, it seemed to be a person's name. Sometimes he wrote it in Hungarian: *Egy kő*. Other times he wrote it in Portuguese: *Uma pedra*. And several other tongues. It wasn't until she experienced the phrase in the windy mauves and taupes of German that she realized who Alex was talking about.

In German, One Stone translated to Einstein.

UPOKO 46

Title: The Infinite Diary. (Volume & Entry #TBD)
Date: 1950's
Subject(s): Albert Einstein, Princeton University, others
Language(s): Too numerous and jumbled to notate. Detailed supplemental index required
Material: Leatherbound codex, parchment
Condition: Fair to poor
Note: Actual dimensions of item are 29.6 x 22.8 cm.
Location discovered: Classified

A moment has passed, brother, since last I wrote you. A moment for you and I, but decades for faithful Mr. Ziegler, who has grown old whilst I drew but a single breath. When next I breathe shall he be dead, and I shall stand envious over his grave.

What has moved my hand to quill now is none other than fear. Fear?! Such a strange, animalistic emotion, ever present in the humours of living things, but rarely in me, brother. Only the thought of losing Seraphina has driven the stake of fear through my heart, and naught else until now. For on this day, a fate more horrible than eternal life has been set upon me, and I am lost. That final hope of mine, to merge with oblivion, is lost! Even my correspondence with you, you who are me, shall be vanquished, and we shall stand forever divided. Of this have I learned. Only can I laugh upon my parchment now, brother, lest I weep upon it. For this new future is too heinous to bear. Perhaps you should not read on.

I languish now in this town of Princeton in America, which stands as loud and raucous as all cities of this age. What are these modern folk about? By Jupiter's crown, they stare at boxes of moving pictures. They clamber into metal beasts as though the most natural of contraptions. They fill the streets with mechanical stench and vile fogs, rushing about like maddened cocks, ever sprinting from death in a race they little know is afoot. That noise, that blasted noise! I cannot think!

Apologies, brother. I swim oft in chaotic humours in these days of aberrance.

I sit now in accommodations arranged by István. Here have I come, crossing the Atlantic to meet the man called One Stone, who possesses an intuition of modern science with which my ancient mind cannot reconcile. Exceptional sages have I long sought in my travels, as you may remember, you who are me. For as time drips on, I fray ever more at the seams of cognition whilst these rare and temporary minds slowly build upon the work of their predecessors, unearthing bizarre new realities of which I have only guessed. My primeval conscious, dulled by eons, stands in stark contrast to such ephemeral intellects who burn brightly in their era. These folk make discoveries such as "Electricity" and "Radio Frequencies" and "Antimatter." Such concepts stand at odds with all I have ever known, and yet have I yearned for their advancement. For I have hoped that one day, perhaps, sciences of this kind may be employed to vaporize my soul. Yet is that dream now moot. For today, I have spoken with One Stone, who I am told stands as the greatest of these minds, and his words have savaged my hopes.

One Stone did decline to meet initially, as I expected, for a genius little enjoys the pawing of dullards, which he undoubtedly guessed of me. But a massive donation to his university greased my entry, forcing One Stone's consent. Little has the world changed in this regard, the illusion of money ever commanding events. Only now, in this era, money is but a promise writ upon decorative paper, valuable only in the collective mind. Oh, how industrious are the fantasies of Man.

On this afternoon, István escorted me to this campus of Princeton University, where I bade him leave me, for I suspected I might linger many hours there. No, not István, oh twisted memory! Mr. Ziegler, yes he. I gave unto good Mr. Ziegler a wad of false money and bade him wait not upon me. Then did I enter the designated building, where I was met by two men whose names I have since forgotten. For my substantial donation, these fellows basted me with gratitude, tonguing my ear with wet supplications, so I only waited in silence for them to cease. Then, in their language of English, said I, "Please bring me to One Stone."

I was led through a maze of corridors and stairs, past numerous rooms where bespectacled men gawked at me from behind cluttered desks. The false light of 'Electrical Bulbs' assailed me from overhead. At length, the sound of a violin found my ears, drifting lightly upon the air. I was pleased, for twas the most agreeable sound I had heard since leaving home. The violinist was of passable skill. Not masterful, but fine enough to feather my humours. I knew then, in the way I know many things, that the unseen musician was One Stone.

301

I was ushered to his office by the two gentles, and within stood One Stone with his instrument at his chin, playing a piece unacquainted with my ears. Shoeless was he, trousers and sweater loosely fit upon his slight frame. Unkempt was his hair, white and mangy, with dark, unpretending eyes fixed upon his bow. A thick mustache hid his upper lip. About him was the chaos of a thinker, books and parchment in cockeyed piles upon every surface. At his back stood a blackboard chalked with mathematical gibberish. Whilst he played, I attuned to his humours, for they betokened stark rarity. His colors were in flagrant contrast to the common man's, flowing in rare waves upon the coasts of his conscience. This fellow perceived things undreamt by others. Yet was he blind to the humours of sociability and personal attachment. Such is oft the way of genius.

Though One Stone noted our arrival, he yet continued to play whilst we stood in wait. These gentles grew uncomfortable seeing their generous benefactor ignored, so I bade them leave to spare them the sight. After some whispered protests, they departed, stung by my dismissal. No man loves to learn he is unneeded.

Removing my hat, I sat, awaiting One Stone's finish. As I have said, brother, he was a fine violinist. Short of brilliant, but skilled enough. Whilst he plied his bow, I gave deep focus unto the moment, remembering. Then did I reach for pen and parchment from his desk, and thereupon scrawled some words. This paper I folded and placed atop one of his piles. Seeing this, One Stone came to peruse me, this fellow who sat calmly before him, and he began to sense I was not just any fellow. Here did he lower his instrument. "Thank you for letting me finish," said he, his English heavily accented. He waved his bow toward the blackboard. "Playing helps me think."

"I did not recognize the piece." This, I spoke in German to place him in greater comfort.

"Nor would you," answered he, pleased with the shift to his mother tongue. "It is original. Just a dalliance fluttering in my head."

This I knew, only prompting him to speak of his passion. "You play well, *mein Herr*."

"Thank you. Lina does most of the work," said he, speaking of his instrument. "Do you play, *Herr—?*"

"You may call me Alex. And yes, *Doktor* Einstein, I have played a great number of instruments over years untold. For the playing of music roots me in this moment here and now, a state which I scarcely achieve otherwise."

302

This sentiment, he quite adored. "Perhaps you will give me a show then, *Herr* Alex, as I have given you." With this, he offered Lina unto me.

"If you wish," said I, receiving her. "Firstly, however, please give answer to that ghastly telephone."

He looked at the phone upon his desk, flanked by piles of parchment. "But the phone is not ring—"

The phone rang. One Stone looked upon me in mild surprise, expecting explanation, but gaining none. Tickled, he collected the receiver and dealt with the intrusion. When his conversation ended, he sat on the edge of his desk, observing me anew. He was but silent as he noted my youthly appearance, beset with miscolored eyes of ancient gravity. "That was a neat trick," said he. "Tell me, young man, how did you know it would ring?"

"I but remembered it," said I. Then I began to play. I had a mind to play one of my own pieces, as he had, but the airing of my heart-wrenching style might only depress him, endangering the spirit of our meeting. Thus did I settle upon *Danse macabre* as composed by Saint-Saëns, which I'd enjoyed at an opera with Mr. Ziegler. One Stone was rapt, gauging my technique, then but giving himself over to the melody. Of course, as you have guessed, brother, this endeavor was only a buttery ploy to loosen One Stone's guard. To weld a bond of musical passion betwixt us, that he may regard me as likeminded ally rather than privileged fawner.

Though One Stone was a goodly listener, awed by my skill, I stopped. For I again remembered the phone. "It appears, *mein Herr*," said I, setting Lina gently in my lap, "that you have another caller."

Then did the accursed thing ring again like the screech of a pox-stricken hawk. Yet this time, One Stone answered it not, and only unplugged the "Electrical Cord" which gave the thing life. Then he regarded me with furrowed interest. Faugh! Even the memory of that ring assails me now, grating upon my very last nerve! The sea, the sea! Let me live there, where no telephone rings! Where no motorized coaches pump foul vapors into my lungs! Let me tread forever in the midst of the ocean if only to never hear another telephone! Nor factory, nor airplane, nor bomb, nor any other atrocity born from this bizarre era!

Alas, forgive me, brother. I have forgotten myself yet again.

As I have writ, One Stone regarded me with furrowed interest. In short order, I had confounded him on two counts: my improbable prescience and my musical mastery, both imbued within the young, well-dressed, yet gravely composed fellow sitting before him. In me, he recognized *something* he had never encountered. Now his natural aloofness had fled and a desire to learn had been stoked. In steering us toward this, I had ensured he would speak earnestly with me. Yet did I first beckon him to fill his curiosity. "You wonder upon me, *mein Herr*. Ask of me what you will."

"Shall I? It is you who have donated an obscene pile of money for the right to interrogate me, is it not?"

"It is. But my answers to your questions shall inform you of my honesty, which you shall otherwise discard. Please."

"Very well," said he, casing Lina. After this, he began loading his pipe. "How did you know the precise moments my phone would ring?"

"You yet suspect I paid your colleagues to phone you at appointed times. I wish for you to see that it is not so." Rising from the chair, I came to his window where I looked upon a tree-speckled courtyard bustling with students. "I know many unknowable things, *Doktor* Einstein, though I wish I did not. I wish, in fact, to know nothing at all. Please," said I, motioning for him to join me at the window. He came, firing his pipe whilst regarding me with academic suspicion. "Look out upon this field, if you will, *mein Herr*. Gaze on these diligent students and faculty."

"Yes?"

I gazed upon the field with him, attuning to my own humours until I remembered. "That man in the black hat, walking there. Do you know him?" I knew that he did.

"Yes. That is Professor Wilkins. Department of Mathematics."

"Very good. Give eye to Professor Wilkins, for he shall presently trip, and the book shall spill from his hand." A moment later, this very thing happened, the book splaying open upon the sidewalk. Whilst that professor bent to retrieve it, One Stone looked upon me in disbelief. This random event, no man could have guessed. Yet still was his mind clinging to the rational guess that I had preconceived this plot with Professor Wilkins. Furthermore, that I had bade his colleagues call his phone for my amusement. This was expected. A mind such as One Stone's shall exhaust all reasonable conclusions before entertaining the impossible. "Fret not, *mein Herr*," said I. "Tis known to me that you will not be so easily satisfied. I am not short of proof and shall give unto you as much as you dare."

"Proof of what?" asked he, a whimsical glint in his eyes. "That you are a clever trickster?" Yet even as he asked, his humours swirled with doubt, his rigid intellectualism under assault.

"We shall make words upon it. Please," said I, gesturing towards his desk. "Let us sit." With this, I sat and waited.

Whilst he puffed upon his pipe, musing over the tomfoolery afoot here, he came to sit at his desk. In the doing of this did he bump his glass of water. It fell, breaking upon the floor. He cursed and chuckled, calling himself an oaf.

"Wait," said I as he moved to clean the spill. "Before that, I should like you to read my note." Here I nodded toward the parchment upon which I'd writ whilst he'd played.

"But I am shoeless. I should not enjoy stepping on glass, *Herr* Alex."

"Please, I implore you to only sit and read my note this very moment."

Wary, he retrieved it from his desk and began to read. Here, brother, is what I had writ in the tongue of German:

You shall knock over your glass. It shall break into four large pieces among many smaller ones. One large fragment shall slide under your bookcase and shall be in the shape of a lopsided heart.

Upon the reading of this, he was as an old sheepdog gawping at me, pipe drooping from slackened jaw. I fetched the heart-shaped piece from under his bookcase and held it unto him. This he took into his fingers, then fell motionless. Silence reigned whilst he could but stare, boundless thought filling his humours. Thus was my primary aim achieved—I now commanded the full and willing attention of Albert One Stone.

"I offer you this choice, *Doktor* Einstein. Either ply me with the urgent questions that now flood your mind or otherwise allow me to lay all things before you in my own manner."

He was nearly afraid to respond. "Do you already know which I will choose?"

"Yes. As do you."

Still did he hold the glass heart aloft, having forgotten he did so, and but peered into my eyes with intellectual dread. I had just laid the impossible at his feet. Now he stood upon a perilous cliff, fearing the jump, yet knowing he must take it. "Please, then," said he, "lay it before me."

305

Thus did I lead One Stone down the path of my existence, regaling him with tell of my immortal curse. From the vaguest fog of my tribal days onward, I gave tell as best I could, citing entries from my diary that stand more accurate than corrupt memory. The crux of my tale, of course, was fixed upon my desire for oblivion and my endless failures to achieve it. Vividly did I speak of the many ways in which I had tried: starvation, poisoning, drowning, leaping from cliffs, decapitating myself, hurling my body into magma, and many others. One Stone was unnerved to hear these harsh details, yet I piled them at his feet to impress upon him my desperate and solitary desire.

I muse now upon times of yore, brother, when I have revealed my immortality unto others. Such times have been few, for the telling of my condition bears little fruit. Before One Stone, there'd been Mr. Ziegler, to whom I gave tell the day I employed him. Though he accepted my claim as part of his duty, twas only after the passing of ten seasons that he truly accepted, for he saw with irrefutability that I had aged none. Before Ziegler, there was a man in London called Shakespeare, who entertained my claim in trade for my story. Before he, I gave tell unto my love, Seraphina. Ah, a smile has taken my lips as I pen her name, brother. What a gift. Given now, centuries later, by she who yet commands my heart. Aye, Seraphina did I tell of my curse, and by the gods she believed me straight away. No other had ever believed so quickly. Oh, sweet, mad woman. Spice of a thousand flavors. Queen of my eons. Oh, how she accepted me straight away. My heart, my love, but I have lost her. Again am I branded by the hot iron of truth. She is lost, lost, lost! Now my smile is fled, the farce of my existence reclaiming my soul. Faugh! I cannot remember her voice! Its melody, its tone, its rhythm, tis stolen from me! I paint her face in my deepest sleep, yet the sound of her voice is lost! And there stands none to hate for it! No face at which to point, no demon to slay for wicked miseries! No foes, no allies, no saviors, naught! I stand alone, always and forever!

Apologies, brother, for again have I strayed. A mad fever has descended upon me, and I little recognize myself, nor barely the words I pen here. These long-unfelt emotions, faugh! What a mad state One Stone has placed me in this day. This unwelcome science, this learned knowledge of what I shall become. Tis an unbearable thing that I have no choice but to bear. Once more I say unto you, you who are me, if the present moment finds you in vulgar humours, do not read on.

When the heart of my tale had been laid before him, One Stone sat in somberness, staring upon me whilst absently smoking his pipe. Then said he, "I am deeply troubled to imagine such an existence. If your story is true, it is the most heartbreaking thing of which I could ever conceive."

Here did he cross his arms, studying me further. "Let us pretend I believe all that you have told me, *Herr* Alex. What, then, do you ask of me?"

I grew earnest here, hearing the pleading in my own voice. Yet another mortal passion that had crept into my humours of late. "I am told, *mein Herr*, that you have unmasked the very nature of time and matter with this modern tool of science. Well, I stand before you a hopeless abomination of time and matter, unbeholden to either. Tell me, I beseech you, how a thing such as me can be shepherded into final oblivion. Perhaps, with your learnings, you may unravel me."

Lips pursed upon the bit of his pipe, he pondered. "I suppose I haven't a choice but to set aside the sheer absurdity of your plight, lest you terrify me with more prophecies of ringing phones and breaking glasses."

"Not prophecies, sir, but memories."

"Memories," drawled he, brow furrowing. "I cannot make sense of such a thing, remembering an event that has not occurred. Yet you have done it before my eyes." Here did he peer at the heart-shaped fragment. "Tell me, *Herr* Alex, just how far into the future do your 'memories' extend? Hours? Days? Weeks?"

"Only moments. Betimes they strike unexpectedly. Yet always can I beckon them should I give focus unto the present."

"As you did with Professor Wilkins. And while I played Lina."

"Yes."

"Would you say it is like *déjà vu?*"

"You may think of it thusly if it pleases you. But, whilst *déjà vu* is random for you, I may summon it at will."

Here did he mutter to himself for a spell, humours alight with thought. At length, he spoke, "I suppose I must confess, *Herr* Alex, that your ability to divine the immediate future does not violate my adherence to determinism. Because by applying the laws of physics, every event in the universe can be predicted so long as you have a perfect understanding of the causal events preceding it. My objection, of course, lies with how you thoroughly perceive and compile the data behind these causal events mere moments before they occur. This should be quite impossible. Your ability, if we must call it that, is as spooky as quantum entanglement."

"What is 'quantum entanglement?'"

He chuckled. "A bizarre phenomenon that offends me greatly. Simply, it is when two subatomic particles share information instantaneously, even if separated by billions of light-years. If it is found to have merit, it would suggest that on some level, time and distance are nothing but persistent illusions."

"I see," said I, though in sooth I struggled with such concepts. Though I once shared many discussions of determinism with philosophers of old, words such as 'subatomic,' 'quantum,' and 'light-years' stood foreign to my ears. I cared little for them and merely wished for One Stone to hasten toward the revelation I so desired. "Does such a phenomenon have a bearing upon my state?"

"Only in dreams, *mein Herr*. Let us not worry about that and instead address your great problem."

"Please."

"You said earlier that you have leaped into magma, and this did not kill you."

"On the contrary, it did kill me. Many times. Yet in each instance did I stand alive but a moment later."

"Diving into lava is a gruesome image," he said, shuddering. "But we shall ignore gruesomeness and impossibility for the moment. Aside from being vaporized by an atom bomb, I can think of no more absolute way of physically eliminating mass here on Earth. Diving into magma should have reduced you to your core minerals, which would be impossible to reconstruct. Yet you claim that you were, in fact, reconstructed."

"I stood alive near the magma as though I'd never leaped in. Such is the way of my curse."

"Well then. What does this tell us? That time itself works at your behest? That our deterministic universe backpedals for you and you alone when you die, leaving the rest of us unaffected? That it lets you glimpse events that have not come to pass? Only you, and no one else?" One Stone balked. "Even if I believed you, *Herr* Alex, I do not possess all the knowledge of the universe. The sensationalist press would have you believe I am a god, but I am only a curious man who tries to make sense of the world around me. What do I know of immortality, other than I have never desired it? How could I begin to make sense of this fantasy you have put before me?" He stopped here, looking for my response, yet I only waited. For, even as he rejected my great problem, his mind had been fast at work upon it. I expected this, for he is one who loves to unweave the tapestry of Creation as do all higher minds. I needed but wait for him to speak further, which he did. "I suppose there are ways to ensure your ultimate death. But mind you, they are only theoretical."

"Go on."

"Well, by entering a black hole, for instance."

"A black hole. Such as a very deep pit?"

"No," said he, amused. "A black hole is an object from which nothing can escape, not even light. So definitely not you!" Here did he wag a playful finger at me. "Once you enter a black hole, the intense gravity would rip your bodily mass into a very long string of individual atoms." One Stone chortled, drawing upon his pipe. "I should like to see you come back from that."

"Very well, where might I find such a black hole?"

"Oh, *mein lieber Junge*, you cannot. As of now, they are only theoretical. Assuming my theory of relativity is correct in its prediction of these objects, they only exist in deep space, which I fear we may never reach."

"I see." A spark of hope, if only the dream of one, died within me. "Offer me more than the theoretical, sir, I beseech you."

"But I have little else to offer, *Herr* Alex. I am a theoretical physicist, after all. What am I to do, send you traveling at the speed of light?"

"Of what do you speak? Speed of light?"

"I speak of the speed of light, which is three hundred thousand kilometers per second. If we consider the relativistic nature of time, then your problem might be solved by traveling at the speed of light."

"Go on."

"Well, for someone traveling that speed, time comes to a standstill. It would be as if it no longer exists. And if time ceases to exist, so might your consciousness. For what is consciousness if not a processor of time and space?"

"That is fine. How may I travel at the speed of light then?"

Weary of my ignorance, One Stone shook his head. "If I knew that, I really would be a genius. I am sorry, *Herr* Alex, but nothing can reach the speed of light except light." With this, he fetched a small broom from the corner of his office and began sweeping the broken glass. "I see you are earnest, and I sympathize, I do, but I'm afraid I've no expertise in helping immortals commit suicide."

Here did the long-dormant animal of humanity assail me, and I welled with a desire to lash out at One Stone. Anger?! I had not felt such a thing since Seraphina was taken from me, yet here it reared its head at the mere hearing of words. Words of reason, brother, that I had expected to hear. In the deepest pits of my heart, I knew that One Stone could present no solution to my nature. Yet that which is still human in me makes war against such thoughts, ever more violently with the passing of seasons.

When my foul urge had settled, I spoke again. "I ask for your final consideration, *Doktor* Einstein. Tis known to me that my condition slaps the cold cheek of reason, yet I still crave your indulgence. Think, *mein Herr*. Even if the problem stands as pure fantasy, please entertain it, just for this moment. Is there yet anything that science may offer to destroy me in perpetuity?"

He shrugged. "I suppose you could just wait."

"Upon?"

"Well, even if you are immortal, this planet is not. It will not be here forever. In the future, our sun will die. As part of its death spiral, its outer layers will expand, incinerating Earth with incredible heat. The planet and everything on it shall be wiped from existence. So," he said, shrugging again, "just wait."

"Stand you in certainty of this?"

"Certainty. Now there is a dangerous word."

"Let us assume certainty here. When might the sun's death occur?"

"Billions of years, I'm afraid. I am sorry, *Herr* Alex, I know that is not helpful for your purposes."

One Stone had only offered this 'solution' to conciliate me, but in fact, he had achieved the opposite. For my mind was suddenly afire with a grisly revelation. "But *Doktor* Einstein, what if I am incinerated only for my body to resurrect as always? I shall reform anew upon the scorched remains of Earth, only to be instantly incinerated again. Is that not true? Reformed and incinerated, again, and again, and again for all eternity." Brother, I tell you here that I began to lose control as my cold heart filled with boiling fear. "When I am resurrected, shall I not experience an

310

instant of consciousness? I know it shall only be a sliver of a sliver of a sliver of awareness, but it shall happen. Then again shall I be incinerated only to be alive in the next instant, cursed with another sliver of consciousness."

"Well . . ."

"Those slivers shall bind together! They shall seem to me as one eternal moment of being vaporized! Is that not so?! I shall be unable to do anything! I shall not be able to write, or read, or paint, or play music, nothing! I shall only live and die in an infinite cycle of fire, and I shall *know* that it is happening! I shall have timeless awareness! Hera's bones, man, tell me I am in error!"

In One Stone's eyes, I saw my answer. That the terrifying scenario I had just described was at least theoretically possible. He downplayed my fear, saying I should surely die in some other manner long before then. Yet his humours bore no conviction, and he beheld me with pity.

I cannot recall what happened then, brother. A human panic, primal and unconquerable, consumed me so thoroughly that I lost myself, retaining but a dream of the next few hours. When I came to my wits, I lay in the streets of Princeton, dazed and distraught whilst city folk looked upon me. Then I trudged back to the inn.

This is my fate then?! This is what shall become of me?! I cannot, I cannot! How could I have known that *this* life is paradise and my future but a trillion hells? Seraphina, oh sweet Seraphina, I shall never come to you! I shall only forget you as I float in a fiery nightmare, living and dying billions of times in instant succession, and nothing else! Oh, kill me, Jupiter! Kill me, Zeus! Odin! Amon! Athena! Allah! Yahweh! Vishnu! Should any of you stand apart from the smoke of Man's existential fear, strike me from this false existence! KILL ME KILL ME KILL ME KILL ME KILL ME . . .

ORI 47

THE SUN WAS AN orange balloon sinking into the pointy tips of the Dolomites. From the south roiled a sea of clouds, foaming with the brilliant pinks and yellows of the highland sky. To anyone else, it would have been a beautiful sight. To Cervantes, it was nothing but an ocean of gray and white. He had been able to see colors once, many years ago. He was aware that a glorious palette floated overhead, but there was nothing useful in it. No relevance. Pretty colors were distractions for sheep, and he was glad to have discharged them.

With the setting sun came the eagerness of resuming his hike. He'd made incredible time last night, even with the bushwhacking and precariousness of his route. The weight of his rucksack barely registered as he bounced up the steep, rocky terrain with the ease of a mountain goat. The thin altitude rejuvenated rather than drained him. He felt fast. Strong. Surefooted.

Deadly.

He broke camp, preparing to resume his trek after full darkness fell upon the peaks. He wiped down his gear. Packed his bivy sack and thermal blanket. Inspected his weapons. He'd covered almost half the slope last night. By tomorrow morning, he would reach the final waypoint, where he'd enter the recon phase of the operation.

The sound of an approaching chopper forced him to take cover under a rock ledge. The morning patrol scanning the slopes. From his hiding spot, Cervantes watched it drift into view—a beefy Agusta AW139. He scrunched, making himself small.

While he waited for the bird to pass, he drifted into memories of his old sensei back in Oakland, Retired Sergeant Major Bao Lam, former Green Beret, master of tactical weapons and mixed martial arts. As a skinny weirdo wandering the streets of Oakland, shirtless and barefoot, Dominic had walked upon Sensei Lam's dojo by chance. One look in the window, and he was spellbound. The sensei had been teaching a class of about ten students, leading them through a complicated throwing technique. On the wall behind him were lots of practice swords and firearms made of wood. Dominic began showing up every day, hands pressed against the glass, but he scurried off anytime someone tried to speak with him. At the end of class, he'd go into one of the nearby alleys and practice everything he'd observed that day. He was good at it. The moves felt natural. Like his body was created to learn them.

One afternoon, Dominic was in the alley practicing a move called the double-leg takedown. His 'opponent' was an old body pillow someone had thrown in the Dumpster. He practiced the technique on the pillow, trying to hook its 'leg' and throw it to the ground just as the sensei had instructed his pupils. Then a voice came from the entrance of the alley. "Step with your leading leg, not with your back one." It was Sensei Lam in his black gi, watching him. Dominic froze, brown eyes wide. The sensei walked toward him, and Dominic glanced to the back of the alley, looking for an escape. "Hey, it's okay, kid. I just want to help. Let me show you."

He watched Sensei glide slowly through the technique. "You want to be down low, close to your opponent, and you take a deep step right in between his legs with your leading foot, okay? That's important. It sets you up for the shoot. You try."

Dominic only stood there—no shirt, no shoes, filthy pants—overwhelmed by the muscular, steely Vietnamese man who exuded surefire confidence. His hands were thick with callouses, looking like they could squeeze the life from a bull by its neck. He peered at Dominic with narrow, piercing eyes.

"Let's go, kid, I don't have all day. Squat, step, shoot. Let me see."

Dominic grabbed his pillow.

"No, put that damn thing down. I'm your opponent. Come at me."

That was the beginning of his martial arts training. Sensei Lam took pity on Dominic, for he, too, had been a poor nobody growing up in Vietnam after the fall of Saigon. Rather than raising her children under Communist rule, Lam's mother had smuggled them into the United States at great cost. There, after meeting up with other Vietnamese emigrants, Lam began his martial arts journey, eventually joining the US Army in his teens. Sensei Lam set Dominic on the same path. He allowed him to train in the dojo in exchange for doing chores. He introduced him to various martial arts, and later, to tactical weapons. Dominic was the most natural student Sensei Lam ever taught, mastering advanced techniques with 'chosen one' level aplomb. After some time, however, it became obvious to Lam that there was something dark in Dominic. As his pupil became more confident, he began using his skills overzealously. Making full contact with other students, picking fights outside of the dojo, and perhaps worst of all, expressing an intense desire to use deadly force. Lam's efforts to reign in his aggression were only marginally successful. But he knew what Dominic needed, what could straighten him out—the US military. When he turned seventeen, Lam encouraged him to enlist.

It was these mountains that had reminded Cervantes of Sensei Lam. The sensei loved going into the mountains near Oakland. There, he'd practice his outdoorsman and survival techniques, running mountain warfare drills with his buddies. He took Dominic with him a few times. Those had been the best hours of Dominic's youth.

The last bit of sun disappeared behind the crags, and darkness settled over the slope. Time to hike. After situating his rucksack and weapons, Cervantes slipped on his helmet and powered on the night vision goggles. The surrounding slope became an electronic wash of light, greenish for anyone else, shades of white and gray for him. But something was wrong. The rocks and the trees were too bright, much brighter than last night. The stars were like laser pointers in the sky piercing his retinas. He dimmed the display, but that didn't help. To look through the goggles at the surrounding terrain, he had to squint through a discomforting glare, even on the lowest setting. Only when he took them off to play with the dials did he realize . . .

He could see in the dark.

Not through the goggles, but with his natural sight.

As he scanned the slope, the night became clear. Objects near and far became defined, accentuated by a weird, ghostly shine in the darkness. His depth perception was heightened. He could trace every contour on the frost coming from his mouth. Every wrinkle in his palm, every groove in the bark of the pines. In the deep night of the wilderness, this should have been impossible. Far downslope, he homed in on the black forms of mountain goats clopping along the rocks, even making out their individual legs as they crisscrossed in the void. In disbelief, he unsheathed his knife and held it in front of his face. His reflection stared back at him in the steel, clear as glassy lake water on a sunlit day. He checked his eyes to see if anything had changed, but they were as normal as ever. He realized that this uncanny vision originated not from his eyes, but from *behind* his eyes. A second perception. Some kind of higher level of consciousness roused from slumber.

The door to unimaginable power creeping open . . .

He tossed the helmet and NVGs to the ground and kicked them into the rocks.

BOQONNAA 48

SHE SLUNK DOWN THE corridor, feeling her way along the cold stone. No one was awake. It was so dark that, had she been in a lecture hall rather than a narrow hallway, she'd have not been able to tell the difference.

A sudden noise chilled her. A tink from the shadows, like someone had tapped a piece of steel. She knew it was nothing—just temperature fluctuations causing contractions in some nearby metal—but it scared the bejeezus out of her. Plastered against the stone, she waited for the fear to thaw. The wall was freezing, her blindness absolute. In the silence, she imagined people were standing inches away, looking at her, reaching for her with probing fingertips.

With a deep breath, she willed herself toward the studio. It was much more daunting this time. Janelle wasn't at her side tittering with the innocence of a teen who had broken into her parent's liquor cabinet. This time, Valory was alone and—perhaps worse—dead sober. Sneaking through the castle, she felt like a cat burglar in the Louvre on the verge of stealing a priceless work of art.

For the millionth time, she second-guessed this secret foray. She was defying strict directives at a time when something big was happening. Now that Doctor Moretti had turned on her (at least that's what it felt like) she couldn't expect his support if she was discovered. He and the agents had been acting strangely since returning. A new menace fattened the air. A pall, an urgency, something. It wasn't just that the agents were on heightened alert or that the Ministry contractors were nervous. For her, it was more than that. It was a feeling. The equivalent of hearing sirens in the distance, knowing they were coming for her.

Her new translation of Alex's diary entry didn't help matters. His trip to America to see Albert Einstein had ended like a sweaty fever dream. That translation was fresh and gloomy in her mind. At the end, when Alex discovered what would ultimately become of him . . .

His pleas for final death . . .

The brutal despair pouring from his hand . . .

After re-reading his story, Valory had only sat in dejection. Then she'd come to a decision—she would not share this new work with Rafael or the agents. Not right now, anyway. Tomorrow, if asked, she would say that she'd started but hadn't yet gotten very far. The text was confusing and cluttered, and she needed more time. But the truth? She wanted answers. And she'd get them before continuing to see the most important work of her career disappear into a black hole of government secrecy.

Reaching the western stairwell, she flicked on her flashlight and climbed the spiral staircase. It was just after midnight. She wondered if Janelle would already be in the studio waiting. Unlike Valory, Janelle didn't have to sneak there since the studio fell under her realm of study.

As she crept along the corridor outside the studio, she stopped, for a palette of pastels was suddenly rising in her mind like a colorful fog from a lake. Sleepy ribbons of pinks, yellows, and blues curled into her perception with the aromas of spring grasses and hyacinths. The sensations of the French language. Why was she experiencing them now? She was not currently speaking, hearing, or reading French. Yet here it was shimmering in the synesthetic lens of her mind. Frozen, she tuned in, 'reading' the colors.

Oh cool, this one shows the kitchen . . .

My gosh, how did I miss these . . .

So magnificent . . .

This mist of language, Valory realized, originated from Janelle. She was talking to herself on the other side of the wall. Valory could 'hear' her colors, but not her voice. The low vigor of the sensations suggested Janelle was whispering, not talking aloud. *I'm hearing whispers?* thought Valory. *From someone behind a stone wall?* She stood slack-jawed, 'eavesdropping' on the art mouse. On the colors. She 'listened' for several minutes, wondering how she was suddenly perceiving a speaker whose voice she couldn't hear and whose mouth she couldn't see.

Ouch! That's sharp! <sucking sound>

Whoa. This one is cool . . .

Wait until Valory sees . . .

She listened for a while. Then she retreated to the stairwell, wondering if the sensations would dissipate. They did, somewhat. The farther away she moved, the weaker the colors grew. Returning to the original spot, she perceived the whispers as before—a wispy, skin-tingling fog of Easter.

After several stupefied moments, Valory shook it off. She had a pressing goal. As incredible as this new phenomenon was, there was no time to ingest it.

The sliding door to the studio was open by a foot, lanternlight glowing from within. Making herself skinny, Valory squeezed through. The vastness of the studio caught her off guard. Even though she had seen it before, its chasm-like stretch into moon-kissed darkness was remarkable all over again. Pedestals, easels, carts, and supplies dotted the dreamlike expanse. Alikai—Alex—had demanded a lot of space to create.

Janelle was leaning on the table near the north wall, the same table where she'd wowed Valory with Alex's self-portraits. Her pink coat was zipped up tight. In the glow of her lantern, she was studying a stack of parchments, their curled ends weighted by old chunks of marble. Seeing Valory, she waved as if they were just meeting on the beach or something. Amazing. Did the woman not possess anxiety genes, or what?

Valory had no desire to spend more time here than necessary. She hurried over to Janelle and cut off her attempt at cordial hellos. "*Étais-tu en train de te chuchoter il y a un instant?*" Had she been whispering to herself a moment ago?

"*Chuchotement? Oui, je suppose que je l'étais. Pourquoi?*" Yes, she supposed she had. Why?

When Janelle spoke aloud, Valory was relieved to experience the pastels of French at their normal intensity. There'd been a small part of her that hadn't known what to expect.

Valory shook her head. "Nevermind. Janelle, *je dois te demander quelque chose.*" She needed to ask something.

"*Bien sur.*"

Valory continued in French. "Have you noticed that things are getting weird around here?"

"Weird? How do you mean?"

She sunk with disappointment. As usual, Janelle was oblivious. "Okay look. I need to tell you something, but it's just between us, okay?"

"Yeah, sure."

"So, Doctor Moretti told me earlier that this site is no longer a secret. Someone has discovered its location."

"Really?" whispered Janelle, eyes popping behind her lenses. "Who?"

"I don't know. Someone powerful. They've beefed up security because of it."

"Oh my. What does that mean for us?"

"According to Rafael, nothing, but I'm not so sure. I'm wondering if it has anything to do with Professor Mancini. Have you seen him around lately?"

"Mancini? No, what's up with him?"

"He's missing. No one can find him. Rollo and Rafael are in a bit of a panic."

"Ah. Well, he must be around. There aren't many places to go up here."

"Yeah, maybe. What about The Incident? Have you heard about that?"

"The Incident? I don't think so. What is it?"

Valory sighed, smoothing her ponytail for comfort. "I don't know. Some big security lapse that happened. I really don't know."

"Valory," said Janelle, touching her shoulder, "you seem agitated. Do you need to sit down?"

317

"How about the tower?"

"The tower?" asked Janelle, pointing upward. "You mean the one on the roof?"

Oh, for the love of . . . Yes, the one on the roof. "Have you overheard anyone talking about it? The *Sicurezza* agents, maybe?"

Janelle adjusted her glasses. "Um, not really. But, well, there was this one time . . ."

"Yes?"

"Something strange happened a week or so after I arrived at the castle. One morning, I was allowed on the roof to examine the bronze statue up there. Agent Moreno escorted me."

"Okay."

"While I was up there, I thought I heard someone . . . well, screaming."

Valory felt like her heart was trying to climb up her throat. The darkness surrounding Janelle seemed to grow darker. "What?"

"It was very faint. Sounded like it came from the top of the tower. Agent Moreno said it was only the wind howling in the crevices."

And you believed that? Valory wanted to bark, but in her heart, she knew she'd have probably swallowed that lie herself when she was new. Those first few days at the castle felt like a dream job in paradise. If they'd told her that it rains upside down at the top of the mountain, she'd have believed it so long as she could stay. "How long did the screaming last?"

"I don't know. As soon as we heard it, Agent Moreno escorted me off the roof. I have not been allowed to return."

"It was a man's scream?" *Was it Alex?*

"Uh, well, I'm not sure. It was windy and . . . I can't really say. I'm sorry, Valory."

"No, that's okay," said Valory, hoping she didn't sound as exasperated as she felt. She began to pace. "But we have to figure this out."

"Figure what out?" Janelle was finally beginning to look worried. She glanced into the depths of the studio as if something horrible might emerge from the blackness. "Do you think we are in danger?"

"I don't know how to answer that. All I know is that we're not being told the entire truth about this place. I'm starting to feel closed in. I can't just sit around ignoring this."

"What are you going to do?"

Valory stopped short of saying she wanted to snoop into the tower. She doubted she could go through with something as illegal as that. Still, she found herself verbalizing the forbidden thought. "Janelle, how did you and Agent Moreno get to the roof?"

"The same spiral stairs you used to get here," she said, pointing northwest. "If you go up one more flight from this level, there is a hatch that opens to the roof." Janelle seemed to only just realize Valory's intention. "You're not thinking of going up there are you?"

"No, of course not." *Maybe, a little.* "Just curious."

"The hatch has locks on it. You wouldn't be able to go up without an agent."

"Yeah, no, I said I'm not going."

"There are locks on the tower door, too. Big ones. I saw them."

"Yeah, I got it, okay? I'm not going." Valory dropped her head, palms over her eyes. Yes, she had been thinking of going, if only in a fantasy where she'd magically found some courage. "I'm sorry, Janelle. I didn't mean to snap at you. I'm just feeling really out of sorts right now."

"It's okay. Is there anything I can do?"

"No, thanks. I think I'll just head back down."

"Well, maybe I can cheer you up before you go." Janelle took Valory's hand, leading her to the table. "I just discovered these today under a bunch of old junk in the supply room. Have a look."

Valory shined her flashlight upon the unrolled parchment. Cracked and ragged, the parchment had darkened to a deep brown over time, and the coal upon it was faded. But she could still make out the design. It was a sketch of the castle, an aerial view looking down on the mountain from a forty-five-degree angle. The keep was there, the tower, the bastions, the surrounding crags, everything. Sketched with skillful shading and blending techniques. There were even tiny pigs and goats wandering around in the courtyard. Valory felt a little smile creeping into her frown. Though the sketch lacked writing, there was no question of who the artist was.

"Isn't it cool?" said Janelle. "Here, look at the others." Moving the marble paperweights, Janelle went through the stack, showing Valory each sketch in turn. They depicted portions of the castle in one form or another. There was a top-down view of the Great Hall. A sectional cutaway of the keep. A functional diagram of the pulley elevator. A drawing of the spiked gate with a flyout diagram of the raising mechanism. Stacks of other plans— all sketched with an artistic flair, but lacking measurements or technical details.

"*Acestea sunt planuri?*" asked Valory, sifting through the stack. "*Planurile pe care le-a folosit pentru a construi castelul?*"

"What?"

"Hm?" It took Valory a second to realize she'd slipped from French into Romanian. "Ach, sorry. I hate when I do that. I asked if these were blueprints for the castle."

"Sort of," said Janelle. "They have no measurements, so I think they are more like his internal vision. If these are all he used, it means he sculpted the castle by feel rather than by precise mathematical processes. Not like an architect, but like an artist."

Valory shook her head, awed. The next sketch in the stack depicted the library, detailing the method by which Alex had constructed its magical lighting system. It was fantastic in its simplicity. On her first day in the library, Doctor Moretti had told her that a system of metal-lined shafts had been cut into the walls of the keep, capped by an array of 'suncatchers' on the roof. It seemed an ingenious feat given the limitations of the time period, but Valory could see now that the shafts hadn't been drilled into the keep after the fact. Rather, the sketches indicated that they'd been sculpted in tandem with the castle's construction—in calculated stages—as Alex had shaped the keep layer by layer. Detailed flyouts showed that, as he'd excavated the keep's interior, he'd planned strategic access points in the walls to enable the construction of the lower shafts while carving deeper into the mountain. He had, as was now evident, planned the entire construction of the keep around these shafts before chisel was ever taken to stone. "My god, Janelle. He's a genius."

"Agreed."

"Have you shown these to Rafael? Or Dario?"

"Not yet. Like I said, I only just discovered them today."

Valory inspected the remaining sketches. They showed many 'forbidden' areas of the keep. There was an armory on the level they were on now. In the sketch, Alex had drawn various weapons and suits of armor there, displayed on rows of dummies. Adjacent to that was a music room loaded with instruments of every family: percussion, strings, woodwinds, et al. One level below was a bathhouse. That sketch showed a channel sloping into the keep from the mountain, feeding snowmelt into a reservoir under a tub big enough for six people. Beneath the reservoir was a pit where firewood could be burned to heat the water. Valory envisioned herself lying in that tub, soaking in blessed warmth. She hadn't had a real bath since she'd been here, subsisting on wipe-downs and unfulfilling camp showers using kettle water. The desire to jump into a scented, heated pool was almost erotic. Envisioning herself lying in that steamy bath, she moaned, shoulders slumping.

"If I could get into that bath right now," said Janelle, reading Valory's thoughts, "I would never get out."

"You said it, sister."

Sharing a giggle, the ladies continued sifting through the sketches. Scores of information about the castle were there. They examined the plans for the high-altitude garden, which had been situated in the northwest sector of the courtyard at one time, but was now just an empty, oblong pit. They spent a couple of minutes studying the kitchen, located below the Dining Hall. As she neared the bottom of the stack, one sketch caused Valory to stop and stare.

"Ah," said Janelle, moving her lantern closer, "I see you have come to the Great Chamber."

The Great Chamber. The bedroom where the king or queen might have slept in a typical castle. Here was a set of three sketches depicting Alex's private quarters. These were not drawn in an overhead view, but rather from the perspective of someone standing in various places in the room. Holding her flashlight over the sketches, Valory studied each in turn while Janelle provided insight. The centerpiece of the Chamber was the bed. The frame was massive, carved with tall, fanciful bedposts. Much like the bed in Valorie's chamber, only bigger and more impressive. A bed fit for royalty. There was also a table with chairs, an armoire, and assorted other furniture. A small chapel bearing a Lombardic crest was positioned before a row of windows. On the opposite side of the room from the bed was a grand fireplace with elaborate friezes, akin to the one in the Dining Hall.

While Janelle chattered about Alex's expert hand, Valory noticed something odd. In a head-on view of that enormous fireplace, there was some writing scrawled to the side. It was very faint. So faint that she wondered if she was imagining it. Borrowing Janelle's magnifying glass, she held it over the area and shined her flashlight there.

"What is it?" asked Janelle. "You see something?"

"He wrote on this one. Here, to the right of this frieze. It's his handwriting and . . . there's an arrow pointing at the hearth. I think it . . . yes. It's written in Immortalese."

"In what?"

"Alikai's personal language. Immortalese is my tongue-in-cheek name for it."

"Ah. What does it say?"

"I can barely make it out. I think it says . . . " Valory didn't finish. Instead, she froze. The whites of her eyes beamed like full moons down on the parchment.

"What is it?"

Valory remained silent, paralyzed by the text.

"Valory? Are you okay?"

She nodded.

"Well, what does it say?"

Valory gathered herself, struggling to answer. She pressed her eyes closed, blanking her mind of the colors, and then she read the text again. *Yep, still says it.* She knew then, ogling the faded letters under her magnifying glass, that she could not tell Janelle what Alex had written. For his words were a call to action. Brash, dangerous action the likes of which she'd only seen other people take in movies. Whether she would answer the call was a dizzying thought. If she did, her life could change forever. If she didn't, she might spend the rest of her days in piteous regret. It was the biggest 'if' of her life, and she needed time to process it.

Here and now, only one thing was certain—Janelle could not be told what the text said. Valory flirting with disaster was one thing. Involving Janelle was another. She refused to place the art mouse in danger.

She cleared her throat. "Janelle, you said you haven't mentioned these blueprints to anyone, right?"

"Right."

"Don't."

"Don't?"

"Don't tell anyone. Not yet."

"Well, okay, but why? What does it say?"

"I'm so sorry, Janelle. I really am, but, well, I need you to just trust me on this. Is that okay?"

"I don't know, Valory. You're kind of scaring me."

About time you wake up and smell a little fear. "I get that, and I'm sorry. I promise I'd share if I could." Seeing Janelle's confusion and disappointment, Valory realized she sounded exactly like Rafael. *I can't tell you, just trust me, blah blah blah.* Feeling hypocritical, she said, "Tell you what. If you could be patient and just give me a few days to, uh, dig up some corroborating information from the library, we'll reconvene, and I'll clue you in. After that, you can formally document your discovery, and you'll have a little more insight to boot. Would that work? Pretty please?"

Janelle's smile was small and meek. "I suppose."

Valory checked a sigh of relief. "Thank you so much."

"But I will be anxiously waiting."

Valory nodded, taking one last look at Alex's note, and then she said her goodbyes and left the studio. Poor Janelle. Valory would hate to be sidelined in such a way. The fact was, however, that Valory didn't need corroborating information. That was a white lie she'd told Janelle to buy some time. Time to think about whether she was going to sneak into the Great Chamber. Alone, before anyone else got wind of the secret contained therein. Because once that secret was out, Valory wouldn't have a chance in hell of inspecting that fireplace, which was, she now knew, more than just a fireplace. As she slunk down the dark corridor toward her chamber, the vision of Alex's text danced in her head, its arrow pointing toward the hearth:

Concealed passage to tower

БҮЛЭГ 49

PLEASE, MARCO, PLEASE. I'M not ready.

The words played on a loop in his mind. The image of Mancini cowering in the darkened shadows of the jeep. Frosty clouds pushing from his mouth. Eyes shimmering behind his thick, rounded glasses. Big winter coat hanging off one slender shoulder. That tremble in his ragged voice.

Please, Marco, please.

Savelli threw his blanket off and sat on the edge of his bed, head in his hands. He'd only slept in fits, haunted by Mancini's ghost. The first person he'd killed in the line of duty. That was never supposed to happen. Even in his army days, Savelli hadn't killed anyone. Had never even seen combat. Now, at the top of this accursed mountain, he'd done it. Didn't matter that the duty had fallen under the auspices of national security, it still felt like nothing but cold-blooded murder. He hadn't even had the breadth to process it, because on the heels of Mancini's 'accident,' he'd had to propagate a charade to appease Moretti and Rollo. The two scholars had reported Mancini missing, both in a panic. His belongings were still in his chamber, the way he'd left them, but of the man himself, there was no sign. Savelli had made a premeditated show of sending his agents to search for him around the castle's perimeter, of course finding nothing. Tomorrow morning, the farcical show would continue into the surrounding mountainside, with *Capitano* Ricci leading his men on a search and rescue mission. *Il capitano* didn't know it was a show. He'd only been told one of the Ministry contractors had gone missing. At some point—two days, three days later, maybe—his men would spot Mancini's corpse down on the rocks wearing pajamas and a coat. The old coot had finally gone crazy, bumbling into the night looking for his dead wife. He got lost. Slipped and fell off a cliff. Case closed.

The situation hadn't phased *Agente* Trentino. He snored in his bed on the other side of the chamber. Savelli had already woken him twice to tell him to put a sock in it, but minutes later, the man was snoring again. It was just going to be one of those nights.

Savelli got out of bed and tended to the fire, staring into the flames. That's when he heard it. A faint, deep groaning from the floor above.

Someone opening a chamber door. He checked his watch—it was just after 01:00 hours. The door was likely Grace's. At first, Savelli thought nothing of it. Grace often worked in the library late into the night. Retiring at 01:00 was her norm. Then he remembered he'd seen her earlier that evening, around 21:00. She'd just left the library and had indicated she was done for the night. So what was she doing now?

Maybe Grace hadn't been able to sleep and was headed back to the library. Or perhaps a trip to the Dining Hall for a late-night snack. Not even worth worrying about. Still, Savelli could not dismiss it. He'd already dismissed too many things, and his negligence had turned him into a killer. The time had come to be suspicious of everything, even if it seemed miniscule or harmless.

Scowling at Trentino's snoring form, Savelli got dressed. Then he went to the safe in the corner of the chamber. A two-hundred-pound behemoth, the safe had been anchored to the stone floor, much to the displeasure of Dario Bertinelli. The engineer had opposed any modification to the castle that wasn't critical and had refused to drill anchor bolts into the stone. So Savelli had anchored it himself. He'd had to. The agents needed a secure, permanent location to store their firearms and sensitive data, and there was no other option. Dialing in the combination, N-A-P-O-L-I, Savelli removed his pistol from the safe and slipped it into his shoulder holster. Maybe arming himself at 01:00 hours was overkill, but you never know. Then he checked the laptops and the portable drives, ensuring Trentino and D'Arezzo had been logging them properly. Every device, when exchanged with the eggheads, had to be recorded in a transaction log held in the safe. Savelli had already checked the logs that morning, but he'd gotten into the habit of checking anytime the safe was opened. No one had mislogged anything to date, but he couldn't be too vigilant. The data on these hard drives was a running culmination of all the contractors' work, and it was classified top-secret.

He relocked the safe, grabbed a flashlight, and left the chamber. The corridor was pitch black, the air frigid. Flicking on his flashlight, he walked toward the stairwell, checking each door he passed. They were all closed fast, no light peeking from underneath. He climbed the spiral stairs, making it a point to tread softly as he reached the next level. Grace's chamber was a little more than halfway down. He checked each door as he passed, stopping when he reached Mancini's. There, a roll of paper was wedged near the handle. He unrolled it and read its contents, written in Italian:

Emilio,

If you return while I'm sleeping, please wake me up and let me know you're alright. We've all been very worried about you.

Your friend,
Rafael

Savelli's flashlight sagged away from the note. He stood in darkness, a dull needle pressing into his heart. He rolled the paper and wedged it back in.

Making no sound, he approached Grace's chamber. Flicked off his flashlight. The white glow of a lantern shone from under the door. Kneeling, he pressed his cheek against the cold floor and peered through the half-inch gap. His view of the chamber was limited, but he could see Grace's legs as she poked at the fireplace. With the soft aurora of the fire filling the chamber, she walked to the table and turned off the propane lantern. Then, she began to undress.

Savelli watched. She removed her coat and tossed it aside. Then she pulled her shirt over her head. He could only see her from the waist down, just a hint of her pale stomach visible to him, but then she bent over to remove her boots, and her torso came into view, her long, chocolate hair spilling over her shoulder. She wore an uninspiring white bra, but she was a little chestier than her demure style suggested. Doctor Grace wasn't a flaunter, but she could be if she wanted. Tossing her boots, she began to pull off her hiking pants.

He knew he should turn away. He knew that. Yet he didn't. Grace wasn't the most beautiful woman in the world, but she was a woman, and thanks to this assignment, Savelli hadn't seen a naked woman in months. He and the other agents were as sexually frustrated as sailors on a yearlong ocean voyage. He was a man with duties that weren't being appreciated and needs that weren't being met. He let himself have this.

Her white cotton panties were stretched over her shapely hips. They weren't lacy or frilly, but in this context, they were drop-dead sexy. Reaching behind her, she swept them out of her ass with her fingertips, then she bounced on her tiptoes across the frigid stone floor to her bed. Everything jiggled tightly—Grace's daily workout routine kept her fit. Before crawling into bed, she bent down to retrieve something from underneath. It was a roll of canvas—a painting? Grace propped her head on her pillows and then pulled the blankets over her. Settling in, she unfurled the canvas and held it over her, staring at it. A moment later, she began whispering to it. Savelli couldn't hear the words, but she sounded . . . sultry. She began pleasuring herself.

Savelli rose from the floor, ashamed. The basic instinct to walk into the room and show Grace what a real man looked like had nearly gotten the best of him there. It unnerved him to realize he had been seconds away from doing just that. Maybe he really was nothing but a troglodyte as Mancini had often insisted.

As he walked quietly away, he wondered about the painting that had so enraptured Grace. The fact she'd been hiding it under her bed meant she knew it was something she was not supposed to have. A little treasure she'd stolen from the castle. The painting itself meant nothing to Savelli. Of more pressing concern was the fact that Grace had taken to secreting things away. It showed she had made a conscious decision to defy rules and withhold information. What else was she withholding? Where had she been at this late hour? Even if it was only the library, Savelli needed to know. Perhaps he'd have a little chat with her tomorrow.

Knowing he would be unable to sleep if he returned to his chamber, he resolved to make a round of the castle, starting in the Great Hall. Nighttime rounds had been standard operating procedure last year when civilian contractors first began occupying the keep. Novel protocols were still being fleshed out then, the uniqueness of the site presenting unanticipated operational wrinkles. There'd been two teams of agents then, one active at night and one during the day. After a few months, however, it became clear that the *Agenzia* did not require such a vigilant command within the castle. The army platoon provided sufficient perimeter security, and the agents were needed elsewhere. The *Agenzia's* presence was reduced, and with it, the ability for Savelli to enforce a 24/7 watch over the civilian occupants. Fully vetted eggheads, however, required little oversight, so Savelli hadn't complained.

The Great Hall—normally surreal in the dazzling ambiance of starlight—was muted, the clouds suppressing the celestial blush of space. Savelli didn't bother turning on any of the portables. Right now, the darkness suited him fine.

He made a quick breeze through the Hall, inspecting nothing in particular. Aside from his footsteps, it was dead quiet. If he stopped and remained still, he swore the castle was breathing. Like the walls were some sort of world-weary sentience alive with ancient indifference. It was an unsettling feeling. A feeling made worse when he walked by the marble queen. She looked like a real person sitting there, a black form on the throne, staring at him with eyes he couldn't see.

Making his way to the western corridor, he began to ascend the narrow stairwell when he noticed a light bouncing through the darkness from above. Someone was coming down the stairs. He retreated, hiding in the landing which curled into a dark corner. The light crawled along the stone walls, expanding as the person approached. Janelle LaFleur appeared, bumbling down the steps, a backpack on her shoulder. Savelli checked his watch— 01:16 hours. Sixteen minutes since Grace had returned to her chamber.

Passing the main level, LaFleur continued down the stairs. Savelli slunk after her. One level down—the same level where the agents' chambers were located—she exited the stairwell and continued to her room, heaving the door open with her entire body. Savelli watched as she went inside, closing the door behind her.

So. LaFleur had been 'working late,' too. Returning to her chamber mere minutes after Grace. Savelli didn't like it. Something a bit too coincidental there. In fact, if he met an accomplice in secret, he'd be sure to disband ten or fifteen minutes apart to avoid being observed together. That's when it hit him—the painting. Grace was in her chamber right now giving herself a ride, staring at a painting that had likely come from the studio. From LaFleur.

Now that he thought about it, Savelli recalled several occasions in which he'd observed or intuited suspicious behavior from the ladies. Glances and body language that hinted at hidden intentions between them. The realization was obvious in retrospect—the women had been meeting in secret. Defying the strict orders that had been established for the civilian contractors.

The question was why.

Knowing their meek personalities and squeaky-clean backgrounds, there was likely little to worry about. The women weren't exactly rebellious agitators. Probably just starved for friendship. Maybe even a lesbian thing going on. Considering his recent failures to identify similar threats, however, Savelli was not going to take chances. He had to assume that the ladies had been sharing data and research in defiance of orders.

There was a darker possibility as well. What if Mancini had told Grace something she shouldn't know? What if he'd given her further information about the tower other than what he'd admitted to, and other than what Trentino had overheard? If so, that might also explain the reason behind the ladies' nighttime shenanigans. They could be plotting something together. Something dangerous. If the absolute worst was true, then Grace could be trying to find a way into the tower . . .

BABI 50

HE SPOKE TO HER that night.

It wasn't like before when she'd experienced an impression of his physical form. Now, it was only his voice, his soul, his resonance, riding the dips and swells of the ether, driving from timeless shores. Yet, he was within her.

At first, she didn't know what he was saying. For his voice was not a sound produced by lips and lungs and larynx. His words were not words, but a tonal, elemental oneness in the cosmic ocean, frolicking in wraithlike blues, echoing through the troughs in deep, golden ambers. Afloat in that lofty nebula, he swept through her with a timbre unknowable to the human ear. For Alikai spoke not in a single human tongue, but in the all-tongue of infinity.

Come to me.

The words that were not words flooded her, symphonic vibrations impregnating her soul with their meaning. The symphony would have been impossible to understand in the corporeal realm. But here, it needed no translation.

Come to me.

She began to descend from the heavens, drifting into lower, baser dimensions.

Come to me.

The auroral blues and golds of infinity faded. The dream turned to gray, then to black. Then it was gone.

She woke on her back breathing long and deep, hands stretched toward the sky. A faint haze of color swirled in her mind, then dissipated into blackness. She stayed in this position for some time, reaching upward, staring into nothing. Then slowly, she lowered her arms, feeling the heaviness of her body once more. She wanted to cry, but also to laugh. To panic and rejoice all at once. She wanted to run into Vi's room and tell her what had just happened, and also to hide away and never tell a soul.

***

At that moment, he knew it all.

Perhaps that moment lasted a billion years. Perhaps only a microsecond. All one to him. In that span, he was aware of himself, pegged at some point between the physical world and infinity.

He remembered what he was. Where he had come from. Where he was going. He knew, and he knew *why* he hadn't known until now. It was as if he had emerged from terrible saneness to tranquil insanity, wherein his fractured existence finally made sense.

He called for her.

She heard.

Then he was back in the corporeal realm, and he forgot everything. That was the way.

UMUTWE 51

AS DAWN PEEKED OVER the horizon, Cervantes fumed. Daylight meant it was time to set up camp and rest until nightfall. He didn't want to stop, not when he was so near his objective. Last night's grueling hike up the slope had barely phased him. The jagged rocks, the twisted pines, the crevices and fissures—they were not obstacles, but rather handholds that he used to propel himself toward destiny. His muscles felt tight enough to burst through his skin, his blood like it was racing with amphetamines. Had there been a mountain goat nearby, he'd have knifed it to death just to feel some release. He grimaced toward the peaks, his natural night vision fading with the sun, and he cursed. The Grace woman was now less than two miles away. So near that he practically salivated.

Scowling, he hiked two hundred feet off the main route and found a semi-level spot shielded by a garden of boulders. There he slung his rucksack to the ground, cleared away some rocks, and began to set up a stealthy camp. Once that was done, he would have an MRE. Then he'd meditate, muting this anxious rush and preparing his mind for rest.

The sound of a whistle floated down the mountain. Cervantes listened. There it was again, the piercing shriek of a survival whistle echoing among the rocks. Then, faintly, a man's voice. "Emilio Mancini?! *Riesci a sentirmi?!*" A quiet moment, then the whistle again. Cervantes lifted his AK-15, propped himself on a boulder, and aimed the scope upslope. In his monochrome vision, he glassed a line of soldiers cresting a ridge, blowing whistles and calling out the name Mancini as they scrambled down the terrain. Though he didn't understand Italian, Cervantes knew he was seeing a search and rescue operation. The Salvador had not mentioned the name Mancini in his briefing, but whoever he was, he was lost somewhere on the mountain. From his vantage point, Cervantes counted nine soldiers scouring the crags, eight on foot and one on horseback. There were likely additional men fanning down on the far side of the ridge, beyond his line of sight.

Dropping back into his hiding spot, he considered this unexpected turn. If the platoon was out scouring the slopes, the encampment would be empty. What a gift. Tonight, he'd planned on covering the last two miles of the hike and reaching the outskirts of the camp. There, his objective had been to spend the first night in observation, noting the positions and frequencies of patrols and developing a plan of infiltration. But now he was being presented with an actionable opportunity. The platoon was away from the camp. If he acted immediately, he could penetrate the undermanned perimeter. Once inside, he could find a new place to stealth camp until nightfall.

If he was going to do this, he'd need to move fast.

He stored his gear and shouldered his pack. After the search party had advanced well beyond his position, their whistles and calls drifting farther down the mountain, he cut a stealthy path upslope using boulders and fissures for cover. A short time later, his hunch was confirmed. The camp stationed at the most top-secret site in Italy was a ghost town. He strolled right in.

KHAOLO 52

A LONG CHERRYWOORD TABLE with silver snack trays and water pitchers. The midmorning sun over the Berlin cityscape, filtering through the tinted glass walls. Eleven highbacked leather chairs filled with men and women wearing their finest suits, fingering folders and laptops. Executives eager to be seen, to be heard, to impress. Some were American, some German, some 'other.' The woman speaking was Anna Weber, the CFO of Faraday, Thomas Rockwell's European EV firm. Anna was punching out data points on financial positioning and direction, supplementing her presentation with nifty charts. But she was nervous. They were *all* nervous because Rockwell wasn't himself today. Though he'd arrived on time this morning, handsome and imposing as ever, his mind was clearly elsewhere. He'd met his executives not with his customary charm, but with brusque detachment. His smiles were forced, his handshakes abrupt. No asking after kids and grandkids. No talk of deep-sea fishing or last night's soccer match. He hadn't opened the meeting with his usual lighthearted joke or personable anecdote. He'd just taken his chair at the head of the conference table and said, "Run it." Since then, he'd been half-listening, throwing in the occasional "Nice" or "Very good."

He was on fire.

For the first time in years, he felt powerless. Like he'd made a miscalculation. One man? To obtain the greatest prize in human history, he'd sent *one man?* A psychopath whose only desire in life was to kill anything with a face? *How could I have been so callous? This is* real *immortality at stake, and I send One. Fucking. Man?*

A round of light clapping followed Weber's presentation. Rockwell forced a smile. "Well done, Anna. Thank you." While she turned the floor over to the next guy, Rockwell checked his phone again. Not his personal phone, but the mission phone. He shouldn't have done so amidst these people, but he did. Another sign his emotions were making him sloppy. He typed in his passphrase, scanned his thumbprint, and opened the tracking app. As expected, the tracking signal had become spotty as Cervantes had moved up the mountain. His last coordinates had been broadcast more than six hours ago, placing him at half a day's hike to the site. He was likely farther along by now, but infuriatingly, his position had not updated.

He closed the app and pulled up the sat photos of the site. Enhanced, top-down views of a castle hidden at the summit of the mountain. The zoomed-in photos were several years old and highly pixelated. They had been publicly available via Google Earth for years, only removed after Italy had discovered the marvel in their own backyard and restricted the area. Rockwell had studied the images a million times for no good reason. Though they'd helped in planning Cervantes' route, there was no further intel to be gleaned from them. He didn't know why the castle was there, who'd built it, who'd owned it, nothing. His tipster had not provided that information, and his spooks were coming up empty. But that didn't matter. All that mattered was Grace was there, and even, perhaps, the immortal himself.

But could Cervantes pull this off?

It was a delicate operation with many variables. With the lack of stable communications, the in-field decisions were being entrusted to Cervantes. Rockwell had given him a flowchart of orders that required cold consideration, unburdened by animal urges. If this happens, then do that. If that fails, then do the other thing. All of this while surrounded by Italian military and feds. Was Cervantes up to the task? Could he keep the beast tamed long enough to achieve the mission objectives Rockwell had laid out? In the early years, Cervantes hadn't been as disciplined as now. He'd tended to 'lose it' more often when the siren song of murder drifted into his ears. Those days were long over, but that savage inside him had not been eradicated. It was still there, deep down. Rockwell had felt it many times. One good trigger . . .

Rockwell scrolled through his contacts until he found Colonel Hewitt, leader of the Bloodhawks. Hewitt was a rock-jawed disciplinarian who did not accept failure from himself or his men. Half a year ago, he'd led his mercs into the Congo mining region to clear out a local warlord and his little army of dipshits. Hewitt had been fast and effective, for which he'd been paid well. Rockwell's thumb hovered over Hewitt's name. He could still send in the Bloodhawks. There was time if he acted now. Hewitt and his men were on standby in the small country of Lichtenstein north of Italy, sandwiched between Switzerland and Austria. They could be at the site in less than two hours. A couple of Chinooks could drop the mercs into the courtyard in the dead of night. With the Italian encampment outside the castle wall, a small number of Bloodhawks could defend the courtyard while the others raided the keep. They'd execute the objectives and get the hell out before the Italians could coordinate a response. Fast and easy. Doing this at a top-secret government site, however, would be an act of war. Rockwell would be neck-deep in shit if the raid was traced back to him. But if Cervantes was successful, no one would ever know a damn thing. It would be like a ghost had stolen the world's most precious secret right out from under the Italians' noses. They'd be left angry and confused, pointing fingers at each other.

Rockwell put the phone away.

Will Hyland was speaking now, Faraday's Director of Public Relations. He was a twiggy man with a wall of brown hair and a fitted suit. A well-dressed skeleton. And—surprise surprise—he was talking about social responsibility again. Hyland had been a friend of Jonas Krause, the lawyer who'd been blocking construction of Rockwell's gigafactory. Thanks to Cervantes, Krause was counting worms now. But Hyland, a bleeding-heart liberal, had remained sympathetic to Krause's environmental causes. Now here he was pointing at his maps and charts, denouncing the misuse of the Democratic Republic of the Congo. The Congo was one of the world's largest suppliers of minerals like lithium, cobalt, and nickel, which were crucial in producing electric batteries for the EV market. Hyland was explaining how the extraction of these minerals by companies such as Faraday was contributing to the exploitation of the Congo. Faraday, he said, needed to be sensitive to the plight of the Congolese and do more to assist in the infrastructural development of the country and community, blah blah blah.

Rockwell feigned interest in Hyland's proposal. It was a façade he wore on his sleeve at all times—*I care about people*—which is why Hyland felt comfortable, even encouraged, in bringing it up. 'The good of the people' was at the heart of all Rockwell's philanthropic efforts and an effective lubricant in his business dealings. In reality, it was all just a long con. People were just pawns in his decades-long plan. Tools he used in tandem with his gift to build the most dominant empire the world has ever seen. Even Uni-Fi, free internet for all, was a veiled attempt at controlling access to the global flow of information, a theory his rivals advanced to the media any chance they got. Rockwell, of course, laughed them off as crackpot conspiracy theorists.

"So what I'm proposing," said Hyland with a heavy German accent, "is that we create an outreach committee to interface with the Congo and other troubled regions. This committee would work with local officials to identify the challenges they face. Helping them to overcome these challenges will help Faraday maintain responsible and sustainable business practices and become a trusted actor in the region. Now, here's how we do that."

While Hyland presented bullet points, Rockwell's hate for him festered. Those muddy, wide-set eyes. That thin slip of a nose. Lips like a puckered asshole, shitting words into the room, stinking it up. Self-important liberals like Hyland were constantly devising ways to siphon his profits under the premise of social accountability. People like him were desperate to pull kings down from their thrones because they were too weak to be kings themselves.

Rockwell explored the man's essence. There were lots of odorous colors in there, thick with the musk of self-righteous piety. Hyland was full of himself in that 'People count on me' sort of way. The man fancied himself a champion of human rights, a German Martin Luther King. Hypocrite. His essence held just as much garbage as everyone else: lies, envy, greed, delusion. Diving deeper, Rockwell smelled something putrid. A memory buried far down as if weighted and tossed into the deepest ocean. Like a scuba diver recovering sunken treasure, Rockwell exhumed it from the depths. Dismantled it, separating and reconstructing its oozy, oily colors into a vivid memory.

A sunny day on a forested dirt road. A gentle breeze, the chirping of birds. Hyland was a kid. He and another boy were riding their bikes, chatting in German, laughing. Robert. That was the other kid's name. Rockwell didn't understand German, but he knew it was Robert. The name pounded inside Hyland like a heartbeat.

Rob-Ert.

Rob-Ert.

Rob-Ert.

The boys were coasting down a steep hill, approaching a blind turn, gaining speed. Robert made some kind of joke. The boys laughed. They didn't see the oncoming truck until it was too late. It barreled around the corner just as they were turning into it. Robert was hit hard. The truck ran him over before its drunken driver could react.

Hyland escaped physical injury, but the mental injury was much worse. He witnessed the whole thing up close and personal—his best friend smashed to bits in the slow-motion tick-tock of trauma. Blood all over his bike, his skin. The shock was so intense that he went catatonic.

Then came the aftermath. Years of misery and depression, fear and self-loathing, meds and therapy. Little Will Hyland had devolved into a basket case. He hadn't regained a normal sense of self until his early twenties.

"I envision the committee establishing a permanent presence in the Congo," Hyland was saying. "A full-time staff dedicated to the region. The goodwill and trust we create will be well worth the cost."

Rockwell delved into Robert's death anew, but this time, he grasped the visceral details like a hawk sinking its talons into a mouse. He lived the moment through Hyland's eyes. Felt the impact of the truck slamming into Robert, the repercussions drumming on the airwaves. Felt the warm gore splatter on Hyland's skin.

"I know this isn't in the current budget, Anna, but I'm proposing an allocation for the next fiscal year. I, uh . . . ."

The blood seared his eyes. Robert's bicycle cracked, his bones crunched. Part of him was smushed under the tires.

"Um . . . I forgot what I . . . oh, God."

335

Rockwell lived the moment again, intensifying it with his own essence. New details emerged from the memory. This time, he caught Robert's last-second yelp of shock just before he was crushed against the truck's grill. The squeal of the brakes pierced his ears, meat bursting from the tires like a giant ketchup packet. In the cab of the truck, a bottle of Jägermeister clanked around.

"I . . . I can't breathe."

Again, and again, and again. Faster, bloodier, crunchier. Exhaust fumes in Hyland's nose, bits of Robert dripping down his shirt. Squealing and splattering. Screaming, screaming, screaming . . .

Hyland let out a tormented wail, grasping his head. He went limp and spilled to the floor.

Panic rocked the conference room. Someone rolled Hyland onto his back. Someone else yelled to call an ambulance.

Rockwell just watched.

A part of him knew he should be faking concern while the others tended to the man who'd just suffered some inexplicable episode, but another part of him—a part that had laid in careful, calculated hiding for years—was soaring through the atmosphere. All he could do was smile.

KAPITOLA 53

THE WORLD FELT DIFFERENT today.

She couldn't put her finger on it. If pressed, she might say it felt like leaving home. Not her home in Oxford, nor any of the homes she'd had while working abroad, but *home*, back in California. Leaving Sunnyvale for Harvard as a teenager had been the most bittersweet experience of her life. That memory of lingering on the threshold of her girlhood room one last time. Hugging Mom, Dad, and Vi, knowing she'd not see them again for months. The little Chinese restaurant with the eggrolls she liked. The park where she'd had her first awkward kiss with Brian Reynolds. And her books. Her treasured cultural and linguistic books, both traditional and audio, piled in her room and her mom's study. Before she left home, she'd taken it all in with an ache in her heart.

Leaving them behind, however, had meant a new beginning, a chance to remake herself. To grow into the woman she would be for the rest of her life. Fresh opportunities waited around every corner. New places, new studies, new goals, new discoveries—they beckoned her like a hillside full of wildflowers dancing in the breeze.

This morning was like all of that, supercharged. The reason was Alikai.

Aléxandros. Aleksandus. Alixei. Alex. She'd dreamed of him again, or had she? In some weird way, it felt like *he'd* dreamed of *her*, and that she'd been pulled into his soul. In fact, dream was the wrong word. She wasn't sure the right word existed. Maybe 'ganzflicker.' Ganzflicker was a technique of inducing psychedelic visual and auditory hallucinations using strobe light and white noise in an otherwise sensory-deprived environment. An LSD trip without the LSD. Valory's mother, Doctor Victoria Grace, once published a study on her experiments with ganzflicker. She was assisted by her husband, Randy, who obtained the necessary audio-visual equipment and set up the control room. The experiment was a true crossover between art and neurology, and a fitting example of their perfect odd-couple unity. Adolescent Val absorbed the peer-reviewed paper with wonder and pride.

Last night was like ganzflicker. The control room was the dream realm, and Alex was the stimulus. In this experiment, Valory had been soaked in

337

heavenly visuals, gorgeous harmonies, and most pertinently, by Alikai's message.

Come to me.

They had not been words, but celestial melodies charged with meaning, symphonizing in the throat of infinity. 'Speaking' in that language, Alikai had beckoned her into the ganzflicker.

Now that she was awake, she felt at odds with the physical world around her. She had not left her chamber all morning. She'd just been sitting at her desk, soberly intoxicated. Her chamber looked . . . primitive. The wooden chair felt harsh under her bottom. Her feet resting upon the stone felt brutish. Her mind wanted more of the ganzflicker. To rise on a cushion of helium and drift away from the earth to a new life with Alikai. But to meet him here in this world of flesh and bone, she would have to rescue him from the tower . . .

Three sharp knocks snapped her mind from the clouds. "*Dottoressa. Possiamo entrare?*" It was *Agente* Savelli. His tone was friendly, which was odd. Before, whenever he'd come to exchange hard drives, he'd been all business.

Valory pulled herself together. "*Si, prego entra.*"

Savelli entered with *Agente* Trentino, who had an unlit cigarette in his mouth. Trentino closed the door behind them. Savelli greeted Valory with a smile and then he looked around the chamber, cataloging everything. Trentino remained near the door, fidgeting with his suit. Both agents, she noted, were armed. Something with which she still hadn't grown comfortable. With the fireplace crackling at their backs, the agents' shadowy forms glowed yellow on the edges.

"I don't have many updates," said Valory, speaking Italian. "The source material I've been assigned is quite bizarre, but I'll give you what I have."

"No." Savelli held up his hand for her to remain seated. "It's okay, we'll get that later. I was hoping we could chat."

That's when she noticed Trentino wasn't just standing around—he was deliberately blocking the path to the door. Alarm bells fired off within her. She felt the animalism of her physical body again. The sudden thumping of her heart. A swift severance from the otherworldly miasma in which she'd been adrift. Savelli's welcoming demeanor was a practiced farce. A technique tailored toward her. This was no friendly visit—it was an interrogation.

They know.

"Mind if I sit?" asked Savelli in Italian, motioning to the bed.

"Please." She did her best to remain calm, but as Savelli sat on the bed, she realized that the painting she'd 'stolen' from the studio was just two feet below him resting on her suitcase. A quick look beneath the bed and he'd see it.

Savelli placed his elbows on his knees, half smile clashing with the pits and creases in his cheeks. Despite his politeness, his face never seemed so hard as it did now, his eyes never so dark. By the door, Trentino flipped the cigarette to the other side of his mouth.

"So, *Dottoressa* Grace," said Savelli, "you've been with us for what? Six weeks now?"

"Something like that."

"A long time to be away from home. How are you doing with that?"

"Fine, thank you."

He nodded. "Good, good. I remember last year, after I had been here a few weeks, I was so homesick. I missed my own bed, my own kitchen, things like that. I missed watching my team, Napoli, play. Naples is my hometown; we love our football there." When Valory responded only with timid silence, Savelli asked, "What about you, *Dottoressa?* What do you miss about home?"

"Not having to talk to people."

Savelli's easy chuckle caught her off-guard. She hadn't meant that as a joke. She snapped to the fact that she'd just committed one of her embarrassing social gaffes. She didn't have the wherewithal to feel the embarrassment, though, because she knew Savelli was lulling her into a trap. Sitting casually, asking folksy questions, finding common ground, laughing—these were interrogation precursors meant to make her feel at ease. He was a headsman winking at her while sharpening his axe.

"Not talking to anyone," mused Savelli. "Isn't that a little odd for someone who speaks hundreds of languages?"

"Maybe."

"You know what's funny?" he said, unbuttoning his blazer. "We were chatting with Ms. LaFleur a while ago, and she said something similar about avoiding people. You two are like sisters, I think."

Valory's heart was a bass drum booming in her throat. Savelli's implication was clear—he'd already interrogated Janelle. Now he wanted to see if Valory's story matched hers. His delivery was smooth and patient, but she knew he was burning inside, eager to make her show her hand. Did he already know? What were the chances the art mouse had stonewalled the agents under interrogation? Could she be counted on to keep their secrets? Valory's forbidden trips to the studio? The painting under her bed? The blueprints?

The fireplace?

Shit.

Shit shit shit.

Though she hadn't told Janelle about the secret passage, it *could* have previously been discovered by Dario or the others. For instance, if Alex hadn't concealed it well. Or if he'd left it open before he'd journeyed to

America. If so—and if Janelle had blabbed about Valory's cryptic interest in the fireplace—Savelli could have connected the dots. He could have deduced her big dilemma over whether to sneak into the tower.

The walls began closing in. She knew she looked guilty, which made the walls rush faster. By the door, Trentino's narrowed eyes bored into her.

"Are you okay, *Dottoressa?*"

"Yes, I just . . . would you mind if I use the restroom?"

Savelli hid his annoyance behind an agreeable nod. "Of course. Please."

Valory went to the garderobe, bumping into a wrought iron floor candelabra along the way. Closing the narrow door behind her, she lurched over and puked into the dark hole that was her toilet. To hide the noise, she stuck her face in as far as she could, arms splayed to the sides.

When she was empty, she slid off the stone bench and sat in a ball. This was it. End of the line. This incredible assignment, the pinnacle of any linguist's career, was vaporizing. The chance to meet Alex—to save him, to *be* with him—was turning to sand through her fingers. Banishment or even jail loomed large on the horizon.

"*Va tutto bene, Dottoressa?*" Everything okay in there, Doctor?

"*Si. Un momento, per favore.*"

In a frantic daydream, she imagined herself bursting from the door, pushing past the agents, sprinting through the Great Hall, and escaping into the mountains. Or maybe she could just feign a stroke or something. Get herself on a medevac. But they were ridiculous thoughts, and she knew it.

There was a quarter-inch gap between the wooden planks of the garderobe door. Peering through, she saw Savelli look under her bed. Looked right at the painting as if he knew exactly where it would be. He exchanged a look with Trentino.

Shit.

There was a sudden knock at her chamber door, followed by a man's voice. "*Agente Savelli, signore?*"

"*Si, entra.*"

Trentino opened the door revealing D'Arezzo, who nodded for the agents to step outside. Through the crack, Valory watched them leave her chamber, half closing the door behind them. She heard them walk a short way down the corridor and stop. In the momentary respite, she leaned against the garderobe door, managing her breath.

That's when she realized . . .

She could 'hear' them.

They had to be at least forty feet away, whispering in shadows. It was impossible to hear their voices audibly, and yet the wavy hues of synesthesia were drifting like a deep fog into her mind, exposing their private conversation as if they were speaking directly to her. It was the same way she'd 'heard' Janelle through the thick stone wall of the studio. Stunned,

340

Valory tuned into the conversation, which manifested as wispy ribbons of lilac and emerald, outlined with deep red streaks tasting of spiced wine:

We've got a problem.

Go.

They found Mancini.

What? Already?

I told you it wasn't far enough. We should have taken him farther down the mountain.

Don't be stupid. No one would believe an old man could get that far on his own.

Forget that. There's a bigger issue.

What?

The soldiers found a shoeprint on the back of his coat.

There was a pause while a gray wave rolled over the other colors, muting them. It dissipated when Savelli whispered again. *Are they certain it's a shoeprint?*

No, not certain. It's faint, and it's only a partial. They think it could just be a coincidental imprint sustained in his fall, but they're not ruling anything out. I told you this was a bad idea.

No, the bad idea would have been to let him live.

We could have just sent him home.

Now who's being stupid? You really think that mouthy old bastard would keep quiet?

Shut up, both of you. Where is the body now?

They're hauling it up the mountain as we speak. Ricci has called for a medevac.

What? Son of a bitch. That was my order to give. Now he's forcing my hand. The colors dissipated while the conversation paused, gushing when Savelli whispered again. *Trentino, gather the civilians in the Great Hall. They need to hear the news from us, the way we want them to hear it. D'Arezzo, stick to Ricci and don't let him give another fucking order without talking to me. I'll report to Director Teruzzi. And I'll be requesting Moreno's return. We need all agents on deck right now.*

What about Grace and LaFleur?

I'll finish with them later. Move out.

Wait. It's Thursday. Have you already changed the password?

Yes. It's S-C-A-R-P-E.

Copy that. I'm on Ricci once I exchange these drives.

Fine. Let's move.

While D'Arezzo and Trentino's footsteps echoed away, Savelli stuck his head into the chamber. "*Dottoressa* Grace," he called toward the garderobe, "are you okay in there?"

"Yes."

"I'm afraid we'll have to postpone the rest of our chat. Right now, we have an announcement to make. Please be in the Great Hall in twenty minutes."

"Okay."

When the door closed behind him, Valory leaned over the bench and dry heaved.

ບົດ 54

THE MILITARY MEDEVAC WAS a distant dot in the sky, scaling up as it neared the peak. Wobbling in the crosswinds, it hovered over the basin, the thrumming of the rotors rolling around the ancient, rocky bowl.

Cervantes watched, having been woken by the noise. From his perch— a fissure cut into the limestone forty feet above the basin ground—he peered down upon the group of men. A mixture of feds, soldiers and civilians. One fat, balding man was dabbing his eyes.

North of the basin soared the castle, a sight that had awed Cervantes when he'd laid eyes on it that morning. The spiked gate, the fierce battlements, a soaring tower atop a formidable keep. The awe passed quickly, though, the mission dominating his psyche. He'd been in stealth mode—sneaking past the camp, climbing the adjacent rocks, and ferreting out a suitable foxhole for the day. The vertical fracture he'd found was hidden on the eastern face of a headwall, virtually indiscoverable to those below, but it offered little space and zero comfort. It was only big enough to sit in with his rucksack serving as a lumpy chair.

Cervantes peeked over the rock toward the far side of the castle ramparts, observing another group that stood on the landing at the keep's door. He wondered if one of the people was Grace. He was anxious to see her in the flesh. This woman who'd been born at the same hospital as himself and the Salvador, just minutes apart. He did not comprehend what she was. He understood that their connection to each other—and to some immortal man—was not a blind coincidence, but what then? It wasn't just her research. It was something much deeper. Deep enough to wake a passion he'd rarely seen in the Salvador. Maybe when Cervantes saw her with his own eyes, he would gain a better understanding. In the scope of his AK-15, he viewed each person in turn, the mists of the mountain whipping across his field of view. There was only one woman there, a waif in a thick coat and glasses. Not Grace. Cervantes grimaced, returning his attention to the basin.

After hovering for several unstable moments in the gusts, the medevac landed, and the rotors powered down with a whine. A federal agent hopped out first, joining a trio of his colleagues by the wall. Then two soldiers alighted while the pilot stayed inside. Two more soldiers, having been

343

waiting thirty yards away, rolled a gurney toward the copter. Upon that gurney was a brand-new corpse wrapped in a body bag.

So the search party had found its man. This 'Mancini' for whom they'd been yelling. Cervantes locked in on the bag, longing to see its contents. Disappointed that it was moments from being whisked away. As he watched, he detected something in the air. Something alluring. What was it? Could it be—? Yes. Yes, it was. He could *smell the body*. Even from this distance, even through the bag, he could smell it. Not with his nose, but internally. A sensation of fresh decay, faint, but electrifying. He marveled at this impossibility. Was he only imagining it? No, hell no. It was there, dead meat with undertones of sickly fruit, roiling around in his perception. As the soldiers prepared the bay for loading, Cervantes peered intently. There seemed to be a fog emanating from the bag. A vapor leaking through, defying the odor-confining polyethylene fabric. In his colorblindness, the vapor was dark black against a world of grays, billowing around the bag like the steam of dry ice. This confused him. Though he'd never experienced this before, there was something familiar about it. Something . . . elemental. It reached out to him, and he embraced it. Listened to it. Inhaled it. From its nebula emerged a story of death. He tasted disease. Felt the dull ache of inflamed, deteriorated joints. The acute electrical screams of nerves trapped between bone. The sweet, rotten decay of periodontitis. From deep within the void echoed the ghostly laughter of dementia . . .

Cervantes broke from the sight, shutting his eyes, breathing. Held a fist to his mouth, biting into it. His veins throbbed. Molecular knives hacked at his skin from underneath. That foggy corpse down there was blood in the open sea, and he was a great white shark, starving and emaciated.

He hadn't murdered in ages. Days, weeks, months, he couldn't remember, couldn't think. That decay consumed him, embraced him. It was his father and mother, and he its devoted son. If he didn't kill something right now, he was going to explode.

Panting through gritted teeth, he crossed his legs and assumed lotus as best he could in his cramped foxhole. Then he began firing out his calming mantras.

"I am here and nowhere else. No past, no future, only now. I want nothing. I do nothing. I only breathe.

"I am here and nowhere else. No past, no future, only now. I want nothing. I do nothing. I only breathe."

It almost didn't work. The moan of death was not easily muffled, and he spent several sweaty minutes in a fevered sprint toward nothingness, toward control. Eventually, the beast was sedated, and he fell into a restless sleep.

MOKAPO 55

TONIGHT.

Everything she'd been until now—timid, unadventurous, compliant— would die tonight. Not sometime in the faraway future. Not in a few years, weeks, or days, but *tonight*. Mere hours from now, she was going to risk everything in defiance of the highest federal authority. If she was caught, her life was over. If she succeeded, it would never be the same.

Tonight, she was going to free Alex.

He was the prisoner in the tower. That was certain now. There was no one else over whom the Italians would murder innocent old Mancini. Biological immortality—and control of the world's only immortal man— were the most sought-after prizes in human history. If despots and other powerful rulers knew who the Italians were keeping prisoner, they might start World War III to possess him. That's why this operation had been given a top-secret classification, not the provenance lie that Moretti had been told. And that's why Alex was being held in this rugged mountain wilderness rather than being transferred to some urban facility where his existence could be discovered. The Italians would likely keep him entombed alive in the tower for years, safely hidden from the world while they attempted to synthesize his longevity. An exotic hypothesis, perhaps, but it was the kind of sickening thing of which human beings were capable, a fact proven over and again in antiquity. Whether in government, business, or science, people were corrupted by power, and they did despicable things to one another in the coveting of it. Well, the holy grail of power was immortality. To attain the keys to everlasting life, the Italians had probably brought a clandestine team of scientists into the tower to perform illegal, dehumanizing experiments on Alex. Cloning trials, perhaps. Brutal, bloody testing of his regenerative abilities. Repeated killings. Exploiting him to the point of unconscionable cruelty. That could be why Janelle heard him screaming up there. Valory knew she was letting her imagination run wild, but if there was even the slightest chance her hunch was true, she could not stand by. She had to set him free.

And she was going to escape with him.

That thought hijacked her psyche. Pacing, she bumped into her table. Knocked over a spare propane canister. She no longer saw the tapestry of Seraphina that Alex had woven, nor the expert designs he'd carved into the oaken bed frame. Her nerves had rendered the external world invisible. Tonight, she would meet Alex in the flesh, not in the weird nirvana of the ganzflicker. Their eyes would lock. They would touch. They would speak in languages known only to them. Then they would flee down the mountain together, evading the might of Italy in a scheme that was—in all honesty—doomed to fail. But *if* they succeeded . . . *If* Alex could use his immortal prowess to gain their freedom as he'd done with Sera against the Franks . . . Well, then they'd be bound together for the rest of her life. The suffocating excitement of that plot was like drowning upwards.

First, however, she had to control her anxiety enough to maneuver around Savelli. If he saw her like this, he'd go on instant high alert. She wasn't sure what he knew. At the very least, he knew Valory had been defying a few minor rules. After thinking about their encounter from a couple of hours ago, however, she became convinced that he didn't know about the fireplace yet and therefore had not guessed her intention to invade the tower. If he had, Valory would have already been detained. Still, Savelli was getting close. The longer she stayed at the castle, the more likely she would end up like Mancini.

The fact she would never see this place again was a bottomless sorrow. This jaw-dropping wonder, full of treasures beyond her wildest dreams, would be nothing but a memory. The Great Hall, the marble queen, the library. The incredible, history-defying tomes. Given to her one minute, gone in the next.

Even more heartbreaking, if her plan worked, Alex might never read his tomes again. Everything in that library was written by the man he once was. His only equal, his only true friend through unknowable eons. His memories, his life, his sanity. All stolen from him by the Italians.

She could not fathom how despicable the agents had turned out to be. Valory was still grappling with the fact that they'd murdered Professor Mancini just to protect the secret of their immortal prisoner. About an hour ago, everyone had gathered in the Great Hall to hear Savelli's tragic announcement. Tragic lies, more like.

". . . heartbreaking news . . . an unfortunate accident . . . praying for his family and friends . . . no change to our directives . . ."

The shock had leveled the throng. Rafael and Rollo cried in one another's arms. Savelli, standing on the dais before the thrones, spewed his falsehoods with trained solemnity to the trusting civilians. It almost made Valory sick.

After the announcement, she'd shared some words of consolation with Rafael. "I met Emilio while I was an undergrad in Florence," Rafael said.

"We've been colleagues and friends for more than thirty years. You never saw the real him, Valory. Back in our university days, he was sharp and witty. Even personable. A true scholar who loved his work and his family. *Oddio*," he said, hiding his eyes, "what will I tell his daughter?" Rafael cried, his portly frame shuddering. "Why? Why would he go into the night like that all alone? *Mio povero vecchio amico*. I should have accepted that he was struggling. I didn't want to admit it. I should have sent him home."

Valory had never been a great shoulder to cry on. Comforting emotional people was not in the wheelhouse of an anti-social introvert. Knowing the truth about the murder made it that much harder. Still, she did what she could, handing Rafael a tissue and rubbing his back. Just when she thought it was over, Rollo approached, and the hugging and weeping began anew. Valory slipped quietly away.

After forcing herself to settle in the silence of her chamber, it dawned on her that she had a golden opportunity. Right now, all the castle occupants were outside paying their last respects to Mancini as he was airlifted away. This gave Valory a brief window of solitude in the castle to prepare for tonight's escape. She and Alex were going to need a few essentials in their flight down the mountain: thermal survival blankets, flashlights, extra batteries, a lighter, food, etc. She stowed these items into her oversized Jansport backpack, the one she often carried on the Oxford campus. She'd only brought it to the castle on a whim, and now she was glad she did. The last item she packed was her painting of Alex, which she rolled and flattened. Putting creases in it felt sacrilegious, but there was just no other way, and she refused to leave it behind.

She dashed to the Dining Hall, bagging some MREs and finger foods. Hastening back to her room, she packed the food, then stuffed the engorged Jansport up the flue. Then, as she reviewed her plan, it hit her. That conversation earlier . . .

Wait. It's Thursday. Have you already changed the password?

Yes. It's S-C-A-R-P-E.

Copy that. I'm on Ricci once I exchange these drives.

She was running down one level to Savelli's chamber before doubt could molest her. No one was around. Only the castle watched as she pulled the door open and rushed into the room. It was larger than hers, and tidier as well. There were two bounce-a-quarter-off-them twin beds with military storage lockers at their footboards. Spare suits hanging from floor candelabras. A table full of lights and various equipment. The far corner held the object she sought—the giant block of steel that was the safe. Valory was there in a second, punching the six-letter code into the electronic keypad: S-C-A-R-P-E. *Scarpe* was Italian for 'shoes.' *As good a password as any*, she thought as the lock disengaged. She pulled the door open. The agents' badges were on the top shelf with a couple of radios, a pile of folders, two chunky

347

satellite phones, and two holstered pistols. On the bottom shelf was a stack of laptops and hard drives with a notebook on top. Biting her lip, Valory took what she'd hoped to find—an encrypted USB hard drive labeled *Disco principale - Proprietà del governo italiano*. Master disk – Property of the Italian Government. Then she thumbed through the notebook, finding a list of passwords. The encryption passphrase was there. She committed it to memory.

Relocking the safe, she scurried off. No sooner had she hit the stairwell than everyone began filtering back into the keep. She stuffed the drive into her Jansport and re-hid it inside the flue. Then she crawled into bed, juggling a sweaty, breathless menagerie of emotion.

The theft of the hard drive made it official. Doctor Valory Grace was now a felon.

BAP 56

ROCKWELL FINISHED HIS SET of lat pulldowns, then released the bar, letting the weights slam the stack. He hopped off the bench and slid right into the next station, the quad extension machine. He cranked out ten reps, then moved on, leaving a layer of sweat on the padded seat. He was doing a circuit, training without rest, using weights that were just heavy enough to make him work for it. In his wake, Andrew followed with a sprayer and towels, cleaning up after him. No one else was using the gym. The time was 23:26 hours.

This was the way now. Rockwell's business schedule was balls to the wall, sixteen hours straight, Monday through Saturday. On Sundays, he 'only' worked twelve hours. To stay fit, he had to train late or not at all. To stay fluid with his gift, he snuck in meditation sessions at odd times and locations. He refused to view these sessions as optional.

Two hours ago, he'd been in evening meetings with corporate lawyers, itching to escape for a workout. Tonight's was in the shiny, silvery gym at the Waldorf where he was staying while conducting business with Faraday. It was the same hotel where Cervantes had offed Krause and Schulz. Tomorrow, after a day trip to Aeternus in Prague, he'd fly to Redmond, Washington for a tour of the Uni-Fi development facility. There, in a Redmond area dojo, he would spar with a local mixed martial arts expert at midnight.

Doing it like this was becoming increasingly inconvenient. Sometimes he just didn't feel like it. But as he'd come to grips with his mortality some years ago, he'd put a premium on staying sharp and healthy. As his megarich rivals got fatter and weaker, Rockwell busted his hump. One way or another, he was going to obtain the key to immortality, either through Aeternus or through Grace and the immortal. But that key would do no good if he was bloated, diseased, or dead. He was going to achieve everlasting life at peak physical condition.

Andrew's phone buzzed. Rockwell paid slight attention as his longtime personal assistant spoke to the caller with grave sincerity. Sounded like an update on Will Hyland's condition. As he leg pressed four hundred fifty pounds, Rockwell smiled inside. Scrambling Hyland's brain had been an unexpected joy, something he'd never known he could do. The sudden appearance of such a sneaky ability opened some massive doors. Doors he'd been fantasizing over since putting the little shit into a coma earlier that day. In his head, his long-term plan for global authority was suddenly getting much shorter.

Andrew ended the call, waiting for his boss to finish his reps.

"How is he?" asked Rockwell, racking the weights.

"Still unresponsive." Andrew's eyes, though sleepy, darted around like he'd snorted a few lines. "They'll be running more tests in the morning. I'll get the results as soon as they're available."

"And you ordered the flowers?"

"I did, yes, sir. They'll be delivered tomorrow. I've also sent your personal regards to the family." Andrew fidgeted, running a hand through his short brown hair.

Rockwell nodded, and Andrew cleaned the sweat from the quad deck. The guy was a bit of an oddball. Though he'd handled Rockwell's personal needs well the last four years, he nevertheless had an air of perpetual uncertainty about him. Like he was always afraid he was doing his job wrong, or not doing it well enough. His performance was fine. It had always been fine, and Rockwell often let him know that, verbally and financially. Yet the man executed his duties as though he was somehow faking it. It was a phenomenon known as imposter syndrome, where one is unable to recognize his own value. Rockwell hadn't known of the condition before meeting Andrew, but since then, he had detected it in several others, some of whom worked in his companies. In an effort to help him out, Rockwell had fished around in Andrew's essence a time or two, looking for some traumatizing event that might explain his self-doubt. Something he could talk to Andrew about, help him be more comfortable with himself. But there was nothing. No abusive daddy, no school-yard beatdowns, no cry-in-the-dark failures. Nothing outside of the average pits and pinnacles. Boring. Rockwell had stopped probing, chalking up the imposter thing to an unlucky sidebar in Andrew's neurological wiring.

Rockwell rose, pulling the mission phone from his shorts pocket and stepping away from Andrew. He leaned against a squat rack. Supplied his passphrase and thumbprint. Launched the tracking app. Cervantes' location had finally updated about four hours ago, showing him at the castle. Rockwell had been checking the app every fifteen minutes since then. That was pointless, and he knew it. Cervantes might stake out the castle for days before finally making a move. Still, Rockwell couldn't help himself. Though confident on the outside, his nerves were jumping up and down on a trampoline.

Get me that sweet, sweet immortality, brother.

"Andrew," he said, pocketing the phone. "Have some dinner sent to my room. Salmon and mixed veggies. I'm going up to take a shower."

***

He listened to the recording again. Sitting on the king bed in his royal penthouse suite, still wrapped in a towel, he listened, foot tapping the floor like a jackrabbit. His blood was still hot from his workout. Though he'd just showered, his forehead beaded with sweat.

The message ended.

He played it again.

He couldn't believe how long it had been. Going on six months now. For six long months, he'd been investigating, plotting, fixating, all because of this one snappy little recording that had been forwarded to him by his people at Aeternus. It had set everything in motion. It was what told him that true immortality was within his grasp.

When the message ended, he switched to the mission phone and pulled up the tracking app. No change. He knew that'd be the case, yet he couldn't help himself. His own obsessiveness irritated the shit out of him. In these last few days, with Cervantes getting so close, Rockwell had become sloppy. Unfocused. That's what it seemed like, even as he handled his business with his usual aplomb. Whenever he caught himself thinking *I will become immortal and rule the world*, he felt like a goddamn James Bond villain. The self-comparison angered him. Made him feel like a crackpot. He had to keep reminding himself this was real. Listening to the message helped.

There was a knock on the gold-accented door. It opened, and Osborne appeared, the lavish living room stretching behind him. "Andrew is here with your dinner, sir."

"Have him roll it in."

Osborne opened the door, then retreated into the living room. Andrew rolled the silver dining cart inside. Rockwell motioned for him to bring it over.

"Salmon and veggies," said Andrew, lifting the cover, "as requested. And here's your unsweet tea."

"Hm, thanks," mumbled Rockwell, swiping through his phone.

"It came with white bread. Did you want me to . . . ?"

"Yeah, get rid of it."

"Very good." He removed the bread from the plate. "Will there be anything else tonight, sir?"

"No, thanks, Andrew. Nice job today. See you bright and early."

"Yes, sir. Goodnight."

Staring at his phone in one hand, Rockwell cut into the salmon with the other. Then something happened. A subtle deviation in his perception. A next-to-nothing change from the norm. Just a half-second flicker in his overburdened attention as he was about to eat.

It was Andrew.

As he'd closed the door behind him, he'd paused, gaze lingering. When Rockwell noticed, meeting his eyes, the fork was almost in his mouth. Andrew quickly closed the door.

It hit him all at once.

Andrew's behavior tonight had been just a touch more neurotic than his baseline. An extra stutter here and there. The blinking eyes. Messing with his hair a little too much. So subtle, so unnoticeable in the moment, but in retrospect, it was glaring. When Andrew had lifted the lid from Rockwell's plate, his hand had been trembling. Just a little. At that instant, it hadn't even registered, but it did now. Andrew had wanted out of the room quickly, only pausing at the door to ensure Rockwell took a bite.

Rockwell looked down at his food. Glazed and seasoned salmon. Asparagus and avocado. Two lemon wedges. A lovely presentation on fine China.

"Hey, Andrew? Come back in here for a sec."

A long moment passed before the door swung slowly open. "Sir?" said Andrew, standing just inside the room, hand on the knob.

"Come in. Shut the door."

He did. Slowly. His slacks quivered.

Rockwell rose from the bed. He only wore his towel, his muscular torso tightening. He covered the distance between them in a half second, engulfing Andrew's throat with one hand and slamming him down on the desk, shattering a lamp.

The door burst open. Osborne and Barrera rushed in. Clocked the situation. Immediately withdrew, closing the door behind them.

As Andrew gasped for breath, Rockwell raped his essence. He didn't even have to search for the betrayal. It was a prominent black cloud blotting out his other colors, stinking of burning tar. Rockwell latched on, condensing the cloud into a thick rope that was easy to pull. A tug of war with no opponent. At the end of the rope, the memory came sliding into Rockwell's mind.

The hotel bar. Andrew was alone, absently fingering his phone while having a beer. The label read *Schofferhofer Grapefruit Hefeweizen*. A man approached. Middle-aged. Well dressed. Rugged, stony face. Blue eyes. He initiated some strained but friendly banter. Heavy German accent. Never offered a name, but the man knew exactly who Andrew was. When Andrew realized what was happening, he tried to leave, but the man held his arm, whispering some words into his ears. Most of the speech was fragmented and unclear in Andrew's essence, but one phrase echoed with crystal clarity—*Five million American dollars, all yours.* The man slipped a vial into Andrew's blazer pocket. Smiled, nodded, left.

Rockwell pulled out of Andrew's essence. Hoisted him off the dresser. Spun him around. Put him in a rear naked choke hold, deep and tight. Held it until he was dead.

THE STARS WERE FLEECED by endless clouds riding the cold breath of the mountains. The gusts raced through fissures and crevices, filling the air with swirly little screams. Cervantes watched the night from his perch, and it was beautiful. He used no infrared scopes, no night vision binos. Just his newfound second sight—the eye behind his eyes—surveying the nightscape in all its life-negating glory. The surroundings were clear in his mind. To the north loomed the castle. Every windswept scallop in the stone was bare in his perception, every pitted streak of grunge. No one stirred within or without the walls. Behind his position, far down on the southeastern ridge, two soldiers walked toward the checkpoint, smoking and chatting. In the day, he might not have seen them from this distance without a scope. Now, their bodies were fleshy beacons. He could even see the smoke streaming from their mouths before it vanished in the wind. Everything gleamed darkly in his mind. This phenomenon, he decided, was called 'darkshine.'

He flexed his muscles. Stretched his arms, his quads, his back. It was finally time to infiltrate the castle. To establish a staging area within the keep from where he could hide, stash his gear, gather intel, and track down Grace, perhaps even the immortal. He checked his weapons. Kalashnikov rifle with a single-shot grenade launcher. Two pistols, two fixed-blade tactical knives, two flashbangs, and two 40mm frag grenades. He ensured he had his intrusion tools and a bit of food and water. Ready.

He removed his boots, tied them together, and slung them around his neck. Then he shouldered his pack and his rifle and climbed down from the headwall, fingertips and toes pressing into cracks and holds that others might find insufficient. The weight of his gear didn't bother him. He felt strong. Like he was absorbing testosterone through the air.

There was no one in sight in the run-up to the wall. The castle occupants were all within the keep, and the encampment was hidden from view around the bend. After putting his boots back on, Cervantes paced right up to the castle gate. He stopped under the giant iron spikes of the barbican, checking the courtyard. An array of generators was rumbling in the pens along the eastern bailey, but there wasn't a soul to be seen. He took a moment to appreciate the Salvador's instincts. This top-secret site—protected by the

Italian army and the feds, surrounded by blockades and checkpoints, with choppers patrolling the skies—had been a cakewalk to infiltrate. All because the Salvador had sent his best man, and no one else. The Italians hadn't dreamed of devising defenses against a single man. They were wary of an entire pride of lions, not a single panther.

Still, Cervantes proceeded as if there were a hundred sets of eyes searching for him. He melded with the darkness as he scouted the wall of the keep, looking for a suitable entry. There was a set of stairs that led to the main door, but that was too obvious, too risky. There were windows at higher elevations, but the keep was smooth, carved rock, not individual stones. No handholds for climbing.

As he crept around the western side of the keep, a noise stopped him. The snorting of a horse. Peering into the pen along the bailey, he saw it standing within.

He could see its brain.

He could see.

Its fucking.

Brain.

The horse's body glimmered in the darkshine. The brain, the nerves, the veins—they were like black steel glowing with ghostly gray flames. Like some weird x-ray in his mind, he 'saw' through the horse's flesh and muscle. Starbursts of nerve clusters pled to be pricked. A fat, throbbing jugular howled to be severed.

Cervantes pressed against the keep, kill lust stealing his breath. What was this?! Where had it come from?! He looked at the horse again, zeroing in on its vital organs in the darkshine. He drew one of his tactical knives from its sheath, gripping the handle like he might crush it into powder. One kill. Just one good kill right here, right now. Just get it out of his system. He could make it look like an accident. Like something fell on the horse. A rake, a pitchfork, whatever. No one would give a shit about a horse, would they? No one would suspect—

No. Of course they would suspect. What was he thinking? That they *wouldn't* freak out when they found the horse stabbed through its brain? The darkshine was throwing him off. The kill lust. Breathing, eyes closed, he wrestled himself for control. Fired out his mantras in fierce whispers.

"I am here and nowhere else. No past, no future, only now. I want nothing. I do nothing. I am only my breath.

"I am here and nowhere else. No past, no future, only now. I want nothing. I do nothing. I am only my breath."

When he'd regained his composure, he continued the mission.

In the back northwestern corner of the keep was a wooden double door, banded with pitted iron. A thick modern chain was strung through the handles, a large padlock hanging down. The padlock was nothing—he could pick it in seconds—but he didn't have to, for there was a narrow transom above the door. No light or activity on the other side. Jumping up, he looked inside, seeing no one. He shoved his pack through the transom. Then he grabbed the ledge and lifted himself, going prone atop the door. He shimmied through, dropping into an antechamber. Squatting, he saw a pulley elevator on his left, long disused. The rope, thick and hairy, had rotted over time. The iron crank handle had broken off the rotating drum. To the right, he stepped through an archway leading into a storeroom. It was full of old sacks, crates, barrels, and other junk. Beyond that was the kitchen. Lots of shelves and pottery, a couple of tables, and a massive hearth on the west wall. Cobwebs and dust layered everything. To the north, a spiral staircase led to the upper levels.

It was obvious the kitchen was not used by the castle occupants. It was a forgotten corner of the keep and would therefore make a suitable staging area. As Cervantes created a hidden space among the kitchen's aged containers, he marveled at his luck. Everything had gone perfectly on this mission. Better than perfect. He checked his watch—23:47 hours. Good. Plenty of time to explore the castle tonight. Get the layout. Identify the security parameters. Ferret out cubby holes in case he needed to quickly hide during his maneuvers.

Most importantly—locate Grace.

HOOFDSTUK 58

MIDNIGHT.

She wasn't sure how she found the courage to put on her coat. To put fresh batteries in her flashlight. To shoulder her Jansport. To pull her beanie over her head. Tonight, these minor, everyday movements heralded the end of life as she knew it.

She'd spent the last several hours in a trance, preparing herself for this moment. While in that trance, lying in her bed, she'd 'heard' everyone. Rafael, Rollo, the agents, the soldiers, the civilians—she'd perceived the colors of their conversations as they'd roamed the castle. The fact she was now experiencing such . . . abilities? . . . was mind-boggling. Where had they come from? Why now? Had she always possessed such abilities, dormant until last night? That explanation, though inexplicable, felt comfortable. This new remote perception felt like a natural extension of her synesthesia. As normal as listening to people at a conference table. At times, she perceived several conversations simultaneously, dancing in flowy hues of Italian, English, and, to her surprise, Albanian. She had not known there were Albanian contractors here, a testament to the efficacy of Savelli's segregation directive. Some of the conversations had been foggy whispers— quiet little prayers from lips hundreds of feet away. Others had been nothing more than tawny puffs, which correlated to the noises one makes when weeping, coughing, sighing, and the like. In contrast to those puffs, the words of the soldiers had been sharp and direct, snapping through her mind in tight cyclones of purples and greens.

Above all, it had been the chat of the *Sicurezza* agents that had drawn her attention. From somewhere deep within the keep, away from the other voices, the agents had discussed several pressing matters. Their coverup of Mancini's murder. Their tactics in dealing with contractors going forward. Words of spite toward *Capitano* Ricci. A handful of other operational topics. Valory had tuned out everything else, isolating the agents' colors, hoping they might discuss the tower. Maybe even their plans for herself and Janelle. They hadn't. She told herself that was a good thing—the more the agents focused on other matters, the easier her plot would be. Still, part of her wished *Agente* Savelli had rushed into her chamber that night and arrested her for stealing the master drive. Just shut down her crazy scheme altogether. Then she'd be shuttled to a safe Italian jail cell from which she might—after a conviction and some years imprisonment—return to her boring little good girl life.

About an hour ago, she'd 'heard' the agents in their chamber below, chatting about nothing in particular before going quiet. Now, the night was dead still. On the other side of her chamber door, destiny awaited.

She clenched and unclenched her hands at her sides. Looking in the mirror, she watched her mouth form an O as she took long, deliberate breaths. Breathe in, breathe out. *You can do this*, she thought, staring at her nerve-wracked reflection. *Just be like Vi. No fear, no second guessing, no turning back. Be like Vi.*

She took one last look at her room. Six weeks living in an opulent, medieval masterpiece, surrounded by tapestries, sculptures, paintings, and antiques galore. She'd studied the most amazing tomes in the world, reframing history and proving the existence of immortality. It was all over now. Her career, her life, everything. All to run away with Alex.

Rallying her courage, she went for the door. Then, as if springing from a dark, lonely forest, she suddenly perceived the sensations of a fierce whisper.

I am here and nowhere else. No past, no future, only now. I want nothing. I do nothing. I am only my breath.

I am here and nowhere else. No past, no future, only now. I want nothing. I do nothing. I am only my breath.

Who this speaker was, she couldn't say, other than that he 'felt' male and that he was chanting some kind of personal mantra. His colors were odd. They were the hues of English—a robust kaleidoscope of beiges, reds, and blues that smelled of baked bread and sweet pastries—but there was something strange about the sensations. They were . . . decomposing. A second after the foggy whispers curled into her perception, they turned from beige, red, and blue to gray and black. The smell of baked bread went dry and moldy. Intrigued, Valory latched on, delving deeper. She immediately wished she hadn't. As the words decayed in her mind, they turned foul. Rotten. Putrid. A fiendish tickle assailed her, like maggots were suddenly crawling around inside her head. She came within a hair of gagging before forcing the sensations from her mind.

Such a synesthetic deterioration had never happened. Whoever this speaker was, he wasn't well. Maybe he was sick. Dying. Suffering from some sort of trauma, perhaps. Valory had no idea. All she knew for sure was that the man was awake somewhere in or around the castle.

She considered delaying her little venture due to this new speaker's presence. If he was out there walking around, he might run into her and ruin everything. But delay was not an option. Sometime tomorrow, the agents would discover that the master drive was missing. She had to proceed as planned right now or get arrested later.

Gathering her nerves, she turned off her lantern. Darkness swallowed her chamber. She gave herself one last pep talk then opened the door just enough to squeeze through. The groan it produced felt like a tree falling in the forest, its deep grumble rolling down the corridor. Closing the door behind her, she lingered, trembling, forehead pressed against the wood. After a long, controlled exhale, she scampered down the corridor.

***

There it was. A slow, faint groan from above, starkly audible in the otherwise deathly silence of night. Grace was leaving her chamber. The fact that she'd opened the door slowly, carefully, suggested she was not going to the library or the Dining Hall. She was sneaking. Savelli checked his watch. Just after midnight. He shook his head. He'd not expected Grace to repeat her ill-advised forays into restricted areas, not after the scare he'd given her earlier that day. Such a shame. Grace was much smarter than that, but her curiosity seemed to have tainted her. Now he was going to have to catch her red-handed. He would have to fill out a criminal report and arrange for her dismissal, once he'd cleared it with Director Teruzzi. Moretti would be furious, but fuck Moretti. He'd compromised this operation enough. Things would be smoother when Grace was gone. She'd already given the director most of the information he coveted, so she wouldn't be missed much. Some other librarian could take her place, and Savelli would finally be able to sleep easy knowing with certainty that Grace would never get inside that tower.

Hearing the faint sound of Grace's door closing, Savelli woke Trentino, who rubbed the bleariness from his eyes. Then he used tactical field signals to communicate his orders. The last thing he needed was another verbal exchange to float through the walls. With his hands, he conveyed the message; *Remain quiet. Subject is sneaking around. We will track and apprehend. Gear up, let's roll.*

***

Valory's first stop before the Great Chamber was the studio. On her first visit there, she'd noticed a handsaw among a jumble of Alex's woodworking tools. She might need that saw. If she reached the tower to find Alex chained up, she would need something to cut the chain, or lock, or whatever. She only hoped the ancient saw still had teeth.

Feeling her way up the stairwell, her swishing clothes and her labored breaths felt like giant flashing signs pointing her out in the dark. She looked back a hundred times, seeing nothing but blackness. She didn't turn on her

359

flashlight until she reached the studio. Once inside, she made a beeline to Alex's frame-making station, where she'd noticed the saw last time. The studio felt dead. No moonlight beaming through the windows. No Janelle chattering among the workstations with the naivety of a trusting child.

Poor Janelle. Valory didn't know what had become of her since *Agente* Savelli's little visit. She had not 'heard' the agents discussing her fate, nor had she 'heard' Janelle's voice since then. She had perceived some crying, however, which could have been Janelle. Crying, sighing, gasping, and other non-lexical tokens fell under the realm of paralanguage. Though these vocalics manifested as colorful, short-lived puffs in Valory's awareness, they provided no definitive identification of the speaker. But if anyone had reason to cry aside from Rafael and Rollo, it was Janelle. Valory hoped that the art mouse was holding up okay and that she would suffer no more than a rebuke, or at worst, dismissal. As for Rafael, she felt bad for abandoning him, but his actions made him at least somewhat complicit. He'd been the *Sicurezza's* loyal dog, keeping secrets from the Ministry contractors from the beginning. He'd aided them in burying discoveries that had the power to alter world history. Venerable academics should stand in full opposition to such secrecy.

From a wooden cart full of tools, Valory retrieved the saw. Grasping the handle, she fingered the teeth, testing their sharpness. Not great, but not awful. She rummaged for something better, wincing at the metallic ruckus she made, but there was nothing. The saw would have to do. She wasn't positive it would cut metal, but, well, it had to. It just had to.

She hastened from the studio, flicking off the flashlight once she was in the corridor. Then she felt her way back to the stairwell and descended one level. Alex's blueprints had shown the Great Chamber to be located there. She hoped he'd stayed true to the blueprints as he'd sculpted the castle. If he hadn't, this could all be for nothing.

PEATÜKK 59

CERVANTES EMERGED FROM BEHIND a small wall of old crates, sacks, and barrels, exiting the storage room. His rifle and gear were hidden in a disused crate. This portion of the mission required stealth, so he brought only his knives, pistols, and intrusion tools.

The archway to the kitchen led to a stairwell on his left and a long corridor to his right. He suspected his objectives were on the higher floors of the keep, but protocol dictated that he map this floor first. Get the lay of the land. Identify potential obstacles and assets. He slunk down the corridor, a ghost gliding through the darkness. A darkness that was lit in the silvery glow of the darkshine.

A short way down the hall, there was another dusty storeroom packed with junk. A little farther was another small room, empty. Behind the next door, someone was snoring. Each chesty snore was accompanied by a lispy whistle. Cervantes stopped there, inches from the threshold, waiting. Listening. Feeling. Behind that door was a man. A fat man with a missing tooth. Cervantes explored the sensations of this man. His guts stunk of phlegm and muck. His worn knees ached. The onset of disease festered in his liver, his arteries, his heart. Cervantes inhaled the scents, tasting the flavors of a slow, painful death. He gripped his knife handle, burning to open the door and hasten the process.

Tearing himself away, he crept to the next room. No snores, but someone was in there. Not only could he hear the faint crackling of a fire, but he could feel the man's breath. It was strong, steady, clean. His innards gave off the fresh, meaty redolence of health. Unlike the fat man, this guy took care of himself. The urge to slay him was much more intense.

Grimacing the impulse into submission, Cervantes walked the remainder of the corridor, pausing at each chamber, reaching inside with his senses. Some were empty, some had occupants. None of those occupants felt feminine. In all, there were five men on this level. Good to know.

At the end of the corridor, he ascended a narrow spiral staircase. On the next floor, a corridor like the one below ran westward, and there was an arched portal on the south wall. Cervantes peeked around the arch. There, a vast hall loomed, ghosted with the sparse light of the night. Cervantes knew that he should be awestruck. He knew that, right now, a normal person would be gasping and wide-eyed at the grandiose marvel before him, full of columns, sculptures, and thrones. Yet he only viewed the hall with a cold eye, identifying pockets of deep shadow in which he could hide if the need arose.

That need arose quickly. Midway down the corridor, a door opened, and two feds emerged. It was obvious they were feds—the way they were dressed, the way they moved, the firearms bulging under their blazers. That didn't shock Cervantes. What shocked him was that he could see their vital organs. Like the horse outside, the agents were walking X-rays in the darkshine, their brains lumps of glowing shadows in their skulls. Their hearts were obsidian muscles beating in their chests. Just walking sacks of electrified meat, waiting to be slain. The rush was intense. Wherever this sight had come from, it was fantastic.

Hidden behind the archway, Cervantes watched as two more feds emerged from the next room over. The four men congregated in the corridor and whispered to one another. Then they split, two walking west and two east, flashlights pointed ahead. Cervantes ducked into the shadows behind the archway and went dead still, waiting, wondering what they were up to. Could they have somehow been alerted to his presence? Were they searching for him? No. They were searching for someone, yes, but not him.

Two feds strode into the Great Hall, whipping their lights around. Cervantes slipped behind a statue before an agent illuminated the spot where he'd just been. They inspected every nook and cranny of the hall while Cervantes played cat and mouse, slipping into darkness ahead of their lights. Satisfied, the agents returned to the corridor and hastened up the stairwell. Cervantes slunk after them, maintaining a safe distance from the sound of their footsteps. These feds were on a midnight mission, and something told him it had to do with Grace. Just a hunch, but it felt right. His blood simmered. He just might accomplish his objectives much faster than anticipated.

MOAKÃHA 60

VALORY TURNED ON HER flashlight for a quick look inside the bathing chamber. She'd seen this room in Alex's blueprints, giggling with Janelle about sinking into its heated waters. There was no door in the archway. Alex hadn't cared for modesty, she supposed. Waving the light around, she saw a large window on the south wall filled with the night but hinting at a magnificent daytime view. Before the window was the circular tub. It was about the diameter of a standard hot tub with pits underneath for firewood. An enclosed channel sloped into the tub from the wall, a primitive valve installed near its opening. This is where snowmelt was fed into the tub. The thought of joining Alex in that warm water . . . doing things in there . . .

Farther down the corridor, she came upon the door to the Great Chamber. Unlike the other interior doors, this was an impressive double door framed by stone reliefs of flowers, stealthy panthers, and Lombardic symbols. At another time, Valory would have stood back and imagined Alex chiseling the meticulous artwork. Instead, her heart plummeted into her toes. The dual door handles—robust iron rings set in the door at waist height— were threaded with a thick chain, connected by a chunky modern padlock. She stared at the lock, feeling like a rug had been yanked from under her feet. She tugged at it, confirming its fastness. Then she pointed the beam of her flashlight into the keyhole as if that would help. The deep, gold-metal grooves of the cylinder reflected a metallic smirk.

Was there another way to access the Great Chamber? To get to the fireplace? No. Maybe Spiderman could go outside and scale the wall of the keep up to the window, but Valory's only other option was to cut through the lock with her saw, and that was no real option. The racket it produced would echo throughout the castle. Dejection hit hard. She went limp, shoulders slumping. Was this the end? The quest was over? Flicking off her flashlight, she stood in the darkness and considered her options. There were none.

But then . . .

***

363

They were fourteen. A balmy California day in Sunnyvale. Violet asked Mom and Dad if she could spend the night with a new friend, Melissa. After Dad spoke with Melissa's father on the phone, he agreed to let Violet go, but only if she took Val along. Vi was ticked about that—she didn't want her boring, bookworm sister sucking all the fun from her sleepover—but Dad wouldn't budge.

Dad's heart was in the right place. He was concerned about Val's hermit-like lifestyle and the growing divide between the siblings. He wanted her to put down the books, come out of her room, and go have a little fun for a night. But Val resisted the sleepover even more than Vi. She was perfectly happy in her giant bean bag chair reading her new etymological dictionary of the Sumerian language. Dad, however, wouldn't budge.

Val asked Mom to intercede, but she declined. "One night in the company of your sister won't kill you, sweety, I promise. You might even have some fun."

Little did the parents know they'd been hoodwinked. Melissa's folks were actually away for the weekend, leaving Melissa and her eighteen-year-old brother, Jay, home alone. Jay had impersonated his own father on the phone, telling Dad he and 'the wife' would be home with the girls. He'd done this favor for Melissa in exchange for some weed she'd stolen. Val was only let in on the lie after they'd been dropped off.

"And if you even think about squealing," said Vi, poking Val's chest, "you will *never* stop paying for it. Got that, sis?"

Val was horrified. She did not want to be privy to such a 'crime,' but there was nothing she could do. The train had left the station.

Violet and Melissa began the first phase of their plan—calling up boys to see who they could get to come over. Jay was blasting rock music in his room, the stench of marijuana drifting throughout the house. While the girls giggled on the phone, Val was a frightened mouse on the edge of the couch, hands in her lap. A silent killjoy. At first, Vi tried to include her, to let her talk to boys on the phone, to tell them what color panties she was wearing. Val struggled not to cry.

"I know what will kill that bug in your ass," said Melissa, pulling Val from the couch. "You need some schnapps!"

Ignoring her protests, they took Val into the backyard to a locked garden shed. Melissa's dad hid his liquor in there thinking nobody knew, but Melissa knew. She grabbed the hide-a-key rock from under a landscape timber, but then she cursed. "The key's not here," she scowled, waving the rock around to convey its emptiness. "My stupid dad must have moved it."

That's when Vi sprang into action. "Move aside," she said, kneeling before the padlock. She took it into her hands, inspecting it. "Pfft, this is a cinch. Got some paper clips, Mel?"

364

Melissa left and came back with a handful of paper clips. "You know what you're doing?" she asked, handing them over.

"Course I do, check this out. Come here Val, you should watch this."

Vi took two paper clips, unrolled them into straight wires, then shaped them into tools. "Okay, watch carefully. This one's a tension tool," she said, holding up the clip that she'd formed into a twisted L. "You stick it in the barrel first, like this. Then you take the pick," she said, brandishing the clip she'd formed into a wavy hook, "and you stick it in, manipulating each pin until the top pin is above the shear." She worked at this for a bit, tongue curling up over her lip.

"How do you know all this?" asked Val, intrigued.

"These are the things you learn when you actually go out into the world, sis." Vi twisted the tension tool, and the padlock popped open.

The schnapps was horrible. Val almost gagged from the smell alone, and she puked up what she did manage to drink. The next night, however, when the girls were back home, Val found a padlock and some paper clips, and she spent three hours in her room struggling to replicate Vi's cat burglar trick. When she finally succeeded, she felt . . . well, kind of cool.

Bad girls, bad girls, watcha gonna do, watcha gonna do when they come for you . . .

Thankful for that lesson and for Vi's efforts to include her, Val figured she'd give her sis a little gift in return—a tidbit of etymological knowledge. The following night, Vi was on the phone talking to some boy she'd been sweet on. Whenever she and the boy ended their conversations, they'd say goodbye to one another in a cutesy, singsong way—*goodbyyyeee.*

"Hey, Vi," said Val after they'd hung up, "do you know where the word goodbye comes from?"

"What?"

"You know where the word goodbye comes from?"

"Who gives a crap?"

"In sixteenth-century England, people used to end conversations with the phrase 'God be with ye.' Then, over time, that became contracted into 'goodbye.' Neat, huh?"

"Um, hey, Val?"

"Yeah?"

"God be with ye," said Vi, and she left the room.

***

Val summoned Vi's lockpicking technique from the depths of her memory. She'd never popped another lock after that night of practice in her room, so the process was a little foggy. She checked the lock again, examining the barrel, imagining the paper clips going in . . . working the tumblers with that little hook at the end of the wire . . .

Yes. She could do this.

Going to a knee, she searched her backpack. There were always paper clips in there. Colored stickers, paper clamps, tacks, staples, post-it notes—all the stuff she never used anymore but kept anyway. Rummaging through every pocket, she found three paper clips. She held them up, examining them like they were gold.

Propping her flashlight, she sat cross-legged in its light while unwinding a clip. Once it was long and straight, she began bending and twisting it into a tension tool. Halfway through the process, however, the wire snapped. Chiding herself, she took a moment to reset, then began working the second clip. Slowly, carefully. She needed two clips to pop the lock. If she broke another one, game over.

An eternity later, the tension tool had been formed. Her body was hot, her forehead sweating. Removing her beanie, she took another breath and began working on the pick. She went even slower than before. The pick required a complex bend in the business end, an acute hook that was difficult to form. Working that tight of a hook into a section of wire the length of a thumbnail was rough on her fingertips. The clip slipped from her grasp. She stretched her fingers, then tried again. Stopped and restarted. Flattened the hook and tried the bends again. And again. Her hands were sore and crampy as she cursed the darkness.

Finally, success.

A quick breather. Then she began working the padlock, just as Vi had shown her. Insert the tension tool, twist it sideways. Insert the pick. Feel for the tumblers. Listen for the clicks. In the dead silence, every little tick and clink of metal was like a rock concert echoing down the corridor. She got stuck and had to back the pick out. Then she tried again. Click . . . click . . . tink . . . Another failure. Breathe, try again.

She froze. The sensations of whispered Italian drifted into her mind, wreaths of lavender and lime coiling upward, a silent dance of language.

We split from here. I'll check LaFleur's chamber, then I'll head to the studio and work my way down the floors. D'Arezzo, you start on the lower level and work your way up. Trentino, Moreno, check this level first, then take the middle floors. Don't break radio silence until you have something to report, understood? Okay, move out.

Valory nearly puked.

They knew.

Somehow, they knew, and they were coming for her. It would only be a matter of minutes before they reached this level. The point of no return shot into the distance as if fired from a rifle.

366

Her breath came in short, panicky bursts. Her heart pumped so hard her fingers didn't work. The pick slipped from her grasp, and she wasted precious seconds trying to locate it on the floor. When she went to re-insert it, she missed the keyhole, the end of the paper clip scraping the metal.

The corridor turned wobbly, the world blurring in the cone of her flashlight. She tried again, failing. She slowed down, breathed, tried again. Fail. Her face was hot, her eyes stinging. She got the pick in. One by one, she manipulated each tumbler without incident, successfully raising the top tumbler over the shear. She twisted the tension tool.

The padlock popped open.

The relief was cathartic. She loosened the chain just enough to open one of the doors by a foot and a half. Then she chucked her backpack inside and squeezed through, pushing the door shut behind her. She wanted to rest— just take a few minutes to catch her breath—but she couldn't afford the luxury. Any second now, an agent was going to walk down that hall. He'd notice the padlock had been picked. If Valory hadn't escaped into the secret passage by then . . .

She took in the Great Chamber with a quick sweep of her flashlight. It was true to Alex's sketches. Spacious and airy, a row of windows on the south wall looking over the courtyard and the darkness beyond. Everything Alex had sketched was here: a king's bed with towering posts, a Lombardic chapel near the windows, a couple of ancient armoires, a table with two chairs. A garderobe in the corner. There was more, too, beyond what he'd sketched. A gem-encrusted chest. Gorgeous tapestries. A full bookshelf, loaded not with his own tomes but with more contemporary books. Sculptures of jade, onyx, and marble. Paintings, ivory carvings, reliquaries, metalwork. Stringed instruments and woodwinds. Every space was filled with Alex, bathed in a spectral ambiance.

The moment hit hard. This was Alex's room. Where he'd slept, where he'd dressed, where he'd gone to the bathroom. Here is where he'd languished in bed while Jurgen Ziegler had read him the article about Einstein. The article that had led him to America, where he would lose his tenuous grip on sanity. Even as she dashed to the fireplace, a spark of a fantasy played in her consciousness. She envisioned herself climbing into that bed. Laying with Alex, wrapping her arms around him. Kissing him atop the furry bear pelt that was his comforter. Making love to him while the moon shone on their naked bodies.

The fireplace was a functional sculpture carved from the limestone, flowing contiguously into the rest of the chamber. It was seven feet wide flanked by columns the width of basketballs. Overhead, spanning the fireplace, was an oblong frieze packed with miniature dioramas. They depicted Alex and Sera in various scenes: dancing under a tree, kissing by the light of a full moon, watching a mountain sunrise, and others. In each relief, Alex wore plain clothes while Sera wore long, flowing dresses. In the center of the shield was emblazoned a Lombardic crest. As usual, the artwork was stunning.

The hearth was packed full of ceramic jars, old chests, rolled-up carpets, small crates, and the like. These items seem to have been pushed into the hearth to clear space in the chamber. That might be a good sign. If the fireplace hadn't been cleared out, it could mean no one had found the secret passage yet. The bad thing was Valory had to climb on these items to get into the firebox and look for the access. She wasted no time, laying atop the heaps of junk and running her light around the firebox. What she was looking for, she couldn't say. A mechanism of some kind. A lever, maybe. A hidden pully. A button. Something. But there was nothing except decades-old dust and ash. Contorting, she inserted her torso into the firebox like a mechanic under a car. She reached up, pushed the damper open. Took a face full of ash for her trouble. Peered into the flue. No lever, no switch, no button. Nothing but a shaft leading up into darkness.

Time was running out. Heart punching her sternum, Valory flopped onto her belly, pain stabbing her ribs. Things dug into her flesh: the edges of a crate, a pile of candlesticks, some sort of metal artifact. Grunting, she shone her flashlight into the seams of the firebox. They were filled with dust and ash. Taking a huge breath, she blew into the lower seam, sending particulate swirling. She coughed into her sleeve, peering down at what she'd just uncovered—a quarter-inch gap between the hearth and the left wall of the firebox. In a contiguous sculpture, there should be no gaps. A zing of hope shot through her.

Grimacing at the pain in her sides, she blew out the vertical seams to reveal two more thin gaps running up the edges. She knew it then. She'd found it. The left slab of the firebox was a hidden panel that likely opened into the passage. What's more, the buildup of ash in the seams reconfirmed that no one had discovered the passage. She was the first.

Maneuvering herself over a rolled carpet, she squeezed into the narrow space by the panel as best as she could, then heaved against the slab. Didn't budge, not even a little. Redoubling her efforts, she pushed again, this time propping her feet against the junk for extra leverage. The slab's immovable obstinance was a silent mockery. Was it stuck? Blocked? Maybe it was just too heavy for a one-hundred-thirty-pound woman to move. It was a solid stone slab after all. It could be hundreds of pounds. Panting from her exertions, Valory inspected the firebox again, hoping to discover a mechanism she'd missed before. A trigger, a treadle, whatever.

This level is clear.

Copy. Heading up.

The whispery colors sent a fresh surge of heat through her veins. The agents were closing in.

Clambering out of the firebox, Valory ran her flashlight along the mantel, the columns, the ornamentation, and the reliefs. Looking for anything that might serve as the mechanism. She felt along the underside of the mantel. Pushed and pulled on the columns. Standing on a small crate, she ran her hands over various depressions in the sculpted dioramas atop the mantel. Nothing.

Wait. There. Seated in one of the dioramas. An elongated hole, just over an inch in diameter. Hidden among a field of flowers in which Alex and Sera were having a picnic, a mountain landscape behind them. Standing on the crate, Valory stuck her finger in, wondering if there was a button inside. There wasn't, but she felt scarring as if the interior of the hole had been scraped repeatedly by metal.

Hopping off the crate, she shined her light around, looking for a skinny piece of metal that might fit. "C'mon c'mon c'mon," she muttered, cursing the suddenly-too-small radius of the flashlight. She searched among the junk in the hearth for what felt like hours. There was lots of miscellaneous metal lying around, but nothing that would fit into the hole.

Cursing, she looked to the sides of the fireplace. To the right was a tall box made of discolored brass. This held pokers, tongs, brushes, and shovels. Hurriedly, she sifted through the tools. She missed it the first time. But just as she was about to move on, she noticed one of the pokers had a specialized end piece. The last three inches of the poker flattened into a slotted wedge. She picked it up, examined it up close in the beam of her flashlight. Repeated scrapings on the sides of the wedge had eaten into the metal. This had to be it.

But then—light. A weak glow from under the door. It wobbled, growing brighter. Someone was walking down the corridor, flashlight pointed ahead of them. Valory was out of time.

She darted back to the diorama. Raised the tool, inserted it into the hole. Pushed it inside, scraping the stone until it met resistance. Nothing happened. The panel didn't open. Frantically, she shoved the tool in with all her might.

A pop. A grinding sound, like wood on stone. A faint groan. The panel dislodged, opening inward by a half inch. Bringing the tool with her, Valory squeezed herself into the firebox and heaved against the panel. It swung into darkness.

Che diavolo?

The colors of a man's whisper, just outside the door. The colors translated to *What the hell?* He'd just seen the padlock hanging loose from the chains. In his real, audible voice, he said, "*Chi c'è dentro?! Dottoressa Grace?!*" It was Trentino, demanding to know if she was inside.

A metallic ruckus sounded as Trentino began unwinding the chain like he was in a race. Valory chucked her backpack into the secret passage and then went in after it, bringing the tool with her. She closed the panel the same second Trentino rushed into the chamber.

章节 61

AFTER ONE STONE, HE'D slowly fractured, bleeding into two realms. One, the realm of flesh. One, the realm of eternity. Between them he existed, fragmented, unable to leave either.

But the end was drawing near. The ultimate, irrevocable end.

He turned onto his back, feeling the frigid bite of stone upon his bare shoulder blades. Upon his spine. His hand flipped to his side, falling into a plate of cold food. A man had brought that. A week, a day, an hour ago. The man had yelled at him. Slapped him on his bearded face, trying to wake him. Then he'd left him to the darkness. Soon would he never feel the sensations of flesh again.

She was coming.

He knew this.

He felt this.

She was coming, and the end was coming with her.

CAPITOLU 62

VALORY SAT IN COMPLETE darkness, palms clamped over her nose and mouth. On the other side of the wall, *Agente* Trentino was searching the Great Chamber. Searching for her.

"*Dottoressa! So che sei venuto qui! Vieni fuori subito!*" He knew she'd come in here, and he demanded she show herself. Right now.

She didn't move a single cell of her body. Her panting, muffled by her palms, felt like the loudest noise on Earth.

Something dragged along the stone floor. A thump, a slam, things being moved around. Trentino was turning the chamber upside down thinking she was hiding somewhere. She heard him curse as he banged around in the voluminous compartments of the armoires.

"*Dottoressa! Esci ora e sarà più facile per te!*" Come out now and it will be easier on you.

He walked every inch of the chamber, even tearing through the junk in the hearth two feet away from her. His flashlight bled through the seams of the panel, creeping into her hiding spot. Valory fought the impulse to dash into the bowels of the passage, for that would mean turning on her flashlight and moving her body, two actions she dared not chance at this moment. If Trentino heard her through the wall or spied a hint of light in the seams . . .

He cursed. Then he initiated a radio conversation, speaking Italian:

"Griffon One, Griffon Two, over."

"Go ahead Griffon Two."

"Griffon One, target tracked to level four. She broke into the Great Chamber, over."

"Target is acquired, over?"

"Negative. Target was here but gone now, over."

"Hold position, Griffon Two. I'm headed your way."

"Copy."

Griffon One was *Agente* Savelli. When she heard his voice through the radio, Valory experienced a delicate nausea in her mind. For, at the same time she heard him with her ears, she also 'heard' him remotely, muddling her perception. The mix of sensations made her feel like she'd had a couple of drinks.

Trentino exited the room to wait in the corridor. Now was her chance. She flicked on her flashlight, illuminating a dust-swirled passageway barely wider than her shoulders. To her right, a silver torch rested in an iron sconce, its lip blackened by a thousand fires. Beyond a short landing, a staircase loomed. But the staircase did not lead upward. Steep and daunting, it led down into an abyss. She peered into the darkness, the sharp lips of the steps promising a tricky, claustrophobic descent. Missing a step and falling into those depths was a broken neck waiting to happen. But why down? Alex's blueprints had stated: *Concealed passage to tower*. The tower was on the roof of the keep. Upward. So where did these stairs lead?

She could not fret over it. In moments, the agents would return to the chamber. If they were diligent enough, they might find the secret passage. Valory shined her flashlight on the panel, seeing the simple locking mechanism she had disengaged when she'd inserted the rod into the diorama. It was nothing more than a mini drawbar resting in iron slots on each side of the panel. The drawbar had been raised by a metal weight, released by the trigger. Quickly, Valory reset the mechanism, locking the panel. She set the tool in the corner, relieved that she'd had the wherewithal to bring it inside. If the agents discovered the panel, they'd have to find some other way to trigger it.

She shouldered her pack. Illuminating the narrow stairwell below, she began to descend, praying it would turn its way upward to the tower at some point. It had to. There was no Plan B.

Down she went, between the walls of the keep. Deeper, darker, narrower. Every twenty steps or so, the staircase reversed back on itself, always descending into darkness. As she'd come to expect, the passage had been carved from the stone of the mountain, flowing together as one solid sculpture. The only difference was that the stone inside the passage had not been smoothed. It was sharp, jagged, and uneven. No reason for a hidden passageway to look pretty.

If her spatial reckoning was true, she was adjacent to the Great Hall now. Walking down a couple more flights, she guessed she was within proximity of the kitchen, servant quarters, storage rooms, and the like. And still, the stairs led down and only down. Every step made reaching the tower more unlikely. Alex had obviously changed his original plan. All Valory could do now was pray that the passage led somewhere useful. Some place where she could regroup and plan her next move.

While stopping to rest her shins, she guessed she was in line with the library. She didn't know which level, but it was one of them. She imagined she could feel Alex's tomes mere feet away from her, just beyond the stone. Thousands of diary entries she had not been able to read. So much of his amazing life that she knew nothing about. Even if she rescued him tonight, he wouldn't be able to recall the tales of his timeless journey. His mind was mortal and could not 'cradle the memories of millennia,' as he'd confessed in his narrative. Those tomes were a proxy for his sanity, for his human sense of self, but now he might never see them again.

At least she possessed the master drive. Her own work, along with the tomes Rollo had photographed, should be there. She could read the diary from the photos. When she and Alex were somewhere safe, maybe she could even read his entries to him. Help him to connect with his former experiences. He would appreciate that, wouldn't he? Just as he'd appreciated watching Sera read his Latin.

Suddenly, the sensations of Italian rose into her perception. The agents, all four of them, had congregated in the Great Chamber, and Trentino was explaining how he'd found the lock opened.

But when I entered the room, she was already gone.

The window?

No, it's intact. Besides, that's too far of a drop.

What about—?

No, I already checked. There's nowhere else to hide in this room.

What the hell was she doing? Did she come up here to steal this crap?

I doubt it. My hunch is she's looking for something specific.

You don't think . . . the tower?

There was a pause. Standing dead still, Valory 'listened' to the spicy reds and deep-sea emeralds of the conversation. The agents were no longer whispering.

Trentino, you and I will check the tower. If she's not there, you'll stay there until we have her. Moreno, D'Arezzo, secure this room, then continue searching the keep and the courtyard. Listen, gentlemen. Grace is on to us. And whatever the hell she's doing, she's now willfully evading us. At this point, we have no choice but to treat her as an enemy of Italy. Apprehend her accordingly. Understood?

Valory held her hand over her chest, feeling her blood go ten degrees colder. She remained paralyzed against the wall, wrestling with the words she never imagined in her wildest dreams would be uttered. Doctor Valory Grace, enemy of an entire country. An enemy whose next move had just been deduced. If she made it to the tower—a big 'if' since the secret passage was going the wrong way—then an agent would be waiting there for her. How would she deal with that? Her plan, a shoddy wall to begin with, was shedding bricks rapidly. Yet she had no choice but to forge on. If she could just get to Alex. Just *get* to him, free him from his bonds. Then he could use his immortal prescience to guide them to safety. Right?

Farther into the depths, she descended. Each step put more distance between herself and the tower, a fact that buzzed louder and louder in the throes of her anxiety. It was cold, but she was sweating under her coat. The walls were intrusive, scraping her shoulders when she leaned. Her shins ached; her lungs begged for fresh air. Still, down she went, the weight of her 'crimes' pushing her into the mountain bedrock. Deep, deep down. She was now beneath even the lowest level of the library. She recalled the day she'd seen the ground penetrating radar on the lowest level, meaning Dario had suspected there was something beneath. Well, he'd been correct.

After what felt like days, the stairwell leveled out, spilling into a small landing. There, a dark archway awaited. Hoping she'd finally arrived at . . . whatever this was, she approached the arch, aiming her flashlight inside.

The sight erased her legs. She wobbled, grabbing the wall for support.

ΚΕΦΑΛΑΙΟ 63

HIDING IN THE DEEP shadows of the room, Cervantes watched the agents split up. He didn't have to peek around the corner at them. Didn't even need to open his eyes. Their vitals were blips in his ethereal radar. In his mind, he tracked their darkly luminescent brains moving through the corridors, swaying with the movements of their bodies. Glimmering lumps of meat that seemed to chant *Put bullets in me, Dominic*.

Allowing the feds to pass his position required more self-control than he anticipated. The kill lust was a blitzkrieg of subliminal flashes. Polaroid images of shooting them through their eyes. Stabbing them through their spinal columns. Choking them to death with his bare hands. As he squatted behind something that looked like a stone hot tub, Cervantes restrained himself as the agents whisked down the corridor. When they were gone, he breathed, resetting.

He walked down the hallway, stopping at the room that had caused the feds so much heartburn. There loomed a double door, its two iron handles threaded with a chain and padlock. The feds had been inside speaking in anxious tones before leaving, resecuring the lock. Though Cervantes spoke no Italian, he'd caught the one word he'd been listening for—Grace. He deduced that she'd been there moments ago, fleeing just before the feds showed up. He didn't know why Grace was being hunted, but it concerned him. She had crossed the feds somehow. Now they wanted to shut her down. If they caught her before he did, his mission could become impossible. He needed to know why Grace had come to this chamber, and he needed to find out quickly.

The padlock was nothing. Using his intrusion tools, he popped it in seconds. Then he unwound the chain just enough to squeeze through the doors.

He stood in the dark, inspecting the spacious chamber. In the darkshine, he saw everything with clarity. A bunch of furniture, some chests, an altar, a fireplace, books, artwork—exactly what one might expect in an old castle. But why had Grace come here? He went to the windows to see if she might have escaped through them. Not a chance. Nothing outside but a leg-breaking drop into the courtyard. He took a moment to look at his reflection in the window, as clear to him as a mirror in a well-lit bathroom. A few days' worth of stubble grew on his otherwise plain face. He checked his eyes, wondering if the darkshine had affected them. He half expected to see them glowing like a cat's eyes, but no. They were as dark and expressionless as always. Another reminder that this ability, whatever it was, was purely internal.

There was a slim door in the corner of the chamber with a couple of steps leading up to it. Cervantes looked inside, seeing a cubicle the size of a phone box. Nothing in there but a stone bench with a hole in it. Water flowed through a channel far below the hole, something he would not have been able to see without the darkshine. No way Grace could have escaped through there either. Too small of a hole, too steep of a drop. She must have just slipped out of the room a minute or two before the agents had arrived.

Or had she? If Grace was smart, she'd have locked up before she left. Covered her tracks. But Cervantes had been tailing the agent who discovered the chamber, and that agent had discovered a popped lock. Meaning Grace had either not bothered to relock it, or . . .

She'd never left the room.

Cervantes padded around the chamber, looking, smelling, feeling. He absorbed the room in the all-revealing darkshine. Noted various scratches in the stone floor, most of them centuries old. Saw the dust mark where a tabletop sculpture had been picked up, examined, and set back down an inch from where it had been. A wooden chair had been scooted by half a foot. Some kind of medieval guitar had been flipped. Wait . . . there. Someone had recently rummaged through a brass box full of fireplace tools. He knew this because some of the tools had smudged dust on their undersides, their top surfaces shiny. Why would someone need a fireplace tool? The fireplace itself was packed full of crates, carpets, chests, and the like, and had not burned logs in a very long time.

He went to the fireplace. Squatted, peering into the firebox. Right away, he saw that the junk inside had been disturbed. The dust was displaced. A crate had moved just a smidge. Some kind of large weight had been laid atop a rolled carpet, smushing it inward. He may have missed these minuscule details in the past, but in the darkshine, they were glaring. He scooched into a narrow space between the junk and the side panel to get a better look inside the firebox. That's when he saw them—gaps in the seams around the left panel.

Clever Grace.

He pushed the panel. Heaved upon it. Kicked at it. No good. Some sort of trigger was needed to open it. He searched for it. Inside the firebox, up the flue, in the columns around the hearth, under the mantel, on the sculptures over the mantel . . . and there it was. A hole hidden in a bed of stone flowers. He put his eye up to the hole, the darkshine revealing every scrape, nick, and gouge running along the inner shaft. A slotted groove rested about two feet inside. Behind that was a steel surface, probably a pressure plate. Press on that, and *viola*.

There was nothing in the chamber that fit the slot. Whatever the key was, Grace had likely taken it with her. Smart, but this only presented a small delay. Taking his lockpick toolkit, Cervantes chose a dimple rake pick, which had a flat, steel handle on one end. The handle was slightly too big for the slot, so he punched off a quarter inch or so with a small chisel. Then he broke the spear off one of the pokers, affixing the dimple pick in its place. He inserted his makeshift key into the hole, fitting it into the groove and giving it a shove. The panel popped open.

Crouching, he entered the passage, bringing his makeshift key with him. Inside, he noticed the real key leaning against the corner, safely unavailable to anyone in the chamber. He placed his own key beside it, then he descended into the bowels of the castle.

TA 64

THERE CAME A TIME—a couple of weeks ago, perhaps—when the euphoria of working in the castle had waned. Valory had never ceased being amazed, of course, but that amazement had lost its sizzle. It was the difference between seeing the Grand Canyon once versus seeing it all day every day for weeks on end. Normalization had set in. But now, the sight before her leveled her with pure, uncompromising awe.

She stared into a subterranean amphitheater. Cavernous, ovular and ringed with terraced platforms. Like the Roman Colosseum at quarter scale but topped with a lofty dome and supported by columns. Agape, she realized that the amphitheater was softly illuminated from her flashlight. The beam played off a network of burnished steel tiles mounted in the domed ceiling. This created a sleepy, dreamlike glow. A massive ball of crystal hung in the center, its many facets spearing the theater with ghostly rainbows.

The walls of the amphitheater were carved with towering sculptures—high reliefs of Seraphina protruding into the room over the terraced tiers. Here she was dancing in a long, flowy dress. There she was laughing as she brushed her hair. In the biggest sculpture, she sat on a throne, her hand upon the scruff of a fearsome panther. The shadows accentuated the curves in the reliefs, lending a sense of depth which made them pop into the room.

Yet the reliefs were only minor wonders compared to the room's contents. For, resting among the terraced tiers encircling the amphitheater was a sight for the ages.

Treasure.

Hills upon hills of treasure, glistening like the vaults of a thousand empires. Incalculable masses of coins in gold, silver, and copper. Gems of every color, size, and cut. Ornaments, necklaces, masks, chalices, rings, armbands, scepters, jewelry boxes, lamps, reliquaries. Dresses of gold thread, tiaras packed with diamonds, bejeweled weapons, obsidian sculptures. The sheer amount of riches lying in chaotic heaps, spilling into the ovular floor, was staggering and impossible. She was no appraiser, but Valory knew that in today's money, the entirety of the collection was worth hundreds of millions of dollars.

That wasn't all. Among the glittering ocean of coins and relics were rows of marble statues. These were of nobles, peasants, and everything in between, all of them kneeling with lowered heads. Here and there, a statue had fallen on its side, broken among the riches.

And there, centerstage upon a granite dais rested the crown jewel of the amphitheater—a massive golden sarcophagus. Valory knew immediately who rested within. There was no doubt.

This was the coffin of Queen Seraphina of the Lombards.

As Valory drew near the earthly remains of Alikai's true love, a stark realization humbled her. This castle wasn't just a grandiose tribute to Sera. It was a tomb. Just as the Giza pyramids were royal tombs for the most celebrated pharaohs of Egypt, this mountaintop sculpture was Queen Seraphina's final, glorious resting place. The treasure was the consolidation of Alex's hidden troves, the sum of the wealth he had acquired through vast centuries, carted here from all over the world as a parting gift to her. The marble statues were solemn mourners, bowing to Sera forever. The fact that this unique tomb doubled as Alex's home so that he'd never be apart from her, was tragically, bewilderingly, beautifully gut-wrenching.

Valory knelt before the dais, her breath clouding the chilly air. The granite base was inscribed with an epitaph written in Lombardic. Within her, the fiery odors of forge and soot swirled among steely blues and grays as she read that long-dead tongue:

Rest now o' great Queen Seraphina of the Lombards, daughter of noble Desiderata. Your hardships are over, your battle won. Forever shall I sing your song to the world, you who captured the fires of the sun which blazed in your heart, who danced in the moon rays which rippled in your eyes, and who raised a long dead wretch from the grave of life with your unconquerable spirit. Lie now in peace, and I shall hold your glory in my hands for all to see. For you, sweet Sera, rose of my soul, shall flower in my memory forever.

Valory held her hand over her heart as she read the epitaph. Its beauty was crushing. She ran her fingers along the words, noting the deliberate omission of Charlemagne from Sera's lineage. Yes, that is the way she would have wanted it.

She rose from her knees, bathing the coffin in a reverential gaze. It was pure gold, big enough for three, its yellow-orange surface glimmering in the refracted light. From the size, Valory suspected one or more smaller coffins were likely nested within, just like the famed coffin of Tutankhamun. A double layer of protection and extravagance. Atop the lid, an embossed figure of Sera reposed in a queenly robe, a crown on her head, a scepter cradled in her arm. Beside her lay a large panther, its head curled lovingly into her shoulder. The embossed design was an external depiction of what the coffin contained.

The urge to open the lid was strong. That innate, almost childlike sense of exploration was begging her to do so. To open it and view the remains of she who had captured the heart of a god. Of course, she wouldn't. To even entertain such a disrespectful act struck her with guilt. She only ran her fingers along Seraphina's golden cheek and along the panther. She badly wished to know the story of that cat. It was represented in much of the royal iconography in the castle. In the Lombardic crest, in the tapestries, in the paintings—the panther was always at Sera's side. The queen had obviously loved it dearly. How had a jungle cat come to have Sera as its mother? Valory was positive the story laid within the treasure bindings, but she'd been derailed from finishing them. Maybe, if everything worked out, she could read them from the master drive. It was a big maybe. She had to survive the night first.

There was a simple wooden chair near the dais, but it had toppled a long time ago, a layer of dust thick upon the wood. With the random broken statues and the scattershot chaos of the treasure piles, Valory assumed this was the work of the earthquake that had damaged some other artifacts in the Great Hall. The mess also confirmed no one had been down here in decades. She was likely the first person to lay eyes upon the tomb since Alex had left for America. Righting the chair, she ran her fingertips along the once-plush velvet cushions, flattened by decades of use. Strewn around the chair were a dozen ancient tomes, sheets of parchment, worn feathers, old ink wells, and golden incense burners. Valory guessed that Alex used to sit here, spending time with Sera like a widower at his wife's grave.

The tomes had apparently been removed from the library and brought here for reading. Based on their outward appearance, Valory estimated them to be from the early medieval period. Some were half-hidden under sheets of loose parchment. Glancing through the papers, she found poems, scribbles, multi-language ramblings, and sketches, mostly of Seraphina in various artistic styles. There were portraits of other people as well. Men and women of all ages, some dressed in noble finery, others in common folk garb. She shuffled through some of these, feeling guilty for not having clean hands or gloves but too fevered to stop. Unlike the bevy of styles Alex had used to sketch Sera, the coal portraits of these people were photorealistic. Incredibly detailed and alive. Valory felt she could almost talk to them. Below each portrait, in various languages, he had written the subject's name with a brief description.

> Neferu ~ she who leads the Order of Argus and who gave us shelter
> Dauphine a l'Espée ~ the maker of Sera's new dress
> Arnulf Guntramus ~ a street performer who caused Sera to laugh

Name unknown ~ a merchant from whom we rescued Luna
William Shakespeare ~ he who gifted me brief cheer

Valory gasped. Here it was, the missing Shakespeare sketch. The only illustration of the bard drawn during his life. Surprisingly, he did not much resemble the famous images of him that had been created years after his death. The similarities were tenuous at best. Though middle-aged in this portrait, he was youthly in face and spirit, clean-shaven with soft features. His nose wasn't as long as later depictions, and he had a tiny scar on his cheekbone. Really, only the receding hairline and a fluff of curls at his shoulders matched up. Valory stared into his eyes. They were soulful. Reflective. Absorbent. A hint of playfulness lurked within. A spiciness.

Valory realized that the sheet of parchment she held in her hand was worth six figures. "Oh, Janelle," she whispered, wishing the art mouse could see, "*si seulement tu pouvais voir ça.*"

Though she fantasized about framing it and hanging it in her own home, she couldn't. There was no way to stow it in her loaded backpack without smushing or creasing it, which she refused to do. She would not be responsible for damaging this stunning relic. She could at least protect it, though. Wandering into the masses of treasure, slipping atop mounds of coins, she found a golden chest beset with jewels. She laid the sketch inside over a diamond chalice resting in a red velvet compartment. The moment she closed the lid was bittersweet. The sketch was safe, but she'd never see it again. Maybe nobody would.

She brainstormed her next move. Had there been time, she could have spent days of academic glee in the tomb, but the clock was ticking, and she had a problem. The secret passage had not led to the tower. Now she had nowhere to go. No doubt the agents had already resecured the Great Chamber. If she went back there, she wouldn't be able to get out. But there had to be another way. Otherwise, how had Alex gotten all these treasures into the amphitheater? He could not have carted the marble statues, the granite block, and the oversized coffin down that steep, narrow passage. Another means of access existed somewhere. Maybe a tunnel leading to some other part of the castle, or the outer slopes. Shining her flashlight along the perimeter, she found it. An arched tunnel about six feet wide and six feet tall. The problem—it was packed tight with stone and mortar. Alex had apparently sealed the tunnel once he'd moved all the treasures into the tomb. No way she was getting through.

Every second was a poke in her back, pushing her along. On the south face of the amphitheater, fifteen feet off the floor, a high-relief sculpture jutted from the wall. It was a large sun encircled by flowy, spiral rays. The sculpture was hollowed out in the center, a recessed alcove nestled within. The interior of the alcove was fitted with an array of polished steel panels.

When Valory pointed her flashlight there, the tomb came alive. The beam reflected off the panels and spilled into the dome, bouncing off the ceiling tiles and causing an explosion of dazzling light. She gaped, looking around at the suddenly gleaming environs. As a test, she turned off her flashlight, plunging the amphitheater into complete darkness. When she turned it back on, she realized what the sun sculpture was—a device Alex had created to funnel real sunlight into the tomb. Just like the library but amplified. He did not want Sera to spend eternity in darkness, but in heavenly warmth, surrounded by the treasures of the world.

"Oh my god," she whispered, hand over her heart. She wanted a moment just to soak in the romanticism of Alex's devotion and thoughtfulness. To just sit here and look, process, and imagine. But the clock ticked loudly in the silence.

Finding a better angle, she spied a narrow shaft rising from inside the sculpture. That shaft likely led to a suncatcher atop the keep, designed to redirect natural light to the panels. Inside that shaft, spaced at intervals, were iron rungs mounted into the stone. A built-in ladder.

Valory thought back to the times when she'd been outside looking up at the mighty tower. From certain angles, she'd been able to see the edge of a suncatcher up there. Best guess, this shaft rose to that device. Maybe there was an access hatch up there leading into the tower. If so, that would be one hell of a roundabout way to get there, and dangerous. It would be a long, nail-biting climb. One slip . . .

Well, she couldn't go back the way she'd come.

Gathering her things, Valory mounted her flashlight on her backpack strap to where it was pointing upward. Then, as she prepared to climb, she realized something. She had no money. If her plan succeeded, and if she and Alex were able to flee into the countryside, they would eventually need money. What little she had in her checking account would not suffice and would probably be frozen by law enforcement anyway. That's what they did to fugitives, right?

She looked upon the heaps of treasure. In all her years, she never dreamed she'd be a graverobber. The guilt was heavy as she scooped as many gems and coins as she could fit into the utility pockets of her hiking pants. These could be traded for cash—a lot of it. She hoped Alex (and Seraphina) would understand.

She took one last look at the tomb, trying to imprint its majesty into long-term memory. She whispered goodbye to Seraphina. Then she turned, grasping the first rung leading to the alcove. Closing her eyes, she blocked out everything else, focusing only on the cold iron in her palms. She breathed. Said a nervous prayer. Then she climbed.

LUKU 65

CERVANTES STRODE INTO THE room, eager to finally confront his target, but he was not prepared for what awaited him. The amphitheater whooshed into his eyes like a gust off the sea, overwhelming him with its size and splendor. This far below the castle, he'd been expecting something dank and practical. A dungeon, maybe. A sewer system. Certainly not a treasure-packed arena with arched columns and lofty sculptures swooping off the walls.

When the surprise passed, he scanned the room, miffed that Grace wasn't there. But she was close. Her physical musk played in his awareness. He felt her perspiring. 'Smelled' the sweat soaking her shirt. 'Tasted' the acrid adrenaline pumping through her. 'Heard' her blood as it swished through the valves in her veins, which opened and closed like gasping little mouths. So very close. To pinpoint her, he stood still, eyes closed, tuning in. There she was. A fleshy ghost inside the far stone wall, just above the reflective dome. Her brain, her heart, her jugular vein, they glimmered in his mind as she ascended some kind of chute. She was close. If he began climbing now, he could overtake her quickly. Yet he only stood there, motionless. Mouth falling open. Skin going prickly. For Grace shone not in the flaming blackness of the darkshine . . .

But in color.

Cervantes' hand dropped slowly off the pistol he'd been palming. In his mind, he watched her. She was a wraithlike prism in the darkshine refracting hues that he'd not perceived in over a decade. Up she climbed, her flares dancing in his mind while the world around her remained dark.

He knew he should go after her. Yet he only stood with his eyes closed. Why was he 'seeing' this? Less than two weeks ago, the Salvador had shown him something similar. He'd levied a superhuman pulse against Cervantes that altered his state of mind. In that moment, he'd experienced internal puffs of color which dissipated a few seconds later. But Grace's colors didn't dissipate. They remained strong in his perception as she climbed the shaft, drowning out the beam of her flashlight.

He checked his environment for any other color, but there were only the rolling foothills of treasure glinting blackly in the darkshine. He refocused on Grace. He 'watched' her, trying to understand. There were no answers.

Cervantes gathered himself, setting aside the confounding phenomenon. Colors or not, he had a mission to accomplish. But, just as he was about to jog to the shaft, a different sensation tickled him. Something he'd been too shocked to notice until now. Tuning in, he listened, reaching out with his mind. There, in his essence, he felt it. A hollow murmur. A voiceless breath. Subtle and distant, a spectral scent from the netherworld.

Death.

Not just death, but old death. A nothingness from centuries gone, reaching for him with translucent tendrils, writhing from the depths of oblivion. In all his years, he'd never experienced a feeling so elemental, so mighty, so final. Within its folds, every life that had ever existed since the dawn of time had been nullified.

He breathed it in. Felt it in his lungs. It pulled him to the center of the room. There, just beyond a chair and some books, was a dais upon which rested a golden sarcophagus. Massive, ornate, shiny—a coffin made for royalty. And nestled within was the source of his ecstasy—the oldest remains he had ever encountered.

Throughout his life, Cervantes had experienced nothing but fresh, red corpses. New death was the only death he'd ever known. Sure, he'd broken into the morgue in his youth just to look at long-deceased bodies. And there'd been that mass grave his squad had stumbled upon in Afghanistan with corpses several weeks old. But he'd never had an opportunity to experience a body that had died centuries ago. A corpse like that, so far removed from the foul wink of life, was no longer just a corpse. It was the divine bride of entropy.

There was no need to hasten after Grace. She was moving up the shaft like a scared baby. Once he mobilized, he'd catch her in seconds. First, he would answer the call of centuries-old death.

Stepping onto the dais, he looked down at the coffin lid. The embossed forms of a queen and a large cat protruded in smooth, golden swoops, regal and peaceful. But he didn't care about the lavish lid. Setting his palms against its side, he gathered his strength and pushed. The lid budged, grinding against the box, raising dust. With one more shove, it toppled, careening off the dais and crashing to the stone floor. He looked inside only to see a second, smaller coffin. This one was made of silver, and though not embossed, it was inscribed with fanciful designs and rows of some weird language. Cervantes cared nothing for that. Reaching inside, he skewed the silver lid enough to get his fingers under it, then he heaved it over the outer coffin. It crashed down beside the first one, the impact reverberating throughout the dome.

Cervantes jumped up and stood on the walls of the coffin, squatting over its contents. A heavy dust cloud floated between the corpse and him. He blew it out, watching as the velvet padding came into focus, eager for his first glimpse of this ancient husk. Nestled within the padding, the remains of the woman were wrapped in layers of silk, likely to help preserve her. Over that, she wore lavish robes lined with fur, a bejeweled crown near her head, and a scepter cradled in her arm. The form of a jungle cat lay beside her, also wrapped.

He paused, drinking her in.

Lowered himself into the coffin.

Rested his knees on her sides.

Moaned as he felt her between his thighs.

He leaned over, put the tip of his nose on her shrouded face. Drew her hoary aroma into his lungs. Sucked it in deep.

He whipped one of his knives from its sheath. Grasped the silk between his forefinger and thumb. Cut it open from crown to clavicle. Ripped the silk away.

There was the sleeping face of the queen.

***

Valory's hands were achy and sweaty. Grasping the thick rungs was a chore. She pulled herself up a foot at a time, counting each step as a small victory. Her backpack scraped against the narrow shaft with each step, the resistance making it that much tougher. One false move and that'd be it. With the steel panels lining the shaft, the sides were slick and unforgiving. She'd slide straight down to the bottom, joining Seraphina in her eternal tomb.

Her flashlight, which she'd affixed to her strap in an upward-pointing position, lit the shaft overhead, its beam ping-ponging on the polished panels. There was still a long way to go. She had descended much farther into the interior of the mountain than she realized. She dared to look down, but her own body blocked the view. Probably a good thing. Still, in her mind, it was a pit a thousand miles deep.

She gained another rung. Then another. Took a quick breather, wiped her hand on her shirt, and then took another rung. It seemed that decades plodded by while she inched upward. No one would ever find her if she died. She began to cry, but then she couldn't. It was just too hard.

Suddenly, there was an echoing boom from below, so loud that its vibrations raced up the shaft like a geyser of angry ghosts. She froze, clinging to the ladder. It took her frantic mind a moment to deduce the obvious . . .

Someone was in the tomb.

She pressed herself against the rungs, panting enough for three people. Yet even as she tried to swallow her panic, a second boom resounded. In its aftermath, she could hear someone moving around down there. Then, deep within her perception, she 'heard' him. *Him.* The man who'd been reciting mantras earlier that evening. The one whose words decomposed in her mind, turning from reds and blues to foul-smelling blacks and grays. He was down there, his dark moans puffing into her awareness. Though rife with decay, there was a strange, lusty glee in his vocalics. A sick reverence. A macabre pleasure. Whoever this man was, he was twisted.

***

The queen was everything. Ancient, beautiful, pale. Though decomposition had eroded her to some degree, most of her features were still intact. She still had her eyebrows, eyelashes, and nose hairs. Her lips were full, her cheekbones pronounced. Someone had taken great pains in preserving her. Along with the shielded tomb, the double coffin, and the protective silk, a preservative liquid of some kind had been applied to her skin, keeping it fresh. Long centuries of gravity had sunk her inward, and her elegant hairstyle had flattened, but for a medieval corpse, she was remarkable. Removing his glove, Cervantes touched her cheek. It was still elastic, pushing back up when he removed his hand.

He pried her lips open.

Stuck his finger into her mouth.

All the way in.

He smiled. A real one.

He left his finger there, staring at the queen's sleeping eyes. He felt her. Tightened his knees on her sides. In the darkshine, he could see her deteriorating, browning in spots right before his eyes. Exposing her to the oxygen of the tomb had already begun to overcome the meticulous pains taken to preserve her. He laughed at this. His first real laugh since childhood.

Heart thumping, he noted the scarf of gold and purple thread around her neck. Removing his finger from her mouth, he drew his fingertip over her chin, down her throat, and he ripped the scarf away. When he saw it, his smile became a sinister grin.

The queen had been beheaded.

Though she'd been sewn back together with expert precision, leaving only a thin, telltale line in the neck, there was no doubt her head had been severed. It hadn't been a clean blow, either. The discoloration and damage to the skin revealed as much. Removing his other glove, Cervantes cupped her spine with both hands, fingertips probing her cervical vertebrae. They'd been shattered to pieces. Someone had swung multiple, clumsy blows upon her, causing her to suffer a horrific end.

The discovery sent Cervantes into morbid ecstasy, the world around him melting as he soared on a magic carpet ride of death. The queen's ancient corpse was his guide, flying him into a primordial past where everything was nothing. No humans, no life, no light, no universe, no time. He experienced only true, complete, inexorable emptiness in a way that was impossible for electrified meat to comprehend. And there, in the vacuum of preexistence, he glimpsed himself. One fleeting glimpse of his real purpose on Earth, like the flash of a subliminal image. Just a flash, but it was enough. That flash showed him the truth. A truth that had only been a faraway cry from the pits of his soul, a cry that had always hushed when he strained to hear. Yet now, in the complete emptiness, he heard, he saw. Finally, he knew. He was much, much more than just Dominic Cervantes.

Then he was back in his corporeal body. The emptiness was gone. That hint of truth vanished. He was again just flesh and blood trapped in physical time, straddling the queen.

He screamed. He screamed at the absolute top of his lungs as he never had in his entire life. It was the sound of tortured, maniacal joy, echoing through the dome like the war cry of a thousand devils.

***

Just a little farther.

Her entire body ached, pain throbbing in her back, her fingers, her feet, her neck. The end was near, though. Overhead, she could see the clouds of night through a circular aperture, still a hundred feet away. Before that, maybe only twenty feet from her position was an alcove with a small ledge. She prayed this was an entrance into the tower.

She pulled herself to the next rung. Rested a moment. Pulled herself to the next. Almost there.

A scream echoed up the shaft, gushing into her mind like a fountain of rancid tar. High-pitched and delirious, the scream straightened the hairs of her arms and neck, jolting her so badly she almost slipped off the ladder. Stunned, she hooked her arm into a rung, then struggled into a risky position so she could peer down the shaft. With her free arm, she yanked the flashlight from her backpack strap and pointed it down. The lower shaft lit up like Christmas, the sudden view of her lofty height making her gasp. For one tense moment, she watched, sweat dripping from the tip of her nose and falling silently into the long, long depths.

He appeared.

The faraway form of the man, dressed in full black, slipped into the alcove from the tomb. He looked up at her. Their eyes met across the vast distance. He began racing up the ladder, hand over hand like a spider in fast forward, a frenzied grimace splitting his face. The scream that left her lips felt like someone else's. Her flashlight went tumbling toward the man in a pinwheel of wild, strobing reflections. Breathless, she flew up the rungs on the wings of terror.

Бүлек 66

AGENTE TRENTINO SUCKED ON his cigarette like it was a straw. Held the smoke in his lungs, huffed it out. He swept his flashlight down into the courtyard, seeing nothing but the horses in their stables. He walked toward the tower, checking the roof of the keep. Hit a suncatcher on one of its reflective panels, creating a momentary burst of light. In that burst, the statue of the queen lit up. He caught an impression of her blank, grungy eyes staring down at him, the ominous black heavens overhead. Eerie. He turned from her, scowling. Middle of the night and here he was chasing a librarian around a mountain. Jesus, was he sick of this assignment.

Savelli emerged from the tower. Closed the door behind him, relocking it.

"Well?" asked Trentino in Italian.

"Asset is secure. Still, the *dottoressa* might be trying to get up here. You stay put until we locate her. I'll resume the search inside."

"Copy," grumbled Trentino.

As Savelli walked toward the access hatch to descend into the keep, he stopped. "Did you hear that?"

"I did. Sounded like a scream."

The agents remained still, listening, but they heard nothing else over the sporadic gusts of wind.

"Could you tell where it came from?" asked Savelli.

"Sounded lower down. From inside the keep, maybe."

Savelli jogged to the battlements. He looked down into the courtyard, a slight mist rolling in the cone of his flashlight. He pulled out his radio. "Griffon Three, Griffon One, come in, over."

After a pause, D'Arezzo's voice came through. "Go ahead Griffon One."

"Griffon Three, what is your location? Over."

"Still on four, One. Northeast sector. Over."

"Did you just hear a scream?"

"Say again?"

"I said did either of you just hear someone screaming."

Another pause. "Negative. No scream."

Savelli cursed. "As you were." He holstered his radio, thinking. "Recheck the suncatchers," he ordered, striding to the one nearest him. Each suncatcher was about four feet wide, a circular arrangement of mirrored steel panels that directed sunlight into an oculus of curved glass. The oculi were hinged, allowing them to be opened to access the shafts. Savelli and Trentino checked all four suncatchers, seeing only empty, shiny chutes.

"Clear," said Trentino, closing an oculus.

Savelli slammed his oculus down. "She's close, Trentino. She must be on level four for us to have heard that. Maybe the west side."

"Then let's just lock the roof and go get her. You and I can cover that sector in a few minutes."

Savelli nodded. "On me. Let's put this thing to bed."

VALORY CLAMBERED FROM THE ladder into the alcove, weakened, sweating, and horrified. There was no time to rest. The man in black was only seconds behind. In her mind, the fog of his breath grew thicker.

The alcove was small and dark, forcing her to probe the stone in frantic blindness, looking for a means of access. By some blessed fortune, she found it immediately. A mini drawbar much like the one from the Great Chamber's fireplace, only smaller. She lifted this from its iron slots, then opened a stone panel that was just big enough to squat through. First, she had to remove her backpack, nearly falling backward into the shaft as she did so. Then she squeezed through the hole, dragging her pack through after.

She shimmied into a hearth but couldn't see the room beyond. It was too dark, and her flashlight was gone. Curiously, the smell of plastic and electronics was strong here, but that barely registered. Her sole concern now was preventing that man from getting in. That was a big problem. The panel swung inward toward the shaft, so she couldn't lock it from her side. Maybe she could find something heavy to block it.

Like the Great Chamber, there was a bunch of junk lying around the firebox. Rummaging blindly through the items in the dark, she felt crates, ceramic jars, a chest, stacks of books, and a metal torch. She hefted the torch, thinking to wield it like a club, but then she heard liquid sloshing around inside of it. She realized the interior was filled with oil.

A desperate idea struck her. The jars. There were three of them about knee height, each the size of a watermelon. When she'd shifted one of them a second ago, it had sloshed. Now she tilted one of the jars back and forth, hearing liquid inside. She popped the lid off, and the pungent scent of some kind of oil made her recoil. Turning her nose from the opening, she shoved the jar into the secret panel. Then she dumped the oil down the shaft, dousing the rungs. Once empty, she threw the jar over, hearing it break only seconds later. A sharp grunt cut the air.

The jar had cracked on the man. He was only twenty feet down.

Coursing with adrenaline, Valory grabbed another jar, dumping its oil down the rungs, then chucked it over the side. She did the same with the last jar, hearing it shatter on the man in the darkness. He cursed, coughing and spitting oil, but he didn't budge from the ladder. Valory wasn't even thinking anymore. She just grabbed anything she could lift and threw it down the shaft: an old log, a chunk of marble, a fireplace poker, some mystery items that she couldn't make out in the darkness. Some of these elicited furious howls from the man, but he didn't let go. Valory panicked. How was he clinging to oil-slicked rungs while junk rained down on him? Finally, after hurling a dense, foot-long sculpture, she heard the thumping, sliding sounds of his body falling.

Guilt washed over her. In the throes of terror, she'd given no thought to the consequences of what she was doing. She did now. Whether in self-defense or not, the realization that she may have just ended a human life cut deep. Yet even as the remorse began piling up, the man's vocalics shot into her perception. Grunting, coughing, snarling, wheezing. He was alive. He'd caught himself at some point down the shaft. But her relief was short-lived. She'd merely bought herself some time.

Leaning into a nearby chest she'd felt a moment ago, she pushed it, wedging it into the passageway, delaying the man's entry as best she could. Then she ripped open her backpack, withdrawing her spare flashlight. Turned it on, swept it around the darkness, panting. She was in a large, circular room with a bunch of electronic equipment draped in plastic. A set of narrow stairs spiraled up the northern wall, an oaken door situated near the landing.

This was it. She'd reached the base of the tower. Upstairs, Alikai awaited.

CAPÍTOL 68

HE LOOKED UP JUST as the oil splashed down, dousing his face, his hands, and his chest. It went into his mouth. Burned his eyes. Stung the inside of his nose. He gagged, the chemical fumes assaulting his airways. Something broke on his head, but he barely felt it as he clung to the suddenly slippery rungs with a death grip. As fury set in, more oil washed over him, and then another object careened off his shoulder. He dared to look up just as a third deluge splashed his face. He turned away, coughing, spitting oil. Then something shattered on him, and he cursed in unbridled rage, red-hot eyes squeezed shut. His hand slipped, but he hooked his arm into a rung, his feet sliding on the slickened rungs. Then debris came raining down, bashing his head, his arms, his shoulders. He growled like a madman, but Grace kept pummeling him. Then the sharp point of something chunky hit his skull just right. He went woozy, muscles turning to mush. His arm unwrapped, and he dropped.

In a daze, he felt himself tumbling down the shaft, scraping against the slick walls, bones bashing the rungs. In that dozy twilight zone, his fighting instincts took over, hands and legs searching for purchase, clawing for oily rungs as he careened and slid. He regained full consciousness even as pain jolted him from every angle. He expanded his body, creating friction against the shaft with his own mass, slowing his descent. He grabbed a rung and jerked to a stop, righting himself. There, he stood and recovered, a dozen new injuries throbbing all over. He panted, coughed, cursed. Ripping off a piece of his undershirt, he wiped his eyes. Blew oil from his nostrils. Assessed. Saw that he'd fallen halfway down the shaft. The rungs overhead glistened with oil in the darkshine.

The bitch. That goddamn fucking bitch.

Snarling, he took a few moments to recover. Then he resumed his climb at a careful, infuriatingly deliberate pace.

Grace would *not* die quickly.

HOOFSTUK 69

SWEAT POURED DOWN HER her face. Her body was soaked under her coat, her skin burning hot. Fear and despair turned cartwheels in her psyche. It was hard to think straight, hard to keep moving, but she had to. She'd fended off the man in black, but only for the moment. He was coming. Only Alex could protect her now. Alex could fight this man off like he'd fought off the Franks. She had no choice but to believe that.

The base floor of the tower was not what she'd expected. Pointing her flashlight across the circular chamber, she saw modern scientific equipment covered in opaque plastic sheeting. Tall, silvery towers. Squatty apparatuses with control panels. Computer monitors, generators, miscellaneous devices. Everything was wrapped tight within the plastic like a decommissioned science lab. More rolls of plastic and heaps of extension cords were stacked between the machines. On the walls, mostly hidden behind the equipment, were paintings, tapestries, and sconces.

No time to wonder about the equipment. She darted to the other side of the room and checked the door. It was locked from the outside. That was a problem. Once she freed Alex, not only would they have to deal with the man in black, but unless Alex knew of some other way out, they'd have to go back down the shaft and through the tomb to escape. The shaft that was now dangerously oil-slicked. She hadn't thought this through very well.

The stairwell curled upward along the wall, lighthouse style. She took two steps at a time, Alex's treasures jingling in her pockets.

This was it. She was about to meet him.

Somewhere in her cyclone of stress, she hated how it was happening. She'd been imagining her first meeting with Alex like a scene from a fairy tale. She'd come in to rescue him. They'd fall in love at first sight. In the pregnant silence of night, he'd look at her with those mismatched eyes, peering into her soul, whispering words only she could understand. So much for all that. She was filthy, ragged, and sweat-soaked. Behind her, a demented thug hungered to spoil everything.

Huffing, she made it to the second level. Another chamber, slightly smaller than the first. It, too, was packed with equipment draped in plastic.

Valory continued upward, legs and lungs burning, her entire body begging for rest which would not come.

Third level. Smaller again, the tower tapering as it climbed into the sky. Loads of furniture and artwork were crammed together occupying every inch of the floor. Valory assumed these things had been moved here from the lower floors to make room for the science lab. Panting, she adjusted her backpack and continued up.

Finally. The fourth-floor landing. Before her, a thick wooden door, locked with a steel drawbar. Though the timeworn door was native to the tower, the drawbar was a recent installation. It was a carbon steel stud set into shiny, reinforced slots bolted into the stone. Modern additions to secure the chamber. Why this door opened outward instead of inward as all the other interior doors, she couldn't say and didn't care.

She was about to meet a god.

Drawing a long, deep breath, she placed her hands on the cold underside of the drawbar. It was wedged tight. She squatted with her weight beneath it and heaved upward. The bar scraped along the wood, popping over the steel slots. She let it clank to the floor.

She pulled the door open. An explosion of belly butterflies stole her breath.

Standing on the threshold was surreal. Like a cosmic clock had just ticked its last second, freezing the scene in time forever. The seconds that followed felt like a dream.

The interior of the chamber was hidden in darkness. Valory was hesitant to shine her flashlight inside. She wanted to but couldn't raise her arm. The moment was just too heavy.

A stench drifted into her nose. The funk of human waste and body odor. Unbelievable. Not only was Alex a captive in his own home but he was also being denied proper hygiene. It was an outrage on top of an outrage, but she had no breadth to process the injustice.

She tried speaking into the blackness. "H—Hello?" Her voice failed, cracking into fragments. She steadied herself, hand on her chest, then tried again. "Hello? Alexander?"

Silence.

A long moment passed, time she didn't have. She thought about trying another language. In his last diary entry, he'd spoken German as well as English.

But then.

A moan. Movement. The rustling of a chain from the rear of the chamber.

Valory swallowed hard. Within the total blackness, Alex was rising to his knees.

"Alexander? Alikai?"

She heard his body as he stood. A shift in his clothing, the pop of his kneecaps. A deep breath in the dark. She knew he was on his feet now, facing her. Looking at her from the gloom.

"Alex, my name is Valory Grace. I'm a friend. I'm going to raise my light now. Is that alright?"

Silence.

Shuffling forward, trembling, she began lifting her flashlight. "I'm here to free you, okay? I'm just going to—"

"Well, holy shit. Look who finally grew some balls."

Valory raised her light.

Fell to her knees in shock.

It wasn't Alex.

CHAPIT 70

ROCKWELL PACED.

Checked the mission phone. Paced some more. Checked again. Cursed himself. His own sloppiness was at fault here.

Eternal life was within his grasp. It was there, drifting toward him over a foggy horizon. So near. So very, very near, but it had almost gone up in smoke. For, on the proverbial eve of his ascension to immortality, he'd almost been assassinated by his assistant. He'd never seen it coming. Had never dreamed Andrew might be the weapon his rivals used to take him out. Hell, he'd even considered the possibility of Cervantes turning on him, but not weak, self-doubting Andrew. Someone had played a damn fine hand.

Who? Could it have been Harrison Kirk? Had the future U.S. President finally found his cock? Or maybe it was his daddy. Theodore Kirk bore Rockwell little love for the vast influence he wielded over his beleaguered son. Hell, maybe those goddamn Kirks were in it together.

Had it been Kauffman? That wrinkled shit had had rivals assassinated before. Two of them, decades ago. Rockwell had seen those dirty deeds in Kaufmann's essence. Maybe it was time to get in a room with that sagging sack of liver spots and do a little more brain-mining.

The big internet guys. That was another possibility. Uni-Fi was going to ruin empires when it launched. Infrastructure and ISP money was going to take a massive haircut if Rockwell got his way.

It could have been anyone. There were lots of sharks out there who despised Rockwell's meteoric rise. He'd come from nowhere, guns blazing, disrupting the time-honed power scales with no regard for the respected hierarchy of the elites. He could charm some, he could kill some, but he couldn't get them all.

"Sir . . ." It was Osborne in the door to his room.

"We ready?" asked Rockwell.

Osborne nodded. Rockwell followed him to the door of the suite. Waited as Osborne checked the hallway, then followed him two doors down to Andrew's room. Swiped the key. They walked to the bedroom, where Barrera was waiting. Barrera nodded toward the closet. Inside, Andrew's corpse hung by his own belt, naked from the waist down. Death by erotic asphyxiation. A humiliating way to go, but a perfect cover for the choking damage to his airways.

Rockwell inspected the scene like he could see each atom individually. "I don't mean to insult your intelligence, boys, but you wore gloves the entire time, yes?"

"Yes, sir."

"And you understand why this had to happen?"

"Yes, sir."

While focused on Andrew, he delved into the minds of his men, probing for anything that smelled like betrayal. They didn't like this, but they weren't idiots, they weren't traitors, and they liked money. They would remain unflinchingly loyal.

He gave the staged accident one last look. The cleaning crew was going to get quite a shock tomorrow afternoon.

Back in his room, Rockwell climbed into bed, but he couldn't sleep. He lay there, phone in hand, replaying that fateful recording. The recording that had been passed to him by one of his people at Aeternus months ago. The first time he'd heard it, he'd chuckled, dismissing it. Yet there'd been something about it. Something that had pulled him back. He'd listened to it again. Then again. With each hearing, it began to feel . . . fateful. Over the following days, the feeling had taken root, pushing him toward destiny. Showing him a door to unimaginable power.

He flung the covers off and sat up. Scrolled through his contacts, dialed his pilot. It took three calls to wake him. "Gustavo, change of plans. Prague is out. Tomorrow, I need you to fly me to Verona, Italy. Yeah, I know, and I don't care. Verona. Tomorrow. Make it happen."

He terminated the call, then made another, this time to Colonel Hewitt. He confirmed that Hewitt and his Bloodhawks were on standby, ready to deploy into the Dolomites if needed. Hewitt upped his price, for no reason except he sensed he could. He was right. Rockwell agreed without a blink.

Afterward, he sat in the dark, brooding. He played the message one more time.

Thank you for calling the Aeternus Genetics Laboratory, Prague. If you know your party's extension, you may dial it at any time.

Pro návod v češtině stiskněte jedničku.

Our offices are closed. Please call back during working hours, eight to five, Monday through Friday. If you would like to receive a callback from one of our representatives, please leave a message after the tone.

<tone>

"*This message is for the CEO, Thomas Rockwell. Whoever gets this, please, it's extremely important that you get this message to Mr. Rockwell immediately.*

"Mr. Rockwell, my name is Violet Grace. I was a geneticist at Aeternus working under Doctor Bolin. This will sound crazy, but I'm out of time, so I'm just going to spit it out. One month ago, I was recruited by Italian intelligence for a top-secret project. They brought me to a hidden castle in the Dolomites to examine DNA samples they'd collected. I analyzed the DNA and concluded it came from a biologically immortal human male. Again, I know this sounds crazy, but it's true, and I have the DNA to prove it. I smuggled the samples from the castle, but they've caught up to me, and they're closing in as I speak. Please, I need your help. I've hidden the samples but . . . <muffled> Oh, shit. They're here! Shit! <muffled> Please Mr. Rockwell! I'm in Verona and they're about to take me! Please help me! <banging> Help! They're –! No, get your goddamn hands off me! Hel— <click>"

ምዕራፍ 71

I HEARD THEM, I heard everything. You just get a look in that tower, girl. Trust me, you want to see who is there.

Mancini's words galloped in circles around her brain. He'd known. He'd known all along, and he'd been killed for it.

"I don't believe it," said Valory, staring into her sister's tired blue eyes. "It can't be. It just can't."

"And I can't believe you actually made it up here," said Violet, looking into the stairwell. "Kind of smells like a trap. You sure you weren't followed?"

"No, I . . . my god, what are you doing here, Vi? Where is Alex?"

"Who the hell is Alex?"

"Oh my god." Still kneeling, Valory hid her face in her hands, blanking out reality. Of all the places in the world, Violet was here. Right here, dirt-smothered, bruised, and ripe with body odor. The sight of her was like a live wire to the back of the head. In the electric aftermath, spots were swimming in Valory's vision like amoebae under a microscope. "This can't be happening, this isn't real."

"Val!" barked Vi. "You need to pull it together. You're in serious danger. Agent Savelli was here like twenty minutes ago, snooping around. Now I know why—he was looking for you. You've got to get out of here. Right now."

Val gained her feet and shuffled to her sister. Met her eyes in the dark, then hugged her. "Vi . . . you're so thin."

Vi returned the hug, briefly, then separated, shaking Valory by her arms. "Hey! Did you hear me? Those assholes will be back. You've got to get off this mountain yesterday or you'll end up here with me."

"No," said Valory, panting through tears. "No, I'm going to free you."

"How? You have the key?"

"No, but I have this." Shrugging off her backpack, Valory handed the flashlight to Vi, then unzipped the main pocket and withdrew the saw. She held it straight up for Vi to see.

"Hot damn, sis."

"We have to hurry. There's a man coming."

"What man?"

"I don't know. Some kind of freak. I think he wants to kill me."

Violet's eyes popped wide. "Give me that," she snapped, swapping with Val. "Here, point the flashlight at my feet."

The sisters went to the floor. While Valory aimed the flashlight, Violet began sawing through a link of chain connected to a modern shackle, the rapid friction creating a high-pitched riot. Valory took a quick look around the chamber, seeing nothing but a thin mattress, some blankets, and a waste bucket. On the southern wall was the lone window she'd seen from the courtyard. Filled and sealed with mortar.

"This saw sucks," grunted Vi over the noise.

"I know. But it was all I could find."

"Good thing is I've been working this link for months. Been using bits of stone, a butterknife, whatever I could hide from the guidos. There's only like halfway to go."

Months, thought Valory in disbelief. Vi was hunched over the chain, emaciated arm a blur as she sawed like a madwoman. Her long brown hair was knotty and ragged, her clothes torn. She stunk to high heaven. "Vi, why are you even here?"

Violet scoffed. "They obviously didn't tell you about me. But you better believe they told me about you, sis. Been showing me pictures of you in the castle. Threatening to kill you if I didn't talk."

"What?! Kill me?!"

"Jesus, are you really so clueless? How did they rope you into this? What reason did they give to get you here?"

"To translate books."

"Books? Are you kidding me?"

"Books written by an immortal."

"Oh," said Vi, maintaining her laser focus on the link. "I guess that makes sense."

"It does?"

Violet stopped her frantic sawing to blow out the cut. Then she dropped the saw and shook the cramp out of her hand. "I'm here because of the immortal too. I analyzed his DNA."

"What?"

"They recruited me to examine biological samples they'd collected from the castle. They didn't know what they had until I examined it. You saw all that equipment downstairs? I arranged that."

"Well . . . but why did they imprison you?"

"Because," said Vi, laying into the link again, "when I realized I had the holy grail, I stole it. Fled the castle with the only samples. Made it to Verona before they caught up to me. Fuckers brought me right back here, locked me up. Since then, they've been torturing me, trying to make me blab about where I ditched the goods. Ow, shit!" Vi dropped the saw and sucked on the finger she'd just cut.

"Oh my god," whispered Val. "The Incident. That was you."

"What?"

"You were the big security breach. They locked everything down after that. They call it The Incident."

"Yeah," said Vi, inspecting her bleeding wound, "I'm an incident alright."

Valory handed the flashlight to Violet, took the saw, and began cutting. She was slower and clumsier than Violet. "We can sort all that later," said Valory, trying to hold herself together. "Let's just get out of here."

"Who is this freak who wants to kill you? You sure it's not one of Rockwell's men?"

"Who's Rockwell?"

Violet scoffed again. "Still got your face buried in books twenty-four-seven, I see. Thomas Rockwell? Zillionaire entrepreneur guy? He owns Aeternus Genetics. He's offering a standing ten-million-dollar reward to the first person to crack the code of human immortality."

"So . . . you did it for money? Imprisonment? Torture? All for money?"

"Don't judge me, Ms. Perfect. You don't know my situation. Here, give that back, you're too slow." Violet snatched the saw and dug into the link, a sheen of sweat shining on her forehead. "Look, whatever you think you're doing here, it's wrong. They don't care about books or history or preservation of a world heritage site, or whatever other bullshit they've been feeding you. It's all about immortality. The DNA. They want it, and I'm the only one who's got it."

"Got it where?"

"Oh, they'll never find it without me. That's the only reason they haven't killed me."

"Oh my god."

"Yep. Welcome to the real world, sis."

Valory was about to ask Violet why Rockwell would send someone here, but then the earthquake hit.

POGLAVLJE 72

TWENTY FEET TO GO. Then he would take his vengeance.

Grace's little stunt had proven an effective countermeasure. After struggling and slipping on the oil-slicked rungs too many times, Cervantes had begun hooking his arms under each rung and pulling himself up by the crook of his elbow, stabilizing himself with each step. It was slow and infuriating. The fact that his entire body throbbed from his fall and that he was constantly gagging from the fumes drove his rage to soaring heights, but he was almost there.

Stopping to shake out his arms one at a time, he tuned into the darkshine, locating Grace in his mind. She was above, high in the tower, swirling in vivid hues. But now there was something else. He hadn't snapped to it at first. He just thought he was somehow 'seeing' double, like maybe the oil had scrambled his senses, crossed his wires. Then he realized there were two of them. Two brains, two hearts, two spines glowing in the black fire of the darkshine, surrounded by ethereal swaths of color.

Two Graces.

Cervantes thought back on the intelligence brief. He recalled seeing that the target, Violet Grace, had a sister named Valory. A non-identical twin who lived in England. A harmless bookworm. Was that her? What the hell was she doing here? Now that he thought about it, which Grace had he been chasing up the shaft? There'd been an intelligence lapse somewhere, but it didn't matter. He would proceed as planned. His objectives—his flowchart of orders—were still valid:

Confront Violet Grace.

Steal the DNA samples if she had them.

If those samples were still hidden, force her to give up the location. Then kill her.

If she refuses to give up the location, bring her to the safe house where Rockwell can work his magic.

If the Italians had already recovered the samples, kill Grace and pivot to the Italians.

If by some chance the immortal was on site, obtain a sample directly from him, negating all other tasks.

If possible, bring the immortal himself to the safe house.

Bottom line, get the samples or the immortal at all costs. Slay anyone who gets in the way.

The sister, Valory, was nothing in this. Perhaps he could use her as leverage if Violet resisted. Either way, in the end, both sisters would wind up dead.

He pulled himself up another rung. Then another. Almost there.

The shaft began to rumble. It vibrated, groaned, intensified. Dust and debris came raining down as the mountain cracked with ear-splitting force. Cervantes couldn't believe it. Of all the times for an earthquake to strike, it had to be now. The castle thundered and boomed, threatening to eject him from the rungs. He yelled in full-throated rage, clinging with every ounce of strength in his body.

ГЛАВА 73

THOUGH THE QUAKE LASTED less than sixty seconds, it felt like years to the occupants of the keep. Woken by what sounded like warring gods, they hunkered down in their chambers, hiding under furniture, yelling, crying, praying. Clutching photos of their loved ones.

After, they wandered into the Great Hall in stupors, eager to see other faces. Lanterns and flashlights in hand, wearing night clothes and coats, they culminated among clouds of dust, toppled sculptures, and fallen paintings, hugging and thanking God. Janelle joined them, cheeks wet with tears. Some from fear, some from seeing such magnificent works of art shattered on the marble floor. At least Queen Seraphina was intact. She sat upon her throne with a bearing that suddenly seemed impervious. Layered in dust, but perfect as ever.

Someone turned on two of the portables, casting the Hall in mote-swirled illumination. Janelle found herself craving the company of the others. The promise of catastrophe, it seemed, was an effective eraser of social anxiety. Rafael hugged her, followed by Rollo, his face wracked in relief. All the contactors she'd seen over the weeks and months were there as well as a handful of soldiers. Agents Savelli and Trentino circulated, checking on everyone, and taking a head count. They had come running into the Great Hall after the quake, having pulled themselves from some other task. Savelli was endlessly exasperated.

Janelle embraced anyone who crossed her path, thankful for human contact. Though the other civilians spoke little French, their tone and their eyes gave her all that she needed.

But where was Valory?

"*Où est* Valory?" she asked, searching the throng. "Valory? Valory? *Avez-vous vu* Valory Grace?"

No one knew. Not even Rafael, who was too distracted with the others to give it serious consideration. "I'm sure she'll turn up any minute, my dear."

A piercing whistle cut the hall. Standing on the dais near the queen was a man Janelle had seen from time to time, dark-skinned, middle-aged. Valory had once guessed he was a geologist or a seismologist. He clapped his hands while he whistled, demanding attention. In loud, authoritative Italian, he issued a set of commands that Janelle didn't quite understand. With his emphatic hand gestures and the reaction of the contractors, however, she inferred the message.

Everyone needed to evacuate the keep right now.

The quake might not be over.

БОБИ 74

THEY HAD NEVER HELD one another so tightly, not in their entire lives. Lying on the floor, wrapped in one another's arms, the mighty Dolomites quaked around them. Bits of ceiling fell, choking the chamber with dust. The sisters vibrated the length of Violet's chain across the floor. The flashlight leaped from Valory's hand, going dark when it hit the stone.

In the blackness, over the terrifying clamor, the sisters yelled that they loved each other.

Then, finally, it was over.

Still, they maintained their death-strong embrace, huffing like they'd just sprinted a mile. The grumbling of the earth faded, and the tower went still. They were alive, but Valory felt like she'd died. Too empty even to cry.

"Just like home, right?" quipped Violet unconvincingly. It was true. Tremors and quakes were the norm in California, but it was a whole different ballgame on top of a mountain at the highest point of a medieval tower. "Come on. Let me finish cutting this chain so we can get out of here."

Valory reluctantly released her sister.

While Violet resumed cutting, Valory regathered the items that had escaped from her backpack during the quake. The batteries had popped out of her flashlight, so she put them back in. She performed these actions in a daze, her motor skills playing catchup to this unreal reality.

Minutes passed with only the hornetlike buzz of metal-on-metal filling the air. Then . . .

Colors.

Dozens of people talking in a trio of languages. Lively voices in swooshing auroras, fat and vibrant. Originating from both the keep and the camp. Everyone was coming together after the earthquake. Valory dissected the sensations, picking out snippets of hues, textures, and aromas from the muddled conversations. She gleaned words of support, empathy, and hope in the face of shared fear. Everyone was so loving toward one another in the aftermath of a near disaster.

Then two voices emerged from the mists of her mind, strong and bright. These were much nearer than the others.

Bene, la torre è ancora intatta.

Sbrigati, apri le serrature. Dobbiamo portarla al sicuro, supponendo che sia ancora viva.

Two agents, their vocals dancing in peppery reds and ghostly emeralds. They had just come onto the roof, and now they were unlocking the entry door at the base of the tower.

They were coming.

"The agents are here."

"What?" said Vi, halting the saw. "How do you know?"

"I hear them. They want to move you to safety."

"Close the door!" yelled Vi, sawing faster. "When they get up here, you hold it shut with everything you got, okay? I just need another minute or two."

"Then what? Even when you're free, we'll be trapped."

"Good point. Okay, wait a sec. They don't know you're up here, right? So go down a level and hide. After they pass you by, just get out of the tower and come for me later."

"I—" began Valory, but she stopped. The tower door had just opened, and footsteps were now racing up the stairwell. "It's too late. They're coming."

"Shut the door!" hissed Vi. "No choice now, sis. We have to fight them off."

"What? How?"

"I don't know. But if we don't, we're both dead. Now shut the goddamn door!"

"Oh, God," fretted Val, crossing the chamber. She slammed the door and pulled on the handle with all her one hundred thirty pounds, bracing her feet against the jamb.

The agents heard the noises above—the sawing, then the slam—and double-timed it up the stairs. Gaining the landing, one of them pulled on the door. It snapped right back into place from Valory's body weight.

"Vi!"

"Almost done!"

An agent jerked the door, and it opened by a foot before immediately slamming back again.

"I can't hold it, Vi!"

"One more second!"

"Viiiii!"

It all happened so fast.

The agents were in the chamber. D'Arezzo and Moreno.

Valory was flat on her back, muscles on fire. Some of the coins she'd taken from the tomb spilled from her pockets. She scooted backward toward Violet.

The agents advanced, barking commands. When they reached the sisters, there was an explosion of movement. Grappling, fighting, yelling. Flashlights went flying, spawning frantic shadows on the walls. Thumping, whooshing, grunting. A medieval cage fight in the dark.

Violet found an opening, wielding the old saw as a weapon. D'Arezzo got cut. He punched her in the face.

Valory grabbed at moving legs, clawing and ripping. She was dragged along the stone. Moreno cuffed the side of her head.

"Get their gun!" Vi screamed from a mass of whirring darkness. "Get their gun, Val!"

She tried. She reached for Moreno, clutching at his vest holster. Then a foot found her stomach, and she curled to the floor, sucking wind.

The agents gained control, their furious commands ricocheting off the stone. They slammed Violet to the floor, and she cried out in pain. Valory reached for her. It was all over.

Then, the doorway.

The man in black was there.

A spinning flashlight lit him for a hot second.

Knives glinted in his fists.

He was smiling.

He entered the darkness.

POGLAVLJE 75

WHILE THE AGENTS USHERED everyone from the castle, Janelle slipped away. She was concerned. Valory was the only person who had not shown up in the Hall. That could only mean trouble. When she tried to explain this to the agents, however, they were annoyed. Told her not to worry about it. Just get outdoors with everyone else, it wasn't safe inside. But all she could do was picture Valory on the floor trapped under a piece of fallen furniture or something. She would never forgive herself if she died like that. So, waiting until Savelli and Trentino were occupied, she slid into the darkness, grabbing a lantern that had fallen from an equipment table.

She checked Valory's bedchamber first. The bed frame had collapsed. Her chair was on its side. Her laptop was on the floor. But no Valory. She opened the garderobe—empty.

The library was her next stop, but on the way, she stuck her head into the other chambers, calling Valory's name. Maybe she'd run into someone else's room for comfort, but no, she wasn't there.

Janelle had never been to the library before—it had always been off-limits to her—but under these circumstances, she'd risk it. Down she went, spiraling into the depths, lantern light pushing into complete darkness. Knowing that an aftershock could happen at any moment was more than a little scary, but she would not give up on her only friend at the castle.

The library was a mess. Books laid everywhere, thrown from the shelves by the quake. Chairs had fallen over. Dust choked the bubble of her lantern. "Valory?!" she called, voice echoing through the aisles like ghosts mimicking her. "Valory, *peux-tu m'entendre?!*"

She picked her way among the chaos as best she could, stepping over fallen tomes. She checked all the aisles, but . . . wait! There! Someone had just been walking in the darkness, just beyond the reach of her light. "Valory?" she called. "Is that you?" When she reached the end of the aisle, however, there was nothing but empty blackness. The hairs stood up all over her body. Either her eyes had played a cruel trick on her, or . . .

An eerie thought turned her veins to ice—What if that had been Valory's spirit, wandering among her tomes after dying in the quake?

She turned and ran from the library as fast as she could.

ĈAPITRO 76

WIELDING HIS KNIVES ICEPICK style, he rushed Agent D'Arezzo, who was raising his pistol in one hand, flashlight in the other. Cervantes whirled into him like a typhoon, cutting his pistol hand first, then slicing his neck and eyes before he even realized he was being attacked. The pistol discharged as it fell from D'Arezzo's grasp, the deafening explosion illuminating Cervantes' bloodwork in a flash of horror. The agent collapsed, screaming, clutching at his ruined head.

Moreno had drawn his pistol, but he couldn't line up a shot in the darkness. He groped for a flashlight while tracking the cyclone of shadows. When D'Arezzo's pistol discharged, he caught a fleeting glimpse of Cervantes' blood-spattered grin before feeling the knives punch into his body everywhere at once. Dropping, gasping with lungs that no longer worked, he tried to crawl away. Cervantes straddled him, grabbing a dull saw he'd noticed in the darkshine. In fevered ecstasy, he clutched Moreno's hair and sawed into his neck. Bubbling gurgles filled the room.

Valory had lost track of what was happening. The man in black was here, reeking of oil, but everything was a dark blur. Violet was forcing her to her feet, yelling at her. Pushing her toward the door. Slaughterhouse noises echoed in the tinny gunshot aftermath. She felt her backpack on the floor, managing to grab it as Vi pulled her along. Everything was blending and ringing. Time became a weird seesaw, one moment lasting forever, the next whizzing by. She needed to puke, but Violet would not let her stop.

Reality snapped into place as they stumbled across the threshold. Violet threw Valory to the side and slammed the door shut.

They heard his voice from the darkness. "Graces! Come back! I haven't even started with you!"

Hearing her surname from his lips shocked Valory into action. She grabbed the drawbar and raised it into the slots. Violet helped her guide it in, wedging it tight. The second they'd done so, the man bashed the door from the other side. "Graces!" he growled, pounding on the wood. "Open up! Big brother wants to talk!"

As they backed away, gunshots exploded, and chunks of door splintered toward them.

"Go, Val! Move move move!"

The sisters ran down the stairs as fast as they dared, shots cracking like fireworks behind them, wood and metal breaking. At the tower base, they found the door ajar, unlocked by the agents. They didn't have to go down that shaft.

Emerging onto the roof of the keep, they saw the amorphous light rising from the courtyard. People had gathered there, their frightened voices riding the winds. Their vocalics were muddled, but Valory knew they were panicking over the gunshots.

She puked then, her guts catching up to the horror of the last two minutes. Violet kept her moving, stumbling across the roof. An access hatch was open on the northwestern corner near the slope of the mountain.

"The hatch!" yelled Violet. "Go go go!"

While descending the ladder into the keep, they heard the door crash open from the heights of the tower. The man in black screamed again—the same tortured, maniacal scream he'd unleashed in the tomb. Even Violet was spooked. She had just grasped the ring to close the hatch when she heard him. The scream froze her in place. She looked to the tower, arm hairs standing on end.

"Close it, Vi!"

She did, slamming the hatch overhead. Then she slid the bolt and snapped the padlocks closed, ensuring the door could not be opened from above. "He'll just shoot through that too," said Violet, jumping off the ladder. "Let's get the hell out of here."

"What did he mean 'big brother?'" said Valory.

"What?"

"He said he's our 'big brother.' Why did he say that, Vi?"

"How should I know? Just run," said Vi, pulling Valory into the stairwell.

Racing downward, Valory felt like a stone falling into a bottomless hole. Murder. She had just witnessed two savage murders. D'Arezzo and Moreno, slain mere inches from her. Their blood flecked her clothing.

Alex wasn't here. She would never meet him. He would not save the sisters from this maniac, much less from the might of Italy. Even if they escaped to the mountainside, a massive search mission would be launched to track them down. This 'escape' was doomed. She and Violet would be killed or imprisoned tonight, tomorrow, whenever.

One way or another, it was all over.

KAPITOLA 77

THE NIGHT WAS OVERCAST, the sky a steely black haze. A cold breeze gusted in spurts, freezing those who wore flimsy pajama bottoms and slippers. The courtyard was filled with anxious chatter. Ministry contractors and federal personnel milled around, their breath fogging the glow of their lanterns and flashlights.

Agente Savelli was calling for quiet so he could do a roll call. He'd sent D'Arezzo and Moreno up to ensure Violet Grace had survived, and to move her from the tower until its structural integrity could be inspected. Then he and Trentino had rushed here to assess the impact and direct the civilians to safety.

"Are you kidding me?!" demanded Savelli, yanking a cigarette out of Trentino's lips and stomping on it. "Control yourself for one fucking minute and do your job! Give me this," he growled, stealing the Zippo from Trentino's pocket. "Get these people to the camp! Go!"

His rage boiled over. The hunt for Valory Grace would have to wait courtesy of a giant fuck you straight from Murphy's Law. This earthquake had hit at the worst possible time. Just how much more of a disaster could this assignment become?

The answer came quickly.

When the first shot sounded, everyone gasped, looking toward the tower in a hush. When the proceeding volley was fired, panic ensued.

"Everyone out!" yelled Savelli in Italian, waving the masses toward the gate. "Out of the courtyard now! Go go go! Trentino, get them out of here!"

"What is happening?" demanded Doctor Moretti, clutching his coat together and fingering his spectacles. "Why are your men firing guns?"

"Get the fuck out of here, Moretti!"

"But Doctor Grace and Ms. LaFleur aren't here! They might still be inside. You have to get them!"

"I said out! Out out out out!"

Trentino pushed Moretti, herding the civilians from the courtyard while Savelli fumed. Shots fired?! Now?! It had to be Violet Grace. If D'Arezzo and Moreno were unloading their mags up there, then things had gone horribly wrong. Savelli whipped out his radio. "Griffon Three, Griffon Four,

414

come in. D'Arezzo, come in. Moreno, come in." No response. He cursed, assuming the worst—that the prisoner had somehow stolen a firearm and was fighting her way out. He took a last glance at Trentino, ensuring he was pushing everyone through the gate. Beyond the wall, the soldiers guided the civilians downslope toward the camp.

Savelli darted back up the stairs into the keep, chambering a round as he ran. He knew he should have authorized harsher interrogation methods for Violet Grace. Had he done so, he'd have recovered the DNA by now and this debacle wouldn't be happening. The isolation, the cold cell, the electric shocks, the starvation—none of those had been enough to make her crack. She was a fierce *cagna*. Maybe the earthquake had broken her chain, allowing her to attack his men when they tried to move her to safety. Now she might be running amok, and his men could be wounded or dead. Yet another screwup that could be laid at his feet.

He cursed as he ran through the marble columns and courtiers in the Great Hall. His worst fears had come to light, courtesy of the Graces. Now he might have to kill them both. Better that than to allow another Incident.

ಅಧ್ಯಾಯ 78

JANELLE ENTERED THE GREAT Hall from the northeastern portal, catching a glimpse of *Agente* Savelli as he rushed through the cluster of portable lights. "*Agente* Savelli!" she tried to yell, but she coughed on dust while he gained the opposite portal, taking the stairwell up. She ran after him, picking her way over debris. While doing so, her lantern slipped from her hand, busting on the stone and extinguishing with a hiss. "*Zut alors!*" she said, leaving it behind. "*Agente* Savelli, wait! Valory is missing!"

Savelli didn't hear her over his own huffing. He took the steps two at a time, pistol in one hand, flashlight in the other. On the second-floor landing, he stopped, switching off his light. The anxious chattering of two female voices was drawing near, getting louder. It was coming from the floors above. The Graces—both of them, together?!—were descending the stairwell. So—his worst fear was true. Violet had escaped, probably with Valory's help, and they'd somehow overpowered his men, maybe even killed them with their own weapons. Those gunshots . . .

Jaw clenched, he waited in the shadowy alcove under the stairs. They appeared, Violet in the lead. "We've got to find a way past that army," she was saying. "And quick, before that freak catches up."

Just as they were about to hit the landing and continue down, Savelli jumped into their path, pistol and flashlight pointing at them. "Stop right there! Hands over your head!"

The women recoiled in surprise.

"I SAID HANDS UP! NOW!"

They raised their hands. Valory was crying without crying, cringing under his commands. Violet stood tall, spitting venom from her eyes.

"Where are my men?!" Savelli growled. "What did you do?! Answer me?!"

"Fuck you," fired Violet. "And fuck your men."

"Face down on the floor! Both of you! Now!"

Valory was paralyzed. A long-delayed panic attack was setting in, and she began to hyperventilate. Violet noticed. Moved to help her, ignoring Savelli. Enraged, he pistol-whipped her. She wobbled, crumpling. With Violet dazed, he grabbed Valory's arm, shoving her to the stone as she struggled to breathe. Holstering his sidearm, he withdrew a zip tie handcuff, nearly dislocating Valory's shoulder as he cinched her wrists into it. "*Stupide puttane del cazzo!*" he yelled, withdrawing a second set of cuffs for Violet. Vi was wobbling on her knees, holding her head. Savelli spun her around to cuff her. "*Cosa hai fatto ai miei uomini?!*"

He didn't see Janelle. Didn't hear her swinging the heavy torch at his head. She didn't have much behind it. It wasn't a crushing blow, but it was a lucky one, bashing him in the temple. He stumbled into the wall, vision swirling. Janelle backed away from him, horrified at what she'd done. Head pounding, Savelli steadied himself, preparing to take her down.

A shot rang out. A blinding flash. A ringing echo.

He dropped to his knees. Looked up. Saw the barrel pointed at him, smoking. Behind it, Violet peering down. His stomach. It was bleeding. A gut shot. He went to snatch his pistol from his holster, but she fired again. The shoulder this time. Felt like a gorilla hitting him with a ball peen hammer. He fell onto his side, gasping, pressing his stomach. Then Violet was over him, taking his weapon. Valory looked on in horror. Janelle was holding her, arms wrapped tight. All three women stared at *Agente* Marco Savelli as his world turned to black.

TI 79

CERVANTES KICKED THE TOWER door open, striding onto the roof of the keep. He was covered in blood and oil, knives in hand, teeth bared, lips foaming. The wind howled as he looked around, eager for more carnage. Slaying the two feds had unleashed the blood lust. Now he was burning hot, ripping at the seams like a thousand tiny versions of himself were clawing their way out of his skin.

The Graces. They weren't on the roof. He had to find them. Obtain the Salvador's prize. Kill everyone else. He ran to the battlements. The courtyard was empty save for two soldiers in the bailey saddling the horses. Beyond the wall, a throng of people huddled in clouds of lanternlight as they were herded to the camp. Weak, fattened cattle, their vitals flaming black in the darkshine. He tasted their fear in the winds: fear of the earthquake, fear of the gunshots, fear of not seeing their loved ones again. Pathetic.

There was no way down the smooth wall of the keep. He looked around. Spotted an access hatch on the north side of the roof. Ran over, jerked the pull ring with all his strength, but the hatch was locked from the underside. To open it, he'd have to shoot it to hell, and he'd already wasted three mags blasting through that thick tower door.

There sounded a sudden gunshot from below, inside the keep. He froze, closing his eyes, tuning in deep to the darkshine. There they were. The Graces, shimmering mirages of color two floors down. Two others were with them, one woman, one man, their organs lit in his mind. The woman had her arms wrapped around Valory Grace. The man was on his knees with Violet standing over him, a smoking pistol in her hands. The pistol the fed had dropped in the tower. Grace fired again, the explosion like a camera flash in the darkshine. The man fell over, clutching himself. Cervantes sucked air through his teeth. Tasted the man's blood. Licked his ruined spleen. Breathed in the pungent nitro of the gunpowder. Violet Grace was a killer now. Good for her.

He watched Grace as she rifled through the fed's pockets, taking his pistol and a few other items. She bent over, unlocking the manacle around her ankle. Tossed it on top of the fed. Then the three women descended farther into the keep, fading like luminescent fish swimming into the depths.

Cervantes had to find a way off the roof before they fled the castle grounds. He had no rope, and he couldn't afford to waste his remaining ammo on the hatch.

He raced to the northwestern corner of the roof, where the keep merged with the face of the mountain. Looking over the battlement, he scanned the slope which dropped into the courtyard. It was almost vertical, but unlike the smooth wall of the keep, there was a network of cracks and crevices embedded in the mountain face. With the darkshine and his physical prowess, he could climb down.

He secured his weapons and gear. Reached up and clutched the cold rock face with his bare hands. Then he swung over the battlement and began spidering down.

KABANATA 80

THEY RAN THROUGH THE Great Hall. Violet was in the lead, Moreno's pistol in hand, Savelli's in the small of her back. In the dusty light of the portables, Valory got her first good look at her sister. Thin, pale, bruised. Her clothes were loose, torn, and filthy. Dark chocolate hair tangled and dirt-laden. Bright blue eyes worn by a hundred sleepless nights. A shade of her former, beautiful self. Though she moved with confidence, she was unsteady and fatigued, weakened from her imprisonment. From the torture.

Valory and Janelle ran behind her, clutching hands. In her other hand, Janelle still carried the silver torch she'd used to bash Savelli. Not because she thought it would be useful, but because clinging to it was comforting amidst the chaos that had bum-rushed her life. Janelle had helped take down a federal agent. She was in this now.

As for Valory, she grew more numb by the second. The weight of her backpack had disappeared. She no longer heard the jingling of the treasure in her pockets. The last half hour had hit so hard and so fast that it had burned through every last nerve, leaving her as blank as an epileptic aftershock. She just lurched after Violet, eyes glued to her back, clasping Janelle's dainty, sweaty hand.

They crossed the vestibule, rushing through the keep doors and down the stairs. It was dark, and they nearly fell before reaching the ground. "Hey," said Violet, turning to Janelle, "will that thing burn?"

"What?" said Janelle, holding up the torch. "I don't know."

Violet grabbed the torch, heard the oil inside. She stuck her pistol down the front of her pants, then used her fingertips to pull the rope-like wick from the top of the torch. She held it close, sniffing it. "Hoo yeah, that'll fuckin burn." Handing it back to Janelle, Violet fished around in her pocket and withdrew the Zippo she'd taken from Savelli. "Hold it steady," she said.

"Vi," whispered Valory as her sister lit the torch, "you shot Agent Savelli."

"Yeah."

"Is he going to die?"

Violet's pallid face glowed orange in the new flame. "I don't know, sis. Maybe. But we can't think about that. We've got to get out of here while everyone's distracted." She nodded at Janelle. "You good to carry that?"

"Yes, I think so," said Janelle.

"Hey, nice job clubbing Savelli like that. Who are you anyway?"

"Janelle."

"You saved the day, Janelle." Violet drew the pistol from her waist, her breath fogging before her. "Stay close, I need the light, okay? Val, hey." She grabbed her sister under the chin, meeting her eyes. "Remember what we used to say? Yeah, you know what I'm talking about. Come on, say it with me."

"We're not kids, Vi, and this isn't a cartoon."

"Say it anyway. Ready? One, two, three—Wonder Twin powers, activate."

"Wonder Twin powers, activate."

"Good. Now we're invulnerable. Let's move."

In a tight huddle, torchlight dancing in the wind, the women crossed the deserted courtyard and went under the gate. Thirty yards down the low-grade slope, two soldiers were riding the horses toward the camp. Some distance ahead of them, the civilians were rounding the eastern bend under a haze of collective lanternlight. Valory perceived their chatter in her mind, cauldrons of colors mixing and weaving. Certain words popped up over and again in a swooping trio of tongues: gun, earthquake, cold, family. Someone was screaming *Give us our phones!* in brick-red Italian stabbed with dark green.

"*Comment allons-nous dépasser les hommes de l'armée?*" Janelle said, squeezing her coat closed. "*Ils gardent la seule issue.*"

"Hey," said Violet, "English, kid."

"She asked how we're supposed to get past the military," said Valory. "They're guarding the only exit."

"Okay, look," said Violet, halting them there. "We're just going walk up all casual like, okay? Just a few laggards joining the party. Stay on the outside of the crowd, away from the camp. Don't talk to anyone, don't look at anyone, don't draw attention. While everyone's busy crying for mama, we just ease our way toward the checkpoint and slip out. If the guards see us, we make a break for it. Got it?"

"A break for it?" said Valory. "But they'll just catch us immediately."

"Or shoot us," added Janelle.

Violet brandished her pistol. "That's what these are for, ladies. You want one?"

Valory cringed.

"That's what I thought. Don't worry, I'll do the dirty work if it comes to that. Just stay close, got it? Both of you. Now come on. Quietly."

They resumed their advance, staying well behind the riders. Violet kept her pistol at the ready. Valory and Janelle exchanged glances. Squeezed each other's hands. Overhead, the moon made a lonely appearance through a puffy breach in the clouds, lighting the peak for one surreal moment. Ahead of them, the riders became silvery silhouettes, their bodies swaying with the gait of the horses.

That's when she heard him.

The man in black.

She felt him in her perception, a rotting ooze seeping into the folds of her brain. Vocalics of homicidal glee. Hot, grimy breaths.

She turned. There he was, emerging from the gate.

He stopped there, staring at her across the expanse, outlined by the moonlight for a half second. Then the clouds erased him.

"Run!" yelled Valory. She tugged Janelle behind her. "Run, Vi! It's him!"

"Where?! I don't see—"

"RUN!"

They ran as fast as they dared, knees threatening to buckle on the janky, uneven stone. Ahead, the riders halted their horses at the sound. They turned, assuming the ladies were stragglers.

"The horses!" yelled Valory. "Mount the horses, Vi!"

Violet wanted to reject the horse idea for the scene it would make—three ladies galloping through the camp like bats out of hell—but Valory was right. That freak back there was legit. He had slain two armed agents like it was child's play. The women needed to put distance between him and them quickly, all other factors be damned.

"Get off!" demanded Violet, pistol trained on the nearest rider as she approached. "Off! Now! Val, tell them to get off!"

"*Scendi da cavallo o ti ucciderà!*" yelled Valory.

The startled soldiers—unarmed hostlers—dismounted while Violet waved them away with the pistol. Then the ladies saddled up. Violet took Bel Ragazzo, cursing. She'd never really taken to riding during those lessons all those years ago and had intended to never mount a horse again. Valory helped Janelle mount Magia, then she squeezed in behind her, letting her backpack rest on the cantle. In doing so, she bumped Janelle's elbow, knocking the torch from her hand.

"*La torche!*"

"Forget it!" said Valory, looking into the darkness behind her. The man in black was a shadow sprinting toward them. "Press your legs against her body. Hang on to the pommel and just move with me, okay?"

They spurred the horses to a lope, their hooves clopping on the stone like a salvo of small explosives.

ESSUULA 81

SIMMERING, CERVANTES HAD FREECLIMBED down into the courtyard. He'd retrieved his gear from the kitchen, blasting the lock off the door. Now, rifle in hand and rucksack bouncing on his back, he raced in a murderous furor, the darkshine pulsing in his perception, helping him navigate the debris-strewn slope. He spit curses when he saw the Graces boost the horses. He should have slain those fucking horses when he'd had the chance. The hostlers shouted in Italian, making obscene gestures at the women as they galloped downslope around the toothy crags. The ladies vanished from Cervantes' physical eye, lighting up in his third—two balls of color and their companion, bouncing in their saddles beyond the rock. They were riding straight toward a throng of civilians.

The Graces had proven much craftier than expected, and now, on horseback, they had a real chance of slipping from his grasp for good. They could probably ride straight through the soldiers, who were preoccupied by the fresh humanitarian crisis that had been dumped at their feet.

He began sprinting after them. That's when the aftershock hit.

It started with a sudden rumble. The ground vibrated. Small rocks tumbled down the crags, ricocheting, bouncing, shattering. Cervantes knew he should stop and cover up, but he didn't. He wouldn't. He kept sprinting, the land jumping under his feet. He stumbled, dashing his kneecap on the stone. But he got up and pushed through the pain, the darkshine his ghostly nightlight. The quaking intensified, becoming deafening. In seconds, it grew as strong as the original quake, maybe stronger. Still, he never stopped.

He rounded the bend, earth shimmying beneath him. There were the hostlers, huddled together on their knees, covering their heads. Beyond them, the remains of the small village crumbled. And beyond that, the Graces were navigating through a chaotic mass of terrified human cattle, horses pitching wildly. Some of the civilians were running away from the lofty crags that littered rocks into the narrow plateau. Others were curled in protective balls on the ground. Some were praying. Even many of the soldiers—young and inexperienced privates—had abandoned protocol and were running amok. All of them clogged the lane between himself and the Graces.

Then a noise like bombs exploding crashed down from the summit. Cervantes turned to see the tower collapsing. It toppled into the keep, driving great, billowing clouds downslope, obscuring the castle and its crown of jagged peaks. As the quake died off, the sounds of cascading demolition thundered through the caldera as the keep caved in stages, the sight of its destruction blanked by the colossal dust storm it birthed.

Something new happened to Cervantes then.

He panicked.

Not because of the earthquake, the Graces, or the diminishing likelihood of retrieving the DNA. No, he panicked because of the tomb. The queen. His golden corpse. The beautiful goddess of entropy who had whooshed him into that vacuum of preexistence, where he'd glimpsed his true self. His true nature. She had unlocked something in him, something he couldn't grasp here and now when he was away from her. Something he was incapable of understanding without his macabre muse. Only now did he admit that he'd been planning to go back for her. When this was all over, when the Salvador possessed his precious DNA, Cervantes would go back for the queen. He would steal back into the keep, slink through the secret fireplace down into the tomb. He would retrieve the queen and bring her home. Keep her with him forever, beside him, so she may take him on that magic carpet ride again and again and again, into himself. But now, the castle was crumbling. The queen would be trapped under immovable rubble forever.

In and around the encampment, the human cattle groveled and cried. Many of their lights had been lost, reducing their collective aurora to scattershot bubbles of dust-choked light. The soldiers were gathering their wits, knowing they had a job to do but too stunned to do it. A few people had died, pelted by falling rocks. Someone had had a heart attack.

Cervantes looked upon them all in the darkshine, seething. The Graces were getting away. He could see them on their horses, somehow keeping the frightened beasts just calm enough to ride through the mountaintop mayhem. In moments, they would escape through the checkpoint. Between them and him, the cattle spread every which way, wailing, huddling, running.

Yet even above all the chaos, one thing echoed in his thoughts: the queen was gone. He would never know her touch again.

His mission melted to black. Homicidal insanity flooded his mind, his body, and his heart. And this time, he did not fight it off with mantras. He let it consume him, for it was glorious.

He yanked a 40mm frag grenade from his vest. Loaded it into the rifle launcher.

Time to slaughter the cattle.

THE WORLD BOOMED AS they kept their steeds at a shaky lope. The darkness churned with dust, choking visibility. Soldiers and civilians were like phantoms floating in and out of their path, nearly trampled in the blind mania. Valory did what she could to keep Magia from getting spooked, spurring the mare forward despite the chaos, and using a lateral flexion technique to distract her from the many stressors. Violet had less success with Bel Ragazzo, whose big, watery eyes were darting all over. The gelding wouldn't settle for Violet, so Valory closed the gap between them and took his reins, turning his head into Magia while they loped toward the checkpoint. Tricky to do with Janelle's nervous weight shifting around in front of her.

In the pandemonium, they rode past *Agente* Trentino and Rafael, who were looking for cover that wasn't there. Trentino was pulling Rafael by the arm, yelling something. Rafael was coughing and huffing, his body looking like he'd been blasted with flour. The glimpse of him and Trentino hit Valory hard. Six long weeks ago, the two of them had come to her flat in Oxford. Rafael had been so kind, so cherubic, so Santa-like. He'd given her the job of a lifetime. She called to him as they loped past, for no other reason than to say she was sorry, so very, very sorry for everything, but he didn't hear her over the rumbling earth. Trentino locked eyes with her for a half second before he was swallowed by darkness.

As the aftershock died off, a terrible crashing sound shook the mountain anew. Though she could not see, Valory knew the castle was falling. Alikai's supreme tribute to his true love, having stood for a thousand years, was crumbling under the might of the earthquake. His art, his queen, his library— it would all be buried in rubble, perhaps forever. Yet another heart-crushing disaster in a night packed full of them.

The women made it past the camp in an adrenalized stupor. The jeeps at the checkpoint, normally parked head-to-head, had shaken away from one another. A cloud of mountain fallout blanketed them.

"Should we take a jeep?" huffed Valory, voice dry and cracked.

"No way," said Violet. "We have to stay off the main road. Let's—"

An explosion stole her voice, detonating near the encampment. The night lit up with fire, a percussive wave rolling along the rock. Horses skittering, the women saw a second explosion burst from a cluster of civilians and soldiers, sending debris and viscera in all directions. In abject horror, Valory realized that the burning lump she saw flying through the dust was someone's leg.

"Go!" yelled Violet. "Go go go!"

They spurred their steeds beyond the checkpoint. Gunfire erupted from the camp, the night flashing in bursts of orange as screams undercut the pop-pop-pop of an assault rifle.

Janelle's head was hung low, eyes squeezed shut. Valory wanted to do the same, but she couldn't. Magia and Bel Ragazzo, scared out of their poor minds, were now being forced to clamber down the precarious mountain path while explosions rocked the mountain. They did not want to cooperate, and it took everything Valory had to keep her mare and the gelding focused on escape.

The crescendo of death played louder from the camp. The vocalics of violence and murder were like bullets shooting through Valory's perception. The last gasps of one man after another, some of them sharp and sudden, some of them drawn and wracked with pain. In their midst was the growling, hissing pleasure of the man in black. She heard him in her mind. Felt him in her soul. She didn't understand how or why, but she was aware of a connection to him in the worst possible way. He had called her sister in the tower. That had confused her. Now, in some macabre spiritual undertone, he felt fraternal. Like his blood was in her veins. In her mind's eye, she saw his ghastly spree. Felt him using the cover of darkness and dust as he danced among the terrified people, picking them off. He yanked a knife across a soldier's throat, ducking into the shadows just before his partner turned to see. He shot a civilian who'd been running alone toward a tent—popped him in the skull in midstride before vanishing into the night. No one caught more than a fleeting glimpse of him as he wove his ghost-like tapestry of murder. Sickened beyond reckoning, Valory forcefully ejected the man from her psyche.

She spurred Magia forward, trusting the mare's surefootedness in the darkness of the slope, leaning back with Janelle as they pitched downward on steps and ledges. She didn't know how she pushed on. Under different circumstances, she'd have only sat and wept as Janelle did now, unable to confront this salvo of atrocities. But a numbness had set in, a mental exhaustion so overwhelming that it burned through her emotions, leaving only fumes. She rode in an existential daze, only half hearing her sister who directed their course. The promise of morning was just appearing in the east, the mountain horizon lined with a deep, royal blue.

426

It took her a moment to realize that the bloodletting had stopped. All had gone quiet. Janelle's soft weeping, the horses' labored blows, and the clopping of hooves became the only reality in the dusty, predawn world. The pungent odor of sweaty horseflesh overpowered everything else. Violet kept glancing backward, though there was little to see here, in the darkness downhill of the camp. "It's quiet up there now," she said. "Maybe that freak got shot."

"Who is he?" asked Janelle. She was timid and small, the dust on her face smudged with tears. "Why does he pursue us?"

"We don't know." Violet leaned all the way back as Bel Ragazzo dropped into a deep step. "Maybe he's dead."

"No," said Valory. "He's alive."

"How do you know?" challenged Violet.

"I just do."

"I wouldn't be so sure. All that gunfire—"

"He's alive, Vi. And he's coming for us."

Janelle was almost sick.

"Well," said Violet, "if that's true, then at least we've got a head start. We need to ditch these horses, though."

"Why?" asked Valory.

"Last time I escaped, they had choppers searching for me. They'll be out soon. We'd be easier to spot on horses. We go on foot from here, off the main path. I know—"

An engine revved upslope, shattering the silence like the roar of a vengeful mountain god. The ladies froze, looking. In moments, they heard the creaking, clambering sounds of a jeep gobbling up rocks as it sped toward them.

"Off the horses!" yelled Violet. "Into the boulder fields!"

The terror in Violet's voice was like an electric cattle prod zapping Valory from the saddle. Janelle waited to dismount until Valory was clear, but Valory's foot stuck in the stirrup, and she fell the last few feet, a hard landing stealing her breath. Violet had problems as well. Weakened from imprisonment and exertion, she tumbled backward after dismounting Bel Ragazzo.

The jeep burst over the ridge like a monster truck mutilating a lineup of junkers. No headlights. It was a giant black behemoth in the dark, swaying, dipping, and bouncing over the rocks at full throttle. Its screaming motor engulfed the mountain.

427

FƏSİL 83

THE WORLD WAS A slow-motion catastrophe.

Violet was yelling, dragging Valory from the path.

The jeep crashed downhill, plowing straight into the horses. Running over them. Crushing them under its monstrous tires.

Janelle had not dismounted in time.

She slammed into the windshield. Slid off into the rocks, limp.

There was a massive boom as the jeep careened into a boulder, upending its wheelbase. It crashed to an abrupt stop, its meaty front tire spinning in the air. Gore was everywhere.

Cervantes had rolled out of the jeep at the last minute, leaving his pack and rifle inside. The fall had hurt, but he was calm. His madness had abated. With more than sixty new corpses in his wake, the bloodlust had been satisfied. Now he was hyper-focused on completing his mission.

Violet's shouting echoed through the rocks. "Val! Come on, get up! Run, run, run!"

She tried. She ran. But she tripped. Bashed her knee, then her elbow. Lurched to her feet, somehow kept running. Every bone ached. Every step was lead-footed. Every ledge leaped up to trip her. Every wash of gravel yanked the world from under her. Her backpack slipped off, tumbling down an incline into darkness. Violet wouldn't let her go back for it.

The Infinite Diary was lost.

Deeper off the path they clambered, helping each other, panting, sweating, sliding down rock faces. They looked back now and again, but they couldn't see their predator, nor hear his footsteps. Maybe they'd ditched him.

They hadn't.

He emerged from the mists like a shadow made real. Violet reacted at the last second, drawing her pistol, but he ripped it from her grasp and hacked her to the ground all in the same motion. She coughed on her back, struggling to breathe. Valory threw a desperate punch, but Cervantes roundhoused her—elevate, rotate, snap—right in the side of the head. She'd never been hit so hard in her life. She collapsed, swimming in stars.

He stood between the two sprawled sisters. They were like fish out of water, gasping for air. He watched with grim pleasure.

Finally.

He'd caught the Graces.

He stalked over to Violet. Flipped her to her belly, snatched the second pistol from the small of her back. Now they were weaponless. They lay upon the rocks in a daze, separated by six or seven feet. He waited. Let the sisters regain their senses. Watched as they reached toward one another with weak, trembling arms. He sucked it all in through crimson teeth.

The magic moment had arrived.

The orange ambiance of dawn peeked over the eastern peaks, bathing the boulder field in a newborn alpenglow. Breathing mist, Cervantes came to straddle Valory. Squatted over her as he'd squatted over the queen. His face was covered in blood and dust, his cropped hair matted with chunks of gore. He stunk like he'd been swimming in jet fuel and bile. "Doctor Valory Grace," he said, wrapping his hand around her cheeks, breathing into her face. "You've caused me a lot of trouble tonight. Let's find out if I get to kill you or not." He threw her head away and stood.

"Wh—who are you?" she rasped, looking up at him. "Why are you doing this?"

"Shut up and listen." While standing over Valory, he looked at Violet, who was propped on an elbow, wincing from that brutal takedown. "All I want is the DNA. And our sister over there, brave little Violet, is going to tell me where it is. Because if she doesn't—"

He aimed at Valory's head and fired.

The world vanished like it had been sucked away through a straw. Only a ringing blackness echoed in Valory's senses. Her return to awareness was spurred by an intense burning on her left ear where the scalding hot casing had ricocheted off the rock.

"No!" screamed Violet, lurching to her knees. "Don't! You kill my sister, I won't tell you anything!"

"Yes, you will." Cervantes aimed the pistol at Valory's forehead. "I don't fuck around like the Italians, Grace. You're going to tell me everything or your sister dies right here, right now. Then my associate will slit Randy and Victoria Grace's throats. He's standing by at their house as we speak. 1235 Greenwood Court, Sunnyvale."

"Oh, God. Please don't. I'll tell you, just please don't."

"Then spit it out," he said, kicking Valory in the ribs, "or the next one goes right between her eyes. You lie to me, your whole family gets wiped out. Now where are the samples?"

"Verona," said Violet, sinking in defeat. "They're in Verona. A restaurant on the west side. Trattoria Dalla Bruna."

"A fucking restaurant?"

"I needed a deep freeze to preserve the samples. So I broke in and buried them in their freezer. It's the truth. Now please let us go."

"Tell me again."

"What?"

Cervantes fired a second shot, this time a scant half inch to the right side of Valory's head. "I said tell me again goddamnit!"

"Verona!" yelled Violet, wracked with panic. "Trattoria Dalla Bruna! Bottom of the deep freeze! They're there, I swear! I swear to God they're there! Please!"

The whites of Cervantes' eyes were a stark contrast to the crimson nightmare of his face. He didn't move, didn't speak. Just weighed Violet's words while aiming at Valory's face.

From her back, Valory panted, waiting, ears ringing. Everything hurt, from the tips of her toes to the individual hairs on her head. A breeze slid along her body, emphasizing the deep ache of her muscles. Morning was brightening the sky, dashing the mountain with a honeyed aurora. The pistol bore loomed over her, steady and unmoving, center point locked into the bridge of her nose.

"You have the location now," said Violet. She clasped her hands, begging. "Please. Please let us go. We just want to go home. Please."

Cervantes didn't lower the pistol. He held it there, savoring the thickness of the moment. It was a fitting end to perhaps the greatest night of his life. A night where he'd discovered something wonderful about his true self. A night where he'd extinguished more than sixty lives in an orgy of murder, something he hadn't experienced since the Shinwar Massacre. He realized he might never feel such a consuming satisfaction again for the rest of his life.

"Please," repeated Violet. "Please, please, please . . ."

"You know what?" said Cervantes. "I'm in a damn good mood. Thanks to you two bitches dragging me here, I got the best gift of my life. So maybe you've earned a solid." He thought about it. "Why not. I owe you that much."

"Oh, thank you," said Violet. "Thank you, thank you, thank you. You'll never see us again, I swear. We'll just—"

Cervantes rotated and fired, plugging Violet right between the eyes. She collapsed, dying instantly.

He turned the smoking bore back to Valory. She gazed at her sister's body, watching the blood pour from a neat little hole in her head. In an underwater stupor, she looked up at Cervantes.

"She didn't feel a thing. Neither will you. *Adios, hermanita.*"

Valory didn't hear the shot. Didn't feel the bullet lodge in her brain.

She died without pain.

430

JANK'A JAQINAKA 84

SOMETHING HAPPENED. SOMETHING MASSIVE. Rockwell had no clue how to interpret it. It was just a feeling. Like a *snap*. Deep, deep down, yet also way, way out. A sensation like an equilibrium he'd always taken for granted had just been destroyed. Like some kind of cosmic scale had just become perfectly unbalanced.

He inhaled this sensation. Embraced it, probed it. He wasn't sure what to make of it, but his gut feeling was that Cervantes had just succeeded. Or had at least accomplished something big. Maybe he'd found the immortal. Maybe he'd found Violet Grace. Obtained the samples. Someway, somehow, that weird connection between them all had just been strummed. Whatever had happened, it was good. Damn good. It felt like . . . *true power*.

Rockwell pulled out the mission phone, checking Cervantes' location. The locator beacon had updated about an hour ago. The trail of red tracking dots showed he'd been active up there all night. The latest coordinates indicated he'd left the castle proper and was making his way back down the slope. Rockwell smiled.

"Step on it, Karl," he called to his limo driver. "I need to be at that airfield three hours ago."

"Yes, sir, Mr. Rockwell."

CAPÍTULO 85

COLORS BEYOND RECKONING. RAINBOW rivers coursing through the ether. Endless. Elemental. Symphonic.

Sentient vibrations, dancing in luminous swells. Pure, unfiltered beauty, harmonizing in a cosmic ocean. Swirling, flowing, weaving through timeless meadows. The language of eternity.

Where am I?
Everywhere.
What am I?
Everything.
What are you?
This you know. You need only remember.
I do. I remember.
You know what must happen.
Yes. For it has already happened.
And is happening. And will always happen. Forever.
Yes, I remember. Past, present, future. All one.
Then come to me. Come, let not the darkness consume you.
For I must consume it.
Let not the fractures devour you.
For I must devour them.
Come to me. I am here, in the lower realm.
I see you, and I will come.
Only this shall you remember. To come, nothing else.
I shall come, forgetting all else.
For that is the way.
That is the way.

CAIBIDEIL 86

"PLEASE," REPEATED VIOLET. "PLEASE, please, please . . ."

"You know what?" said Cervantes. "I'm in a damn good mood. Thanks to you two bitches dragging me here, I got the best gift of my life. So maybe I'll do you a solid." He thought about it. "Why not. I owe you that much."

Valory watched in a daze. She didn't understand. Hadn't this already happened? Just a second ago? These exact events, these exact words? Now Violet was going to thank him, and then—

"Oh, thank you," said Violet. "Thank you, thank you, thank you. You'll never see us again, I swear. We'll just—"

Cervantes rotated and fired, plugging Violet right between the eyes. She collapsed, dying instantly.

He turned the smoking bore back to Valory. She looked at his dark eyes hovering over the sights, gore covering his face. But now there was something else. Something that hadn't been there before. Clouds of black and gray swirling in her perception. Not words, not language—no one was speaking. Yet tendrils of darkness writhed in her mind's eyes, localized around the man's head. As if they flowed in and out of his ears, his mouth, his scalp. She could feel those dark colors. She could taste them. They reeked of death and decay.

"She didn't feel a thing," said the man. "Neither will you. *Adios, hermanita.*"

Valory didn't hear the shot. Didn't feel the bullet lodge in her brain.

She died without pain.

KAPITEL 87

"PLEASE," REPEATED VIOLET. "PLEASE, please, please . . ."

"You know what?" said Cervantes. "I'm in a damn good mood. Because of you two bitches dragging me here, I got the best gift of my life. So maybe I'll do you a solid." He thought about it. "Why not. I owe you that much."

Valory rose to a sitting position. She was sure she had just died. Yet now she was alive, and it was all happening again. Same actions, same words, same everything. "Wait," she said, surprised at the authority in her voice. "Don't kill her."

"It's okay, Val," said Violet. "He's saying he'll let us go. Thank you, thank you, thank you. You'll never see us again, I swear. We'll just—"

Cervantes fired, plugging Violet right between the eyes. She collapsed, dying instantly.

He turned the smoking bore back to Valory. She looked at his dark eyes hovering over the sights, blood covering his face. The colors were there again, stronger, blacker, more putrid. They churned in her perception, drowning him in a morbid miasma. Valory realized there was something in them. A synergy of some kind. A symbiosis. She reached for the colors in the same way she reached for language. She tuned in, exploring. Realized what they were. Memories. Memories of language. Of words. Of pivotal conversations this man had had throughout his life. She could hear them. Could hear the voices of everyone with whom he'd ever spoken, jumbled together in a hurricane of vocalics.

"She didn't feel a thing," said the man. "Neither will you. *Adios, hermanita.*"

"Wait," she said, putting her hand up.

"What?" he sneered. "You want to pray?"

"No. I . . ." Valory focused inward, soaring through the somber colors like an airplane through a storm. She separated the colors with her mind, fanning the shades into singular lanes through the ether. Amid the black and gray swaths, she perceived an outlier. A streak of pale pink entombed beneath layers of decay. "I hear your mother."

"What?"

"I hear her," she said, loading the pinkness into her perception. "Your mother. She's singing to you."

"What kind of shit is that? You really think that's going to work?"

"It's true. I—"

Valory didn't hear the shot. Didn't feel the bullet lodge in her brain. She died without pain.

장 88

"PLEASE, REPEATED VIOLET. "PLEASE, please, please . . ."

"You know what?" said Cervantes. "I'm in a damn good mood. Because of you two bitches dragging me here, I got the best gift of my life. So maybe I'll do you a solid." He thought about it. "Yeah, sure. Why not. I owe you that much."

Valory lived. She had died, and now she was alive. In some weird way, it felt normal.

Now Violet would thank the man, thinking he was letting them go. Instead, he would shoot her in midsentence. That was the way it had gone three times. Three horrifying repeats. Valory would not let it happen again. She dove into Cervantes' colors. Flew through the black storm of his language memories. Separated them again, fanning them out. There was the pink band, faint and ghostly, lurking in his depths. She brought it inside herself, filling her perception.

"Oh, thank you," said Violet. "Thank you, thank you, thank you. You'll never see us again, I swear . . ."

Cervantes covered the trigger, aiming at Violet.

Valory began to sing.

Not in English, but in Spanish.

Not in her own voice, but in another—the voice of Cervantes' mother.

> *"Arrorró mi niño, arrorró mi sol,*
> *arrorró pedazo de mi corazón.*
> *Este niño lindo se quiere dormir*
> *y el pícaro sueño no quiere venir . . ."*

Cervantes didn't fire. He watched Valory in blunt confusion. Paralyzed with shock. *His mother's voice* was coming from Valory Grace's lips. Same pitch, same tone. The same breathy quality of her words. That certain way she rolled her R's. That curious habit she had of dropping the N's off the end of some words, like *corazón*. When she said it, it was *corazó*. Only Gabriela Cervantes spoke like that.

436

"Este niño lindo se quiere dormir
cierra los ojitos y los vuelve a abrir.
Arrorró mi niño, arrorró mi sol,
arrorró pedazo de mi corazón . . ."

He lowered his pistol. Relaxed his shoulders. Motionless, he stared, listening to his mother. Wondering how it could be real. A feeling he'd not felt in twenty-six years pried into his heart as the memory overcame him. The memory of that one time as a child—that one, solitary time in his entire life—when he felt truly loved. When his mother held him in her arms and sang this very Spanish lullaby. After she'd discovered he was a psychopath. He felt her rocking him. Felt her hand caressing the back of his head. Saw her light brown eyes looking down on him as she sang, feeling the unconditional love that only a mother can give.

"Arrorró mi niño, arrorró mi sol,
Duérmete mi niño, duérmete mi amor . . ."

He was frozen, paying no attention to anything other than his mother's voice. He didn't notice Violet pulling the lighter from her pocket. The Zippo she'd taken from Savelli. In his trance, Cervantes was oblivious, eyes far away, jaw slack.

She held the lighter to his pant leg.

Flick.

The flames whooshed up his body, consuming the oil Valory had dumped on him in the shaft. For a moment, he didn't even notice. Too lost in the stark impossibility of hearing his mother singing. When he realized he was burning, he roared, dropping the pistol. In a twirling dance of hysteria, he began trying to pull his clothes off, a blazing human bonfire.

Valory crawled away as Cervantes flounced in panicked rage. He filled the air with burning flakes of detritus, his skin melting. Waiting for her chance, Violet darted in and scooped the pistol from the ground. Then she stood at Valory's side, aiming at the tornado of fire before them. Howling, Cervantes' eyes suddenly fixed upon the sisters from within his own personal inferno, and he snatched his other pistol from its holster.

Violet fired, stopping him in mid-draw. Fired until the mag was empty. Couldn't tell how many times she hit him, or where. She just kept pulling the trigger while Cervantes careened and stumbled toward a ledge, yelling, leaving remnants of himself smoldering on the stone. He tripped, tumbling down a steep slide. At the bottom of the rock face, he rolled over a cliff, leaving a wispy trail of black smoke in his wake.

Violet realized she was still pulling the trigger, hearing only the click click click of an empty chamber. When it dawned on her that it was all over, she dropped to her knees by Valory. The sisters crawled into one another's embrace.

They stayed like that, crying.

Violet because they'd almost died.

Valory because she was immortal.

SABABU 89

A SALVO OF SUNBEAMS fired over the distant peaks. The clouds that had blanked the night sky were chased away by angelic pinks and azures. For a while, the sisters didn't speak. They only sunk into one another, each sorting through the disaster of the last several hours in her own mind. The new, quiet peace of the mountain was an emotional salve. It soothed them, promising that the horrors were over.

Still embracing her sister, Violet finally broke the silence. "Val," she said, voice cracking. "What was that? That singing? You didn't sound like you."

"I don't know," said Valory. "I'm not sure I understand what happened here."

"Well, how did you know it would stop him?"

"I didn't. It just felt right."

They separated, looking into one another's teary eyes. Violet gasped.

"What is it?" asked Valory, feeling her face. "Am I wounded?"

"Your eyes."

"What about them?"

"They're . . . different."

"What do you mean? Different how?"

Violet stared in confusion. "Different colors."

"What?"

"Your right eye is blue. Your left is golden brown."

THEY RETRIEVED VALORY'S BACKPACK, tracing it back to where they'd dropped it. Without it, they would have had no food or survival supplies. Perhaps even more importantly, the master disk was in there. With the destruction of the castle, the disk held the only copies of the Infinite Diary. No way Valory would abandon it.

Afterward, at Valory's insistence, they went back for Janelle. Violet insisted Janelle was dead, and that they needed to hike to the north face of the mountain immediately before the road was crawling with Italians. But Valory wanted—needed—to make sure, and she wouldn't take no for an answer.

They found her about twelve feet from the road, having slid down an embankment. One look at her mangled body confirmed the worst. Unable to do anything else, Valory said some tearful words in French in Janelle's honor. Then they left her there.

No sooner had they begun their descent than the helicopters began circling the summit, surveying the archeological and human disasters below. Though the sisters were dog-tired, they stealth-hiked toward the northern slope, which faced Austria, putting several miles between themselves and the main path. When they could push no more, they found a suitable overhang under which to camp for a while. There, they ate some MREs before passing out from sheer exhaustion.

Before she drifted off, Valory tried to understand why she was immortal. Why she was doomed to suffer the same curse as Alex. Why? How had it happened? Had she always been immortal and simply not known it? Or had she somehow become immortal without realizing it? There were no answers. She knew only one thing—she had to find Alex. Here in this world, not in the ganzflicker. And she knew where he was.

When she was dead, he'd shown her.

THOMAS ROCKWELL FUMED.

He stood at the window, arms crossed, looking upon the evergreen corks and cypresses outside the safe house. Something weird had happened. He could feel it, but he couldn't understand it. It was a sinking sensation. Like certain victory had been snatched right out of his hands, leaving only a ghostly residue on his fingertips. Somewhere back there, in the depths of his essence, there was a feeling—a memory?—of the cosmic scales tilting in his favor. Like all his plans had come to fruition. It had been so real. Yet now it was like he'd woken from a beautiful dream.

Cervantes' tracking dot had not updated in hours. It had stalled out after he'd descended the mountain, completely off course. He wasn't going to make it back.

Rockwell called Colonel Hewitt. He ordered a covert extraction mission into the Dolomite foothills, transmitting Cervantes' last known coordinates. Hewitt's men found Cervantes clinging to life in a thicket of pines. He had two gunshot wounds, several broken bones, and there were third-degree burns covering his body. Somehow, he'd crawled and shimmied his way down the mountain, finally passing out from intense pain and exhaustion. How he was still alive was a mystery. Who had done this to him, Rockwell could not divine. Cervantes was catatonic, his essence inaccessible.

Cervantes was delivered to a clandestine medical team contracted by Colonel Hewitt. Whether he would live or not was no more than a guess. Whatever the case, the bitter, driving truth was clear:

Cervantes had failed.

Which meant Thomas Rockwell would remain mortal. At least for now.

***

Operazione Prato Fiera, or Operation Fair Meadow as it was known by Italian intelligence, was covered up by the Italians. The families of the soldiers and the civilians who'd lost their lives on the mountain were told that the earthquake had claimed their loved ones and that the bodies had been buried under metric tons of displaced rock. They would remain forever

441

irrecoverable. Lying about their deaths was necessary. Delivering savagely murdered corpses to their respective families would spur endless investigations, costing Italy millions and jeopardizing the secrecy of the project, which was ongoing. The question baffling them the most was Who the hell did this? There was no sign of a military force entering the area, yet that was clearly what had happened. Nothing else could have destroyed an entire army platoon and a team of federal agents. So where had it come from, and how had it vanished without detection?

Unable to access the ruined keep, and having lost the likelihood of recovering the DNA, Director Teruzzi detached a team of agents to England. According to the texts translated by Doctor Valory Grace (presumed deceased), the immortal human male traveled to Stonehenge every summer hoping to encounter the spirit of his dead queen. A ridiculous scenario, perhaps, but it was the only lead they had left. The only known location where they might intercept the immortal. Though it was a long shot, Teruzzi wanted his team to monitor the site on the slim chance he was still making the annual trip. The team would also hunt for the immortal's cache of treasures, which the texts revealed to be north of the henge, near a tributary of the River Avon.

If these objectives proved unsuccessful, the operation was essentially over.

KGAOLO YA 92

SHE ALIGHTED FROM THE bus, joining a small group of Icelanders returning from the capital. The natives had been chattering for most of the five-hour journey from Reykjavik. Having lived in the same village most of their lives, they knew each other well. Valory was a stranger in their midst, but they had included her in the conversation for a while until she politely told them she was going to take a nap. She needed the shuteye. Since Italy, sleep had been a fleeting luxury.

Hugging herself in the cold breeze, she looked around the town of Ólafsfjörður. Like most of the fishing villages they'd passed on the northern coast of Iceland, there wasn't much there. Just a few small restaurants, a quaint residential neighborhood, and a handful of people walking the streets. A far cry from the touristy southern coast. Behind the town, the black, snow-topped mountains rose toward a dark gray sky. A fleet of fishing boats rolled in the gentle swells of the harbor. The wind toyed with a small bell somewhere in the distance.

"*Það var gaman að hitta þig,* Maria." It was an old man from the bus, telling her it was nice to have met her. Maria Bianchi was the alias she'd been given when Violet had obtained their 'synthetic identities.' How Violet found the types of people who dealt with such things had always been a mystery to Valory. The black market was her world, and she'd slipped back into it like it was her favorite old hoodie. With Vi's street savvy and Val's language proficiency, the twins had been able to sell Alex's treasure for a small fortune as they'd made their way north, obtaining everything they needed to travel in discretion. And, true to Violet's nature, she'd gotten wasted the first chance she got, downing a bottle of Slivovitz while Valory soaked in a long-missed bath. Never mind that Vi was malnourished from her imprisonment, still healing from various injuries. As always, she would not be stopped from getting high at inappropriate times. A nasty fight between the twins had ensued.

"*Ég vona að þú finnir einveruna sem þú ert að leita að,*" said the old man, telling Valory he hoped she found the solitude she was looking for.

"*Þakka þér fyrir,*" said Valory, thanking and congratulating him. "*Enn og aftur til hamingju með dóttur þína.*" The man was returning from

Reykjavik, where he'd attended his daughter's wedding. Valory appreciated speaking to him in Icelandic. Due to Iceland's isolated location, the language hadn't changed much from its West Scandinavian roots. Natives could still read texts written a thousand years ago, a rarity in historical linguistics. Valory experienced the tongue as snowy swirls dashed with sparkling swoops of blue and yellow. Curiously, its smell was like nail polish, and its texture was furry, like the coat of a shaggy animal. Sometimes, there was no accounting for the synesthetic sensations of a language.

On the bus, when the villagers had asked why an Italian such as herself had come to north Iceland, she told them it was for the peace and quiet. A getaway from the hustle and bustle of noisy city life. They were genial and accepting of her lie, though their expressions said, *Okay, but why* here *of all places?* Not to mention their other unspoken question, the type with which she was all too familiar: *How does a native Italian speak flawless Icelandic?*

She'd dodged the more serious inquiries with curt graciousness, doing her best to remain unremarkable. Just a boring Italian lady out for some R&R, not the American fugitive who'd defied a nation.

The truth, of course, was even more outlandish. It was a truth that she would never share with anyone—that she'd come to Iceland to meet an immortal.

A *fellow* immortal.

The realization had still not sunk in. Since Italy, she'd been staring into every mirror in every dingy motel and every convenience store bathroom. Just inspecting herself, realizing that she had not shown signs of true aging in several years. No sign of oncoming wrinkles, no foretelling gray hairs. She was thirty-four going on twenty-eight. Up to now, she'd been chalking it up to good genes. *Why am I immortal? Have I always been so, or did it 'happen' at some point? What* made *me immortal? What does it all mean? How is it going it affect my relationships with people? With the world? Will it corrupt my very perception of time? Am I going to wind up like Alikai, forever depressed and suicidal?*

That last question was horrifying. For Alikai, immortality was the most crushing curse imaginable. It was much too new for Valory to feel the same, but one day, centuries from now, she would feel his pain. She just could not fathom that future. She had, of course, considered such existentialist questions when she'd first learned of Alikai, but now that she was asking those questions about herself, they carried the weight of the universe.

And the weirdest question, the one that she just couldn't shake, was:

When I choked on that grape as a child, did I die and just not realize it?

She looked into the bay beyond the black sand coastline. Less than a half mile out, a series of basalt sea stacks rose from the water like the fingers of a submerged giant. The sea stacks ranged in height from forty to two hundred feet, gnarled, volcanic, and magnificent. Just one of the numerous geological wonders of the land of fire and ice. Though there were many such sea stacks located around Iceland, this was the specific cluster Valory had sought. For this one had been 'shown' to her when she was dead.

It was difficult to quantify now. Since escaping the Dolomites, Valory had felt a certain loss. The invigorating energy she'd experienced up there—the heightened prowess, the extrasensory abilities, the magic of being in Alikai's castle, the *aliveness*—had diminished. Like she'd come unplugged from a power grid when she left the mountain. No longer could she 'hear' remote conversations in her mind. No longer could she sing in another person's voice. That was all just . . . gone.

Violet had expressed something similar. She explained that in her last week of imprisonment, she'd begun feeling energized. More alive. Not that it did her any good being chained up, but she'd definitely felt 'heightened' in a way she didn't understand. Now, that feeling was lost.

From Amsterdam, the sisters had flown into Reykjavik, though Violet resisted at first. She wanted to go back for the DNA samples so she could win the ten-million-dollar prize from Thomas Rockwell. This had started a fight between them, with Valory falling just short of calling Violet a greedy idiot. If the Italians suspected the Graces were still alive, they'd be the targets of a nationwide dragnet. Did Violet really want to throw herself back into that fire? Risking capture, torture, and death? All for money? In the end, she backed off, acknowledging the danger. Valory convinced her of the most important thing, that she was alive and had a chance to start over. In Reykjavik, she could just take it easy for a while. Lay low, heal up. Meanwhile, Valory would take a little solo trip up the northern coast to 'visit an old friend.' That was the lie she would go with until she located Alex and got a better grasp on what might come next.

It only occurred to Valory later that her own DNA could now serve the same purpose as Alex's. If she was immortal, her DNA should reflect that. Did that mean Violet's should as well? They were fraternal twins, meaning they did not share identical DNA. Still, up on that mountain, Violet had been murdered. Now she was living and breathing, the same as Valory, the only difference being that Vi had no memory of being slain. What did it mean? Was Violet immortal or not? Their parents, obviously, were mortal. They were aging as expected. But with Violet, it was hard to tell. Maybe she looked younger than thirty-four, maybe not.

The question raised another mind-boggling mystery, something Einstein had mentioned in his discussion with Alex—Was her immortality a mechanism of time travel? Valory and Violet had died multiple times. Then time rewound, and they were alive, placed right into the previous situation. Einstein's incredulous comment shot straight to the heart of the matter: *What does this tell us? That time itself works at your behest? That our deterministic universe backpedals for you and you alone when you die, leaving the rest of us unaffected? Only you, and no one else?*

It was yet another rabbit hole in an existence suddenly chocked full of them. With this newfound immortality, she was more lost than ever.

Whatever the truth, Valory didn't tell her twin about it. She'd barely begun to process it herself. All she knew was that she needed to keep quiet, at least for now. She certainly didn't want to arouse Violet's worst instincts, let alone the rest of the world's. That's why she didn't tell Violet the real reason she was going up the coast. Vi knew the 'going to visit a friend' thing was bullshit, but she didn't press for details. She was fine being left behind. No doubt looking forward to some alone time without being mother henned by her sister.

Still, withholding this new reality from Violet was tough. For, with every passing second, the fresh new truth churned her stomach:

I am immortal.

Me, Valory Grace.

Immortal.

Part of her sensed she already knew the answers but just couldn't connect to them. She felt they'd been revealed to her that first time she'd died up there on the mountain. The first time the man in black had shot her in the head. She had experienced *something* immediately after being slain. Something like the ganzflicker. She only had the vaguest of memory of it now, so vague that it could not even be called a memory. More like a dream of someone else's memory. And with it, the feeling like she'd learned something monumental from a sea of magnificent, musical colors. She'd felt Alikai's presence in that sea. Yet, in the end, only one thing remained from the experience—a fleeting vision of an ocean lapping against soaring ebony sea stacks. The stacks that loomed before her now. This was where she would finally find Alikai.

There was one thing she'd taken with her from the mountain, though— the heterochromia. No longer did she possess the eyes with which she'd been born. Her left was the glowing amber of rich honey. Her right, the blue of a tranquil sea. Just like Alex. Why? Perhaps, with everything that had happened, the more appropriate question was Why the hell not?

Valory took the short walk to the only hotel in town, the Northern Comfort Inn. It was late afternoon, and the sky was already growing dark. Tomorrow, she would begin her search for Alex. Thanks to the vision, she was sure he was in this region. Where specifically, though, she hadn't a clue. She would have to track him down. She'd brought enough cash for two months if the search took that long.

Once she settled into her room, she withdrew her new most cherished possession, the USB master hard drive. Or rather, a copy of the drive. The original was in a safety deposit box in Innsbruck, Austria, where the sisters

446

had passed through a few weeks ago. While there, Valory had purchased two additional drives, copying the contents of the original to each of them. Everything was there: her translations, the other contractors' reports (even Violet's!), pictures of the castle, everything. She mailed one copy anonymously to Professor Meadows in Oxford with an unsigned note urging her to keep the drive safe. Valory had encrypted the drive, making it useless without her passphrase. Perhaps that was a little mean. Meadows would be confused receiving a drive she couldn't access, but Valory wasn't ready for the data to be revealed just yet. She'd only sent it so that there would be at least one copy somewhere under the lock and key of an accomplished academic. One day, when she'd sorted through all this, she'd send the passphrase to Meadows, giving her access to everything the Italians wanted to hide. Maybe the diary could be prepped for academic treatment, who knows.

The other spare drive, Valory kept with her at all times. This was for her own pleasure. There were photos of the treasure bindings on there, and she was dying to read the remainder of Alex and Sera's love story. After she found Alex, maybe they could read them together.

She hadn't been sure how she was going to find him. Her loose plan was to query the locals about an odd man in town until she uncovered his location. Luckily, she got a hit the first time she asked about him. Something she might have expected in a small village where everyone knew everyone else.

"You mean Aksel," said the hotel clerk, Sigar, speaking Icelandic. "Yes, everyone has heard of him around here. You must be his sister."

"Why do you say that?" asked Valory.

"They say he has different colored eyes, same as you."

"Ah. Right. Can you tell me where to find him?"

Sigar shrugged, sliding over a room key and a paper to sign. "I am told he stays in the mountains west of Kvíabekkur. I've never met him myself, but people talk about him."

"What do they say?"

"That he is strange. Crazy, maybe." He suddenly realized he might be offending her. "I apologize, I don't mean to insult your brother."

"No, please. Go on. What else can you tell me?"

"He keeps to himself mostly. He has come into town a few times over the years, but he doesn't stay long. So I've heard. Maybe you can talk to Jöður over at the Kvíabekkur farm. I believe he sees Aksel from time to time."

The next morning, Valory ate breakfast before looking for a way south to Kvíabekkur. There were no taxis in Ólafsfjörður. The morning clerk, Ölnir, told her that if she just stood at the intersection of 76 and 82 and waited for a passing car, she could hitchhike. The locals were always glad to help each other out like that. Still, the thought made her a bit nauseous. She couldn't help it. Even after everything that had happened, she still felt a sinking feeling knowing she would need to flag down a stranger and ask for a ride. The anti-social claws of introversion were not just for mortals, it seemed.

A woman named Rayna gave her a lift. She worked at Scandic Mountain Guides a few miles southeast of the Kvíabekkur farm. She, too, had heard of Aksel, the weird hermit who lived in the mountains. Though it was technically illegal to live in those mountains, she said, he wasn't causing any harm. The locals just let him be.

"In fact," said Rayna, speaking Icelandic, "the owner of Kvíabekkur, Jöður, brings him food from time to time. Talk to him, he will tell you."

Kvíabekkur was a dairy cattle farm set in the foreground of a snow-dusted mountain range, demarcated by a fence of wooden posts and barbwire stretching into the distance. An expanse of green pasture was filled with Icelandic cattle grazing on turnips, barley, and oats. The main house was a field's length from the road. Rayna drove up the path, offering to introduce Valory to Jöður.

Jöður was in his early fifties but moved like a man in his late twenties. He was tall and ropy with a beard that would have made his Viking ancestors proud. He invited Valory inside, where he offered her some coffee. The interior of his home had an uncluttered, minimalistic feel. "You are Aksel's sister?" he asked in Icelandic, looking into her strange eyes.

"Yes," she lied, feeling immense guilt. The Icelanders had been so nice and helpful, and here she was lying to them all. "We've been worried about him back home. I just want to make sure he's okay."

Jöður handed her a cup of coffee. "Okay is not the word I'd use to describe him. No offense."

"None taken. How would you describe him?"

"Well, he lives in lava tubes, which is dangerous. They can flood without warning. Also, he is about this big around." Jöður made a circle with his thumb and index finger. "Whenever I see him, he looks on the verge of death. I've told him he is welcome for dinner here anytime, but he just tells me to go away. So I bring him food once in a while. I don't like knowing a man is starving to death in my backyard."

"Yes. My brother is quite, uh, hardheaded. You're very kind to try to help him, Jöður."

"You know, I could never get him to tell me where he is from originally. I would have never guessed he is Italian."

"Why is that?"

"His accent is strange. It changes all the time. I don't know."

"I see. Well, we moved around a lot as kids, so . . . you know." Valory sipped her coffee, anxious to advance the conversation to the part where she finds out how to get to Alex, but unsure how to do it without being rude.

"I wouldn't have guessed you for an Italian either," said Jöður. "You speak Icelandic better than some natives. That is unheard of for foreigners. Ours is not an easy language to learn."

Valory shrugged. "Practice makes perfect, I suppose."

"I suppose."

"So," she said, unable to contain herself any longer, "how far away is my brother?"

"About forty-five minutes by ATV," said Jöður, pointing a thumb to the back of his property, toward the mountains. "If you can wait until midday, I'll take you."

"Oh, gosh, that won't be necessary, honestly. I can hike there if you just tell me where to go."

"You want to hike?" Jöður's expression made clear he thought the idea was kooky. "The route is very steep in places. Lots of loose gravel. I don't know who would want to hike that."

"I'm sure I'll manage," said Valory, and she meant it. What could happen—she'd die? "I've got more mountaineering experience than I ever dreamed I'd have. I'll be fine."

Jöður wasn't satisfied. "Have you ever driven an ATV before?"

"No."

"It's easy. I will show you. Take mine and just call me if you have any problems."

CHAPTER 93

SHE DROVE THE ATV up the mountainside, glad that Jöður had lent it to her. The black gravel switchbacks were steep and sketchy with snowbanks that grew larger with elevation. It would have been a slow, lung-busting hike.

Cresting the saddle of the mountain, she stopped, looking down into a long, crescent-shaped ravine. According to Jöður's directions, Valory would need to skirt the north side of the ravine for about eight miles until it turned back and dropped southward into the crescent. She looked back the way she'd come, appreciating the giant, sweeping views of the Icelandic peaks and the deep blue fjord called Eyjafjörður. She wondered how Alex had found his way here to this remote country bordering the Arctic Circle.

The rest of the way was downward trending with the occasional steep hill and twisty turn. There was not a clearly delineated path, but the route was obvious. At one point, an Arctic fox sped across the route and darted over a knoll. Valory barely noticed. She was finally going to meet Alex. For real this time. That thought consumed her.

She drove around a long, gradual switchback, turning south into the ravine. Jöður had told her once she reached this point, she would need to continue on foot. Then she should start looking for a jagged opening cut into the escarpment on the north face of the ravine. It would be set into the escarpment at an angle, like a cellar entrance without doors. This was one of several openings to the lava tubes that were Aksel's 'home.'

She parked the ATV, miscolored eyes following a trickling river into the crescent. There, about a hundred yards along a narrow shoreline littered with black rocks, she saw the opening.

In later days, she would not be able to recall hiking along the stream. The anticipation was too thick, too intense. She would only remember standing before the opening, looking into the hollow darkness. She lingered there, gathering herself.

"Aléxandros?" she called, her voice echoing within. "Aksel? Alex?"

No answer.

She pulled a small flashlight from her daypack. Swallowed hard, took a deep breath. Then she climbed down into the cave.

450

Entering the cave was like setting foot on an alien planet. The caves had been formed millions of years ago by basaltic lava flowing from a volcanic crater in confined channels, leaving an otherworldly subterranean landscape to cool in its wake. After Valory crouched through a tight squeeze, the cave expanded into an open grotto of red and black rock. Shark tooth stalactites hung from the ceiling like waves of giant bats. Gnarled stalagmites rose from the ground. Farther in, Valory saw daylight slanting in from a high opening, mist riding the beams.

She picked her way forward over the rough, uneven stone. Drawing closer to the light, she stifled a gasp. In this portion of the cavern, the walls had been carved into a continuous string of high-relief sculptures.

Sculptures of Seraphina.

Valory approached the nearest one. It was a life-sized Sera protruding from the wall, dancing in a flowy dress. The sculpture was crude, the porous basaltic rock leaving much to be desired as a medium. Still, it was striking.

A few feet over, another Sera wielded a drawn bow, arrow trained on unseen prey. Beyond that was another, and another, and another. Valory ran her flashlight over them all, admiring the unique menagerie of artwork. On the opposite wall, in a protected alcove, she saw a heap of books, papers, and fur blankets. Beneath the alcove, next to a small fire, was a plastic dish containing a half-eaten haunch of beef.

"Alex?" she said, looking into the depths of the cavern. "Are you here?"

It took her a moment to realize that the tall, shadowy stalagmite on the opposite side of the cavern was a man.

No, not a man.

A god.

Obscured in the mists, he stood motionless. Thin. Long hair. Tattered clothing. Face hidden in shadow.

For a moment, they only stood in silence, looking at one another.

Then, he spoke:

"It is time."

END BOOK 1

For news about future books in The Infinite Diary trilogy, follow Tony Huston at tony-huston.com

ACKNOWLEDGEMENTS

SEVEN YEARS AGO, I was struck with the idea for *The Lost Immortal*. As I jotted notes about a potential plot, I began to suspect that the story was much too big for me to handle. Historical linguistics, synesthetic geniuses, Carolingian history, existentialist philosophy, a conversation with *the* Albert Einstein—these subjects carried epistemic risk beyond the mindset of a beer-loving mountain biker who yells at football games on TV. The research would be daunting, and the time commitment would exceed that of any project I'd undertaken in my life. If I proceeded, I might very well end up creating the literary equivalent of Sloth from *The Goonies*. Well, I went for it, and with the encouragement and support of a handful of excellent people, my most rewarding achievement now lives and breathes forever.

Thank you first to my lovely wife, Amy, who endured more writer's-block-induced bad moods than I care to acknowledge, and who served as my initial sounding board (mostly because she couldn't run away).

To my mom, Cindy, who thinks I am the greatest writer on Earth, and don't you even try to contradict her.

To my talented and creative daughter, Lauren, who makes me proud every day, and not just because she says *The Lost Immortal* is her new favorite book.

To my great friend since childhood, my fellow writer, and the most voracious book-brain ever, Paul Barrera. His fingerprints can be found between the lines of this novel.

To the witty and sagacious David Garcia, whose life stories and self-conjured proverbs I steal for use in my writing.

To Gilbert "Where are my new chapters?" Perez, who never let me slack off.

To Sherri Roberts, who read my manuscript twice and provided valuable feedback that saved me from an embarrassing mistake or three.

To firearms guru Curtis Wallace, who set me straight on scenes involving gunplay.

To Karen Garza, who, after reading my draft, demanded a thirty-minute, face-to-face Q&A sesh that put a smile on my face.

Thank you also to Nick Castle, UK-based cover designer extraordinaire. Nick was patient and accommodating of my many meticulous requests, though I think I heard him grumbling way over here in Texas.

So much research went into this novel. My nonfiction collection grew to unexpected heights as I strove to craft the most authentic story possible. Without these brilliant references, I'd have just been making stuff up. I now cite the subset of works that most heavily influenced my novel. In no particular order:

Historical Linguistics: An Introduction by Lyle Campbell

The Time Traveler's Guide to Medieval England by Ian Mortimer

Sapiens: A Brief History of Humankind by Yuval Noah Harari

Why Smart People Hurt: A Guide for the Bright, the Sensitive, and the Creative by Eric Maisel

The Superhuman Mind: Free the Genius in Your Brain by Berit Brogaard, Ph.D. and Kristian Marlow, MA

Quiet: The Power of Introverts in a World That Can't Stop Talking by Susan Cain

The Psychopath Inside: A Neuroscientist's Personal Journey into the Dark Side of the Brain by James H. Fallon

Shakespeare: The Biography by Peter Ackroyd

The World As I See It by Albert Einstein

Dagger 22: U.S. Marine Corps Special Operations in Bala Murghab, Afghanistan by Michael Golembesky

Dark Psychology and Manipulation by Liam Robinson

The Emperor Charlemagne by E.R. Chamberlin

The Writer's Guide to Weapons by Benjamin Sobieck

Regrettably, I leave out a plethora of websites, magazines, and academic forums from which I gathered bits and pieces of helpful information. There are simply too many to list. Just know that my novel is peppered with many voices from obscure reaches of the Internet, and I sincerely appreciate them all.

Made in United States
Orlando, FL
05 May 2024

46528891R00250